Praise for *ARNS and the Man*:

"Amusing, sardonic political and social satire that brims with wordplay legerdemain and oddballisticelaboratified name invention. Trenchantly twisted and good fun." – John Shirley author of *A Song Called Youth: Eclipse*

"I don't often read science fiction but when I do, Ira Nayman's *ARNS and the Man* is near the top of my list. Wacky, surreal, bizarre, and all too close to reality, Nayman spins a web of satirical hilarity ripped from the headlines." – Terry Fallis, two-time winner of the Stephen Leacock Medal for Humour.

"Ira Nayman rivals Walt Kelly for the skilled and joyous administration of near hallucinogenic word play as an antidote for the madness of our political process. And unlike the brave possum of Okefenokee Swamp, the truths of *ARNS and the Man* were crafted by someone wearing pants." – Hugh Spencer, author of *Why I Hunt Flying Saucers* and *Extreme Dentistry*

"Ira skewers American politics in a way only a Canadian can, with absurdist wit and wisdom. Short humorous Fake News articles that know they're fake and relish in their lies. (Or ARE they?) Makes me once more jealous of our neighbors to the north." – Michael A. Ventrella, author of *Bloodsuckers: A Vampire Runs for President*, among other things

"Reading an ARNS book is like going head-to-head with an selection of thirty three and a third disconnected Wikipedia entries filtered through seven layers of artesian coffee filters woven from at least three more fibers than permitted by the historic laws of any major religion in a blender made of a strange kind of cotton candy spun from titanium anodized in fairground colours with blades made of live sharks while simultaneously tap-dancing to a Steve Reich composition based on the absolute value of the square root of pi. In other words, simply and elegantly the most entertaining way ever invented to invert your brain over a platter prepared with roasted apples and a variety of field mushrooms for your own delighted consumption. Also, a hilariously skewed take on the Trump administration." – Jen Frankel, editor, *Trump: Utopia or Dystopia*, author, *Undead Redhead*

Ira Nayman

Idiotocracy for Dummies

The Alternate Reality News Service,

Ira Nayman, Proprietor

This is a work of fiction. Any resemblance to real persons, places or things is…inevitable, really, given the nature of the multiverse. However, the probability of any resemblance to real persons, places or things in your particular universe is vanishingly small, and must, therefore, be considered coincidental.

DEDICATION

Yep. That is certainly what it takes to finish a book. Any book. Even this book. Especially this book, which is really three, three, three books in one. Not to mention making it available to the public, which must count as dedication squared. Dedication on top of dedication – that is what you're holding in your ha –

What? This is supposed to be the kind of dedication where people important to the creation of this book are thanked? Oh. Okay. I can do that.

Idiotocracy for Dummies is dedicated to my family, especially my father, whose unwavering support for my writing career has made this and my other books possible. It is also dedicated to my Web Goddess, without whom it very likely would not exist.

Finally, I would like to dedicate this book to the men and women who serve Donald Trump, and the American President himself, without whom none of this would have been necessary.*

ACKNOWLEDGEMENTS

I would like to thank Hugh Spencer for the graphics that were at the heart of the three original volumes' covers, and Gisela McKay, who took all of the elements I handed her and made those covers, and this one, something unique and special.

In addition, I have been remiss in not thanking the people who gave of their time and blurbiage to the first Vesampucceri collection, *Arns and the Man*. Your kind words may not have increased my sales appreciably, but they make me think that I may not have been completely wasting my time with this whole writing thing.

* Yes, I know that that is a line from the Firesign Theatre. It's probably not the first I have used; it probably won't be the last. If one must steal, one should always steal from the best.

CONTENTS

FORWARD

Reflections on a Time of Madness

1. So, umm, yeah. Fucking Donald Trump. FDT – the opposite of fine flower delivery. Fucks up everybody's special days.

The Alternate Reality News Service (ARNS) started as a science fiction feature. No, really. Go back to the first couple of books and you will see. Sure, it was satirical, so there was some social and political commentary thrown into the mix, but there were robots and artificial intelligences and even the occasional spaceship. Science fiction.

In the seventh book in the series, *Futures in Mirror Are Closer Than They Appear*, there was a chapter devoted to a universe where the United States of Vesampucceri was the world leading idiotocracy, which, as you might imagine, was rule by the stupidest. As I started working on the follow-up, I figured it would have a similar mix of articles.

Then, FDT happened.

There was something every day. Collusion! Corruption! …Some… other bad thing starting with "co!" Scandals that would have ruined any other politician were met with a shrug and a contented grin. Kleptocracy? FDT is in it for the money, so why shouldn't everybody in his administration be? Sex scandal? FDT denies everything, but grins like a little kid who has stolen his first porn magazine from the corner store. (He grew up in more technologically innocent times.) And, the whole Rusher thing? Rusher? He never met her!

I found that I was writing articles about the FDT administration. A lot of articles. Like, really a lot of articles. Ordinarily, I would write and publish one ARNS article a week. I had to start publishing two ARNS articles a week, not to keep up with how much I was writing, but not to fall too far behind: I was writing anywhere from two to five ARNS articles a week.

Put it another way: each ARNS book contains 80 articles. Ordinarily, they would take about 80 weeks to accumulate. *ARNS and the Man*, book eight in the series, was written in less than half that time. I held back releasing it for three or four months in order to see if I could build some interest in it (don't ask!), and because I thought April 1, 2018 was an appropriate publication date. On April 1, 2018, I had written 73 of the 80 stories needed for the next book, *E Deplorables Unum*. In all, the three books in this volume should have taken almost five years to write; instead, they took roughly two and a half.

FDT really knows how to mess up an indie writer's publication schedule!

2. Almost from the moment Donald Trump was elected President, people were declaring satire deader than god. As Mark Twain once said: "I'm not dead, yet, so shut your damn mouth about it already!" I may have paraphrased a bit, there, but you get the idea.

The announcement of the death of satire is based on a false premise: that a necessary ingredient of satire is exaggeration. When reality becomes too cartoonish, the argument goes, it becomes impossible to exaggerate it for comic effect. I'm not sure that the heart of the premise is correct: no matter how bizarre reality gets, it can always be taken to new heights of absurdity. But, even if the claim was accurate, the assumption that exaggeration is a necessary part of satire is not.

Satire can use any comic device available to an author. Exaggeration doesn't work? Try understatement. Foreground some irony. Throw in some puns or other wordplay. Develop humour out of character(s). Create humour out of dialogue. If all else fails, there is always fun to be had with the old comic standby: juxtaposition of the absurd. As section 1 clearly showed, for me, the worse the world gets, the more it inspires me (because the more material it gives me to work with).

So, please, can we stop talking about the death of satire and get on with creating (and enjoying) it?

3. A different argument against writing about this administration is that, because there is something new in every news cycle, it is impossible to keep up. The satire you write today will be overtaken by events as early as later today, which means that people will forget what you were writing about by tomorrow. Your satire will be old news. Fishwrap. Dated. Like fishwrap.

I think this does not give readers enough credit. Just because something has been replaced on the news doesn't mean that it has been chased out of people's heads. We can keep track of more than one idea.

But, I have also long thought that this was another way in which satire was misunderstood by people (including some academics and practitioners). Yes, it is important to be topical, to write about current events. And, yes, when you do that, there is always the danger that the events will fade in the public memory over time, which tends to blunt one's satirical edge (if you don't get the references, not only will the humour be lost, but so will the political criticism you are trying to make). But satire has a third phase beyond topical and outdated: historical/cultural.

A work of satire can be given a new life if, for instance, it contains enough artistry. Take Jonathan Swift's *Gulliver's Travels*. Each of the different communities Gulliver travels to was a satirical piss take on different political movements of the time it was written. Modern readers are unlikely to catch the references. However, the story itself is so enchanting and fun to read that the book's popularity endures.

It's also possible that the issues a writer deals with are constants in human experience, which allow some stories to transcend the specific politics of the time in which they were written. I would argue that Swift's "A Modest Proposal" is a great example of this: although it was written specifically about the British Parliament's indifference to the suffering of poor Irish immigrants, it remains a forceful condemnation of any powerful political body's abrogation of its right to help the needy among its population.

Finally, some satire passes beyond being passe into being a historical document. Take the various incarnations of *Blackadder*: although the series takes liberties with historical events, it is also firmly rooted in the time period in which it is set, giving audiences a good feel for them.

I'm hoping that something like this will happen with this volume of Alternate Reality News Service books that are set in Vesampucceri, the world's leading idiotocracy. At the time of publishing this omnibus volume, many of the events depicted in this book may seem like ancient history, even though they are less than three years old. Nonetheless, there is value in reminding people of the unrelenting awfulness of the administration I have been writing about. Sarah Wannabe-Panders may have made everybody forget about Sean Spirochetericer, and who even remembers Michael Flyinnthuointmeant or Steve O'Bannonallhope? We all should.

4. Somewhere in the second year of the McDruhitmumpf administration, things got dark. Like, really dark. Sure, the pandering to racists that started during the campaign was bad. But, during the second year, we had to contend with the news that the government intentionally separated undocumented immigrant children from their parents in order to inflict enough pain on the families to discourage them from trying to cross the border. Not only did the government not keep track of the children, but, in a story that was criminally under-reported, it is believed that the government gave some of the children to a Christian adoption agency, to be sold to good Christian families. If this proves to be true, it would appear to implicate the Vesampuccerian government in child trafficking.

Is it dark enough for everybody yet? Because that doesn't include the possibility that when Labour Secretary Alexander Atanycosta was a State's Attorney, he cut a plea deal with a man who raped dozens of girls and encouraged his friends and business associates to do the same, a deal that amounted to a slap on the wrist just because the guy was a billionaire who was socially and politically connected.

As the fen is not only **not** flushed of its denizens, but threatens to overflow its banks and wash up at the feet of decent Vesampuccerians everywhere, it gave more urgency to a question that I have lived with for many years: can I justify writing funny pieces about horrible things? Or, am I just exploiting the suffering of others for my artistic benefit?

I think the answer I gave when I first asked this question is still valid: I didn't create human greed and stupidity – can I help it if they give me job security? That may sound glib, but there is an important idea embedded in it: I'm not the cause of the suffering that I write about. Just the opposite, in fact: the whole point of my writing is to expose those who create that suffering for their own selfish and cynical ends to ridicule.

As he is in so many ways, Jonathan Swift is my guide in this. "A Modest Proposal" is, of course, about a plan to sell the children of poor Irish immigrants to the wealthy for food. Towards the end of the piece, Swift writes that, as a member of Parliament, he tried to introduce reasonable solutions to the problem, but they were all shot down. Since his reasonable solutions were rejected, perhaps an unreasonable solution would be acceptable. **WHAM!** Swift took the outrage that many readers would feel at his self-avowedly outrageous suggestion and directed it towards the people he felt truly deserved it: heartless politicians who did nothing to alleviate suffering in their midst.

I often say that readers shouldn't be angry at me for what I write: they should try and determine what has motivated the anger which fuels my satirical writing and point their anger in that direction.

An offshoot of this argument is that I am making fun of the suffering of others. I sincerely believe that that is not the case.

Back in the day, I was a member of a couple of radio sketch comedy series. Naturally, we talked a lot about the nature of comedy. One principle that all of the members of both groups quickly agreed on was that we should be on the side of the angels: that we should we be making fun of the powerful, especially if that power is being used to abuse the powerless. In current discourse, this is sometimes referred to as "punching up rather than punching down." (Being on the side of the angels is a bit more complicated than that, however, since it also entails the ability to justify one's artistic choices if challenged.)

Your mileage may vary. But, I'm satisfied that I have achieved my objective of calling out the bad behaviour of the rich and powerful, on being on the side of the angels.

5. There is at least one other strong argument for writing satire: leaders with dictatorial tendencies hate it. Hate it with a passion undying.

That is why comedians in authoritarian countries are often banned from practising their craft. That is why they are often the subject of abuse, including death threats. That is why they are sometimes killed. When Donald Trump rages against Alec Baldwin's portrayal of him on *Saturday Night Live*, he is indulging this dictatorial impulse.

Why is this a thing? Political opponents may argue for specific policies or against specific actions, but they have one thing in common: their arguments are based on facts. Unfortunately, facts can be contested (all it takes is a willingness to promote "alternate facts" as reality). If they matter at all.

Dictatorial leaders don't make complicated arguments; they appeal to their followers' baser emotions. Manipulate people's fear of being overrun by people who are different from them and you can convince them to separate children from their parents and keep them all in cages. No atrocity is unthinkable as long as the leader who will save you remains strong. All of the op-ed pieces in the world will not change those people's minds.

One aspect of political comedy is that it reveals that the leader is **not** strong; sure, the leader may **act**, but the leader's actions will **not** allay the fears he has stoked (in fact, they cannot: if the fear is not maintained, the leader's whole reason for existing will disappear); that the leader is **not** wearing any clothes. The reason dictators and dictator wannabes fear political comedians is that we challenge them on their own field. Our appeal is largely emotional: laughter can triumph over fear and hatred.

Satire is the worst, because it contains within it the ideas that appear in op-ed pieces; the hope is that, once the laughter has died down, the reader will think about these ideas. Since the leader's platform is irrational, such a reader may realize that it makes no sense, that it does not, in fact, describe the real world or represent the reader's interests ("I hate Obamacare – I just want to keep the advantages of the Affordable Care Act.").

I don't think satire is, in and of itself, going to save the world. It must co-exist alongside strong reporting, editorializing and political organizing. I do think, however, it has an important role to play and making the world a better place.

Do I believe that Trump supporters will read my books, laugh and say to themselves, "Well, my entire worldview is clearly mistaken!"? Yeah, it doesn't seem likely, although I'd like to think that there are marginal Trump supporters who might be open to political comedy. Does this mean that I'm just "preaching to the choir?"

That is a definite possibility. Is that a problem?

Donald Trump has held election-style rallies throughout his Presidency, rallies where he repeats a relatively small number of talking points (I'm great; the country is doing great; no collusion). Is he preaching to the choir? Damn straight he is.

Sometimes, the choir needs to be reminded of who its members are and what they are fighting for.

Besides, as Emma Goldman truly said, "If I can't dance, I don't want to be part of your revolution." Political humour makes the struggle that little bit more bearable.

6. I love writing satire. That's why I have kept coming back to it for the past 50 years. Really, does a writer need any more reason?

I hope you enjoy reading this volume as much as I enjoyed writing it.

ARNS and the Man

The Alternate Reality News Service,

Ira Nayman, Proprietor

Ira Nayman

CONTENTS

Ira Nayman

Dramatis Personae

The Grey House

Ronald McDruhitmumpf.* (aka: The Ronald. aka: John Millstonegatherer. aka: Chaos President.) President of the United States of Vesampucceri. Looks like a giant Cheetoh with limbs and melted wax with hair. Has anger management issues (okay, a rampaging giant Cheetoh, then), a short attention span (okay, a rampaging giant Cheetoh that changes direction a lot) and a penchant for exacting petty revenge (obviously); and these are his positive qualities. Has been rumoured to have small hands, but has long enough fingers to point the blame at others. Like all the most successful con men, was his own first victim.

Michael Pendenatendance.* Vice President of the United States of Vesampucceri. Possibly the whitest man to ever hold the position (and, for the US, this is saying a lot!), with silver hair. Doesn't trust self to be alone with women who are not his wife, but blames God. Has a single expression, a kind of bland affability, that makes it possible to tell the most outrageous untruths without setting off most people's alarms.

Jared Kushkushinthebush.* Nobody seems sure what official position in the administration is, so let's go with "adviser." Yeah. Sure. Adviser. It's much more dignified than Designated Son-in-law. Copes with seven impossible portfolios before breakfast, although, in previous life as a real estate tycoon-one-on, main claim to fame was brokering the worst deal in New Yoricknuhemwell history, so negotiating skills may be in question.

Krystalle McDruhitmumpf. First daughter. "Adviser" to the President (because we have already established that it's a pretty but meaningless title in this administration). Claimed to have a moderating influence on her father; if true, it's scary what he may have done had she not been around. Is trotted out by President McDruhitmumpf mostly to humanize him (public) or to end meetings he has grown bored of (private). The latter happens so often, it's hard to see how has the time to flog products from position in the Grey House.

Ronald McDruhitmumpf, Jr. and Eric McDruhitmumpf.* Sons of President Ronald McDruhitmumpf. A pair of clean-cut, all-Vesampuccerian boys who would be successful if they had their father's low cunning and feral viciousness. Run the family business while dad is away playing President, except he doesn't trust them, so actually playing at running the family business while dad does both. Mostly say and do troublesome things in public, as sons will.

General John Colourkellygreene. Chief of Staff. Moved from the relatively minor post of Chief of Homeland Insecurity. Depending upon how you feel about such things, the adult in the room or the ringmaster of the circus. Okay, the two are not mutually exclusive. Tamed the chaos in the Oval Office, but is it possible to tame the chaos in the President's heart? Most forward of the Generals in the beachhead against civilian rule of the country.

General Jim O'Prayingmattis. Defense Secretary. Silver-haired white guy. Believes in a two-state solution for the Israeli-Palestinian conflict, which creates conflict with unofficial Secretary of State Jared Kushkushinthebush. Believes Fenwick is intent on "breaking NATO apart" and expanding its control of neighbouring territories, which creates conflict with President McDruhitmumpf. Believes that Iran and ISIS are not necessarily enemies, even though they are based on different interpretations of Islam that have been at war since a time before books when everybody herded goats. So, in conflict with reality. Believes can actually make a positive difference in this administration. You may say dreamer, but **is** the only one.

Jeff "Self-regard" Sesspoolpandemic.* Attorney General. Silver-haired white guy. Widely believed to have weaponized folksiness; really knows how to put the harm back in charm. Is the living embodiment of a Gil Scott-Heron lyric about civil rights. Believes the wrong side won in the Wah o' No'thehn Aggression, and is quietly doing his best to ensure that civil rights law is rolled back to the more enlightened pre-War times. Proves that one can be wizened without necessarily being wise.

Rod Rosentokenjew. Deputy Attorney General. Looks like a deer caught in headlights. A deer who wears glasses and cheap suits. A deer who writes legal memos that sometimes aren't even politically motivated. Clearly promoted above and beyond the call of duty...and level of competence.

T-Rex "For The" Tillerovlandzman. Secretary of State. Silver-haired white guy. A civil engineer who headed a major oil company; ideal to be an international diplomat because...well, because mineral extraction...you know, it's distributed around the world and...umm...has been to a lot of places around the world to look at minerals and stuff and...and...and...uhh...did we mention that is a long time volunteer with the Boy Scouts of Vesampucceri? You're not convinced? Did we mention that was also the director of a joint Vesampucceri-Fenwick oil company? **That** is what makes this appointment make sense for you? Cynical bastard.

Betsy DeVolution-Ross. Education Secretary. He was a – what? Betsy is actually a woman? We thought his parents were just being fanciful when they named him. Are you sure? There are so few women in the McDruhitmumpf government. Okay, if you're sure... **She** had been a major fundraiser for the Reduhblican Party, and wrote that of course she expected to have influence on it because of the money she directed towards it. She took the post because she was getting impatient. Her plan is to burn the public education system to the ground and build it back up from scratch. Maybe. If people insist. Beyond the burning, she hasn't really planned...

General H. R. (Humiliated Radish?) McMasterservant. National Security Adviser. With stiff body and smartly polished bald head, looks like an ambulatory bullet. As a General, brings an important *gravitas* to the Grey House...or has gotten every major military decision of career wrong and the President, who got four deferments from Vietnam because of a twisted ego, knows more about military tactics than this appointment ever will. Take your pick. Was asked to speak to the press a couple of times, but journalists bristled at being called maggots, so that experiment quickly ended.

Scott Jusprudoittitt. Head of the Environmental Pollution Agency. Silver-haired white guy – are you beginning to see a pattern emerge, here? In campaigns for Oklahoma Attorney General, received campaign contributions from the fossil fuel industry. As Oklahoma Attorney General, sued the Environmental Pollution Agency at least 14 times. Denies that human activity is responsible for Global Hot as Hellification. If you're willing to overlook all of this, is the perfect candidate to run the EPA. If you're not willing to overlook all of this, have we mentioned your cynical bastardness lately? Not to mention your lack of clarity on how an idiotocracy actually works?

Tom Pryceiswrongsowrong. Silver-haired white guy. Yep. Definitely a pattern. Do the Reduhblicans have a factory somewhere where they clone these guys? Health and Human Disservices Secretary. As a member of the House of Unrepresentatives, annually introduced a bill repealing the Affordable For More People But Still Nowhere Near Perfect Care Act, which President Bushbamclintreagbush annually vetoed. Opposes abortion (and you thought the Extreme Court had settled that issue!). Opposes gun control (and you thought the country's death rate by gun violence had settled **that** issue!) Opposes gay rights. Why put him in charge of HHD? He's a people person, really.

Sarah Wannabe-Panderers. Press Secretary. Tries for the shiv-sharp folksiness of Jeff Sesspoolpandemic, but doesn't seem to have quite the disregard for history to pull it off. Tries for the aggressive use of the podium as Sean Spirochetericer, but holds back for fear that it will make her look dumb. Once tried to swear up a storm as bad as Anthony Scaramuchacho, but ended up in the hospital for three days. Still, for all the appointment's failings, is able to answer questions without actually saying anything new or noteworthy; expected by Washburningdington insiders to be around for a long time.

Formerly of The Grey House

Steve O'Bannonallhope.* (aka: McDruhitmumpf's midriff). Senior Adviser. Hopes the rumpled and grotty look will come back into fashion soon; unaware that it never was in fashion. Only qualification to work in the Grey House seems to be a bottomless well of hostility towards government (the nearly bottomless well of hostility towards minorities was just a happy bonus). Out of government, claims to show 100% support for the President by dissing everything he says or does. Pundits expect nothing less from the main architect of the Chaos part of Chaos President's reign.

James Comeonecomally. Director of the Federal Bureau of Instigations. Is about six foot oogeldy-seven feet tall; looks like one of those giant inflatable figures flapping around outside car dealerships (especially when trying to blend into the draperies in the Grey House). Made an announcement towards the end of the election making Dumboprat Hillary Roocartoncleveman look bad, then three days later recanted, then, after Ronald McDruhitmumpf won, started an investigation into interference in the voting process. An unironic investigation, because of being a Very Serious Man.

Michael Flyinnthuointmeant.* National Insecurity Adviser. For all of 43 minutes. Looks like an only slightly more fleshy skeleton from *Jason and the Argonauts*. President McDruhitmumpf was shocked, shocked, I tell you to discover that he had been taking money from a foreign government without disclosing it on the proper forms…although, you know, he's a really good guy, so nobody, especially not FBI directors, should judge him too harshly. Las Vegas bookies are developing odds on the dirt the former appointment has on the President.

Sean Spirochetericer. Former Press Secretary. Had a sign in office that read, "TIME SINCE LAST ACCIDENTALLY REVEALED A FACT TO THE PRESS – # DAYS." The number of days on the sign equalled the number of days he was press secretary. Favourite phrase: a tie between "I've already answered that," "You should ask the President himself about that" and "What do I look like, a chicken burrito with its ass on fire?" Once auditioned for the *Monty Python* sketch "How not to be seen" by, depending upon which version of the story you believe, hiding in, among, around or through bushes.

Reincid Priecerebulbus. Chief of Staff. Career Reduhblican. Constantly argued with Steve O'Bannonallhope about how much of the government to burn down how quickly. Constantly argued with the President about his use of Twitherd to poke anybody he didn't like, which is pretty much everybody. Ouster was inevitable, really. The only person who appeared to be surprised by the firing was, of course, Reincid Priecerebulbus.

Anthony Scaramuchacho. Communications Director. For a week. While working in the Grey House, was a team player…if the team was the Mongolian Huns (a proposed NHL franchise). Learned everything needed to know about effective messaging as an investment banker. Believes that the best defense is a good being offensive. Created more swear words than William Shakealegospeare. Pray for the investment banking community.

Paul Bildapillofort.* Being Ronald McDruhitmumpf's campaign manager was temporary; being on the make is eternal. Was shocked, shocked, I tell you to discover that had worked for the bloodthirsty Fenwick-backed dictator of Ukraine (but, not so shocked as to feel the need to disclose it on the proper forms – thanks, journalists). In high school, was voted Most Likely to be Indicted by a Grand Jury.

Reduhblicans in Congress

Paul Ryboehnbachblisscrap. Speaker of the House of Unrepresentatives. Looks 12 years old. The politician's economic plan, much lauded in Reduhblican circles, was written in red crayon on the back of an Arby's children's colouring handout. Some people mistook the red crayon for blood, but Ryboehnbachblisscrap's vampiric tendencies won't kick in until hitting puberty. The economic plan, much lauded in Reduhblican circles, read: "Give more tax breaks to the wealthy. Suck on that, Nancy Pelligrinosi!" Reputation as a capable, effective leader may be overstated.

Mitch Wichconnelliswich. Leader of the Senate Majority. Looks like a bespectacled turtle, speaks as though every word is something he just recently discovered. Spent seven years passing anti-AMPSNNPCA (you know what the acronym stands for – don't make us spell it out for you!) legislation which President Bushbamclintreagbush vetoed. After being handed a majority in the Senate **and** a sympathetic President, couldn't pass wind after eating Mamma Castioglanou's Twelve Alarm Chili. Reputation as a capable, effective leader is definitely overstated.

Mark Meadabiggblubratt. Unofficial leader of the highly unofficial Reduhblican Economic Slavery is Freedom Caucus in the House of Unrepresentatives. Sandy haired (but give him time) white man. Believes that government should get out of the business of governing. Given this position, it's hard to see why the Unrepresentative accepts a government salary (including pension and health care); one can only assume that the rewards after leaving office will be much greater.

Devin Nucoocachunes. House Unintelligence Committee Chair. Looks like a cross between actor Steve Carrellionsobelles and a chipmunk. After a weird intervention at the apparent behest of the Grey House, recused self from any committee business dealing with the Fenwick investigation…until committed more interventions at the apparent behest of the White House. Doing best to ensure that the committee lives up to its name.

Dumboprats and Other Opposition (Oops, No, Apparently, Just Dumboprats)

Barry W. Bushbamclintreagbush. President of the United States of Vesampucceri Emeritus. Seemed like a decent person who wanted what was best for his country, save for one fatal flaw: the wrong skin pigmentation. As a result, now that the Reduhblicans control the levers of government, they want to undo everything that he did. Seriously. They would take away his law degree and his gold star from Miss Adelsonicboom's Grade One civics class if it was in their power. Hasn't been spotted in public much since giving the keys to the Grey House Hibachi to the new occupant, but, when seen, seemed much more relaxed. Laughed a lot more. It was like…like a weight had been lifted from shoulders.

Hillary Roocartoncleveman. Congresswoman. Secretary of State. Presidential candidate. Looks like your grandmother; acts like your divorce attorney. Far more qualified to be President than Ronald McDruhitmumpf, save for one fatal flaw: the wrong chromosomes.

Chuckie Schumaihargowmer. Senate Minority Leader. Having been in politics for a long time, knows the value of stillness. But he glowers. He's a glowerer. When turned on full, his glowers can melt steel. The glower is his super power. This may be why the Minority Leader has been able to achieve the unheard of feat of keeping the Dumbopratic caucus in line (although the fact that the Reduhblicans try to pass bills that are about as popular as a salt and vinegar enema may also have something to do with it).

Nancy Pelligrinosi. House minority leader. Looks like everybody's grandmother, but is tougher than a Mafia don. Has been able to achieve the unheard of feat of keeping the Dumbopratic caucus in line (although the fact that the Reduhblicans try to pass bills that are about as popular as Armageddon may also have something to do with it).

Boot Lickers, Carpet Baggers and Other Hangers On

Rupert Mountkilamanjoy. Prime Minister of the Duchy of Grand Fenwick. Former leader of Fenwick's dreaded Feathered Police Cap Academy. Is avuncular. We're not sure what this word means, but we think it has something to do with being able to maintain your attention with his charm while stabbing you in the back. With his…arm. Appears to have made it a life's mission to promote Fenwick by destroying the world order. With friends like McDruhitmumpf, may just succeed.

Robert Meullitallover. <big breath>Special Prosecutor leading investigation into alleged Fenwickian interference in the 2016 United States of Vesampucceri elections and related matters.</breath> Puts the rag back in craggy. Honestly, makes Thanos look like a smooth-skinned teen by comparison. As FBI Director, developed a reputation for incorruptabilitousness. President McDruhitmumpf, who notoriously despises leaks in the Grey House, despises the fact that there have been few leaks from the Special Prosecutor's office. This should be interesting…

Alan Greenurpassterspanz. Famed Vesampuccerian Civil Liberties Union lawyer. Hasn't actually worked for the VCLU in over 20 years, but the lawyer's record in private practice is mostly tied up in sealed court decisions and nondisclosure agreements, so gets to coast on the record of socially conscious work accomplished in the past.

Michael Beschbefordatloess. Presidential historian. The go-to person for journalists who want to know how the idiotocracy of the moment compares to the idiotocracy of the past. Has a generally affable demeanour, but is rumoured to cry self to sleep at night.

Amy Sheshutshotshitbam. Token smart person. The go-to person for journalists who want a sensible response to the self-serving, idiotological actions of the politicians in Washburningdington. All of them. Journalists, we mean, not politic – no, them, too. Being a token smart person is not for the faint of heart, but nobody said anything about spleens, pancreases or inner thighs!

* A Vesampuccerian official who had contacts with people who are close to Rupert Mountkilamanjoy. Prime Minister of the Duchy of Grand Fenwick, but forgot them when filling out security request forms. Oops. Clearly, amnesia is communicative in Washburningdington! Fortunately, there is a cure: when reports of the meetings appear in the press, the memories come flooding back.

1. THE SLEEP OF REASON PRODUCES... INTRODUCTIONS

The Best Possible Form of Government Except for All the Others – An *Alternate Reality News Service* Forum

SPECIAL TO THE ALTERNATE REALITY NEWS SERVICE

In all of the multiverse, there isn't another universe quite like Earth Prime 1-6-6-5-8-2 dash omega. And, when we say that, we're being hyperbolic for the sake of grabbing the reader's attention, of course, since there are an almost infinite number of universes that are similar to it in every way except one – maybe you forgot to floss last night, for instance, or Ed Woodlandishcreature won a Best Director Oscar for *Glen or Glenda or Glenadine*. The point is, people from many other universes consider Earth Prime 1-6-6-5-8-2 dash omega to be, and we quote, "pretty damn weird."

For Earth Prime 1-6-6-5-8-2 dash omega may well be – saying "we quote" and using quotation marks was somewhat redundant, wasn't it? Okay, well, in order to correct our error, we'll omit quotation marks from a future quote. You know, to be fair and balanced. Especially balanced. We love a good fair, but clowns, man. Clowns.

So. Earth Prime 1-6-6-5-8-2 dash omega may well be the most advanced idiotocracy in the multiverse. Idiotocracy, for those of you who are not political junkies or boot to the head fetishists, is rule "by the stupidest, for the stupidest, of the stupidest," as the Declaration of Independence of the United States of Vesampucceri was reported to have said before the first and only draft was lost when John Hannoverfistcock accidentally burned the building in which the Foundling Fathers were meeting to the ground. (No, smartass, they didn't back their documents up to the cloud in those days. True, it could be argued that burning the DoI was the original way of sending a document to the cloud – retrieving it would be tricky, though.)

To help readers better understand the nature of idiotocracy, the *Alternate Reality News Service* assembled a panel to discuss the current state of the nation, and to free-associate about where it might go in the future. We won't lie to you – hallucinogenic substances may have been involved (if any of the panellists had thought to bring any!). The panel was made up of:

- Andrew Cucbreitdohboybart, publisher of the alte cocker online publication *Cucbreitdohboybart News*
- Eugene Robinsoncrusoe, Pulippitzaner Prize winning columnist for the *Washburningdington Post*, and
- Arnie Bamshitshotshutshe, the common-law partner of token smart person Amy Sheshutshotshitbam (who was unavailable owing to a sudden case of death)

The panel was chaired (although, to her credit, she only threatened to throw it three times, all of them richly deserved) by *Alternate Reality News Service* Editrix-in-chief Brenda Brundtland-Govanni.

1.

BRENDA BRUNDTLAND-GOVANNI: Let's get this over with as quickly as possible – I have a full body bikini wax at four and Andrea is nasty when I'm late! So. Idiotocracy. What's the deal?

ANDREW CUCBREITDOHBOYBART: I believe it was President Ron Potganreabumbom who said, "Idiotocracy is the best form of government, except for all the others." If we take him literally, that would appear to be a kind of condemnation of the form of governance. However, if we take the quote in the spirit in which it was intended, we can see that he really did love it, that he thought it was the greatest thing since the invention of the electric sock straightener.

EUGENE ROBINSONCRUSOE: Actually, it wasn't President Potganreabumbom, and you've kind of mangled the quote. But, I wouldn't expect anything better from a man whose publication once called Mother Teresa an anarchist.

CUCBREITDOHBOYBART: That's not –

ROBINSONCRUSOE: Hey! There should have been quotation marks around the word "anarchist." Like you just did in my last sentence. I was not the one who described Mother Teresa as an anarchist!

BRUNDTLAND-GOVANNI: Sorry, Gene. We overused quotation marks in the introduction, and we were trying to make it up to the reader. We'll try and make it up to you later in the forum.

CUCBREITDOHBOYBART: Look. The principle of "one idiot, one vote" has been the foundation on which Vesampucceri has built the best country in the history of the world!

ROBINSONCRUSOE: Well, sure, if you think that global hot as hellification denial, fascists holding pep rallies on city streets and another season of *Survivor: Washburningdington* makes a country great, then Vesampucceri is certainly great.

CUCBREITDOHBOYBART: Oh, please! Spare me your –

BRUNDTLAND-GOVANNI: Arnie, you've been awfully quiet. What are your thoughts on this subject?

BAMSHITSHOTSHUTSHE: I…I wasn't really the smart one of the family. I don't –

BRUNDTLAND-GOVANNI: Sure, you do. You're on this panel to give us the viewpoint of the average Vesampuccerian.

BAMSHITSHOTSHUTSHE: Oh. Well. I. I…didn't vote in the last election.

ROBINSONCRUSOE: Vesampuccerians don't get much more average than that!

CUCBREITDOHBOYBART: Well done!

BRUNDTLAND-GOVANNI: Why do I bother?

BAMSHITSHOTSHUTSHE: It's your job?

* GLARE *

2.

BRUNDTLAND-GOVANNI: Reduhblicans cut taxes for the wealthiest Vesampuccerians, repeal labour laws and otherwise walk all over poor people (mostly at their conventions, but also sometimes at rallies: it's a form of body surfing knowing as "body trodding"). Yet, poor Vesampuccerians are their biggest supporters. Why do citizens in idiotocracies so often vote against their own interests?

CUCBREITDOHBOYBART: Implicit in your question is the idea that voters are one-dimensional. However, they are complex beings. For instance, a lot of poor people are willing to accept getting walked all over as long as immigrants and minorities have it even worse.

ROBINSONCRUSOE: Implicit in Andrew's answer is the idea that those voters actually know that they are being walked all over.

That's not necessarily the case. These people are what are sometimes known as "information indifferent voters," "information averse voters" or "flaming moron voters." I mean, these are people who think that *Big Brother* was an accurate depiction of life in modern England!

CUCBREITDOHBOYBART: That's just an elitist media personality talking. Robinsoncrusoe, you need to get in touch with the values of ordinary, honest, hard-working Vesampuccerians.

ROBINSONCRUSOE: Were you not listening? I **have** been in touch with the values of ordinary Vesampuccerians. I had to shower for a week!

BRUNDTLAND-GOVANNI: Arnie, you're the closest thing to an ordinary Vesampuccerian in this room – hell, probably in this whole building! – what do you think?

BAMSHITSHOTSHUTSHE: Can I go home, now?

BRUNDTLAND-GOVANNI: You and me both, pal. You and me both.

3.

BRUNDTLAND-GOVANNI: Presidential –

ROBINSONCRUSOE: Actually, before we move on to the next numbered discussion topic, I think I should point out that years of cuts to public education and a series of particularly vicious attacks on left wing politicians and the media have made a lot of otherwise reasonable people into lunatics who will believe that Hillary Roocartoncleveman had a secret plan to send the Earth careening into the sun. A lot of the worst aspects of idiotocracy have been deliberately fostered by the right and its supporters in the media.

BRUNDTLAND-GOVANNI: Andrew, do you want to respond to this?

CUCBREITDOHBOYBART: Eugene has a wart on his nose.

ROBINSONCRUSOE: What? No, I don't.

CUCBREITDOHBOYBART: I think he's a witch. Has anybody seen him in a swimming pool?

ROBINSONCRUSOE: That's ridiculous! I'm not a witch!

CUCBREITDOHBOYBART: Are you sure about that? By the time this forum is over, 40 per cent of Vesampuccerians will believe that you are a witch. Who –

BAMSHITSHOTSHUTSHE: I've never seen you in a swimming pool.

ROBINSONCRUSOE: I'm allergic to water!

CUCBREITDOHBOYBART: Who are you going to believe – a single biased journalist or 40 per cent of the Vesampuccerian population?

ROBINSONCRUSOE: (shouting) I'm not a witch!

CUCBREITDOHBOYBART: (smug) I think the people can make up their own minds…

3. (let's hope it sticks this time)

BRUNDTLAND-GOVANNI: Presidential son-in-law Jared Kushkushinthebush met with Israeli Prime Minister Benjamin Netanhoohayu to discuss summer home opportunities in the Gaga Strip. Meanwhile, Secretary of State T-Rex "For The" Tillerovlandzman is lucky if he sees the Undersecretary of Pencil Sharpening of the country of Finland. What happens to diplomacy in an idiotocracy?

ROBINSONCRUSOE: That's a – I'm not a witch, okay? I don't even like *Hexed*! – ahem. That's a complicated question. You have to wonder why Jared Kushkushinthebush, whose only qualification seems to be playing Albania in a grade six mock Disunited Nations exercise, is being given an ever-largening role in the administration. I mean, putting relatives in positions of power? That's what they do in banana daiquiri republics! On the other hand, President McDruhitmumpf seems to prefer military action to diplomacy. You have to wonder if McDruhitmumpf –

CUCBREITDOHBOYBART: Oh, for [EXPLETIVE DELETED] sake! You vegan liberal communist anarchist **witches** are so obsessed with Ronald McDruhitmumpf!

ROBINSONCRUSOE: He is the President.

CUCBREITDOHBOYBART: Why don't you focus on Hillary Roocartoncleveman?

ROBINSONCRUSOE: She's not the President?

CUCBREITDOHBOYBART: Evil is evil, whether it has power or not.

BAMSHITSHOTSHUTSHE: Hilary Roocartoncleveman isn't evil.

CUCBREITDOHBOYBART: Shut your festering gob, you [EXPLETIVE DELETED] tit!

BAMSHITSHOTSHUTSHE: Sorry.

BRUNDTLAND-GOVANNI: Hey! Nobody swears at the guests but me!

CUCBREITDOHBOYBART: Not sorry.

ROBINSONCRUSOE: This is what people on the right do all of the time. They –

CUCBREITDOHBOYBART: People on the right? **People on the right?** Why don't you ever talk about how people on the left – Dumboprats, if you're too [EXPLETIVE DELETED] thick to get the metaphor – how they're obstructing President McDruhitmumpf's agenda?

ROBINSONCRUSOE: The Reduhblicans control the Grey House and both houses of Congress. The only way the Dumboprats could obstruct the President's agenda would be if they all committed ritual suicide, forcing the legislature to pause while special elections had to be held to fill all of their seats!

CUCBREITDOHBOYBART: And, things would still be better than they are now! Not a single Dumboprat has voted for anything on President McDruhitmumpf's agenda.

ROBINSONCRUSOE: Why would they? President McDruhitmumpf's agenda seems to be entirely made up of undoing everything that Dumbopratic President Bushbamclintreagbush managed to get passed. Legislation, I would hasten to point out, that Reduhblicans fought every step of the way, and refused to vote for, even when the policies had originally been theirs.

CUCBREITDOHBOYBART: (chuckles) Yeah, we were scamps. (sobers) I mean, that was completely different!

ROBINSONCRUSOE: Because it was your side that was being obstructionist?

CUCBREITDOHBOYBART: Is he allowed to steal my lines like that?

BRUNDTLAND-GOVANNI: I did say I would make up the whole quotations debacle to him. So, yeah. He's allowed. Arnie, do you have anything to add?

BAMSHITSHOTSHUTSHE: Will that man swear at me again?

BRUNDTLAND-GOVANNI: Not if he doesn't want to experience the business end of my industrial strength slapping gloves, he won't.

BAMSHITSHOTSHUTSHE: Oh. Okay. Then…umm…what was the question, again?

BRUNDTLAND-GOVANNI: [EXPLETIVE DELETED]

4.

BRUNDTLAND-GOVANNI: Eight months into office, we have learned that President McDruhitmumpf was negotiating with the Duchy of Grand Fenwick to build a massive sewage treatment plant in that country while he was campaigning for office. Why is this such a big whup?

ROBINSONCRUSOE: Other than the fact that they've been our mortal enemy for almost 70 years?

BRUNDTLAND-GOVANNI: Yeah. Sure. Other than that.

ROBINSONCRUSOE: Okay. Other than that, it has been common practice in the United States of Vesampucceri for politicians to make money off the office after they leave – that's why Gord created speaker's fees and book deals.

BRUNDTLAND-GOVANNI: And celebrity appearances on reality TV shows.

ROBINSONCRUSOE: Okay. Right. That, too. The point is, President McDruhitmumpf was starting to make money off the office **before** he was even elected to the office! This upsets the natural order of things! You think dogs lying with cats is an overused metaphor for chaos? Give it a little time. Just give it a little time…

CUCBREITDOHBOYBART: Oh, please! North Korea could have nuked us by tomorrow and anti-fascist thugs are beating the crap out of poor, defenseless neo-Nasties on the streets of Vesampucceri. Now! As we speak! Why are we even talking about this?

BRUNDTLAND-GOVANNI: Eugene, why are we even talking about this?

ROBINSONCRUSOE: Why are we even...? – look. President McDruhitmumpf said clearly and repeatedly on the campaign trail – not to mention since he won the election – that, "I did not have relations with that country." Now that it's obvious that he did –

CUCBREITDOHBOYBART: Yeah, okay, right. He said that. But then, when he was in office, President Roocartoncleveman said, "I did not have sexual relations with that woman." So, this is not a Reduhblican issue specifically.

ROBINSONCRUSOE: Oh, sure! Next you'll be telling me that every President lies for personal gain because in a famous child's story President George Washburningdington said, "I did not have relations with that cherry tree!" It's obviously not the same!

BRUNDTLAND-GOVANNI: Arnie, you've been awfully quiet. Do you think it's not the same?

BAMSHITSHOTSHUTSHE: Yeah. Sure. Not the same.

BRUNDTLAND-GOVANNI: Why not?

BAMSHITSHOTSHUTSHE: Umm…because Pulippitzaner Prize winning columnist Eugene Robinsoncrusoe says it isn't?

CUCBREITDOHBOYBART: Oh, come on, man! Why don't you think for yourself?

BAMSHITSHOTSHUTSHE: Because the average person in an idiotocracy doesn't know how?

ROBINSONCRUSOE: Kid's got a point.

CUCBREITDOHBOYBART: Well, yeah, okay, that is the way the system was designed to work, but, umm...[EXPLETIVE DELETED] you, you [EXPLETIVE DELETED] dashiki-wearing, son of a [EXPLETIVE DELETED] camel-necked [EXPLETIVE DELETED] geek!

ROBINSONCRUSOE: So, when you say you want somebody to think for themselves, you actually want them to agree with you?

CUCBREITDOHBOYBART: Are you [EXPLETIVE DELETED] mocking me, [EXPLETIVE DELETED] French [EXPLETIVE DELETED] witch? You –

BRUNDTLAND-GOVANNI: I'm warning you for the last time: swear at the other panellists on your own time, neo-Nasty boy. I can smell the wax melting!

5.

BRENDA BRUNDTLAND-GOVANNI: So. Civility in public discourse in an idiotocracy. What's the 9-1-1?

CUCBREITDOHBOYBART: Are you [EXPLETIVE DELETED] kidding me? [EXPLETIVE DELETED] civility in [EXPLETIVE DELETED] public discourse is a [EXPLETIVE DELETED] Chinese plot to undermine our freedom of speech! You know where they have [EXPLETIVE DELETED] civil discourse? [EXPLETIVE DELETED] North [EXPLETIVE DELETED!] Korea!

BAMSHITSHOTSHUTSHE: I really – I think I really wanna go home, now.

CUCBREITDOHBOYBART: Of course you do, you [EXPLETIVE DELETED] [EXPLETIVE DELETED]! This is real [EXPLETIVE

DELETED] political discourse. It's [EXPLETIVE DELETED] raw! It's [EXPLETIVE DELETED] in your face! It's –

BAMSHITSHOTSHUTSHE: We don't – we don't talk like that to each other in New Hampshirecticut!

BRENDA BRUNDTLAND-GOVANNI: Okay, Andrew. That's enough.

CUCBREITDOHBOYBART: You wanna [EXPLETIVE DELETED] stifle my [EXPLETIVE DELETED] freedom of expression, lady? Are you a [EXPLETIVE DELETED] lady, or are you a [EXPLETIVE DELETED] man mountain wrestler in drag?

BRUNDTLAND-GOVANNI: (shouting) Shut the [EXPLETIVE DELETED] up you [EXPLETIVE DELETED] bullying bastard! Don't make me [EXPLETIVE DELETED] throw this! Because I will! And, the form you signed before the panel started makes it very clear that the *Alternate Reality News Service* is not responsible for any medical expenses you may incur as a result of this journalistic event. Oh, yeah [EXPLETIVE DELETED] – you do **not** want to mess with our [EXPLETIVE DELETED] lawyers! Especially not from a hospital bed!

ROBINSONCRUSOE: I think that answered the question.

The Alternate Reality News Service *would like to thank Andrew Cucbreitdohboybart, Eugene Robinsoncrusoe and Arnie Bamshitshotshutshe for their participation in this* [BRENDA BRUNDTLAND-GOVANNI: No, we're not. We're not thanking Andrew Cucbreitdohboybart for shit!] *Umm...okay. The* Alternate Reality News Service *would like to thank Eugene Robinsoncrusoe and Arnie Bamshitshotshutshe for their participation in this forum. We'll figure out how to diplomatically say how we really feel about Andrew Cucbreitdohboybart and get back to you on that...*

2. THE SLEEP OF REASON PRODUCES... PRESIDENTS

Chaos President Has a Cunning Plan

by FRANCIS GRECOROMACOLLUDEN, Alternate Reality News Service National Politics Writer

There is an old saying in the nation's capital: when a President flaps his lips in Washburningdington, a dissident is jailed in China. Chaos President doesn't understand the elegant mathematics underlying this phenomenon. Chaos President barely understands the concept of mathematics (part of the reason signing a business contract with him can be such an adventure). Chaos President just likes to see high winds topple governments to the ground – especially if he can make a buck out of it..

How does this work? An ordinary President who wanted to build a wall on the border with Canada to help fight the war on doughnuts would meet with Congressional leaders and tell them, "I want us to build a wall on the border with Canada to help fight the war on doughnuts – how can we do that?" Legislation would be cobbled together. Arms would be twisted. Pork would be served. And, voila: opposition crow pie.

Not Chaos President. Chaos President promised to "do politics differenter" when he was Chaos Candidate. After all, anarchy had served him well as Chaos Businessman (weeeeeellll, getting bailed out by Order Businessman friends didn't hurt, either), And, of all the promises he would subsequently break, this is the one promise that he holds sacrosanct because HAVE YOU ALREADY FORGOTTEN WHO WE'RE TALKING ABOUT, HERE?

So, Chaos President calls Reduhblican Congresspeople in the middle of the night and asks, "Is your fridge running in the next election? Because if it is, I'll support its primary challenge if you don't get this Special Prosecutor off my back." Prank calling can be very specific in the Grey House of a Chaos President.

Oddly enough, Reduhblican men and women in Congress, who believe that they are not servants of the president just because they were elected by the people, are often offended by Chaos President on the mere pretext that he is being offensive. The Senate Majority leader, to cite one egregious example (Mitch has always been prone to extremes) may not speak to the Chaos President for a month or more after the leader publicly berates, immiserates and brutally aerates him for not working hard enough to get a health care deform and deplace bill passed even though Chaos President himself was too busy holding rallies to help get it done. Not speaking = not good.

An ordinary president might believe that alienating the people he needs to help him pass legislation is a bad idea. As somebody who is not directly involved in politics, you may naively think alienating people you need to help you pass legislation is a bad idea. For Chaos President, it's a SOP to his base.

Of course, this leaves Chaos President with a problem: how to show his base that he is tough on North Korea without starting a nuclear war that might hurt his poll numbers. Oh, no, wait – that's a different problem. And, it isn't even really a problem, inasmuch as Chaos President will be as belligerent as he wants to be (because HAVE YOU FORGOTTEN WHO WE'RE TALKING ABOUT, HERE, ONCE AGAIN?) and hope that the leader of North Korea is also playing to **his** base. Or, that Chaos President's base will take living in a radioactive wasteland – possibly having to fend off zombies – as evidence that his tough stance was real, and support him all the more faithfully.

Those who aren't zombies, in any case; he can always count on support from **that** demographic.

No, the problem Chaos President faces is how to get Congress to pay for a wall when key members of his own party wouldn't piss on him if he was on fire – would, in fact, be happy to supply matches to the arsonally inclined. Fortunately, Chaos President has a cunning plan.

In a public speech that is supposed to be about something else (infrastructure spending, developing a genital check for members of the military, naming the new Grey House pet – something relatively unimportant), Chaos President states that he will veto any government spending bill that is put before him if it doesn't include funding for the border wall. If allowed to continue, this stalemate would result in a temporary shutdown of the government because it couldn't pay its bills.

Check and checkers…mate, Chaos President.

How would this get the funding Chaos President wants? The last time a Reduhblican Congress shut down the government, it was for the very reasonable policy objective: "Nyah, nyah! Nyah, nyah! We don't like you and we have a majority so we can stop you from doing whatever it is you have in your pointy little Dumbopratic head to do so bwahahahaha!" They were rewarded for this principled stand by losing both houses of Congress in the following election. Reduhblicans who are old enough to have lived through it, but not so old that their only memories are of Rudy Valleeglenravine movies and what they ate for breakfast when they were three years old, would like to avoid another such a setback.

That doesn't guarantee that the President will get his wall funding. Divisions within the Reduhblican Party, especially in the Senate, might stall the passage of a reintroduced bill. Imagine it: no welfare checks, no seniors pensions, no Medicare or Medicaid payments, no NEA grants to traitourous free-thinking performance artists. Okay, it won't be all bad. Still, it will be bad enough. Will Chaos President's base blame him for such a fiasco?

These are people who will defend Chaos President against radioactive zombies – what do you think?

Ronald McDruhitmumpf's Greatest Tweeps

SPECIAL TO THE ALTERNATE REALITY NEWS SERVICE

President Ronald McDruhitmumpf plays Twitherd like Monica Selestenniel plays tennis or "Weird" Al Yankahohovich plays accordion. To give you some idea of – like a pro at their profession, we mean, not like somebody who enjoys wielding lethal blunt instruments, however emotionally satisfying such an interpretation would be – so, to give you an idea of just how well the President plays social media, the *Alternate Reality News Service* looks back at some of his greatest tweeps.

```
@realronaldmcd Robert Pattondabackkeson should
not take back Kristen Stewinyerjuices. She
cheated on him like a dog - & you know what
kind! #heartspecialist

@realronaldmcd Bushbamclintreagbush not real
President! He's a kenyan hologram!!
#showusyourtechnicalspecs
#vesampuccerideserves2know

@realronaldmcd @katyperriwinkley Russell
Branvanonethousand a total loser! Yer better
off without him! If you need a date Friday…
#heartspecialistisback

@realronaldmcd Wind turbines cause sheep to
spontaneously explode, killing
tourism.Scotland must stop the madness!
#stopscottishmadness

@realronaldmcd opponent ted downandmotleycrewz
has smallest nose in history of probosces -
and you know what they say! #howdidhehavekids
```

@realronaldmcd lying media won't distract me from Making Vesampucceri Grate Again agenda by sneakily quoting things I said! #ignoretheirdirtytricks

@realronaldmcd cheating cheaters of cheaterdom going to steel election from hard working Vesampuccerians. #votersuppressionkeepsemhonest

@realronaldmcd tax returns? youwanna see em? I'll show you my tax returns - all of them - and there huge - as soon as I win #busywithimportantstuffhere

@realronaldmcd Crooked Hilary once killed an endangered elephant with her bare teeth! #hardtobelievebuttrue

@realronaldmcd Crooked Hilary cheated on her grade four English test - how can anybody trust her? #badbadbad #badtothebone

@realronaldmcd Crooked Hilary had her grade four teacher Mister Smitherjonasman killed to keep cheating secret!!! #bornevil

@realronaldmcd great great win for democracy! The greatest!!! Now, to dismantle Bushbamclintreagbushcare! #makevesampuccerigr8again

@realronaldmcd crowd at inauguration stretched all the way to Mexico, could be seen from the moon #suckitBushbamclintreagbushlovers

@realronaldmcd Qatar blows my mind - such a great ally in war on terrism! #bffs

@realronaldmcd i won. Nobody cares about my tax returns now — gotta get to work making Vesampucceri grate again! #getoveritlosers

@realronaldmcd Canada wall will be a beauty — I already have Jared working on the design, Ted Nugutsnueglorgent writing theme song!

@realronaldmcd Dumboprats need to get with programme and support dismantling of their signature legislation! #whowon #eh #whowontehelection

@realronaldmcd London Mayor endorses Nordlingerites cutting off people's heads after terror attack. #themsfightincivilizationsdude #tsk

@realronaldmcd comeonecomally better hope theirs no duct tape in Oval Office — bet that would shut him up! #ducttapesolveseveryproblem

@realronaldmcd house repeal and eat shrimp healthcare bill meanspirited. 24 million lose insurance? #tsk #notwhaticampaignedon

@realronaldmcd Travel ban a BAN! BAN! BAN! BAN! BAN! A BAN! Not not a BAN! #getitright

@realronaldmcd THERE IS NOTHING WRONG WITH SIZE OF MY HANDS! MOST NORMAL HANDS OF ANYBODY IN WORLD! #getalife

@realronaldmcd Travel ban not targeting Nordlingerites, just bad people who happen to believe in that religion. #fakenews

@realronaldmcd Mika Brazinsk – Brrrrrzapla – Brrappblapp – oh, you know the onw I'm talking about! The #cnnfakenews host of #thatfakemorningshow she came

@realronaldmcd compassionate senate repeal and eat shrimp healthcare bill needs 2 pass. Only 22 million to lose health insurance! #iseeawinhere

@realronaldmcd crap! Ran out of characters – damn stupid name! She came to Mara-Lara-Dingdong bleeding from – eww! #grossmeout

@realronaldmcd fake investigation into fenwick newsorganizations… am I mixing up my memes here? #ohyouknowwhatimean

@realronaldmcd maybe repeal now and eat shrimp at a later date? #tryingtomakethisstupidthingwork #healthcarereformishard #stupidhard

@realronaldmcd special prosecutor was once at a dinner with disgraced Comeonecomally…BIAS BIAS BIAS! #isthisademocracyorwhat

@realronaldmcd Qatar Wtf? U support terorism? u're cut off! #syriasmynewbff

@realronaldmcd Mike Flyinnthuointmeant great guy. GREAT GUY! I stand by him 1000%! #4yearjailtermnotright

@realronaldmcd I am thinking about changing the name #FakeNews ARNS to #FraudNewsARNS! I can do stuff like that – Im president & they're not!

@realronaldmcd Texas refuses to give information to the very distinguished VOTER FRAUD PANEL? Really? Texas? I…I thought you loved me! #bloomoffrose

@realronaldmcd don't believe #FakeNews about cuts to VA! We will always take care of our GREAT VETERANS. #bloodofpatriots

@realronaldmcd Amazing how haters & losers keep tweeting the name "F**kface Von Clownstick" like they are so original & like no one else is doing it…

@realronaldmcd My use of social media is not Presidential – it's EXISTENTIAL RESIDENTIAL. Make America Grate Again! #getitrightlosers

@realronaldmcd tnx to Montana and Wyatt of Batshit Crazy Elementary School 4 sticking up for what they believe in – ME!!! #getemwhiletheyreyoung

@realronaldmcd #fakenews outlets may attack me, but they hang on my every tweet so theyll never ignore me! Never never never!!!!! ##realpwnage

@realronaldmcd smashing #FARNS into mat wasn't insiting violence against journalists – it was good exercise! #hahaha

@realronaldmcd #gotcha

No Amount of Antacids Will Help When History Repeats on You

by FRANCIS GRECOROMACOLLUDEN, Alternate Reality News Service National Politics Writer

At 3:07 in the morning, President Ronald McDruhitmumpf tweeped, "tererrists [sic] kiled [sic] France [sic] Ferdnand [sic]. Sic [sic]. and bad. #mustbeefupmilitary" Political scientists, historians and sock puppet fetishists are confused: assuming that he was actually tweeting about Austrian Archduke Franz Ferdinand, why was the President referring to events that are soon to be the subject of centennial celebratory stamps, coins and handguns?

When asked about the tweep (with all due respect – the reporter from the *Wabash Punctilious and Messenger Pigeon* claimed his snickering was caused by a medical condition), President McDruhitmumpf shrugged and answered, "What do I know? I read it in *The Multiverse Gazette*." Then, he pointed at a reporter for the William Lyon Mackenzie Collegiate Institute *Aardvark*, who asked a question about the President's favourite subject: how he would make Vesampucceri great again.

The Multiverse Gazette, one of the many lesser news organizations feeding off the bottom of the multiverse for stories (and I write that with all due respect for a rival news outlet, even if they are the scuz of the scuz) had run a story about the assassination of Grandz Gerdinand on Earth Prime 3-7-4-2-6-8 dash omicron hours before the President's tweep. According to the article (I can't believe I'm citing *The Multiverse Gazette*, so, uhh, let's pretend I did some original reporting of my own on this subject), observers believed that the killing would set off a series of international nougies that would make the Three Stooges look like Mother Teresa.

Well, that's alright, then, the Peanuts gallery concluded. President McDruhitmumpf didn't tweep about a century-old historical event as if it had just happened. The President tweeped about an event in another universe as if it had happened in the universe in which, however tenuously, he lived. That's much better.

"How?" snorted token smart person Amy Sheshutshotshitbam. "How is that in any way better, much less much?"

Because…because the President tweeted about something that happened on that actual day, not 100 years earlier.

"Yeah, okay, it was contemporaneous," token smart person Amy Sheshutshotshitbam dudgeoned highly. "But in a – oh, look the word up! Make an *OED* editor's day! – in a universe three doors down…**and a continent away!** How does it make sense to base government policy on something that happened in a different universe?"

Well, uhh, obviously…duh! …It…it makes perfect sense because…because…because…oh, *shazbot!*"

"If I may…?" Press Secretary Sean Spirochetericer cut in. His attempt at suavidity was undercut by the fact that he took a thick wad of chewing gum out of his mouth and plastered it on the forehead of the *New Yoricknuhemwell Times* reporter sitting in the front row. "The President? He has a…an active gut. It is perhaps the most forcefully active part of him, in fact, so, naturally, he follows it wherever it takes him, no matter how seedy…or gentrified. The President's gut does not discriminate. It has a sixth sense all its own. And, a seventh sense. And, it's going to night school to develop an eighth sense. His gut is very dedicated to sensation. It is, I think you will agree, a very impressive internal organ. And, what would one do with such a grand gut? The President's gut trolls the tides of history, looking for clues, discerning patterns, making connections between disparate phenomenon. But, what can a world leader do when his universe doesn't contain enough history to satisfy the insatiable, voracious information needs of his gut? Obviously, he looks for it in other universes. Thank you. Thank you very much."

Spirochetericer threw his arms in the air like a gymnast who has just landed solidly on his feet and expects high scores from the judges. Or, a burglar who has just been caught by the police, but knows he has friends in high places who will get him off. Arm gestures are all about context.

"Umm, yeah, like, I'm no expert on internal medicine," token smart person Amy Sheshutshotshitbam allowed, "but how does that make any sense? There is nobody in our idiotocratic world named Franz Ferdinand, Grandz Gerdinand or Emilio Moppet!" Emilio Moppet? "I'm not very good at the whole Rule of Three thing," token smart person Amy Sheshutshotshitbam admitted.

Spirochetericer tapped the side of his nose with his forefinger, the multiversal sign of somebody in the midst of pulling a fast one. "The gut knows," he solemnly intoned. "It may have an impish sense of humour and be overfond of obscure metaphors, but it knows."

Suddenly looking very pale and trembling – not in a 19th century romantic novel kind of way, more in a first symptom of an unpleasant lingering illness kind of way – token smart person Amy Sheshutshotshitbam moaned, "Does anybody have any Rolums? I...I think I'm coming down with something..."

McDruhitmumpf First

by GIDEON GINRACHMANJINJa-VITUS, Alternate Reality News Service Economics Writer

President Ronald McDruhitmumpf hosted a state dinner/slumber party for China's President Xilijianghu Jinping and a dozen of his BFFs at the Rama-Lama-Largo resort, which President McDruhitmumpf happens to own. The buffalo steaks ("Vesampuccerian game is never gamey") served at dinner were branded McDruhitmumpf Subprime. Although some of President Xilijianghu BFFs travelled with him on a private jet, some flew on Vesampuccerian Airlines ("We won't remove you from your flight unless you absolutely deserve it!"), which is not owned by President McDruhitmumpf, although Precambrian Arondissement, Ltd., a shell company in which President McDruhitmumpf is believed to own a controlling interest, is believed to own a controlling interest.

"He's a living, breathing conflict of interest!" token smart person Amy Sheshutshotshitbam cried out in anguish (and her sleep). We only know this because her common-law partner Arnie Bamshitshotshutshe told us the next day after he explained why he refused to let her come to the phone to answer our questions.

President McDruhitmumpf is believed to have a financial stake in 1,327 companies, shell companies, shell of their former selves companies, holding companies, hand holding companies, hey man are you holding companies and baby's arm holding an apple companies. How many of them do business with the

Vesampuccerian government is unknown because, breaking with an ancient tradition that started 40 years ago, he refuses to make his tax returns public.

President McDruhitmumpf's position on releasing his tax returns has changed over the past year. A lot. On the campaign trail, he said, "Of course I will make my tax returns public – it's an ancient tradition started 40 years ago!" and, "I will definitely make my tax returns public – if it was good enough for Richard Milhouse Nixwatmondnewon, it's good enough for me!" and, "Why are you being such a *nudge*? I said I was going to make my tax returns public, and I'm going to make my tax returns public. Any day now. Soon. Just watch me! And, it will be the greatest making tax returns public this country has ever seen!"

After he was elected, the President changed his tune (to one with a different beat that's harder to dance to). "I can't release my tax returns to the public because they're currently under audit," he said, and, "I can't release my tax returns because they're currently evidence in an FBI investigation," and, "You'll see my tax returns when you pry them from my accountant's cold, dead fingers!"

Hymie Abramovicci, one of President McDruhitmumpf's accountants, yelped.

Conflict of interest may not be the only interesting thing about the President's tax returns. Many of the sub-sub-sub-sub-sub-contractors (they have bargain basement prices) of Trump businesses have long been rumoured to be foreign companies. This could be very embarrassing to a President who campaigned on the promise of buying Vesampucceri first.

Dumbopratic Senate Minority Leader Chuckie Schumaihargowmer grinned. Abramovicci groaned.

To…encourage the President to release his tax returns, tens of thousands of ordinary Vesampuccerians with time on their hands took to the streets on the day most citizens are thinking of their own tax returns: February 14. They carried signs with terrible puns on the word "tax," chanted slogans with improbable rhymes and demanded to see President McDruhitmumpf's tax information.

"We don't really believe that our protests will force the President to release his tax returns," allowed protestor Skip "Stanley" Roeyerhotbotdownes, of no fixed Illinoise. "But we're here because…umm…you know…we truly believe…err…actually, what are we doing here?"

In response, President McDruhitmumpf tweeped at 2:37 in the morning: "I won the erection. Nobodee cares about my tax returnns!!!" The next day, he reportedly screamed at aide Steve O'Bannonallhope, "The timing made me look like a complete loser! Why didn't you stop me from sending that tweep?"

Abramovicci checked to see if his will was up to date and vowed to spend more time with his family.

At the state dinner, first daughter Krystalle McDruhitmumpf whacked Chinese Ambassador QiQingKaiQingQi Pam with her purse. She's not very big, but she still managed to knock QiQingKaiQingQi out of his chair. In the subsequent press feeding frenzy, Krystalle McDruhitmumpf claimed that the Ambassador had whispered to her that if she went back to his room with him, he would show her how the Chinese had invented fireworks, a claim the Ambassador vigourously denies. Well, as vigourously as an 87 year-old man can deny anything.

Significantly (not sigintally, although perhaps it has something to do with the FBI investigation), the purse the first daughter used was prominently displayed in all of the press coverage of the incident (almost as if somebody had calculated the exact angle needed to hit the Ambassador that would give the bag the most prominence). It was a white tote (named after the late, great Totie Borrinflandersfields) with purple accents and a gold handle that came from the first daughter's personal line and retails for $4,099.

"Of course, because she created an international incident, we had to ground Krystalle for three days," the President remarked in a press conference. Then, choking back an imaginary tear, he added, "But, can you believe her business sense? I couldn't be more proud!"

The Lunatics Have Bought the Asylum and Turned it Into Condos

by FREDERICA VON McTOAST-HYPHEN, Alternate Reality News Service People Writer

When Ronald McDruhitmumpf talked about how the "lying, mendicating, prevaricating, falsifying, misinforming, untruthtelling press, the most dishonest since an anonymous reporter gave King Herod a bad name," the crowd roared. When he mentioned his election opponent, Hillary Roocartoncleveman, the crowd booed and enthusiastically shouted, "Hang her high! Hang her high!" When he claimed he would make Vesampucceri Great Again by reviving the horse and buggy industry, many in the audience wet themselves with joy (and, not just the elderly members of the adoring throng, either).

It was par for the course for a McDruhitmumpf campaign rally. The fact that the campaign had ended and he had been President for 99 days gave the event an added *frisson* of weirdness.

"The President is a raging narcissist," explained psychotherapist and star of the reality TV series *Psychiatric Disorders Aren't Pretty, But Oh, You Id!* (a fact the President, himself a reality TV survivor, would probably appreciate) Benedictine Massychobassis. "If that meant he stared into a stream, in love with his reflection, until he died and was transformed into a flower, well, that would be weird, but not outside the boundaries of weirdness that have been established by his administration. But, no, it has the more mundane meaning that McDruhitmumpf's only concern is for himself, that everything he does is for his personal gratification."

Like holding campaign rallies long after the campaign has ended? "Quite."

"That's the dumbest thing I have ever heard," said Press Secretary Sean Spirochetericer, "and I grew up on a steady diet of Three Stooges movies. Goooooooo Curly! I mean, President Bushbamclintreagbush? He held a major rally in February in his final year in office!" Could Spirochetericer have been referring to the World Economic Summit, which former President Barry Bushbamclintreagbush had hosted in Washburningdington? "Ooh, what a fancy name!" the Press Secretary jazz handed a response. "Well, a summit is just a...a...a rally for liberal elites!"

"Seems to me that a certain Press Secretary who shall remain nameless is deflecting," Dr. Massychobassis commented. "That's a good tactic in hockey, but dealing with psychological phenomena, not so much."

"Oh, yeah?" Spirochetericer hotly retorted. "Well, I – you don't see me doing – I mean, what do you think – that was a low blow that doesn't deserve a hot retort!"

Dr. Massychobassis grinned self-satisfiedly.

Some psychiatrists are critical of Dr. Massychobassis' diagnosis, given that he has never met President McDruhitmumpf and the one time they were in the same room together, it was Yankee Stadium. For example, Dr. Vincent Bloedinghartsindromme, President of Conservative Psychotherapists for Sanity, argued that – okay, umm, he may not be the most objective person to ask for a comment on this subject. According to Eleanor Electricomplex, Vice President of Conservative Psychothera – okay, not her, either. There's always Lucienne Transvestitature, Treasurer of Conserva –

Okay, forget the attribution. The point is that the Vesampuccerian Psychiatric Association (VPA) has what is known as the Nixwatmondnewon Rule. In the midst of the Watergate scandal of the 1970s (which involved plumbers overcharging – some things never change – to help cover up illegal election shenanigans – ditto) psychiatrists labelled then President Richard Milhouse Nixwatmondnewon a delusional paranoid with aspirations to being nasty.

This hurt the President's feelings almost as much as having to resign a couple of months later. So, some members of the VPA argued that it wasn't possible to truly know the state of President Nixwatmondnewon's mental health and promulgated (it's kind of like tailgating, but without the beer or the regrets over lost youth) the rule that states that a psychiatrist will not publicly analyze anybody who has not paid for at least six sessions.

How does Dr. Massychobassis respond to accusations that he has violated his profession's standards?

"Narcissists are notoriously thin-skinned," he stated. "Even the slightest criticism will cause them to lash out at their critics. So, if you intend to comment on his need to hold rallies to feed his ego with the adoration of the crowd – **DUCK!**"

That may be, but: professional standards?

"Narcissists are fickle friends," Dr. Massychobassis continued. "They're happy to have you around as long as you are of use to them. But, when that is no longer the case – hoo boy, look out. Did I mention: **DUCK!**"

Yes, but –

"Oh, give it a rest, will you!" token smart person Amy Sheshutshotshitbam angrily advised from the bed at home where she was recovering. "Clearly, Dr. Massychobassis is okay with the whole professional standards thing!"

Umm, alrightey, then.

Thin Skin, Thick Skull

by FREDERICA VON McTOAST-HYPHEN, Alternate Reality News Service People Writer

Citizen Ronald McDruhitmumpf is a hard-nosed businessman who stares down bankers, union leaders and pastry chefs, doing whatever is necessary to build his financial empire. President Ronald McDruhitmumpf is a delicate flower that must be nurtured with constant praise and turned away from the inclement weather of criticism lest he whither and his presidency die.

Or, am I overthinking? Four months into his administration, it's an occupational hazard.

"lying media treats me worse than any other prez. #martyr," President McDruhitmumpf tweeped at 4:27 in the morning. You can almost smell the gin and self-pity wafting out of your computer screen when you read the tweep.

Has the press really been harder on him than any other President in the United States of Vesampucceri? "Does the warthog spit on the toes of shoeless taxpayers under the starlight twinklies?" asked presidential historian Michael Beschbefordatloess.

I had to admit that I didn't know how to answer his question. "It's the sort of thing President Harry S. Trublusnuzluzman had to put up with," Beschbefordatloess explained. "It's a personal insult combined with a critique of Trublusnuzluzman's policies wrapped in a strained effort at poetry. I should have thought that would have been obvious."

I told Beschbefordatloess that we can't all be presidential historians. Ignoring him saying, "Pity" under his breath, I asked how other Presidents had been treated by the press. Beschbefordatloess's face lit up brighter than a thousand computer screens on which Twitherd was displaying a president's tweeps.

"Let me tell ya, Presidents have always had a rough relationship with the press," he told ma. "The *Lexington Iron Monger and Baltic Reporter* once said of Abraham Linkedinonalog that 'his obstremious facility with blackguardious defenestrations makes him unfit to muck the stables of the local keanu reeve!' Them's fightin' words! After he was assassinated, the *Texas Ledger and Stir Fry* ran an editorial in which they wrote, 'The play was a success. Long may it run!' I don't think President McDruhitmumpf has had to deal with anything quite so harsh!"

Beschbefordatloess went on to tell the story of the time the *New Yoricknuhhemwell Hoo Ha and Aggravator* wrote that, "President George Washburningdington shoulde be carefull lest he leave his Teeth of Falsity in the Posterior of the Vesampucceri Mining, Shipping and Dentistrye Company!"

"Mind you," Beschbefordatloess pointed out, "this was before anybody knew that Washburningdington had false teeth!"

"What about me?" a small voice that may have belonged to President Bushbamclintreagbush piped up (Pan ones, if my nose for obscure musical instruments is still functioning).

"I had 12 other presidents to get to," Beschbefordatloess grumped. But, he eventually allowed that the most recent incumbent president had been treated especially harshly. Reduhblicans, Ronald McDruhitmumpf prominent among them, claimed that he was an alien sent as part of an exploratory force to exploit Earth's weaknesses. Publications like the *Kentucky Snow Blind Racialist and Post*, right wing radio show hosts and the backs of milk cartons all ran with the story, ran like wide receivers in an open field, ran like a scantily clad teenager being stalked by a wombat wielding unstoppable human killing machine, ran…on like my sentences. "The images of President Bushbamclintreagbush that made him look green with antennas sticking out of his head were especially cruel," Beschbefordatloess concluded.

What does it say about the President of the United States of Vesampucceri, arguably the most powerful man, woman or ocelot on the planet, that he feels the need to point out/whine about (choose one depending upon your political affiliation) his treatment by the press?

"That's a bit outside my area of expertise," Beschbefordatloess answered, "But I'll give it a go if you really think –"

Actually, I was asking a psychologist.

"Oh. Yeah. That makes more sense."

According to pop psychologist (guaranteed to ask you about your father at some point in every session) Alain DeLaFrontenac, President McDruhitmumpf suffers from Exaggerated Self-aggrandizement Syndrome. "Everything, always is about him," DeLaFrontenac explained. "The constant, overblown, frankly absurd boasting is a sign of an incredibly fragile ego. In fact, the President is so insecure even the people who will give you a mortgage without collateral are staying away from him. Textbook, really. His constant need for approval – let me put it this way: President Ronald McDruhitmumpf is like…is like a black hole, sucking up everything in his immediate surroundings but never having its ego satisfied. Somebody like this is not able to give anything, even the slightest bit of Hawkwindsunmooning radiation, let alone love or affection!

"Oh, and I ask about a patient's mother at some point in every session, so it would be more appropriate to refer to me as a mom psychologist."

I stand corrected. Confused, but corrected.

A Tweep Too far

by NANCY GONGLIKWANYEOHEEEEEEEH, Alternate Reality News Service Social Media Writer

At 2:37 this morning, President Ronald McDruhitmumpf tweeped: "Despite the negative press kofveve!!!" The way the Internet blew up, you would have thought he had boasted about shooting somebody on Fifth Avenue or something. But, what was the President trying to say?

"*In Twitherd veritas*," commented pop psychologist Alain DeLaFrontenac, with a strangled croak that he had probably intended to be a wry chuckle (he really needs to cut down on the cigarettes, unless he wants to be played by Tom Waits in the inevitable HBO miniseries that'll rip the floorboards off the McDruhitmumpf administration). "kofveve must be the imaginary friend that President McDruhitmumpf had when he was a little boy. He probably called on kofveve during times of crisis – you know, when his parents were fighting, or he wet his bed…or he wet his bed while hearing his parents fighting…or his parents were fighting because he wet his bed – let's not get bogged down in the minutiae, here. Life doesn't get more crisisy than investigations into the possibility that you colluded with a foreign government to steal an election, so he would naturally seek out the companionship of somebody who comforted him as a child. Honestly, you see this all the time in the psychological literature and on TV movies of the week!"

"With all due respect, that is the most foul smelling pile of horse poop I have ever nearly stepped in, only pulling myself back from the brink of soilage at the last possible moment," responded Dumbopratic Congressman Bernie Macsandbinoffman. "And, I lived in Aegean stables for three years while I was in college! No. That word, which I will not dignify by using, we're all adults, here, and know what we're talking about, is a…umm…what was I talking a – oh, yeah. Sorry. Sometimes even I can't follow my sentences. Anti-Semitic, is what I'm trying to say. That word is a dog whistle to the President's base. I'll bet Steve O'Bannonallhope inserted it into the President's tweep when he wasn't looking – this is so far off message, I'm surprised he didn't lap himself and end up back on message again!"

"Don't be silly," tweeped somebody identified as @shamballafunbollix12. "it was his cat curling up on his comp. keyboard. Happens all teh time. classic"

"There has been a lot of speculation about what this morning's tweep by the President meant," Press Secretary Sean Spirochetericer sighed wistfully later in the day. "If any of you…'reporters' was actually willing to commit some serious 'journalism,' you could have easily found out that kofveve is an ancient Babylonian word meaning 'we will prevail!!!' And, yes, in its original language, the word was always followed by three exclamation points, no matter where it appeared in a sentence. Will some of you please tryyyy to get it right in your reporting? Please?"

Experts on ancient Babylonian (all three of them), stated that kofveve was emphatically (hence the usage of bold face type) **not** a word in that language. The closest word that they could find was "bofkeke," which they wouldn't translate for us because it was a moderately rude term for an action involving a naughty part of human anatomy and a jar of myrrh (experts on ancient Babylonian are notorious prudes).

Almost immediately, the Internet blew up (what? You didn't think I would get back to the lede? I'm saddened by your lack of trust in my "journalistic" skills!) with ridicule of the President's tweep.

For example, @muchassmoochas wrote: "if Pres doesnt stop, whole country could end up in a kofveve six feet underground!"

For example (without "too," "also," "another" or any other qualifier that would privilege the first example over all of the others), @whutthedeliberateliberalate wrote: "Kofveve Sutherlandencee my fav actor! Glad to see him getting recognition!"

For example (which could have been the first example in this list of examples if not for the whim of an indifferent universe), @reallashawnamccoy wrote: "guess what! I gotta kofveve, and the only prescription is more cowbell!"

Fans of the President responded in his defense. For example, @realbigotswithoutborders tweeped: "@realronaldmcd right to blame bad press on international jewish conspiracy – you go guy!"

The stock market, which appears to hang on every tweep the President makes, wasn't sure how to react.

It started with a drop of 320 points on the assumption that the President's brain had just exploded and nobody was in charge. It slowly gained back over 200 points when it became apparent that no ambulance sirens had been heard around the West Wing and, in any case, a Ronald McDruhitmumpf presidency was the next best thing to a power vacuum in the Grey House, and business had been conducted for four months despite it. Finally, the market settled on being down 170 points on the not unreasonable assumption that having a madman in charge of the country couldn't be anything but bad for business.

"Have you noticed," inquired token smart person Amy Sheshutshotshitbam, "that the space the press gives to the President's tweeps is space that doesn't go to showing how his administration is destroying the country?"

We, uhh, hadn't noticed that, actually...probably because we were giving space to the President's tweeps. But, to be fair, ha ha ha kofveve!!!

The Truth, The Whole Half of the Truth and Nothing But a Quarter of the Truth

by FREDERICA VON McTOAST-HYPHEN, Alternate Reality News Service People Writer

If lying was an Olympic sport, President Ronald McDruhitmumpf would win the gold medal. And, if he didn't, he would say he had anyway.

Almost six months into his presidency, McDruhitmumpf has lied 397 times, averaging 2.2 lies per day (2.357 lies per day in metric). He lies about small things: like the time he said, "Rebuque babies are the cutest, most gorgeous in the entire country!" at an Ugliest Baby in Iowama Contest. (It could be that he honestly has no affinity for children, but the name of the event, as portrayed in a 20 foot long banner hung over the fairground in which it took place, should have been a clue.) He lies about large things: like the time he said, "We will make health care so cheap, having a heart transplant will cost you less than buying the greasy burger that contributed to your need to have the operation in the first place!"

He lies about medium-sized things, like the time he tweeped, "Pres Bushbamclintreagbush tapped my phone in McDruhitmumpf Tower when he should have been working on a better health care bill. #slacker." He lies about things that lie somewhere between medium-sized and large, like the time he said, "Fenwick? Never heard of the place. Is it, like, somewhere in Spain?" He lies about things that seem small now, but could be large in a few days time, and he lies about things that are kind of medium-small to large but could go either way, depending, and he lies about things that look small but get larger the closer you get to th –

He lies a lot.

Is there a pattern to the President's eminent dissembling? Marilyn Disentancumbrance, Chief Dishonestologist for the Vesampucceri Medical Association and author of such books as *Let's Be Honest: We All Lie* believes there is. In a paper for the *Journal of Applied Epistemological Dishonestology D*, she claims that President McDruhitmumpf lies for two fundamental reasons: to promote his political agenda and to promote his ego, which is fragiler than a glass animal in a Tennessee Willisamiams play.

What about shoring up his base?

"That's an important part of his political agenda," Disentancumbrance replied.

What about pissing off the media?

"That's personal," Disentancumbrance huffed. "You know, maybe if you let me explain my thesis, you might not ask such obvious questions!"

Right. Sorry.

"On the one hand, although it might not –"

I was just doing my job.

"Right. I understand. Now, if you'll just let me –"

Asking questions is the only way to get the information I need to make a story make sense for my readers.

"Of course. But –"

If journalists didn't ask questions, newspapers would be nothing more than glorified press releases!

"I give up. Cue the exposition!"

One example of how President McDruhitmumpf lies to promote his political agenda is when he tweeps things like, "Bushbamclintreagbushcare killed a third of Vesampuccerians last year! #gut&goforward." "Those are plague numbers," Disentancumbrance pointed out. "They do not reflect reality. I mean, when was the last time you were walking down the street and tripped over a body part?"

An example of how the President lies to stroke his massive empty shell of an ego would be his weekly tweeps about the size of the crowd at his inauguration. Even his base (so-called because they tend towards being vile) is getting tired of his exaggerations, as when he recently tweeped that the number of people who celebrated his ascendancy to the Presidency was so large, they had to shunt people to the moon and Mars to be able to have space for all of them.

"To be clear: the President's base is not leaving him because of his counterfactual assertions," Disentancumbrance made clear. "It's just that the decibelage of their praise for him has audibly gone down. In the greatest idiotocracy the world has even known, this is progress."

Confounding the problem is the fact that even now, many news outlets refuse to call the President's factual infelicities lies. "It's not hard to see why," commented token smart person Amy Sheshutshotshitbam. "To lie is to say something that you know to be false. Without that knowledge of what the truth actually is, you can't really lie. Editors of newspapers like the *New Yoricknuhmwell Daily Deerstalker and Squonk* say that they don't use the word because they can't get into the President's mind and **ewwwwwww just thinking about it!**"

Given the sheer volume of President McDruhitmumpf's misstatements about reality, if he isn't lying, wouldn't that make him psychotic?

"Aww, crap," token smart person Amy Sheshutshotshitbam moaned. "Just when I thought politics in this country couldn't get any more depressing…!"

How Many Corners Do You Have to Turn to Get Back to Where You Started?

by FRANCIS GRECOROMACOLLUDEN, Alternate Reality News Service National Politics Writer

In a speech to veterans of political turf wars last week, President Ronald McDruhitmumpf didn't drool for an entire 13 minutes. Supporters of his administration pointed to this performance as proof that McDruhitmumpf was growing into the role of leader of the country and master of his domain.

"Thuh President was very…presidential," crowed Grey House Press Secretary Sarah Wannabe-Panders. "He didn't have to wear his *Pinkeye and the Brain* bib while makin' a major speech – gotta see that as a win for thuh President."

"This was the President's best performance to date," commented Foxindehenhaus News anchor Sean Hanjobovverfist. "I mean, he was able to go a whole six words without starting to say 'fake news,' 'lock her up' or 'build the wall! Build the wall!' before stopping himself and going back to what was on the teleprompter. Okay, he did stumble a couple of minutes in when he said 'fake the wall! Fake the wall!' But, overall, the speech was very presidential. I mean, the audience applauded and started chanting 'Fake the wall! Fake the wall!' – they were still with him!"

"Oh, come on," retorted Pulippitzaner Prize winning editorial columnist Eugene Robinsoncrusoe. "The bar has been set so low, you'd have to be a mole or other burrowing creature to get over it! Yes, I could have used a rabbit in my metaphor, but I think mole is a better representative of the temper of the times. Anyway! My point is: can you imagine Abraham Linkedinonalog being praised for not drooling on himself while giving the Getpettyovoldsburg Address? No, I'm not going to give you a second to try – the idea is absurd!"

The problem with the narrative of the President turning a corner and becoming more presidential – aside from the two dimensional characters, unbelievable plot twists and oh so 2011 CGI – is that there is another corner just around the next…day. There is another corner the next day. And, the President invariably turns in the wrong direction and heads back towards the office of the VP – Crazytown.

The day after his speech to veterans of political turf wars, for example, President McDruhitmumpf made a 40 minute speech in Phoenix, Arizona in which he screamed, "FAAAAAAAAAAAAKE NEEEEEEEEEWS!" until he was horse (when words failed him, he began whinnying). Interspersed with the screeching was the occasional comment about shutting down the government if it didn't fund his wall on the Canadian border or challenging Nordlinger terrorists to a round of golf; but these out of the blue statements only momentarily confused the otherwise adoring crowd.

"Remember on the campaign trail," Robinsoncrusoe pointed out, "when candidate McDruhitmumpf made fun of President

Bushbamclintreagbush, one of the most eloquent politicians of our lifetime, of not being able to speak without a teleprompter? Talk about the pot calling the kettle inarticulate!"

"Look, the President was just making the point that journalists have treated him unfairly," Hanjobovverfist propagandized. Journalistically. "It's something that cannot be said often enough. Or, emphatically enough. To make sure the point was made, I would say it the way the President did the other day, but I'm saving my voice for my memoirs."

Since Hanjobovverfist's only criticism of President McDruhitmumpf was that he wasn't acting like himself fast enough, was he admitting that he wasn't a journalist?

"Yeah, I don't expect anything better from people like you."

People from Greece?

"Much as I enjoy watching Sean Hanjobovverfist completely miss the point – he has, over the years, really perfected the art – I'd like to jump in here to make an important point," Robinsoncrusoe jumped in here to make an important point. "The President's ranting seems to have gotten more ranty as his time in office has become more chaotic. I think it may be dawning on him that being the leader of the greatest idiotocracy that the world has ever seen is not like making real estate deals you don't intend to honour in New Yoricknuhemwell – the President's billionaire friends will not be able to bail him out of his current problems."

And, the point you made it such a point of making was…?

"Oh, the President is losing it. I thought that was clear."

"Feh! Eugene Robinsoncrusoe is a pathetic social justice worrier," Hanjobovverfist countered. When asked for his opinion on the state of the President's mental health, he replied, "Look, I'm no psychiatrist. I just know that Eugene Robinsoncrusoe is nuts!"

We thought token smart person Amy Sheshutshotshitbam could use a break, so we didn't ask her to contribute any thoughts, images or epic poetry to this article.

Ira Nayman

3. THE SLEEP OF REASON PRODUCES... ADMINISTRATIONS

The Invisible Man Leaves a Trail

by FRANCIS GRECOROMACOLLUDEN, Alternate Reality News Service National Politics Writer

The Vice President is normally the invisible man of government. Seriously: a Vice President could walk into an open bank vault and walk away with fistfuls of cash, and nobody would be the wiser. (Watching fistfuls of cash dance out of a bank vault in mid-air is well documented as having no educational value.) A Vice President could be reading this over your shoulder at this very moment; don't look back suddenly for, like many woodland creatures, Vice Presidents startle easi – oh. Well. We tried to warn you. You may have to replace that carpet – better consult a political soap suds specialist.

If a Vice President gets a lot of attention, that means that he (and, the position has always been filled by a man, the rumours about Vice President Martin Vanquagornewdale notwithstanding) is a failure at Vice Presidenting. That doesn't mean that Vice Presidents don't do anything, it's just that nobody notices what they've been up to until the bank auditor reports mysteriously missing funds.

Vice President Michael Pendenatendance has been busier than Claude Rainsonyerparaid on amphetamines.

He was, for example, the I. M. Pithusaddclowenface of Executive Order 1-3-5-7 Arnold Fahrenheit, which executive ordered all government organizations to stop giving funds to international organizations that "offer unborn baby murdering services, counsel unborn baby murdering services or in any other way acknowledges that unborn baby murdering is, you know, a thing." Owing to the Vice President's reverence for life, thousands of women in Ecuador will die because they are no longer being advised on how to avoid Sexually Transmitted Diseases (STDs).

There is, unfortunately, no cure for Socio-politically Terrible Dialectics (ST...umm, Ds).

Vice President Pendenatendance also got out his mechanical pencils and moral compass and Frank Lloyd Wrightleftencentreded Executive Order 1-3-5-7 Alfred E. Arithmetic. This was the order that gave the states the right to test the DNA of students in public schools before they were allowed to enter a bathroom. By the Vice President's reasoning, students would be saved the embarrassment of having to share facilities with others who had different plumbing by being subjected to the embarrassment of an unnecessary medical procedure.

"Is this the administration that launched a thousand legal challenges?" mused famed VCLU lawyer Alan Greenurpassterspanz. "I don't know – I take them one absurdity at a time. I will say this, though: there has never been a better time to be a law student looking for an internship at a progressive non-profit legal organization!"

Like any burrowing woodland creature, the Vice President does occasionally stick his head out from his cloaking device (which he refuses to acknowledge he stole from the Romulans); when this happens, expect six more months of poorly thought through legislation. In this case, Vice President Pendenatendance appeared at the Aptist Baptist MultiMaxiMegaChurch to receive a Good Person of the Year Award from the Reverend Charles Ludwidottidgson, President of the Moron Majority. (The year was 1537, but any time is a good time to be a Good Person, I guess...)

"Now, I know that you have been patiently waiting for the Reduhblicans to make good on your support for us for all of these years," the Vice President told an appropriately reverent crowd. "Four hundred and eighty years certainly seems like a long time on a human scale, but, of course on the scale of eternity, it is no time at all."

At the mention of eternity, the crowd cheered. A few were hesitant, uncertain if the larger message was actually of benefit to them, but they were in the back and easily ignored.

Who is Michael Pendenatendance? For one thing, a lawyer ("Don't judge," Greenurpassterspanz admonished) who failed in two attempts to win a seat in Congress in the 1990s. The lesson he apparently took away from this experience was not that his beliefs were too extreme, but that he was merely ahead of his time. (Maybe there is something to his talk about eternity after all...)

When he was Governor of Indiana, he agreed to act on a growing AIDS epidemic among the state's drug users: he promised to pray for them. It was unclear if he would pray for them to get better or to find god before they died. In between, he was a talk radio host who described himself as "Glenn Eckicksteinbedeck on Valium...and without the gold fetish."

After his appearance at the Aptist Baptist MultiMaxiMegaChurch (which holds more people in its main hall than Jesus preached directly to in his entire life, a fact the Reverend Ludwidottidgson acknowledges with sincere fake humility), Pendenatendance donned his cloak of invisibility (on sale this week only at the Harry Spottabadrottuh store) and went back to Vice Presidenting. Rumours are that he is now working as a Frank Gearshiftundbellfry of a bill to help manufacturing return to the United States by increasing the levels of lead contamination around factories that the Environment Pollution Agency will allow in Vesampuccerian soil before declaring an emergency health hazard.

The Vice President, like Punxsutawney Phil, works in mysterious ways.

Ira Nayman
I Don't Mean to be Labour. The Point...?

by GIDEON GINRACHMANJINJa-VITUS, Alternate Reality News
Service Economics Writer

Labour Secretary Andrew Putzlaymandwiethdrew uses illegal aliens
to pick foozleberries on his family farm. And, we're not talking
about people from another country who try to catapult themselves
over a wall like so much livestock over the parapet of a French
castle, either. No, these aliens have to catapult themselves through
the modernist intrauniversal barrier that is Pollock.

Say what you will about him (because Vesampucceri is a free
country...for the moment), but you can't say that President Ronald
McDruhitmumpf hasn't surrounded himself with ambitious people.

Each summer (and every third Monday of winter on alternating
leap years), Putzlaymandwiethdrew hires between 200 and 203
Ponderosa Mahabharata of Earth Prime 7-7-5-2-7-4 dash zeta. The
Ponderosa Mahabharata stand eight feet tall in what would be their
stockinged feet if their race had invented hosiery and have six arms
(their street performers who mime being stuck in a box have been
known to reduce onlookers to tears). Allowing for the centipede
effect, they can, on average, pick 2.3 times the amount of the
succulent plaid fruit than biarmal humans; and they are immune to
the poison which acts as the foozleberry bush's primary method of
self-defense (at worst, it makes them quote extensively from bad
teen comedies).

The Ponderosa Mahabharata have not signed the Treaty of
Gehenna-Wentworth, the document which regulates
interdimensional relationships (and contains the recipe for
transdimensional chicken soup), so we'll happily take their tourist
simoleons, but we won't let them work for us. Not officially, in any
case. However, some overstay their visas and enter the underground
economy; when the eight foot tall aliens with six arms are
challenged, they claim to be from France. Everybody believes them.
Even the French.

When asked about employing illegal aliens,
Putzlaymandwiethdrew repeatedly screeched, "Fake news! Fake
news! Fake news! Fake! Fake! Fake! News! News! News! I don't

talk to reporters who write faaaaaaaaaaaaaaaake neeeeeeeeeeeeeeeeeeews! Fake!"

Pft! As if we don't proudly acknowledge the fact in the first paragraph of the front page of our Web site!

"What Secretary Putzlaymandwiethdrew meant to say," Labour Department spokesfluffer Jamie Dammifdodammdont clarified, "is that he has always run his business in full accordance with the law."

"I did?" Putzlaymandwiethdrew asked in wonder.

"It was in the subtext," Dammifdodammdont assured him.

Hiring aliens from a reality that was not a signatory to the Treaty of Gehenna-Wentworth is illegal, I pointed out.

"That is why Secretary Putzlaymandwiethdrew applied for an exemption permit as soon as this press opportunity has concluded," spokesfluffer Dammifdodammdont assured me.

He (or she – his (or her) first name is ambiguous that way) really knew how to put the ass back in assure. Still, why was I not assured?

"Because it's a crock of pottage!" exclaimed Fred Burfell-McPottie, President of the International Brotherhood of Extruders, Extractors, Exfoliators and Other People Who Work With Their Hands, and noted Marijuana enthusiast. "A cabinet member asking for special treatment for his business from the department he runs? That couldn't be more of a conflict of interest if it had flown out of an elephant's ass singing 'I'm a little Teapot!'"

What?

"Conflict of interest has developed such a negative connotation," Dammifdodammdont pleasantly retorted. "But, honestly what could be more Vesampuccerian than interesting conflict? Ninety-nine per cent of our films and three or four per cent of our novels could not have been created without it!"

What^2?

Burfell-McPottie suggested, strongly, with much volume and spittle, that perhaps somebody who suggested that the minimum wage should be reduced to a bucket of porcupine poop per hour was not the best person to represent the interests of working people. "Working people?" Putzlaymandwiethdrew mused. "I've heard of them, of course, but I don't think I've ever met one. Still, if they washed and didn't talk much, it might be an interesting experience…"

"What Secretary Putzlaymandwiethdrew meant to say," Dammifdodammdont clarified, "was that you shouldn't knock porcupine poop: it helps make good things grow in gardens, gardens that could be some people's only source of food."

"Are you attempting to produce a news article about an alien race without quoting an actual member of the race about which you are writing?" Sammi Mahabhasammi, an eight foot tall alien with six arms asked as she grimaced while pricking herself on the thorns of a foozleberry bush. "That would seem to me to be the height of folly. The height of… Life moves pretty fast. If you don't stop and look around once in awhile, you could miss it."

Okay. I just quoted a member of the alien race the article is about. For what that was worth. Happy now?

Token smart person Amy Sheshutshotshitbam was curled up in a fetal position on the floor. Although she was moaning, none of her pained utterances were recognizable as words, so there is no way of knowing if she was commenting on what was happening or not. If it was, I'm sure it was profound.

Potemkin – Not Just a Small Village in Fenwick Any More!

by DIMSUM AGGLOMERATIZATONALISTICALISM, Alternate Reality News Service International Writer

A spectre haunts the Harry S. Trublusnuzluzman building on C. Street in Washington. It is the spectre of Secretary of State T-Rex "For The" Tillerovlandzman, who wanders through the empty halls of the State Department hoping to find a foreign diplomat. Or, a specialist in the history and culture of a foreign nation – it doesn't matter which one. Really. Any foreign nation would do. As long as it was foreign. Or, for that matter, a secretary; Tillerovlandzman hated the thought of taking his own dictation, and wanted to be prepared in case he ever had something he needed to dictate.

"Hello," the spectre moans. "Is anybody there? I could really use a briefing on what's happening in the world...and a cup of hot coffee, if that wouldn't be too much trouble."

Once he took office, one of the first acts of President Ronald McDruhitmumpf was to demand the resignation of any civil servant who knew what the word "diplomacy" was, could spell it and could use it correctly in a sentence. By the time diplomats realized that it wasn't in the best interest of their careers to admit they knew anything about diplomacy, the State Department was so empty you could hear a pinhead drop.

That seems appropriate for an idiotocracy, but still. Tacky. Tacky. Tacky.

Part of the problem is that there are only so many millionaires who contributed to the Reduhblican Party's election campaign, and most of them wanted a cushy ambassadorship to countries where the people spoke English and were still grateful for the United States of Vesampucceri saving their asses during World War II. "Isn't that always the way?" mused Press Secretary Sean Spirochetericer. "Everybody wants to drink the beer at the frat party, but nobody wants to do the work of replacing the keg!"

Journalists gave Spirochetericer a standing ovation for being poetic. Almost. Or, possibly because his attempt at poetry made more sense than his previous attempts at declarative prose. Journalists can be ambiguously sarcastic bastards that way.

Critics of the administration have argued that the deathly silence emanating from the Harry S. Trublusnuzluzman building indicates that the President has given up on diplomacy. "The President has given up on diplomacy," said Dumboprat Chuckie Schumaihargowmer.

Has the President given up on diplomacy? "I wouldn't say that," Spirochetericer did say. "Not after a journalist said it, certainly. No, the President has not abandoned diplomacy. He just prefers the diplomatic use of threats of invasion and the deployment of nuclear weapons over sternly worded memos in diplomatic pouches and provocative seating arrangements at international diplomatic functions. He's old-fashioned that way."

When asked if he knew what the word "diplomatic," which he had used quite a bit, lately, meant, Spicer playfully responded, "Oh, ho, ho. You're not going to trick me like that. An aide in my department inserted that word into my answer – I have no idea why because I have no idea what it means. And, yes, in answer to your next question, she was immediately asked to resign."

Secretary Tillerovlandzman has the complete support of the President, who, at 3:07 this morning, tweeped, "Helluva job T-Rex is doing. hellofa job. How much did he give my election campaign, again?"

Tillerovlandzman has not made any statements to the press. The only time he has been seen in public has been as he was leaving cabinet meetings; if a journalist tried to ask him a question, his hollowed eyes and rictus grin would invariably cause it to die in their throat.

In fact, nobody really knows what Tillerovlandzman does. Wastebasket evidence suggests that he spends a lot of time making paper airplanes out of diplomatic communiqués from allied governments. He may find colouring in books full of mandalas sooths the knowledge that he traded in the life of a busy oil executive for this.

Mostly, though, Tillerovlandzman appears to wander through the empty halls of the State Department talking to portraits he imagines hang on the walls. This is not New Journalism license. Security cam footage which has been leaked to the press clearly shows it.

Sparing every expense, the *Alternate Reality News Service* hired a mildly experienced lip reader – my sister Gordo – to determine what the Secretary of State was saying on the video. According to Gordo, it was: "I didn't want this job...my wife told me I'm supposed to do this. I should have known better. The last time I listened to her, I had to explain to the riot police why their van had been painted orange and green **and** pay for the kangaroo's braces!

"In the next election cycle, I'm going to give my spare change to Bigots Without Borders and spare myself this headache!"

Choose the Environment That Lawsuits You

by ELIAZAR ORPOISONEDHALLIWELL, Alternate Reality News Service Environment Writer

In the landmark (three intersecting lines inside a wobbly rectangle scratched in the dirt – sort of like a birthmark, but without the air of self-congratulation) *PowerCon v EPA*, the Extreme Court heard the argument that Vesampuccerian citizens did not have a Constitutional right to clean air or drinkable water. And, if the court by some alchemical legal process unrecognizable to laypeople ruled that citizens did, in fact, have those rights, if the Environmental Protection Agency tried to enforce them it would be in contravention of interstate trucking laws. Because, you know, pollution doesn't respect state borders. You econuts have been saying that forever, right? How does it feel to have the argument thrown back in your faces? Hunh? Hunh? Hunh? It doesn't feel that great, does it?

The Extremes unanimously laughed them out of Court. In the ruling, Chief Justice John Robalthomkenlia wrote: "We have not laughed in this *extremis* since we attended a private screening of *Hot Tub Time Machine*! Well, all except Justice Thomustomtombrap. Humourless bast – I mean, reprobate. Bastard has a specific meaning in the law that does not, to our knowledge, apply in this instance."

Expect Justice Thomustomtombrap's dissent early next week.

The last laugh may be on the Extreme Court, however. President Ronald McDruhitmumpf has tapped (without the messiness of having to hammer a metal spigot into a tree) Scott Jusprudoittitt, one of the most vocal members of the conglomerate of oil companies, coal miners unions and cosmetic manufacturers that brought the lawsuit, to head the EPA.

"That is – the most – last – outrageous – aarrrgh!" token smart person Amy Sheshutshotshitbam bitched (and we use that word in the most non-gendered way possible). "They may as well call it the Environmental Pollution Agency!"

"Environmental Pollution Agency?" Jusprudoittitt grinned. "I like it. Yeah. It has a ring to it. Think I'll suggest it to the boss the next time I see him."

Token smart person Amy Sheshutshotshitbam fainted.

As an Oklahoma Senator (expect an NHL franchise to be announced in the next couple of months), Jusprudoittitt opposed any law that would mitigate the effects of Global Hot as Hellification. "There is a dentist in Dubuquerque, Iowana who does not believe that Global Hot as Hellification is a thing," he argued on the floor of the legislature (his chair was being recovered at the time). "And, dentists are scientists, right? I mean, they have to know a little science to become dentists, right? And, anyway, he did a great job of fitting me for a mouth guard when I was gnashing my teeth so badly that I was having trouble sleeping, and that counts for a lot with me. What I'm saying is that the science of Global Hot as Hellification has not been settled to the satisfaction of everybody with an even tangential relationship to science, and, until it is, we should be skerpeptical, if not downright denialsome of the idea."

Jusprudoittitt's first act as head of the EPA was to lift restrictions on the use of plutonium in macaroni and cheese. "Plutonium is a well known preservative," he explained. "It has a shelf-life* of 10,000 years. And, as a bonus, it will change the colour of the cheese just enough that it will be less tempting for grade school kids to use cheesy macaroni to create dioramas of the President's hair."

His second act as head of the EPA was to repeal all regulations regarding the extraction, transportation or cultivation for personal use of oil. "Half the members of cabinet are former oil company executives," Jusprudoittitt explained, "and have smoked their share of their own product. So, as you might imagine, this was their number one priority. I adopted this measure second so as not to give the appearance of a pro-industry bias."

When it was pointed out that his second act was signed less than five seconds after his first, Jusprudoittitt responded, "Well, obviously, I wasn't **that** concerned about not giving the appearance of a pro-industry bias!"

Had she been conscious while I was doing the research for this article, token smart person Amy Sheshutshotshitbam might have asked hard questions about putting somebody in charge of a government agency who is radically opposed to the agency's mandate. As it was, she briefly awoke so that she could faint a second time.

* Jusprudoitttt likely meant half-life, so this should probably have been marked as his error, not ours. However, [sic] partied its ass off last night and called in [sick], so we're going to have to let the error stand unidentified.

Taking the Piss to a Whole New Level

by FREDERICA VON McTOAST-HYPHEN, Alternate Reality News Service People Writer

Special adviser to President Ronald McDruhitmumpf Steve O'Bannonallhope has been removed from the National Insecurity Council. This is not a drill! I repeat: this is not a drill! It's for realz! Teacher's pet Steve O'Bannonallhope has been removed from the National Insecurity Council.

Sources within the Grey House confirmed that the reason for the ouster was that O'Bannonallhope and Jared Kushkushinthebush, President McDruhitmumpf's favourite adviser who also happens to be his son-in-law, had gotten into a pissing match behind the West Wing. All over the lawn. And, up the side of the building. Gross. And, bad for the plants. But, apparently, that's the way politics is played these days.

"The President appreciates a vigourous debate about the issues," Press Secretary Sean Spirochetericer dug deep into his toolbox of pat responses and pulled out 23-B Apple Orchard to address the question of what happened. "But, trust me, he draws the line at the smell of ammonia outside his window!"

"Och, aye, whull, Press Secretaruh Sean Githead didna ha' ta resod thuh grass and repaint thuh side o' thuh buildin', now, did he?" Grey House Groundskeeper Willie disagreed. We assume he disagreed from his tone of voice; we didn't actually understand a word he said.

Kushkushinthebush and O'Bannonallhope have been at loggerheads (an archaic term that refers to the even more archaic act of cutting off the head of a logger and burying it in the remains of a forest that has been fully clearcut to appease the arboreal gods;

naturally, the loggers argued vociferously over who most deserved to have the honour foisted upon them) ever since they both entered President McDruhitmumpf's inner circle. They have a fundamental disagreement over the role of government in civil society: Kushkushinthebush believes there is one, O'Bannonallhope doesn't. Civil society, I mean; nobody knows if either actually has a position on the role of government in it.

So. When Kushkushinthebush suggested that the tax code be simplified to cut the effective rate rich people had to pay (I didn't say that the role of government in civil society that he envisioned would necessarily be a positive one), O'Bannonallhope argued that they should abolish taxes. Kushkushinthebush wanted to roll back the regulations governing the stock market enacted by the Bushbamclintreagbush administration; O'Bannonallhope demanded that the stock market be abolished and replaced by autonomous corporate fiefs. And, so on. On just about any issue, the extremity of Kushkushinthebush's position would look like a four year-old's tea party when compared to that of O'Bannonallhope.

Conflict was inevitable, really.

It didn't help that O'Bannonallhope called Kushkushinthebush a "cuck" (a popular term among the malt-right – yes, alcoholic beverages are involved whenever one of them appears in public – which either refers to a small cucumber or, if the person drinks a lot of alcoholic beverages, a small gherkin). Kushkushinthebush never gave any sign that he understood what the term meant, which infuriated him all the more.

President McDruhitmumpf, whose book *The Art of Confusion*, which contained 437 pages in random order, copious spelling errors and words that were not in any identifiable language (so, basically, a longer version of one of his tweeps), is said to thrive on chaos, but even he was fed up with the feud, telling O'Bannonallhope to "Get 'er done!" The redneck right was impressed that the President could quote one of their comedians, but that was short-lived when it dawned on them that the President had ordered their darling (in a purely platonic way, of course, because homophobes) to work things out, but not his son-in-law.

"You know," said token smart person Amy Sheshutshotshitbam through gritted teeth (she should really get those sanded down or something), "the more attention you give to the personalities that are clashing in the Grey House, the less attention you give to how its policies are screwing the average Vesampuccerian."

"Thank you," I humbly responded.

"You're wel – what?"

Rumour has it that O'Bannonallhope threw a hissy fit when the President asked him to end the conflict, threatening to take his ideological ball and go home. Typical firstborn behaviour. Meanwhile, Kushkushinthebush batted his angelic eyes and rhetorically asked why O'Bannonallhope had to be so darn mean to him all the time. His place as the second born was cemented by the fact that O'Bannonallhope always looked like the stubble fairy visited him every morning **after** he shaved.

"Thah's all fine and wuhl," Groundskeeper Willie grumped, "but it dinna replace the burnt roses, do it?"

A Political Tease That Titillates No One

by FREDERICA VON McTOAST-HYPHEN, Alternate Reality News Service People Writer

Is Cartwheel Brandewpagemacher the stupidest man in Washburningdington? Vesampucceri? The world? (I could expand further, but that would get us into questions about alien IQ, and that is more properly the realm of science fiction.) He works very hard to make it seem easy to give that impression – or does he? – but could it all be an act? Could he, in fact, be a strategic genius? Could I stack my lede with more questions? Was the last sentence a way of padding the number of questions in my lede? WILL NOBODY STOP ME?

[Stop. Brenda Brundtland-Govanni, Editrix-in-Chief]

Thank you!

Last week, the *Washburningdington Post* reported that Brandewpagemacher was the subject of a FIFA warrant (so-called because the subjects of them tend to become political footballs). You know how the Federal Bureau of Instigations is not allowed to surveil (literally: place a security shroud over) Vesampuccerian citizens? A FIFA warrant is when the FBI explains how really, really, really, really, really important it is to tap the phones and watch the comings and goings of a Vesampuccerian citizen; and, because of the five reallys rule, the court cheerfully tells them that of course you can, and thanks for asking so politely!

The FBI reportedly sought the FIFA warrant to surveil Brandewpagemacher because while he worked for President McDruhitmumpf's election campaign (as a central strategist or go-to guy for coffee and bagels depending upon who you're talking to), he was being paid by the government of the Duchy of Grand Fenwick. This is referred to by the FBI as "suspicious behaviour" in public and "Sweet Mary, Mother of Jesus, is a foreign power trying to interfere with our election? The integrity of our whole system of governance is under attack! Oh, shit! Oh, shit! Oh, shit! Oh, shit! Oh, shit!" in private.

Other people who contributed to President McDruhitmumpf's election efforts who were subsequently found to have ties to Grand Fenwick have either disappeared from the public eye (*a la* Paul Bildapillofort, an unsavoury dish, indeed); or lied to Congress about their connections to Vesampucceri's Cold War enemy and cuticled (because they were hanging on to their careers by their fingernails) themselves from the investigation of the McDruhitmumpf campaign's connections to Grand Fenwick after they were given a position in the government anyway (yes, I'm looking at you, Attorney General Sesspoolpandemic, in a very can't look away from a car crash kind of way!).

Not Brandewpagemacher. No, he appears in public every chance he gets and hints that he might, maybe, some day, you know anything is possible so don't give up, hope tell his side of the story, but never quite reveals anything newsworthy. Or, mildly interesting.

The following exchange on MSNBC is typical:

CHRIS CARFAIRINDRUGHAYES: The obvious question is: who hired you to work on the McDruhitmumpf campaign?

CARTWHEEL BRANDEWPAGEMACHER: People want more than the obvious these days, and, and, and, gribble gribble amberswatch, they deserve more, don't you think?

CARFAIRINDRUGHAYES: Oh. Umm. Okay. I think…I think they deserve to know if the Duchy of Grand Fenwick stole the election for Ronald McDruhitmumpf.

BRANDEWPAGEMACHER: Oh, ha ha ha you big silly!

CARFAIRINDRUGHAYES: Cartwheel, who hired you to work on the McDruhitmumpf campaign?

BRANDEWPAGEMACHER: You know, Chris, there are a number of ways that I could answer that question. Spiritually, I think it could be argued that the universe directed me towards the campaign. Albrachim garfluie! Philosophically, we are mere grains of sand blown this way and that with no purpose or control over where we end up…being an indispensable part of a team. Stoogily – quingqling clocket – we're all just an eye poke away from the big nyuk nyuk nyuk in the sky. Grumpy cattily, we –

CARFAIRINDRUGHAYES: So, you're saying that, of the many ways you **could** answer my question, you'll go for any except the one that actually **would** answer my question?

BRANDEWPAGEMACHER: You know, Chris, schnaft schnozzer magic jojo, there are a lot of ways I could answer **that** question…

Throughout the interview, Brandewpagemacher coyly batted his eyelashes and grinned like somebody who knows the murderer is in the house, but doesn't want to give that knowledge away to the police officer at the door.

Although the impression Brandewpagemacher gives is of somebody whose brain has no apparent connection to his mouth, not everybody is convinced. "He's sending a signal to President McDruhitmumpf," argued token smart person Amy Sheshutshotshitbam's common-law partner Arnie Bamshitshotshutshe. "He's saying: 'Don't feed me to the wolves, or I'll make sure that you're on the menu, too.' It's brilliant, really."

Is it, though? Is it really brilliant? Is the man who went on the cooking show *Meat the Press* and said, "I – umm – that is to say – what a good question, but I flibble, flibble, flibble fetang!" really some kind of genius?

I suspect we'll need an independent investigation into the ties between the McDruhitmumpf campaign and the Duchy of Grand Fenwick to find out.

The Southern Gentleman's Recusal Refusal

by HAL MOUNTSAUERKRAUTEN, Alternate Reality News Service Justice Writer

"Wuhl, suh, ah done reckon that what muh deah depahted daddy used ta say afo' he up and disappeahed on us without so much as a by y'all's leave oah faeh thee well maht just be apropos in this heah cihcumstance. Seems theah was this heah ahmadillo, see, what wanted ta scale Everest with nothin' moah than a tea strainah and a 1947 Buick El Nino. Course, that was thuh convahtible with thuh foah on the floah clown masks whut –"

When I pointed out to Attorney General Jeff "Self-regard" Sesspoolpandemic that my article hadn't actually started yet, he drawled, "Don' give it a second thought, son. Have you nevah seen a Southern gentleman get intah charachtuh befoah? Go on. Do what ya need ta do – I'll be ready when y'all need me."

Umm…okay.

As shocking as the firing of Federal Bureau of Instigations Director James Comeonecomally was (easily 10,000 volts – somewhere between sticking your finger in a light socket and sitting in an electric chair), details of how the decision was made are even more disturbing. One that has been buried in the coverage is that Attorney General Sesspoolpandemic was consulted before President McDruhitmumpf made the decision to downsize (so called because of the parka the fired person would have to wear to keep him warm in the remote post where he would be banished to) Director Comeonecomally. The reason that is problematic is –

"Wuhl, now, mah pappy always used ta say that if you can't pull thuh poahk outten the woolens in time foah summah calvin', you –"

I hadn't gotten to the part that required a response from you, yet, Mister Attorney General.

"Wuhl, recuse me."

Exactly. When he was going through the confirmation process in the Senate, then citizen Sesspoolpandemic testified under oath that he did not know of any contacts between the McDruhitmumpf campaign and the government of the Duchy of Grand Fenwick, which has been accused of interfering in the Vesampuccerian election. "I did not have relations with that country," he said. After his confirmation, it was discovered – hee hee, oops – that Sesspoolpandemic himself had met twice with Grand Fenwickian Ambassador Sergey Kismekillmeyack.

"Wuhl, we talked mostly abaht golf and who was gonna be thuh new host on *Thuh View*," Attorney General Sesspoolpandemic explained. "If we had discussed anythin' havin' ta do with national secuahty, wuhl, of coahse ah would have said so in mah confahmation hearin'. Ah was raised better'n that – Ah'm not a bahbarian, ya know!"

Almost there, Mister Attorney General.

"Wuhl, recuse me."

Wuhl. I mean, well, exactly. When newly minted (not only was he shiny, but he looked like he could be valuable) Attorney General Sesspoolpandemic's meetings with the Ambassador during the campaign became public, he recused himself from anything having to do with the Grand Fenwick investigation. To the extent that the firing of Director Comeonecomally was about his handling of the Grand Fenwick investigation, Attorney General Sesspoolpandemic's participation in it would seem to be in violation of his recusal.

Attorney General Sesspoolpandemic? Now would be a good time to respond.

"Wuhl, of coase it would," Attorney General Sesspoolpandemic responded. "Of coase it would. See, my daddy? He was a hahd man, but faih. When any of his children picked theah noses with theah feet, he would admonish them to use theah finguhs instead. 'Sorry, daddy,' we would say. 'Please recuse us foah ouah uncouthness.' So, you see, I know exactly what recusin' mahself mea –"

"Oh, that's just insane!" came an anguished cry from token smart person Amy Sheshutshotshitbam. "For a politician to recuse himself means to have nothing to do with legislation or a policy that he has a vested interest in! Attorney General Sesspoolpandemic lied to Congress when he said he had no meetings with representatives of the Duchy of Grand Fenwick! He lied when he said he would recuse himself from anything having to do with Grand Fenwick! And, now, he's lying about not knowing what recusing himself means!"

"Wuhl, recuse me," Attorney General Sesspoolpandemic said, "but interruptin' a public official tryin' tuh explain hisself on a mattah of national impohtance is downright rude!"

Is constantly interrupting a journalist trying to write a story good etiquette?

"Wuhl, Ah may be a southuhn gentleman," Attorney General Sesspoolpandemic responded, "but that does not mean that Ah am anybody's beahskin showah mat!"

Dumb as a Post Box, But Loyal

by FRANCIS GRECOROMACOLLUDEN, Alternate Reality News Service National Politics Writer

It has been 18 months since Walter Shaloubalaban, the Chair of the Department of Ethics and Light Inebriators & Snacks, resigned six months before the end of his term, saying, "This was the great privilege and honor of my career," with his mouth, but, "I'm going to have to take a six month long shower to feel human again!" with his eyes. Now, it appears that President Ronald McDruhitmumpf has finally nominated somebody to take his place.

Press Secretary for the time being (just sayin') Sarah Wannabe-Panders, looking like she had just swallowed fly pate on a low sodium cracker, said, "The President has always been clear that his commitment to ethics in government is, to quote the man himself, yuuge. I'm goin' ta get in trouble for sayin' that in our meetin' later, but it was the best way to describe his position. And, anyway, he doesn't have a copyright on the word, so anybody should be allowed to use it – uhh, he **doesn't** have a copyright on the word…does he? That would explain – okay, whatever. The point is, this wasn't just any old appointment for the President, so he wanted to be sure to get it right. If that takes 18 months…has the President copyrighted any other words that I should know about?"

The candidate for the position is named The Smijodoenesiths. If it looks to you like a mailbox, the sort of thing that you would find in front of farms on rural routes in Callaban County, Montalbana or Nanobozho, New Mexico, well, that's because that's what it is. It's a bright red mailbox on which somebody has painted over The Smijodoenesiths in white, not quite obscuring what was underneath, and painted crude eyes and a mouth in its place.

"Have you seen the candidate?" asked Senate Minority Leader Chuckie Schumaihargowmer. "The stake on which the mailbox rests has been shattered at the bottom. It's as if some kids were joyriding on a back route, maybe drinking a little even though they aren't of what you would call legal age, shooting at mailboxes – which, don't get me wrong, is their NRA-given rite – and they managed to hit this one in the stake. Only, instead of sending this mailbox to the scrapheap, the Reduhblicans have nominated it for Ethics Commissioner! Believe me, I can't wait until the confirmation hearing – this candidate doesn't have a leg to stand on!"

At 2:37 this morning, President McDruhitmumpf tweeped: "Ds better not obstruct nomination of DELIS chief, or they'll taste bitter defeet in 2020!" Given recent procedural changes, about the only thing Senate Dumboprats can do is hold their breaths until they turn Smurf. Anticipating this move, at 2:41 this morning, President McDruhitmumpf follow-up tweeped: "Smurfs are powerful, mystical creatures. D's Smurf strategy brilliant, but doomed. #imbrillianter!"

Little is known about The Smijodoenesiths – the government is rumoured to be keeping it in a closet until the confirmation hearings, "The Smijodoenesiths has been sharin' a room with its brother-in-law, a broom, and its best friend, a tennis racquet," Press Secretary Wannabe-Panders stated. "They've been livin' together for many years, and they are very happy with the arrangement. So happy, in fact, that they engage in spirited hijinks all the time! I mean, it's a regular *Three's Company* in that closet! So, if you are implyin' anything negative about the candidate's living arrangements, **cut it out!**"

How is a mailbox supposed to answer questions at a Senate confirmation hearing? "Through an interpreter," Press Secretary Wannabe-Panders explained, as if the point's obviousness made her embarrassed to say it out loud. As if she hadn't said a dozen more embarrassing things out loud in the previous ten minutes.

"Does anybody believe that the McDruhitmumpf administration is serious about ethics?" asked token smart person Amy Sheshutshotshitbam, who seemed to take her own question too seriously, so perhaps it evened things out. "No, no, no!" she insisted. "The Law of Rhetorical Averages does not apply to this situation! Just because I'm serious doesn't mean – can we please stick to the point, here? President McDruhitmumpf and members of his family and inner circle are making fortunes off his administration! Of course they don't takes ethics seri – GAAACK"

Token smart person Amy Sheshutshotshitbam got Blue Man Group in the face. Not so much Cirque de Soleil is interested in buying your act to market in China; more, being rushed to Caesar's Sinai Hospital (in Vegas) for a possible brain implosion.

Everybody at the Alternate Reality News Service wishes her a speedy recovery.

4. THE SLEEP OF REASON PRODUCES... POLICIES

Red State, Red Face

by FRANCIS GRECOROMACOLLUDEN, Alternate Reality News Service National Politics Writer

Like many people of his income bracket (the embarrassing end of the middle class), on call assembly-line worker Manny Posifrazitronic was surprised that the first bill President Ronald McDruhitmumpf's signed into law was that anybody whose name contained more than five syllables must report to a government office once a week to be beaten about the head and shoulders with rutabaga stalks.

"The Ronald promised that he would clear the beach of driftwood," Posifrazitronic ruefully commented as he held an ice pack to the side of his head. "If I had known that this is what he intended to do, well, I would have voted for him anyway, but at least then I could have used my Bushbamclintreagbushcare to get steroid injections in my head!"

Abolishing the Affordable For More People But Still Nowhere Near Perfect Care Act (popularly, and even more unpopularly known as Bushbamclintreagbushcare) was President McDruhitmumpf's second act in office.

I pointed out that President McDruhitmumpf repeatedly promised on the campaign trail to do exactly what he did. Not only was it a major part of the Reduhblican Party platform, but Kid Knee Stonecoldasdover, the only musician to play at the President's inauguration (which had the virtue of allowing everybody to make it an early night, or would have if the President hadn't decided to fill the additional time with his campaign's greatest hits), wrote the song "Beat People With Funny Names About the Head and Shoulders With Rutabaga Stalks" to celebrate the policy.

"Yeah," Posifrazitronic grudgingly allowed, **"but I didn't think he actually meant it!"**

"About the only thing we didn't do to promote the rutabaga policy was take out a billboard in Times Square!" crowed Special Adviser to President McDruhitmumpf Steve O'Bannonallhope, his voice dripping with the kind of contempt you would reserve for a 12 year-old caught drinking Scotch older than he was, desperately trying to make the most of it before the bottle was snatched from his hand. "And, I wanted to. You have no idea how much I wanted to! That would have shown those east coast, tofu-loving, animals over humans, capitalism-hating libtards something!"

When I asked him what, exactly, such a billboard would have shown the east coast, tofu-loving, animals over humans, capitalism-hating libtards, O'Bannonallhope went off on a 20 minute rant leavened with so many profanities I had never heard before that I wondered if he would be eligible for his own supplement to the *OED*.

Meanwhile, in red states across the nation, Vesampuccerians who voted for President McDruhitmumpf are experiencing three card Monte player's remorse. "The Ronald was hiding his intentions in plain sight!" said Cruella deVolvo-Lorraine, an aspiring trouser presser of no fixed IQ. "How was I supposed to know that he was going to repeal my Bushbamclintreagbushcare just because he gave out cookies at his rallies that contained fortunes that read: 'I'm gonna repeal Bushbamclintreagbushcare, make Vesampucceri great again!' Now how am I supposed to pay to get my tragically hip surgery?"

Not everybody is disappointed with President McDruhitmumpf, however. Demi-thaumatic-dramaturge Eugenie IOUnescaf couldn't have been happier. "Bushbamclintreagbushcare was a Communist plot to weaken Vesampuccerians by making us physically stronger! I couldn't be happier that President McDruhitmumpf burned it to the ground, put the ashes into a rocket and shot them into the sun! If market forces can't get me treatment for my gall stones, I don't deserve the freedom to live a pain-free life!"

Whoa! Somebody's got a lot of stones. Of a gallic nature.

Then there's David Duchastempecker, former Grand Visor of the Korrupt Klown Kollege. "Going after people with more than five syllables in their name is a great first step – we certainly don't want **their** kind mixing with our kind! But, it's only a start. Soon, we will have to [EXPLETIVE DELETED] the [EXPLETIVE DELETED] [RACIAL SLUR DELETED]. And, the [EXPLETIVE DELETED] [RACIAL SLUR DELETED] who are sapping this country of its precious bodily fluids will have to be [EXPLETIVE DELETED] immediately after. That's how the world will know that we will do whatever it takes to preserve our [EXPLETIVE DELETED] freedom!"

Apparently, profanity is the new orange.

Given the current state of stunned remorse, why did so many people vote for President McDruhitmumpf in the first place? "Oh, that's simple," explained pop psychologist (his most well-known work is *The Five Things Your Father's Soda Choices Reveal About You*) Alain DeLaFrontenac. "They are what we in the pop psychology biz categorize as CFMs: Complete Ferking Morons!"

When pressed, DeLaFrontenac insisted that his expletive was not deleted because he was speaking in the name of * SCIENCE *.

"Oh, wait," Posifrazitronic responded. "I know why I voted for The Ronald. He didn't have the contempt that the Washburningdington elites have for people like me."

"I think I'm going to be sick," token smart person Amy Sheshutshotshitbam moaned. I was wearing my second favourite business suit, a piece of apparel that had been washed only 27 years ago, so that seemed like a good place to end the article.

Ira Nayman
Is It Hot as Hell in Here, Or is it Just – AAAAAAH! OOOOOOW! AAAAAAARGH!

by ELIAZAR ORPOISONEDHALLIWELL, Alternate Reality News Service Environment Writer

It was a typical speech to the Oil Grower's Association of Texas that featured one of President Ronald McDruhitmumpf's favourite themes: global hot as hellification is false science news propagated by the Communist government of Slobonia and traitorous Vesampuccerians to force the country to bankrupt itself buying solar panels. The fact that he could not name a single Vesampuccerian traitor and that there is no such country as Slobonia was only of interest to the dwindling number of people in this idiotocracy (government by the stupidest) who clutched for dear life to "facts."

Just as he was getting to his favourite part (although how valuable that description was is open to debate, given that pretty much everything the President says is his favourite part), about how solar panels kidnapped and ate the babies of random dingoes, President McDruhitmumpf's hair caught fire.

"I thought it was a halo," said Mignon Duprelecilly, who had attended the outdoor rally with his wife Piotr. "Swear to glob, it looked like the President was filled with the holy spirit. Then, he started screaming. Not speaking in tongues, mind, just hollering like an animal in intense pain. Then, that there Vice President Michael Pendenatendance strode onto the stage – slowly, deliberately, cause that's his way – and sprayed President McDruhitmumpf with a fire extinguisher. I tried to convince myself that it was holy foam blessed by the Pope hisself, but when the paramedics ran onto the stage with a stretcher, well, I knew that something weren't quite right..."

President McDruhitmumpf was rushed to The Nearest General Hospital where, after being given the third degree by the admitting nurse, a second degree black belt treated the first degree burns over 63 per cent of his head.

Scientists are divided over what happened. Those who believe that President McDruhitmumpf's hair is natural suspect that something in the gel he uses to keep it at an unnatural angle ignited in the intense sunlight. Those who believe his hair is an artificial construct – possibly of alien origin – believe that something in the headpiece itself spontaneously combusted.

Whatever their differences, 97 per cent of scientists agreed that global hot as hellification was definitely to blame for the…tragedy might be an overstatement…let's go with bad thing that happened. (The other three per cent were too busy watching *The Big Bamboo Theory* to respond to the survey.)

"Nonsense!" retorted (in the legal rather than scientific sense) Press Secretary Sean Spirochetericer. "First, the President's hair did not catch fire. Second, if it did catch fire – which it didn't – it had nothing to do with global hot as hellification: it was because he fell asleep while smoking in bed!"

Spirochetericer is allergic to follow-up questions – they make him break out in aggressive rhetoric and podium thumping – so he called on a different journalist for the next one. Her question was about whether it wouldn't be better to build a moat along the border than a wall – it would certainly boost the Florida alligator industry. This meant that Spirochetericer never did have to explain how the President fell asleep in a bed while giving a speech in a stadium in Texas.

Later in the same press scrimmage (with all of the grunting and bodies flying in all directions and concussions that the league refuses to acknowledge that that implies), Spirochetericer suggested that anybody who wanted to know the government's position on global hot as hellification could find it on the government's Web site. Now, I'm a trusting soul. I went to the government's Web site. Several hours later, I had not found any information on the issue, but I did have to swear allegiance to the country at least six times and sign several documents that make Microsquish's End User Licence Agreement look like flash fiction.

I can hear President McDruhitmumpf laughing from his hospital bed.

At 3:07 in the morning, the following tweep appeared on President McDruhitmumpf's official Twitherd account: "Slobonia pres Glumpenfidditchov used space-based magnifying glass to attack me for stand on phony GHaH. lol Loser!"

Token smart person Amy Sheshutshotshitbam responded, "Does anybody have a paper bag? Paper bag, anybody? Anybody? I'm not kidding, people: I'm really gonna be sick, here!"

The President is expected to make a full recovery. The environment, not so much.

Ouchers Hurt Us All

by MAJUMDER SAKRASHUMINDERATHER, Alternate Reality News Service Education Writer

Education Secretary Betsy DeVolution-Ross' plan to give parents of children enrolled in public school education ouchers has run into some unlikely opposition: the far right of the Reduhblican Party.

"More and more, we're finding that our members can't read," said American neo-Nasty Maxamillian Greibflischflachulah. "I mean, we had to publish the latest edition of *People We Hate* as a colouring book to maintain their interest. It was embarrassing. Piotr can't draw worth a shi –"

Greibflischflachulah blamed the education system.

"Hey, don't blame the education system," DeVolution-Ross countered. "Yeah, most of our schools are so starved for funds that the buildings are shakier than Jell-O in a blender during an earthquake. And, yeah, sure, teacher pay is so low that high school graduates would rather work with old farts greeting people in Prison-Mart than going on to getting a degree in education. And, yeah, sure, okay, some schools have so few resources that nuclear power plant models at science fairs are made of paper clips and chewing gum wrappers (preferably with the chewed up gum inside). I grant you all of that.

"Still, the education system is not to blame for illiteracy in this country. Absent fathers are. Bastards."

If the education system (using the term so broadly that if it was an antibiotic it could cure a wide variety of STD (Sophistry Transmitted Diseases) is not to blame for illiteracy, why create a national oucher programme? "I don't want to piss off the neo-Nasties," DeVolution-Ross explained. "They're mean!"

Ouchers have been the holy grail (cue the coconuts) of Reduhblican education policy since Potganreabumbom palled around on the set with monkeys. Put simply, families are given coupons worth about $10 (23 piastrums at current cross-temporal exchange rates) and told that they cannot redeem them for burgers and fries at the cafeteria of their local MultiMaxiMegaMart, that they must put them towards the cost of enrolment in a school they want their children to attend. After five to 18 repetitions of this message, it finally sinks in to most parents that they cannot, in fact, redeem the coupons for burgers and fries at the cafeteria of their local MultiMaxiMegaMart, at which point most tear them up in frustration and/or try to eat them. (I was told by many subjects I interviewed for this article that they go down reasonably well with ketchup.)

They have been called ouchers because finding out how little value they have is like a punch to the gut, although, given the ultimate use many people find for them, indigestion may also be involved.

"How is that supposed to help anybody learn?" moaned Dumbopratic Party gadfly (that insect sure gets around!) Bernie Macsandbinoffman. "Oh, sure, I suppose eating the oucher will give your child enough energy to learn something that day, but how will it help them in the long term?"

Of greater importance, an oucher would only buy parents 12 minutes of class time or three chapters of a textbook in any school worth sending their children to. "Yeah, yeah, I was getting to that," Bernie Macsandbinoffman grumped.

Of course, this inconvenient truth is offset by the fact that such schools can usually be found in a different neighbourhood/city/state than the students who need them most. Travel costs can eat up their ouchers faster than a family of moths at a fabric buffet in your closet. "Oh, come on!" Bernie Macsandbinoffman angrily mumbled, "I would have said that if you had just given me the chance!"

Honestly, poor parents would be better off eating the ouchers. Ketchup makes everything taste like chicken (if the chicken had been drowned in ketchup).

Is DeVolution-Ross the best person to craft education policy, in this country? After all, the first time she stepped foot in a public school was the day after her confirmation. "It was…nice," DeVolution-Ross, trying to say something positive about the experience, failed miserably. "It had…walls. And, doors. Mostly. And, I'm pretty sure I saw a book, although, honestly, I hustled through there so fast that it could have been a small dog."

Students from Patrick Dumpsterdivery Junior Low School in Texas had planned to protest DeVolution-Ross' appearance, but, not being able to tell time, they got to the school between three and seven hours after she left. This did not stop White House Press Secretary Sean Spirochetericer from accusing the children of being paid $15 each by George Soroboraros to disrupt DeVolution-Ross' tour of their school.

The irony that that non-existent payment was more than the school ouchers was lost on him.

If she hadn't been indisposed with an undisclosed illness, token smart person Amy Sheshutshotshitbam might have suggested that it was absurd to put somebody who had no experience with, and, indeed, seemed antagonistic to the public school system in charge of it. "What can I say?" DeVolution-Ross might have responded, grinning. "I came by my ignorance honestly – I was home schooled!"

Not My Deportment

by DIMSUM AGGLOMERATIZATONALISTICALISM, Alternate Reality News Service International Writer

Fareeq "Ted" al-Matalalall thought it was a joke. A joke with a confusing setup and a poorly worded punchline, but a clear attempt at humour, nonetheless. After all, when was the last time somebody from Delaware, Mississippi was arrested on charges of allowing a camel in his care to go unconstrained in a public place and spit in the eye of a government official?

al-Matalalall wasn't laughing when he found himself on a plane headed for the Middle Eastern country of Aqqa Velveeta. (Not that he had been laughing in the first place, the joke teller having poor diction and acutely bad timing, but he **really** wasn't laughing on the plane, where he had been given a middle seat between a baby and a real estate agent.)

al-Matalalall had been the victim of an Executive Order signed by President Ronald McDruhitmumpf that anybody with an unVesampuccerian sounding name who has been convicted of a crime be immediately transported to a country that also has an unVesampuccerian sounding name. When it had been pointed out that al-Matalalall hadn't been convicted of a crime, only accused of one, White House Press Secretary Sean Spirochetericer tightly clutched the official press secretary podium (reinforced for those days when the press are getting…you know…fresh) and stated, "So, ICES agents may have been a little…overzealous. Still, I think we can all agree that deporting people with unVesampuccerian sounding names is the key to keeping us all safe!"

When it was pointed out that it wouldn't necessarily be safe for the people who were being deported to countries with a less forgiving approach to foreigners than ours (yes, they do exist), Spirochetericer broke off a piece of the podium and, waggling it at the reporters, responded, "Doesn't anybody want to ask me about Krystalle McDruhitmumpf's line of topless and bottomless bathing suits? I think your readers would be much more interested in that than some boring old administrivia…don't you?"

The next 12 questions were about Krystalle McDruhitmumpf's line of topless and bottomless swimwear. Journalists can be patriotic that way.

"There are so many things wrong with this case that I don't know where to begin!" exclaimed famed VCLU lawyer Alan Greenurpassterspanz. When, 93 minutes later, it became clear that he really wouldn't be able to find a place to begin, I decided to jump in with some exposition.

al-Matalalall had been accused of breaking a law that had been enacted in 1835 because municipal Reeve Steve Goode-Gauleemollee nearly lost an eye when a camel that had been brought to Vesampucceri by showman P. T. Smithsoniation to promote Smithsoniation's Magicke Elixir chewed through its rope and ran amok. When the dromedary was found three days later masquerading as a government peg leg inspector, the camel was put down (in the local press). Smithsoniation had been the only person to have been charged under the act in over 177 years.

"Yeah, that's a good place to start," Greenurpassterspanz agreed.

It is also true that al-Matalalall did not own a camel, had never been seen in public with a camel and, as far as anybody could tell, had never been within 703 miles of a camel. He had once seen a camel on the nature documentary show *Mild Kingdom* when he was but a wee sprat of a deportee, but it was chased down and graphically torn apart and eaten by a lion. A, err, sand lion. Al-Matalalall was so traumatized by the show that for years he would start crying if anybody innocently used the word "hump" in a sentence.

"Yes. Absolutely. That," Greenurpassterspanz enthusiastically concurred. "Can you begin to see why I was having so much trouble beginning?"

There is also the fact that ICES may have confused Fareeq "Ted" al-Matalalall with Fareeq "Bill" al-Matalalall, an Iowan native who had also never seen a live camel in his life, although he had once owned a brown Beano Baby with orange and yellow streaks that could have been a camel. Or, a unicorn with its horn on its back. Or, a large, strangely misshapen platypus. But, it did spit. Sort of. If you soaked it in water overnight and squeezed really hard. Even then, it was more of a light dribble than a forceful oral expulsion of saliva.

"I wasn't aware of that," Greenurpassterspanz goggled, writing furiously on his legal notepad (he assured me that he hadn't bought it on the black market). "If I had been, it would have made it even harder for me to figure out where to begin!"

"They seem to be determined to get rid of Vesampuccerians with unVesampuccerian names by any means necessary," commented token smart person Amy Sheshutshotshitbam through gritted teeth, clutching her stomach like it was Sean Spirochetericer's podium. She should see a doctor – the woman did not look at all well.

Spirochetericer disagreed with the token smart person's assessment. "We wanted to ensure that it was…you know…legal, so we spent twice as much time crafting this Executive Order as we did the first Executive Order about people with unVesampuccerian sounding names – the one that the Extreme Court was so unfair to, so mean and…and…and petty to. You know, twice as much time as…" Then, he mouthed the words, "…the one we don't talk about."

When it was pointed out that the President took no time at all crafting the first Executive Order, Spirochetericer exasperatedly pointed back: "Why do you think we…" Then, he mouthed the words, "…don't talk about it?"

On the phone, al-Matalalall told me, "I don't know what to do – I've never been outside of Mississippi in my life! You wouldn't happen to…do you have any idea where I might be able to get a thin-dish, deep-crust pizza in downtown Aqqa Velveeta City?"

Why Wait For Christmas When You Can Have the Gift of Coal All Year Round?

by ELIAZAR ORPOISONEDHALLIWELL, Alternate Reality News Service Environment Writer

As part of his plan to Make Vesampucceri Great Again™, President Ronald McDruhitmumpf has signed an Executive Order rolling back many of the environmental protections put in place by his predecessor (known around the Grey House as "He Who Shall Not be Named"). Central to the President's plans is "a return to manufacturing the coal-powered automobiles that were such a vital part of making Vesampucceri great in the first place." The fact that the United States of Vesampucceri never made coal-powered automobiles, or that the only coal-powered car – the Imperial Ocelot made in the Duchy of Grand Fenwick in 1912 – was a disaster, did not in any way dampen his enthusiasm for the idea.

According to President McDruhitmumpf, the Executive Order, "Is important to the future of Vesampucceri. Oh, so important. It will bring jobs back to the country.* It will help us grow our economy.** And, it will insure the country's energy independence in the future! *** Oh, I love being me!"****

At the signing press opportunity at the headquarters of the Environmental Pollution Agency, the President was surrounded by over a dozen members of the coal, oil and nuclear energy industries. The only black thing anywhere near him was the lump of coal that rested symbolically on the table near his signing pen (Presidential Adviser Steve O'Bannonallhope threw a temper tantrum to have it removed, but he was overruled).

One of the people on the stage was Wilbur Rossinantehead, Secretary of Commerce and founder of the International Coal Group. Could his grin be described as cat who ate the canary, all of the food in its bowl, all of the food in the bowls of its three siblings and the ham sandwich you foolishly left on the table while you went into the other room to see why your cellphone was making that strange sound, a chirruping meat grinder version of "We Are the Champions?"

"You might say that," Rossinantehead said with an offhand toss of his hand. "I couldn't possibly comment."

"This is going to fail in spectacular new ways," token smart person Amy Sheshutshotshitbam cooed lovingly to herself.

"Actually, while I hate to disagree with a token smart person, I must disagree with Amy, a...a token smart person" said famed VCLU lawyer Alan Greenurpassterspanz. "This is going to fail in a pretty mundane old way: it will be tied up in the courts until the final stages of global hot as hellification make the whole thing moot."

As with the other court challenges to President McDruhitmumpf's policies, his tweeps are expected to be used to prove his bad faith. "GHaH? Chinese hoax, people. eet the food, not the conspiracy!" he once tweeped. "Think of the jobs well create," he also tweeped, "when the air is so black you can't see a executive order an inch from you're face!" Oh, and then there was this one: "The war on coal is over, people! Over! We bombed the enemy into submission. Unconditional surender Have I mentioned how much I love being me?"*****

"And, people complain that the President's tweeps are counterproductive!" Greenurpassterspanz grinned.

"Coal powered cars?" mused Generic Motors CEO Mary T. Barrarraboomdee. "I know we're supposed to be innovative and all that, but we've never produced anything like it. I mean, where would we find the specs for something like that? I'm thinking a steampunk novel – anybody got any recommendations?"

Notes

* Nope. Thanks to automation in the coal mining industry, removing obstacles to the use of coal is only expected to create 11 new jobs. Not even a dozen. This is less than a rounding error in unemployment statistics.

** Wrong again. Thanks to Bushbamclintreagbush – yes, we dare speak his name! – era regulations, the economy is committed to renewable energy sources: many power plants have turned to natural gas, much of it supplied by citizens on a heavy bean diet, and many more are planning to in the near future. It will be hard to integrate coal into this new – ahem – environment. The effect on the economy is likely to be a rounding error of a rounding error.

*** Nyuh unh. Ain't enough coal in the world to stop Vesampucceri from importing oil. Looks like the President wants to beat his own *Guinness Book of World Records* record for most misstatements in a single press opportunity!

**** Okay, finally the President got something right. As if it wasn't obvious.

***** Yeah, you may have mentioned it once or twice. It's okay to stop now. Really. Feel free to stop at any time. The sooner, the better.

Law and Order: Washburningdington

by HAL MOUNTSAUERKRAUTEN, Alternate Reality News Service Crime/Court Writer

The problem with being a law and order candidate who has graduated (with barely passing grades, but the board of education still gave him a diploma!) to a law and order President is that you need lawlessness and anarchy for your domestic agenda to make sense. Trying to be a law and order lawmaker when crime rates are going down? Awkward.

"NY is criminal Dizznizzfizzlizzeyland," President Ronald McDruhitmumpf, never one to shy away from an abyss of awkward, tweeted at 3:27 two mornings ago. "cant walk block w/o tripping over corps. SAD"

"The President's…communication reminds me of Times Square in the 1970s," New Yoricknuhemwell City Mayor Bill dennuiBlaseohoh chuckled. Then, quickly sobering, he added, "Uhh, but that was then. And, then was a long time ago. Today, I mean right now, New Yoricknuhemwell is safe, safe, safe. Safer than your bathroom at home!"

"Like they don't have bathrooms in New Yoricknuhemwell!" scoffed Press Secretary Sean Spirochetericer, bringing his fist down on the podium that everybody in the room respected. Bringing it down hard.

In fact, murder, assault, and aggressive thumb-rising and "Ehhhhhh"ing have all declined in New Yoricknuhemwell over the past decade. Even the nature of criminal activity has changed: muggers now hand out cards with "How'm I doin'?" on the front and a 1-800 number on the back that armed robbery customers can call to rate their experience. And, get victimized again if they're foolish enough to give out their credit card information; but at least they'll be in the right place to lodge a complaint.

"Oh, these are just facts," chirped McDruhitmumpf administration's spokesmoralandintellectualvacuum KellyAnne Conwaytwittiest. "Who are you going to believe – the police who have painstakingly been gathering statistics for, like, ever, or what the President knows in his heart to be true?"

"Uhh, the police?" Mayor dennuiBlaseohoh responded. "Seriously, is that even a question?"

Apparently, it is to the 34% of Vesampuccerians who told a Rasputinmusson poll that they somewhat, a little more than somewhat, a lot more than somewhat, more than somewhat but less than lots, a little more than lots, a lot more than lots, more than lots but less than a great deal, a great deal, a little more than a great deal, a lot more than a great deal, more than a great deal but less than a huge heaping amount, a little more than a huge heaping amount or a lot more than a huge heaping amount believed that President McDruhitmumpf was right on crime. (Even in an industry renowned for flakiness, Rasputinmusson's polling methods are considered eccentric.)

Nobody quite knows why the President chose this moment to pick a fight with his home town. On the campaign trail, he wasn't so specific about the locus of internal evil. At 2:37 on October 22nd, for example, he tweeped: "gang violins up in bad neighburhoods – you know the ones I mean, don't pretned you dont!" The President's (appropriately called) base knew what "bad neighburhoods" he was referring to: predominantly black areas, especially those that were tragically situated in Dumbopratic states.

"This is just another example of government by distraction," explained token smart person Amy Sheshutshotshitbam on the afternoon of her release from hospital. "When something appears not to be going President McDruhitmumpf's way – like, say, revelations that the Federal Bureau of Instigations was investigating his campaign's connections to the Duchy of Grand Fenwick – he distracts from it – by, for instance, announcing that he is finally going to get rid of Bushbamclintreagbushcare. When Congress torpedoes that, he distracts attention from **it** by announcing a ban on travel from seven…or, maybe six countries that has nothing to do with the fact that they are predominantly Nordlingerite, nope, nyunh uh, whatever gave you that silly idea, they just…looked at us the wrong way, is all, and, for the good of international amity, we can't let them get away with it! …Anyway, when the courts strike down his travel ban, for whatever reason – or, maybe, no good reason at all other than the need to pander to his, there's that word again, base – he distracts from **that** by insulting New Yoricknuhemwell. There are so many levels of distraction in play that it makes *Inception* look like *Tiny Talent Ti* – wait, where…where have I heard that before?"

"The idea that this is government by distraction is absurd," retorted Spirochetericer. "We are clearly focused on the issue of tax reform, which has been the President's priority from the moment that he was elected!"

Distraction or not, President McDruhitmumpf's comments have real consequences. "My grandmother Phernwoodomina refuses to go out in public now," Mayor dennuiBlaseohoh pointed out, "and as the close relative of an elected official, she has an armed guard. Imagine how people I'm not related to must feel!"

The Fog of Fog

by MARA VERHEYDEN-HILLIARD, Alternate Reality News Service War Writer

"weir takin teh gloves off now – bad people better be scarred!" President Ronald McDruhitmumpf tweeted at 3:47 yesterday morning.

Nobody is sure what he meant. Optimists would like to believe that he was thrilled that winter was over, and that he looked forward to not having to wear mittens. Others hoped he was saying he was planning on taking the metaphorical boxing gloves off and working with Congress to make real progress on solving the problems the country faced, but they were doubtful: President McDruhitmumpf, who had never used a metaphor in his life, wouldn't know what one was if somebody took a laser and etched the word "metaphor" on the back of his eyeballs.* Perhaps he intended to signal to security officials that it was now accepted government policy to slap suspected terrorists with woolen hand coverings.

He probably wasn't referring to the gloves that poor little Tommy al-Faroukdesade was wearing when an air raid on his neighbourhood in the Iraqi town of Mosul blew his hands off. Not literally, in any case.

In the last week, civilian casualties in Mosul have gone through the roof – or, at least, they would have if the roof hadn't been blown away in an air raid last month. Perhaps as many as 200 civilians were killed in the bombing raid that took poor little Tommy al-Faroukdesade's hands, making it the worst instance of civilian deaths** at the hands of Vesampuccerian-led forces since the US first sent troops to Iraq in…umm…well…

"1991," whispered token smart person Amy Sheshutshotshitbam.

"We knew that!" we responded. "We just…get a little confused by anything that happened before yesterday, is all."

The rise in the death toll of innocent people suggests that the rules of engagement in the War on Nouns, Terror Campaign have changed. The old rule was that the Vesampuccerian military would try to limit civilian deaths…if anybody was paying attention. Now, even that fig leaf seems to have become just so much *Greek dolmades*.

"First of all, they're not people, they're foreigners," Grey House Press Secretary Sean Spirochetericer tried to correct me. "And, secondly, they don't die, they…umm…"

"Casualt?" somebody in the back of the press room suggested. The voice sounded suspiciously like token smart person Amy Sheshutshotshitbam.

Missing the irony,*** Spirochetericer grunted, "Exactly. They don't die, they casualt. And, no, to address the elephant in the room,**** the rules of engagement in a war zone have not changed. They –"

"Have just been casualted?" the somebody in the back of the press room that sounded suspiciously like a token smart person offered once again.

Spirochetericer frowned. "Is that even a word?" he asked.

When asked why, if the rules of engagement haven't changed, so many more peop – "Uhh, uhh, uhh," cautioned Spirochetericer – sorry, so many more foreigners had been…casualted in the fighting in Mosul, the Press Secretary replied, "I don't know. Maybe IWISH***** advised people in Mosul to throw themselves in front of the bombs of coalition forces to make us look bad. If it was a choice between that and listening to one of their endless speeches about the horrors of freedom, well, I know which fate I would prefer!"

As soon as the press conference was over, in an apparent effort to bolster what his Press Secretary had said, President McDruhitmumpf tweeted: "Ah lahk eeeeeegth." Nobody could figure out how this achieved its apparent objective.******

<u>Notes</u>

* Taking into account his intellectual sloth, smart money in Vegas was on the assumption he would rather look around the etching than look the word up in a dictionary.

** The term casualties seems so…casual, doesn't it?

*** The whole administration should be on a strict regimen of irony supplements.

**** This was ungracious of Spirochetericer. The African bush elephant in the room had a name, Eloise. And, although she had a tendency to bellow her questions in order to be heard over the din, most often they were sharp and insightful. Frankly, the Washburningdington press corps could use more elephants like her.

***** IWISH (also known as Duhesh) is an acronym for "Death to the Infidels as Long as it Doesn't Interfere With My Internet Connection." They are the biggest organization claiming to fight for Nordlingerites in the Middle East since coalition forces destroyed the last three biggest organizations claiming to fight for Nordlingerites in the Middle East.

******I've been advised that I missed an opportunity for reader engagement by abandoning poor little Tommy al-Faroukdesade in the fourth paragraph. The problem is that he isn't adorable – especially now that he has no hands, he's more confusing platypus than playful panda – so readers likely won't feel much empathy for his situation. And, anyway, he now makes a living selling his services to wealthy foreigners as a…umm…you know that box thing with arms sticking out that martial artists use to train on? What do they call that? Dangit! I bet token smart person Amy Sheshutshotshitbam would know! Well, he rents himself out as one of those. How relatable is that?

Building a Bridge to the 19ᵗʰ Century…
And Walling Ourselves In

by ELIAZAR ORPOISONEDHALLIWELL, Alternate Reality
News Service Environment Writer, and FRANCIS
GRECOROMACOLLUDEN, Alternate Reality News Service
National Politics Writer, with a little bit by HAL
MOUNTSAUERKRAUTEN, Alternate Reality News Service Legal
Writer thrown in for flavour

In his 20 minute address on the Paris Accord on Global Hot as
Hellification, President Ronald McDruhitmumpf's hand kept
touching his hair, as if he needed reassurance that it hadn't caught
fire. It made him look like a teenage boy on a date, but not in an
appealing way.

"Environment good," President McDruhitmumpf speechified.
"Jobs better. Vesampucceri out of Paris Accord. Don't like Japanese
cars. Especially if they're made in France." He then spent 19
minutes, 37 seconds railing against the media's coverage of the
Fenwick scandal.

President McDruhitmumpf has made no secret of the fact that he
wants the United States to return to being a world leader in the
production of coal, the miracle fuel of the 1870s. While coal isn't
specifically mentioned in the Paris Accord (it would be like setting
rules for buggy manufacturing in an Auto Pact), the Hellhot Gases
(HHG) its use puts into the atmosphere are definitely regulated by
the Accord. Oh, my lordy lord, are they regulated by it.

This is just the latest example of the McDruhitmumpf
administration's experiment in ersatz time travel. Labour Secretary
Andrew Putzlaymandwiethdrew has been quietly changing
workplace labour laws, making it legal for corporate leaders to whip
employees as long as the switch they use is no thicker than three
thumbs (a Biblical thumb allowing for inflation). Combined with the
abolition of minimum wage laws and Welfare benefits, workplaces
will come to resemble the Dickenjaneprimariesian sweatshops of the
1880s, but without the literary merit and good ventilation.

Another example of Vesampucceri moving forward into the past
involves foreign relations. Apparently, the McDruhitmumpf

administration doesn't believe in them. It's not just that President McDruhitmumpf demands that NEATO members pay more for their defense or he will throw them under the bus…iness end of a group photo op. The fact that the State Department is staffed mostly by tumbleweeds strongly suggests that diplomacy is not in the president's vocabulary (along with the words tact, sensitivity or, for some unknown reason, exfoliation – he has used the word in sentences, but it seems to mean something completely different to the President than it does to the rest of us).

As the United States pulls out of an international leadership role, President McDruhitmumpf's foreign policy looks more and more like the isolationism of the 1840s, when the only foreign entanglement the government could left ventricle (its stomach being only partially formed at the time) was how to keep Texas out of Mexican hands.

When not busy not recusing himself from anything to do with the Fenwick investigation (except for the important or entertaining bits), Attorney General Jeff "Self-regard" Sesspoolpandemic has been dismantling national laws, giving more control over the justice system to states. Thanks to this, Alabama will allow jurors to consider whether a defendant's name ends in a vowel while determining guilt, and Utah has added stoning to its list of acceptable forms of capital punishment. This takes them back to 1879 and 1883 (BC) respectively.*

Sesspoolpandemic has also been instrumental in crafting rules that would allow states to allow businesses to opt out of health care provisions for religious or moral reasons. So, for example, if a CEO believed that there was no such thing as spleens because they were not mentioned in the Bible, he could refuse to insure his employees for splenectomies. If a different CEO believed that all human beings are sinners who deserve to be punished for their moral transgressions, he could arrange to omit anesthetic from their health insurance. Or, if a CEO was opposed to heart bypasses – ostentsibly for moral reasons – well, you get the idea. The country could return to the 1810s, 1830s or 1870s, depending upon which state you happen to live in.

The main target of this change is female contraception medications. Along with rules limiting affirmative action, action on gendered pay discrimination and discrimination in hiring practices, the social regressives in the McDruhitmumpf government seem to be succeeding in making women BFF (Bare Footed and Fecund). They are definitely not women's BFFs. Choose your least favourite period of the 19th century as a reference.

And, of course, Stand Your Ground laws have all but made duelling in parking lots legal. Welcome back to the 1920s – best be careful what you say in public. Especially to strangers.

"Jethro Tullaladidah was a prophet!" token smart person Amy Sheshutshotshitbam said. Sometimes, token smart people can be enigmatic that way.

* Not that such changes in the law should be treated with respect. English can be awkward that way.

Middle Vesampucceri Meets the Middle East (At the Extremes)

by SASKATCHEWAN KOLONOSCOGRAD, Alternate Reality News Service Religion Writer

President Ronald McDruhitmumpf has signed his eleventh Executive Order banning travel from six predominantly Nordlingerite countries…and France.

"I've got a good feeling about this one," the President crowed at the signing ceremony. "The courts aren't going to overturn this one. It's been weeks…a week…well, almost a week…a few days, for sure since I talked about how bloodthirsty the Nordlinger religion is, so there's no way they can say its a religious ban. This Executive Order is bulletproof!"

To drive the point home, the Executive Order wore a heavy, military-grade vest.

"It's like President McDruhitmumpf read Samuel Huntdownandkillem's book *Them's Fightin' Civilizations*," commented Senate Minority Leader Chuckie Schumaihargowmer, "and took the wrong lesson from it."

"Actually," MSNBC host Chris Carfairindrughayes corrected him, "it's like he heard somebody talking about Samuel

Huntdownandkillem's book *Them's Fightin' Civilizations* on Foxindehenhaus News, only he didn't quite hear what it was actually about correctly."

"No," insisted pop psychologist Alain DeLaFrontenac, "it's more like somebody in his office drafted a one page memo about what they said on Foxindehenhaus News about Samuel Huntdownandkillem's book *Them's Fightin' Civilizations*, only they didn't quite get the point."

"That's not exactly right, either," Token smart person Amy Sheshutshotshitbam argued, "it's exactly like somebody reported to the President about the one page memo about what they said on Foxindehenhaus News about Samuel Huntdownandkillem's book *Them's Fightin' Civilizations*…only the message the President heard was a garbled version of what was in the book."

"Well," Senate Minority Leader Schumaihargowmer summed it up. "Any way you look at it, it's not good."

"Oh, lighten up, people!" said Reduhblican Senator and McDruhitmumpf surrogate (if asked, he would happily bear the President a child) Chuck Gasleygrassteahee. "What the President said was just words! Words are easy to say. But, if you want to judge him, you should judge him by his actions!"

When it was pointed out that the President's actions pretty much matched up with his words, Gasleygrassteahee grunted and muttered, "You would have let me get away with that sophistry if I was KellyAnne Conwaytwittiest – she makes it look so easy!"

The problem with the argument that the travel ban was not motivated by religious animus is that a large percentage of the Reduhblican base is motivated by religious animus. "Oh, I don't hate Nordlingerites," said retired (but he was good about getting out of bed to talk to me) stealworker Tommy Boy Allvespuccinuts. "I mean, they're greedy, shifty, untrustworthy people with low standards of personal hygiene, but, other than that, they're…well, pretty rotten bastards, really, who should be sent back to where they came from and stop threatening honest, hard-working people such as myself."

Allvespuccinuts voted for McDruhitmumpf…twice. "Yeah, I would have voted for him a third time," Allvespuccinuts explained, "but my fake moustache fell off just as I was giving the people running the polling station the name of my dead uncle. Next time, I'm using Krazy Glue!"

Why did Allvespuccinuts vote so…enthusiastically for McDruhitmumpf? "Law and order."

"I came to this country with next to nothing," said Tareeq Alfazzuba – I mean, Alfalfalooza – no, actually, that is to say Azzafalafel – dammit! Why do foreigners have to have such difficult names? – said Tareeq A., a member of The Church of the Bed Hidden Nordlinger. "I worked hard, and now, 37 years later, I have almost next to nothing. See how far I have come? I'm living the Vesampuccerian Dream!"

I asked Tareeq A. if the fact that he had dark skin and a beard long enough you could build a stairway halfway to heaven with it might have something to do with the fact that certain Vesampuccerians feared him. "So, I haven't been able to afford a shave in years," he answered, "and used soap isn't as effective as I had hoped it would be. Is that really a reason to hate me?"

Weeeeeellll, that and the fact that Nordlingerites have claimed responsibility for terrorist attacks around the world.

"That's ridiculous!" Tareeq A. exploded. "The main – exploded? Really? Of all the verbs in the English language that could be related to speech, that's the one you're going to go with in this context?"

Would you prefer "blew up?"

Tareeq A. sighed. "Look. The primary tenet of our faith is that when faced with a potential conflict, no matter how minor, we find a bed to hide under until the whole thing blows over. Anybody who commits an act of violence in the name of Nordlinger is perverting the faith!"

"Exactly!" Allvespuccinuts exploded (without, you will notice, complaint). "It's a religion of perverts! I say ban 'em all and let the Disunited Nations sort 'em out!"

Ira Nayman
The United States of Vesampucceri Does Not Qatar and Run

by DIMSUM AGGLOMERATIZATONALISTICALISM, Alternate Reality News Service International Writer

Ronald McDruhitmumpf's behaviour on his recent trip to the Middle East has some people asking, "Mister President, are you on crullers?"

At 2:37 the morning after he returned, the President tweeped, "Qatar sponsors terrism. Bad bad people. I support SA blockade bigly!"

"There are two problems with the President's position," commentalyzed Senate Minority Leader Chuckie Schumaihargowmer. "Of course, there are more than two things wrong with the McDruhitmumpf administration. Way more than two things wrong with the – let me put it this way: you would need a quantum computer to calculate all the things that are wrong with the McDruhitmumpf administration. Still, I am but a single human being, finite and fallible, with all of the limitations of –"

Jumping ahead: one of the problems Senator Schumaihargowmer has with President McDruhitmumpf's position is that the United States of Vesampucceri just signed an agreement to sell $110 billion worth of military equipment (as part of the "Make Vesampucceri War Industries Great Some More campaign) to Saudi Arabia. The Saudi Arabia that supports radical Nordlingerite groups like Duhesh with arms and a shoulder to cry on when their relationships aren't going well? Right. **That** Saudi Arabia.

"...ike to think that, despite my human frailties, once in a while something I say does appertain to the subject at – oh. You made my point without me? Yeah, okay, I get that you have word limits so that was probably a good idea," Senator Schumaihargowmer commentambled. "The problem is that the human mind is far too easily distracted by any shiny object that – ooh! Well, will you look at that? Is that a Yellow Bellied Bipartisan Sucker? It kind of reminds me of a hot dog I had in college, but without the three pronged silver riding breeches!"

Jumping ahead (and stepping to the right), it seems odd that the government would condemn one state supporter of terrorism while rewarding another. In response to repeated questions on the subject, the Grey House stated: "It's a beautiful day. The sun is shining. A gentle breeze is blowing. You shouldn't be worrying your pretty little head over trivialities like this! You should be out enjoying yourself. I would recommend poisoning pigeons in the park – so cathartic!"

That's what I get for trying to get a straight answer out of a building!

Meanwhile, Senator Schumaihargowmer was commentusing: "…without knowing if the boy genius would vote for increased lead contamination testing for starlings, skylarks and red-breasted festering warblers. Still, despite our propensity for distraction, the human mind has the ability to focus with laser-like precision on the task at hand. For instance, I couldn't help but notice that you had gotten ahead of me once again. Understandable, if a little insulting. I'm on top of the issue we are supposed to be discussing, you know. The third problem with the President siding with Saudi Arabia against Qatar is –"

Stepping back a little, the **second** problem with the President's condemnation of Qatar is that the country is home (in the sense that it lives in the basement, blares loud music at all hours of the night and communicates with everybody else who lives there with great reluctance – and, no, I am not projecting my problems with my teenage son onto this political situation!) to the al-Acheelat Maror airbase, the largest Vesampuccerian military base in the Middle East. An airbase Vesampucceri sends planes on bombing runs against Duhesh from and, you know, actually fights terrorism and stuff.

Why would the McDruhitmumpf administration jeopardize the War on Nouns (Terrorism Division) in this way? "The future is cloudy," the Grey House claimed. "Try again later."

"It was the glowing orb," said @leftisrightdeskjokey, who goes by the name Dwight Kefauvesteser when not on twitherd. "It got the president all kafuffled!"

Going forward – no, back – no, not that either. Umm, going in whatever direction gets us where we need to be at this point in the article, Kefauvesteser was referring to the start of President

McDruhitmumpf's Middle East Getting to Know You, Getting to Know All About You Tour 2017. While in Saudi Arabia, the President, Saudi King Salman Abdulazizi and Egyptian President Abdel Fattah al-Sisisenor put their hands on a glowing white beach ball while staring blankly into space. "Oh, sure," Kefauvesteser wrote on Farcebook, "they **said** it was to open the Saudi Arabia Global Centre for Strategies to Combat Extremist Ideology (And Irony). But, it's really a mind control device! Oh, yeah! Mind control device, baby! It vibrates at a frequency that relaxes the brain of anybody who touches it! Then, boy Howdy Doody, then they're susceptible to any suggestion the last person they spoke to puts into their heads! It explains a lot, doesn't it? DOESN'T IT?"

"Oh, please!" Senator Schumaihargowmer commentplained. "If I had a machine that could do something like that, I can think of much more entertaining things to make the President do than this!"

We wanted to get a bit ahead to write about what the Senator was getting at, but we couldn't stop thinking about all of the entertaining things **we** could make the President do if we had one of those humming orbs...

5. THE SLEEP OF REASON PRODUCES... LEGISLATION

Health Care to Die For

by LAURIE NEIDERGAARDEN, Alternate Reality News Service Medical Writer

Speaker of the House Paul Ryboehnbachblisscrap has claimed that the Reduhblican replacement for the Affordable For More People But Still Nowhere Near Perfect Care Act (aka47: Bushbamclintreagbushcare) will save the government "a gazillion dollars in the first seven months, three days, 14 hours and 36 minutes," money that will help people. Okay, primarily military contractors and private prison corporations if the planned 54 gazillion dollar military budget increase is passed. But, they're people, too. Broadly defined. If you squint.

Speaker Ryboehnbachblisscrap crowed: "This will be the biggest change in the nature of Vesampuccerian government since George Washburningdington refused to hold cabinet meetings unless everybody in the room could prove they had wooden teeth!"

What goes mentioned less frequently (if, by less frequently, I mean not at all) is the fact that changes to the Act would mandate at least 24 million Vesampuccerians to catch Bubonic Plague.

"Who do you think is gonna get it in the neck from these changes?" asked Dumbopratic Congressman Bernie Macsandbinoffman. "The poor and those with pre-existing deadly communicable diseases – we're talking those in our society who are least able to fight off the Bubonic Plague – that's who!"

Technically, the department of Health and Human Services recommends that citizens be oculated in the arm or shoulder; otherwise, Macsandbinoffman has a point. A sharp one. Which, I suppose, is useful when you're trying to needle the government.

Some Vesampuccerians who voted Reduhblican are outraged by the policy. "I was told that horrible, rotten, no good Bushbamclintreagbushcare was going to be gotten rid of, but that I would be able to keep my health care under the fantastic, great, whiter than white Affordable For More People But Still Nowhere Near Perfect Health Care Act," groused Caucasus, Alabama unemployed *Remington Steele* worker Augie Filamentbuster. "If I had known that they would be getting rid of both, well, I would probably have still voted Reduhblican, but I wouldn't have been so darned enthusiastic about it!"

When I pointed out that the Bushbamclintreagbushcare and the Affordable For More People But Still Nowhere Near Perfect Care Act were the same thing, Filamentbuster said, "No they're not!" so loudly that people three booths down spilled their beer. Fortunately, they spilled it into each other's mouths, so it didn't go to waste.

Sensing discontent among their base (in every sense of the word, including those from chemistry and sports), some Reduhblican Congresspersons' support for the legislation is thinner than a male stripper's thong. Piercing the bubble of self-regard that clung to him like cheap perfume, President McDruhitmumpf's aides finally impressed upon him that his health care bill (which was really Speaker Ryboehnbachblisscrap's, but Ryboehnbachblisscrapcare doesn't have the same ring as McDruhitmumpfcare) could be defeated in Thursday's planned vote.

President McDruhitmumpf sprang into action: he tweeted, "hated Bushbamclintreagbushcare bill has to go. Bad! Bad! Bad! Bad! baaaaaaaa!" Then, he surprised everybody by holding a closed door meeting with Congressional leaders in which he reportedly shrieked, "You [EXPLETIVE DELETED]'re gonna make me look bad! Not gonna happen. Not gonna [EXPLETIVE DELETED] happen! Anybody who [EXPLETIVE DELETED] votes against my [EXPLETIVE DELETED] health care plan can expect me to campaign vigourously **for them** in the next election. You've seen my [EXPLETIVE DELETED] dismal approval ratings. Imagine what **that's** gonna do to your [EXPLETIVE DELETED] re-election chances, [EXPLETIVE DELETED]s!"

Rumours are that Speaker Ryboehnbachblisscrap will postpone the vote until the onset of the next ice age.

"You have to think that if he loses the vote on Thursday," pundited MSNOBC pundit Claire Febrilondalong, "the President will lose a lot of support among people who confuse bluster with strength. This could hamper enacting the rest of Paul Ryboehnbachblisscrap's agenda. And, it would deal a serious blow to the President's feelings. The consequences are mind-blowing!"

When it was pointed out that if the legislation was passed, millions of Vesampuccerians would die horrible deaths, Febrilondalong sniffed and replied, "Can we please focus on what's important, here?"

Token smart person Amy Sheshutshotshitbam moaned, "Could this be why I've been feeling so bad, lately? Have I gotten pre-Bubonic Plague in anticipation of the passage of this legislation? No. No, that's idiotcratic thinking. And, yet…it makes a certain amount of sense…so seductive – yes, there's an obvious conspiracy against token smart people to complete the idiotcratic agend – ah, but, no! No, I need to resist such groundless theorizing! If I don't, I'll become just like…**them!**"

After a moment's reflection, she added, "Does anybody have any aspirins? This whole health care debate is giving me a headache!"

Apparently, Going Ballistic is an Option

by FRANCIS GRECOROMACOLLUDEN, Alternate Reality News Service National Politics Writer

Senate Reduhblicans have pulled the trigger on the ballistic option. No, that doesn't mean that they have rained Hellfire missiles down on the offices of the Dumbopratic opposition (although the thought made Reduhblican Easter office parties the most lively they've been in years). No, they changed the rules for approving Extreme Court nominees: where it used to take a super majority (a majority that could only be overcome with Kryptonite) of members of the Senate, now all it takes is a simple majority (a majority with an IQ of less than 70) of Senate Reduhblicans.

Dumbopratic Senate Minority Lea – you know, upon a moment's reflection (I haven't been able to look into a mirror since the Habitant pea soup debacle when I was four years old – I hope you appreciate the sacrifice I make for you, my treasured readers), it occurs to me that this action isn't really dramatic enough to qualify as "ballistic." I mean, it's not like there will be enough destruction of property to make insurance agency executives wake up in the middle of the night with the involuntary sweating hodaddies or anything. But, hey – you try writing an attention-catching newspaper lede in these times of 24 hour cable screaming punditry and political fake bloggery and…and…and…

Anyway.

Dumbopratic Senate Minority Leader Chuckie Schumaihargowmer considered the situation carefully. "This was a very short-sighted decision," he admonished when he had finished weeping. "Some day, god and gerrymandering willing, Dumboprats will once again have a majority in the Senate. Then, we will be able to get our nominees approved without any support from the opposition. You just wait and see, boy. Some day."

Reduhblican Senate Majority Leader Mitch Wichconnelliswich needed no time to consider the situation, carefully, sloppily, adumbratedly or any other whichway. Grinning, he said that he would let the full implications of the changes sink in before responding to his <verbal air quote>respected</verbal air quote> colleague.

This comes after the Reduhblicans had made it impossible for former President Barry W. Bushbamclintreagbush to fill the Extreme Court vacancy with his own candidate, Justice Merritt Cinnamondgarfunckle. The majority on the Senate Injustice

Committee held meetings at random places in Washington for over a year to avoid holding a hearing with Justice Cinnamondgarfunckle. Locations were chosen by having the committee chair throw darts at a map of DC; he only informed the majority Reduhblican members an hour before the meetings, leaving the bewildered Dumbopratic committee members wandering the streets in the hope of accidentally stumbling upon the secret site. One time, Cinnamondgarfunckle found himself across the street from an Injustice Committee hearing, but he only discovered this because he was leaving an IHOP just after the Reduhblicans had adjourned their conclave in the building across the street.

When they recognized him, the Reduhblicans scattered like so much pork in an appropriations bill.

Some critics (on the MSNBC early early morning talk show *Some Critics Argue*) argue that the Reduhblicans stole the Extreme Court seat, an accusation that President Ronald McDruhitmumpf vigourously denied. "Sure, we stoll it," he tweepxulted at 3:47 in the morning. "but we stool it fare & square, so ha ha ha!"

Why does this arcane (but ballistic – let's not forget what got you reading in the first place – ballistic, ballistic, so very ballistic) matter matter? The Extreme Court was divided four-four; the ninth seat (by which I mean the person sitting in it, since, obviously, the seat recuses itself on every issue) could decide a lot of issues. And, Neil Goretexersumsuch, President McDruhitmumpf's choice to fill the vacant seat? He makes Antonin Scoliatosis look like Mickey Monstrousitiness.

"You can kiss *Roeliodingdong v. Watuhfouriday* goodbye for a start," explained famed VCLU lawyer Alan Greenurpassterspanz. "But, better be sure it's a short kiss – to be on the safe side, no tongue – or you'll have to live with the consequences for the next nine months…or 20 years. Were you disgusted by *The Handmaid's Tale*?" Well, guess what? The Reduhblican majority on the court considers it a how-to manual!"

"You say you don't care about that because it only affects women?" Greenurpassterspanz went on. "Do you like breathing air? Because the Reduhblican majority on the Extreme Court will ultimately rule on Environmental Pollution Agency rules that will make breathing feel like eating borscht! Mmm…that reminds me: I have to pick up some beets on the way home after this interview…"

"You say you don't care about **that** because it only affects land-living mammals?" Greenurpassterspanz went on anon. "How would **you** like to live next to an oil rig? They make noise that will keep you up at all hours of the night and probably interfere with your navigational sonar. When you find yourself washed up on a beach, boy will you regret not supporting the land-living mammals!"

Goretexersumsuch is expected to be confirmed after this article goes to press but before the print issue comes out, so choose your favourite tense. How can the Senate majority get away with this? "Dumboprats govern," token smart person Amy Sheshutshotshitbam sagely commented. "Reduhblicans rule."

When we asked her to elaborate, elucidate and/or possibly perform another verb ending in "ate," the token smart person noticed that it was time to take her anti-anxiety meds, after which she needed to have a good long lie down in a dark and quiet room. We may ask her to *ate again in a week or two.

Push Me Pull You Politics Us

by LAURIE NEIDERGAARDEN, Alternate Reality News Service Medical Writer

Imagine you are on a teeter totter with seven of your closest friends (or, since it may be a stretch to believe that a businessman/politician of your stature has any friends, let alone that many, seven employees that you have involuntarily volunteered – on their own time – for this thought experiment). The problem is that when the fourth person on one side (say, the right) gets on, they throw the fourth person on the opposite side (the other right) off. When the fourth person on the other right side tries to get back on, they throw the fourth person on the right off again. And, so on.

Now, imagine that 210 of your best friends/poorly compensated employees are doing this. Only, they aren't your friends/employees, they're members of the House of Unrepresentatives. And, they aren't on a child's playground amusement ride, but trying to pass a health care repeal, reform and remonstrate bill. Under these circumstances, it should be easy to see why there would be very little teetering, and absolutely no tottering.

"I love the smell of withdrawn legislation in the morning," crowed Mark Meadabiggblubratt, the unofficial leader of the Reduhblican Economic Slavery is Freedom Caucus, a far right group that believes...well, the name pretty much sums it up, doesn't it? "It smells like...ideological victory."

"Well, we tried," shrugged a disconsolate (after this debacle, he had to know he would never be an ambassador to a foreign nation) Speaker of the House Paul Ryboehnbachblisscrap, "but we just didn't have the votes. Next time, we'll try something simpler, like tax reform!"

Or, not. Having had a weekend to mull it over, Speaker Ryboehnbachblisscrap and the Grey House floated a new health care reform, repeal and recriminate bill meant to win over members of the Economic Slavery is Freedom Caucus. Now, instead of 24 million Vesampuccerians being given Bubonic Plague, the number would be 37 million, and, on top of that, many of them would now be mandated to be given HIV, the virus that leads to AIDS.

"This is the free market working as it should," Meadabiggblubratt grinned.

Or, not. Again. This time, the or, not refers to the problem that for every vote the Reduhblicans gain from the Economic Slavery is Freedom Caucus by making the bill harsher, they lose a vote on the other right side of the party. Seriously: if the one to one correspondence was any more perfect, a thousand postmodernist theorists would throw up their hands in defeat, burn all of their maps and go into organic farming.

"I've heard from my constituents," said Reduhblican Unrepresentative Marcus Atavistical. "Boy, oh boy, have I heard from them. Frequently. And, loud. Often incoherently, but the volume really sends its own message. And, that message is: I will lose my seat if I vote for a health care bill that will force them to get HIV. My conscience is clear."

Further lowering the desire of Reduhblican Unrepresentatives like Atavistical to vote for the bill is the fact that it has little chance of being approved by the Senate. This would be like the teeter totter being caught up in a tornado and all of your friends/employees being thrown miles away from the playground. And, if nothing else, politicians are very up on natural disaster preparedness for their careers.

"hc reform failure fault of Dumbs," President Ronald McDruhitmumpf tweeped at 3:47 in the morning. "not 1 voted to repeal their guy's signature legislation. SAD!"

"Umm…why would we?" House minority leader Nancy Pelligrinosi asked with a twinkle in her eye (she should really have an optometrist look at that).

In seven years of opposition, the Reduhblicans claimed that the Affordable For More People But Still Nowhere Near Perfect Health Care Act (known as Bushbamclintreagbushcare because life is too short) would cause " a tear in the space/time continuum that would allow demons from other dimensions to attack Earth!" and "spots to appear all over your body! Big, round ones! Purple!" and "a revival of *Mork and Mindy* starring Gilbert Gottfriedchickenlegs!" In all the time they were attacking the AFMPBSNNPHCA, did they craft a carefully considered plan to replace it?

"Does it look like they crafted a carefully considered plan to replace it?" Unrepresentative Pelligrinosi goggled. Oh, yeah, she definitely needs to get her eyes checked.

As we were about to ask for her opinion, token smart person Amy Sheshutshotshitbam wondered if her health insurance provider would consider politics-induced exhaustion a preexisting condition. As a result, her blood pressure spiked and she was unable to offer a coherent thought on the issue.

When the Teeter Totters

by LAURIE NEIDERGAARDEN, Alternate Reality News Service Medical Writer

The House of Unrepresentatives has done the unthinkable: they have passed a bill.

A couple dozen of them (including three women, two blacks and as many as five under the age of 60 – there's nothing anybody can teach the Reduhblicans about diversity!) congregated on the Grey House lawn to celebrate the passage of the bill. A marching bad (the Millard McFilmadgoonie High School Golly Gee Club was so terrible that my computer threatened to shut down if I described them as a band) spontaneously appeared in front of them and balloons fell on their heads – an odd occurrence considering there was no ceiling to drop them from.

"Phew!" exulted Speaker of the House Paul Ryboehnbachblisscrap.

The phew-inducing bill was the Reduhblican repeal, replace and rerelevant response to the Dumboprats' Affordable For More People But Still Nowhere Near Perfect Health Care Act (known as Bushbamclintreagbushcare for reasons that are lost to history, as the bill may soon be), so while the Reduhblicans were celebrating, the Vesampuccerian people? Not so much.

"Everybody in the country will have better health care at a lower cost," President Ronald McDruhitmumpf boasted. "And, if you don't believe me, just ask the Secretary of Unicorns!"

No need. Everything President McDruhitmumpf said was true… as long as you disregarded the actual facts.

In order to get votes from the Slavery is Freedom Caucus, the Reduhblicans had to make their first effort at a repeal, replace and remonstrate bill even more Draconian (while not bringing to mind the Surreal-Malfoysance character from the Harry Potter movies). At least 24 million Vesampuccerians would be given Bubonic Plague under the old version of the bill; nobody knows how many additional millions will be added by the new bill because it wasn't scored (music to opponent's ears) by the Congressional Office du Budget (COB) before the vote was taken.

One new provision in the bill that passed gives states the power to send those over the age of 60 or those with a permanent disability out to sea on ice floes. "Local governments are in a better position to care for people than the federal government," explained Mark Meadabiggblubratt, the unofficial leader of the Economic Slavery is Freedom Caucus. "And, anyway, whose gonna miss a few doddering old fools and gimps?"

Those set free on ice floes will either die or survive on a diet of kelp and bitter memories. Either way, the money saved by not covering them will go to a worthy cause: tax cuts for the wealthiest 400 families in the country. Including the McDruhitmumpfs. Possibly. You never know. Crazier things have happened. Hell, crazier things happened less than an hour ago.

Last week, we reported that a health care reform, repeal and redline bill had no chance of passing the House because for every Slavery is Freedom Caucus member the leadership won over, it would lose a moderate. Whu haaaaappen? "Paul Ryboehnbachblisscrap promised that we wouldn't actually have to read the bill," explained Congressman Antoine Delapanburggies. "I was so grateful – those things are boring! – I offered to buy him a beer, but he said he would rather have my vote on the bill – he can be very focused that way – and how could I possibly say no?"

President McDruhitmumpf said that his contribution to the effort was to threaten to primary challenge any Reduhblican who voted against the bill and promise any moderate Reduhblican who voted for the bill a date with a *Playboy* model at Rama-Lama-Largo. There is no reason to believe that he could make good on either, but that likely wouldn't occur to the kind of politician who would vote for a potentially toxic bill that they hadn't read. Neither is there reason to believe that the President actually did what he said he would, but that wouldn't deter the kind of journalist who accepts assignments with ludicrous deadlines.

According to presidential historian Michael Beschbefordatloess, celebrating the passage of a bill in the House is unprecedented. "You celebrate the actual passage of laws. This law has to go to the Senate, which will undoubtedly make changes to it. Then, the two houses of congress have to meet to merge the two bills into one. Then, both houses have to pass the amended bill. It's like celebrating the creation of an atomic bomb after you've managed to get fire from rubbing two sticks together! There hasn't been anything quite like this since Grover Cleaverhatchetland celebrated the –"

I cut him off there because I wasn't writing a book. And, the whole ludicrous deadline thing.

Token smart person Amy Sheshutshotshitbam had a jaundiced view of the legislation (her doctors were having trouble diagnosing her condition and had begun clutching at straws). "It's a pyrrhic victory – the Reduhblicans' majority in the House will go up in flames," she commented. Then, she checked her body to see if it was still female. "Life!" she moaned. "It's a preexisting condition!"

Spinning Dross Into...Shinier Dross

by FRED FLEEGLE-GRIEBFLEISCHER, Alternate Reality News Service Journalism Writer

President Ronald McDruhitmumpf has been hit with the biggest setback of his administration...this week. The House approved an appropriations bill that would fund the government for the next six months. By optimistic projections. With asterisks. And a headwind. President McDruhitmumpf had threatened to put on his big veto panties (which his government paid $399 for even though anybody can get them at WoolMart for $4.99 a pair) if the bill did not include a billion dollars to start building a wall on the Vesampuccerian/Canadian border.

The bill crossed the President's desk without funding for the wall, and he went pantyless.

Although Washburningdington has the memory of a flea that has undergone CIA brainwashing experiments, enough Reduhblican Congresspeople remembered 2007, the last time the party shut down the government by refusing to fund it; in that case, it was over the fundamental principle that they wanted to catch up on the current season of *Lost*. As a result, not only did support for the Reduhblicans plummet (senior citizens are not sufficiently supportive of Reduhblican policies to be willing to forego their pension checks – who knew?), but *Lost* made even less sense at the end of the season than it had at the beginning.

"Yeah, nobody wanted a repeat of that fiasco!" exclaimed Speaker of the House Paul Ryboehnbachblisscrap. "Even with the coming revival of *Twin Peaks*!"

Of course, setbacks don't phase the President...they send him into a volcanic rage. So, was lava pouring out of his ears when this happened?

"Is the President disappointed that Congress didn't give him the funds he had requested to start building the wall?" Press Secretary

Sean Spirochetericer rhetorically asked. "Of course the President **isn't** disappointed that Congress didn't give him the funds he had requested to start building the wall!" Press Secretary Spirochetericer rhetorically answered. "President McDruhitmumpf has fulfilled his promise to the Vesampuccerian people by already starting to build the wall without those funds!" Press Secretary Spirochetericer rhetorically...rhetoricked.

To prove his point, Press Secretary Spirochetericer put images of a pile of straw, a pile of wood and a pile of bricks on the screen in the press room. "Ladies and gentlemen," Press Secretary Spirochetericer did his best P. T. Barnonendbayleys impression, "These are pictures of the wall on the border between New Yoricknuhemwell State and...umm...Vancouver...State. Or, wherever. It's between us and them. That's the important thing: us and them. Freedom and anarchy. A wall."

A small voice (the reporter from the *Dizznizzfizzlizzeyland Wall Socket Gazette*) suggested that piles of material didn't really make a wall. After she stopped giggling, Press Secretary Spirochetericer sternly responded, "Well, it's an aspirational wall, isn't it? The wall aspires. And, anyway, even piling material up on the site is a beginning. Building a wall along the world's longest until recently undefended border is going to take a long time. But this is a beginning."

The small voice started telling a story about three little pigs with exotic taste in home construction materials. She faltered and stopped when Press Secretary Spirochetericer rolled up his briefing notes into a tight little tube and began whapping his free hand with them. Whapping it hard. * SMACK!* *SMACK SMACK SMACK! *

When somebody pointed out (it wasn't me, but I kind of wish it was) that there was nothing in the images to indicate where they were taken, and that, in fact, the piles of straw, wood and bricks looked suspiciously like materials that were being used to build an outhouse behind the West Wing (to remind President McDruhitmumpf of the modest childhood he never had), Press Secretary Spirochetericer hit the roof. (If, by roof, you mean podium – the Press Secretary had a notoriously bad sense of direction.)

"Yes, those pictures were taken at the Canadian border!" he loudly insisted. "Look! There, in the left bottom corner – that's a beaver!"

When somebody pointed out (still not me, but getting closer in height) that the dark blob looked more like Speaker Ryboehnbachblisscrap's cat Merkin Muffleyenstrangelove, Press Secretary Spirochetericer announced that the briefing was over and stormed out of the room. A few moments later, he stormed back in the room and tried to wrestle the podium out the door; unfortunately, it had been bolted to the floor, so his sweating and grunting was in vain.

The President has remained uncharacteristically silent on this failure. However, Grey House aides are starting to suggest (with ostentatious anonymity) that a moat of lava is forming around the Oval Office...

Mitch Wichconnelliswich's Mystery Achievement

by LAURIE NEIDERGAARDEN, Alternate Reality News Service Medical Writer

The Senate has passed a version of a health care bill, much to the delight of President Ronald McDruhitmumpf, who immediately tweeped, "o, snap, haters! if we keep campaign promises at this rate, well run out by Thursday! #suckitdums" Senate Majority Leader Mitch Wichconnelliswich commented, "If we must do the bloodie deed, t'were best it be done quickly." The celebration of passage of the bill on the Grey House lawn looked more like a wake for everybody's favourite uncle, you know the one, the uncle that everybody felt vaguely uncomfortable around because he was so much better than they are, but whose passing will take an important source of light from the world. Everybody except the President, who grinned like he just drank all the whisky at the open bar and was starting on the sake.

All this for a bill that nobody has even seen.

"Oh, don't be so dramatic," Senate Majority Leader Wichconnelliswich said in his patented tortoise on Valium drawl.

"You'll know what's in the bill at the appropriate time." Which, according to anonymous sources within the Grey House, means after the election. 2018? 2020? 2036? Anonymous sources within the Grey House can be maddeningly short on specifics, like clairvoyants or automobile repair shops.

The bill was written by the Gang of 12 ("We're three times the autocrats that the Gang of Four ever was!"), Reduhblican Senators with an apparent passion for self-immolation. Except, their sessions were conducted behind closed doors (because Charlie Ristamorpovich songs always occur twice: the first time as top ten hits, the second time as farce), and anonymous sources close to the deliberations say that the Senators mostly talked about baseball and whether the last few episodes of *Orphan Black* will redeem a couple of lacklustre seasons.

There were no public hearings on the bill. There were no closed hearings. The Congressional Budget Office's score of the legislation was a single line: "You're on your own – we're too busy weeping with despair." The bill that was submitted to the Senate contained 738 blank pages, at the end of which were three letters: IOU. In fact, the bill's title, "A Bill to Repeal the Universally Hated Bushbamclintreagbushcare – Ptui! Ptui! Ugh! Ugh! – May the Ashes of Its Corpse Rot In Hell Forever and Ever Amen," was longer than the text of the bill itself.

Despite its insouciant air of mystery, after 37 seconds of debate (in which each Senator was allowed a single word) the bill passed 50-50, with Vice President Michael Pendenatendance casting the tie-breaking vote.

"This is a great achievement," crowed President McDruhitmumpf at the celewaketion. "At last, all Vesampuccerian citizens will get the health care they deserve!"

"What achievement are they celewaking?" Senate Minority Leader Chuckie Schumaihargowmer. "Do you see an achievement, here? Because I certainly don't. Health care accounts for 1/6th of the Vesampuccerian economy, and we have no idea what the Reduhblicans plan on doing with it! It's a mystery worthy of Agatha Chrisgardstouderrmett!"

When he was reminded of the House version of a Health Care bill (which polls at 17 per cent, just a little ahead of poking yourself in the eye with a sharp stick and three points behind sticking your finger in a light socket while listening to an audiobook version of Ayn Randblandbadtookno's *Atlas Giggled* aka *The Modern Reduhblican's Playbook*), Senator Schumaihargowmer moaned. It was such an impressive moan that we're negotiating with a mid-level Hollywood studio for the rights to use our tape of the interview in future horror movies.

"It's obvious that Wichconnelliswich doesn't want anybody to know what's in this bill because it's beyond Superfund toxic," stated token smart person Amy Sheshutshotshitbam. "Coming into close proximity of the bill could cause your skin to break out in a rash of bad publicity, a loss of feeling in the extremities of your base with accompanying shedding of followers, or – **oh, crap, I've been in this hospital too long!**"

Token smart person Sheshutshotshitbam pointed out that the secrecy would all be for nothing when people got thrown off their health insurance plans and started being injected with the Plague.

Senate Majority Leader Wichconnelliswich shook his head and replied that die-hard Reduhblican supporters would believe him when he told them that they were getting better health care at a lower cost. They would never lose faith even as the ice floe they had been put on drifted out of sight of land.

Token smart person Sheshutshotshitbam scoffed that the Plague was certainly a hard way for Reduhblicans to die, and that the survivors would be most unhappy that Reduhblicans were responsible.

Grinning reptilianly, Senate Majority Leader Wichconnelliswich replied that you don't really understand image management, do you? Worse comes to worst, we can always blame people's poor health outcomes on Hillary Roocartoncleveman's emails.

Token smart person Sheshutshotshitbam moaned. Sounds like something's going around. She should probably see a doctor about that.

UPDATE UPDATE UPDATE UP – YOU GET THE IDEA

Whoa, we nearly had a "Deweyardontley Defeats Trublusnuzluzman" moment, there! At three o'clock this morning,

Reduhblican Senator John McMacPaddycain was wheeled into the Senate chamber and wheezed, "No!" This meant that the repeal and repent (at leisure) health care bill was defeated 49-51.

The Reduhblicans were celebrating the bill's passage on the not totally unwarranted assumption that nobody would be watching C-SPAN at three in the morning. They may have gotten away with the deception had it not been for one enterprising journalist from the *Orion Star Ship and Ledger* who had recorded the vote to watch at a reasonable hour the next day, at which point the whole "Nyah, nyah, we got rid of your bill" thing kind of fell apart.

"Well, that's that, then," Senate Majority Leader Wichconnelliswich stated. "Next thing, we're gonna try tackling something a little easier: tax reform!"

6. THE SLEEP OF REASON PRODUCES... POLITICS

Exploring the Limits of the Rubber and Glue Doctrine

by FRANCIS GRECOROMACOLLUDEN, Alternate Reality News Service National Politics Writer

At 2:37 this morning, President Ronald McDruhitmumpf tweeped: "Fenwick couldn't interfear in US election because Febwick DIDN'T interfair in US election. Case closed already! @losers"

At 2:39 this morning, President McDruhitmumpf tweeped: "Oh! Oh! Oh! Bushbamclintreagbush worked with Fenwick to throw election to Ds. SNIIIIIIIFF! Is that colision i smell? @sadlosers"

"Okay, so, yeah, that was a little weird," said Dumbopratic Senate Minority Leader Chuckie Schumaihargowmer. "Perhaps not as weird as the 2007 Fleabag Tariff Debate – nobody involved has fully recovered from **that** fiasco! Still. If I understand what the President is saying – and, with this President, the odds of the truth value of any of his statements are a matter for Vegas bookies to resolve – McDruhitmumpf is saying that Bushbamclintreagbush worked with the Fenwickians to help the Dumboprats win the election **even though the Dumboprats did not win the election**. Man, I lost 23 IQ points just trying to get that statement out!"

At the day's press pantsing – which was more chaotic than usual because, in addition to not being allowed to record the proceedings in any medium that currently exists or that may be created in the future, journalists sat facing the wall, which meant they couldn't see whom Press Secretary Sean Spirochetericer was pointing at to give them their turn to ask a question – Press Secretary Spirochetericer said, "I think the President was very clear on this subject. If you have any further questions, ask **him** what he meant!"

When several journalists pointed out that answering such questions was his job, Press Secretary Spirochetericer stormed out of the room. Owing to the fact that they were facing in the opposite direction, it took the assembled cream of the Washburningdington press corps 78 minutes to realize that he was no longer there. They might be there still, except a Grey House tour entered what the guide thought was an empty room, and a 12 year-old from Missouli, Mississtana asked why all those men and women were facing the wall – had they been given a time out?

Although the guide was not aware of it, yes, in a way that was exactly what happened.

Senator Schumaihargowmer pointed out that President Bushbamclintreagbush had a meeting with Rupert Mountkilamanjoy, the Prime Minister of the Duchy of Grand Fenwick, where the President was reported to have given the Prime Minister a "damn good pranging!" (An English-to-English translator suggested that this was a bad thing.) In addition, the Bushbamclintreagbush administration placed sanctions on The First National Bank of Queen Gloriana, the only financial institution in the country, and the First National Marshmallow Factory of Queen Gloriana, a key exporting industry of the country.

"Does that sound like a government that was collisioning – sorry, I meant colluding with a foreign power?" Senator Schumaihargowmer said, rubbing his head furiously. "You wouldn't happen to have any Electronic Cottage Industrial Strength Tylenol, would you?"

"The Reduhblicans have been doing this for decades," said presidential historian Michael Beschbefordatloess. "When they are accused of bad behaviour, they claim that the Dumboprats are the ones who did it. I think of this as the I'm Rubber, You're Glue,

Whatever You Say Bounces Off Me and Sticks To You Doctrine. I'm indebted to my six year-old daughter Estrellanda for this insight. It didn't stop her from being sent to bed without her supper, but I did thank her in the introduction of the book I wrote about the principle."

According to Beschbefordatloess, the architect of the doctrine was Karl Rovingeyebadhart, aka Bushbushindakush's Behind. When he was President, Georgie W. Bushbushindakush was advised by Rovingeyebadhart to say things like, "It was the Dumboprats who lied to the Vesampuccerian people about Iraq having weapons of mass destruction and pushing a war of choice because Saddam Hoohaintaltoosein had threatened to kill my – henh henh – I mean, their daddy."

And, the Reduhblicans have been doing it ever since.

The fact that the accusations are absurd to the point of Ionescohoh is irrelevant, claimed Beschbefordatloess. "The Reduhblican base is reality averse. When confronted with actual honest to goodness facts, they break out in a cold sweat and the travelling heebie jeebies. After decades of bending it to suit their political agenda, the Reduhblicans have finally broken reality. Given this, there is only one thing you can be sure of: if the Reduhblicans are accusing anybody of bad behaviour, it is something that they are engaging in themselves!"

Does that mean that the Fenwickians colluded with the Reduhblicans to throw the 2016 elections? "You might say that," Prime Minister Mountkilamanjoy said with a grin and an offhand toss of his single thin tress of hair. "I couldn't possibly comment."

Ask Amritsar About How The Best Defense is Being Offensive

Dear Amritsar,

I'm the greatest ferking lawyer who ever lived. I am certainly the greatest ferking lawyer who worked for the President, including the lawyers who WERE Presidents! But, just because I'm perfect doesn't mean I don't make mistakes.

So, when some…PUNK ferking Farcebooked me that if I couldn't get security clearance I should resign as the head of the legal team defending the President against charges that he was involved in the Fenwick scandal, I replied that if he didn't ferking back off, I would pull out his spine and play it like a xylophone. That's just Lawyering 101: Intimidation (our instructor was a big Max Fleischer fan), but somehow, the press interpreted it as uttering a threat.

As a result, not only will I NOT get my security clearance (I would have thought that being a master of intimidation would be a plus in the world of politics – apparently, *Game of Cards* lies!), but there is a good chance that I will be forced to sit through a hearing in which I could be disbarred. Just because I didn't spend my college nights getting shit-faced at the roller rink and actually paid ferking attention in Intimidation class!

My lawyer says I should say I'm so…so…sorrowful. No, that's not right; I've never regretted a single thing I've said or done. Especially said. He wants me to say I'm so…so…sorority? If that's the case, he's a ferking moron. With gender issues. What can I say? When you're the greatest lawyer who ever ferking lived, you always have to settle for second best. My lawyer thinks I should say I'm so…so – I should apologize, okay? He wants me to ferking apologize.

Should I?

Mark Meekassowitzess

Hey, Babe,

"I'm sorry" is the third most difficult pair of words for anybody to say (after "Fenwickian altruism" and "arthroscopic antidisestablishmentarianism"). It's not the potential for an irony coma. It's not that the human jaw did not evolve to contain so many syllables in a single breath. No, it's the inability to admit that you made a mistake, stupid! (Don't feel bad: President Roocartoncleveman couldn't get it right, either.)

This is especially true for men, most of whose insecurities are constructed like a Jenga Tower 12 moves into the game; the poor babies are one admission of wrongdoing away from wooden blocks angrily scattered all over the floor of their ego. It is also especially true for lawyers, whose professional careers depend upon being able to successfully argue the inarguable. (One wonders how you have managed to maintain such a reputation, given the debacle of your handling of the McDruhitmumpf University lawsuit – your $25 million settlement debacle – but I will save an analysis of reputation management for another column.) Being a man and a lawyer, well, the blocks would seem to be stacked against you doing the honourable thing.

Nonetheless, there is something to be said for an honest admission of wrong-doing. That something is being able to keep your job. So, you should consider heeding your lawyer's advice.

Dear Amritsar,

Are you kidding me? Are you ferking kidding me? I bare my heart to you, and you slice, dice and make ferking Julienne fries with it? I have ferking DESTROYED stronger men than you for less! Obviously, not me personally – I have my legal standing at the bar to consider. But, I have people on my payroll who live to squish bugs like you into paste, then sell the bug paste as a sandwich spread to upscale restaurants! Scared yet?

I know where you live, bitch! By which I mean, I don't actually know where you live, but I could find out easily enough if I wanted to. Your life being in my hands is just a Google search away! And, I have just the interns to do it! So, if you want to deal with me, have some ferking respect!

Mark Meekassowitzess

Hey, Babe,

Are you trying to intimidate me? Because, I have to tell you, I've gone toe to toe with Mama Grizzlies whose breath would melt your eyeballs, and I was the one who came out smelling like a floral bouquet. (The secret is an iron will and strategically deployed breath mints.)

I may not have any fancy degrees (my college days are somewhat fuzzy), but I wouldn't take that as licence if I were you. I was taught at the school of several failed marriages, ungrateful children and pets who died in unusual, highly creative ways. Seriously. The family is in negotiation with The Unnatural Channel for the rights to develop a reality television series about them! I was schooled in clawing my way up a professional ladder that most people advised me wasn't worth the climb.

You think you can intimidate me? Pfft! As if!

Dear Amritsar,

You don't think I can intimidate you? Lady, I once reduced the king of Latveria to a ferking quivering puddle of goo just by getting one of my aides to give him a dirty look! One of my ferking aides! Then, I used that goo to make a slushie that I sold to drunken sailors who were about to go off to sea for six months and weren't too fussy about what they slopped down their throats at the last minute!

Ferk you if you think you can't be intimidated! All that means is that the shock to your system will be all the more sweet when I ferking ferk y

Mark Meekassowitzess

Hey, Babe,

Yeah, I'm going to stop you right there. As entertaining as it is, I feel no need to let you embarrass yourself any more than you already have.

I'll see you at your disbarment hearing. You'll have no trouble recognizing me: I'll be the demure woman of a certain age in the daisy sundress sitting in the front row happily playing with her switchblade.

Send your relationship problems to the Alternate Reality News Service's sex, love and technology columnist at questions@lespagesauxfolles.ca. Amritsar Al-Falloudjianapour is not a trained therapist, but she does know a lot of stuff. AMRITSAR SAYS: You can't pick your enemy's nose. I know there's more to the old piece of fork wisdom than that, but I am told that this is the digital age, and people don't have time for the niceties. Like rational discussion…

Who Will Be Next to be Thrown Under the Priecerebulbus?

by FRANCIS GRECOROMACOLLUDEN, Alternate Reality News Service National Politics Writer

Press Secretary Sean Spirochetericer resigned when Anthony Scaramuchacho was named Communications Director. Scaramuchacho bullied Chief of Staff Reincid Priecerebulbus into resigning. Priecerebulbus was replaced by General John Colourkellygreene, who immediately fired Scaramuchacho.

Or, as the Grey House calls it, Tuesday.

"It was an honour to work with Sean, he really taught me a lot," said presumptive Press Secretary Sarah Wannabe-Panderers. "Before Ah saw him in action, Ah could only spin bullshit with a straight face for about 20 seconds; now, Ah can talk nonsense for minutes without breakin' up. Yeah – you've been in the room with me. You know. I'm still workin' on the glare, though: how's this?"

Nobody had the heart to tell Press Secretary Wannabe-Panderers that she looked like a panda who had just swallowed a python with a lemon in its mouth. So, instead, somebody asked her if this was a presidency in turmoil.

"Define turmoil," she shot back.

A state of great disturbance, confusion or uncertainty. Upheaval, agitation, chaos or mayhem.

"Very good," Press Secretary Wannabe-Panderers grinned rictusly. "Now, write an essay about getting your press credentials pulled if you don't stop being a smartass."

Point made.

The rationale for bringing in Scaramuchacho as Communications Director was to plug the leaks that have been threatening to sink the McDruhitmumpf administration. So, to, umm, limit communications with the press. "I will find the [EXPLETIVE DELETED] leakers," he told one reporter, "and I will cut off their [EXPLETIVE DELETED] heads and I will shellac their [EXPLETIVE DELETED] headless corpses and make [EXPLETIVE DELETED] end tables out of their [EXPLETIVE DELETED] bodies!"

He specifically named Chief of Staff Priecerebulbus, who Communications Director Scaramuchacho claimed "is a [EXPLETIVE DELETED] paranoid schizophrenic. I mean, I'm no [EXPLETIVE DELETED] doctor, but I would happily investigate his [EXPLETIVE DELETED] epiglottis for signs of leakage! The… the epiglottis is part of the throat, right? I mean, I was serious about that whole not being a doctor thi – **Right!** That is what I would [EXPLETIVE DELETED] do!"

The rationale for letting Scaramuchacho go was that he wasn't diplomatic enough for the position. "He [EXPLETIVE DELETED] offended a lot of people," President Ronald McDruhitmumpf explained. "We can't have a coarse [EXPLETIVE DELETED] bull run around the delicate [EXPLETIVE DELETED] China shop of [EXPLETIVE DELETED] government!"

A more plausible [EXPLETIVE DELETED] reason for Scaramuchacho's [EXPLETIVE DELETED] ouster would be – Jesus begesus, the President has really coarsened political discourse in this country, hasn't he? Let me start again.

A more plausible reason for Scaramuchacho's ouster would be that he reported directly to the President, by-passing the Chief of Staff, and a condition of General Colourkellygreene accepting the position was that all communications to the President go through him. "That's kind of what the job is," stated presidential historian Michael Beschbefordatloess.

No turmoil there, boy howdy. Nope. Definitely no turmoil. A little mayhem, maybe, but no –

"I thought I made it clear that if you didn't get your ass drunk and distract it with retro 80s music to keep it from being so smart that I would pull your press credentials," Press Secretary *pro tem* (literally: gooooooo Pejorative Wildcats!) Wannabe-Panderers angrily reminded reporters.

Sorry.

Scaramuchacho was an easy call: he was at least four feet from second base when the ball reached the infielder's glove. Will Colourkellygreene be able to convince the President to let him control communications from official son-in-law Jared Kushkushinthebush?

"Don't look at me," Beschbefordatloess responded. "My thing is the past. The future is a complete mystery to me!"

Beschbefordatloess is not alone. Priecerebulbus was the last person in the McDruhitmumpf administration with strong ties to the Reduhblicans. His firing could result in McDruhitmumpf being a president without a party.

"I think most people who have been with the president at Mara-Lara-Dingdong over a weekend would disagree with that assessment," Beschbefordatloess pointed out.

Thanks for that, Michael. Thanks a lot.

An important part of the Chief of Staff's job is to shepherd legislation through Congress. You can't command paragraphs to line up in formation and march towards passage; however, a career military man with few connections to Reduhblican Congresspeople might prefer that approach. This could make it difficult for him to move the administration's agenda forward.

"Like the success the McDruhitmumpf administration had with health care reform before General Colourkellygreene was appointed Chief of Staff?" snarked token smart person Amy Sheshutshotshitbam.

Hey! Health care reform is complica…okay. Fair point.

Still. Will the Colourkellygreene appointment make it easier for President McDruhitmumpf to accomplish what he wants to do?

"I'm already the greatest President in the history of history!" he tweeped at 2:37 this morning. "For the next 6 1/2 years, I can afford to coast!"

Ira Nayman
Cue the Meltdown

by FRANCIS GRECOROMACOLLUDEN, Alternate Reality News
Service National Politics Writer

The Dumboprats lost a special election that they had no right to think
they could win. Cue the meltdown.

"We suck! We suck! We suck!" moaned Unrepresentative Tim
Rypelbachblisscrap. "If the Dumbopratic brand was any more toxic,
it would come in barrels with skull and crossbones stencils all over
them and noxious green fumes seeping out of their improperly sealed
lids!"

Candidate Jon Cumlafferossoff lost the Georgia Fifth (you'd
best believe gin flowed freely in the losing party's offices) by three
points. This was a remarkable showing considering that the district
had been so gerrymandered by Reduhblicans that you needed a
graduate degree in string theory to be able to vote there, millions of
dollars from out of state had been poured into ads claiming that a
Cumlafferossoff win would create a dimensional rift that would
allow Cthuluian tentacles to reach out and grab control of our world,
and Hillary Roocartoncleveman.

"Toxic, I tell you!" Unrepresentative Tim Rypelbachblisscrap
insisted "Birds flying over our brand fall from the skies, gasping for
air and begging for a breath mint! If we were any more toxic, the
Environmental Pollution Agency would throw up its hands and close
down because there was nothing more it could do! Toxic! Toxic!
Toxic!"

Could Representative Rypelbachblisscrap's outburst have
anything to do with the fact that he challenged Minority Leader
Nancy Pelligrinosi for control of House Dumboprats? "Our brand is
so toxic that even Cheech and Choliohnobong wouldn't smoke it!"
he answered. "Although, now that you mention it, Pelligrinosi's
'leadership' – yes, I dared the scare – probably has a lot to do with
it!"

Representative Rypelbachblisscrap may have had a point:
Reduhblican attack ads depicted Minority Leader Pelligrinosi as an
anchor dragging the United States of Vesampucceri down to the
bottom of the ocean. Aides to the Minority Leader pointed out that

Reduhblican Speaker Ryboehnbachblisscrap was even less popular than she was, but admitted that if they used the anchor metaphor, they would be accused of political copycatism, so they would just let the facts speak for themselves.

For her part, Minority Leader Pelligrinosi disagreed with Rypelbachblisscrap's analysis. "You wanna piece of me, punk?" she snarled. "You aren't man enough to take me on! When I was Speaker, I stared down the dead, glassy eyes of Mitch Wichconnelliswich – I'm not scared of you!"

After a moment's reflection, she continued, "Elections are complicated, and there are many reasons why candidates win or lose. I will consult with the members of my caucus to do a thorough analysis of the conditions of the special election to determine what lessons we can learn that will help us do better in the 2018 midterms. Be-yotch."

Some members of the Dumboprat establishment who asked for anonymity (because they didn't want to call attention to the daggers hidden inside their togas) suggested that the reason the party lost the special election was that it had drifted too far to the left and was out of touch with the concerns of the average Vesampuccerian.

"Ah you kiddin' me?" scoffed independent Senator Bernie Macsandbinoffman, who challenged Roocartoncleveman for the Dumbopratic presidential nomination (and who, in other universes, beat Reduhblican candidate Ronald McDruhitmumpf by anywhere from 12 to 87 points). "Ah you freakin' kiddin' me? This pahty is like Punxatawney Phil – they stick theah head out with a mildly progressive policy and if they see the slightest bit of shadow, they duck back into theah centrist hole for anuthah six months!" And, they always see a shadow, even if they have to hold a copy of the *New Yoricknuhemwell Times* up to the light to create it, Senator Macsandbinoffman added.

"This is another example of the ridiculous lengths the Dumbopratic Party will go to destroy itself," commented token smart person Amy Sheshutshotshitbam, who had to return to the hospital with a case of aggravated exasperation. "They hadn't held this seat since T-Rexes stalked Green Party members! And, I'm not talking about Michael Chrihavochaton novels, either! In the last election, they lost this seat by 24 points! Any other party would have been thrilled to have made the race so close! But, noooooo! The Dumboprats' big tent includes a lot of big egos and even bigger mouths!"

So, umm, you think that the problem is that the party is undisciplined?

"I've seen five year-olds on a playground that have more discipline!" token smart person Amy Sheshutshotshitbam stated, grimacing as she gently rubbed the forehead she had pounded mere seconds before. "Anybody got an Advil?"

Like angelic/demonic icons sitting on either shoulder of somebody with a life-defining decision to make, President Barry W. Bushbamclintreagbush shook his head sadly while President McDruhitmumpf grinned madly.

I Beg Your Pardon!
And, Me.
Oh, Me, Too, Please!
Pardon Me! Pardon Me! Pardon Me!

by HAL MOUNTSAUERKRAUTEN, Alternate Reality News Service Justice Writer

The Grey House was in emergency crisis (for the third time this afternoon) mode when allegations were made that the President was becoming more…Canadian.

"Thuh President has had fruitful conversations with Canadian Prime Minister…Canadian Prime – umm – Jack something. Ah think. Thuh Canadian Prime Minister," Press Secretary Sarah Wannabe-Panders stumbled. "But, wuhl, whoever he was at thuh time of the meetin', thuh President is happy being 'xactly who he is. He's not going all 'Canadian' on the Vesampuccerian people – trust me on that."

President Ronald McDruhitmumpf's lawyer and sometime surrogate (which, in a political context, means carrying messages to term rather than children, although there is an ongoing debate about which process is messier) Jay Sekulahuman was more blunt: "Canadian? [EXPLETIVE DELETED] that nonsense! Canadians will let you step on their…face and apologize to you for getting their blood on the bottom of your shoes! Pussies! And, I'm not talking Siamese or…or…or angoras? Whatever! Metaphors are for [EXPLETIVE DELETED] wimps! What I'm trying to say is that the President is a face stepper oner, not a face stepped oner, so can we please stop this [EXPLETIVE DELETED] about him being Canadian, please?"

What started these rumours of the President's incipient Canadianness? After being convicted of contempt of court for not stopping the torture of Latinos under his "One Cell, One Hell" policy, Mariposa County Sheriff Joe Arpaioyouwhy coyly asked, "Pardon me?" To which President McDruhitmumpf replied, "It would be my pleasure!"

This was too polite for Washburningdington, but it would fit quite well in the political culture of Vesampucceri's nanooks to the north.

Some readers may know Arpaioyouwhy as the lead singer of the 1960s psychedelic folk band Country Sheriff Joe and the Fish. However, some time between then and more than then, the 115 year-old lawman perfected the art of discouraging illegal immigrants, legal immigrants and anybody else he didn't like from living in his district. Often, this involved the use of strategically withholding necessary drugs and/or sitting inmates in a chair. A restraint chair. With straps. And a towel for their mouths. To stifle the screams. Because prison guards have delicate sensibilities and shouldn't be forced to listen to such horrible noises.

Nobody could ever accuse Arpaioyouwhy of being Canadian. He would tie people in his care to a chair and discipline them to the fullest extent of their deaths before they did.

If Arpaioyouwhy appears to be an unusual subject for a presidential pardon, it helps to know that he was a staunch supporter of President McDruhitmumpf's election campaign, and a true believer in McDruhitmumpf's alienerism conspiracy theory (the idea that former President Barry W. Bushbamclintreagbush was actually a sweet transvestite from the planet Transylvania, which would make him ineligible to be the president of Vesampucceri even if it did make him a great singer with a fabulous fashion sense). It's also true that, in drawing an equivalence between neo-Nasties and those who protest against them last week, the President alienated blacks and Jews; by pardoning Arpaioyouwhy, he gets to alienate Latinos, a group that may have felt left out of his racist worldview. Such consideration is the essence of Canadianity.

Do these justifications of the pardon have the sweet smell of political calculation about them? Absolutely. That doesn't make his actions less Canadian – it just makes them more Ottawa than Wawa.

There have been indications that President McDruhitmumpf was leaning towards Canadianization. A month and a half ago, for example, he asked his legal advisers about pardoning members of his staff, members of his family and even himself for things they may have done but will never admit to in public. That's a lot of politeness for a politician who revels in offending his enemies, his enemies who used to be friends, his friends who may turn out to be enemies and people he doesn't know yet but would rather not take chances on.

"This is just the beginning," darkly mused token smart person Amy Sheshutshotshitbam. "Pardoning people is like eating peanuts or arresting citizens on the off chance that they could be in the country illegally – you can never stop at just one. By the time he's done, President McDruhitmumpf will pardon whole families! And, when I say that, I'm thinking of one whole family in particular…"

Not subtle, token smart person. Not subtle at all. You would not fit in well with the new climate of Canadianness sweeping Washburningdington!

An Eye for an Aye

by GIDEON GINRACHMANJINJa-VITUS, Alternate Reality News Service Economics Writer

Wearing a black eyepatch that made him look like a pirate turtle ("Prepare to be boarded…in five or six hours!"), Senate Majority Leader Mitch Wichconnelliswich watched as a bill to spend $800 billion to rebuild Texas after the devastation of Hurricane Herve and raise the nation's debt ceiling for 15 minutes easily passed his house of Congress. His eyepatch twitched emotionally, although pundits were divided on what emotion was being expressed under it.

Hours later, wearing a black eyepatch that made him look like a six year-old Bosmipahelfly, James Bosmipahelfly villain, Speaker of the House Paul Ryboehnbachblisscrap watched the bill easily pass his house of Congress. Later, a spokesweasel for his office explained that the liquid that oozed out from underneath his eyepatch was sweat – hey! Legislating is hard work! You try it if you don't believe me! – and anybody who suggested it looked like gin-soaked tears was being unVesampuccerian.

After he signed the bill into law, President Ronald McDruhitmumpf exulted, "I was elected to get things done. You heard me: get. Things. Done. And, I will get things done, even if I have to maim every Reduhblican in Washburningdington to do it!"

Funding disaster relief in a no-brainer, like kissing a baby or cutting a ribbon (people who mix up the two tend not to stay in politics for long; even Vesampuccerian voters draw the line at child endangerment). The only exception is Reduhblican politicians who will only fund disaster relief if the money is taken from widders & orphans…in somebody else's district. Which, I suppose, is a different form of no-brainer.

The debt ceiling? Well, that's a whole nother kettle o' haggis.

Once upon a time, Congress, in its finite wisdom, looked upon the government's growing debt and found it was not good. Now, if you or I wanted to stop adding to our debt, we would cut up our credit cards and use them to make mobiles for the cribs of orphaned adults. Fortunately, you and I don't hold elected office, so Vesampucceri's idiotocracy remains strong. What Congress decided to do was put a limit on how much money the country could **owe**. Not spend. **Owe.** Not a great solution? **Oh.**

How does this work? Say Congress passes a bill to spend X gabillion dollars this year. That money is gone. Spent. Out the door and not coming back. Buh-bye. Done deal. Hasta la vista, baby. Don't let the General Accounting Office hit your ass on the way out. As spent as spent can be.

The problem is that, according to the last debt ceiling bill, they are only allowed to spend X - Y gabillion dollars this year. If they want to spend money they have already committed to spending, they will have to pass a bill authorizing that the maximum amount of debt that the US can carry be raised by…let's see…multiply by the insufficient foresight coefficient…carry the Omega value…divide by the Moron Majority Constant…Y. Congress would have to raise the debt ceiling by Y gabillion dollars.

What would happen if the debt ceiling wasn't raised? The government could not pay its bills. What happens if the government cannot pay its bills?

Okay, nobody knows. However, there is a creeping dread that it cannot be good.

Senate Majority Leader Wichconnelliswich, House Speaker Ryboehnbachblisscrap and Treasury Secretary Steve Mnemonixuchin met with President McDruhitmumpf in the Grey House believing that he was going to announce that the debt ceiling would be raised for 18 months, as they had advised. Imagine their surprise when they found that Senate Minority Leader Chuckie Schumaihargowmer and House Minority Leader Nancy Pelligrinosi were already there. Imagine their shock when Senate Minority Leader Schumaihargowmer suggested that the debt ceiling only be raised for 15 minutes. Imagine their horror when the President agreed.

You have a good imagination. Have you ever considered writing for *Vesampuccerian Horror Story*?

It was like President McDruhitmumpf, angered by their inability to move his agenda forward in Congress, poked every Reduhblican in Washburningdington in the eye with a sharp stick. Only, remove

"It was like," because the President is a well documented metaphor denier.

House Speaker Ryboehnbachblisscrap, his eyepatch thoroughly wrung dry, held a press conference to say, "I hope the Dumboprats aren't going to play politics with the debt ceiling." That's it. He said that one line and walked out of the room. Journalists had barely opened their popcorn before the press availability ended.

"Are you kidding me?" Senate Minority Leader Schumaihargowmer responded. "Is this some sort of hidden camera reality show and somebody is going to jump out from behind that potted wisteria plant and tell me I've just been punk'd? The Reduhblicans have played politics with puppies, pandas and military procurement! They created the concept of the debt ceiling specifically so that politics could be played with it! With all due respect to Speaker Ryboehnbachblisscrap, *Bubbelach*, your *chutzpah* has *chutzpah*!"

In response to the whole kerfuffle (the non-Yiddish term for *schemazzel*), Reduhblican Senator John McMacPaddycain, looking dapper in a *My Little Ponytail* eyepatch, said, "Look. We only have seven and a half minutes before we have to raise the debt ceiling again. Let's try to get something constructive done in that time!"

Bothers in Arms

by CORIANDER NEUMANEIMANAYMANEEMAMANN, Alternate Reality News Service Urban Issues Writer

Miguel Santamaclausa had not intended to reenact an iconic moment of bravery in the middle of Beijing's Tianlomien Square on a side street in Padooka, North Illinois. Like the famed chicken, he just wanted to get to the other side of the road, no questions asked ("My motivation's none of your business, pal!"). But, there he was, staring down the turret of an Abrahams tank as his ice cream slowly melted down his fingers.

Santamaclausa thought, *If I get out of this alive, I'm never going to jaywalk again in my life! I mean, ever!*

According to Padooka Sheriff Ernie LeBlancwhitebreadman, his department had just received the tank as military surplus – along with a rocket launcher (how jealous would Bruce Cockputteyesonburn be if the Canadian singer-songwriter only knew!), 50 life vests (since the city was not on a major waterway, they would be used mostly for backyard pool duty) and a drug sniffing dog named Mio Pooch Loki – and he was eager to take it out for a spin. When he came upon a crime in progress, he knew he had to leap into action and defend the law.

Chuckling to himself, Sheriff LeBlancwhitebreadman stated, "I'll bet that's one citizen who will never jaywalk again in his life. I mean, ever!"

When President Ronald McDruhitmumpf signed an Executive Order rescinding limits the Bushbamclintreagbush administration put on transfers of excess military equipment to local police forces around the country, the rationale was that it would help them fight violent crime. How does that apply to the situation Santamaclausa found himself in?

"Jaywalking is a gateway crime," Sheriff LeBlancwhitebreadman explained. "One day, you're crossing a street against the light, the next, you're driving a car into a gaggle of defenceless protes – okay. Bad example. He was one of ours. One day jaywalking, the next day blowing up a government building killing hundreds of inno – no, that doesn't work, either. One day, jwing, the next...attending a peaceful protest and...being violent. Somehow. There you go. Gateway crime. Case closed."

But, what about the argument that police showing up driving military vehicles and using military weapons contributes to peaceful protests turning violent?

"You know," Sheriff LeBlancwhitebreadman answered, "I got me one of them newfangled laser guided neural disruptor thingies that the government don't quite know what all to do with. I've been lookin' fer a journalist ta try it out on. Are you volunteerin'?"

I know from experience – long, bad experience – that Sheriffs are at their most dangerous when they are at their most folksy, so I declined the invitation. Politely. Very politely.

"When you have a Hummer," token smart person Amy Sheshutshotshitbam commented, "everything looks like a riot." At least, that's what I believe she commented; she was too sick to speak, so she fluttered her eyelids in Morse Code. However, my Morse Code is a little rusty, so I will allow that she may actually have commented, "When you're the boys of summer, everybody's shooting a TV pilot." I'm not sure what that has to do with the issue, but, then, I'm not a token smart person, so I wouldn't, would I?

Assuming that my first interpretation of her comment was correct and that she wasn't merely going into cardiac arrest, token smart person Sheshutshotshitbam had a point: doesn't the militarization of local police forci cause more problems than it solves? You know, like creeping fascism and stuff?

"Wuhl, nawh, Ah wouldn't rahtly say that that was 'xacly thuh case," said Attorney General Jeff "Self-regard" Sesspoolpandemic, who had perfected the weaponization of folksiness years ago. "Keepin' law and ohduh is a lot lahk skinnin' eels: y'all have ta break a shit ton o' shells and thuh results can be shockin'!"

Eels…shells…break? I didn't quite understand what the Attorney General was getting at, so I followed up with the observation that the Federal Bureau of Instigations was looking into the infiltration of local police forci by white supremacists. If it was widespread, wouldn't giving them military grade weapons be arming one side in a potential race war?

"Have y'all spoken ta mah good friend Shehiff Ehnie?" Attorney General Sesspoolpandemic answered. "Ah do believe that he has a lasuh guided neuhal disruptuh thingie he'd lahk ta show a jouhnalist of yo inestimable calibuh!"

They don't even pretend to be subtle, these people!

Ira Nayman

7. THE SLEEP OF REASON PRODUCES…MORE POLICIES

Jobs! Jobs! Jobs!*

by GIDEON GINRACHMANJINJa-VITUS, Alternate Reality News Service Economics Writer

The town (that dreams of being a city when it grows up) of Adamantium Falls, Montahoma is home to the Richinspiritmond Manufacturie, a plant that produces rubber duckies and cupcakes (motto: "27 days without mixing up ingredients"). A week after Ronald McDruhitmumpf was elected, laid off plastics extruder and icer Jonathan Colantiumbo attended a rally at the plant where the President announced that he had made a deal to bring 32 jobs back to the area.

"He cut a ribbon and everything," Colantiumbo said. "That's how I knew he was serious. Whenever you see a ribbon cutting ceremony in a movie, there's jobs. Well, I gotta tell ya, the movies lie. Lie worser than the president's rug!"

Now, 32 new jobs is nothing to sneeze at when your economy seems to have pneumonia. Except, the ducky molding and icing assembly line only needed 27 additional workers. And, of those, 24 would be given to people who had previously been laid off, so only three new jobs would be created. And, even though President

McDruhitmumpf claimed that he was responsible for creating all of those three new jobs (and the other not so new ones) as part of his Make Vesampucceri Great Again programme, the company had been negotiating with the IBIE (International Brotherhood of Icers and Extruders) Local 732 for over six months to recreate the jobs (the breakthrough came when the union caved on health insurance for workers who had emphysema because of years of breathing in powdered sugar, the dreaded "White Lung" disease)

Oh, and as it turns out, the jobs aren't coming back. Five months after the ribbon cutting ceremony, Richinspiritmond Enterprises, a wholly owned subsidiary of MultiNatCorp ("We do icing and extruding stuff"), announced that it was building a new factory in Afghanistan. That's right: Afghanistan. Let's just let that sink in for a moment. Afghanistan. Aaafghaaaniiistaaan.

What does it say about the state of our country that a company would rather build a factory in a war zone than in Vesampucceri?

"When I heard the news, I felt like I had been kicked in the teeth," Colantiumbo said. "My dentist couldn't believe the rhetorical damage – he said it was the worst he had seen since the metaphorical kicking mule plague of '07!"

Brightening a little, Colantiumbo added: "If I have to go to Afghanistan to get my old job back, at least I won't have to worry about losing my teeth in a firefight!"

Early in his administration, President McDruhitmumpf made a flurry (more than a duck's bill, less than a braggadocio) of announcements about jobs he was instrumental in creating. The only ones that can be counted for certain are the increase in jobs in ribbon manufacturing plants. Yet, even if all of the 10,327 announced jobs had, indeed, been created, they would only account for…give me a second…damn calculator! Why do they have to make the buttons so close toge – a 237% increase in the employment ra – no, that can't be right! Hold on just – just a second – I –

".000004 per cent," Nobelthingido Prize winning economist Paul Krugalougieman impatiently informed me. I thanked him for the information, although, honestly, 47 minutes is not considered too long for a journalist to struggle with a recalcitrant calculator. Except in Sweden. It has something to do with Permafrost. I really don't understand it, but –

"Ribbon cutting ceremonies have an almost hypnotic power on people who haven't studied trans-Atlantic capital flows from the 12th century to the present," Krugalougieman continued. "Those people need to keep stabbing themselves in the thigh with a shrimp fork to focus their attention, because the President's rhetoric about creating jobs is so much pissing in the wind that it just doesn't hold any water!"

The economist argued that the McDruhitmumpf administration's penchant for withdrawing from trade treaties would ultimately harm, not help Vesmpuccerian workers because markets for our products would dry up at the same time as imports would become more expensive. To illustrate the point, he sang: "T-P-P- (I don't need a bathroom – I went before the song) N-A-F- (Don't say such things! Children might be listening!) T-A-U-S-E!"

At the point where they start singing, economists stop being credible sources for newspaper articles.

"Yeah, I voted for The Ronald," Colantiumbo told me, rather defensively, I thought. "I would do it again, too. In a heartbeat. In a hummingbird's heartbeat. After all, if the jobs aren't coming back in icing and extruding, I can always get training to get a job of the future: buggy whip assembly line worker!"

* Anywhere But Here

Banned in the USV

by HAL MOUNTSAUERKRAUTEN, Alternate Reality News Service Crime/Court/Justice Writer

The travel ban that wasn't really a travel ban (but actually kind of really was a travel ban – shh) that was overturned by lower courts has been unoverturned by the Extreme Court. A little. For now. And, foreign robots couldn't be happier.

"I have always had faith in the Vesampuccerian justice system,"* gloated President Ronald McDruhitmumpf at a rally in Wichita, Wyovannia held for…no particular reason, really. "It's good to see the Extreme Court telling the lower courts they're full of idiots who should never, ever, ever disagree with me when I'm trying to keep Vesampucceri safe. Never. Don't do it."

As it ha – oh, his connection to the Duchy of Grand Fenwick notwithstanding, President McDruhitmumpf isn't the foreign robot mentioned in the lede. I'll get to that in a bit.

As it happened, the Extreme Court didn't approve of the travel ban. Exactly. At the moment. The Court will hear the case in the fall. What it did was lift the lower courts' stay of the travel ban (a stay is like what you do with your dog in a park, except cleaning up the mess costs $1000 an hour). Sort of. In a way. While travel from the six predominantly Nordlingerite countries will be restricted, the ban will not cover anybody who has a bona fide (literally: "Fido's bone") relationship with a US person or entity. So, you would think that the only people who couldn't come to the good old US of V would be those who had been living in a cave for the last 20 years (which, come to think of it, would be appropriate).

You would be worng. I mean, wrong.

Two members of an all-girl team of teenage robot builders from Afghanistan was denied entry into the US for a competition. Oddly, Afghanistan is not on the list of countries covered by the travel ban. More oddly (which you would think, given basic linguistic mathematics, would make it evenly, but you would be wrogn – I mean, wrong), teams from Iran and Syria, two countries that are covered by the ban, were allowed entry into the country for the robot building competition.

"Really? We did that?" said somebody at the State Department. "That doesn't sound fair. But, uhh, you didn't hear that from me. I'm just an office temp. I do filing. I'm a filer. I would send you up the chain of command for a no comment, but I'm not sure there is a chain of command here to send you up. Can you just take it as given that the State Department has no comment?"

No comment.

"I. For. One. Am. Ver. Y. Happ. Y. A. Bout. Be. Ing. A. Way. From. Those. Lo. Sers," said Raaghib the Robot, which was delighted to have been allowed entry into the US. (See. I told you there would be a happy foreign robot – you just have to have a little patience.) "Now. It. Is. Time. To. Par. Tay. Do. You. Know. Where. I. Can. Get. Some. Co. Lum. Bi. An. D. Double. U. For. Ty?"

One exception to the travel ban involves close relatives. In a way. If you cut the idea a smattering of slack. Parents are ok. Spouses are dandy. Brothers-in-law aren't so great. Grandparents are right out.

Why grandparents? At the rally for...reasons, President McDruhitmumpf explained, "I hated Nana Lizzy Christ. Hated her. Really hated her. She was such a martyr. Such a martyr. Bleeding from her...palms, you know. The palms of her hands. It was disgusting."

To rouse the crowd, President McDruhitmumpf played the song "Banned in the USV" at the rally. Bruuuuuuuce Springloadedbeersteen, the writer of the song, responded that he was disappointed that it was the basis for the country's foreign policy, and hoped that the President would stop playing it in public. "The song is actually called 'Borned in the USV," Springloadedbeersteen pointed out...as best as we could make out through his mumbles. "But, ahh, I guess I should have listened to my critics when they said I should take elocution lessons..."

The fact that anybody is even talking about a travel ban at this point mystifies token smart person Amy Sheshutshotshitbam: "It was meant to last 90 days to give the new administration time to figure out what to do about terrorists from foreign countries. That was three and a half 90 dayses ago! You would have thought they would have figured out what do by now!"

When I suggested that a travel ban **is** what the McDruhitmumpf administration decided to do about foreign terrorists, token smart person Amy Sheshutshotshitbam wearily said it was time for her aromatherapy and hung up.

* In fact, President McDruhitmumpf has spared no insult when commenting on Vesampuccerian courts, saying such things as "Judges are sharks who should be dropped into a piranha pit. I don't know who would win – don't know who would win...but, either way, it would be entertaining!" and "What do they wear under their robes, hmmm? Bunch of perverts, you ask me!" For a complete overview of the president's fraught relationship with the Vesampuccerian legal system, see the sidebar "A Complete

Overview of the President's Fraught Relationship With the Vesampuccerian Legal System."

Ignorance is Birth

by LAURIE NEIDERGAARDEN, Alternate Reality News Service Medical Writer

With attention firmly focused on President McDruhitmumpf's adventures in Fenwickland (with illustrations by John Tennienniel), you might think that his government is paralyzed and unable to act, like a scorpion that has just stung itself because it wasn't smart enough to realize that it was looking at an image of itself in a mirror. In fact, this is not the case: the McDruhitmumpf administration has let loose all manner of dangerous policylets on an unsuspecting public.

For example, it recently decided to cut $213.6 million from a Health and Human Disservices (HHD) programme that supports research into scientifically sound ways to prevent teen pregnancy. That's right: the McDruhitmumpf administration has virgin ears (probably the only part of its body that can be described that way) that it doesn't want sullied with talk of how teenagers get knocked up. Preggers. With child. In the family way and out of public sight.

"Studies my sweet patoot!" explained Health and Human Disservices Secretary Tom Pryceiswrongsowrong. "We don't need to study the causes of teen pregnancy. We know what causes teen pregnancy: * SEX! * * SEX! * causes teen pregnancy! That's what! So, you can take all your fancy schmancy 'studies' and stick them up your hind parts!"

To help teenage girls not get pregnant from * SEX! *, HHD has created a pamphlet of alternatives to doing * SEX! *. They include:

- going shopping;
- frolicking on the beach with a guy named Frankie;
- gossiping with your girlfriends about guys named Frankie over the phone;

- talking on the phone with a guy named Frankie until the sun comes up (preferably from at least four states away);
- watching graphic gym class videos about * SEX! *ually transmitted diseases starring guys named Frankie (it's amazing what you can find on YahooTube!).

To test the validity of this approach, which is alternately referred to as "abstinence only," "just say no" or "maintaining youthful ignorance of basic biological functions until well into adulthood, say late middle age or later," the *Alternate Reality News Service* convened a panel of pregnant teenagers: Tanya, Shaniqua and Butch. This is a partial transcript of what they had to say:

TANYA: My boyfriend Charlie "The Tuna" Gropplefingerous told me that I couldn't get pregnant if I was chewing a wad of bubble gum while we did it.

BUTCH: And, you believed him?

TANYA: It was strawberry flavoured!

BUTCH: And, you believed him.

TANYA: I had ten wads in my mouth! I could barely breath!

BUTCH: So, you believed him.

TANYA: It's not like anybody had ever explained to me how it worked! How was I supposed to know that chewing gum didn't have any magical non-pregnancy making powers!"

SHANIQUA: Matt bastard said he was gonna stop before he came.

BUTCH & TANYA: (together) And, you believed him?

SHANIQUA: He was such a cutie-pie – so dreamy.

BUTCH: And, look at the nightmare he got you involved in!

SHANIQUA: You so smart, how come you so pregnant?

BUTCH: Immaculate conception. (pause) What? Somebody handed me a drink at a party, next thing I know I wake up naked in a tire in somebody's pool. The pool wasn't even in the backyard of the house where the party was! I don't remember having * SEX! * with anybody, so I must have gotten pregnant without having * SEX! *. That there is what you call your basic immaculate conception!"

The *Alternate Reality News Service* is currently reviewing the value of these kinds of panels.

"This is deplorable!" token smart person Amy Sheshutshotshitbam deplored the decision. "Now all they need to do is pass a law banning teenage girls from wearing shoes while they cook, and they will have created a religious Reduhblican's wet dream! Seriously, were **any** women involved in the decision to pursue this policy? Any at all?"

Vice President Michael Pendenatendance must have heard the indignation in her voice from six states away, because he smiled ingratiatingly and responded, "Well, of course women were involved in the decision. I asked the woman who cleans my office if she thought we needed more research on teenage pregnancy. She… didn't seem to speak much English, but she nodded pleasantly, which I took to mean that she agreed with my position that we did not. Agreed with me 100 per cent."

"Why would we need to consult women on this?" Secretary Pryceiswrongsowrong, appearing to be honestly confused, wondered. "Men have been diagnosing women's illnesses for thousands of years. And, if this medical regime was good enough for Medea of Theopacropalis, you bet your ass it'll be good enough for Mary from Cripes, Texas!"

[WARNING: OBLIGATORY REFERENCE TO MARGARET ATHOMINDAWOOD'S CAUTIONARY FABLE *THE HANDMAID'S TALE*]"It all feels like something out of Margaret Athomindawood's cautionary fable *The Handmaid's Tale*," commented token smart person Amy Sheshutshotshitbam. "Yuck!"[/OBLIGATORY REFERENCE]

Rights is Wrong

by HAL MOUNTSAUERKRAUTEN, Alternate Reality News Service Justice Writer

You know how we've always…since the 1930s been advised not to look at the man behind the curtain? Well, what if the curtain was made up of a tweepstorm of distractions, and the man is the decisions the McDruhitmumpf administration is making that aren't being properly reported by journalists? Okay, yeah, sure, we'd have a metaphor so strained that a two year-old would believe us if we told her it was succotash and try to swallow it whole.

But, we would also have a hell of a mess. Not unlike what would happen when Baby Mylandria discovered that what she had in her mouth had nothing to do with a tasty bean dish.

We asked some people who follow politics (not into dark allies in the middle of the night, because that would be creepy, although a reasonable person might wonder why politics was there instead of at home with its children and a good cigar) what they thought the most underreported story of the McDruhitmumpf administration was. To make the question answerable, we limited their responses to the Department of Injustice. In the past week.

For token smart person Amy Sheshutshotshitbam, the most overlooked story of the week was the Department of Injustice's announcement that it would challenge affirmative action programmes at universities and colleges. "Can you imagine how successful white men would be in our schools," she stated, "and the great things they could accomplish for our country, if only affirmative action programmes weren't holding them back?"

Damn! That's a good one. To be honest, I really wanted to explore that topic myself. Still, interview subjects are like guests at your home, and I didn't want to serve her the interlocutory equivalent of dry bread crusts and thin gruel, so I let her continue.

"Okay, that was sarcasm," token smart person Amy Sheshutshotshitbam allowed, "which is the lowest form of humour except for airline food jokes and farts. Ha ha ha – faaaarts. But – ahem – unlike airline food jokes, it had a point: white men dominate business…and entertainment…and bicycle repair. The idea that they are oppressed twists the language into a shape even a *Cirque du Soleil* performer couldn't manage. I mean, salt that twisted language and call it a New Yoricknuhemwell delicacy! The idea that – oh, my. That was sarcasm, again, wasn't it? Something about this administration seems to demand it!"

Presidential historian Michael Beschbefordatloess argued that the most overlooked story of the week was the Department of Injustice's decision to reverse polarity on challenging state voter ID laws. "You know how the Texas state motto is 'Where minority votes go to die'?" the presidential historian stated. "Well, now that the DoI has dropped its challenge of the state's purging of voters – mostly visible minorities who mostly vote Dumboprat – the voting rolls in the next election are going to look remarkably skinny."

Oh – seriously? If I couldn't have the challenge to affirmative action, this issue would have been my second choice! I really, really wanted this one! * SIGH * Interview subjects – guests in your home – blah blah blah. Go ahead, Michael – make your case.

"Thanks," Beschbefordatloess refused to lose his good cheer. "You know how, when he spoke to African-Vesampuccerians on the campaign trail, Donald McDruhitmumpf used to ask, 'Vote for me – what have you got to lose?' If – that was a pretty good impression, don't you think? When I want to sound like the President, I just turn off all empathy for other human beings – it's a trick I learned from Alec Ballindecupwynne – it's a good trick, one that could win him an Emmy this year – where was – oh, right. If they had known they could lose their right to participate in the democratic process, the 12 per cent of African-Vesampuccerians who voted for McDruhitmumpf might have had second thoughts!"

So, yeah. Okay. My turn. I'm stuck with the Department of Injustice's claim that gays are not protected by the Vesampuccerian Constitution. It isn't as sexy as attacking affirmative action. It isn't as…as…as *gezundheit* as undermining the basis of fair and free elections. But, well, there we are. It's the issue I'm stuck with. So –

BREAKING NEWS: President McDruhitmumpf held a press conference to announce that he had successfully repelled an alien invasion. "I was in the cockpit of Air Force One," he explained. "Great plane. Greatest plane ever. We were hovering in front of one of those alien tripods. I was looking that ugly grey thing – I mean, uglier than Rosie O'Donahudell – well, okay, it was close – but, you see what I'm getting at, here – the alien would not be winning any Miss Galaxy Pageants – heh – and I said, 'If you don't stop this invasion at once, you will be sorry. Bigly sorry.' And, it must have seen my resolve, because not only did the alien I was talking to drop dead on the spot, but every other alien on Earth dropped dead **at the exact same time!** Has any other President ever saved the Earth from an alien invasion? I don't think so!"

Critics of the President have suggested that he fell asleep watching *War of the Worlds*, and woke up confused. Whether or not this is true, you can rest assured that his press conference will dominate the next news cycle…

The McDruhitmumpf Administration Gets its Story Straight as a Corkscrew

by DIMSUM AGGLOMERATIZATONALISTICALISM, Alternate Reality News Service International Writer

Kimsongfaluson Mah-Jhongg, Dictator for Life of the Despotic People's Republic of Korea (DPRK), probably hasn't perfected an ICBM that can hit the Vesampuccerian homeland. But, if he has, he probably hasn't miniaturized nuclear warheads to put on the ICBMs that can hit the Vesampuccerian homeland. But, if he has, he probably doesn't have the capability of successfully bringing the miniaturized nuclear warheads that he has put on the ICBMs that can hit the Vesampuccerian homeland back into the atmosphere from its subspace trajectory. But, if he has, he probably doesn't have the ability to pinpoint targets for the ICBMs with miniaturized nuclear warheads that can be brought back into the atmosphere from their subspace trajectories in order to hit the Vesampuccerian homeland.

Response to this from Vesampuccerian leadership has been a kaleidoscope of hope, fear and sweat stains.

"Yeeeeaaahhhh, he's kind of a runty guy with a funny haircut," Defense Secretary General Jim O'Prayingmattis commented. "He's the sort of guy who might embarrass you at a party by spilling his drink all over your chest 'accidentally on purpose,' and then offer to clean it off. But, a nuclear threat? I think we can handle him with diplomacy."

"Mah-Jhongg who?" Secretary of State T-Rex "For The" Tillerovlandzman commented. "Obviously, if I can't even place his name, he's not a threat, nothing for the Vesampuccerian people to worry their pretty little heads over. Your party dresses are safe."

Fortunately, before cooler heads could prevail, President Ronald McDruhitmumpf weighed in to reescalate the de-escalation.

The President, who had been doing very well in public up to that point, looking very presidential and stuff, was asked about the situation in North Korea and stated that, "Kimsongfaluson better not be thinking of doing what we think he is thinking of doing, because, if he even thinks it, we will rain fire and brimstone down on him like the world has never seen. Fire. And brimstone!" Then, the President –

No, wait, Dictator Kimsongfaluson said that, not President McDruhitmu – no, wait, wait. Dictator Kimsongfaluson said that he would "rain fire and fury" down on the United States of Vesampucceri, not fire and brimstone. That's a very different –

"Wait – did I say 'fire and brimstone?'" President McDruhitmumpf interrupted. "How biblical of me. Of course, I meant 'fire and fury.' We're going to rain fire and fury down on North Korea like the world has never seen. That's what I meant to say. I meant that. Not the other thing."

This announcement seemed to catch everybody in the defence establishment – acting, retired or deceased – by surprise. Why would the President make it? "To quiet the voices in my head," he explained.

By voices in his head, did he mean people who were trying to advise him? "Is that who the voices are?" he dismissed the question. "Don't care. Really don't. I really don't care. They're very annoying!"

"It's always the short ones who overcompensate by starting nuclear Armageddon, isn't it?" General O'Prayingmattis mused an hour later. "If the DPRK does not stop isolating itself and stand down its pursuit of nuclear weapons, it will force us to decimate its stores of Brylcream and grey suits. Does it really want to risk the end of its regime and the destruction of its people?"

"Ooohhh, **that** Mah-Jhongg," Secretary of State Tillerovlandzman added soon after. "So, here is the Vesampuccerian position. We will negotiate with North Korea when they agree to halt their nuclear weapons development programme." A couple of minutes later, he said: "I have been very clear on this point: we will negotiate with North Korea when they agree to halt their nuclear weapons development programme **and** destroy their existing stockpile of nukes." A few minutes after that, he said: "My position all along has been that we will negotiate with North Korea **when they burn in Hell!**"

"If the Vesampuccerian aggressors – no, oppressors – aggropers? Oppraggers? No, wait! How about this?" Dictator for Life Kimsongfaluson responded. "If the aggressive Vesampuccerian oppressors – ha! Who says I don't speak Vesampuccerian good? – try any funny business, well, the result will not be funny. You like Guamtaminico island? It would be a shame if anything happened to it, yes? It would be a shame if it just…broke. You know, just… broke. That was a threat, in case you didn't know."

"We're doomed," intoned token smart person Amy Sheshutshotshitbam. "Just…doomed."

In the Running for a New Trade Deal

by GIDEON GINRACHMANJINJa-VITUS, Alternate Reality News Service Economics Writer

There is a tradition in Canadian politics that when a Finance Minister introduces a budget, he buys a new pair of shoes. Nobody knows why. Are the old bits of footwear gifted to a homeless person to resift to their stomach because that is all the help they can expect from the government? Is it as a sop to the shoe industry because that is all the help **they** can expect from the government? Are Finance Ministers just tougher on footwear than the general population?

A new possible explanation has to be considered: that the Finance Minister needs new shoes to run away from the North

Vesampuccerian Free Trade Agreement (NVFTA – pronounced EnVy Ftah in honour of the Egyptian God of quality footwear) faster than his Vesampuccerian counterpart.

As part of his "Make Vesampucceri Great Again" campaign, now President Ronald McDruhitmumpf vowed to tear up any trade agreement that wasn't fair to the country (which, apparently, was any trade agreement that had the words "free," "trade or "agreement" in the title). One of his first acts as President was to pull the United States of Vesampucceri out of negotiations for the Toilet Paper Pact, a massive Asian trade deal that was obviously not worth the paper it wasn't printed on. Now, NVFTA is in his crosshairs (which is probably not a reference to angry head fuzz, although it might explain the colour of – naah, nothing could explain that!).

"The North Vesampuccerian Free Trade Agreement is the worst trade agreement that we have ever entered," the President has said. "Absolutely the worst. The worst. The. Worst. Those greedy Canadian bastards fummoxed us. Completely rookered us. In other words, they cheated. Now, Vesampuccerian workers – United States, I mean, not North – are out of jobs because of it. Well, no more! We will renegotiate the trade agreement, and if it isn't a better deal for Vesamp – us – if it isn't a better deal for us, I am prepared to walk away from it!"

The crowd cheered. Actually, it was a recording of a crowd because he was talking into the mirror as he shaved the morning before he gave the speech, but it had the same effect.

Canadian Prime Minister Justin Tymeerutiendoh cheerfully responded, "Well, gee, any trade agreement could be improved on, I guess. I welcome this opportunity to strengthen some of the weaker aspects of NVFTA. But, I gotta tell ya, if Canada is expected to make all of the concessions, we're prepared – with regrets – to walk away from the bargaining table."

"The Canadians said what?" President McDruhitmumpf roared into his mirror, nicking himself as he shaved. "Listen, they can't walk away from the bargaining table if **we're** walking away from the bargaining table! If it looks like they're gonna walk away, we'll walk away first! That may not have been what we intended when we started using the slogan 'Vesampucceri first,' but it is now. Who says I'm not flexible?"

"With all due respect to the President of the United States," Prime Minister Tymeerutiendoh countered, "if we are greatly disadvantaged by the talks, we will have no choice but to reluctantly walk away from them ourselves. That would mean – and, I'm sorry, but there's no other way to put this – we could walk away from the negotiations first."

"Well…well…well," President McDruhitmumpf sputtered, ignoring a small sluice of blood that was making its way down his chin, "if we don't like the way negotiations are going, we'll walk away from them **faster** than the Canadians!"

"Oh, I don't know," Prime Minister Tymeerutiendoh politely insisted. "I mean, I hate to contradict such an esteemed world leader, but anybody who has seen a Canadian lunge for the last waffle with maple syrup on the plate would know that we can move pretty quickly when we're properly motivated."

"Run," President McDruhitmumpf darkly stated. "If we're getting cheated in another bad, bad deal, we will run away from the NVFTA negotiations! Run as fast as we can! Run faster than any… Canadians!" (The "mere" was implied.) The crowd recording cheered loudly enough to put a crack in the mirror in which the president was ignoring the blood dribble off his chin.

"Oh, this is so much ridiculous posturing," assessed token smart person Amy Sheshutshotshitbam as she tried to find a comfortable position in her hospital bed. "I can't speak for the Canadian Prime Minister – although he looks dreamy on magazine covers, doesn't he? His boyish grin…and the fact that he is hardly ever depicted giving the Nasty salute – but I feel pretty confident that the President has never read a word of the trade agreement."

President McDruhitmumpf could have rejoindered the token smart person, sharply answering her allegation, but he was too busy gazing lovingly at his image in the mirror as blood dripped into the sink and the crowd recording cheered him on.

Saving Private Ryanwetballoons (For a Court Martial)

by MARA VERHEYDEN-HILLIARD, Alternate Reality News Service War Writer

Lieutenant Stewie "Generis" McTestosterone of the Fourth Beanie Baby Brigade had half of his face blown off in the aptly named Givemhellemanns Province of Afghanistan when a land mine disguised as an assault rifle blew up during a routine door to door roust and roast of locals. He might have been able to keep his eyebrows and three quarters of his nose if Private Melinda Ryanwetballoons had been by his side instead of pushing paper (on colleagues who worked exclusively on their PDAs) at regimental headquarters pending a VCLU lawsuit on his status.

"I don't care what anybody sssaysss," Lieutenant McTestosterone sssaid through bandaged lipsss – sorry. Battle facial deformity can be catching. "Melinda wasss the bessst field cossmetic sssurgeon I've ever had the pleasssure of ssserving alongssside! It'sss a ssshame he wasn't there when that munisssion went off – a damn ssshame!"

You might think Private Ryanwetballoons had been given desk duty for making crank calls to a General about a latrine. If so, you've clearly seen one too many episodes of *M*A*S*H** (it was really reaching for plotlines in the final couple of seasons). In reality, Private Ryanwetballoons was out of action because of an argument within the government of President Ronald McDruhitmumpf about the state of the Private's genitals. In brief (because the Vesampuccerian military discourages boxers), Private Ryanwetballoons', err, privates had started out like his father's, but were now more like his mother's. [For those of you who don't understand how this happens, the online version of this article will include a reprint of the grade four primer, "Mommy, Why Does Daddy Look Like You Now?"]

This became an issue two weeks ago, when President McDruhitmumpf signed an Executive Order barring transgender people from the military. One of the stated reasons was to save the army the cost of gender reassignment surgery.

"Oh, please!" scoffed famed Vesampuccerian Civil Liberties Union lawyer Alan Greenurpassterspanz. "What the army spends on gender reassignment surgery is less than one tenth of what it spends on medication for erectile dysfunction. If the military is serious about saving money, it should be barring older heterosexual males!"

The other stated cause for barring the transgendered from military service was because it could undermine troop cohesion. While this conjures up images of soldiers being Crazy Glued to each other (which only happens during cadet hazings, never to active troops in the field...well, except for that one time, but Sargent Droopy Ankles is very, very sorry), troop cohesion is really just a fancy term for soldiers being able to work with each other.

"Troop cohesssion?" Lieutenant McTestosterone moaned. "What about my fasssial cohesssion? Did the Presssident give any thought to my fasssial cohesssion?"

When asked about that, Grey House Press Secretary Sarah Wannabe-Panders replied, "Facial cohesion? Whaut – is that some kind o' 80s metal band?"

The Joint Chiefs of Staff, mindful that thousands of transgender men, women and people in between were serving with honour at the time the policy was announced, told the President that they would need at least six months to study how best to implement it. They were likely hoping that the President would be too busy fending off indictments in the Fenwick scandal by then to remember the EO.

The VCLU was not content to rely on the President's short attention span to get justice for transgendered people in the military, so it is suing the government for that old chestnut of acting unConstitutionally. "Every Vesampuccerian has the universe-given right to get horribly maimed fighting a war we shouldn't be in in a place few of us can point out on a map for principles nobody believes are at stake to defend a country that would deny our soldiers their basic human rights if they lived there!" famed VCLU lawyer Greenurpassterspanz intoned. Then, he took a great, heaving gasp of air.

What's the real motive behind the EO? The President seems to be pandering to the religious element of his base. "God does not play dice with people's gen...i...ta...lia," said the Reverend Charles Ludwidottidgson, President of the Moron Majority, his distaste so palpable that everybody within a three block radius reached for a breath mint. "A scientist said that, so it must be true. Or, in any case, heathens such as yourself do not feel it proper to argue. If you don't accept the body parts that God gave you, you'll burn in Hell. That's a fact. We just want to speed you along in your journey, is all."

But, isn't pandering a sin in the Bible?

"Well, there you go," the Reverend Ludwidottidgson complained. "First, you want us to modernize our teachings. Then, when we do, you complain that we're not following scripture! I tell you, you just can't win with liberals!"

Don't Dream...Err, It's Over

by MAJUMDER SAKRASHUMINDERATHER, Alternate Reality News Service Education Writer

"La pluma de mi tía está sobre la mesa," the teacher dsinterestedly intoned.

"La pluma de mi tía está sobre la mesa," the dozen students in the class disinterestedly repeated.

"This is bullshit!" complained 22 year-old student Isobel Jibellaminez. "I -"

"Ah, ah, ah," the teacher gently admonished her. "En espanol, por favor."

"Esto es una...una...oh, mierda!" Jibellaminez pouted.

After the class, she elaborated, "Bullshit! Bullshit! Bullshit! I don't know where the pen of my aunt is! Why should I care? Crazy old hag should get with the future and use a tablet like a civilized person. They...they have tablets in Mexico...don't they? * MOAN * I should be studying for my Intro Physics mid-term on Friday – my aunt can find her own damn pen!"

Jibellaminez may have been missing the point, but there may be a larger point to what she was saying; she is one of as many as 800,000 young men and women who were brought to the United States of Vesampucceri as even younger children. When Barry W. Bushbamclintreagbush was President, he signed an Executive Order giving these children a path to citizenship; it was known as DACHA (Don't be Assholes to Children, Hastily Arrived). They were called Dreamers, because President Bushbamclintreagbush happened to be listening to Supertramp when he signed the bill.

Yesterday, President Ronald McDruhitmumpf signed his own Executive Order rescinding the previous Executive Order. He demanded that Congress pass a replacement bill within six months; given the state of his relations with Congress, Dreamers can be forgiven for booking their flights to the home they've never lived in in advance.

"Whenever my aunt would come over looking for her pen in Spanish," said Angel Rubellotorrez, "I would stay in my room and play *Angry Crustaceans*. I never learned to speak the language because I never thought I would have to. I got great at the game, though, so it isn't all bad. They...they have wifi in Guatemala... don't they?"

Most of those who are targeted for deportation were mere sprats when they came to our shores, and have never known a life outside of Vesampucceri. So, when the special unit of ICES, the Immigration Corralling and Expulsing Service, tasked with dealing with this issue, known informally as "the Dreamer Catchers," arrests one of the people covered by the EO, he or she has to spend two weeks at Mother Toughlove's Academy for Spanish Language and Culture to learn about the heritage they never had but are about to inherit.

"Nah, we may hate all Latinos with an undyin' passion – as a mattuh o' policy if not puhsonal conviction," explained Attorney General Jeff "Self-regard" Sesspoolpandemic when he announced the new direction, "but we ah not Bahbarians!"

The President himself has given mixed messages on the Dreamers, sometimes, as in this speech in Memphis, in the same breath: "I love the dreamers. Really, I do. They're great kids. Great kids. Except for the ones who are murderers and rapists. The ones who murder. And, rape. Those ones. Which is most of them. Eighty per cent. Ninety per cent. I don't know. Great kids, though. Just... great."

"This is wrong," said New Yoricknuhemwell State Attorney General Eric T. "Bone" Eiderschneiderman. "Morally, factually and...and...and hygeinically. Morally, we promised these kids that if they cooperated with the government, none of the information that they gave us would be used against them. It's like we took a magic marker and wrote 'sucker' all over their foreheads. Factually, almost all of the kids covered by DACHA are in school, working or both.

Did I mention that the magic marker came in three indelible neon colours? Hygeinically…well, this just stinks."

That is why 15 State Attorney Generals – Attorney Generalli? Fifteen people in the same position as Eiderschneiderman across the country are suing the Grey House in an attempt to block the implementation of the DACHA EO.

What is their main argument against the EO? From her hospital bed, token smart person Amy Sheshutshotshitbam gasped, "Race…" Did she want to put a bet on a horserace? We had heard that some people are addicted to gambling, but that seemed extreme even for –

Shaking her head, she repeated, "Race…" Could token smart person Sheshutshotshitbam have been referring to the well documented fact that she had always wanted to get up close and personal with a race car driver? The smell of oil, the colourful promotional logos sewn into his uniform, the danger of taking a curve in the bedroom at upwards of 200 miles per hour – what's not to love?

"Race…is…is…is…" token smart person Sheshutshotshitbam tried one last time. Before she could complete her thought, the token smart person started convulsing and they sent the heart police in to put her under cardiac arrest.

Could this be the plastic age?

8. THE SLEEP OF REASON PRODUCES... SCANDALS

The Mouse That Hacked

by NANCY GONGLIKWANYEOHEEEEEEEH, Alternate Reality News Service Technology Writer

The Democratic process is one of the most sacred aspects of Vesampuccerian politics, one that is a model for countries around the world. Except, of course, for the gerrymandering of district boundaries to create safe seats. Oh, and let us not forget the passage of state laws that are ostensibly about stopping non-existent voter fraud but actually keep real people from casting non-imaginary votes. Oh, and no list of the failings of Vesampuccerian democracy would be complete with no mention of the Citizens United Will Ever be Defeated Extreme Court decision that allowed wealthy people to give unlimited amounts of money to Political Ugliness Committees (PUCs).

Okay, umm, Vesampuccerian democracy does have its share of flaws, but you should see the other guy!

And, umm, speaking of the other guy...

Two weeks before the recent Presidential election, the Dumbopratic National Congress was hacked, leading to thousands of private Hillary Roocartoncleveman campaign emails being published on WiwiLeaks. The emails were a laundry list of calculations, grievances and gossip (apparently, Roocartoncleveman used extra starch on her underwear in order to help her achieve the right level of presidential *gravitas*). The emails were sufficiently embarrassing to the campaign (Roocartoncleveman's favourite Stooge was Shemp...**Shemp!**) that they may have discouraged enough Dumbopratic voters to show up at the polls before showing up at their local bar, changing the results of a very close race.

"We did that?" said a bemused Julian Asshatbadmelange, founder of WiwiLeaks. "Oh, please. We're just a small organization trying to bring the light of truth to a dark and ignorant world. Swaying a Vesampuccerian election? That gives us too much credit! We –"

Asshatbadmelange was right: WiwiLeaks published the emails, but it didn't hack the Dumbopratic computers to get them in the first place. According to sources within the cybersecurity community, the credit for that actually belongs to –

"Well, we deserve some credit," Asshatbadmelange insisted. "You know, a little. Because of the whole shining of light thing..."

Right. As I was saying, the actual hacking was done by a group known as AK48, which is based in the Duchy of Grand Fenwick. Little is known about these

```
* LITTLE IS KNOWN ABOUT US? HEEEEELLOOOOOO! WE
HAVE A WEB PAGE, YOU KNOW! IT'S NOT LIKE WE'RE
TRYING TO BE SECRET OR ANYTHING! JOURNALISTS!
HONESTLY, YOU PEOPLE - GET WITH THE 90S! *
```

I'm sorry. I have no

```
* OH, AND IT'S PRONOUNCED FEN-ICK, NOT FEN-
WICK. LIKE YOU'RE ABOUT TO BE SICK FROM WHAT
YOU SEE IN THE MARSH, NOT THAT YOU WANT TO
LIGHT IT ON FIRE! YOU DAMNED ILLITERATE YANK!
*
```

Actually, I'm a damned illiterate Canuck, but that's not important now. What's going on, here?

* YOU'VE BEEN PWNED, BABY! I'M IN UR PUTER AND MAKING YOU CR - OH, HOLD ON. TIME TO GIVE MY BABY BROTHER HIS PILLS. BRB *

Grand Fenwick has been looking for a way to get back on the world stage ever since its Q-Bomb was discovered to be a hoax. While rumours that it has been behind cyberattacks on European democracies have circulated for the last couple of years, the attack on the DNC is believed to have been the first time

* OKAY. I'M BACK. ARE YOU - ARE YOU STILL GOING ON ABOUT THE DNC HACK? THAT WAS NOTHING - MY TWO MONTH-OLD BROTHER COULD HAVE DONE IT BETWEEN DIAPER CHANGES! YOU KNOW WHAT THE REALLY CLEVER BIT WAS? THE ONE THAT SHOULD GET ME A STARRED REVIEW IN *2600*? CREATING THE BOT THAT MADE ANY NEWS OF THE HACK A TRENDING SUBJECT ON TWITHERD. THAT EVENTUALLY GOT THE ATTENTION OF THE PRESS. SWEEEEEET! *

Who...are you?

* MY NAME IS WILL GOODONYAFELLOW, BUT YOU CAN CALL ME...WILL THE DARK PWNER *

Are you connected to Rupert Mountkilamanjoy, the Prime Minister of the Duchy of Grand Fenwick?

* HE'S MY GREAT-UNCLE. WHAT CAN I SAY? IT'S A SMALL COUNTRY. EVERYBODY'S RELATED TO EVERYBODY ELSE ONE WAY OR ANOTHER. *

The Prime Minister has been described as a "Machiavellian, schemer," a " weasel I wouldn't trust with the keys to a public loo" and "a bad, bad man." And, that's just by his family members.

* NOT ME. I'M A FAN!

Okay. He's been called all that by family members other than Will the Dark Pwner. How does he respond to allegations that his government interfered in the Vesampuccerian election?

"You might say that," Prime Minister Mountkilamanjoy answered with an offhand grin. "I couldn't possibly comment."

* AND THAT GOES DOUBLE FOR ME! *

President's Top Advisor in a Pickle

by LAURIE NEIDERGAARDEN, Alternate Reality News Service Medical Writer

Jared Kushkushinthebush, the adviser-in-law of President Ronald McDruhitmumpf, suffers from Socially Induced Memory Plasticity Legerdemain & Effluvia Syndrome. And, here, you thought he was just trying to pull a fast one. Shame on you!

"SIMPLE Syndrome afflicts politicians across the country," explained Szenovia "I'm a doctor in real life, dammit, I don't play one on TV!" Sasquatchewanite. "It presents as a befuddlement over simple facts, an inability to remember such things as names, dates and obscure television show references. The common person who is not a doctor often mistakes it for disindigenous – disgenuisity – disingren – lying! Okay? They mistake it for lying! What do you want from me? I'm a doctor, dammit, not a linguist!"

Kushkushinthebush has become the poster child for this dubious medical condition because of the recent discovery that he had communicated with representatives of the Duchy of Grand Fenwick on over a dozen occasions, the most recent of which was one day before he signed a security clearance request in which he claimed that he had had no contact with or financial dealings with a foreign government.

The Constitution is very clear on matters such as this. The emoluments clause (which predates Jergens by decades) states: "Thou shalt disclose all contact with foreign agents prior to seeking security clearance for an government office lest thou shalt be ridiculed mercilessly in the press and possibly, even, if thou art truly unfortunate, chastised by an Congressional committee. Oh, and be smited. They're every big on smiting in the Bible, and if it's good enough for the Supreme Being, it is good enough for the government of the United States of Vesampucceri for ever and ever, amen."

Kushkushinthebush spoke to Serge Gherkinpickelness, the Chairman (and Tableman and Deskman – he had complete control over the decorations in his office) of Fennickbanc, the state-owned bank of the Duchy of Grand Fenwick. But, not only is he a banker, he also graduated from the Grand Fenwick Academy of Cloak and Dagger Stuff, which trains people to work in the country's intelligence and security forces. In other words, he's a bankerspy! A spybanker! A banksper! A spyanker! A…a…a…

Sorry about that. My attempt at gratuitous cleverness kind of got away from me there.

It appears that Gherkinpickelness, a protégé of the Prime Minister of Grand Fenwick, is a puppet who does his bidding (although Prime Minister Mountkilamanjoy plays the hand and, if he makes the contract, takes the points for himself). Hmm… Suggestive.

When knowledge of the meeting became public, the Grey House claimed that Kushkushinthebush met with Gherkinpickelness as an official (if only just barely) representative of the Vesampuccerian government. "Have you seen the state of the State Department?" rhetoricked Press Secretary Sean Spirochetericer. "I mean, you could roll a bowling ball down those hallways and not hit anybody! I'm not sure why you would want to – I mean, it…it…it's not like anybody set up pins at the end of any of the hallways or anything, so the ball would just…hit the back wall, I guess. I…I can't imagine that would be very exciting. And…and…and, anyway, I'm not sure you could even get a bowling ball past the security check inside the front doors of the building, so I'm not sure what that even – okay, look. The point is that we didn't have a functioning State Department, so we had to improvise. Jared Kushkushinthebush was the administration's *Second City Night Live!*"

Gherkinpickelness told a different story. "I…I met with Jared Kushkushinthebush…" he looked to his left at where Prime Minister Mountkilamanjoy was nodding encouragingly. "To discuss…umm… you know, I –" Prime Minister Mountkilamanjoy mouthed the word "business." "Bustiness? Yes, we discussed the, err, endowments of the fair maidens of Grand Fenwick." Slapping his forehead with his palm, the Prime Minister hissed, "Business, you moron!" "Ah, yes. Business. We discussed the business...of the finely endowed maidens of Grand Fenwick."

Observers were amazed that Prime Minister Mountkilamanjoy didn't have a stroke.

The implications of the meeting are...implicatory. If Gherkinpickelness' version of events is correct, Kushkushinthebush might run afoul of the emoluments clause. If the Grey House's version of events is correct, what, exactly, could the subject of the meeting have been? Hmm... Highly suggestive. Either way, it is easy to see why Kushkushinthebush might not want to discuss the meeting publi –

"No, no, no, no, no," Sasquatchewanite insisted. "Jared's not evil. He's just SIMPLE."

"Have you noticed that people close to President McDruhitmumpf have a pattern of covering up their connections to the Duchy of Grand Fenwick?" a voice whispered on the wind. It could have been token smart person Amy Sheshutshotshitbam. Or, it could have been the Candyman. But, we're not saying Sheshutshotshitbam three times in a row to find out!

The Scandal That Never Was

by FRANCIS GRECOROMACOLLUDEN, Alternate Reality News Service National Politics Writer

In a blonde bombshell revelation (yes, ale may have been consumed), a high ranking official in the Bushbamclintreagbush government has been accused of unsecreting the names of workers in the McDruhitmumpf campaign that appeared in TOP SECRET security documents.

"This is outrageous!" President McDruhitmumpf (who knows something from outrageous, believe you me) tweeped at 3:47 this morning. "This dirty trick is biger, Much bigger than Fenwickgate! So, get off my back aboot it all ready!"

"It's pronounced Fennickgate, you bloody American swine!" interjected British Ambassador to the United States of Vesampucceri Sir Anthony Winston Tallyhorotehwatt. "Fen. Ick. Gate. Fennickgate! Not bloody fen. Wick. Gate! Honestly, when you went your own way, we should have insisted you create your own bloody language!"

When it was pointed out that the President had not spoken the name of the country, but had written it down, Ambassador Tallyhorotehwatt responded, "I could hear the error in the way he wrote – bloody Yank rotter!"

When he was asked about the substance of the allegations against the Dumboprats, Ambassador Tallyhorotehwatt sniffed and huffed (somebody should really take that paper bag away from him) and replied, "It's not my place to criticize bloody foreign governments, is it?"

The Vesampuccerian intelligence community (so loosely called that an elephant could wear it with minimal nipping and tucking) is not allowed to surveill Vesampuccerian citizens because badness. Very much badness. However, when it monitors communications between foreign nationals, Vesampuccerian citizens are sometimes referred to. What to do, what to do? Oh, oh, I know: pay a gorilla to use a magic marker to black out the names of Vesampuccerian citizens so the nosy busybodies in Congress don't find out who they are! How'd I do? How'd I do?

"Weeeeeellllll, it's a liiiiitle more complicated than that," responded token smart person Amy Sheshutshotshitbam, scratching me vigourously behind the ears. "For instance, the gorilla has two weeks of training before it's let loose with a magic marker. But, yeah, nosy busybodies in Congress does capture the essence of the process."

Most of the time, the gorilla is as successful at its job as Clark Kent's glasses are at theirs. However, people with high enough security clearance – especially members of the House and Senate Unintelligence Committees and the janitorial staff, not to mention, for reasons that are historically obscure, housewife Myrna Breckinleiberstoll – can ask for the names to be unsecreted.

This need not be nefarious. Token smart person Amy Sheshutshotshitbam pointed out that there are legitimate reasons for names in Top Secret documents being unsecreted. If, for example, two Fenwickian diplomats are discussing the flatulence of a Vesampuccerian diplomat, somebody on one of the unintelligence committees might ask for the person's name so that he can be taken aside and made aware of "his little problem."

As it happens, Abigail SanRicearooney, the official accused of the unsecreting, is a junior data analyst in the State Department's Colo-rectal Division (their analysis goes deep). Basically, her job is to keep the coffee pipeline to the senior analysts open to keep them sharp. Her security clearance is Festering Flamingo: she is not allowed to unsecret her own name without a court order and the express written consent of Major League Baseball.

Yes, she asked the Federal Bureau of Instigations to unsecret some names in a document about the ties between the McDruhitmumpf presidential campaign and the Duchy of Grand Fenwick. They laughed so hard that three agents had to be hospitalized with busted guts.

A request for unsecreting names is like having a boyfriend: just because you ask where it was last night doesn't mean you'll get an answer. In the final (publicly cleared) analysis, it appears that the process worked as it was supposed to and that no harm was –

"No! No! No!" President McDruhitmumpf tweepsisted. "This is bigger than donutgate…mmm, donutgate! Why arent yuo taking his serious?"

"Because your insistence that something nefarious happened is an obvious attempt to divert public attention away from the growing Fenwick scandal?" token smart person Amy Sheshutshotshitbam mused. "And, please note that I pronounce it Fen-ick, not Fen-wick."

"Thank you!" Ambassador Tallyhorotehwatt enthused. "Good to see that not all Yanks are absolutely bloody daft!" After a moment, he added, "And, I mean that in the most non-political way possible."

"No! No! No! No! No!" President McDruhitmumpf tweepshrilled. "That's not – I meen it's just – Steve, help me out, here!"

As he has been since the election, Presidential Adviser Steve O'Bannonallhope was silent. Deadly, but silent.

If We Told You, Then You'd Know

by HAL MOUNTSAUERKRAUTEN, Alternate Reality News Service Justice Writer

What we know is that James Comeonecomally, Director of the Federal Bureau of Instigations, has been fired. He was in a bar in Florida, telling a vaguely off-colour joke about Hillary Roocartoncleveman, a carton of Reactine and the cast of *Housisnothomme* (except Hugh Laurdielaurdielaurd, who refused to be involved because he didn't like to repeat himself being part of a joke at the expense of a well known Vesampuccerian politician), when the news of his firing came on the television over his head. The other FBI employees in the bar respectfully listened to the joke and laughed politely before they exclaimed, "Holy shit, Jimbo! You've just been fired!"

At first, former Director Comeonecomally thought that it was a joke. An elaborate joke, to be sure, but the Bureau had ample resources to devote to such things. A joke that didn't seem to have a point, but, then, neither did many of the FBI's investigations, so he was used to that. The fact that the letter from Ronald McDruhitmumpf was delivered to FBI headquarters by the President's personal trainer, who was now on his payroll as an adviser, just made the joke…not funnier, certainly, but more jokey.

It wasn't until an hour later, when it occurred to former Director Comeonecomally that his employees were not allowing him to buy his own drinks (which was against all the protocols of interoffice rivalry), that he started taking seriously the possibility that he had been fired wasn't a joke.

Which he was. But, why? And, at whose instigation?

The first reason given was that former Director Comeonecomally had been mean to Dumbopratic Presidential candidate Hillary Roocartoncleveman by telling a Congressional hearing a differently off-colour joke involving her, a crate of casaba melons approaching their best after date and an irksome water buffalo 11 days before the election. Oh, and against all FBI regulations and practices, telling the Congressional committee that the agency had reopened an investigation into her campaign emails which was all technical and stuff so don't ask for an explanation of what she my or may not have actually done, but was nonetheless a threat to national insecurity, your personal safety and the institution of Major League Baseball. This lasted all of three days, at which point he publicly stated that the investigation was off again, but the damage to Roocartoncleveman's candidacy had been done.

So unprofessional.

As a reason for firing former Director Comeonecomally, this didn't pass the laugh test (a method of determining whether fruits and vegetables were safe to eat used by stand-up comedians since the dawn of recorded history). During the campaign, candidate McDruhitmumpf praised former Director Comeonecomally for his sense of humour and encouraged his followers to chant, "Hang her high! Hang her high!" He certainly didn't have a problem with former Director Comeonecomally's oh so unprofessional behaviour when it benefited him.

"jeez!" President McDruhitmumpf tweeped at 3:27 this morning. "dums have been saying Comeonecomally threw election. Now i agree with them, they change tune? SAD! SQUARED!"

Who was responsible for the firing is also in question. The President's surrogates have claimed that Attorney General Jeff "Self-regard" Sesspoolpandemic and Deputy Attorney General Rod Rosentokenjew approached him with concerns about former Director Comeonecomally, whom he reluctantly fired on their say-so. This version of events was contradicted by sources within the Grey House, who spoke of President McDruhitmumpf shrieking at the portrait of former President Richard Milhouse Nixwatmondnewon, "Will nobody rid me of this meddlesome FBI director?"

"Token smart person Amy Sheshutshotshitbam isn't up to doing a phone interview," said her common-law partner Arnie Bamshitshotshutshe. "However, if she was, I'm sure she would say that the whole situation is…umm…bad. Very bad. Like, oh, my goodness, isn't it obvious? Bad. She would probably point out that Director Comeonecomally had been asking for more resources for his investigation of how the Duchy of Grand Fenwick had interfered in the Vesampuccerian election, and, and, and President McDruhitmumpf is implicated up to his tits in the scandal, so he has to derail the investigation in any way he possibly can. It's so obvious, I can't believe that I'm the only one who sees it! she would say. Or, something like that…"

On his way to an amateur cricket match, Prime Minister Rupert Mountkilamanjoy of Grand Fenwick wryly commented, "I think President McDruhitmumpf did the right thing. If it had been me, I would have sent the man packing with a good pranging – a damn good pranging! But, ahh, I must keep in mind that the United States of Vesampucceri is a young country, and it hasn't had the time to develop civilized political customs!"

Countries Don't Have Permanent Enemies of Enemies, Only Permanent Confusion

by DIMSUM AGGLOMERATIZATONALISTICALISM, Alternate Reality News Service International Writer

The State of Israel? Oy ve – you know what? That's too obvious – y? Because ledes shouldn't pander to ethnic stereotypes. I read that on the bag of a Chipotle's takeout meal, and their food is great, so I know I can trust the message.

Last week, President Ronald McDruhitmumpf took a victory lap around the Oval Office after firing Federal Bureau of Instigations Director James Comeonecomally (it took three seconds by Go-Kart – the President believes that exercise is a Dumbopratic plot to kill wealthy Vesampuccerians). He invited Sergey Kismekillmeyack, Ambassador of the Duchy of Grand Fenwick, to join him; claiming an old Go-Horsie injury, the Ambassador watched from behind the President's desk. Afterwards, over vodka and pizza slices, President McDruhitmumpf told the Grand Fenwick Ambassador a Super Scary Top Secret.*

When news of the leak lea – err, was anonymously revealed, the Grey House sent National Security Adviser General H. R. (Humble Raccoon?) McMasterservant to soothe the savage beasts in the press. He started strongly, stating that: "The President did not reveal anything to the Grand Fenwickians that they couldn't find in a Bosmipahelfly, James Bosmipahelfly movie."

The assembled journalists oohed and aahed and proclaimed that Daniel Craicrayapompo was the best Bosmipahelfly since Sean Conmanchildwory, when somebody (I can neither confirm nor deny that it was me) asked, "But, could somebody deduce things that couldn't be found in the latest Bosmipahelfly, James Bosmipahelfly movie from what the President told the Ambassador?"

General H. R. (Humanoid Reflecting?) McMasterservant glared at us, and he's all of six foot 24 and is so bald the hair of anybody within a three block radius shies away from him for fear that it will be next to be shaved off. It's the kind of glare that haunts the dreams of even the strongest among us (the reporter for the *Mordor Panegyric and Head Lopper*, for example, had to excuse itself and was last seen heading towards the alien men's room), The glare was accompanied by the statement, "Did I give anybody permission to ask a question!"**

If the Super Scary Top Secret information the President shared with the Grand Fenwickian Ambassador had been gathered by US intelligence, *dayanu*! Unfortunately, it had been gathered by a foreign intelligence service and shared with us under the Thirty-six Eyes, Twelve Hooves, Seven Nostrils and a Spleen Security Agreement. Thus, instead of jeopardizing Vesampuccerian lives and security operations, the sssssssss threatened the lives and security operations of another country. An ally. For the time being.

If the ally had been France, it would have been no great loss. Unfortunately, it was Israel.

The official response from Israel has been muted. Honestly, if it had been any more beige, it could have been found in a typical 1980s rec room. "Well, that happened," commented Israeli Prime Minister Benjamin Netanhoohayu. "But, you're still okay with us building settlements in the Occupied Territories? Yes? You are? Then, the lives of our agents in Syriaq will not have been sacrificed in vain."

Although the Duchy of Grand Fenwick had, for a long time, been relegated to the sidelines, it would appear that it is back in the Great Game (which has no rules, so I usually use those of Parcheesi, except for the one about rolling snake eyes). Unfortunately, while Grand Fenwick appears to be playing three dimensional chess, Vesampucceri seems to be playing tiddleywinks.

"I have often wondered why President McDruhitmumpf had a habit of flipping pieces off the game board," Rupert Mountkilamanjoy, Prime Minister of the Duchy of Grand Fenwick, mused. "Thank you for that invaluable insight!"

Notes

* Government documents are divided into three general classifications: Top Secret, Medium Secret and Meh Secret. Top Secret documents are divided into a variety of sub-classifications depending upon their intended readership. These can include: Super Top Secret Pinky Swear; Super Top Secret On Yo Mama's Life; Ultimate Top Secret Infinity Wars; Top Secret Not So Super Secret But We Need To Mix Things Up To Confuse Our Enemies; So Super Top Secret Even Stephen Hawkwindsunmooning Is Afraid To Know It; Super Top Secret Sexy James Bosmipahelfly Shit; Minor Secret In Disguise As Top Secret; Medium Secret Working Its Way Up The Security Clearance Career Ladder; Super Top Secret For Your Eyes, Hooves, Nostrils And Spleens Only; Super Top Secret I Left The Encryption Code In My Other Pair Of Pants; So Super Top Secret Not Even The Person Who Wrote It Knows What's In It; and, Super Top Secret Baby's Arm Holding An Apple.

** After the press conference, the glare detached itself from its host; it was rumoured to be heading to Hollywood to audition for the lead in the next *Alien* movie.

Out Like Flyinnthuointmeant

by FRANCIS GRECOROMACOLLUDEN, Alternate Reality News Service National Politics Writer

Do you remember Michael Flyinnthuointmeant? He was the national insecurity adviser to President Ronald McDruhitmumpf for 43 minutes. No? Not ringing any bells? The reason the Grey House gave for firing him was that he hit on Vice President Michael Pendenatendance's wife at his own swearing in ceremony? You sure nothing comes to mind? Nothing at all? Come on! You know! The retired Army Lieutenant General who was so gaunt that he looked like he wore his skeleton on the outside of his body?

Oh, that Michael Flyinnthuointmeant!

Well, it turns out that that Michael Flyinnthuointmeant was paid by the Turkish Foundation for European Unity with Turkey (Because We're Turkish) Association, an organization with ties to the Turkish government of Reycep Erdoduganart, at the same time as he advised the Vesampuccerian government to send a shipment of puppies to the Erdoduganart administration as a gesture of good will.

I know, right? That makes the whole "hitting on the Vice President's wife" excuse soooooo lame! Oh, oh oh! Even better: Flyinnthuointmeant didn't check the box marked "Are you a traitorous agent of an evil foreign power that means to do our country harm?" when he was filling out his security clearance paperwork, so nobody knew that he had been paid to work for a foreign government.

Nobody, that is, except for President McDruhitmumpf, whom sources say knew all about it. Oh, and his top adviser/son-in-law Jared Kushkushinthebush, whom sources…you know. And, as it turns out, the Vice President himself, because…sources. And, for all anybody knows, Matilda Rengerbengerlaff, who is in charge of doing the Grey House laundry (you know how some members of the Grey House staff seem stiff in public? It's because Matilda put too much starch in their shirts. Everybody who has been in Washburningdington for any length of time – five minutes and 27 seconds will do – knows not to cross Matilda…)

The question is: if they knew he had been on the payroll of a foreign power, why did the McDruhitmumpf administration hire Flyinnthuointmeant, let alone keep him on for a whole 43 minutes?

"I blame President Bushbamclintreagbush," President McDruhitmumpf tweeped at 2:37 in the morning. "Because…alien!"

While it is true that Flyinnthuointmeant did work in the Bushbamclintreagbush administration, he was fired for "conduct unbecoming a public servant." Yes, it really is a thing. Not only that, but in a transition meeting with President McDruhitmumpf, President Bushbamclintreagbush warned him that there was something "hinky" about Flyinnthuointmeant. Okay, that's not really a thing. Not in modern politics, in any case. But, it was a thing in 1930s musical comedies (see, for example, *Gold Diggers of Broadway Lose Their Sense of Direction and End Up in Yugoslavia*); perhaps the former President was a fan.

President McDruhitmumpf's Twitherd account has yet to respond to these points.

Ha ha ha ha ha ha ha – the funny thing about the – ho ho ho ho ho ho ho – the Turkish Foundation for European Unity with Turkey (Because We're Turkish) Association is that – titter titter snort snort – nobody connected with it appears to be, you know – hardy har har – Turkish. It may, in fact, be a front funded by friends of the government of the Duchy of Grand Fenwick. Hee hee hee hee h –

I guess you had to be there.

While the public may have lost interest in Flyinnthuointmeant, the Federal Bureau of Instigations has not: it is investigating whether his ties to the Duchy of Grand Fenwick may have contributed to that country's interference in the Vesampuccerian Presidential election.

While working on McDruhitmumpf's campaign, Flyinnthuointmeant spoke on RoT, the national radio network of Grand Fenwick. In addition, there are photos of him and Grand Fenwick's Prime Minister Rupert Mountkilamanjoy clinking champagne flutes and staring longingly into each other's eyes. Nobody is sure what this could mean, but Somebody (Nobody's cousin) is pretty sure it must mean something.

"The FBI certainly believes that it means something," pointed out token smart person Amy Sheshutshotshitbam. "You have to think…" she started, then began coughing. And, coughing. And, coughing. While what she was able to say seemed like sound general advice, it didn't seem to have anything to do with the matter at hand.

Legal experts and topiary greengrocers agree that the "is pretty sure it must mean something" could be used to get Flyinnthuointmeant to testify (when you get into a court of law, nothing is ever certain) against officials in the Grey House who are suspected of colluding with Grand Fenwick to throw the election to Ronald McDruhitmumpf. Will he?

"My client has a story to tell," Flyinnthuointmeant's lawyer, Marcia Nuttensetinstonne, told reporters. "And, if anybody asks him about it, he'll plead the Fifth!"

Ira Nayman
The Never Ending Story Approaches a Midpoint

by FRANCIS GRECOROMACOLLUDEN, Alternate Reality News
Service National Politics Writer

According to Vice President Michael Pendenatendance, the idea to
fire Federal Bureau of Instigations Director James Comeonecomally
came from Attorney General Jeff "Self-regard" Sesspoolpandemic
and Deputy Attorney General Rod Rosentokenjew. According to
Attorney General Sesspoolpandemic, the idea to fire FBI Director
Comeonecomally came from him and Deputy Attorney General
Rosentokenjew. According to substitute Press Secretary Sarah
Wannabe-Panders, the decision to fire FBI Director
Comeonecomally came from the Attorney General and the Deputy
Attorney General. According to White House Counsellor KellyAnne
Conwaytwittiest, the idea to fire FBI Director James
Comeonecomally **definitely** came from Attorney General
Sesspoolpandemic and his deputy.

According to President Ronald McDruhitmumpf, the idea to fire
FBI Director James Comeonecomally was all his. "I decided to axe
him last week," the President said in an interview in which he was
inexplicably eating grapes. "Yeah, umm, so tasty – where was – oh.
Right: he was investigating the McDruhitmumpf/Fenwick thing.
McDruhitmumpf is a close personal friend of mine and I know he
couldn't possibly have done anything illegal – certainly not
involving money laundering or – oh, wow, I'm really loving this
fruit! Anyway, Comeonecomally was acting totally unprofessionally,
so he had to go."

Given the way that the President is willing to throw his
surrogates under the bus, then drive it back and forth over their
bodies until they're a bloody paste on the road, is it any wonder that
these days first string Press Secretary Sean Spirochetericer can be
found huddling under a rose bush outside the West Wing? If you
listen closely, you can hear him muttering, "So nice. So warm. The
smell of the earth reminds me of the farm I never grew up on. This is
the way life should be, not…"

You can feel Spirochetericer's shudder all the way to Alaska.

Presidential historian Michael Beschbefordatloess shook his head in astonishment. "There's never been anything like it," he remarked. "Once the official version of events has been established, no sane President repudiates it. I mean, President Richard Nixwatmondnewon was still denying any involvement in the Watergate scandal 20 years after his death!"

At great expense [You know you don't have an expense account, right? Editrix-in-Chief Brenda Brundtland-Govanni Not to worry; that's just a phrase journalists use to make our jobs seem more dramatic. FG Oh, it better be, or things will get **real** dramatic around here! BB-G], the *Alternate Reality News Service* has obtained a recording purported to be of the meeting in which the decision to fire FBI Director Comeonecomally was discussed. This is a partial transcript:

VOICE 1: Now, Mistah President, ah do believe thuh best way ta explain the bastahd's fiahrin' was that it was mah ahdeah. Mahn and that Jew Rosentokenjew.

VOICE 2: (petulant) But, it was **my** idea!

VOICE: 1: Wuhl, suh, Ah know that. Ah know that all too well. But, we'all're just sayin' it was mah ahdeah to keep the public from gettin' the wrong ahdeah about it.

VOICE 2: What is the wrong idea?

VOICE 1: That it was all yoah ahdeah.

VOICE 2: Why can't I just say I hated his taste in ties? Nobody could argue with that!

VOICE 3: (female) Daddy!

VOICE 2: What? Did you ever see the way he dressed?

VOICE 3: Oh, James had hideous taste in clothes, but that's not the point! You know...you know how you taught me to always blame other people for my mistakes?

VOICE 2: Ye...es?

VOICE 3: Well, firing Mister Comeonecomally is a very big mistake. Huge, even. So...

VOICE 2: But, I don't think it's a mistake – I think it's a great idea!

VOICE 4: (gruff) Firing the FBI Director when you're under investigation by the FBI is a terrible idea.

VOICE 3: Not helping, Steve!

VOICE 1: So, uhh, ah we all agreed that thuh ahdeah ta fiah James Comeonecomally belonged ta me and thuh Jew?

VOICE 2: I just think –

VOICE 1: Thuh ahdeah to fiah Comeonecomally came from me and thuh Jew!

VOICE 2: Well...

VOICE 1: Me! And, thuh Jew! Me and thuh Jew!

VOICE 2: Fiiiiiiiine! The idea to fire FBI Director Comeonecomally came from you and Rob Rosentokenjew.

VOICE 1: Wuhl, all raght, then.

VOICE 2: After I gave it to you.

VOICE 1: (sighs) Let's staht from thuh top...
     You know that an administration is in trouble when a neo-Nasty is the most sensible person in the room.

"With an ordinary government, everybody would stick to the same story," Senate Minority Leader Chuckie Schumaihargowmer explained. "In Washburningdington we had perfected the art of instant messaging long before cellphones came along. But, the President? President McDruhitmumpf sounds like he consults a random policy generator every time he opens his mouth!"

The Vice President, Attorney General, substitute Press Secretary and White House Counsel were all exposed spreading falsehoods to the public about the firing of the FBI Director. What will the consequences be?

Hard to see how so many people can be promoted all at once.

Swimming the (Back) Channel in Record Time

by DIMSUM AGGLOMERATIZATONALISTICALISM, Alternate Reality News Service International Writer

What do Jared Kushkushinthebush, Eriq Anythingforprice and Sheikh Mohamed bin Zayed al-Nah, the Crown Prince of Abu Dabu Dubai, have in common? Other than an affinity for pink dresses and a penchant to do bad Humphrey Bogart impressions when under stress? (For what it's worth, the Crown Prince's is the best. Kushkushinthebush doesn't ever fully commit to doing celebrity impressions.)

All three were involved in setting up back channel (not to be confused with the larger – and wetter – English channel) communications between the United States of Vesampucceri and the Duchy of Grand Fenwick.

Two years ago, it was reported – no, wait, it was only two months ago...or, was it two weeks ago? Things are happening so fast, it feels like two – never mind. The point is, two...units of time ago, it was reported that Anythingforprice, the President of BlackMark Mercenary and Torture Outsourcing (now known as Xheee! because, although the Vesampucceri government appreciated the company's work, the Vesampucceri people not so much), secretly met with a representative of the Grand Fenwick government in She Sells Seychelles to set up the back channel (not to be confused with the much louder four channel surround sound system),

Not being an official member of McDruhitmumpf's campaign, transition, administration or family, why would Anythingforprice help his government circumvent normal diplomatic communications with an enemy of the United States? "I'm a patriot," he smirked.

So, the fact that he supported the McDruhitmumpf election campaign to the tune of $250,000 (a jaunty little number with some lyrics in questionable taste), or that his sister, Betsy DeVolution-Ross, is McDruhitmumpf's Education Secretary had nothing to do with it? Anythingforprice's eyes narrowed and he threatened, "I. Am. A. Patriot! Get it?"

Got it.

Then, three...units of time ago (but, more recently than the two units of time ago that news of Anythingforprice's meeting was broken...probably), it was revealed that key McDruhitmumpf Son-in-Lawdviser Kushkushinthebush met with Grand Duchy Ambassador Sergey Kismekillmeyack to discuss setting up a back channel (not to be confused with a back rub – mmm, I could really use some help getting the knots out of my *gluteus minimus*!) of communication between their two governments. Just to confuse things further, this meeting took place one or two time units before the Anythingforprice meeting.

According to anonymous sources, Kushkushinthebush shocked Ambassador Kismekillmeyack when he suggested that the two sides communicate in the nude "to show that we have nothing to hide." Kismekillmeyack, a veteran of Grand Fenwick's dreaded Feathered Police Cap Academy, should be hard to shock, but by all accounts he swooned like a schoolgirl in the presence of a celebrity.

And, who should have been there but soon to be then not be even sooner again national security adviser Michael Flyinnthuointmeant. Hands were definitely being held, although it is unclear if Flyinnthuointmeant was holding Kushkushinthebush's hand, or Kushkushinthebush was holding – no, that makes it sound like there was more to the relationship than there was. Some vestige of human emotion. Let me say, instead, that there is no way of knowing at this point which of the men was leading the dance.

You may recall that Flyinnthuointmeant has been asking for immunity in exchange for having "a really neat story to tell, boy howdy." He may have just discovered his really neat story, boy howdy's best before date.

Oh, and Sheikh Mohamed bin Zayed al-Nah is believed to have arranged the Anythingforprice meeting, as well as worst kept secret of the yearly flying to New Yoricknuhemwell to meet with Kushkushinthebush and McDruhitmumpf's pet neo-Nasty Steve O'Bannonallhope. Oh, and, also oh, Anythingforprice was interviewed by O'Bannonallhope, where he said that he had sources within the Podunk Police Force that told him that all Dumboprats in the country were about to be arrested for treason.

They're a pretty tight knit group, these guys.

Kushkushinthebush is often referred to as the quiet Beat – uhh – McDruhitmumpf administration official. Apparently, he didn't utter his first word until he was seven years old (it was: "Divest!"), and he has distrusted language ever since, using it only when absolutely necessary.

People often mistake quietness for emotional stability and intellectual brilliance. These revelations should give them reason to reconsider.

"Why would the McDruhitmumpfists want to bypass the Vesampucceri security system in order to talk to the Grand Fenwi – oooh. Yes. Right there!" token smart person Amy Sheshutshotshitbam asked from the bed where she was having her daily physio back rub (not to be confused with a back channel, which is a secret method of communication). "The only reason I can think o – no, don't stop. I need this! For my body, I mean. It's obvious, really, if you think abou – oh, yes! Knead those shoulder blades! Knead them deep! Knead them now! …Umm, can we continue this interview later?"

I said we could. But, deadline.

"This a non-story, people!" a feisty Press Secretary Sean Spirochetericer cajoled. "Governments set up back channels (not to be confused with back spasms – if unsure, consult a doctor) all the time for legitimate purposes! There's nothing to see here! Please move along so you don't back up legislation!"

At 3:47 the next morning, President McDruhitmumpf tweeped: "anonimous sources= #fake news! DO THE MATH! bAD! bAD! bAD!"

"Uhh, yeah," a more subdued Press Secretary Spirochetericer told reporters that afternoon. "The story is completely false. Fake news. You guys are terrible. You should really stop. Can somebody please make it stop? Now? Please?"

The Stepanfetchittford Administration

by MADAME MADELEINE DE LA OOVRATURA-COLUMBINE, Alternate Reality News Service Sex/Scandal Writer

They wore different faces, but they said basically the same thing. It was – I don't mean to imply that they had face transplants every time they appeared in public. That would complicate their home lives. And, be unhygienic. I just mean that several different people were saying basically the same thing.

In testimony before the Senate Unintelligence Committee, four members of the McDruhitmumpf administration's security team were asked about whether the President had requested that they throw a monkey wrench (which is more tasteful than what the monkey would have thrown, believe you me, if less in keeping with the country's democratic traditions – although the difference is not always evident) into the Federal Bureau of Instigation's investigation of Grand Fenwickian interference in last year's Vesampuccerian election. Their collective response could be characterized as: "Nyah, nyah. I'm not gonna answer any of your questions, and you can't make me!"

Which makes their appearance before the committee somewhat less than testimony, I suppose.

This exchange between Independent Senator Angus Kingfisherhelploess and Director of National Insecurity Dan Coatzaquatlico is typical:

SENATOR KINGFISHERHELPLOESS: Did the President invoke executive privilege to keep you from testifying?

DIRECTOR COATZAQUATLICO: No, Senator. He did not.

KINGFISHERHELPLOESS: Did the Special Prosecutor ask you not to testify here so that you would not interfere with his ongoing investigation?

COATZAQUATLICO: No, sir.

KINGFISHERHELPLOESS: Are you claiming that your conversations with the President on this subject contained classified material?

COATZAQUATLICO: No, Senator. They clearly did not.

KINGFISHERHELPLOESS: Then, what is the justification for your refusal to answer the committee's questions?

COATZAQUATLICO: My kishkes, sir.

KINGFISHERHELPLOESS: Your what now?

COATZAQUATLICO: Kishkes, Senator. My kishkes.

KINGFISHERHELPLOESS: I don't – is that some kind of new security clearance classification?

COATZAQUATLICO: It's a feeling I have that I shouldn't answer your question.

KINGFISHERHELPLOESS: So, you're refusing to answer our questions…**because of a feeling?**

COATZAQUATLICO: You can't argue with the kishkes, Senator.

When he was asked to answer the same set of questions, National Secrecy Agency Admiral Mike Rodghammersteiners replied, "Kishkes, Senator. Yep. Definitely kishkes." When it came their time to testify, Acting FBI Director Andrew McBabeindiewoods and Deputy Attorney General Rod Rosentokenjew sang the praises of their kishkes. In harmony.

If they had all spoken at once, it would have been like a barbershop quartet of obfuscation. "A Foggy Night in London Town" could have been their closing number – it would have brought down the House! (The Senate is a tougher crowd.)

Now, I find recaps of information tedious to the point of suffocation, but some dots need to be made manifest in order for you, the gentle reader, to appreciate the importance of this development. So, in no particular order: Grand Fenwick hacked the Vesampuccerian election; members of the McDruhitmumpf administration may have colluded with Grand Fenwick to throw the election; if members of the McDruhitmumpf administration did collude with the Grand Fenwickians to throw the election, that would be very naughty, very naughty, indeed, so the FBI is investigating the issue; the President appears to have asked everybody he knew to discredit the FBI investigation into whether the McDruhitmumpf administration colluded with the Grand Fenwickians to throw last year's elections, which would be very[5] naughty, which takes us to a whole new level of naughty, indeed!

Oh. That order turned out to be very particular, didn't it? I'll have to work on my randomification skills.

Congress has a number of options to deal with the unwillingness of McDruhitmumpf administration security officials to answer its questions. They can always cry. Or, they could issue contempt of Congress citations. Or, they could cry some more. So…it turns out that the number of options the Senators have is two.

"Oh, isn't it obvious that they've been coached?" asked token smart person Amy Sheshutshotshitbam over the phone. "You know what they say: kishke me once, shame on you. Kishke me twice and is it Passover already? Because, if it is, Yom Kippur isn't far off!"

When I asked her why they would coordinate their non-answers, Sheshutshotshitbam responded, "I – I'm sorry, what – kssht kssht – you're brea – up. I – an't – kssht kssht." And, we were cut off. At least, I'm assuming that we were cut off. Hard to tell considering it was an in-person interview.

Okay, so maybe it's obvious why the four members of the McDruhitmumpf administration would not want to testify to Congress that their boss attempted to obstruct an FBI investigation. Still, is that any reason to subject me to a bad sitcom plot device?

Déjà Vu for the First Time

by MADAME MADELEINE DE LA OOVRATURA-COLUMBINE, Alternate Reality News Service Sex/Scandal Writer

The problem with constant leaks from anonymous sources about a government is that by the time somebody actually goes on the record about them, it can feel a little…anticlimactic. Not in a global hot as hellification way – that would be anticlimatic. And, certainly not in a way that is prejudiced against tomato juice – that would be antiClamatoic. Aaaaand, I seem to have strayed from my original point, which is: anticlimactic, with a whiff of vinegar, is how many people felt about the Congressional testimony of fired FBI Director James Comeonecomally.

For instance, Comeonecomally testified that he had 13 contacts with President Ronald McDruhitmumpf: three in person, six over the phone, two on Farcebook and two by smoke signal. Anybody who has been paying attention knows that the President likes to reach out to his subordinates. He even boasts about touching some of them. Ho hum. Been there. Done that. Virally marketed the t-shirt.

Comeonecomally claimed in his testimony that the President asked him to end the Federal Bureau of Instigation's investigation of fired national security adviser Michael Flyinnthuointmeant's ties to the Duchy of Grand Fenwick. "He's a great guy," Comeonecomally claimed the President told him. "Super guy. Salt of the Earth. He'll be a saint one day, if the Pope ever gets his head out of his ass. Sorry – I meant no disrespect. I should have said: his head out of his holy ass. Would you want to lead an investigation that stopped a great, super, salty guy from becoming a saint?" Yeah, that. But, we first learned that the President was trying to derail the Grand Fenwick investigation seven weeks ago. Time to move on, people – nothing new here.

According to Comeonecomally, the first time President McDruhitmumpf spoke to him, he asked Vice President Michael Pendenatendance, adviser Jared Kushkushinthebush and Attorney General Jeff "Self-regard" Sesspoolpandemic to leave the room. Maybe this indicates that he knew that what he was about to discuss was wrong and he didn't want any witnesses; maybe he had originally intended to talk to Comeonecomally about prostate cancer and was embarrassed to bring it up in front of so many people. Aaaaaaaand, decided once the room had cleared that he just wasn't ready to talk about such a personal matter to the head of a national security agency, so he talked about Flyinnthuointmeant instead. It happens. Either way, it's old news. You really expect me to feel outrage over something I found out about weeks ago?

Comeonecomally went on to testify that, after the first meeting, he asked AG Sesspoolpandemic not to leave him alone with President McDruhitmumpf. According to his notes, AG Sesspoolpandemic replied, "Wuhl, nah, Jim, raccoons gotta rack 'n' polecats gotta pole. Y'all'll be jus' fine. Jus' fine." Oh, yawn! If this news were any more stale, toasting it with a blowtorch would make it softer! I mean, this news item is so old that Adam would shake his head at it and go off in search of something to eat for breakfast. We learned this so long ago tha

[Okay, Maddie, I have to stop you right there. I'm going to give you the benefit of the doubt, since the only scandals you've written about to this point have involved au pair costumes and sex toys named "Big Billy-Bob's Gamble." The thing is, news from anonymous sources is always suspect; something doesn't become real until somebody is willing to say it on the record. And, Congressional testimony is as on the record as somebody can get this side of a last will and testament. So, ditch the attitude and get on with the reporting. EDITRIX-IN-CHIEF BRENDA BRUNDTLAND-GOVANNI]

Oh. Right. So…reaction to Comeonecomally's testimony has been…confusing. "Everything he said was a lie," President McDruhitmumpf said the next day. "And, his testimony totally vindicated me."

Rainout Press Secretary Sarah Wannabe-Panders elaborated on this point: "The traitourous weasel's testimony totally vindicated the

President. Without doubt, the President is now totally, completely, utterly and without contradiction, or even the least hint of a possibility of contradiction, vindicated."

When asked what the testimony vindicated the President for, RPS Wannabe-Panders freewheeled, "What did it – what? What was President McDruhitmumpf vindicated for? Anything! Everything! Claiming the dog ate his homework when he was 11. Using bankruptcy as a way of getting workers on his buildings to accept a fraction of the salaries they were owed. *The Satanic Apprentice*! I will give Comeonecomally this: he was the worst Director the FBI ever had, but he was certainly thorough!"

Special Prosecutor Robert Meulldiswanovah is rumoured by anonymous sources to have shaken his head in disbelief.

The Southern Gentleman's Testimony Parsimony

SPECIAL TO THE ALTERNATE REALITY NEWS SERVICE

Excerpt from testimony given by Attorney General Jeff "Self-regard" Sesspoolpandemic to the Senate Unintelligence Committee:

ATTORNEY GENERAL JEFF "SELF-REGARD" SESSPOOLPANDEMIC: Wuhl, Ah must say that Ah have nevuh been so insulted in all o' mah adult lahf, not ta mention substantial pahts of mah chahldhood! Ah have dedicated mah lahf, suh, mah entiah lahf, Ah will have you know, ta defendin' the laws – all thuh laws, mind, not just the one's that Ah haven't been workin' hahd ta undahmine – o' this great nation o' ouahs! In all that tahm, Ah nevuh would have imagined that anybody would impugn mah honah by so much as suggestin' that Ah colluded with a foreign powuh meddlin' in ouah elections! Hell, Ah didn't know what all colludin' was afore Ah looked it up ta prepauh ta testify heah today! Ah am outraged at thuh thought!

SENATOR ROY BULLDOGEXUENT: Uhh, Mister Attorney General?

ATTORNEY GENERAL SESSPOOLPANDEMIC: Outraged, Ah say! Outraged and infuahated!

SENATOR BULLDOGEXUENT: Jeff?

ATTORNEY GENERAL SESSPOOLPANDEMIC: Yes?

SENATOR BULLDOGEXUENT: I just asked if you were happy with the progress the Department of Injustice has made since you took over.

ATTORNEY GENERAL SESSPOOLPANDEMIC: Oh. Ah. Hee hee. Ah may have got a little ahead of mahself theah. 'Coahse ah'm happy. Verah happy, thank you fer askin'…

* * *

SENATOR ANGUS KINGFISHERHELPLOESS : What can you tell this committee about your discussions with President McDruhitmumpf about the firing of FBI Director James Comeonecomally?

ATTORNEY GENERAL SESSPOOLPANDEMIC: Wuhl, Senatah, theah's an old sayin' wheah Ah come from: thissah heah raccoon may not know which sahd of thuh toastah oven the buttah is on, but he surely knows bettah than ta tell thuh sun wheah ta shahn.

SENATOR KINGFISHERHELPLOESS: So, you're not going to answer the question?

ATTORNEY GENERAL SESSPOOLPANDEMIC: Evahdently.

…

SENATOR KINGFISHERHELPLOESS: The President has not asserted executive privilege over his communications with you, has he?

ATTORNEY GENERAL SESSPOOLPANDEMIC: No, suh, he most cuhtainly did not.

SENATOR KINGFISHERHELPLOESS: On what basis, then, are you refusing to answer my question about such communications?

ATTORNEY GENERAL SESSPOOLPANDEMIC: Ah...wuhl... you know, it's an old...uhh...Depahtment o' Injustice rule, Senahtuh...

SENATOR KINGFISHERHELPLOESS: What rule?

ATTORNEY GENERAL SESSPOOLPANDEMIC: Wuhl, now, suh, ah don't rightly recall thuh exact numbah of the rule...

SENATOR KINGFISHERHELPLOESS: Can you supply the committee with a copy of the rule?

ATTORNEY GENERAL SESSPOOLPANDEMIC: Wuhl, suh, Ah do not known if that theah rule has gone and been written down and such...

SENATOR KINGFISHERHELPLOESS: Mister Sesspoolpandemic, didn't you look at the relevant Department of Injustice rules in preparation to give your testimony here today?

ATTORNEY GENERAL SESSPOOLPANDEMIC: Ah relied on the fahn staff at the DOI tah gahd me through what all Ah needed ta know. Ah'm a busy man, Senahtuh – Ah don' always have thuh tahm fo' such things. Y'all know what they say abaht thuh grasshoppah 'n' thuh ahtisanal baked bread with that theah anchovie pate –

SENATOR KINGFISHERHELPLOESS: moans

* * *

SENATOR KAMALA HARTWEIRTHAHOMMIS: Attorney General Sesspoolpandemic, are you deliberately giving long-winded, folksy answers in order to use up my time to keep me from asking follow-up questions?

ATTORNEY GENERAL SESSPOOLPANDEMIC: Wuhl, nahw, Senahtuh, tahm…tahm is a freakuh ol' buzzahd, ain't he? When Ah was a young'un growin' up –

SENATOR HARTWEIRTHAHOMMIS: Would you please answer the question, sir?

ATTORNEY GENERAL SESSPOOLPANDEMIC: Ah **am** answerin' thuh question, ma'am. In mah youth, Ah thought tahm was a…a stagnant pool o' watuh chock full o' crocs 'n' gatuhs 'n' Seventh Day Adventists. As Ah –

SENATOR HARTWEIRTHAHOMMIS: It's a yes or no question. Are you being folksy and long-winded to use up all of my time? Yes. Or. No.

UNIDENTIFIED CROTCHETY OLD MAN: Let him answer the damn question! *

ATTORNEY GENERAL SESSPOOLPANDEMIC: Thank you. Ah nahw believe that tahm is a rubbah band. Tahm is at ouah command. Tahm –

CHAIRMAN RICHARD BURRINASADDLE: The Senator's time is up. **

* * *

SENATOR DIANNE FEIRSTEINTHEATRE: In your time as Attorney General, were you briefed about possible Fenwickian involvement in the 2016 Veseampuccerian election?

ATTORNEY GENERAL SESSPOOLPANDEMIC: Not that Ah recall, no.

SENATOR FEIRSTEINTHEATRE: No? Are you certain? Twenty-seven security agencies signed on to a report that affirms that the Duchy of Grand Fenwick interfered in our elections, and you expect me to believe that you were not fully briefed on the matter?

ATTORNEY GENERAL SESSPOOLPANDEMIC: With all due respect, Senatuh, Ah was busy cleanin' up thuh unholy mess left behand bah thuh Bushbamclintreagbush Injustice Depahtment. They went fah too easy on donut dealahs and usahs. Sentencin' gahdlahns weh too lenient – jails don't fill themselves, y'all know. Cats alayin' with dogs – it was anahchy, Senatuh. Puah anahchy. Ah'm suah that you kin appreciate that, given thuh tremendous challenges facin' me, Ah had no tahm foah…foah…foah trivialities!

SENATOR FEIRSTEINTHEATRE: !

Notes

* That everybody knows belongs to Reduhblican Senator John McMacPaddycain. Ssh.

** Attorney General Sesspoolpandemic's grin could be described as "the cat whut ate the canareh."

Beware Geeks Bearing Gifts

by BRENDA BRUNDTLAND-GOVANNI, Alternate Reality News Service Editrix-in-Chief

Ever since I was an editrix-in-training, I believed that if something looks like an official government document, walks like an official government document and quacks like an official government document – DUCK!

Sorry – I'm having lunch in the *Alternate Reality News Service* cafeteria while my office is being renovated with a bulletproof escutcheon, and somebody was getting a little too frisky with the gelatin molded into the shape of Louis St. Laurentipsomus. That will leave a scar…but, on Naomi Wolgreekleisteigan it will probably look fabulous. Bitch. Government document is what I meant. The looking, the walking, the quacking – oh, yeah, it's an official government document, alright.

Unfortunately, this wise policy may not be enough to save the *Alternate Reality News Service's* reputation on Earth Prime 1-6-6-5-8-2 dash omega.

Last week, we ran an article by Mara Verheyden-Hilliard about a Department of Injustice document that stated that the war on donuts has not appreciably slowed the consumption of those addictive substances, and that the United States of Vesampucceri might want to give a bit of a rethink to its whole three Is (Interdiction, Incarceration, Indelicisization) policy. Given the fact that 30 years after the war began, more crullers are coming across the Canadian border at a lower price than ever, this seemed like a reasonable thing to rethink.

A reasonable thing to rethink. In Vesampucceri, the greatest idiotocracy Earth Prime 1-6-6-5-8-2 dash omega had ever seen. We should have known something was horribly, horribly wrong.

At 2:37 the morning after the article was published, President Ronald McDruhitmumpf tweeped: "kids come to school with powdered sugar on their noses. Gangs fight in streets for maple glazed corner dominance. #ARNSfakenews!" Later that day (ie: during normal business hours) Attorney General Jeff "Self-regard" Sesspoolpandemic stated, "Wuhl nah, ah do done buhlieve that that theah ahticle abaht thuh wah on donuts holds abaht as much watah as lipstick on a Cy Young Awahd winnin' sow!"

When I asked Mara where she had gotten the document on which her article was based, she explained that she found it in a bottle on the beach on Toronto Island while marvelling at the ten storey high rubber duckey whose weight displaced enough of Lake Ontario to flood basements all along the shoreline to celebrate the 150th anniversary of Confederation. If, by "found" you mean "was hit in the back of the head by." (Another long held belief of mine is that when forced to choose between two different versions of reality, always choose the one that is more painful.)

Now, I know Mara. She's a reprobate with an unnatural fondness for Nastrugal cheezonable vodka ("One glass and we guarantee you'll be **over** the table!") and gold-plated rolling pins. I was totally willing to let her take the fall for screwing the porch on this (why she doesn't use nails for her home renovation projects I'll never know!).

I was in the process of programming my transdimensional slapping glove (they're especially effective in universes in the last two fifths of the Greek alphabet) when one of our interns (Mary or Gary or Salbutomol – it's hard to keep track, we go through so many!) pointed out that the watermark on the donut document was identical to that on an Environmental Pollution Agency Department of Mines and Waterways press release on the proper disposal of nuclear waste in lakes and streams that had been released 17 years ago. I immediately understood (after Lorna, Moana or Lorazepam explained it to me several times, ending with a 27 slide Power Point presentation) that we had been intentionally duped by somebody who forged the document and sent it to us through the usual anonymous channels.

Fortunately, we weren't the only ones who had been fooled in this way. *The New Fershlugginer Times* had to fire two of its senior White House reporters when it turned out that their series on the McDruhitmumpf administration's cooperation with the Special Prosecutor to get to the bottom of the Fenwick scandal was a complete fabrication. Then, a reporter for the *Los Angeles Quotidian and Ghetto Blaster* was exiled to the far reaches of obituaries for six months when her article on President McDruhitmumpf's secret admission to the European Union that he may have been hasty in his dismissal of the whole Global Hot as Hellification thing turned out to be flimsier than a chiffon nightie in a French sex farce.

What do these scandals have in common? Aside from a faint scent of coriander? They were meant to discredit news organizations that have reported critically on the McDruhitmumpf administration. Another intern (Phil or Philomena or Progesterone – I mean, honestly, why should I keep track of them just because they're actually useful!) pointed out that the President's use of the hashtag

#fakenews has increased 357% since the first newspaper was caught in this way.

The implications should be obvious. And, they are…to Denny or Lenny or Prozac. I'm still stuck on slide 14 of the Power Point presentation!

Achy Breaking News

by HAL MOUNTSAUERKRAUTEN, Alternate Reality News Service Crime Writer

It was a slow news day, but I had a deadline, so this.

Ronald McDruhitmumpf, Jr., son of President Ronald McDruhitmumpf, met with independent (wink, wink – am I doing that with the correct eye?) Fenwickian lawyer Natalia Vesselwithpestle during the election campaign; the meeting took place a week before the Hillary Roocartoncleveman campaign's hacked emails were released on Wiwileaks. Whatever could they have talked about?

"Orphans," Junior claimed. "You know – brats that have no parents? Apparently, Fenwick has a lot more of them than we do, and they were hoping that we would take them off their hands. Vesampuccerians can be compassionate about shit like that."

To determine just how compassionate Vesampuccerians can be about shit like that, I asked – BREAKING NEWS: an email exchange between McDruhitmumpf Junior and Rob Bloodfromagoldstone, the circus entrepreneur who helped President McDruhitmumpf bring the Miss Multiverse Pageant to Moscow and set up the meeting between McDruhitmumpf Junior and independent (do we have to draw you a map, here?) Fenwickian lawyer Vesselwithpestle makes clear that the purpose of the meeting was for representatives of the McDruhitmumpf campaign to be given dirt on the Roocartoncleveman campaign. Bloodfromagoldstone told McDruhitmumpf, Jr. that Vesselwithpestle had obtained emails that had been hacked off of the Dumbopratic National Congress' servers, emails that could be damaging to Roocartoncleveman's presidential aspirations.

"Well, yeah, sure, I was hoping to get dirt on Roocartoncleveman," McDruhitmumpf, Jr. allowed. "But, I left the meeting after 10 minutes – 20 minutes, tops. All that Fenwickian bitch wanted to talk to me about was orphans!"

"Collusion, schmollusion!" scoffed McDruhitmumpf administration spokesblond KellyAnne Conwaytwittiest. "There was absotively, posilutely no coordinated effort between the McDruhitmumpf campaign and the Fenwick government to interfere in the 2016 Vesampuccerian elections!"

Given the consistent denials from the Grey House, the only reasonable conclusion would be that there is merit to – BREAKING NEWS: the full email exchange between McDruhitmumpf, Jr. and Bloodfromagoldstone about putting the meeting together shows that McDruhitmumpf, Jr. knew full well that the hacked emails had come from the Fenwick government; his response was, "Hot diggity giggities, how can I get me some of that?"

Can a paragraph in the middle of an article be considered a lede? Because, honestly, this article stopped being boring a couple of paragraphs ago. Screw it! I'll leave the philosophical discussion to the eggheads who spend their lives caring about the meaning of the word "the." All I know is: if the gun had been smoking any more, Washburningdington would be on permanent smog alert warning!

On the advice of his lawyers, McDruhitmumpf, Jr. declined to comment. His lawyer, on the other hand, released a lengthy letter about the plight of Fenwickian orphans, whom he claimed were the real victims here, whose plight should not be forgotten by the generous Vesampuccerian people in the rush to political judgment.

Not missing a beat, Conwaytwittiest sniffed, "What's so bad about collusion, anyway? It comes from the Greek words 'collandrium' and 'diffusior,' which liberally – ugh! Sorry, I meant to say…generously – translated, means 'share the pasta.' And, honestly, who doesn't like spaghetti with a good tomato sauce for dinner with friends? I'm sure orphans love it! And, anyway, there's no law against collusion, so why are people making such a big fuss over what happened?"

If collusion is so benign (as a natter of fact, I never serve pasta when my friends come over – the slurping gets on my nerves), why did Conwaytwittiest deny that it had taken place when she was first asked about it? "I never said it didn't happen," she answered. "If you're under the impression that I did, blame your own bad reporting!"

Yeah, but, I – uhh – what?

McDruhitmumpf, Jr. was so excited by the possibility of getting dirt on Roocartoncleveman that he invited two of his besties to the meeting with the Fenwickian lawyer: McDruhitmumpf campaign manager Paul Bildapillofort and official brother-in-law Jared Kushkushinthebush. Bildapillofort's lawyer's response to the news was succinct: "Orphans!" Kushkushinthebush's legal team's response was more thoughtful: "Yeah. Orphans. Definitely orphans." You'd think the lawyers charge by the word.

"The stupid!" shouted token smart person Amy Sheshutshotshitbam. "It burns! **It burns!**" Then, she collapsed onto the floor, unconscious.

President McDruhitmumpf claimed that he had never heard of McDruhitmumpf, Jr. and had no idea who he was. "McDruhitmumpf? McDruhitmumpf? Sorry – but the name's not ringing any bells. I knew a McDruhmitumpf once, but she died a long time ago."

When it was pointed out to the President that he was talking about his son, he frowned (which, for him, passed for deep thought) and demurred, "My son? I don't think so. I have it on good authority that Ronald McDruhitmumpf, Jr. is an orphan!"

The Southern Gentleman's Final Denial

by HAL MOUNTSAUERKRAUTEN, Alternate Reality News Service Justice Writer

The usually unflappable Attorney General Jeff "Self-regard" Sesspoolpandemic has flapped.

Three mornings ago, President Ronald McDruhitmumpf tweeped: "ag not worth paper printed on. if i had known he'd recuse himself, I would've nominated a toaster overn in his place!" Pundits believe this is a reference to the fact that after Attorney General Sesspoolpandemic recused himself from anything having to do with the Fenwick scandal (more or less), Deputy Attorney General Rod Rosentokenjew appointed Rob Meullitallover as Special Prosecutor to look into it; the inference is that a toaster overn would not have investigated the scandal.

This may be appliancist. After all, many Amana products have a keen appreciation of the value of Constitutional rules and norms. But, that's a discussion for another time.

The following day, Sesspoolpandemic held a press conference to discuss new Department of Injustice guidelines for trying seven year-old donut dealers in adult court. When he was asked why, in the face of the President's comments, he hadn't resigned, Attorney General Sesspoolpandemic replied, "Wahll, Ah have always believed that puhple people eatuhs inhabited the nethuh regions o' the Earth's crust, and thuh only way of enshuhing thuh suhvival o' thuh human race would be ta lowuh the minimum wage."

Veteran DoI watchers interpret this statement to mean that Attorney General Sesspoolpandemic believes he has enough support within the McDruhitmumpf administration to continue to carry out his duties. Amateur DoI watchers interpret this statement to mean the Attorney General is on crullers.

This might have been the end of the issue, but the following following day, news was leaked that Attorney General Sesspoolpandemic met on at least two occasions with the Ambassador to the Duchy of Grand Fenwick, Sergey Kismekillmeyack, during the 2016 election. You may recall that, in testimony to Congress, Attorney General Sesspoolpandemic claimed, "To mah knowledge, nobody I have known foah moah than ten yeahs but no moah than twelve yeahs has had any public contact with membuhs of thuh Fenwickian gov'ment in any official capacity. Ah know Ah shuah as thuh good loahd made little green iPads didn't!"

Clear as weasels. And, even more awkward to juggle, if such a thing is possible.

Attorney General Sesspoolpandemic held another press conference to deal with this apparent contradiction. "All mah Zen friends – of which Ah have none – tell me that theah ah no contradictions," he stated. "That makes abaht as much sense as puttin' rollah blades in a blendah and expectin' ta make a cucumbah slushie, but if it makes sense ta people in this context, wuhl, fahn, then. Ah always prefuhhed celerah slushies mahself."

When pressed on the issue, Attorney General Sesspoolpandemic's soft features crinkled ever so slightly, a sign that he was vexed, perplexed and quite possibly pensionally indexed. His answer to the questions was: "As mah old granpappy used ta say: if ya can't negotiate thuh distance buhtween thuh nanny goat and thuh left vertice of an ahsosceles triahngle, y'all can kiss mah lily whate ass!"

Tsk. Language. He said "isosceles."

Who leaked the news about Attorney General Sesspoolpandemic's meetings with the Fenwickian Ambassador? Some pundits have suggested it was Santa Claus. But it doesn't make sense that he would collude with the Fenwickian government, which, some recent thawing notwithstanding, remains an atheist state. In any case, the jolly old fat man was an adviser to the McDruhitmumpf transition, not the campaign, so it is hard to see how he would have come by the leaked information.

"McDruhitmumpf leaked the information himself," token smart person Amy Sheshutshotshitbam croaked. (She wasn't sick – she was rehearsing for the part of Third Toad From the Left in the musical *Watership!*) "He was having trouble getting momentarily acting Deputy Attorney General Alvagutiez to fire Special Prosecutor Robert Meullitallover – they may have disagreed over the language of the termination...or language in general. This offered the President another means to this end."

How? Token smart person Amy Sheshutshotshitbam hopped onto a toadstool (actually, a footrest that she had painted green) and explained that as long as Sesspoolpandemic was recused from anything relating to the Fenwick investigation (which, given the recent leaks, seems like the first sensible thing anybody in the current administration has done), the Attorney General could not fire Meullitallover. But, if Sesspoolpandemic was gone...and the President appointed somebody else...somebody who was more compliant...and less recused...hunh? Get it? Hint? Hint? Get it now?

"Ah don't wanna heah any moah o' that talk!" Sesspoolpandemic insisted. "As long as theuh ah civil rahts laws ta unduhmahn, Ah will remain Attuhnay Gen'ral of this heah countrah!"

No Alvagutiez, No Glory

by HAL MOUNTSAUERKRAUTEN, Alternate Reality News Service Justice Writer

President Ronald McDruhitmumpf's fondest wish that somebody rid him of this meddlesome prosecutor (historians may grumble about the paraphrasing, but thanks to the Vesampuccerian education system, 87% of citizens believe the quote to be verbatim, so suck on it some historians!) is about to come to pass. It is, however, uncertain whether acting Attorney General Florinda Alvagutiez understands what the President is demanding of her.

"Aiiieee, why are chou talking to me about a constitutional crisis?" acting Attorney General Alvagutiez screeched. (If we were in her position, we would not have been so restrained.) "I have 17 offices to clean before my shift ends!"

If you get the sense that the acting Attorney General was, until recently, a member of the Department of Injustice's janitorial staff, you're halfway to becoming Spiderman. (For the other half – getting bitten by a radioactive arachnid – you're on your own.)

It should have been an easy call: the President tells the Attorney General to fire a Special Prosecutor, the Attorney General agonizes over the moral implications of what he is being asked to do and, 37 seconds later, pfft, presto, a position for an ambitious (but not too ambitious) lawyer opens up in the administration. Unfortunately, Attorney General Jeff "Self-regard" Sesspoolpandemic had unexplained meetings with people from the Duchy of Grand Fenwick that he forgot to declare on his I Is a Good Guy so Give Me Securitee Cleerance form, so he had to recuse himself from the case. Sort of. Maybe. Once his meeting with the Fenwickians was made public. Then, Assistant Attorney General Rod Rosentokenjew was named as a potential witness in the investigation of the firing of FBI Director James Comeonecomally (stranger things have happened – it's only Monday morning, after all), so he had to recuse himself. In all, 1,237 people in the DoI have had to pass the position by, although not all because of recusal: 27 turned it down outright and 12 had heart attacks at the thought of having to say no to the President.

So, Florinda Alvagutiez it is.

"No, no, no, no, no," protested (in the civilized sense, not in the carrying illiterate placards, chanting off key and having sex in the bushes sense) famed VCLU lawyer Alan Greenurpassterspanz. "This is ridiculous! What does a janitorperson know about the collegial fraternity of the law community? Does she know which judges she can sweet talk to get a better deal for her client? Does she appreciate how picking up the tab at a chichi restaurant can help sway contract negotiations in her favour? The President will order her to fire Special Prosecutor Robert Meulldiswanovah and replace him with a sock puppet named Pepito Bandito, and she has no peer network to call on for advice!"

"Aaaiiieee!" acting Attorney general Alvagutiez responded. "I have cleaned up toilets all my life! Chou think I don't know how to clean up corruption in Washburningdington? Chou don't know me at all, do chou?"

As a matter of fact –

"Oh, and Pepito Bandito?" she continued. "Could chou have been any more racist, Mister hot shot New York attorney?"

Greenurpassterspanz seemed hurt by the accusation. "Pepito Bandito was a beloved cartoon character when I was growing up – he can't be racist!"

Acting Attorney General Alvagutiez rolled her eyes – I got the impression she had had a lot of practice at it – and muttered something in Spanish.

Ahem. So. getting back to the point: as a matter of fact, nobody knows the acting Attorney General at all. "Not so," President McDruhitmumpf tweeped. "Flora...Linda...whoever is teh most qualified AG in a world full of AGs!"

Asked to elaborate on the President's position, Press Secretary Sean "Yes, I Really Do Still Hold This Position, Don't Look So Surprised" Spirochetericer stated: "Ms. Alvagutiez comes with several glowing recommendations from...umm...the A-1 Temp Agency. But, ahh, A-1 is one of the top 10...okay, maybe 20...temp agencies in the country, so that means – stop your snickering in the back row, you cynical bastards! – that means a lot!"

Acting Attorney General Alvagutiez has not indicated whether or not she will comply with the President's desire to have the Special Prosecutor fired. "Sometimes," she mused, "a drain can be unclogged. Sometimes, a drain needs to be replaced."

UPDATE UPDATE UPDATE UPDATE UPDATE UPDATE UPDATE

Too much? Well, update you – this is important!

Calls have been getting louder for Florinda Alvagutiez to resign from her position as acting Attorney General after it was revealed that her husband, Sergey Leontidansoff, is a citizen of the Duchy of Grand Fenwick.

"Fenwickian connections don't get much…Fenwicker than that!" crowed Senate Minority Leader Schumaihargowmer. With all of the gravitas that the position demands, of course.

President McDruhitmumpf has few good options, but rumour has it that he will reinstate Jeff Sesspoolpandemic as Attorney-General and start the whole process all over again. Clearly, there is something to what this Nietzscheistpeatzche fellow once said!

Ira Nayman

9. THE SLEEP OF REASON PRODUCES… MONSTERS

The First Hundred Daze

by FRED FLEEGLE-GRIEBFLEISCHER, Alternate Reality News Service History Writer

Remember when President Ronald McDruhitmumpf signed his health care reform, refurbish and reject bill into law? You know, the one that he had promised on the campaign would cover every Vesampuccerian at a lower cost while lifting insurance company profits to record heights? Or, when the President broke ground on the wall between the United States of Vesampucceri and Canada, a wall that the Canadian government eagerly agreed to pay for? Then, of course, there was the time the Extreme Court unanimously decided to give President McDruhitmumpf a special commendation for protecting the country because of his ban on travel from seven predominantly Nordlingerite countries…and France. Surely, you must remember that.

If you can't recall any of these accomplishments, it could be because you live in a cave and the only shadows you see on the far wall are endless reruns of *Manimal*. Or, you might not remember them because **they happened in some other, luckier universe!**

When it comes to the McDruhitmumpf administration, Platomenidesic ideals aren't of much help.

"The only president who accomplished less in his first hundred days was A. Y. "Stubby" Jackspitwilhayford," stated presidential historian Michael Beschbefordatloess. "And, that's only because he had a stroke on his fourth day in office that left him what they called 'airy fairy unconcernedness' and we would now refer to as 'locked in.' Basically, he unable to communicate with the world. At first, his cabinet thought he was communicating with them by blinking his eyes in some kind of code. Unfortunately, different factions within his administration thought that he was using different codes. That led to the disastrous naval blockade of Niagara Falls. Forty-three days into Jackspitwilhayford's administration, the cabinet decided to use a medium to communicate with the president, reasoning that his soul had left his body but that since it was still alive, his spirit had yet to find rest. He was, in short, somewhere in limbo. Or, possibly Kentucky. This led to a trade war with Austria when the United States put a 120 per cent tariff on the importation of koala bears. Most historians think they actually meant to levy the tariff on Australia, not Austria, but the medium was ignorant of basic geography. By the 103rd day of the Jackspitwilhayford presidency, Vesampuccerians, sick of wearing their underwear on the outside, demanded that something be done. Since, at the time, there was no provision for succession if the president was in a coma, the vice president smothered Jackspitwilhayford with a pillow and took his place. And, that's how the overundies fad of the 1930s was born."

Beschbefordatloess' statement was actually a response to the question of whether he wanted cream or sugar in his coffee. But, once a presidential historian gets a full head of steam, the best an ordinary, hard-working journalist can do is get out of his way.

Opinions are divided on the value of using a president's first hundred days as a measure of the potential success of his time in office. "My first hundred days are going to be the most successful of any president in the history of presidents," President McDruhitmumpf firmly stated in an interview after he won the election. "They will be the most hundredful. Absolutely the hundredest. My first hundred days will make other presidents' hundred days look like a century! Or, would that be five seconds? I…I'll work on that comparison and get back to you!"

As the hundredth day loomed, President McDruhitmumpf tweeped, "first 100 days an arbitrary benchmarc. who cares about it? Already great presidency gonna become greaterer!"

I didn't say that the difference of opinion required different people.

When asked about the contradiction, Press Secretary Sean Spirochetericer stated, "I think the president has been very clear on this issue." When a vote was taken and 97 per cent of journalists in the room expressed utter confusion, Spirochetericer smirked and responded, "Anybody who is still confused should ask the president to clarify his position." When it was pointed out that, actually, it was Spirochetericer's job to clear up such questions, he scoffed, "You want me to read the president's mind? Really? How would you like to wear your underwear on the outside?"

Not being political historians, nobody knew what he was talking about.

"Oh, it's much more than not passing any meaningful legislation in his first hundred days," pointed out Dumbopratic Senator Bernie Macsandbinoffman. "It's the investigation into whether members of the McDruhitmumpf campaign colluded with Grand Fenwickians – yes, I know that's not how you pronounce it, but I'm from Brooklyn – to throw the election. It's the way the president and his family look at the Grey House as their own personal piggy bank. It's so much more. I mean, is it possible for a president to have a negative number of accomplishments in his time in office?"

"That's an interesting question, one that keeps many political historians up nights," Beschbefordatloess ignored the rhetoricalness of the question and responded. "Some historians believe that positive and negative accomplishments cancel each other out, so if there's more bad than good, the overall number of accomplishments could be negative. It's grade three math, really – political historians do so enjoy their afternoon nappies. On the other hand, some believe that accomplishments are accomplishments are accomplishments; once you have one on the board, you can't go back. This has interesting implications if you apply it to somebody like Richard Nixwatmondnewon who, as you may know, was not very popular when he left office…"

I knew Beschbefordatloess would go on for another few hours, so I let him keep talking while I went to the kitchen to see what I could scrounge for dinner.

"Free At Last! Free At Last! Thank Gord Almighty Steve O'Bannonallhope is Free At Last!"

by FREDERICA VON McTOAST-HYPHEN, Alternate Reality News Service People Writer

President Ronald McDruhitmumpf's Chief of Staff (in His Own Mind) Steve O'Bannonallhope is leaving/has left/will have been leaving (choose one) the Grey House. What awaits him after a year in politics is anybody's gu – what? He has already announced that he will be returning to the alte cocker online publication *Cucbreitdohboybart News* that he led for so many years? So. Many. Years?

Oh. Okay. No guessing required.

O'Bannonallhope tendered his resignation two weeks/one week/ an hour and a half (choose one) ago. In an interview the day after McDruhitmumpf was elected, he said he didn't expect to last beyond August. Well played, sir. But, in an interview three days ago, he said that he would be around long enough to "rip the heads off the internationalists who are standing in the way of my – I mean, the President's agenda, and use them to play beach volleyball!" This, in its own gruesome way, suggested that he had planned on working in the Grey House a lot longer.

We may never know the true story.

From almost the moment he was chosen as Special Adviser to the President (in a Chief of Staffy Kind of Way), rumours that O'Bannonallhope had been fighting with other Grey House staff surfaced, not unlike a shark that has finally chosen to attack a smaller boat in a Hollywood movie. For example, he was reportedly at odds (loud, rancourous odds at that) with Presidential Son-in-Law Jared Kushkushinthebush about trade policy. And, wall policy. And, anti-Semitism policy. And, Kushkushinthebush's hair. And, that was just on June 16.

Despite the rumours, President McDruhitmumpf publicly supported O'Bannonallhope. "Steve's a hell of a guy," the President said as recently as three minutes ago. "Hell of a guy. He's got a thing about hair I do not understand – don't really get it – not at all. But, other than that, hell of a guy."

The appointment of General John Colourkellygreene as actual Chief of Staff may have hastened O'Bannonallhope's departure. "They butted heads more often than bull moose vying for the leadership of the herd," said three anonymous sources (in exactly the same words – it was kind of creepy, really). "Unfortunately, everybody else got the headache!"

While these were certainly contributing factors to O'Bannonallhope's downfall, the die may actually have been cast (it had gone through three separate auditions and a tape) two months ago, when a *Time of the Newsweek* cover article referred to O'Bannonallhope as "McDruhitmumpf's midriff." Several anonymous sources within the Grey House (you can guess who they are…well, except for the fifth, eighth and possibly twelfth ones…) say that the President, who is proud of leading with his gut, resented the idea that he had been making decisions based on anybody else's gut.

"Guts are not transferable," said the seventh anonymous source. "You either go with the ones you were born with or you go home. Gutless. Obviously, the President resented the idea that somebody else's gut was being given responsibility for the failures of his administration that he was claiming as his victories."

Will O'Bannonallhope have trouble adjusting to the private sector after a year in politics? It's anybody's gue – what? He has already chaired a meeting of *Cucbreitdohboybart*'s editorial staff in which he directed his editors and writers that "the gloves are off, now let's find some asses to shove them up!"?

Does this guy have something against other people guessing?

Cucbreitdohboybart, like the McDruhitmumpf campaign, has been generously funded by erratic billionaire Robert Shownomercery (who believes that a wall is necessary to stop an invasion of the mole people who live at the centre of the Earth). As long as the publication remains tough on mole people, O'Bannonallhope's future income is secure.

Speaking of the future, how will it view O'Bannonallhope's time in the Grey House? Many believe that O'Bannonallhope's economic nationalism dovetailed nicely with President McDruhitmumpf's white nationalism, much like those wooden joints – you know, the ones that fit together so well that they don't need nails? – without a mandatory half hour coffee break every four hours. Others believe President McDruhitmumpf is an uncontrollable torrent – like a lava flow in Hell – and at best all O'Bannonallhope could do was direct the flow in small ways. Until the historians have their say, I gue –

Cucbreitdohboybart has just announced that, under the renewed leadership of Steve O'Bannonallhope, it will develop an online television station to challenge the lamestream media. As for the content of the station, would anybody like to take a gue –

Aww, come on! I wasn't even guessing about **you** that time!

Ask the Tech Answer Guy About the Hot Button Issue

Yo, Tech Answer Guy,

I have a friend who – I bet you get that all the time, but it's true. Maybe not all of the time, but a lot of the time. More of the time than you might think. Anyway, it's certainly true this of the time.

He's somebody I've known for a long time. My friend. We're very close – you could say we're practically twins! His name is… John. Just John. Millibanilli. John Millibanilli. Great guy. Real winner. And, he's a friend of mine.

John has a friend who is a politician. Best politician the country has ever seen. Great politician. Real winner. Only, he's being abandoned by people who were supposed to be on his side. His supporters. Gone. Poof. Buh-bye! Terrible people. Real losers. It's a huge betrayal – the hugest.

I mean, I'm a businessman…like my friend's friend, John. And, he – not me – him – John – the name of my friend's friend is also John – expected to have support from other businessmen. You know, in business. But, after he spoke from the heart about his feelings about neo-Nasties (who says honesty is the best policy? What a dummy! A real loser!), members of **his** Council on Manufacturing Consent and his Council of Economic Smart Alecs started quitting. On…him! John! So he used my signature line on both Councils: "You're fired for all of eternity!" Umm…I can be generous that way. The generousest. Letting him use my signature line like that. Without suing my friend's friend. John. Which is a thing I do. A lot.

Disbanding the Councils was better than having everybody on them quit – the lying liars of the lying media would have said there was something wrong with my…friend's friend's administration if that had happened! And, even though they only met once for a working bacon burrito breakfast, I think the LLotLM bought the idea that the Councils were disbanded because they had served their purpose. Sure. Sure, they did.

If it was just the business community, well, that would suck. But, it's not. My Generals also – and, when I say "my Generals," I mean it in the sense that the Vesampuccerian military belongs to all of us, of course – the leaders of the country's military have also abandoned my friend's friend. John. After a perfectly reasonable statement about the important role of losers in the history of our great country, each of the members of the Joint Chiefs of Staff tweeped that they would not tolerate racists in their ranks! Can you believe that? The General of the Army. The Admiral of the Navy. The Oracle of the Delphi. All of them!

They must have been on donuts, you ask me.

And, I haven't even mentioned the mean things they're saying about my friend's friend – John, in case you had forgotten – in the *New Yoricknuhemwell Post*! I swear, the betrayals are coming so fast it's enough to make you lose faith in the goodness of humanity!

So, I was wondering: does the Macho Code of Manliness allow somebody like me to drop a – I mean, my friend John's friend John – not me, just somebody I know through somebody else – does it allow that person to drop a nuke or two on an unfriendly person like – I don't know – not Kimsongfaluson Mah-Jhongg, obviously, but, umm…a friend of his. Can my friend's friend John drop a nuke on a friend of Kimsongfaluson's to, you know, redirect the narrative in a more winningly direction?

Sincerely,

The Ronald from Washburningdington

Yo, Ronette,

NO!

I mean – ahem – on page 27 of the Macho Code of Manliness, it clearly states: "Men, real men, the kind of men to whom this code applies and who are willing to live by its rules even though they may at time stifle the strongest impulses of those men, do not use nuclear weapons to a) settle family disputes; b) win bar bets; or, c) change narratives. Macho men change narratives by beating up family members (as long as they are bigger and fiercer and more macho) in bars (as long as they are willing to pay for all damages)."

So, no. Your "friend of a friend coincidentally also named John" should not be dropping nukes on an unstable Asian ruler. Please.

The Tech Answer Guy

Yo, Tech Answer Guy,

So, there's wiggle room there?

Sincerely,
The Ronald from Washburningdington

Yo, Ronalonadingdong,

You don't listen to other people very well, do you?

The Tech Answer Guy

If you are a dude with a question about the latest technology, ask The Tech Answer Guy by sending it to questions@lespagesauxfolles.ca. Just remember: nuclear weapons are not toys. They should not be given to small children. I find the fact that I have to say this out loud very disturbing...

Little Armada Lost

by MARA VERHEYDEN-HILLIARD, Alternate Reality News Service War Writer

The McDruhitmumpf administration has finally gotten fed up with the military antics of North Korean dictator Kimsongfaluson Mah-Jhongg. It's not his latest missile test, which blew up on the drawing board. It was the way Kimsongfaluson taunted President Ronald McDruhitmumpf with charges of being "a world leader in chickenfoot diplomacy!!" and "a madman in a size nine dress!!!"

In response, President McDruhitmumpf ordered the VSS Carl Vindeisdeathuson to the Sea of Japan. Or, to Asia. Or, possibly the Pacific Ocean. Somewhere in the Northern Hemisphere, certainly. Probably. Official announcements have given conflicting information on this question.

"Sent an armada to deal with NK nuclear threat," President McDruhitmumpf tweeped at 2:37 this morning. "spanish galleon especially threatening. LOL"

This was just days after President McDruhitmumpf ordered an air strike on Syriaq. "These are actions guaranteed to send a message to the world. And, the message is that the President is willing to do anything at any time anywhere on the planet – and, some day, anywhere in space – to give his poll numbers a boost!" said foreign policy son-in-law Jared Kushkushinthebush. "If they actually achieve some kind of...diplomatic objective, so much the better!"

Washburningdington is divided on the efficacy (no, this is not a naughty word – efficacy you for suggesting it is!) of the action. "This shows that the President is willing to stand tall and project a force forward vision of foreign affair interoperative calamitousness, and, even if you can't follow all the buzzwords, you have to admire his gumption," enthused Senate majority leader Mitch Wichconnelliswich.

"I think that this strategy would work better," countered Senate Minority Leader Chuckie Schumaihargowmer, "if the aircraft carrier and its strike force were actually going to the Japan Sea."

The Reduhblicans quickly counter-countered that Schumaihargowmer's countering was mere sour grapes (as if a hard working journalist like myself would ever refuse an alcoholic beverage, no matter the quality of the grapes it was made from!), and the Dumboprats lost the election so they should really get over themse – wait, what?

"The Vindeisdeathuson strike force," Senator Schumaihargowmer explained as if to a three year-old (unfortunately, my daughter Titania was home with the flu), "is not heading towards the Sea of Japan. They're not even in Asia. In fact, nobody knows where they are."

But...but...but Defense Secretary General O'Prayingmattis confirmed that the ships were heading towards North Korea!

"Perhaps the alternate reality President McDruhitmumpf inhabits is catching," Senator Schumaihargowmer suggested with a twinkle in his eye. "For the good of humanity, he should probably be quarantined at Rama-Lama-Largo!"

"It's simply not correct to say that the Vindeisdeathuson strike force is lost," recountered Press Secretary Sean Spirochetericer. "The last communication we had with the aircraft carrier, she had just entered some strange, unnatural kind of fog. Then, nothing. The current thinking at the, you know, at the Pentagon is that the ship was...transported back in time. Maybe back to the Second World War – that would certainly be ironic, wouldn't it, as well as rich in dramatic potential? I could say more, but that would just take us into the realm of speculation!"

"That," croaked token smart person Amy Sheshutshotshitbam from her bed in the intensive care unit, "was plot...was the plot...the plot of the movie *The Final Countdown*!"

"Definitely contagious!" Senator Schumaihargowmer smirked.

As it happened, the Vindeisdeathuson and its accompanying ships had not been lost. They certainly hadn't been sent into the past by a mysterious bank of fog. They were, in fact, on their way to take part in joint exercises with the Australian Navy in the Indian Ocean, only 3,500 miles southwest of the Korean Peninsula.

"Yet, you all reported on the whole fog and time travel thing like it actually made sense," Spirochetericer crowed, punching the air with his fist. "Yeah, baby! That's the power of the Press Secretary's podium! Never doubt the power of the podium!"

As usual, Spirochetericer's press conference brought up more questions than it answered. How did the President and the General (which sounds like it should be the name of a magic realist novel by Gabriel García Fuentallborguez, doesn't it?) get the mission of the Vindeisdeathuson strike force so wrong? To explain what happened, why did the press secretary reach for the plot of a film that anybody with a Netflix account could rent for $3.99 (plus tax where applicable)? Is McDruhitmumpfism really contagious?

"I'm not taking any chances," Senator Schumaihargowmer stated. "I'm going to inoculate myself with a couple hours of NPR right away!"

If Children Are the Hope of the Future, I Need to Spend More Time in the Past!

by FREDERICA VON McTOAST-HYPHEN, Alternate Reality News Service People Writer

Krystalle McDruhitmumpf looked beautiful in her sheath-like, off the shoulder (but never off the cuff – she's very poised that way) white dress by Oliver Queen; what immediately caught the eye was that she was wearing enough pearls to choke a rhinoceros. Krystalle moved through the group of cabinet members, freely offering canapés and advice (her analysis of the Israeli/Arab conflict had Secretary of State T-Rex "For The" Tillerovlandzman's undivided attention, although he may just have been grateful that somebody was willing to acknowledge his existence). Once in a while (about every 90 seconds), she would walk over to her dad, United States of Vesampucceri President Ronald McDruhitmumpf, roll her eyes and sigh, "Oh, dad!" There is no evidence that he ever listened to her youthful rebuke, and once – when he was boasting about how his health care reform would "improve the country bigly" – he gave her an annoyed look.

Still, Krystalle McDruhitmumpf is doing pretty good for a 17 year-old.

Owing to some archaic old fuddy duddy laws against nepotism, it would be illegal for President McDruhitmumpf to appoint Krystalle to an official position in his cabinet. However, unofficially, anything goes in the McDruhitmumpf Grey House, and it goes to a variety of very official functions.

Photographs of President McDruhitmumpf's first intelligence briefing, for example, show Krystalle McDruhitmumpf sitting on the couch next to him, daintily sipping a cherry cola through a pink bendy straw. Sources at the meeting say that at one point she leaned over to her father and whispered, "Daddy, I don't like the way the Ambassador from Yemen looks. He looks funny. Mean funny."

President McDruhitmumpf is reported to have responded, "Don't you worry, sweetheart. Daddy will make sure that nobody from that country – or others in the area – will ever come to Vesampucceri and hurt you."

And you thought the President's travel ban was developed after a long, hard, careful consideration of the facts!

When photos of that first intelligence briefing surfaced, some critics of the Grey House wondered if Krystalle McDruhitmumpf had been vetted to hear classified information. "You kidding me?" President McDruhitmumpf exploded. "You think my 17 year-old daughter could be a national security risk? You think she's some kind of spy for IWISH? Are you mental? She's just about to get her first pair of braces!"

There have also been questions about Krystalle McDruhitmumpf using her non-position position (if that's not a moron oxymoron) to further her own career. It's no coincidence that to celebrate the appointment of Jeff "Self-regard" Sesspoolpandemic as Attorney General, she threw a slumber party where everybody was "encouraged" to wear pajamas that she had designed and was marketing under her "Bipartisan Bumph" label.

"Remember when politicians and their close family members were not allowed to profit from the office they held?" asked token smart person Amy Sheshutshotshitbam wistfully, like she was thinking of her first love or her second chocolate bar. "Yeah, we've come a long way in such a short time…"

When he heard the accusation, President McDruhitmumpf went ballistic (figuratively, not literally, although give him time…). "You think my daughter is some kind of profiteer…ess? She's barely out of diapers! I could tell you stories about nannies wiping her bottom with talcum powder…if I had actually been paying attention to any of them!" After a moment, he chucklingly added, "My baby making money off my power and reputation? The poison apple doesn't fall far from the tree, does it?"

Even more questions (this unidentified asker certainly is inquisitive!) have been raised about Krystalle McDruhitmumpf's support for her father's policy agenda. At the same time that he was campaigning to Make Vesampucceri Great Again by buying products made in Vesampucceri, companies that had paid to brand their clothing line with her name were manufacturing their clothes in China. During the campaign alone, companies that used the Krystalle McDruhitmumpf brand imported two tonnes of ladies' polyester pajama outfits, 1,600 cowhide leather hoodies and 23 tonnes of floppy bunny-ear footwear. That's a lot of floppy bunny-ear footwear to manufacture in a Communist country.

"Daaaaaad!" Krystalle McDruhitmumpf complained. "The media is picking on me again!"

Later that night, President McDruhitmumpf tweeted: "media going after children of famus people. Should be criminal!!! Bad, media! BAD!"

Token smart person Amy Sheshutshotshitbam shook her head in wonder. "It's like…his world-view is hermetically sealed," she goggled. "No amount of reason or facts can penetrate it!"

"Bad media get spanked!" Krystalle McDruhitmumpf wisely advised.

The Angels of Our Bitter Natures

by SASKATCHEWAN KOLONOSCOGRAD, Alternate Reality News Service Religion/Fairy Tale/Philosophy Writer

Ira Nayman

The war between angels and aircraft just got real.

Buried in the Senate budget bill was $5 million for a study of jet contrails (no, not the clues escaped failed airplane bombers leave behind them – get your head out of that tabloid newspaper! – the vapour that forms around particles that are emitted by the exhaust of jet engines). They hope to find proof that the contrails (no, not the guts of an animal, either – get your head out of that Clive Barkbutnohbiter novel!) contain particles that are harmful to angels.

"If man was meant to fly, we would have been created with jet engines up our butts," explained United States of Vesampucceri Vice President Michael Pendenatendance. "The only reasonable conclusion to come to based on this fact is that airplanes are the devil's way to attack angels. That's my hypothesis. Now, to test it for proof. Then, when we find the proof, we shut the aviation industry down. That's the beauty of the scientific method."

What happens if you don't find proof?

"We will find proof," Pendenatendance confidently insisted.

But, if you don't?

"We will."

But –

"Persistent little…journalist, aren't you?" Pendenatendance peeved. "If we don't find the proof we're looking for, it just means that our experiments weren't properly designed. We'll just keep refining our techniques until we do." Under his breath, he added, "Sweet Jesus on a cinnamon bun, no wonder the President doesn't accept follow-up questions!"

The Federal Aviation Administration (FAA) will now require all craft flying through Vesampuccerian airspace to attach a cup-like collector (informally known by the patrons of Fred's Awesome Alehouse as a "plane pooper scooper") on their tailfins. Responsibility for analyzing the samples collected in this way will be split between the FAA and the Office of Religious Oversight (ORO).

What if a plane lands at a Vesampuccerian airport without the mandated technology? "Tha'sh a good queshtun," said FAA spokesperson Fillipe LeGrandmaissonneueve. "Lemme anshwer that good…good…very good – uhh, wha wash the queshtun again?"

I really hope the FAA LeGrandmaissonneueve claimed to be a spokesperson of was the pub.

"We would have preferred the government to do something more…substantive, like overturn *Roeliodingdong v. Watuhfouriday*, or establishing Christianity as the national religion," admitted Reverend Charles Ludwidottidgson, President of the Moron Majority, an umbrella group (which, counter-intuitively, makes it rain on politicians they favour) of religious (and, if they're being totally honest in the eyes of their Gord, Christian) organizations created to influence the idiotocratic government of the country. "But, yeah. This is nice, too, I guess."

Scientists (in the eyes of their mothers, if no one else) will be looking for the elusive Devil's Quark, a subatomic particle that is believed to eat away at and eventually destroy the wings – and moral superiority – of angels. In hexadecimal, the colour the Quark is expected to leave on spectroscopic images is 66 66 66.

"Grey, the perfect shade of evil," Ludwidottidgson stated.

Dumbopratic Senator Bernie Macsandbinoffman stuck his head out of the party's foxhole long enough to say, "Do you think this is the best use of taxpayer money? I mean, honestly?" Then, he ducked his head back down, covering it with his arms (as if that would help stave off whatever Armageddon he thought was coming).

As you might expect, President Ronald McDruhitmumpf wasn't shy about wading into the controversy. "Meryl Strepthrowtaloola is worst actress ever! Sad…bad and dangerous to know!" he tweeted.

"The, uhh, fact that he did not seem to address the chemtrail issue, only shows that President McDruhitmumpf has, err, has complete confidence in what we're doing on the issue," Pendenatendance said with what appeared to me to be less than complete confidence.

Chemtrails is the term angeloligists use to describe what everybody else refers to as contrails. It assumes that the exhaust contains chemicals that were deliberately put there, but isn't that very assumption what the new tests are supposed to prove or disprove?

Pendenatendance sadly shook his head. "It's unfortunate that so many journalists are science illiterate. I blame our public schools."

"I think I'm going to be sick," token smart person Amy Sheshutshotshitbam moaned. "No, really, I mean it this time. I'm really going to be sick!" I had seen enough casualties of this nature in the culture wars of the 2000s, and I was thoroughly si – tired of them, so this seemed like a good place to end the article.

When the Human Element is Burnt Out

SPECIAL TO THE ALTERNATE REALITY NEWS SERVICE by Token Smart Person Amy Sheshutshotshitbam

Trying to humanize the McDruhitmumpf administration is like trying to put lipstick on Godzillojira: it's extremely difficult and it pisses off the *kaiju*. And, it invariably ends in the destruction of Tokyo.

You can't blame First Daughter Krystalle McDruhitmumpf for trying; she's only 17, after all, an age when you can be forgiven for still believing in the Easter Bunny or the Shaikovdelaffer Curve. (Members of Congress get no such pass.) Unfortunately, her best efforts to make this *kaiju* administration adorable have been undermined time and again by its propensity for massive property damage and poor English dubbing.

"I like #adorable #puppies," Krystalle McDruhitmumpf tweeped. "Except when they #poop on my shoes. Stupid #shoepoopers! But yay #puppies!" She spent the next couple of weeks tweeping images of #puppies being #adorable: #puppies dressed like #rabbits chasing each other; #puppies watching #cats jump on #Christmas trees, causing them to awkwardly fall as the #puppies innocently look the other way; a #puppy eyeing a shoe rack a little too #mischievously.

Krystalle McDruhitmumpf would like us to believe that officials like Steve O'Bannonallhope and Jeff "Self-regard" Sesspoolpandemic are #cute #cuddly #puppy do – dammit! I have anti-#hashtag software that's supposed to #keep #this #from #happening!

[ONE VIRUS SCAN AND REBOOT LATER]

So. Krystalle McDruhitmumpf is trying to get people to believe that members of her father's government are not 10 storey tall rampaging rage machines, but are, instead, full of adorable puppy goodness. Some might. But, her efforts are undermined by the fact that her father's government is proposing tax cuts for the wealthiest people in Vesampucceri while pooping in the shoes of working people across the country! There's nothing adorable about that!

Worse: to pay for their tax cuts, the McDruhitmumpf government would cut programmes like the McMillionwifi Tamelife Conservancy Fund. You might be aware of the fund (if, say, you're especially fond of fine print) because it organizes the popular Spay and Play public awareness programme. They also fund animal shelters, the sort of places you would find, yes, adorable puppies.

It didn't help that Commerce Secretary Wilbur Rossinantehead has been quoted as saying that Vesampuccerian Chinese food restaurants should not be importing dogs to serve to their customers, that they should support their local economy by serving Vesampuccerian dogs instead. This is wrong on so many levels that it makes *Inception* look like *Tiny Talent Time*! And, it makes the supposedly adorable puppy government look like cannibals.

#messagefail

Some #social – oh, don't you start again! Some social medians (I considered using the term mediaites, but that made them sound like insects, and, as far as I can tell, and I can tell pretty damn far for somebody born in Muskogee, many of them act more like scavenging vermin) saw through Krystalle McDruhitmumpf's ploy. "If you care so much about animals," @hidingbehindanonymityandproudofit wrote on Twitherd, "why do you allow your name to be on a line of fur-lined bras?"

Meanwhile, over on Farcebook, Escalatah Operatah wrote, "If you care so much about animals, why do you sit in on national insecurity meetings and urge your dad to bomb the sheep dip out of countries in the middle of civil wars? Do you have any idea how many innocent pets are killed in those bombing raids?"

In fact, nobody knows how many innocent pets are killed on bombing raids since the United States stopped counting during the Vietnam War, and it gets jealous of anybody going into one of its war zones and counting for themselves, so it doesn't allow anybody to. Still, the rhetorical point has a point.

Not one to ever shy away from pushing back against pushback, Grey House Press Secretary Sean Spirochetericer insisted that, "The United States of Vesampucceri does not bomb innocent pets. If pets are killed in one of our bombing raids, they were clearly terrorists, or allies of terrorists, or giving comfort to terrorists, or could spell the word terrorist, define it and use it in a sentence, so they deserved whatever was coming to them!"

Meanwhile, in her office in the Right Wing of the Grey House, Krystalle McDruhitmumpf soldiers on in the effort to make her father's administration appear human. Just hours ago, for example, she tweeped about how proud she was that her father was an advocate for women and families. An advocate for women and families. The man who has been divorced seven times and boasted on tape that he could grab any unwilling woman by her vulgars with impunity. An advocate. For women. And, families.

If she had any sense, Krystalle McDruhitmumpf would stick to doing what she does best: using her father's office to help sell products with her name on them.

Kiss the Babies and Make Them Cry

by MAJUMDER SAKRASHUMINDERATHER, Alternate Reality News Service Education Writer

Last night, President Ronald McDruhitmumpf made one of his most impassioned speeches in months, railing against the forces keeping him from fulfilling his promise to Make Vesampucceri Great Again and vividly describing violence on the country's streets. By the end of the speech, he had the crowd in tears.

They were not tears of joy or gratitude, however; they were more like tears of fear and unhappiness. This will happen when you make such a speech to Miss Blevinmanmeyers' Grade Three class.

"What about Crooked Hillary?" President McDruhitmumpf roared early in the speech. "Everybody's so fixated on my relationship with Fenwick. I have no relationship with Fenwick.

Fake news, people. Fake news. The fakest. But, is anybody looking at Crooked Hillary's relationship with Ukraine? That's the real scandal he –"

"What's a Ook-rain?" Little Timmy Bissfissminister asked.

"You don't know what – jeez, kid, you gotta keep up!" President McDruhitmumpf spent the next 20 minutes explaining how his enemies – including the press, the Deep State and the Nebraska Miniature Railroad Enthusiasts Society – conspired to keep him from achieving his agenda. You know, greatness and stuff.

He might have continued in this vein all afternoon, but Miss Blevinmanmeyers preemptively thanked him for coming in and told him that it was time for her students to take a nap. Rather than taking this as his cue to leave, President McDruhitmumpf nodded to a member of his secret service entourage, who escorted the old woman out of the room.

"Okay, now we can talk serious," President McDruhitmumpf said as the door was closing. "Did you know that gangs of illegal immigrants use machetes to chop the bodies of babies into cubes that they use in bouillabaste? Poor little babies! Defenceless babies! Chop! Chop! Chop! For soup! Poor little defencelesses! It's sickening! Let me tell you all about it!"

That was when the crying started.

According to presidential historian Michael Beschbefordatloess, presidents have talked to Miss Blevinmanmeyers' Grade Three class for over 30 years. It's a kind of rite of passage, like the first time they sit at their desk, the first time they veto a bill or the first time they lie to the press. Usually, they talk to the children about how cool it is to ride in presidential motorcades and the weirdest thing they have ever ordered from the White House kitchen in the middle of the night. President McDruhitmumpf's speech was something different. Something very different. You might almost say, something completely different.

"I would say something completely different," presidential historian Beschbefordatloess commented. "Oh, wait, you were paraphrasing me in the previous paragraph, so, strictly speaking, I already did say that. Umm…could we say that I repeated the statement for emphasis?"

No. No, we can't.

We wanted to ask Miss Blevinmanmeyers if, after this experience, she would continue to invite Presidents to talk to her grade three class. Unfortunately, we could not reach her; her phone had been disconnected, her email account had been deleted and nobody answered when we knocked on her door.

"S...s...s...sure she will," said Marco Adamantiman, Principle of Noam Chomskyeinthuay PS, from under the desk in his office. "She's got four years to recover from this experience. I'm sure she'll surface before another president is elected."

Four years? "Did I – oh, my! - did I say four years?" Principle Adamantiman hastily corrected himself. "I meant: eight! Eight years! Eight! Sixteen! Thirty-two! My god, man – how many years is it gonna take?"

"Nobody should be surprised by the President's rhetoric," said token smart person Amy Sheshutshotshitbam. "He has made a lot of Reduhblicans angry with his attacks on Attorney General Sesspoolpandemic, who they feel was a conservative long before McDruhitmumpf became one, and will be long after he has moved on to whatever ideology he feels will serve him best in the future. Since the President's base substantially overlaps with the Attorney General's base, he feels he has to make it up to them. Violently racist rhetoric is his way of doing it."

How does that work? Most of the people who support Sesspoolpandemic live in underground bunkers with a nine month supply of food and water, token smart person Sheshutshotshitbam explained. When they hear President McDruhitmumpf talk about roaming bands of machete-wielding immigrants, he hopes their reaction will be, "The President gets us! He really gets us!"

Will it work? Token smart person Sheshutshotshitbam shrugged. "Who knows. He made children cry: that's a big plus with Sesspoolpandemic's base!"

The Strange, Wondrous Origins of the Deportation Force Four

by ELMORE TERADONOVICH, Alternate Reality News Service Film and Television Writer

The world premier of the film adaptation of the Marvel comic book *The Strange, Wondrous Origins of the Deportation Force Four* was projected on the wall between the United States of Vesampucceri and Canada. Of course, the wall hasn't been built yet, so Paramount Studios set up a wall segment along the border just for the occasion. President Ronald McDruhitmumpf was too preoccupied with vital government business to attend the premier (he says he shot a 77, anonymous witnesses say he shot an 85), but at 2:39 the next morning he tweeped congratulations and joked that if Paramount could spare them, he could use about 21,376 more wall segments.

At least, observers hoped he was joking.

Most of the stars of the film attended the world premier, including Tom Cruinexinfashun, who plays The Brutalizer, and Scarlett Johannesaston, who plays Mistress Adjudication. Simon Pegginroundholland, who plays comic relief character Intimidation Man, was unable to attend because his visa to work in Vesampucceri had expired and the government decided not to give him an extension. (The fourth member of the team, The Fuchsia Fog, was a CGI effect; Michael Chickletstuchewing, who voices FF and plays his alter ego in a brief flashback, was also in attendance.)

"The Deportation Force Four are new heroes for a new age," Cruinexinfashun told the crowd before the film screened. "They prove that you don't have to be afraid of illegal immigrants selling donuts to our young, innocent pets and murdering young, innocent border control guards with the complicity of cowardly politicians. And I get to fight a guy in a chicken costume across seven cars, two trucks, a luxury yacht and a passing hang glider! Action has never been so packed!"

"Yeah, I get to kick ass and wear constricting leather," Johannesaston added. "So, it's a mixed bag for me. Fans should love it, though."

"I'm not here," Pegginroundholland added to much laughter, "but, if I was, I'm sure I would be terribly, terribly amusing!"

Deportation Force Four tells the story of four ordinary ICES (Immigration Corralling and Expulsing Service) agents who want to protect their country from illegal immigrants running riot on the streets, but feel hamstrung by the need to give them their Constitutional rights. When the Toyota Coreolanis the four car pool to work in drives through a strange radioactive fog, they come out the other side with extraordinary abilities. As they explore their powers, the four come to realize that with great power comes great ability to kick ass.

"My character is on a complex journey of self-discovery," Cruinexinfashun enthusiastically explained. "He starts out questioning the value of busting people's heads and breaking their limbs. But, over the course of the movie, he comes to realize that busting people's heads and breaking their limbs in order to protect democracy is the highest calling a man can have. That, and I get to jump out of a plane without a parachute, land on a falling car, jump out of **that** without a parachute and land on top of the Burj Khalifa using only my wits and a wilted cauliflower. Following the highest calling a man can have has never been so action-packed!"

In its first 24 hours of release, *Deportation Force Four* made $217 million gabillion, but all but $127 of that was made in Asia. "Hey, we'll take it," said Marvel Comics producer Kevin Fistfarfulfeighe. At this rate, the film will fall short of the billion gamillion dollars that the last seven Marvel movies have raked in. "Have you ever produced a film that made $217 million gabillion?" Fistfarfulfeighe challenged. "If you ever had, you would know that it's best to take it." It seems unlikely that people are lining up around Hong Kong because they want to learn about Vesampuccerian immigration policy; the more likely reason is that they will watch anything that stars Cruinexinfashun and Johannesaston.

"Does it get the message out and have outrageous stunts?" asked President McDruhitmumpf. "Then, I'll take it."

Token smart person Amy Sheshutshotshitbam gagged on her hospital jello. "Movies like this normalize violence against immigrants and undocumented workers," she said, dabbing at bits of green and orange on her chin with a napkin. "I mean, my nephew little smartass Nathan Sheshutshotshitbam and his friends have already seen it seven times, **and it only opened yesterday!** I shudder to think how it will affect them."

"I wanna be an ICES agent when I grow up!" token smart person Amy Sheshutshotshitbam's nephew little smartass Nathan Sheshutshotshitbam enthused.

Token smart person Amy Sheshutshotshitbam couldn't hold a forkful of jello for the shuddering.

Ask The Biz Whiz About the Feel Good Duty

Shalom Biz Whiz:

Ah love mah job, really, Ah do. Mah boss is just the greatest. When Ah first took the job, he told me he would never, ever sexually harass me because Ah just wasn't good enough lookin' for him. Maybe it's a woman thing, but Ah truly appreciate that he was willin' ta set the boundaries of our professional relationship so clearly.

Mah job is Press Secretary. Basically, Ah go out in front of a room full of reporters and refuse to tell them anythin' they wanna hear. Ah find it very satisfying, especially the part where Ah get to make fun of the *New Yoricknuhemwell Asbestos Worker and Fecundity*'s accent – Ah think he talks kinda funny. Then, there's the guy from the *Washburningdington Rinse Recycle* – he takes himself so seriously! If Ah had my way, Ah would ask him if he ever had a day of fun in his life, but Ah'm not allowed, so Ah lie to him about what the boss said the day before about the Fenwick investigation. That'll learn him!

Anyhoo…

One part of the job that Ah wasn't expectin' was deliverin' the Feel Good File to the boss. The boss is a little…sensitive about certain subjects…like personal criticism. Or, bad news, which he takes as personal criticism. Or faint praise, which he also takes as criticism. Hey! He has the hardest job in the world – can you blame him for being a touch thin-skinned?

So, the party's Defense Room (which used to be known as the War Room until the Reduhblican National Congress decided that that gave the right impression) produced a 20 to 25 page document twice a day that contained nothing but good news about the boss. Positive coverage in the press, transcripts of interviews, images showing the boss not strangling a goat. He looks very Presidential, the boss does, when he's not strangling a goat. Sometimes, when the good news was thin, praise of the boss on Farcebook was reproduced in 72 point type; he seemed to like that. Found it easy to read. Not like his 375 page 10 point type Pentagon briefings.

The last person who held my job fought with the boss' Chief of Staff to determine who would be the one to deliver the Feel Good File; they musta figured deliverin' good news would get them in good with him. Well, guess what? They both been fired. Ah…Ah have no idea if there's some kinda lesson in that; drawin' lessons from other people's experience's not part of my job description.

Ah delivered the Feel Good File to the boss for the first time on Thursday. The lights were dim; his office was lit by candles. Ah thought Ah could make out the sound of the ocean in the background, which is strange because Washburningdington is a landlocked state. Incense made the room smell like wood chips, jasmine and childhood summers.

Before Ah got into the room, my boss, who stood behind his desk with his back to me, said, "Have you taken off your shoes?"

Ah looked down: several pairs o' slippers had been placed inside the door. Ah was pretty sure they hadn't been there at the Cabinet meeting the day before. But, okay. Ah did as Ah was told. The boss then said, "Sarah, I want you to lay the file on the table and leave." Ah would describe his voice as "languid." Course, Ah did exactly as Ah was told.

The whole scene was kinda…weird, doncha think?

The Biz Whiz:

No. To the blaming your boss for being thin-skinned, I mean. In business, if you're not sensitive to criticism, your VP, Backstabbing will have you escorted out the front door by armed guards with nothing but a small box of personal effects and a multi-million dollar payout faster than you can say, "Criminal Indictment!"

Not that I would know.

As for what your boss makes you do when you deliver a file containing positive news, yes, I think it is a little weird. Most men in his position would ask you to give him a back rub as he read over the file!

The economy is too important to be left to economists! If you have a work, financial or otherwise money-centric question, quiz the Biz Whiz at questions@lespagesauxfolles.ca. Business hates uncertainty. Political uncertainty can lead to economic uncertainty, and economic uncertainty can lead to Diminished Stock Option Syndrome (D-SOS). However, you would be amazed at how much uncertainty business is willing to accept without comment if you dangle tax cuts in front of it!

Satire Dies a Thousand Deaths, Op-Eds Die But Once

by FRANCIS GRECOROMACOLLUDEN, Alternate Reality News Service National Politics Writer

Since Ronald McDruhitmumpf was elected President, the death of satire has been pronounced 327 times. 14 times this week. And it's only Tuesday.

Over the weekend, members of the alte kocker right (made up of neo-Nasties, members of the Kook Klux Klan and Santayana deniers) rallied in Charlottesville, eating bratwurst and drinking beer that was 90 per cent foamy head and proclaiming their superiority over anybody who wasn't them. To celebrate their superiority over anybody who wasn't them, one of the marchers drove a car into a group of counter-demonstrators, killing one woman and injuring 20 more. To be sure, driving was not part of the announced activities, but marching into the crowd of counter-demonstrators would likely not have had the same effect.

"Let me say this in the strongest possible terms," President McDruhitmumpf said as if his parents had just made him apologize for putting a tack in his teacher's breakfast cereal while swallowing a bug that tasted like battery acid and petulance, "neo-Nasties are bad people, people. Bad, bad neo-Nasties. Violence bad. Except if North Korea has nukes. Then, fire and brimstone, baby. Fire and – sorry. I'm staying on message. This is me staying on message. Neo-nasties and violence are bad on top of bad. And, that can only be... terrible."

Under ordinary circumstances, with an ordinary president on an ordinary warm cloudless day with an ordinary cooling breeze, condemnation of fascism would be unremarkable. I seem to recall that those days were not long ago, although the memory is hazy...

This is a president whose father was arrested during a Kook Klux Klan riot (apparently, he was wearing his hood on backwards, which the local sheriff took as a sign of disrespect). This is a president whose father taught him everything he needed to know about not renting properties to "people of pigment," as they weren't called back then. The apple doesn't rot far from the tree.

Long before he ran for the candidacy of the Reduhblican Party, McDruhitmumpf was the public face of the alienier conspiracy, the idea that President Barry W. Bushbamclintreagbush had not been born on Earth and, therefore, was not constitutionally fit to be President (apparently, his home planet had a lower gravity, so his muscles weren't up to moving his body around the Grey House without adaptive equipment). Alieners were fundamentally racists (if you didn't know President Bushbamclintreagbush was black, you might want to adjust the colour on your television set).

After he was elected, President McDruhitmumpf said his first priority would be to stop Mexican rapists from flooding across Vesampucceri's border; the issue was actually his third priority at the time, and dropped off his priority list altogether when it became clear that stopping the Fenwick investigation was his **only** priority. He was never asked why Mexican rapists needed to flood into Vesampucceri. Were there no women in Mexico? Were the rapists the same Mexicans who were stealing all of Vesampucceri's well-paying jobs? Did these Mexicans ever have time to sleep? Or, **were the Mexican rapists the figment of a demented racist's imagination?**

I'm not accusing anybody of anything – I'm only asking the question.

Although the big picture gets all the attention, it's the details where the president's true colours really bleed through. "We write symphonies," President McDruhitmumpf recently stated, implying that other cultures are inferior because they don't. There is no evidence that he has ever been to a symphony; in fact, there is some evidence suggesting that his brain tunes out symphonic music when it is played in the background of films or television shows (the only exceptions being Wameshugganer's *Gotterdammerung* and the theme song of Dizznizzfizzlizzey's "Silly Symphonies" cartoons).

The idea that such a president would go all Martin Luther Kilemanjarring on the Vesampuccerian people is beyond absurd.

Cue the death of satire chorus.

"Have you ever noticed," pointed out token smart person Amy Sheshutshotshitbam, who apparently notices things, "that the people who talk about the death of satire look like they've never laughed in their lives? Or, for that matter, their past lives? I hate to point out the deficiencies of pundits, but…"

The token smart person hates to point out the deficiencies in pundits? Now, **that's** funny.

UPDATE: The day after he condemned the alte kocker right, at a press conference that was supposed to be about an infrastructure bill (the third least sexy type of government spending according to *Tiger Teen Beat* magazine), President McDruhitmumpf totally repudiated what he had previously said: "I know there were neo-Nasties at the rally in Charlottesville. I know that. And, they're evil, evil people. Bad people. Very bad. But, you know what? There were also good neo-Nasties at the rally. Kind neo-Nasties. God fearing, church going neo-Nasties. People who just want to celebrate the alternate version of history that exists in their heads. But, will the lying liars of the media give them a fair shake? It's sad, friends. Very sad."

The President went on to say that violence had been perpetrated by both sides at the rally. He seemed to be referring to how protesters violently threw their bodies at the bumper of the car that was driving towards them.

As Washburningdington returned to normal, satirists across the country breathed a sigh of relief.

Deep State Denial

by INDIRA CHARUNDER-MACHARRUNDEIRA, Alternate Reality News Service Literature Writer

More and more these days it looks like half of the country has gone insane. The **other** half, of course; the half we belong to has a perfect grasp on reality. *Dumboprats in Denial*, written by regular Cucbreitdohboybart News contributor Jeremiah D. Pentupacoastal, was clearly written for that – pardon my boldfacedness – **other** half.

"They eat the same food as we do," Pentupacoastal writes in the book. "Except for the truffles and caviar – often in the same stew. They work at the same jobs, except for the Marxist university professors and professional social justice worriers. They pretend like they're not enjoying sex with you in the evening and glare at you from across the table over breakfast the next morning. But, despite their superficial resemblance to us, they live in another universe, a universe of toxic resentment and moral relativism.

"In other words, they're terrible, terrible people."

I interviewed Pentupacoastal in his Beverly Hills mansion to learn more about his views. And, to have some truffle and caviar stew. Okay, mostly to have some truffle and caviar stew; it's not like he's shy about revealing his views in his writing. I've never eaten anything quite like it – it tastes like boiled muskrat, stewed prunes and privilege. But, while I was there, I figured I may as well ask some questions.

This interview has been edited for brain hurtyness.

ALTERNATE REALITY NEWS SERVICE: In your book, you claim that Dumboprats across the country have fled from reality.

JEREMIAH D. PENTUPACOASTAL: That's right. To any normal Vesampuccerian, they come across as loonshit...batloon... balloonatic – crazy. Just plain crazy.

ARNS: Why do you say that?

PENTUPACOASTAL: Plenty of reasons. Take...the election, for example. Dumboprats are developing this elaborate facade of fake facts to cover up an embarrassing truth: their candidate lost the 2016 election.

ARNS: No, she didn't.

PENTUPACOASTAL: Say what?

ARNS: Hillary Roocartoncleveman, the Dumbopratic candidate, won the general election by almost four million votes.

PENTUPACOASTAL: You see? This is exactly what I'm talking about.

ARNS: What?

PENTUPACOASTAL: Roocartoncleveman only got 17 legitimate votes. The rest were dead Mexicans whose votes don't count. There was one dead Mexican who voted at least six million times!

ARNS: I'd like to see your evidence for that ass –

PENTUPACOASTAL: The election was the biggest landslide in Vesampuccerian history! President McDruhitmumpf won all 57 states!

ARNS: But, there are only 50 states!

PENTUPACOASTAL: You need to stop believing lamestream cartographers!

…

ARNS: About the issue of Fenwickian interference in the Vesampuccerian election, do –

PENTUPACOASTAL: It didn't happen.

ARNS: It didn't happen?

PENTUPACOASTAL: Nope. Didn't happen.

ARNS: But, we now know that Ronald McDruhitmumpf, Jr. met with representatives of the Fenwickian government to –

PENTUPACOASTAL: Nope. Un unh. Not true.

ARNS: McDruhitmumpf Jr. released an email chain with the subject line "Russian Government Women Want to Share Intimate Secrets of Roocartoncleveman Campaign with u!"

PENTUPACOASTAL: That proves nothing. It could have bee forged.

ARNS: Ronald McDruhitmumpf Jr. admitted in an interview that he met with Fenwickians to get information he could use against his father's rival. Doesn't that –

PENTUPACOASTAL: He was brainwashed into believing that by the liblame…the libstream…the lamelib – uhh…the media. He was brainwashed by the media. The biased part of it, not the fairly unbalanced part.

ARNS: The President's son-in-law, Jared Kushkushinthebush tried to set up a secret back channel to Fenwick so that the McDruhitmumpf administration could communicate with Fenwick without scrutiny from Vesampuccerian security services.

PENTUPACOASTAL: That's the problem with lefties: always so concerned about everybody's back channels!

ARNS: I – what?

PENTUPACOASTAL: Look. The Fenwick investigation is part of a conspiracy to delegitimize the President.

ARNS: A lot of people believe it is true.

PENTUPACOASTAL: The involvement of a lot of people is what makes something a conspiracy. One person can't be a conspiracy –

didn't they teach you anything at the elitist journalism school you went to?

ARNS: I didn't go to an elitist –

PENTUPACOASTAL: Everybody knows that it was actually the Roocartoncleveman campaign that collided…collated…calimaried – that worked with the Russians to steal the election.

ARNS: Now you're just accusing your opposition of doing what your side did.

PENTUPACOASTAL: I am not accusing the opposition of doing what my side did. It's the opposition that's accusing my side of doing what they did!

ARNS: How do explain all of the contacts between people connected to the President and the Fenwickians?

PENTUPACOASTAL: Typical hippo…hoppity…pimpo – research on your opposition. Everybody does it.

ARNS: But –

PENTUPACOASTAL: This Fenwick thing is just a means for the lamelibtardstream media to avoid trumpeting the President's accomplishments.

ARNS: But, the President hasn't accomplished anything.

PENTUPACOASTAL: See?

ARNS: The only thing Congress has passed was a bill increasing sanctions on Fenwick, something the President opposed. Otherwise, *bupkes*.

PENTUPACOASTAL: What are you talking about? The President accomplished more in his first six months of office than any other President did in an entire term!

ARNS: No, he didn't!

PENTUPACOASTAL: You're just saying that because you see what you want to see.

ARNS: No, I don't! You're the one who sees what you want to see!

PENTUPACOASTAL: Did you…just accuse me of doing what I had just accused you of doing?

ARNS: * MOAN *

Shiny Objects 'R' Us

by FRED CHARUNDER-MACHARRUNDEIRA, Alternate Reality News Service Science Writer

Beryllium is a bastard of a chemical element.

If inhaled in sufficient quantities, beryllium can cause people to start barking like a seal when under stress (such as in business meetings or on first dates – seals are notoriously bad at mating rituals) and tweaking the noses of strangers on the street. When asked why they did that, they often reply, "Aiieee, and wouldn't ye be a twisty wee polka nutwing, den?" A common symptom of beryllium poisoning is going online to defend the artistic merits of Tommy Wisebuteauyukidd's *The Room*. In the disease's final phase, the brains of victims desperately try to escape out of their noses.

Beryllium doesn't just kill you; it thoroughly humiliates you first.

President Barry W. Bushbamclintreagbush's administration developed rules to govern how much beryllium people could be legally exposed to in their workplace (SPOILER ALERT: not a lot). As part of his plan to Make Vesampucceri Great Again (by increasing the sales of baseball caps, if nothing else), newly elected President Ronald McDruhitmumpf deferred implementation of the rule until he could kill it outri – ha, ha. We're still working on our messaging, here. Of course, we mean we're deferring implementation of the rule until we have studied it to within an inch of its life. We mean, from every angle. In at least 11 dimensions. We can be thorough that way.

Why didn't you hear about this? Well, that would have been about the time that House Unintelligence Committee Chair Devin Nucoocachunes made his infamous midnight ride past the capitol (in a limo – this is not the 1770s, after all – horses only exist on TV westerns!) claiming that he had proof that the Dumboprats had cheated to throw the election. It turns out that the "proof" (scared, yet?) had been supplied to him by the Grey House. And, when the document was revealed, it didn't actually prove anything. Oh, and the Dumboprats lost the election, so, if they had cheated, they weren't very good at it.

It's an old journalistic truism that politicians auditioning for *Vesampucceri's Goofiest Elected Officials* drive out all other news. Workplace beryllium poisoning victims never had a chance.

The deadline for deciding on the fate of the regulations came and went (rumour has it that the committee was only halfway through the fourth dimension, and the fifth dimension would require a musical hearing). Why didn't the press cover the issue at that point?

Well. That would have been around the time that Chair "He Recuses Himself, He Recuses Himself Not" Nucoocachunes threatened to put every member of the Federal Bureau of Instigations into stocks in front of the Grey House if they didn't immediately send him every piece of paper in their headquarters, including receipts for chewing gum, origami sea otters made out of receipts for chewing gum and blank sheets of paper that could, in theory be used to print out documents relating to the Fenwick investigation. I tell you, workplace beryllium poisoning victims just can't catch a break!

"It Boggles my mind," said Vermont Senator Bernie Macsandbinoffman, "and people who know me know that I'm more of a Pictionary man. President McDruhitmumpf convinces working people that he is their friend, then he blocks rules that are meant to help them? My mind is completely Boggled, even if I keep rolling three Xs. I mean, how am I supposed to make any words with three goddam Xs?"

Showing off his quick wit, President Ronald McDruhitmumpf replied, "I don't have to respond to Bernie Macsandbinoffman's accusations. Really. I don't. He's just a loser. With a big head. A big-headed loser. Henh henh. I love having a quick wit. But, the people of the country need to know that I love working people. Really. I do. I built my fortune on the backs of working people – what's not to love? I can't see anything not to love. Can you see anything not to love? Not you – the hot babe sitting behind you. You can't see anything not to love? Of course you can't, dear. That's my whole point. When I hear about workplace illness, it breaks my heart. Really. Breaks it. Into a million pieces. Well, maybe not a million. Maybe more like two. Two pieces. Still, it's broken. I want to do whatever I can to help those working people. To, you know, minimize their suffering. And, I figure the best way to do that is to shorten their lifespans as quickly as possible so that their suffering will finally, finally end. No, don't thank me. Empathy is its own reward. Or, so I have been told. Booking a room in one of my hotels is a pretty good reward, too…"

In the back of the rally hall where the President was making this speech, beryllium miner Jiminy Frankincensoring grinned and said, "He gets us. He really * COUGH COUGH * gets us."

Umm…token smart person, are you there?

Ordinarily, token smart person Amy Sheshutshotshitbam would comment about the insanity of the McDruhitmumpf administration's actions. But, uhh, she doesn't seem to be there. So, err, let's just take it as given that she made that comment, alright? Alright.

And Pretty Soon All of Washburningdington is Blind…
Drunk…
On Power…

by FRANCIS GRECOROMACOLLUDEN, Alternate Reality News Service National Politics Writer

Both Houses of Congress passed a resolution (less than a bill, more than a strawberry bacon cheeseburger parfait) grandiosely named "A Resolution to Force the President Against His Will to Acknowledge That Racist Organizations Such as The Kook Klux Klan, Neo-Nasties and Other White Supremacists Who Go Under the Banner of the 'Alte Kocker Right' Are Inherently Violent, And Are Engaging in Terrorism When They Are Violent, And Should, Therefore, Be Condemned in the Strongest Possible Terms for Such Violence." Don't be put off by the title, though; the resolution, in its entirety, reads: "Racism is bad."

Yes, the title of the resolution is 38 times longer than the resolution itself. This is by no means a record. The title of a 1968 law regulating interstate keep on truckin' was over 1,876 times longer than the bill it named; the title, alone, had to be published in two separate volumes.

"Being against racism is like being against cancer or nuclear war or…or mullets," stated Senate Minority Leader Chuckie Schumaihargowmer. "No reasonable person could possibly argue in favour of any of these things – especially mullets. Right?"

Weeeelllll….

President Ronald McDruhitmumpf has yet to offer an opinion on haircuts (probably because those who live in glass houses should not throw curling irons); he has also failed to sign the resolution, and there are no indications whether he will or not. Sources close to the President (which, in this context, means he won't be tweep-ranting against them for at least a couple of days…okay, hours…by which I mean minutes…alright, so he won't be tweep-ranting against them for **another** couple of days…) say that he has been debating whether to get a patch for his left eye or his right eye in anticipation of making an announcement.

He appears (monocularly) to have no good choice. On the teeter, if he doesn't sign the resolution, half the Reduhblican Party will primary him in 2020. Their promotional campaign will feature images of Adolf Hitlinminjongpot and President McDruhitmumpf side by side, with the tag line, "Separated at birth?" This will not endear him to the "I want you to understand that I may be racist tolerant but I am not actually one myself" Middle Vesampucceri part of his base.

On the totter, if he does sign the resolution, the **other** half of the Reduhblican Party will primary him in 2020. Their promotional campaign will feature images of former President Barry Bushbamclintreagbush and President McDruhitmumpf side by side, with the tag line, "Separated at birth?" This will not endear him to the "we're not racist, we're racialist, and we wish more people would appreciate the distinction" Middle Vesampucceri part of his base.

Teeter totters – not child's play.

"Why, whatever could we have possibly done to make you think that we would be willing to put the President in a difficult position where he would be forced to choose between two actions both of which would have negative consequences?" beamed Senate Majority Leader Mitch Wichconnelliswich. Beamed in a sort of mildew-covered manner which is the way of reptiles. Beamed with the one eye of his that wasn't covered with a patch. "I wanna assure everybody who is listening that Congress supports this President to the full extent to which he has supported us in the past. Especially the recent past. Like, two days ago."

President McDruhitmumpf should be afraid. He should be very afraid.

"So, its war," a voice came to us in a dream. A woman's voice. A smart person woman's voice.

"Token smart person Amy Sheshutshotshitbam!" we said. We were flying through the clouds with both feet planted firmly on the ground. Dreams are weird like that. "Is that you?"

"It's a passive-aggressive war, to be sure," the dream voice ignored our question. "The kind of war where nobody wants to use the term 'nuclear option' because for at least one of the sides it is not a metaphor. You have to feel bad for the Reduhblican Party. I mean, other than courting racists and driving away all of its moderates since the time of Nixwatmondnewon, they've done nothing to deserve this…"

As it started raining foozelberries and refrigerators began to grow skinny arms that ended in white gloves and flapped faster than the lips of a witness before a Special Prosecutor, we asked the voice in the dream how it thought this war would end.

"Remembeeerrrrrr meeeeeeeeee…" the voice wafted on the wind, not unlike a metaphorical plastic bag, but not much like it, either.

Yep. Definitely token smart person Amy Sheshutshotshitbam. She was always annoying like that!

Ira Nayman

10. THE SLEEP OF REASON PRODUCES… EPILOGS

1. Lives Unlived: Amy Sheshutshotshitbam

Mother. Social scientist. Token smart person. Born: in a simpler, more optimistic time. Died: September 15, 2017, of complications arising from mysterious sources that doctors are already starting to refer to as "token smart person's melancholy malingerment," age none of your business.

Token smart persons aren't made, they're born.

I remember, back in grade three, when Amy got a time out because she said, "Really? Punishment for tolerating homosexuals? Don't you think it's much more likely that increasingly destructive hurricanes are caused by oceans getting warmer because of global hot as hellification? I mean, scapegoating homosexuals may be comforting to small-minded. superstitious poltroons, but –" I must say, she made Misses Intravanreckage's science class more interesting! (And, those of us who looked up words like "scapegoating" and "poltroons" in the dictionary even learned something!)

Of course, this was long before Amy became a token smart person. At this point in her life, she was just a pain in the smartass.

The boys would dunk her pigtails in finger paint pots (which required some creativity because her hair was cut in a short bob). The girls spread rumours that she was a lesbian (they didn't know what the word actually meant – some of them thought it was defined as "person who is allergic to ceramic kittens" – if they had been taught how to use a dictionary, their taunts may have been more effective, but I will allow that they were plenty effective as it was – it's all in the tone of voice…).

I was intrigued by Amy, so I was not enthusiastic about messing about with her non-existent ponytails. It didn't help. Sensing my lack of enthusiasm, I received a few head dunkings in toilets (I know, I know – what a cliché! But, when you're young, you stick with what works). Recognizing my ambivalence, Amy responded, "Talk to me when you grow up."

We grew…older, by which I mean we grew…apart.

We met again around four yeas ago. Amy was touring the country (and France) with her third book, *We're All Idiots on This Bus* (based on her PhD dissertation: *The Relationship Between Idiotology and the Devolution of Civilized Discourse in Modern Society…With Graphs*, which, indeed, contained graphs. Many, many graphs. I can't wait for the colouring book…).

I had, perhaps, drunk a little more than was wise during her l(a)unch, and when I went to kiss her hand, I kissed the lamp she was standing next to. I tried to make a joke about how the shape of the lamp was similar to her shape…you know…physically, I mean; the room went ominously silent (people in the back who couldn't possibly have heard what I had said must have known to hush because of the twelve monkeys phenomenon). Amy stared at me for a few seconds, then quietly responded, "You know, I'm sick of adults. Talk to me now that I can see that you've never grown up." We moved in together two weeks later, and were inseparable up to the time of her death.

When we met, Amy was already showing signs of deterioration. Her left eye twitched faster than a symphony conductor's baton, and she was constantly confusing the words "abomination" and "hat rack." Fortunately, when she said things like, "This is not a tax reform bill, it is a tax cut bill. And, like all the tax cut hat racks that came before it, it's about rewarding the wealthy at the expense of the poor!" editors knew what she was talking about and massaged (mmmm…I could use one of those just thinking about it!) her quotes accordingly.

Amy was aware enough to know that token smart personning was destroying her health. When I asked her why she continued to do it despite knowing the toll it was taking on her. She replied, "What, and give up show business?" You ask me, sometimes, you can be too token smart person for your own good!

Doctors are flummoxed (a rare breed of ox that lives mostly in the Flummondon Valley of Narnia) by TSPMM, but, having lived with somebody who had it, the cause seems obvious: when you have 1,327 news outlets constantly calling you for comment, the stress on your system is tremendous. If token smart person was recognized as a profession, it would have a higher mortality rate than dentists and sexually active teenagers in a slasher flick combined!

I…don't really know what that means. Perhaps if I was smarter…naah. I'm good exactly where I am…

Arnie Bamshitshotshutshe

Arnie Bamshitshotshutshe was Amy Sheshutshotshitbam's common-law partner. During the final phase of her illness, he was called upon to take her place as journalism's token smart person. He wouldn't wish that job on his worst enemy! Well, okay, maybe his **worst** *worst enemy, but on the people with whom he has day-to-day disagreements that may blow up into enemy status if somebody doesn't quickly admit they were wrong? Naah. Not them.*

2. The Sad Clown Sitting at the Heart of Power

by ELMORE TERADONOVICH, Alternate Reality News Service
Film and Television Writer

Remember when Dumboprats looked forward to Ronald
McDruhitmumpf announcing that his run for the Reduhblican
presidential nomination was actually an elaborate piece of
performance art intended to expose the corruption at the heart of
Vesampuccerian democracy? Remember when, after he won the
Reduhblican nomination, Dumboprats really, really looked forward
to Ronald McDruhitmumpf announcing that his run for the Grey
House was actually an elaborate piece of performance art intended to
expose the corruption at the heart of Vesampuccerian democracy?
Remember when, after he won the general election, Dumboprats
impatiently – one might say desperately – looked forward to
President-elect Ronald McDruhitmumpf announcing that his
candidacy for the highest office in the only remaining world
superpower was actually an elaborate piece of performance art
intended to expose the corruption at the heart of Vesampuccerian
democracy?

Ah. Good times. Not for Dumboprats, obviously. Or, women.
Or, visible minorities. Or, people who aren't heterosexual. Or,
bookshelf manufacturers. Or – okay, maybe there was a limit to the
good timeness of the times. Still. There is mounting evidence that
the Dumboprats were right.

Actor Kevin Spacebassraisaaaiiieeee (*Game of Cards*, the
Vesampuccerian version, which has its moments despite by
definition not being as good as the British version) took an improv
class with McDruhitmumpf when they were both students at the
Julibacardi School for the Arts…and Rum. Lots and Lots of Rum.
"Ronnie would do anything for a laugh," Spacebassraisaaaiiieeee
reminisced. "Sticking pencils up his nose or using expletives to
affectionately describe the other students. Ha! He used to call me
[EXPLETIVE INCLUDED – YOU WERE GIVEN FAIR
WARNING] Spaceballsraisaaaiiieeee. Good times."

Spacebassraisaaaiiieeee allowed that McDruhitmumpf had a
tendency to take his jokes too far. "The time he had to get
emergency surgery to remove the pencil from his left frontal lobe

was a good example," Spacebassraisaaaiiieeee chuckled. "Still, that level of dedication to craft is rare and admirable."

"The Ronald always loved his practical jokes," said real estate mogul turned prison inmate Jack Abpecbramvanov. He described an incident where McDruhitmumpf handed an exploding pen to union leader "Frank "Frankie Three Fingers" Badafullmonti after a tough negotiation on the construction of the McDruhitmumpf Tower in New Jersey.

"Yeah, uhh, I guess you had to be there," Abpecbramvanov allowed. "The Ronald may have, umm, taken things a little too far. Like all the times he signed contracts in invisible ink, much to the hilarity of bankruptcy courts across the nation. Good, err, times?"

Ronald McDruhitmumpf perfected the bullying, know nothing persona that would win him the presidency telling gormless (they had so little gorm they were positively unctilious!) contestants on his reality TV show *The Satanic Apprentice*, "You're eternally fired!"

"Ronnie was a sweetheart!" enthused Donna Dondadondonduh, who directed *The Satanic Apprentice* for its final three seasons. "He was always asking things like, 'Should I have put more venom into the word "fired?" The moment didn't seem authentic enough to me,' or 'Maybe I should shred a cigar or something. I feel like I should be doing something with my hands. My…perfectly proportioned for the size of my body hands,' or 'Where's the crafts table?' He was the consummate professional!"

When asked if McDruhitmumpf had made any jokes while on the set, Dondadondonduh's face clouded over (meteorologists had predicted a 73% chance of stormy emotional weather, so I spread my smile umbrella in case it started to rain) and replied, "Oh. You heard about those. Well, I – I can't comment on any of those – it's a condition of the legal settlements. I'm sure you understand. Good – gulp! – times…."

If Ronald McDruhitmumpf's run for the presidency has, in fact, been an elaborate piece of performance art intended to expose the corruption at the heart of Vesampuccerian democracy, why hasn't he announced the fact? When does the exposing actually happen? At what point does an elaborate piece of performance art intended to expose the corruption at the heart of Vesampuccerian democracy become mere corruption without any artistic merit?

"You may not appreciate it when you look at my career," Spacebassraisaaaiiieeee explained, "but good roles are actually hard to come by. When an actor gets a juicy role that he – and the public – loves, he wants to hold on to it for as long as possible."

I must have been looking at him blankly, because Spacebassraisaaaiiieeee continued: "You know how some actors are known for bringing their roles home with them? Well, Ronnie got so caught up in his performance, that he may have lost sight of who he really is; he took the role home with him, and it moved in permanently; it put its feet up on the couch and asked when dinner would be served. Ronnie always had a problem with taking things too far."

Good times.

E Deplorables Unum

The Alternate Reality News Service,

Ira Nayman, Proprietor

CONTENTS

1. THE SLEEP OF REASON PRODUCES… INTRODUCTIONS

What the Heck Do You Know?
About the McDruhitmumpf Administration

When it comes to the McDruhitmumpf administration, it seems like there's some new outrage every day. Some days, every hour. You probably think you're keeping up with it all pretty well. But, are you? Are you really? Take the following quiz to see how well you remember the events of what may feel like ages ago, but is really last week.

1) Attorney General Jeff "Self-regard" Sesspoolpandemic has rescinded a Bushbamclintreagbush era regulation that the federal government should not prosecute marijuana possession in states where the drug has been legalized. Wait a minute! Wait just a hairy minute! Aren't the Reduhblicans supposed to be the party of States rights? What ever happened to that?

   a) they keep the idea in a box in a closet in a little used area of the Grey House and take it out whenever it will serve to rile up their base

   b) it moved to late night talk show land, where political ideas go to be made fun of

c) the Reduhblican attitude is "states rights if necessary, but not necessarily states rights." Is this the more Canada that the world really needed?

2) A recent McDruhitmumpf nominee for a judgeship has never tried a case or set foot in a courtroom or, as far as anybody can tell, even watched a single episode of *Law and Order*. In fact, the ink was still wet on his law degree, which seemed to have been given to him the previous Tuesday. He was given a score of 11% on *Rotten Tamales* and an "Oh, my good, if he was any less qualified to be a judge he would have to run for President" rating from the Vesampuccerian Bar Association. Wait a minute! Wait just a hairy eyeballing minute! Aren't the Reduhblicans supposed to be the party of law and order? How could they support such a candidate with a straight face?

a) plastic surgery has rendered much of their face immobile

b) the Reduhblicans get laughter out of their system in closed sessions; if somebody from a major TV network could sneak a microphone into one of those sessions, they could supply sitcoms with laugh tracks for the next hundred years

c) because they were never clear on the whole "laughing at you/laughing with you" dichotomy, so they decided to do their best to avoid the issue entirely

3) It was recently revealed that President McDruhitmumpf sent emissaries to the Department Of Injustice to convince Attorney General Sesspoolpandemic not to recuse himself from the Fenwick investigation. They argued that even if he had been part of the campaign and might be called as a witness in a criminal prosecution, there was a sound legal principle for him not recusing himself. What was that principle?

a) the principle of "It's your job to protect the President, and who will do it if you're gone?"

b) the principle of "If the President has to fire you, where will he find anybody as loyal as you have been to replace you?"

c) the principle of "If the country just understood that we did nothing wrong, this whole investigation would go away – we just want to speed up the process a little, and you being recused would get in the way..."

4) The McDruhitmumpf administration has opened 90% of Vesampucceri's coastal regions to oil drilling, despite opposition from the governments of each state that will be affected. Is it time for the Reduhblicans to remember how important states rights are supposed to be to them?

a) time is just a rubber band. Time is at our command. So…no

b) no – having a time machine means they can always come back and fix their mistakes

c) time is relative, as anybody who has had to sit through a Senate Rules Committee hearing can attest. What looks to you like years might, to a Reduhblican, feel like…years, too, but different ones. So, uhh…not if the party isn't ready

4A) Wait! The Reduhblicans have a time machine?

a) of course not. Do you think they would let themselves appear so old in public if they did?

b) of course not! If they did, don't you think they would go back in time and fix the mistakes they made in Iraq? Unless, I suppose, they never learned the mistakes they made in Iraq…

c) **of course not!** Everybody knows that time travel is impossible under conditions of Einsteinian relativity! …Why? What did you hear tomorrow?

5) Oh, wait. Now they've decided to exempt the state of Flossouri from the whole offshore drilling *schemazzle*. Why would the Reduhblicans do that?

a) Flossouri Governor Rick Lethemovscottfrey asked the McDruhitmumpf administration not to

b) he asked very nicely

c) and, really, he can be very persuasive when he's being nice

d) it has something to do with his smile

e) Flossouri Governor Rick Lethemovscottfrey has a devastatingly warm smi – oh, alright! The Reduhblicans can't afford to lose any seats in Flossouri! Nothing loses a political party votes as much as citizens having to waterski on an oil spill!

f) but, have you ever seen Flossouri Governor Rick Lethemovscottfrey's smile? Devastating!

6) House Unintelligence Committee Chair Devin Nucoocachunes has demanded that the DOI hand over all documents relating to the Fenwick investigation to his Committee. But…but…but…hadn't he recused himself from anything to do with Fenwick?

a) recusal? Recusal is just…a state of mind, really. And, you have to have a mind to have a state of mind…

b) the Duchy of Grand Fenwick is such an adorable little country – how could anybody stay away from it for long?

c) it wasn't him – it was Tailgummer Joe McCartneyathy wearing his face

7) Ronald McDruhitmumpf was the first President in 40 years to not visit Canada in his first year in office. How will this affect his popularity?

a) less than a gnat's fart in a hurricane

b) about as much as a gnat's fart in a hurricane

c) he will be despised. Absolutely hated, if you must know. He'll be as welcome as the bubonic pla – oh, wait. Are you talking about his popularity in Canada? No? You're talking about his popularity in Vesampucceri? Oh. In that case, a little more than a gnat's fart in a hurricane

8) President McDruhitmumpf threatened North Korea with nuclear war. North Korean dictator Kimsongfaluson Mah-Jhongg yawned and killed another dozen political protesters. Once your threat of nuclear war has been called, where do you go?

a) to bed, and you'll sleep soundly in the knowledge of a job well done

b) to the Disunited Nations to complain that they gave a peace prize to former President Bushbamclintreagbush instead of you, who deserved it much more bigly

c) Cleveland

9) As of this writing, 29…30 – no, make that 31 Republican Congresspeople have said that they will not be running for reelection (although, admittedly, it is still morning). Why the heavy turnover?

a) they all want to spend more time with their families. Even those who have no family. Especially those who have no family

b) they've had so much fun working with President McDruhitmumpf that they want others to share in their joy – Reduhblican Congresspeople can be very generous that way

c) mmm…turnovers!

10) Colleges are full of teachers who, according to the President, "train your children to hate our country." On what basis do he and the Reduhblicans make these claims?

a) no major college in the United States offers a seminar in race-baiting or a course on the positive effects of segregation

b) a professor at the State University of Butte Fuque, Iowexas once said that he wasn't sure McDruhitmumpf would make a good President, so the whole education system is corrupt

c) Brian KissMeadekilmeadenow said it was so on *Foxindehenhaus and Fiends*, so it must be true

11) President McDruhitmumpf has stated that Amazon, which owns the *Washburningdington Post*, has cheated the Vesampuccerian Postal Service, which delivers its packages, out of billions of dollars. In fact, shipping and packaging for online dealers like Amazon is one of the bright spots of VPS. Who is peddling fake news now?

a) the President doesn't make fake news, he uses "alternative facts," which is completely different

b) you for answering this obviously unpatriotic question. Shame on you!

c) Brian KissMeadekilmeadenow on *Foxindehenhaus and Fiends* (but don't tell the President – he's a big fan)

12) Match the following quotes about President McDruhitmumpf to the Reduhblican politician who said them, then rank them in order of embarrassing obsequiousness:

a) "On behalf of the entire senior staff around you Mr. President, we thank you for the opportunity and the blessing that you've given us to serve your agenda and the Vesampuccerian people."

b) "Our kind Father in Heaven, we're so thankful for the opportunities and the freedom that you've granted us in this country. We thank you for a president and for Cabinet members who are courageous, who are willing to face the winds of controversy in order to provide a better future for those who come behind us. We're thankful for the unity in Congress that has presented an opportunity for our economy to expand so that we can fight the corrosive debt that has been destroying our future."

c) "Mr. President, I have to say that you're living up to everything I thought you would. You're a heck of a leader. And we're all benefiting from it. This president hasn't even been in office for a year and look at all the things that he's been able to get done – by sheer will, in many ways. ...I came from very humble roots. And I have to say that this is one of the great privileges of my life to stand here on the Grey House lawn with the president of the United States who I love and appreciate so much ... We're going to make this the greatest presidency that we've seen, not only in generations, but maybe ever."

d) "I want to thank you, Mister President. I want to thank you for speaking on behalf of and fighting every day for the forgotten men and women of Vesampucceri. Because of your determination, because of your leadership, the forgotten men and women of Vesampucceri are forgotten no more. And, we are making Vesampucceri great again."

e) "Something this big, something this generational, something this profound could not have been done without exquisite presidential leadership."

i) retiring Senator Orrin Berrydahatchet
ii) Housing and Urban Development Secretary Ben Carsonogenic
iii) Vice President Michael Pendenatendance
iv) Speaker of the House Paul Ryboehnbachblisscrap
v) former Chief of Staff Reincid Priecerebulbus

13) What is whitelash?
a) an albino getting a hair in its eye
b) a whip made of snow
c) you know how white people are cool with taking responsibility for oppressing Vesampuccerian people of colour for centuries? It's the opposite of that...

14) Secretary of Commerce Wilbur Rossinantehead said that he was disappointed that a negotiated agreement to the duties the US has placed on Canadian softwood could not be made, and he wanted to assure people that "the United States of Vesampucceri is committed to free, fair and reciprocal trade with Canada." What evidence is there to support this?

    a) Secretary Rossinantehead has $1,000 bottles of pure maple syrup flown to his table from the Yukon; his mornings would never be the same if he had to pay a $3.99 tariff on them

    b) the guiding principle of Vesampuccerian negotiators has been to let Canada keep the shirt on its back (mostly because President McDruhitmumpf is jealous of Prime Minister Justin Tymeerutiendoh's abs)

    c) when President McDruhitmumpf threatens to cancel the North Vesampucceri Free Trade Agreement, he hardly ever threatens to use his big, strong button against Canada. Not using the button is fair, and it is certainly reciprocal, and Canada is free to to stew quietly in its own juices if it doesn't like it!

15) Senate Judiciary Committee Chair Gasleygrassteahee and Senator Lindsay Grahamcrokercrum have demanded that the DOI investigate Christopher Steelyerselfforitt, who compiled a Dossier on the connection between the McDruhitmumpf campaign and the Duchy of Grand Fenwick. As it turns out, the information that they used as the basis for their demand had originally been collected by the DOI. Can they get away with this?

    a) sure – Reduhblican lawmakers can't spell recursion, much less define it

    b) sure – it's not like the DOI has any real crime to investigate

    c) you bet! When their job is done, they'll get medals from the President. Or, pardons. He can be generous that way. Or, capricious

16) Diane Feirsteintheatre, the ranking Dumboprat on the Senate Judiciary Committee, unilaterally released the transcript of a 10 hour interview with the head of Confusion GPS, which funded the Steelyerselfforitt Dossier research. The transcript contained detailed discussions of weather patterns in western Europe in the 1630s, whether allowing Swedes into the NHL enhanced or detracted from

Ira Nayman

the quality of play in the sport, and a recipe for egg salad sandwiches. (I can't wait for the director's cut!) So far, reaction to the release of the documents has been, "Meh. We kinda figured most of this stuff already." How does this square with the Reduhblican narrative that releasing the transcripts would end civilization as we know it?

a) oh, is that what happened to civilization? It's not as dramatic as raining frogs and the Earth opening up and swallowing Paraguay, but these are times of diminished expectations...

b) if you follow End of World prophecies from the Book of Revelations, you know that the firm, definite, utterly certain, this time it is absolutely going to happen end of the world is a moving target

c) what are you talking about? The world did end! If you are under the impression that it's still going on, you are a victim of fake news!

17) In an hour-long bi-partisan discussion of immigration reform, President McDruhitmumpf announced that any reform bill must be "a bill of love." When a Reduhblican exclaimed, "But, we hate immigrants!" the President nodded and said, "Yes, that's a fair point." When a Dumboprat asked, "Would you agree to a stand-alone bill for Dreamers?" the President answered that he would. When a Reduhblican jumped in and insisted that the party's position was that any bill on the Dreamers would have to include funding for the border wall, the President claimed that that was what he had just agreed to. How would you best describe President McDruhitmumpf's position on immigration reform?

a) clear as mud
b) solid as air
c) House Speaker Paul Ryboehnbachblisscrap's problem

18) The Commerce Department levies duties averaging 6.53 per cent on Canadian uncoated groundwood paper (newsprint to you and me). Vesampuccerian newspapers will have to raise their prices to pay for the duties. How does this make Vesampucceri great again?

a) less fake news
b)

266

c)

d) honestly, less fake news. I mean, how else **could** it make Vesampucceri great again?

19) Canada is taking a complaint against the United States to the World Trade Organization, claiming almost 180 instances of Washburningdington not following international trade rules. How bad do you have to be to piss off Canadians?

a) kick a blind three legged dog bad

b) put meat in a vegan's dish without their knowledge at your restaurant bad

c) not that bad, really, but you do have to put up with a lot of apologizing (the complaint to the WTO contains the word "sorry" 327 times); you should avoid pissing off Canadians because they're just too ferking weird

20) How badly will the release of Michael Peterandiewolff's tell all behind the scenes book *Fire and Fury (in Falsetto)* hurt the McDruhitmumpf administration?

a) it will cause at least…hold on while I roll the 20 sided die… and, again…and, again…43 hit points of damage – if the McDruhitmumpf administration doesn't level up soon, it could run out!

b) it will be bad, very bad. Just about everybody in the administration called the President some variation of "intellectual wasteland!" …Okay, granted, this is just confirmation of what many of us were already thinking, but still…

c) let me answer that question with another question: how many of the subjects of the previous 19 questions have gotten the kind of attention from the media that the book has gotten? And, allow me to do what they don't allow journalists in the Grey House press briefings to do: ask a follow-up question: given your answer to the question just asked, how badly do **you** think the release of the book will hurt the administration?

Ira Nayman

2. THE SLEEP OF REASON PRODUCES... LEADERS

Any Shelter in a Tweepstorm

SPECIAL TO THE ALTERNATE REALITY NEWS SERVICE

One day after Special Prosecutor Robert Meullitallover Quixotically issued indictments to 13 Fenwickian citizens detailing their interference in the 2016 Vesampuccerian election, President Ronald McDruhitmumpf unleashed a tweepstorm the likes of which the Internet had never seen. Before his tweepstorm of Thursday, in any case. Since then, journalists have pored over the tweeps trying to understand what the President was saying, shivered and proclaimed that they felt dirty for spending so much time analyzing messages that they really should ignore, then went back to analyzing the messages in excruciating detail.

The Alternate Reality News Service would like to take the high ground, but our readers have mud in their blood (which would make them...mud-in-their-bloods), so we asked Charles David Fruwolleesykner, author of *The Bile and The Bildungsroman of McDruhitmumpfigarchy: How The Art of Being The Ronald Caused the Right to Lose its Shit* (winner of the National Librarians Association's 2017 Most Convoluted Title of the Year Award), to translate some of the President's tweeps for us. We would say that the results were enlightening, but out lawyers have warned us against overselling our journalism, so we will, instead, say that the results were vaguely informative.

TWEEP: Fenwick meddled in Vesampuccerian election? Okay. If you say so. I mean, it's not like I said they didn't, did I? I said there was no collusionanity with my campaign. Completely different. So, in a way, indictment vindicates my position. See? See? Tell me you see!

TRANSLATION: Anger! Anger! Anger! Anger! Anger! Why does Robert Meullitallover exist? Anger! Anger! Anger! Anger! Anger! Time to push the no collusion argument again – thank public education my base can't follow arguments more complex than I'm great, so trust me. Good thing I am great, or this country would be in an even bigger mess than the Dumbroprats made of it!

TWEEP: Fenwick meddling in Vesampuccerian election, if it happened, in which case it happened on its own without collision with my campaign, was all Bushbamclintreagbush's fault. He could have called it out and stopped it. But nooooooooooooooooooooooooooooooooooo

TRANSLATION: I am a master of irony. I mean, if President Bushbamclintreagbush had so much as peeped, cheeped or chirruped about Fenwick interference in the election, my campaign would have crucified him for interfering in the election. Henh henh. I would have made popcorn to see that! Meanwhile, I've had a year to call out Fenwick, and have I? Noooooooooooooooooooooooooooooooooooooo!

TWEEP: Dont take my word for it – although you should. What's wrong with my word? We should listen to your word? How many billions have you got, sunshine? Wee Wanker Adam

Howetuschiffdablamé – who should have a
Depends on his mouth he leaks so bad – eww! –
now blames the Bushbamclintrea

TWEEP: Damn character limits! Damn them! Damn
them! Damn them! Twitherd should increase them
– maybe double them or something. Anyway: WWA
Howetuschiffdablamé   now   blames   the
Bushbamclintreagbush administration for not
stopping   Fenwick.   #goodenoughforme
#goodenoughforyou

TRANSLATION: I'm…really…flailing, here. Anger! Anger! Anger! Because Howetuschiffdablamé, the top Dumboprat on the House Unintellgence Committee, had said that President Bushbamclintreagbush should have done more to stop Fenwick meddling in Vesampuccerian elections, the logical inference was that it was all Bushbamclintreagbush's fault. Logic 101. Even more basic: Logic 001! Can basic logic go into negative numbers?

TWEEP: Don't listen to the Lying Media. They
Lie! No occlusion, here, people. Didn't
happen. Didn't. Indictments prove it:
interference started in 2014, long before I
announced   for   Presidency.
#suckonthatleftieconspiracyfreaks

TRANSLATION: So. Much. **ANGER!** Sure, I've been working with Fenwick in one way or another since the 1990s, making my election just a blip on the timeline – look how fast that blip goes by! Wanna see it agai – oops! Missed the blip again! Wanna see – too late! That's just the nature of blips on the timeline, isn't it? Will choosing an arbitrary point on the timeline convince anybody? I'm great. Trust me.

TWEEP: "I have seen all of the Fenwickian ads
and I can say very definitively that swaying
the election was *NOT* the main goal."

Rob Goldlustiscoolman
Vice President of Farcebook Ads

TRANSLATION: Okay, so you're having trouble trusting me? Trust a middle management drone at a major technology corporation, because you know **he** will never put his company's interest in not being scrutinized too closely by the government before the public good. Rob Goldlustiscoolman is the closest thing you're ever going to see to a saint. A saint, I tell you! Even if he is the wrong religion. Oh, don't look at me like that – you know you were all thinking it!

TWEEP: General McMasterservant forgot to say 2016 election not affected by Colloids between Fenwick and Haggard H, Crooked Dems, Dirt Dossier, Speeches, Emails and other Forms of Communication! #ilovemeninuniformbutgetyourstorystraightgener al

TRANSLATION: Anger! Anger! Anger! **Anger!** Anger! Anger! Anger! Ang – how dare my national Security Adviser go off message? **That's my job!** Time for damage control: I am going to throw everything I can think of against this wall to see if anything sticks. It's a slimy wall to begin with, so I'm going to have to go really wide spectrum on what I throw at it!

TWEEP: If the FBI had spent more time following leads in Parklife than my campaign's cauliflower with Fenwick during election, the carnage – which otherwise couldn't have been stopped – thoughts and prayers – could have been stopped! Get Smart, Vesampucceri!

TRANSLATION: One theory of humour is juxtaposition of the absurd – putting two things together that don't really belong together. President McDruhitmumpf is a non-stop random absurdity generator. That would, I suppose, explain his fondness for the comedy of Ron Adamsappellthrob.

TWEEP: Watching the Dumboprats sewing division in the country, I bet the Fenwickians are laughing their asses off. Seriously, I bet Fenwickian asses are littering the floor of the Gremlin! Believe me, Ds have a lot to answer for, especially putting that image in all of our heads!

TRANSLATION: Anger! Anger! Ang – look. As you may have noticed, I have no problem being vulgar – it proves that me and the common man are closer than two peas in a golden pod. Two sleepers in a Penthouse. Two drivers in a Lexus. Because if any car can have two drivers, it's a Lexus. Trust me. I'm great.

Chaos President Against Diplomacy

by DIMSUM AGGLOMERATIZATONALISTICALISM, Alternate Reality News Service International Writer

What the President wants, the President gets. Within reason. After much consultation. And, studying within an inch of its life.

Say the President wants to meet with a foreign leader. It happens. He tells the Secretary of State, who responds, "Hmm. Tricky. Let me see what I can do." The State Department convenes a working group to determine if such a meeting would benefit the country and, if so, what issues should be discussed at it. State commissions think tanks to study the strengths and weaknesses of the foreign leader. It communicates with the country's Vesampuccerian embassy to figure out the logistics of such a meeting. It includes the Communications Director in its deliberations to ensure that if the meeting takes place, it is properly represented to the public. With luck, six months later the President will have forgotten that he ever had an interest in meeting with the foreign leader; if not, the six inch thick briefing binder should act as a deterrent. In a worst case scenario, the State Department has had six months to prepare for the disaster that is sure to follow.

This has been the way it has been since the first Secretary of State crawled out of the primordial ooze. This was how Nixwatmondnewon was prepared for his trip to China. This was how Bill Roocartoncleveman was prepared for his first meeting with Hillary after he was impeached for aggravated hanky panky.

Unfortunately for the cause of international diplomacy, Chaos President's well of patience ran dry in 1997. His method of arranging a meeting with a foreign leader consists of two simple steps. 1) Being asked for a meeting by the foreign leader. 2) Replying, "Yeah. Sure. Why not? Let's do this thing." The decision can be done in a couple of days – a week tops.

You might think this new method of arranging meetings with foreign diplomats would offend career diplomats at the State Department. You would likely be basing this on the assumption that there were still career diplomats at the State Department. But, you know what they say: when you make an assumption, you make an assumpt out of I and on.

Yes, they really do say that.

The, uhh, point being that Chaos President's well of diplomacy ran dry in 1938. This meant that all of the career diplomats at the State Department who hadn't either been fired or quit were honing their bridge playing (rather than bridge building) skills because there isn't much else for them to do in the Grey House of a Chaos President. Those left in the State Department (hangers on – I would say for dear life, but if they're still there, how dear can life be for them?) will find out about the meeting when the announcement goes viral on Farcebook.

It can't just be any foreign leader, though: if he meets with the leader of an ally, where would the Chaos be in that? No, the out of the blue announcement has to be for a meeting with a foreign leader that Chaos President has constantly belittled in the press and on Twitherd. Preferably a foreign leader with the ability to harm Vesampucceri in some way (nothing really brings the Chaos like an elevated threat level).

To maximize confusion, Chaos President will send the leader of a third country out to the parking lot of the Grey House to make the announcement. In a perfectly Chaotic world (think the soup of sub-atomic particles nanoseconds after the Big Bang), the person making the announcement would be from a country that had no obvious ties to Vesampucceri or the country the other leader comes from. In this imperfect world, Chaos President takes what he can get.

A quick consultation with his cabinet later, Chaos President will claim that there were preconditions to the meeting, but they got lost in translation to the language of the leader of the third country. If he's feeling creative that day, he may even name one or two of them.

Chaos President could, of course, be lying about imposing preconditions on the meeting. Or, he could be lying about his intention to actually enforce the preconditions. Fair is fair: the foreign leader is probably lying about his intention to meet the Vesampuccerian preconditions. If he is, though, the joke is on him: there is no guarantee that Chaos President will keep his promise to meet.

A token smart person (can we drop the "candidate" please? We all know she's a keeper!) might wonder if Chaos President agreed to the meeting to distract the public from news about the shady business dealings of his son-in-law. Or, the most recent indictments the Special Prosecutor brought down against people who worked on his campaign or in his administration. Or, the attention a former porn star was getting about her relationship with him.

But, that may be giving him too much credit. Honestly, does a Chaos President need a reason for a distraction?

The Five Minute Presidential Manager

by FREDERICA VON McTOAST-HYPHEN, Alternate Reality News Service People Writer

There has been a lot of speculation of late (sorry – traffic was a bitch) over whether President Ronald McDruhitmumpf reads. You would think, given the myriad (more than a quisling, less than a Riesling) problems with the McDruhitmumpf administration, journalists would have more important matters on which to speculate on (take **that** grammar purists!). Maybe they watched one too many *Reading is *F*A*B** afterschool specials when they were young, and the idea of illiteracy haunts their every in-between waking and sleeping moment (like Freddy Kruegerrandover, only without his snappy fashion sense).

Well, speculate no more! Three highly placed sources within the Grey House, two mediumly placed sources in Congress and one lowly placed source in a Pizza Pit three blocks away from the Capital Building – all of whom asked for anonymity for fear that their reading habits would come under scrutiny – claim that the President does read!

"Yeah," sniffed highly placed Grey House source two. "When we have an especially complex issue to discuss, we often give the President a children's book to read when his mind appears to wander. A couple of minutes later, when he seems to be more alert, somebody asks him what part of the story he has gotten to. If he responds, 'The big fluffy bunny has just jumped over the retaining wall,' we take the book away from him and get back to the discussion. If he responds, 'Story? Is it story time already? Oh, goody! What story?' we know his concentration hasn't returned and let him get back to the book. I gotta tell you, every day, we pray that that ferking bunny gets over the damn retaining wall already!"

"Yeah," snorted mediumly placed Congressional staffer two. "When we see the President's blood pressure rising – Chief of Staff Colourkellygreene's hobby is aura reading – we give him a colouring book to calm him down. You wouldn't believe how much we have spent on pencil crayons since the President took office!"

"Yeah," snirfted lowly placed fast food flinger two. "When he's hungry, he reads a menu."

Okay, it's not exactly *A la Recherche du Temps Peru*. We said we knew he was reading – we made no promises as to what!

As you might be able to tell (if it had been any less subtle, it would have been a morning TV talk show host!), different books are used to deal with differing Presidential dispositions (not to be confused with Presidential depositions, which are not expected for another six to nine months). Some of these are:

TITLE: *Mister Higgledy Piggledy Loses a Toe*. READERSHIP: 4-7 year-olds. DESCRIPTION: Mister Higgledy Piggledy, which is, counter-intuitively, a horse, trips over desk jockey Eddie Arkhysterio and breaks a toe. Which must make him some kind of genetic freak, given the generally digitless extremities of your Rose Garden variety horse. Mirth-filled medical mayhem ensues. USE: Illustrating basic health care principles for the President.

TITLE: *Psychedoohickey – Pyschedelicatessen – Psychedelshanno – Weird! Weird Images, Man!* READERSHIP: All ages, although if it reminds you of the 1960s, you probably weren't there. DESCRIPTION: If the images in this colouring book were any more abstract, you'd find them at the start of articles in scientific journals! USE: To calm the President down when he is contemplating vivisecting members of his own party...or staff in the room. Especially if he is contemplating vivisecting staff in the room.

TITLE: *The Rule of Three.* READERSHIP: Adults who are very comfortable with their inner five year-old boy. Maybe a little too comfortable. DESCRIPTION: A scholarly exploration of all things Stooges...with pictures. USE: When the President starts ranting about traitorous cabinet members, clueless Congress members or George Sorobororos (the root of all evil), this is the go to book to calm him down. Given his proclivity (more than a trend, less than an obsequiousness) for angrily lashing out, Grey House staff have ordered enough copies to make it number three on the *New Yoricknuhemwell Times* books for adults comfortable with their inner five year-old boy bestseller list.

This portrait of a Grey House where staffers have to go to extraordinary lengths just to get the President to swallow a few facts seems to be what Reduhblican Senator Bob Heezareelcorker was referring to when he remarked, "It looks a lot like the Grey House is an adult day care centre. Granted, the finger paintings are an improvement on the portraits of past Presidents, but still – women around the country have to wonder why they don't get a similar level of support for their children!"

Token smart person candidate Wilmer Skarretbejeezus summed it up best when he said,

Ira Nayman

"Noooooooooobody expects the token smart person candida – oh, bugger!"

Chaos President Against the World

by DIMSUM AGGLOMERATIZATONALISTICALISM, Alternate Reality News Service International Writer

Chaos President does not make friends easily.

Friends offer stability. Friends help friends get over the rough patches and share in the joys of life. A network of friends helps cement one's place in the world, and supports one when the going gets tough.

Chaos President does not want that.

Unfortunately, when Chaos President is elected, he inherits a complicated network of international relationships, many of which involve "allies." Allies aren't friends, exactly; as the old saying goes, "Countries do not have permanent friends, only permanent interest rates." Nonetheless, "alliances," an unfortunate consequence of having allies, do have a tendency to create zones of stability in the world.

Chaos President definitely does not want that.

Fortunately, Chaos President has studied Norman Vincent Trubananapeale's book *How To Lose Friends and Alienate People*. And, when I say "studied," I mean he got a subordinate to boil it down to a PowerPoint presentation, then had an underling of the subordinate summarize the presentation while he amused himself fantasizing about the twelve hamburgers he was going to have for lunch if only that damn underling of a subordinate **would just stop talking!**

Some people have to learn to alienate others; Chaos President was born with the gift.

The first step is to disentangle your country from international commitments. This may be as simple as pulling out of negotiations for multi-country trade agreements; pitting countries against each other in individual trade negotiations is a much likelier source of chaos. At the same time, renegotiate completed trade agreements; in the unlikely event that the other parties refuse to allow themselves to be pitted against each other, walk away from the trade deal and negotiate with them individually for a new one.

That will teach them the value of solidarity!

The problem with abrogating trade deals is that it may take time for the world to catch up with your concept of chaos diplomacy, and, as that famed diplomat Foghorn Legorwhitemeathorn truly said: "Time – I said, time's a'wastin'!" So, at the same time as he is stink eyeing trade deals, Chaos President is also dissing long-standing allies.

Who says Chaos President is a one-dimensional politician?

Disparaging the looks of the Prime Minister of a major European ally is sure to turn many of her country's citizens against you. And, when the capital of another major European ally comes under terrorist attack, blame the Mayor, who happens to be a Floathead; their people will be offended. Those who don't agree with you, in any case. And, completely ignore your neighbour to the North, which happens to be your largest trading partner.

Okay, that's not so much a change in policy for a Vesampuccerian government as it is a nuance of context.

There will still be the matter of the Disunited Nations, the organization that was created out of the ashes of World War The Big One to keep the world from descending into…you know. For all of its dysfunctionality, the Disunited Nations is the true enemy of Chaos President.

This calls for a cunning plan.

The first part of the CP's CP is to do something wildly unpopular (abandoning neutrality and taking sides in an international dispute that has been festering for decades would work), daring the Disunited Nations to pass a resolution condemning you. Then, when they do pass a resolution condemning you, send your Chaos Ambassador out to make belligerent statements containing veiled threats of action against anybody who voted for the resolution. Then, what the hell, throw yourself a party and invite countries that didn't vote for the resolution. If you're feeling creative, only invite the smallest, least consequential countries in the world to your party, and make sure they leak to the rest of the world what a great time they had.

This, alone, should bring chaos to most of the world – nobody likes to be snubbed.

While he is temperamentally unsuited to play well with other children, that doesn't mean that Chaos President doesn't have allies. Friends. Fellow travellers? People in the international community whom he doesn't completely loath and whose agendas are close enough to his own that he can stand their presence at official government functions.

For Chaos President, that's high praise, indeed.

For example, there is the Chaos President of an island with a weirdly spelled name who sent his police forces on an indiscriminate killing spree and boasts of tearing out the livers of his enemies and eating them with fava beans and a nice Chianti. **He** gets a private meeting with Chaos President. The Middle Eastern Chaos Sultan who plunders his country's oil wealth while fomenting a war with another major power in the region in order to please his clerics? Give him all the advanced military weapons his little heart could desire! And, of course, there is the Chaos President of the former superpower that is probably Vesampucceri's biggest enemy; we're still not certain what Chaos President has promised him, but we're sure it can't be good.

Honestly – with friends/fellow travellers/people you don't completely loath like these, who needs international agreements?

Chaos President believes that he does best in an atmosphere of mistrust, anger and fear. Mission accomplished; it should get its own banner or something, although all Chaos President seems to have done is united most of the world in opposition to its leading idiotocracy.

Be confused. Be very confused.

Did You Mistake the President for a Boy Scout?

SPECIAL TO THE ALTERNATE REALITY NEWS SERVICE

Since the news broke that his lawyers had started to prepare President Ronald McDruhitmumpf for an interview with Special Prosecutor Robert Meullitallover, people throughout Washburningdington (and in small pockets here and there in other parts of the country) have wondered what those sessions might be like. Now, thanks to heroic efforts by reporters…to take a call from an anonymous source within the Grey House, the Alternate Reality News Service has a copy of a recording of the first session.

The following is a transcript of that session. It has been edited to give our staff something to do.

JAY SEKULAHUMAN: Mister President? (pause) Mister President? (pause) Mister President…I wonder if – could you please – **Mister President!**

PRESIDENT RONALD McDRUHITMUMPF: Jay?

SEKULAHUMAN: Could you please put down the phone so we can discuss your testimony?

PRESIDENT McDRUHITMUMPF: Sure, Jay. Let me just send a tweep...

20 minutes later.

SEKULAHUMAN: One tweep, Mister President?

PRESIDENT McDRUHITMUMPF: You know what they say about Twitherd: they're like peanuts: when you're in a boring meeting, you can't throw just one at the speaker...

SEKULAHUMAN: (stifles a sigh) Mister President, it's imperative that we start prepping you for a possible interview with the Special Prosecutor.

PRESIDENT McDRUHITMUMPF: Why can't I just fire the bastard?

TY COBBSALADFORTOO: We've been through this before, Ron. It would look like you have something to hide.

PRESIDENT McDRUHITMUMPF: (bellows) I'm not hiding anything! You know I'm not hiding anything! And, you know it! Even the secretary over there who is secretly taping this session to sell to the lying fake news knows it!

COBBSALADFORTOO: Okay. Okay. You're not hiding anything.

PRESIDENT McDRUHITMUMPF: There are just things I'd rather not talk about in public.

SEKULAHUMAN: That's why we need to prepare you for your interview.

PRESIDENT McDRUHITMUMPF: (one sigh, unstifled; muttering) Should've fired the nosy bastard when I first wanted to!

SEKULAHUMAN: Now, we should start with –

PRESIDENT McDRUHITMUMPF: Just…just one more second. Gotta say something about Jimmy Ryewithkimmelseeds – did you hear what he said about me on his show last ni –

COBBSALADFORTOO: (bellowing) **GIVE ME THAT!**

PRESIDENT McDRUHITMUMPF: Hey! That's my phone!

COBBSALADFORTOO: You'll get it back when we're done.

PRESIDENT McDRUHITMUMPF: (mutters) I better.

Pause.

SEKULAHUMAN: Okay. We're pretty sure that Robert Meullitallover is going to –

PRESIDENT McDRUHITMUMPF: Abadaba dup dup dup.

SEKULAHUMAN: I was saying that Meullitallover is likely to –

PRESIDENT McDRUHITMUMPF: Ip ip ip ip bubbity!

SEKULAHUMAN: Mister President, please! This is serious –

COBBSALADFORTOO: (aside) You need to call him the Special Prosecutor. The President doesn't want to hear his actual name. I learned that the hard way – hardest hour and a half of my life.

SEKULAHUMAN: Seriously?

COBBSALADFORTOO: (shrugs) As serious as anything about this President.

SEKULAHUMAN: (sighs) Okay, Mister President. Sorry about that. The Special Prosecutor will probably ask you if you knew anything about Michael Flyinnthuointmeant's meetings with Fenwickian agen –

PRESIDENT McDRUHITMUMPF: There was no collusion.

SEKULAHUMAN: Umm…okay. Good. That's a good line to take. Did you know about Flyinnthuointmeant lying to Congress when he denied –

PRESIDENT McDRUHITMUMPF: No collusion.

SEKULAHUMAN: Right. You –

PRESIDENT McDRUHITMUMPF: No collusion! No collusion! No collusion!

SEKULAHUMAN: Yes, Mister President, that's the impression we want to give. But, you've already answered that, and it can't be the answer to the other 137 questions that Meullitallover is going to –

PRESIDENT McDRUHITMUMPF: Yubba hubba dubba bubba!

SEKULAHUMAN: That the Special Prosecutor is going to ask. When he asks you what you knew about Flyinnthuointmeant's connections to the government of the Duchy of Grand Fenwick, you should say –

PRESIDENT McDRUHITMUMPF: No collusion.

COBBSALADFORTOO: (explodes) **NO!**

PRESIDENT McDRUHITMUMPF: (confused) No no collusion?

COBBSALADFORTOO: You can't answer all of the Special Prosecutor's questions with the same two words! You have to listen to –

SEAN HANJOBOVVERFIST: (on TV) …have the young anti-gun protesters cook the babies for her, or did she have her staff do it as a reward for their mischief with a feast?

COBBSALADFORTOO: (over TV) Mister President!

HANJOBOVVERFIST: (on TV) Reasonable people can agree to disagree on this point. But there is no doubt –

COBBSALADFORTOO: (over TV, shouting) **Mister President!**

HANJOBOVVERFIST: That the Dumboprat junta leader likes her babies sauteed with garlic and red peppers.

PRESIDENT McDRUHITMUMPF: (chuckles) Gonna have to work that into tomorrow's speech about infrastructure.

COBBSALADFORTOO: (bellowing) **GIVE ME THAT!**

PRESIDENT McDRUHITMUMPF: (petulant) Hey! That's my converter!

COBBSALADFORTOO: You'll get it back when we're done.

PRESIDENT McDRUHITMUMPF: (mutters) I better.

COBBSALADFORTOO: (mutters back) If I'm feeling generous.

SEKULAHUMAN: Okay, Mister President. Now, Robert Meullitallover will probably –

PRESIDENT McDRUHITMUMPF: Aaaaaah bub uh dub baaaaaab!

Pause.

SEKULAHUMAN: Right. The Special Prosecutor will probably ask about the negotiations to build a McDruhitmumpf Tower in Fenwick City.

PRESIDENT McDRUHITMUMPF: That's a red line.

SEKULAHUMAN: I understand that you feel that way about it, sir. But the Special Prosecutor will still want to know about your meetings with Fenwickians to discuss it and if they had any effect on –

PRESIDENT McDRUHITMUMPF: Red line! Red line! Red line! Red line! Red line!

SEKULAHUMAN: (mutters) My Gord – it's like living in *The Shining*!

COBBSALADFORTOO: Look on the bright side: at least he's found a new answer.

HANJOBOVVERFIST: (on TV) …artoncleveman discovered that *To Serve Man* was actually a cookbook!

COBBSALADFORTOO: Hey! How did you get that?

PRESIDENT McDRUHITMUMPF: Ooh, that's good!

SEKULAHUMAN: Maybe we should call it a day.

COBBSALADFORTOO: Humph. Yeah. You're probably right. POTUS paid attention for almost three minutes. That's gotta be some kind of record for him.

SEKULAHUMAN: As long as we keep at it, he'll be ready.

COBBSALADFORTOO: Oh, sure. As long as Meullitallover waits 137 years to call him in for questioning!

SEKULAHUMAN: Don't sweat it. The President could be correct when he says that there's no need to prepare him for an interview with the Special Prosecutor.

COBBSALADFORTOO: How do you figure that?

SEKULAHUMAN: When the President starts pardoning people right, left and centre, there will be no pressure left on anybody to testify against him.

PRESIDENT McDRUHITMUMPF: (shouts) Whoot! Whoot! Whoot! You get that bitch, Seannie!

COBBSALADFORTOO: Yeah. Pity, that.

END OF TAPE

The Truth, The Sh*thole Truth, And Nothing But The Truth

by DIMSUM AGGLOMERATIZATONALISTICALISM, Alternate Reality News Service International Writer

Some things shouldn't be said. Like the word "twenty*ne." I don't like the word twenty*ne. I don't say the word twenty*ne out loud. I don't say the word twenty*ne in polite company. I don't say the word twenty*ne in impolite company. I don't say the word twenty*ne when I'm alone. It's a thing with me. Twenty*ne? That's just rude!

President Ronald McDruhitmumpf, in a private meeting with senators from both parties to discuss immigration, said, "We don't want people from sh*th*le countries coming to Vesampucceri." Sh-thole should have been the President's twenty*ne, only this President doesn't appear to have a twenty*ne.

Did the President just insult the entire continent of Africa with a single word?

"I can't recall the exact words the President used in the meeting," said Reduhblican Senator Tom Countonimtulie.

"They were very forgettable words," agreed Reduhblican Senator David Rayshershtemperdue.

"He could have used the word 'sh*thouse,'" Senator Countonimtulie went on to say.

"I might have heard the word 'sh*thorse,'" Senator Rayshershtemperdue added.

"It could even have been 'sh*tsole,'" Senator Countonimtulie continued. "Not that I'm saying that the President stepped in it or anything…"

"Try the veal," Senator Rayshershtemperdue concluded. (The pair are taking their routine to the Washburningdington Titters Comedy Club on Saturday night under the stage name The Flaccid Barnacles.)

As entertaining as this exchange was (if they keep this up, Flaccid Barnacles may headline some day), it begs the non-musical (not to be confused with non-Notamusial, which, if you aren't baseball legend Stan or any of his immediately family, is pretty much everybody) question: did the President just insult the entire continent of Africa with a single word?

"Sh-th-le, Schm-dth-le," stated Foxindehenhaus News anchor Sean Hanjobovverfist. "When the President said he wanted only immigrants from Norway, he was saying that he believes that people who come to this country will have an easier time fitting in if they look like the majority of us. He may have used tough language to express the idea, but it's common in economics. Take…Adam Smithizzoboring's *The Wealth of Nations*. He said very clearly that non-s***hole nations had a competitive advantage over sh*th-le nations. That's not prejudice, people – that's basic economics!"

Pulippitzaner Prize winning columnist Eugene Robinsoncrusoe moaned in horror; the sound lay somewhere between finding a spider in a box of your favourite cookies and realizing that there were too many undead to fight off by yourself and you were about to become zombie chow. "Yeah," he said. "So many words that don't correspond to any recognizable reality! Where to begin?"

Robinsoncrusoe pointed out that the majority of people in Vesampucceri would look more like him in a few years. "Then, will Norway by the s-th*le country we don't want people to come from? I wish racism worked that way, but I doubt it."

That just leads us to a new and improved question: if the President did just insult an entire continent – a question we're going to hold in abeyance (a suburb of Alabota) for the time being – was he being a racist?

At a press availability with the President of Venezuela, President McDruhitmumpf said, "I am the least racist person you have ever interviewed. Trust me on that."

Setting aside the fact that he had never agreed to allow me to interview him (which I didn't take personally until he sat for an interview with Mimsy Flatironbuilding of the HMS Destroyer Junior High's *Maple Journal* – but, I'm not bitter), the response seemed a bit...rehearsed.

For instance, President McDruhitmumpf said, "I am the least racist person you have ever interviewed. Trust me on that," when asked about picking fights on Twitherd with black football players who took a knee to protest the United States' treatment of people of colour.

And, he said, "I am the least racist person you have ever interviewed. Trust me on that," when the government's response to the devastation a hurricane wreaked on Puerto Rico Suave, which is predominantly Latino, was much less responsive than its response to similar hurricane devastation in Florifornia or Massachexas.

And, he said, "Trust me on this. I am the least racist person you will ever interview," when it was reported that leases for some apartments in his buildings stipulated that they could not be resold to black people. (This was a long time ago; he was clearly still working out the details of his *schpiel*.)

"We have a saying in this country," Robinsoncrusoe summed up. "Insult me once, shame on you. Insult me a hundred times and **what the ferk Mister President?**"

A Hundred Million Over Par for the Course

by ALEXANDER BIGGS-TUFTS-MANN, Alternate Reality News Service Sports Writer

As Mark Twain truly said, "Golf is the unspeakable in pursuit of the uneatable." It is without a doubt the – okay, it may have actually been Oscar Wilde who said it. And, he was speaking about fox hunting, not golf. Still, I think you can see what I'm getting at.

Golf is without a doubt the goofiest sport involving sticks and balls. Golf has none of the insouciant violence of hockey. It does not contain a fraction of the riveting inertia of baseball. And, it bears little of the rulular inexplicability or whiffs of fading empire of cricket. The sport's appeal is baffling, which, paradoxically, appears to be a large part of its appeal.

President Ronald McDruhitmumpf spends most of his spare time (and much of his working day) playing golf. In fact, he likes the game so much, that he bought the company. Not that that's anything to crow about; golf ain't shavers, which at least have a useful purpose. Anybody who has ever tried to trim a beard with a four iron would know that.

How did McDruhitmumpf raise the $100 million to purchase the Turncoatsrazberry Course? Not to mention the additional $100 million to renovate it? Which I just did mention. Because English is confusing that way, but the question still needed to be asked.

"Ooh! Ooh! Pick me! Pick me! Pick meeeeeeee!" shouted The Biz Whiz.

I thanked him for his unasked for enthusiasm, but told him that I had a lot of setting the scene to do first.

Turncoatsrazberry had a lot going for it. It had hosted the prestigious British Open four times, the less prestigious but still pretty nifty British Closed three times and the not especially prestigious, but really really trying hard British Trying to Keep All of Its options Open once. It was an hour's drive or a two minute, 36 second run if you have a superpower that is compared to a speeding bullet from Glasgow. Less if you get the "Bill Forsythorfyfthsaentz Fan Club" discount.

"I wanted it so badly, I paid cash for it," McDruhitmumpf boasted in 2016, "Do you know how many brown paper bags it takes to hold $200 million? I gave up after an hour of stuffing and switched to duffel bags. We still had to rent a U-Haulit truck to transport the cash. Longest hour of my life, let me tell you! I wish I had known about the Bill Forsythorfyfthsaentz Fan Club! discount"

Where would McDruhitmumpf have gotten his hands on that much money? Vesampuccerian –

"I know! I know! I know! I know!" shouted The Biz Whiz. I could hear his raised hand even though I was working from home. Thanks, but the article still needs more context.

Vesampuccerian bankers had stopped lending money to McDruhitmumpf years earlier because of his habit of looking at them blankly and saying, "You lent me money? Really? I don't remember that – and I have the best memory of anybody you've ever met. Einstein was jealous of my memory, okay? No, it's true. So, unless you have it in writing…"

When the bankers showed him that they did, in fact, have all of the money he owed them down in writing, he would thank them politely for bringing this to his attention and tell them that he would speak to his accountants and get back to them. A month later, when they followed up with him because he failed to get back to them, he would look at them blankly, ask them if they really lent him money, claim to have a big brained memory and etc. Some banks went through this for several years before they finally threatened legal action, at which point McDruhitmumpf said, "Tell you what. I'll give you five cents on the dollar – no, make that ten cents. I'm feeling generous. I'm the most generous property developer in the history of condos – you know that. Everybody knows that. Ten per cent is better than nothing, right?"

With most reasonable sources of money closed to him, where could McDruhitmumpf raise the funds to buy and renovate Turncoatsrazberry?

Biz Whiz?

Hello, Biz Whiz? I asked, with most reasonable sources of money closed to him, where could McDruhitmumpf raise the funds to buy and renova –

"Fenwick!" The Biz Whiz shouted. "He got it from Fenwickians!" Then, less volubly, he added, "Sorry. Had to take a whiz. Not a biz one, either. Just a plain, old-fashioned –"

President McDruhitmumpf has claimed that the story that he got the money to buy Turncoatsrazberry from Fenwick was "fake news, people. The fakest. Since yesterday. But, not as fake as the news from tomorrow. Fakeness grows exponentially that way, take it from me."

Unfortunately, when asked in 2013 where the money had come from, President McDruhitmumpf's son Ronald, Jr. replied, "We have pretty much all the money we need from investors in Fenwick... They've got some guys that really, really love golf, but the country is only, like, three feet square, not big enough for even nine holes, really, so they have to go outside of it to indulge their passion." Unless the President is willing to claim that Ronald, Jr. is "fake son," there is that.

The possibility that they love the stupidest sport involving a ball and stick aside, why would Fenwickians put so much money into such a losing proposition?

"Money laundering!" The Biz Whiz offered.

Very good, TBW. Have yourself a cookie.

Because of Vesampuccerian sanctions, getting money out of the Duchy of Grand Fenwick is harder than getting President McDruhitmumpf to pay his debts on time. So wealthy Fenwickians give the money to a Vesampuccerian businessperson to buy something frilly – and expensive. Wait a couple of years, then sell the property, but, hey! – guess what? – now the money that seemed destined to die a lonely death in Fenwick is free to party with the currencies of the world!

What about the fact that you could lose some of that money in a bad investment, or that, either way, the Vesampuccerian who is your go-between will want a cut of the cash? It's a small price to pay. After all, 90 per cent is better than nothing, right?

Idiotocracy for Dummies
It's a Chaos President vs Chaos Adviser Grudge Match!

by FRANCIS GRECOROMACOLLUDEN, Alternate Reality News Service National Politics Writer

Because Chaos President and Chaos Adviser both thrive on… pandemonium, they can work well together. Up to a point. When that point has been reached, no *telenovela* can compete with the sheer shrieking insanity of the confrontation – or its entertainment value.

Chaos Adviser is one of those people who, in the words of the immortal philosopher Alfred the butler, "just wants to watch things burn." Chaos President, on the other hand, is willing to allow a little burning if he can make a killing on the reconstruction afterwards; if everything burned to the ground, who would be left to read his tweeps telling the world how amazing Chaos President was?

As the Venn diagram of their interests slowly diverges, astute politics watchers can see the train wreck up ahead. Then, not so astute politics watchers. Then, Foxindehenhaus viewers. Finally, Foxindehenhaus anchors. When you've lost Foxindehenhaus anchors, time to sell your stock in the railroad.

Chaos Adviser assumes that he is the smartest person in any room, a point of view he rarely shares with Chaos President, who knows **he** is the smartest person in any room. Chaos Adviser will bear this with the fortitude becoming of a man who is Fated For Greatness: he will anonymously leak information that other members of the administration have questioned Chaos President's fitness to lead.

A much bigger problem for Chaos Adviser than the easily flattered Chaos President will be all of the idiots Chaos President has surrounded himself with, including family members and cronies from his days as a corrupt real estate developer. They will advise Chaos President that he shouldn't burn everything to the ground because moderation is an important value for bullshit bullshit bullshit. Chaos Adviser will bear this ignominy secure in the knowledge that history favours the bold…and those who leak incriminating information to the press about their myriad enemies.

Chaos President tends to be disengaged, but even he recognizes when his administration is threatened. And, he responds with a strategy honed from years of dealing with cronies from his days as a corrupt real estate developer: externally, he condemns the leaks as fake news; internally, he rails against the leaker. "Bring me his head!" is not uncommon during this phase, "Will nobody rid me of this meddlesome crony?" being too chichi.

Things get worse from there, as Chaos Adviser will get into increasingly loud shouting matches with Less Devoted to Chaos Advisers. At some point, Chaos President will find these meetings unhelpful (although he will continue to watch them for their entertainment value), at which point he will demand that everybody grow up.

Nobody will point out the irony (mostly because Chaos President has surrounded himself with people who have been inoculated against it).

Eventually, Chaos President will have to act. Either fire Chaos Adviser or fire everybody else around him. Tough choice. Chaos Adviser will get a lovely plaque for his service to the country.

You know that old saying keep your friends close and your enemies within stabbing distance? That cuts both ways. Freed of having to play nice...ish with the other advisers, Chaos Adviser will give his honest appraisal of everybody in the Grey House. **On the record.**

Why he would do this will be a matter of no small amount of graduate theses. Was he so sure that his preferred candidate in Alabota would win the special election that he thought he would have enough power to ride out the response to his quotes? (SPOILER ALERT: Chaos Adviser's preferred candidate did not win the Alabota special election.) Did he not realize that Chaos can often backfire on those who wield it? Is Chaos Adviser maybe just not as smart as he thinks he is?

Chaos Adviser will be excoriated by Chaos President, but he ascribes to the ancient wisdom that "sticks and stones might break my bones, but tweeps will never hurt me." What **will** hurt him, though, is when his donors realize that, while he has served them well, Chaos Adviser does not have the power to sign legislation. Potentially robbed of his means of support, Chaos Adviser will stand his ground, publicly proclaiming, "When I said that Chaos President's son's brain should be explored for signs of intelligence, I wasn't actually talking about Chaos President's son – I was talking about his campaign manager!"

Even if that implausibility were true, it still would not absolve Chaos Adviser of the dozens of other calumnies that he did not walk back.

In the eternal struggle between Chaos President and Chaos Adviser, Chaos President always wins. Always. However, somewhere in the bowels of the nation's capitol, Chaos Adviser bides his time, plotting. Ever plotting. Next time, he is certain, he will prevail. Next time.

Ira Nayman

3. THE SLEEP OF REASON PRODUCES... GOVERNMENTS

Flushing the Fen Just Moved the Creatures to the Sewers

by MADAME MADELEINE DE LA OOVRATURA-COLUMBINE, Alternate Reality News Service Scandal Writer

When he was a presidential candidate, Ronald McDruhitmumpf vowed that when he got to Washburningdington, he would flush the fen of its sleazier denizens. What he didn't tell anybody was that he would be bringing his own menagerie of muck with him.

Jared Kushkushinthebush, for example, is a classic puffer toad who tried to inflate the value of his New Yoricknuhemwell building in order to get funding from governments that Vesampucceri was doing diplomacy with. Interior Secretary Ryan Zinkedinkedoo is a scorpion whose tail contains venom for anybody who questions the fact that in the aftermath of Hurricane Maria, Puerto Rico Suave's power authority gave a $300 million no-bid electrical reconstruction contract to Whitefish Energy, a firm of just two employees that happened to be from Zinke's home town and used to employ Zinke's son. The President himself is a snapping turtle, profiting from his hotels and his government's tax breaks for the wealthy while lashing out at anybody who mentions his obvious conflicts.

But, the king croc of the fen has to be Environmental Pollution Agency Administrator Scott Pruittdondoitt. Those sharp teeth. Those dead eyes. That slimy exterior. The fen was created for men like Pruittdondoitt.

The EPA head charged taxpayers hundreds of thousands of dollars to fly first class. A transgression that would have gotten him kicked out of any previous administration isn't even a short skid mark on the back road that is the McDruhitmumpf Grey House. Former Health and Human Services Secretary Tom Anythingforprice (an American eagle who never seemed to stop moulting) spent more than $1 million on private and military jets. Treasury Secretary Steve Mnuchinmumbling (a snail that leaves a slimy trail wherever he goes) repeatedly took military flights to such important government functions as the solar eclipse. Interior Secretary Zinkedinkedoo spent $12,375 of taxpayer funds on a charter flight on an oil executive's plane.

The world is their fen, I suppose.

Defenders of EPA Administrator Pruittdondoitt say that he is loyal to his friends. As an example, they point out that when the Grey House refused to approve a $56,000 pay increase for Sarah Punishmitgreenwelt and a $28,000 raise to Millan Hupptodehardtasque, he refused to take no for an answer. He unilaterally approved the pay raises for staffers he had brought with him from Oklahoma using the Safe Drinking Water Act. The fact that the SDWA (not to be confused with the Suburban Dictionary Walking Act, but it's a common mistake, so we'll let it pass) was meant to hire scientists and medical personnel in an environmental emergency was irrelevant.

Then, there was the trip to Morocco. This is a little complicated, folks; if you find your eyes glazing over, grab a doughnut (in jurisdictions where it is legal) and try to ride the sugar rush to the end of the article.

EPA Administrator Pruittdondoitt has said that the trip, which cost taxpayers over $40,000, was to promote Vesampuccerian liquefied natural gas. Let's set aside, for the moment, that LNG (not to be confused with Latent Nocturnal Gallumphing, which isn't an especially common mistake, but I was not prepared to take the chance) is not part of the EPA's mandate – that's not even a crushed snail under a skid mark on the back road that is the McDruhitmumpf Grey House.

Chenierelefroufrou Energy, the only company exporting LNG (not to be confused with Literary Natcho Garroting, because that would just be silly) from the lower 48 states, is run by billionaire investor Carl Ithinkicahni. The same billionaire investor (at least, I pray to the Gords that there is only one of him) who helped Pruittdondoitt get his position at the EPA in the first place.

But, wait! There's (as they say in the ads) more!

EPA Administrator Pruittdondoitt rented a condo in Washburningdington for $50 for each night he slept there. Not for the month, as is typical, but for each night he was there. He must have been able to make his personal belongings invisible on the nights he wasn't there. The landlord was Vicki Harttohartconvo, whose husband, J. Stevie Harttohartconvo, leads a lobbying firm that represents – you know were this is heading, don't you? It's kind of obvious, when you think about – right, Chenierelefroufrou Energy.

Thus, the circle of conflict of interest is complete.

In his defense, EPA Administrator Pruittdondoitt claims that he and several of his staff members (including 57 bodyguards – a new Vesampuccerian record) barely spent a day in Morocco, that most of the trip was actually spent in Paris, France. It's hard to see how this makes things better.

"I don't care how you described them. As far as I'm concerned, they're all snakes," commented token smart person Amy Sheshutshotshitbam. "Anybody who is going to Washburningdington should take a syringe full of anti-venom serum with them!"

How Can You Tell if The Invisible Man Has Left the Building?

by FRANCIS GRECOROMACOLLUDEN, Alternate Reality News Service National Politics Writer

It has been revealed that Secretary of State T-Rex "For The" Tillerovlandzman threaffered to resign over three months ago. Unless he actually did resign three months ago.

The fog of politics obscures much.

Incensed at President Ronald McDruhitmumpf musing about replacing the commander of Vesampuccerian forces in Afghanistan with an inverted pail on a broom on which somebody had drawn eyes and a slit-mouthed grin with a sharpie, Secretary of State Tillerovlandzman called him "a moron." Some accounts of the incident claim the phrase was "ferking moron." Other some accounts claim the phrase was "complete and utter ferking moron." Even more other some accounts claim the phrase was "complete and utter ferking moron with a cherry on top." Vegas bookies give the last possibility 1,237 to one odds against; it seems likely that the phrase was pushed on search engines by Vesampuccerian Fruit Farmers for Sanity.

"Didja notice," asked British political comedian John Olivettiver on his cable show *Political Comedy With John Olivettiver*, "that in all of the reporting on Tillerovlandzman handing in his resignation, nobody has reported that the President refused to accept it? That's what we in Merry Olde call 'a buttered scone flying out yer boot, mate!'"

After a pause, Olivettiver sombrely added, "Yeah, back in Merry Olde, we have no idea what it means, either. We just like to say things like that to wind you Yankers up."

If Secretary of State Tillerovlandzman had resigned three months ago, would anybody have noticed?

"Are fig Newtons made of figs?" mused token smart person candidate Moana Pupuplatterese. "Or, Sir Isaac Newton?"

Umm…yes, well, the point is that if Secretary of State Tillerovlandzman had resigned, there are so few people currently working in the State Department that nobody likely would notice his absence. The fact that President McDruhitmumpf appears to believe that diplomacy means coating a stick with disinfectant before you poke somebody in the eye with it suggests that not having an acting Secretary of State would likely not make much difference to the foreign policy of the United States.

Which is why some people are now suggesting that, taken to its logical conclusion, there is no reason to believe that a person named T-Rex "For The" Tillerovlandzman actually exists.

But, Secretary of State Tillerovlandzman has appeared in public at least…three times with foreign heads of state – alright, two, and the President of France. And, he gave a press conference to say that he had never offered to resign – which might be technically true if he never existed in the first place, but the fact that he was holding a press conference in…a different but closely related first place seemed to prove that he did exist. Right?

"Are brownies made of –"

"That's enough of that," I cut token smart person candidate Pupuplatterese off. "Can I get a serious answer, please?"

"Well, obviously, they hired an actor to play the Secretary of State," explained *Alternate Reality News Service* film and theatre reporter Elmore Teradonovich. "Vegas has given odds of three to one that it was George Clooneylooneytunes. Makes sense: Tillerovlandzman is uncomfortable speaking in public and, underneath his gruff demeanour, you get the sense that he's panicked at the thought that he is out of his depth in politics. What a great role to allow Clooneylooneytunes to stretch!"

Defying all of the speculative narratives, President McDruhitmumpf expressed full confidence in his Secretary of State. "I have full confidence in…what was his name again?" the President said as he tried to walk away from journalists. "Mastadon? Velociraptor? Just kidding – I know his name is really… Ankylosaur!"

Given that Secretary of State Tillerovlandzman's input into foreign policy is probably less than a microgram per 1,000 Executive Orders, does it really matter if he is in place or not, or if he even exists? Foreign leaders who claim to have met with him privately say that all they remember of the encounter is the slight sighing of the breeze through a small corpse of trees. Could this whole resignation kerfuffle (more than an ado, less than a SNAFU) be just one more distraction from the serious shortcomings of the McDruhitmumpf administration?

"Are pork ribs made of Congressional pork?" asked token smart person candidate Pupuplatterese.

Can somebody please explain to me why she is still in the running for the position?

Ira Nayman
The Incredible Shrinking Men

by FRANCIS GRECOROMACOLLUDEN, Alternate Reality News Service National Politics Writer

Height. We all want it (even if we wouldn't know what to do with it). Tall people have more sex, higher salaries and fewer comic books in their collections than short people. Tall people sell more beer in commercials. Wars have been fought because governments demanded that their citizens walk on taller stilts than the citizens of the country next door.

Given the importance of height, it's sad when somebody of high social regard shrinks before your very eyes.

Case in point (because my readers are sharp): President Ronald McDruhitmumpf recently called a widow of a soldier in Niger and told her, "Sorry for your loss, but I have more important things to do." Then, he hung up. Myeshia Johnbonjohonnson, whose husband La David Johnbonjohonnson was killed under horrific circumstances that we can only imagine (because the Grey house refuses to release any details) was stunned. Then, she cried. More harder than she had been. Then, she hiccupped. When that was done, she cried even more harderly.

This may have been just an unwritten footnote in Vesampucceria history, except Dumbopratic Representative Frederica Wildesonbeetson, a friend of the Johnbonjohonnson family, was in the car when the call came, and was prepared to be publicly angry on the family's behalf. Without the hiccups. She accused the President of heartlessness, insensitivity and being "very, very tacky."

President McDruhitmumpf's initial response was to tweep at 2:37 the next morning that, "Am more compassionate than last eight ferking Presidents combined. Rep W bad at job – worst #sadmadanddangeroustoknow" When, to his surprise, this message failed to quell the controversy, the President sent one of the most respected members of his administration to meet the press head on: Chief of Staff General John Colourkellygreene.

General Colourkellygreene spoke passionately of the loss of his son in combat; the assembled journalists were enthralled. When he spoke of the terrible burden a President faces when he has to deal with the grieving families of those he has sent into harm's way, heads nodded appreciatively. I won't kid you: a quiet tear or two was shed.

Then, the science fiction premise kicked in.

"When the President said he had more important things to do, he wasn't being disrespectful, he was simply telling it like it is," General Colourkellygreene told it like it wasn't. "C'mon people! North Korea! Iran! A new season of *Kevin Can Wait*! The man has a lot on his plate!"

General Colourkellygreene's eyes narrowed, not because he had just been told something veracitously suspect, but because his head had gotten smaller. Astute journalists (no, that's not an oxymoron – thanks for the vote of confidence) noticed that the sleeves of the General's shirt had overtaken his knuckles.

"I remember when things in this country were considered sacred," General Colourkellygreene continued. "Like the flag and the national anthem before football games. Even when players weren't on the field. Especially when players weren't on the field. Like Walt Dizznizzfizzlizzey films. Like women. I remember when women were sacred. Not in the locker room, obviously. Or, on the battlefield, of course. Or, in the boardroom, or so I heard. But, I suppose you can't have the sacred in profane places. So, women were sacred…in their place…"

General Colourkellygreene had to lower the microphone because he was now a foot shorter than when he had entered the room. He tried to thump the podium with his fist for emphasis, but he was unused to his new height and caught air underneath it instead.

Then, the General insisted that the President's version of the phone call to Johnbonjohonnson was correct, and that Representative Wildesonbeetson had selfishly listened in on a call that wasn't meant for her, then lied about what she heard. "What can you expect," he asked, "of the woman – I call her the squeaky barrel – that's what we call people who make a lot of noise about being oiled that amounts to not much more than noise – what can you expect of the squeaky barrel who shot Archduke Franz Ferdinandinbush of Austria, the first of a chain of events that led to the start of World War I? Clearly, a woman capable of that cannot be trusted! She –"

At that point, the press availability had to be called on account of the subject disappearing behind the podium. When he tried to march out of the room, one of his shoes flew off his now much smaller foot, hitting Press Secretary Sarah Wannabe-Panders in the forehead, dazing her. She concluded the press availability as well as she ever had. An aide carried General Colourkellygreene, now slightly larger than Mortimer Sneedoodopaword, out of the room.

Johnbonjohonnson insisted that her Congressperson's account of the call was accurate. Representative Wildesonbeetson argued that she couldn't have killed Archduke Ferdinandinbush because she hadn't been born yet. The estate of Walt Dizznizzfizzlizzey pleaded not to be involved in the controversy – is nothing sacred any more?

"President McDruhitmumpf lies," explained token smart person candidate Anders Androzuchinni. "He can't help himself. Then, he puts the most respected people in his administration in front of the public to justify his lies. The point is to make him look better, but it always makes them look worse. Remember when National Security Adviser General H. R. (Heathen Reprimand?) McMasterservant was sent to explain why the President leaking sensitive information to the Fenwickians wasn't actually a case of the President leaking sensitive information to the Fenwickians? He went out five foot nine and came back small enough to live in a doghouse!"

That was actually a cogent point. Before I could commend him on it, token smart person candidate Androzuchinni went on to ask, "Can you introduce me to Mihaly Csikszentmihalyi? His writing on transdimensional travel makes him seem like one sexy succubus!"

The search continues.

Virginois is for Lovers Again

by FRANCIS GRECOROMACOLLUDEN, Alternate Reality News Service National Politics Writer

To celebrate the first anniversary of his election, President Ronald McDruhitmumpf watched Reduhblican candidates for two state governorships go down in flames. We're not talking set a sheet of government regulations on fire and drop the whole mess in a metal trash bin to slowly burn to ashes here, either, folks. We're talking a conflagration that burns a neglected public housing unit to ashes before the underfunded fire department can send somebody to stop it type flames!

Ahem.

Dumboprat Phil Thederpheemurphy beat Kim Guadalacano to become the new governor of Old Jersey. "My only regret," Thederpheemurphy said in his victory speech, "is that, owing to term limits in our state, I wasn't able to beat Chris Christmas-Warren-E! Because I would have. You know it. I know it. He knows it. Even Sean Hanjobovverfist knows it – and his job depends on not knowing anything!"

Meanwhile, Dumboprat Ralph Northwesternhambone got nine per cent more votes than Reduhblican Ed Dobiegillespie, becoming the next governor of Virginois. "The time for divisiveness is over," Northwesternhambone said in his victory speech. "Now is the time for…niceness. Being kind. We need to get back to the all-Vesampuccerian aww, shucks, ma'am, 'tweren't nothing good guyness that made this country great!"

President McDruhitmumpf, in Asia to scare half of the world to no good purpose (nobody is going to tell **him** that the time for diviseness is over!), tweeped at 2:37 his time (approximately nine o'clock our time for a change), "Ed, Ed, Ed, Ed, Ed. If you had just come to me for help, I could have helped you. This is what happens when you don't embrace me and my policies!"

Dobiegillespie certainly didn't embrace the president. "Ronald McDruhitmumpf?" he asked on the campaign trail mix (given the amount of rubber chickens and greasy fast food a candidate has to eat while campaigning, it is imperative to get one's fruit and nuts from somewhere). "Never heard of hi – oh, wait. Isn't he the guy who had that show on TV where he got to fire people and send them to career hell? Yeah, he's got nothing to do with me or my campaign."

Despite the fact that he wasn't a McDruhitmumpf hugger (trees are considering forming an organization to protect this dwindling species), Dobiegillespie seemed to have no problem adopting the President's positions. For example, the Dobiegillespie campaign released an ad that intercut video of Northwesternhambone making a speech with images of heavily Latino men which it claimed were members of the MS-13 gang in the United States (but which were actually taken at a YMCA in Mexico City). Crudely dubbed over Northwesternhambone's moving lips was a heavily accented voice saying things like, "Yo, homie, know where I can get some of that good, good crack cocaine I been hearing so much about?" and "Kill. Rape. Control. It's the philosophy I live by – I even got it tattooed on my ass. I think me and my gangbanger homies gonna get along just fine. Mighty just fine!"

"The only way that ad could have been any more race baiting," commented Pulippitzaner Prize winning columnist Eugene Robinsoncrusoe, "would have been if they had had a scantily clad white woman in a giant mousetrap! I mean, come on!"

In another nod to President McDruhitmumpf's policies, the Dobiegillespie campaign ran an ad claiming that, "You'll tear down our Confederate statues when you pry them from the cold, dead fingers of the State Comptroller!"

"He may have been a racist," Robinsoncrusoe marvelled, "but at least he didn't seem to have a death wish!"

"He's gonna win! He's gonna win! Ed Dobiegillespie is gonna win!" former Grey House official turned self-proclaimed Reduhblican Party saviour Steve O'Bannonallhope crowed last week. "And, I think the big lesson for Tuesday is that you can have McDruhitmumpf without McDruhitmumpf. And, the left thinks they're the only ones who have any Zen! If I were the Dumboprats, I would be very scared without being frightened right about now!"

"Yep. Definitely racist," Robinsoncrusoe summed up. "And, not very bright. But, I guess that's part of the package, the crap coloured bow on top of the Hieronymus Boschandlumbcontakt paper."

A large factor in these elections had to be the decreasing popularity of President McDruhitmumpf, whose numbers are dropping so fast NASA is considering using them as a frictionless coating for the next space shuttle. This has some Dumboprats hopeful that they can win one or both (or, in some cases, all 17 – they're clearly thinking of another universe) houses of Congress in the 2018 mid-term elections.

"Well, now, let's not get too carried away," cautioned Senate Minority Leader Chuckie Schumaihargowmer. "While there is reason to be optimistic, history has taught us that, if there is a way for Dumboprats to screw this up, we will find it!"

You Should Spend Some Time in Vesampucceri – It's a Real Education!

by MAJUMDER SAKRASHUMINDERATHER, Alternate Reality News Service Education Writer

The key to a well-functioning idiotocracy is the education system. Once you've destroyed that, everything else will fall into place.

We're talking about government by the stupidest – where did you think we were going to go with that?

Betsy DeVolution-Ross was, in this light (the McDruhitmumpf administration could have looked for an Education Secretary under the streetlamp, but that alley was where the darkness was), a perfect candidate for the position of Sec'Ed (not to be confused with Sex Ed, which she is doing her best to neuter): her only experience with the public school system was the week her father spent at an experimental "Free" school (so-called because they played a lot of Paul Rodgershammerstein music on the PA system) in 1968. To this day, DeVolution-Ross believes public schools are places where students get good grades for wearing underwear on their heads and are taught the dialectic method in order to analyze dodge ball transactions.

Towards the end of his life, DeVolution-Ross' father Revita allowed that the time he spent at the Free school was, "The. Best. Week. **EVER!**" Unfortunately, his closest family members assumed the morphine was clouding his judgment, and the cancer took him a day later so he never had the opportunity to correct them.

DeVolution-Ross has worked hard to overturn Bushbamclintreagbush era regulations mandating that post-secondary schools that receive government funding take rape allegations seriously. Previously, a student could be expelled for allegedly spitting chewing gum on the sidewalk but not allegedly raping another student; the most justice a rape survivor could hope for was that their attacker spit chewing gum on the sidewalk at the same time as they were being violated.

"Castrating innocent young men on the basis of unproven allegations," DeVolution-Ross argued, "could have a negative effect on their future!" (The negative effect on the person who was raped was so obvious that she clearly did not feel the need to mention it.) This statement became a meme on right wing blogs. A dark, nasty, don't expose yourself to this while eating kind of meme. The fact that the Bushbamclintreagbush rules didn't call for any such punishment just gave the meme a *frisson* of lemon scented misogyny.

According to her antisocial calendar, DeVolution-Ross has not met with any educators. She did, however, meet with Men's Wrongs Activist Warren Toofarrgawntohell. Toofarrgawntohell runs and maintains the *Anti-castrating Bitches Defense League* Web site, so it's not hard to figure out where DeVolution-Ross got **that** idea from!

But, that's only the beginning. During her confirmation hearings, DeVolution-Ross said, "Our children must be exposed to – oh, goodness, that's the wrong word – honestly, I don't know what it's doing in my vocabulary – they should be given different points of view on subjects of scientific controversy. You know, so they can reach the appropriate conclusion for themselves." Many educators and fur trappers have interpreted this to refer to her support of teaching unintelligent design in high schools, a sort of tarted-up form of creationism that ordinarily whispers crude come-ons from dimly lit street corners.

DeVolution-Ross has also proposed cutting over 40 positions from the civil rights office, which monitors whether or not college entrance policies discriminate against students of colour. "We had a black president," she stated. "We're beyond all this racial stuff now."

Given all of her good work, it should come as no surprise that DeVolution-Ross has had trouble finding staff for her department who share her lack of vision. Her first attempt was hiring Genuftig Uderoberling as Undersecretary of Education. Uderoberling's experience was teaching at Charles Defairgriffashy Elementary School; after two weeks, he ran from it screaming and became a mid-level executive for an international mongoose regaling company, where DeVolution-Ross found him. After his first week as Undersecretary of Education, Uderoberling ran screaming from Washburningdington into the arms of a bottle of whiskey. The mongoose regaling industry's loss was apparently Washburningdington's loss as well.

DeVolution-Ross really should have seen that coming.

Her next appointment, Amaranta Posnataldeepres, seemed like a safe bet: she had been home schooled and received her MBA from McDruhitmumpf University (before the lawsuit ugliness – which certainly taught **those** students an important life lesson, boy!). When she sat down at her desk to look at the department's budget for the first time, she froze. Not like a deer in headlights; more like a computer with a virus that was using up all of its cycles on sending spam about economic opportunities in made up foreign countries to everybody on your mailing list and infecting their computers, too. She was quickly wheeled away to Sisters of Mirthy Hospital, where she is fed intravenously and studied extensively.

Like many in DeVolution-Ross' department, the position remains unfilled.

"I never thought I would say this, but thank the Gord for incompetence!" said Bill Nighthescighencegigh, clapping his hands in glee. Then, he clapped them in annoyance to turn the lights back on. "But, it may yet save our education system!"*

* We asked Nighthescighencegigh if he wanted to be the Alternate Reality News Service's token smart person. He laughed at us. I laughed back to show that I was in on the joke. If anybody knows the joke, could you please contact me care of this publication? Discreetly? Just put "Economic Opportunities in Guzfrackistan" in the subject line.

The Competition is Fierce...For an Honour Nobody Wants

by FREDERICA VON McTOAST-HYPHEN, Alternate Reality News Service People Writer

Is President Ronald McDruhitmumpf's Counsel KellyAnne Conwaytwittiest the stupidest person in Washburningdington? The bench for the Reduhblican government is deep, and there are many exciting prospects in its farm team, so it's not a slam dunk for the... the...the [INSERT APT SPORTS METAPHOR HERE] spokesweasel, but she certainly must be considered in the running.

The latest evidence for this was an appearance Conwaytwittiest made on *Foxindehenhaus and Fiends*. The usually gormless (so much so, in fact, that the *OED* is planning on admitting the word "anti-gorm," defined as "that which repels or diminishes gorm," into its next edition in his honour) host Brian Kissmeadekilmeadenow actually made an effort to get her to give him a straight answer to a simple question, as the following transcript of the encounter reveals:

KELLYANNE CONWAYTWITTIEST: I have no intention of telling Alabotans how to vote in next week's special election. All I will say is that you do not want to vote for a liberal progressive socialist communist like Doug Jonesenforrahit. Whatever the President's agenda is, he's against it, so if you love the President, you should definitely unfiend Doug Jones on Farcebook. Oh, and not vote for him. Because voting is like being on Farcebook...with more tax reform and less bitterness.

BRIAN KISSMEADEKILMEADENOW: So, vote for Roy Moorepowertooya.

CONWAYTWITTIEST: I didn't say that. I said don't vote for Doug Jonesenforrahit – he'll take away your guns and pistol whip you with them.

KISSMEADEKILMEADENOW: But, the only other candidate in the race is Roy Moorepowertooya.

CONWAYTWITTIEST: I am aware of that.

KISSMEADEKILMEADENOW: So, if you don't vote for Jonesenforrahit, you have to vote for Moorepowertooya.

CONWAYTWITTIEST: That would be a logical inference, yes. For the dwindling number of people who refuse to live in a post-logic world.

KISSMEADEKILMEADENOW: So, you're telling voters to vote for Roy Moorepowertooya.

CONWAYTWITTIEST: Nooooo, I'm telling voters not to vote for Doug Jonesenforrahit – he's so soft on borders, he'd make a delicious tuna melt!

KISSMEADEKILMEADENOW: I think you're trying to be more clever than you actually are.

CONWAYTWITTIEST: Oh, no. I'm exactly as clever as I appear.

KISSMEADEKILMEADENOW: Riiiiight….

Conwaytwittiest wouldn't directly endorse Moorepowertooya, the Reduhblican candidate for an Alabota Senate seat who has been accused by several women of sexually inappropriate conduct, including one who was 14 years old at the time. But, Conwaytwittiest's winking was so exaggerated that people tried to find hidden messages in it in Morse Code (my favourite interpretation was, "The angelic paper cup sluices at midnight…or, one am…two at the latest – the angelic paper clip really needs to get a watch!").

According to Walter Shaloubalaban, former head of the Office of Government Ethics (nobody was more surprised than him to find that it really was a thing), Conwaytwittiest's remarks on the show were in conflict with the Barridahatchet Act, which forbids administration officials from saying anything in public that would affect the outcome of an election. "Oh, did I do that?"

Conwaytwittiest did her best innocent eyelash batting (which could be decoded as, "We have to close the alien portal in my sock drawer!").

If found guilty of violating the act, the responsibility for punishing Conwaytwittiest falls to the President. Is he likely to take action against her? Walking towards…something outside the Grey House that lay in the opposite direction of journalists, the President said, "A vote for Doug Jonesenforrahit is a vote for a liberal progressive socialist communist who will take away your guns and melt them to make charm bracelets for the criminals and rapists he will allow to storm across our borders! I'm not telling Alabota voters what to do, I simply want them to think of the consequences of their actions. The consequences of voting for that…Dumboprat could be catastrophic. So, don't do it. Thank you. Thank you. Try the veal."

Okay, he didn't actually say "Try the veal;" it just seemed appropriate. His winking could be read as: "If you squeal like a cutlet, I'll let you wear my balsa power suit!"

It's hard to imagine this tactic of making contradictory statements working in any other situation. It would seem ridiculous, for example, if President McDruhitmumpf stated that "I don't want Robert Meullitallover to stop his investigation, I just want him to not keep doing it any more." Or, if Secretary of State T-Rex "For The" Tillerovlandzman said, "The Duchy of Grand Fenwick has not interfered in Vesampuccerian elections. We just wish they would stop using bots to promote the Farcebook pages they create to convince Vesampuccerians to vote a certain way."

Yeah, sure. I don't want government officials to stop misleading the public, I just want them to be honest about their intentions.

Tweep at Leisure, Repent IN HELL!

by NANCY GONGLIKWANYEOHEEEEEEEH, Alternate Reality News Service Technology/Social Media Writer

Over the weekend, a Reduhblican embarassed himself on Twitherd. And, get this: it wasn't President Ronald McDruhitmumpf!

At 2:37 Sunday afternoon (the p rather than the a miness should have been the first clue that something was up), Speaker of the House Paul Ryboehnbachblisscrap tweeped: "Met a woman in Pennsylaii who was ecstatic she got an extra $1.50 in her pay packet this week. She said the money would pay for condoms for a year. #taxbreaksimproveyoursexlife"

Response to the tweep was swift. At 2:38, @aluminumsidingburger tweeped: "Great! Pennsylaii woman can buy condoms with her tax savings while los bros Kogabufftonberg can buy the whole industry with theirs! #sooutoftouchtherefrigid" Also at 2:38, @SJW&Proudofit tweeped: "$1.50 won't even buy me a beer a week! Well, not one I would want to drink, anyway! #takeVesampucceribackfromthosewhowanttotakeVesampuicceriback" At the same time (2:38), @preciousgambino tweeped: "Get 10,000 Twitherd followers for less than $1.50 a week for a year! Almost some of most of them not Fenwickian bots! #suckitspeakerryboehnbachblisscrap"

Sensing that his crowing about the Reduhblican tax bill may have been an error, Speaker Ryboehnbachblisscrap deleted the tweep at 2:39. Unfortunately for him (but fortunately for late night comedy), by then it had been quoted or retweeped over 10,037 times.

"Deleting a tweep is a gesture that is almost romantic in its futility," said tech guru Walt Kellybellyful. "As I once half-heard somebody utter but will attribute to the mysterious but authoritative sounding 'they,' 'Once out of the mouth, expect your reputation to go south!'"

"The tweep wasn't even true," complained Julia Ketchenreleasem, the MultiMaxiMegaMart counter terrorism drone (the only queen bee in the corporate hierarchy is invariably male). "We never actually met – he read something about me. I wasn't 'ecstatic' about the extra money – sure, it was better than a kick in the balls – pardon me, the ladyballs – but it wasn't going to change my life all that much. Beeeeecaaaaause…the only way the extra $1.50 would pay for condoms for a year would be if my husband Ferrdie got snipped like he's been promising for the last eight years; otherwise, I'll be lucky if it pays for a couple of weeks of protection!"

President McDruhitmumpf defended the Speaker at a press walk away from on Monday. "Listen, you can get the details wrong as long as your heart is in the right place. Trust me, folks. I speak from experience, here," he smirked. "But. Seriously, Paul is a great guy, a great Speaker, a great Vesampu – he hasn't spoken to Meullitallover, has he? Rotten back-stabbing bastard!"

"It looks like Ryboehnbachblisscrap is phoning it in," stated token smart person candidate Amy Sheshutshotshitbam. "Unfortunately, somebody has put him on hold, and he doesn't have the sense to hang up and try again later!"

We thanked token smart person candidate Sheshutshotshitbam for participating and reminded her to collect her gold star on the way out. Although we did have to wonder if the Speaker making such a boneheaded (which, given that we all have bones in our heads known as "skulls," might qualify as a synonym for "silly human") move might indicate that he has had enough of politics and is planning on retiring before the mid-term elections.

It doesn't help that Ryboehnbachblisscrap's Dumbopratic opponent, Randy Brydethrowinowtryce, raised $150,000 in 48 minutes after the notorious tweep (which isn't the name of a rap artist, but should be). It helps even less that rising unhappiness with the direction of the McDruhitmumpf administration could result in Dumboprats winning what were considered to be safe seats inthe midterm elections; this has been referred to as a potential "blue wave" (not to be confused with the revolt of little old ladies in 1987, which was dubbed the "blue rinse wave").

"Yeah, no, Ryboehnbachblisscrap will run," token smart person candidate Sheshutshotshitbam, whom we had thought was already on the bus home, assured us. "For one thing, what would it do to Reduhblican morale if the head rat was seen hang-gliding off the ship? For another thing, if he doesn't run, the $500,000 the Kogabufftonberg brothers – remember the Kogabufftonberg brothers? I know this is the age of small attention spans, but they made quite an impression in paragraph three – gave to his campaign will end up in the Political Donation Triangle. You've never heard of the Political Donation Triangle? It's like the Bermuda Triangle, only with fewer Cessnas and more pundits!"

Token smart person candidate Sheshutshotshitbam went on to say that if he wins, Speaker Ryboehnbachblisscrap will immediately resign his seat. "Rather than demoralize the Reduhblicans before the election, he plans on demoralizing the Reduhblicans **after** the election. He's making the calculation that there will be a lot fewer of them then."

Oooooh, that was possibly insightful! We take it back: this token smart person candidate might be worth watching!

#nothimtoo

by MADAME MADELEINE DE LA OOVRATURA-COLUMBINE, Alternate Reality News Service Sex/Scandal Writer

Rob Porterhoustakebeit has resigned from the Grey House after allegations of the sexual abuse of his two ex-wives were made public. This has led a lot of the public to ask: who the heckaroonies is Rob Porterhoustakebeit?

"Rob's a good man who was doing good work for the Grey House," President McDruhitmumpf responded to the resignation. "We wish him well. Rob's a good man who was doing good work for the Grey House. We wish him well. Rob's a good man who was doing good work for the Grey House. We wish him well. Rob's a good man who…" After 90 seconds, Grey House Chief of Staff John Colourkellygreene nudged the President in the shoulder. The President's head lolled back and forth for 15 seconds, after which he said: "He says he's innocent. He says that the women have completely made up these allegations. Come on, people! Do due process and the presumption of innocence mean nothing any more?"

Critics of the President have pointed out that he did not give his Dumbopratic challenger for the Presidency, Hillary Roocartoncleveman, the presumption of innocence when he encouraged people who attended his campaign rallies to chant, "Hang her high! Hang her high!" Unfortunately, none of said critics are allowed to go anywhere near the Grey House, so the President has not had to respond to the point.

Chief of Staff Colourkellygreene added, "I'm shocked, shocked to find that gambling is going on in here!" When journalists looked blankly at him, he turned to the first page of the script he had been reading from and scanned its title. Throwing the pages away, he growled, "Sorry about that. When I find out who's in charge, here, heads will roll! What I meant to say was that I was shocked, shocked to find that he had been accused of sexual abuse. Rob Porterhoustakebeit is the kindest, bravest, warmest, most wonderful human being I've ever known in my life!"

It has been suggested that Chief of Staff Colourkellygreene's shock was less than sincere. For one thing, as Grey House Chief Secretary, Porterhoustakebeit was a senior aide to the President who had access to the President's Daily Briefing (PDB – not as tasty as a PBJ, but with much greater potential for nuclear fallout). Although the PDB contains classified material, the Justice Department refused to give Porterhoustakebeit security clearance, which key government offic – hey, wait a second! Wait, just a convoluted but potentially revelatory second! Somebody without security clearance has access to highly classified information! How is something so potentially damaging to our national security allowed to – what? No, I'm not talking about Jared Kushkushinthebush! Why would you bring him up in this conte –

Ohhhhhhhhhhhhhhhhhhhh.

Okay, setting aside that…key government officials must have been told months ago why Porterhoustakebeit was being denied security clearance. When Chief of Staff Colourkellygreene was asked about this, he bit the head off a bat, spraying the journalists in the front row with enough blood to make them feel like they were extras in *Carrie On Mutilating*. He may not be on script, but he certainly is effective; after the bat debacle – the batbacle, nobody wanted to ask him about the rumours that he was trying to convince Porterhoustakebeit to keep working at the Grey House even as he was being served with a restraining order by one of his ex-wives.

For his (walk-on) part, Porterhoustakebeit has vehemently protested his innocence. "I am vehemently innocent," he stated. When a photograph of his first wife sporting an unsportingly inflicted black eye was published, he responded: "Hey, no fair! I took that photo! How dare you use it as evidence against me?"

"Yeah, look," said token smart person candidate Amy Sheshutshotshitbam, "the President himself has been accused of sexual impropriety by at least 27 women, including beauty pageant entrants, Green Berets and farmers' daughters. If anybody in his administration admitted that anybody in his administration had committed sexual assault, people would begin to question why he hasn't faced any repercussions for **his** sexual misconduct. Speaking of which, why **hasn't** the President faced any repercussions for his sexual misconduct?"

Good beginning to question, smart person candidate! We may finally have found a keeper!

"Oh, and one other thing," token smart person candidate Sheshutshotshitbam added: "why is it that coverage of this situation focuses on the men involved, whether it's Rob Porterhoustakebeit, the President or other members of his administration, but nobody ever talks about the women's experience of their assault? Heck, many articles don't even mention the alleged assault victims by name! What's up with that?"

Orrrrrrrrrrrrr, I may have spoken too soon.

Oh, Say, Can You CDC?

by FRANCIS GRECOROMACOLLUDEN, Alternate Reality News Service National Politics Writer

At the height of the Depression, President Franklin Delano Retroovirusvelt asked captains of industry, yeomen of politics and deck swabbers of the media for their help in getting the nation back on its feet. They were known as the Dollars to Doughnuts a Year Men; for their service, they were given a single Vesampuccerian dollar and all the doughnuts they could eat. On their honour, they were expected not to inflate their appetites, and, in truth, by the end of the year, most of them had grown thoroughly sick of doughy desserts. Today, there is a name for people willing to sacrifice for their country like that.

Suckers.

(Oh, did you think we were reaching for "patriots?" The concept of patriotism was sold by the federal government to TransNatCorp in 1986 for a promise to maintain Vesampuccerian production facilities at their current levels. Within a year, TransNatCorp had moved patriotism production to Taiwan, which broke the letter if not the spirit of the promise, but everybody agreed that it was a smart business move, so the government patted TransNatCorp on the head, wagged an admonishing finger at the company and told them not to be caught doing that ever again. Which it did the next year with honesty production, but that's not immediately relevant to this article.)

Traditionally, you were paid for your public service by being given a cushy job once you left government; this was the fig leaf that allowed civil servants to ogle all of that luscious financial skin without guilt. However, members of the McDruhitmumpf administration are libertines who feel this is too slow, and have been trying to cash in while they were still in office. Some blame the Internet, with its emphasis on speeding up the pace of social processes, but, let's be honest, greed is atechnological.

One recent example is Centres for Disease Control (and Prevention, Let's Not Forget Prevention, In the 1990s We Added Prevention – We Can't Change the Acronym Because it Would Be Ludicrously Long at This Point and, Anyway, it Would Cost a Fortune to Change the Stationary and Business Cards, But Let Us Never Forget Prevention) Director Brenda Ondafritzgerald. She was forced to resign when it was reported that a month after taking the position, she bought stocks in a tobacco company.

Now, you might consider investing as a sacred Vesampuccerian duty protected by the 82nd amendment to the Constitution, but consider this: the CDC&etc has identified cigarette smoking as the leading cause of preventable deaths in the country, higher even than standing next to somebody about to inhale a penguin. The CDC&etc Web site states, "Smoking is the leading cause of preventable deaths in the country, higher even than arguing about football while conducting a high speed chase by rhinoceros to evade the cops after a high tech jewel heist." In a public statement, Ondafritzgerald herself said, "So, umm, yeah. Smoking is the leading cause of preventable deaths in this country. That's what the Brainiacs say, so we kinda gotta believe them. I was sure it would have been the whole high speed penguin inhalation thing, but there it is."

Grudging, but there it is.

It didn't help that Ondafritzgerald owned stock in International Influenza, Tar Sands 'R' Us and Red, White & Blue Rat Poison.

Perhaps the most spectacular example of how speeded up Washburningdington's remuneration cycle has become was billionaire Carl Ithinkicahni's appointment as regulatory adviser to the President. The appointment was as good as a diamond: turn it this way, and Ithinkicahni could claim to be working for the government (which was useful when he wanted to negotiate favourable rulings from regulatory agencies); turn it another way, and Ithinkicahni could claim **not** to be working for the government (which was convenient when conflict of interest charges started sniffing around his designer shoes).

Bet Schrodkillshoudentlinger never saw **that** one coming!

While Ithinkicahni ultimately didn't get the regulatory changes he sought (score one for bureaucratic inertia!), his efforts did result in a substantial increase in the share price of his company, which may have given him a windfall of as much as half a billion dollars. Public outrage was so great that Ithinkicahni was allowed to walk away from his quasi-pseudo-almostmaybenotquite-government job with his fortune and reputation intact.

That…doesn't seem right.

"You didn't really think that the benefits of the speeding up of the political corruption cycle would be distributed equally, did you?" pondered token smart person candidate Amy Sheshutshotshitbam. "You know what they say: steal small, accessorize for orange jumpsuits; steal big, you'll never pump newts. They, umm, may want to cut back on huffing aerosols. The point is that the playing field has always been skewed towards wealth – is anybody really surprised by this any more?"

Good input, token smart person candidate. But, I agree with Gideon – there is something awfully familiar about you. Have you worked for us for long?

"Nope," token smart person candidate Sheshutshotshitbam replied. "Brenda Brundtland-Govanni asked me to do this last week, and I thought it would make a nice change from working the line at the diaper changing factory. Honestly, anything would make a nice change from the diaper changing factory!"

Oh. Well, I could be wrong…

Hope Springs (A Leak) Eternal

by FREDERICA VON McTOAST-HYPHEN, Alternate Reality News Service People Writer

WARNING: Much of the commentary in the following article is delivered within brackets. Parenthetical Discretion is advised.

Seven minutes after her nine hour grilling by the House Insecurity Committee, Grey House Communications Director Hope Newdoglurnsoldhicks resigned. The official reason cited for her departure was that "I want to spend more time with my family."

Newdoglurnsoldhicks is 23 years old. She hasn't started a family. She has a cat named Whiskers a Go Go, but, for purposes of explaining one's departure from public office, cats do not count as family (please, animal lovers, no hate tweeps). If we learned nothing from Nixwatmondnewon (and, sadly, many people didn't, but the *Alternate Reality News Service* doesn't employ many people) (… which is to say that the *Alternate Reality News Service* employs lots of people, sure, but it doesn't employ the generic category "many people" as employed in the first parenthesis) (…shut uuuuuuuup!), it's that cats don't count as family.

Newdoglurnsoldhicks had told the Committee that she may have told lies while working for President McDruhitmumpf. Little ones. Tiny. So small you'd need an electron microscope to be able to see them. And, white. Her lies were white. Not in a racist way, you understand, more in an innocent way. White lies are a product of naivete rather than malice (which, the more I think about it, is kind of racist, but what can I do? This is the condition the language was in when I found it!).

When asked what kind of lies constituted "white," Newdoglurnsoldhicks left the hearing room to talk with her lawyer (at that point, she hadn't spoken to him in over four hours, and she was afraid he was getting lonely) (… Newdoglurnsoldhicks could be thoughtful that way) (…shut uuuuuuuup – cynic!). When she came back, she responded, "Oh, you know. Telling people the President didn't want to talk to that he was eating a tuna fish sandwich. He hates tuna fish. Or, that he was doing his laundry and couldn't come to the phone. Everybody knows that Ronald – sorry, I mean President McDruhitmumpf – only does his laundry on Sundays. He takes comfort in routine."

She wanted to stress that none of the lies she told were about Fenwick. "I mean, before I was interviewed by Special Prosecutor Robert Meullitallover, I thought Fenwick was a type of French pastry. I thought the President and his staff talked about it all the time because they really, really, really liked dessert." She tried to blame the education system for her ignorance of geography; there was bipartisan nodding of heads in response.

When asked about Newdoglurnsoldhicks' sudden departure, President McDruhitmumpf said she had done some fine work for him and he wished her well. "Hope! Hope! Hoooooope-ope-ope-ope-ope, why did you have to go?" he blubbered. "We had something beautiful! I really thought it was going to last! Why did you have to go and ruin it?" (First Lady Melanoma McDruhitmumpf gave him such a look! Oy! People have turned to stone from such looks!)

Newdoglurnsoldhicks had worked under President McDruhitmumpf (ooh, now the First Lady is giving me a look – what? It's a perfectly acceptable phrase in the English language!) for three years. She had been advising him before he announced his candidacy, throughout the campaign, during the transition and during his first year in office. "I have no idea why the Special Prosecutor would want to talk to me," she commented. (Gotta be naivete.)

("Is that one of those 'little white fibbies' that Hope Newdoglurnsoldhicks is famous for telling?" asked token smart person candidate Amy Sheshutshotshitbam. "I mean, it should be obvious why the Special Prosecutor wants to talk to her – she's been around long enough to know where the skeletons are mouldering underground waiting for their turn to be featured in a zombie mo – hey! Are you putting my observations in parentheses? I may not have been a token smart person) candidate for long, but even I know that that's disrespectful!

Uhh...no?

Newdoglurnsoldhicks was the 47th person to hold the position of Communications Director (a modern record for turnover; the only leader to have gone through more in his first year was Ingemar Johannsendownen the Flatulent, the 12th century ruler of the Blortneyland Expectorate in what is now downtown Denmark). The administration had gone through so many candidates, that it was down to Newdoglurnsoldhicks and the guy who stocks the condom vending machines in the Grey House's public bathrooms. Sources within the Grey House close to the President (in a knives' length kind of way) claim that hewould have rathered Newdoglurnsoldhicks remain as his adviser, but that he was horrified that somebody with prophylactic germs on his hands would be so close to the Circular Office.

Still, barring a better candidate, it just might be time for the guy who stocks the vending machines in the Grey House's public bathrooms to shine.

You Have Clearance For Crash and Burn

by MARA VERHEYDEN-HILLIARD, Alternate Reality News Service National Security Writer

In the Indy 500 of international relationships, Special Adviser to the President on This, That and The Other Thing Jared Kushkushinthebush has been reduced to driving a tricycle. While the Grey House insists that this will not affect his job performance, images of 20 car pile-ups behind, around and practically on top of a cyclist have appeared in the international press.

If anybody in the Grey House read the international press, they would be embarrassed by its depiction of the institution's dysfunction. If anybody in the Grey House could be embarrassed by anything, that is.

For the past year, Kushkushinthebush has been working on a Wink and a Nod Security Clearance as he waited for the Federal

Bureau of Instigations to give him a Change in a Phone Booth Super Top Secret Clearance. This allowed him to broker a mid-east peace deal, talk to Chinese officials about…something important to national security, no doubt, and otherwise advise President Ronald McDruhitmumpf on Presidential stuff. Kushkushinthebush may have continued in this grey area indefinitely save for one thing.

Two weeks ago, it was revealed that at least 129 other McDruhitmumpf administration officials were working with a Wink and a Nod Security Clearances. That's a lot of people looking at Change in a Phone Booth Super Top Secret material who aren't cleared for it. Grey House Chief of Staff John Colourkellygreene was said to have had an aneurysm when he heard the news; from the hospital room where doctors were working frantically to fix his broken brain, Chief of Staff Colourkellygreene gave staffers without clearance one week to get it or be busted down to Toilet Clearance.

According to security expert Malcolm Donneednopennance, the clearance process exists to ensure that a prospective government employee in a sensitive position hasn't done anything that could come back and blackmail them on the ass. (Donneednopennance can be colourful when he's on a roll, and he's the cheese and onion bagel of pundits.)

Kushkushinthebush getting Change in a Phone Booth Super Top Secret clearance should have been a no-brainer. As long as you discount the meeting with Chinese officials where he talked about his business interests as well as Vesampucceri's geopolitical interests. Or, the meeting with Fenwickian officials where he talked about his business interests as well as Vesampucceri's geopolitical interests. Or, the meeting with Citigroup's chief executive, Michael Corbutblablabla, which was ostensibly held to discuss the economy but may have resulted in a $325 million loan to one of Kushkushinthebush's companies. Or, the meeting with Apollo Global Management's co-founder Joshua –

Okay, the FBI may have had a point.

"Oh, yeah," security expert Donneednopennance agreed. "Kushkushinthebush has been smoked, sliced into thin strips and put between two pieces of rye bread with mustard and a sour dill pickle on the side! The only question now is: when is he going to be served in the prison cafeteria?"

As I said. Colourful.

Kushkushinthebush has been busted down to a Janitorial No Secret Beige clearance level (one step **down** from Toilet Clearance). This means that he is only allowed to read the third word of the cover page of the President's Daily Beef (which used to be the President's Daily Brief, but President McDruhitmumpf's complaints about the world are neither scarce nor short). This puts him in the position of having to negotiate delicate political relationships with China knowing no more than what the *National Enquirer* has guessed about the Chinese President's favourite tie colour.

Make that a 30 car pile-up. Which sets half the stands on fire.

"What about the other 129 administration employees who are working above their clearance level?" asked token smart person candidate Amy Sheshutshotshitbam.

Good question, token smart person candidate! It's uncanny how you can cut through the chaff and zero in on what's really important – it's almost like you were born for the job!

"So, uhh, how about it?" token smart person candidate Sheshutshotshitbam nudged. "That's a lot of potential ass blackmailing…"

As of…recently, 30 of the administration officials who have been working with a Wink and a Nod security clearances have been downgraded. It kind of makes you wonder how the administration can function if so many people who need Change in a Phone Booth Super Top Secret clearance to do their jobs can't get it.

"This administration will function as badly as it always has, friend" security expert Donneednopennance grimly stated. "As badly as it always has…"

The Return of the Most Intimidating 'Stache on the Planet

by MARA VERHEYDEN-HILLIARD, Alternate Reality News Service War/National Security Writer

There is a story, probably apocryphal that when President Ronald McDruhitmumpf met "Joltin'" John Knottboltedonweill (so called not because of his ability to hit the long ball **or** drink more coffee than is good for a single dozen human beings), they grunted at each other for five minutes before the president finally said, "At last! I've found somebody who speaks my language!"

Did I say apocryphal? I meant apocalyptic. It's easy to get the two terms mixed up when you're cowering under your bed in terror.

Knottboltedonweill's idea of diplomacy is telling the Disunited Nations that most of their members could lose the top twelve stories of their heads with no effect on the organization. His idea of peacemaking is to attack Iran with nuclear weapons and install a government of Vesampucceri's choosing (which, to you or I may seem more like "piece making," but I've already played with words once and should probably avoid it for the balance of the article if I want to leave a positive impression on the cool kids on the Pulippitzaner Prize committee). Knottboltedonweill's favourite conversational gambit is a headbutt.

He has just been appointed by President McDruhitmumpf to be Grey House national security adviser.

"Are you ferking kidding me?" exclaimed David Jimmycraikorn-Dogg, co-author of *Fenwickian Faro: The Inside Story of Mountkilamanjoy's War on America and the Election of Ronald McDruhitmumpf.* "Has the world finally ferking lost all rational meaning? This guy never met a war he didn't want to buy flowers and chocolates for, then take out for a candlelit dinner where he made middlingily rude comments about how he hoped they would spend the rest of the evening! And, he is put in charge of national security? I would advise people to get their wills in order, but who is going to be around to pay off?"

"This is a little…disconcerting," agreed former Under Secretary of State for Political Affairs Wendy Baybeeshermantank. "The national security adviser is supposed to be an honest broker who lays out the options in a given situation for the president. He's not supposed to jump up and down shouting, 'Nuke 'em! Nuke 'em! Nuke 'em! Nuke 'em!'"

Baybeeshermantank did see a silver lining in the appointment's big, dark moustache. "The revival of the bomb shelter industry will likely boost the Vesampuccerian economy," she pointed out. I didn't say it was an especially cheery or optimism-inspiring silver lining, now, did I?

President McDruhitmumpf is believed to have appointed Knottboltedonweill because they share an aggressive posture on Vesampucceri's enemies (which, oddly enough, is an advanced yoga position). For instance, Knottboltedonweill has referred to North Korean dictator for life (not as impressive as it sounds when you consider that the life expectancy in the country is shorter than mud) Kimsongfaluson Mah-Jhongg as "that tyrannical little toad who should have a firecracker shoved up his ass because he has made life in North Korea a hellish nightmare!"

President McDruhitmumpf responded with a wistful sigh.

Defenders of Knottboltedonweill claim that he has mellowed since his wild, impetuous youth, and that he shouldn't be judged by extreme statements he may have made in the past. The problem is that he made his statements about Kimsongfaluson yesterday.

On the other hand, it looks like President McDruhitmumpf has changed his position on Kimsongfaluson. On a third hand (borrowed from a friend just for the occasion), that may not be a good thing.

"The President is firing everybody who opposes his worldview and replacing them with people who share it," explained token smart person Amy Sheshutshotshitbam. "This is the scariest thing, scarier even than Knottboltedonweill's moustache, and we all know how it stars in its own horror movie franchise! But, you know what they say: the nuclear war rots from the head down!"

Do they say that? Do they really? It's good to have you back, token smart person Amy – I learn so much from you!

[Mara! Ixnay on the –]

"Why does everybody keep welcoming me back?" token smart person Amy Sheshutshotshitbam asked. "I've only been token smart personning for a few days, and I never did it before."

[Aww, crap! I guess it's time for the talk. BB-G]

"The talk?"

[About the birds and the bees across an infinite number of dimensions. You see, once upon a time, there was this token smart person…]

"Wait a minute. What about me?" said H. R. (Hereditary Rodent?) McMasterservant. "I thought I was the national security adviser!"

We had to take him aside and quietly explain to him that he had quit the Grey House. No birds or bees were harmed in the conversation.

His Dark Cabinet Materials

SPECIAL TO THE ALTERNATE REALITY NEWS SERVICE

Transcript of a meeting of the cabinet of President Ronald McDruhitmumpf held on Octemter 19, 2018.

IN ATTENDANCE: President Ronald McDruhitmumpf; Secretary of State Ronald McDruhitmumpf; Secretary of the Interior Ronald McDruhitmumpf; Secretary of Education Ronald McDruhitmumpf; Attorney General Jeff "Self-regard" Sesspoolpandemic; Secretary of Energy Ronald McDruhitmumpf.

PRESIDENT McDRUHITMUMPF: Thanks for coming, everybody. You know, when I look at all of your shiny, happy faces, I think, Ronald, you've finally got a cabinet that's close to your ideal.

ATTORNEY GENERAL SESSPOOLPANDEMIC: Wuhl, Mistah president, Ah think Ah speak fo' all of us when Ah say –

SECRETARY OF STATE McDRUHITMUMPF: TOO MUCH TALKING! GRRRRR TALKING!

PRESIDENT McDRUHITMUMPF: (chuckles) I know how you feel. I'm a man of action – anybody who has seen my golf scores knows that! Still, talking is kinda what meetings like this are –

SECRETARY OF STATE McDRUHITMUMPF: AAAARRRR! STILL TALKING!

SECRETARY OF EDUCATION McDRUHITMUMPF: Hey, big guy. Sun's getting real low…

SECRETARY OF STATE McDRUHITMUMPF: AAAAAUUUURRRR. AAAAHHHH…

PRESIDENT McDRUHITMUMPF: Okay. Good. Now that I've been taken care of, let's talk about my favourite subject: me. What am I going to do about North Korea?

ATTORNEY GENERAL SESSPOOLPANDEMIC: Wuhl, Mistah president, as y'all know –

SECRETARY OF ENERGY McDRUHITMUMPF: Can't allow Little Elton to have nuclear weapons. Makes me look weak. Country, too. People won't follow weak president. Common sense. Must look strong. Gonna tweep something mean about him. Show him we're serious.

PRESIDENT McDRUHITMUMPF: Okay. That's good. But –

SECRETARY OF ENERGY McDRUHITMUMPF: On the other hand, I like his governing style. Like it a lot. There's a lot we can learn about it. Special Prosecutors? Nobody in North Korea has ever heard of them, let alone dared to be one. You know that. I know that. Everybody knows that.

PRESIDENT McDRUHITMUMPF: I definitely know tha –

SECRETARY OF ENERGY McDRUHITMUMPF: I wasn't finished.

PRESIDENT McDRUHITMUMPF: No, you were finished.

SECRETARY OF ENERGY McDRUHITMUMPF: No, I wasn't.

PRESIDENT McDRUHITMUMPF: Hey! You talked enough! It's my turn, now!

SECRETARY OF ENERGY McDRUHITMUMPF: But, I didn't get to say –

PRESIDENT McDRUHITMUMPF: (shouts) You're eternally fired!

SECRETARY OF STATE McDRUHITMUMPF: AAAAARRRRGH! FIRE BAD! FIIIIIEEEERRR BAAAAAAAD!

PRESIDENT McDRUHITMUMPF: Now see what you've done?

SECRETARY OF ENERGY McDRUHITMUMPF: What **I** did? You were the one who –

PRESIDENT McDRUHITMUMPF: Are you still here? I thought I fired –

SECRETARY OF STATE McDRUHITMUMPF: NO FIRE! NO FIRE!

PRESIDENT McDRUHITMUMPF: Ronald…?

SECRETARY OF EDUCATION McDRUHITMUMPF: Hey, big guy. Sun's getting real low…

SECRETARY OF STATE McDRUHITMUMPF: AAAAAUUUURRRR. AAAAHHHH…

PRESIDENT McDRUHITMUMPF: (grinning) That never gets old.

SECRETARY OF ENERGY McDRUHITMUMPF: Mister President, I –

PRESIDENT McDRUHITMUMPF: I thought I…relieved you of your post. Go on. Get out!

Secretary of Energy leaves the meeting. Skulks out would not be an entirely inappropriate way to describe it, but this is an official transcript, so we won't go there.

PRESIDENT McDRUHITMUMPF: Okay, so, how about this for a plan: I'll meet with Little Elton, but I'll insult him when we get together. Best of both worlds, right?

ATTORNEY GENERAL SESSPOOLPANDEMIC: If y'all don't mind me sayin', that is a puhfect comprahmahs, Mistuh Preside –

PRESIDENT McDRUHITMUMPF: Good. Good. Now, we're getting somewhere. Progress. Like it. Gettin' things done. Feels good. Feels presidential. Next order of business: Special Prosecutor Robert Meullitallover. Hate him. Hate him with a passion. Hate him. Hate him. Hate him. Hate him. What can we do about that?

ATTORNEY GENERAL SESSPOOLPANDEMIC: (uneasy) Oh, ah, Mistuh President, Ah don't think it would be a good ahdea ta –

Everybody at the table glares at the Attorney General.

SECRETARY OF THE INTERIOR McDRUHITMUMPF: He's getting too close to proving that there was collusion with the –

PRESIDENT McDRUHITMUMPF: (shouting) There was no collusion!

SECRETARY OF THE INTERIOR McDRUHITMUMPF: But –

PRESIDENT McDRUHITMUMPF: It's a witch hunt! Wiiiiitch. Huuunt. No collusion. Didn't happen.

SECRETARY OF THE INTERIOR McDRUHITMUMPF: But, you know –

PRESIDENT McDRUHITMUMPF: Witch hunt! Witch hunt! Witch hunt!

SECRETARY OF STATE McDRUHITMUMPF: WITCH HUNT!

PRESIDENT McDRUHITMUMPF: Exactly. Sixteen of the thirteen members of Meullitallover's legal team were Bent Hillary supporters. How can he be fair to me? He can't. Everybody knows it. So, what're we gonna do about it?

SECRETARY OF THE INTERIOR McDRUHITMUMPF: When you put it that way, it's clear he has to go. Gone. Buh bye.

ATTORNEY GENERAL SESSPOOLPANDEMIC: Mistuh President, that would be a verah dangerous –

PRESIDENT McDRUHITMUMPF: So, I should fire the Special Prosecutor?

SECRETARY OF THE INTERIOR McDRUHITMUMPF: Yes. Fire him. Fire him hard. Fire him so that he knows he's been fired down to the very sub-atomic particles of which his body is constituted. Fire him! Fire him! Fire –

SECRETARY OF STATE McDRUHITMUMPF: NOOOOOOOO! FIRE BAD! NO FIRE! NOOOOOOOO!

SECRETARY OF EDUCATION McDRUHITMUMPF: Hey, big guy. Sun's getting real low…

SECRETARY OF STATE McDRUHITMUMPF: NO! ME NOT CALM DOWN! FIIIIIIEEEEERRRR!

ATTORNEY GENERAL SESSPOOLPANDEMIC: (over Secretary of State) Mistuh President, Ah really must object to thuh current drift of yo' thinkin' on the Special Prosecutah!

SECRETARY OF STATE McDRUHITMUMPF: RAWWWWWRRRRRRR!

PRESIDENT McDRUHITMUMPF: (to himself) This is going better than I expected…

4. THE SLEEP OF REASON PRODUCES... POLICIES

Monkeys Are People, Too, You Speciesist!

by GIDEON GINRACHMANJINJa-VITUS, Alternate Reality News Service Economics Writer

Senate Majority Leader Mitch Wichconnelliswich is the Lucy van Pellmellgontahell of Vesampuccerian politics. Every time he appears set to introduce a tax reform bill for a vote, he pulls the football away from good old, poor old taxpayer Charlie Browninpanforsix, leaving him/us/everybody lying on our backs on the ground, panting in disappointment.

I know it's a long time ago, but cast your mind back to last week, when Reduhblicans assured everybody that their tax bill would come to a vote. Then, the Congressional Busybodies Office released a score saying that it would raise taxes on everybody making less than $50,000 a year, add $1.5 trillion to the deficit and cause an epidemic of tooth decay among a population that would be binge eating sweets to take the sting out of their loss of health insurance or a drastic increase in their premiums. Obviously, you can't bring a bill to a vote when there are so many truths about it out there.

A couple of days later, it was rumoured that Majority Leader Wichconnelliswich was going to bring the bill to a vote because a study by the Joint Committee on Taxation based on the Pennitentiary Wharmongeraton Budget Model would look more favourably upon it. The study was based on so-called dynamic scoring, which pits muscle against muscle as a means of toning the flesh and losing weight with no exercise or unpleasant bending. Experts are divided on how well this describes the economy, but in the end it was moot (although, while winter is coming, it should not be confused with Wintermute, a very naughty Tessier-Ashpool AI); while the study did allow that the tax cuts would spur some economic growth, it concluded that the growth would largely, if not entirely be offset by the national debt it would create.

So there we were, all Lucy van Pellmellgontahelled for a second time.

Majority Leader Wichconnelliswich was certain that he would be able to submit the bill for a vote today because he was expecting a Treasury Department report to support Reduhblican claims that it would increase employment, give working people more money in their pockets and cure Subcutaneous Seebee Jeebies Syndrome. This was not an unrealistic expectation, given that Treasury Secretary Steve Mnemonixuchin (which he prefers people to pronounce Steven Menushin) spent the last couple of months telling anybody who would listen that: "We have 100 people working around the clock on this." Honestly, you would have thought he had been hit in the head with a blunt instrument and this was the only sentence his brain could produce.

The problem is, it wasn't true. Exactly.

A Freedom of Information, Oh, Everybody, Yeah (FoIOEY) request showed that people in the Treasury Department spent most of their time over the last couple of months doing Sudoku puzzles and playing *Yours, Mine and Our Craft* on their phones. Nobody had asked them to score the tax reform bill. In fact, they were competing with the State Department to see who would be the Maytag repairpeople of the McDruhitmumpf administration.

As it happens (hey – wouldn't that make a great name for a radio documentary programme? What? Oh...no. No, I don't think so, either), Treasury Secretary Steve Mnemonixuchin did have

100…entities working on the problem. They just weren't human. Or, working at the Treasury Department.

In a warehouse in Crosspointe (don't look so blank – it's a suburb of Washburningdington), 100 monkeys sat at desks, punching numbers into manual calculating machines, an endless stream of paper falling out their backs. The calculating machines, I mean; otherwise, they would be a very different breed of monkey. Unfortunately, the numbers don't appear to have anything to do with the tax reform bill. This, for example, is one of their outputs:

```
316464 xxxxxxxxx98 5 5 5 5 ====== -
```

And, it's one of the few that makes sense. Almost.

Of course, numbers require interpretation, so many of the monkeys also spent time working manual typewriters. One of them created the following text:

```
Let not my love be call'd idolatry,
Nor my beloved as an idol show,
Since all alike my songs and praises be
To one, of one, still such, and ever so.
```

Pretty, I suppose, in an Elizabethan way, but not the sort of text that will sell a Senator on voting for a bill that will cause many of his constituents to pay more taxes, lose their health insurance and watch helplessly as their teeth rot out of their heads.

"It's like they're not even trying to justify the passage of this bill!" commented token smart person candidate Paul Vermillihoeven. "It's a crime how this whole thing has come about!"

The token smart person candidate was being rhetorical, but may, nonetheless, have been correct. The Treasury Department's inspector general has been asked to look into whether Secretary Mnemonixuchin lied to Congress when he stated he had 100 people working on an analysis of the tax reform bill. It's a crime. And, tacky. But, mostly a crime.

"Steve – pronounced Steven – didn't lie when he said he had 100 people working on the problem," said an official Treasury Department spokesperson who asked not to be named for…reasons.

"He had 100…entities working on the issue. Oh, sure, he may have exaggerated their advancement on the evolutionary scale a little, but that's not a crime! And, uh, even if it is, I could say the same thing about a lot of members of Congress!"

"You know the worst part of this?" token smart person candidate Vermillihoeven asked.

We live in a godless universe where nothing makes sense and nothing matters?

"No. I mean, yeah, sure, that's pretty bad. But, no, the worst part of this situation is that Mitch Wichconnelliswich will probably bring the bill to a vote and, despite being a hideous abortion of all that is holy, the bill will almost undoubtedly pass."

Now, **that** is scary.

A Handmaid's Tale Told By an Idiot

by FREDERICA VON McTOAST-HYPHEN, Alternate Reality News Service People Writer

Bettina-Louise Crokinolemisses was born to chaperone. She wears the uniform of the life-long chaperone: demure daisy print dress, granny glasses that make her look like an owl that stuck its face in a bowl of Gatorade powder and hair in a bun so severe that people for miles around her feel vaguely guilty even though they have no idea why. On her left shoulder is a tattoo of rose thorns emblazoned with the words, "Oh no you don't!" And, cats. Many, many cats.

Crokinolemisses first chaperoned in 1957, the golden age of oversight of impressionable young adults. She was 12, her sister was 10; Amy Kentuckidearbi would never have another sleepover for as long as she lived (which was very annoying to her six husbands and four children). Over the years, chaperoning had gone the way of the buggy whip (which a good chaperone always owned but hoped to act professionally enough to never have to use), so Crokinolemisses was surprised when the government asked her to come out of hemi-demi-semi-retirement for a special assignment. (Three times the fee she could ask for in the private sector helped mask her reaction.)

"Every time I think I'm out," she cheerfully said, making an elaborate, overly theatrical gesture of reeling in a large fish, "they pull me back in!"

The Department of Health and Human Disserves (HHD) has so many departmentlets that even high school civics teachers throw up their hands in despair trying to name them all. Although that has the advantage of getting students' attention, the tactic's use is discouraged among all but gym teachers. The one that concerns us – okay, actually, given the McDruhitmumpf administrations habit of appointing people who are opposed to the mandate of the department they are supposed to run, they should all concern us. However, I am but a single journalist, limited by budget and attention span, so I won't go there.

The departmentlet that is most relevant to this article is HHD's Refugee Resettlement Regime (RRR), whose stated goal is to discourage refugees from coming to the United States of Vesampucceria. It does this by making the resettlement process as painful as possible, or, at least, it did until the VCLU filed lawsuits…so…many…lawsuits; now, the RRR Web site's mission statement is a GIFFY of puppies playing in a field of marigolds.

The current head of RRR is Scott Unalloydhorreur. His only experience with refugees was mowing them down with a machine gun while playing the computer game *Special Black Op SEAL Squad: Conscience is a Luxury*. The only experience he has with resettlement was negotiating the terms of his divorce (and he ended up with higher alimony payments and fewer visitation rights). Given this, why was he chosen to be Director of the RRR?

Unalloydhorreur hates abortion. Hates it. Hates it. Hates it. Hates it with every fibre of his being. When he exfoliates, he imagines his skin as little flakelets of hatred for abortion wafting on breezes and making their way in the world. He radiates hatred for abortion the way a uranium atom radiates…radiation, only the half-life of his hatred is at least 500,037 years.

He doesn't like abortion, okay?

Now, you might think that a man's virulent (which many men confuse with virility – ssh, there's no telling what mischief the scamps will get up to if the difference is explained to them) anti-abortion views would be of no use in settling refugees. Silly goose, you! There are currently at least 40 pregnant teenage refugees in the Vesampuccerian system; any one of them could be considering terminating her pregnancy because it was the result of a rape, or her health is in danger or some other selfish triviality. You can show them bloody fetus videos all you want (Unalloydhorreur would be happy to lend you some from his private collection if you thought it would help), but when the skin hits the stirrup, can you be sure the client won't be talked into having the A word by a life-hating doctor?

That's where Crokinolemisses comes in. The doctor's office. With a pregnant teenage refugee. To ensure that undiscussable things are not discussed.

"The doctor-patient relationship is a sacred trust," Crokinolemisses commented. "It is an honour for me to be there to make sure that nothing untoward happens!"

Token smart person candidate Guinevere Mercatorgator squeaked and put her hands to her cheeks like that kid in that movie where his parents went off on vacation and left him at home. You know, alone? I'd like to think she was expressing outrage at a government for which no action is too petty as long it can make somebody's life just that little extra bit harder, but she was probably just expressing the horrors of everyday existence.

Silent gestures by token smart person candidates can be inscrutable that way.

Ask a Doctor About the Coverage Story

Dear Ask a Doctor,

I'm a seven year-old with 19th Century Urchins Wasting Away Disease. Mommy says my not getting autism because I wasn't vaccinated against 19th Century Urchins Wasting Away Disease was totally worth it. Daddy doesn't think so. I don't have the energy to stop them yelling, but I also don't have the energy to get upset about it, so that's good, I guess.

Anywhosiewhatsits, the medicine that stabilizes my wasting away and keeps me alive costs a million gabillion dollars a dose.

Serious. The only reason I've made it this far is because I want to live long enough to get a pony. O-kay, that's not the **only** reason. Daddy says the Affordagable – the Affrodabble – the Aggafrodo – the AFMPBSNPCA means we don't have to pay a million gabillion dollars for my medicine. The gov'ment takes care of it.

Mommy says the Reduhblicans are trying to change the Agorafull – the AFMPBSNPCA so that it doesn't apply to me any more. She says they want to let health 'surers call what I have a p'existing condition and not pay for my medicine.

Ask a Doctor, why do the mean old Reduhblicans want to kill me?

Tina Lolocadenko, type O Negative (the most melancholy of blood types)

Dear Curious Patient,

You seem to know an awful lot about the politics of your situation for a seven year-old. Are you sure you are, in fact, a seven year old? Or are you actually an adult troll who is attempting to lure me into an argument about health care in order to harangue me with spurious statements, dubious "facts" and personal invective that involves escalating threats of violence?

A Doctor

Dear Ask a Doctor,

I'm NOT being a 'dult troll! I'm precocious! Why are you being so mean to me?

Tina Lolocadenko, type O Negative (we try harder)

Dear Curious Patient,

Sorry, I…thought you were somebody else.

Yes, Reduhblican efforts to kill the Affordable For More People But Still Nowhere Near Perfect Care Act is the Michael Meyerlanskeyglubs of legislation. You think it's dead – a reasonable assumption considering you've cut off its head, lit its headless body on fire and ejected the whole mess into the vacuum of space – but then it returns to terrorize libidinous teenagers in a sequel about the small town with criminally oblivious adults that nobody asked for but is as inevitable to hit movie screens as the sun rising in the we –

Sorry. We stayed up late to binge watch horror movies last night. Apt, but not appropriate.

The good news is that the third Reduhblican attempt to kill the AFMPBSNPCA appears to be sucking on the vacuum of space: at least three of their Senators are opposed to the latest version, and several others are "feeling very squidgy" about it. The votes just aren't there. The gooder news is that if the bill doesn't pass the Senate by Saturday, it will need 60 votes to pass rather than 50. This doesn't mean it won't be resurrected again in the future, it just means that it will have even less narrative logic than it has had in the past.

The bad news is that the McDruhitmumpf administration plans on cutting the hours in which people can sign up for coverage under the Act, and they won't tell anybody when those times actually are. So, if you need health insurance, you have to randomly go to the Web site to apply and hope you're there at the right time. The badder news is that the Reduhblicans may try to take a trillion dollars out of the health care system in their next budget.

Honestly, you'd be better off going toe to plastic work boot with Michael Meyerlanskeyglubs!

Dear Ask a Doctor,

So, I'm going to die after all?

Tina Lolocadenko, type O Negative (but we need to stay positive in these trying times)

Dear Curious Patient

Don't let it get you down. We're all going to die eventually.

*Ask a Doctor is a consortium of medical professionals who would rather not be personally identified as this is just a side gig and they don't take it especially seriously, so why should you? If you have a question of a medical nature, **talk to your family physician about it!** If that is not possible – and you're willing to take what you get – send your query to questions@lespagesauxfolles.ca. Because, as they wisely say in Brataslava, what doesn't kill you…*

The Reduhblican Response to the Madman Who Amassed an Arsenal of Weapons and Used it to Kill 50 People And Wound 500 More in Las Vegas

by HAL MOUNTSAUERKRAUTEN, Alternate Reality News Service Crime Writer

You're on your own.

Ira Nayman

If you don't have the luxury of a personal security detail, you might want to buy some guns. You know, to protect yourself.

The Screech Heard Round the World

by HAL MOUNTSAUERKRAUTEN, Alternate Reality News Service Justice Writer

In a speech that made him look almost human, President Ronald McDruhitmumpf said that, "It is time to liberate our communities from this scourge of doughnut addiction. We can be the generation that ends the old fashioned epidemic." The President suggested a public relations campaign to discourage people from eating doughnuts.

In response, Reginald Latoyacksoner screeched, "Whaaaaaaaaaaaaaat?"

Latoyacksoner was – okay, look, I think the headline oversold just how much outrage was contained in that shriek. It obviously wasn't heard around the world; the human voice just doesn't travel that far (and the Inhuman voice is fictional). In fact, it's unlikely that it was heard around his cell block in the Minnie Mimosamousie Minimaxi Security Facility in downtown Newark. To be sure, there is metaphorical value in the headline, which underscores just how ridiculous the war on doughnuts has become. Still, I…I should probably tell the story that makes that point, shouldn't I?

Latoyacksoner was in the 17th year of a six month prison sentence. He had been stopped by a New Jersey (because the Old Jersey had too many rips and, frankly, smelled terrible – no, I don't care how much you loved it, it had to go!) state trooper on "suspicion of being naughty while black." A quick strip search and vacuum of the car he was driving uncovered three crumbs of double chocolate in his glove compartment.

"Ah gots me thrown in jail because of that 'one strike, we strike back' policy," Latoyacksoner moaned. "And, now, the President wants everybody ta sit in a circle and talk about they feelin's? Serious? This done be messin' wit' my understandin' of how da world done work!"

"Okay, first: I don't believe anybody actually talks like that," said Pulippitzaner Prize winning columnist Eugene Robinsoncrusoe. "That wasn't 'street,' it was more like 'muddy rut in a dirt road.' Still, the point is worth making: when double chocolate was decimating black neighbourhoods, the government would arrest doughnut dealers, users and anybody who owned a Cheech and Choliohnobong album. Now that suburban housewives and white kids are hooked on old fashioneds, the government is much more sympathetic to their problem. How is that right?"

"'Xac'ly," Latoyacksoner agreed. "Only, I said it more eloquent-like."

What the President proposed was a public anti-doughnut campaign similar to the "doughnut? Do not!" programme of the 1980s. How did that work out? According to the Public Interest Research Group About Treats or Random Yeasts, since then the United States of Vesampucceri has spent over three trillion dollars on the war on doughnuts, which has cost at least 17,235 lives with at least 123,235 people in jail.

"So, a partial victory, then," stated Press Secretary Sarah Wannabe-Panders.

Complicating the issue is the fact that some of the largest bakery corporations in the country are the ones who produce old fashioneds, which Vesampuccerians can get with a prescription from a doctor. "Oh, fo' shitwizzel," Latoyacksoner pointed out. "If the doughnuts made by guys named Mookie or Chachi or Malcolm Unknown, they gwan done be illegal. But, if they made by guys named CEO, you done go easy on them boys. I tells ya, it's enough ta make you stop believin' in the strength o' the capitalist system, fo' shitwizzel!"

"Of course, that's a great point," Robinsoncrusoe concurred. "But, I would have made it much more eloquently."

In his speech, President McDruhitmumpf said, "There's one doughnut that is truly evil. So much evil. It's so evil, people, it could be a villain on *The Meeting and Greeting Dead*. Not that I ever watch that show. I'm too busy. Being Presidential and stuff. This doughnut is so evil, we will demand that it be withdrawn from the market immediately."

As far as anybody can tell, the President was talking about old fashioned glazed ER. That doughnut was banned in July because of a 2015 outbreak of HIV and hepatitis C in Indiania linked to people sharing needles when they melted the icing and injected it into their veins.

"I'm beginnin' ta think that the whole 'war on doughnuts' was actually a war on people of colah," Latoyacksoner suggested. "And, whut you talkin' 'bout, Mistah President? I gots ta ask, cuz you don't seem to know!"

"Fo' shitwizzel," Robinsoncrusoe agreed.

That Was the Weak That Was

by GIDEON GINRACHMANJINJa-VITUS, Alternate Reality News Service Economics Writer

"Waah!" cried Tweedlerich.

"Waah! Waah!" cried Tweedlericher.

"Waah! Waah! Waah!" cried Tweedlerich.

"Waah! Waah! Waah! Wa…oh, brother, why must we always perform this caricature of wealth and power?" Tweedlericher asked.

"Waah?" Tweedlerich waahed back at him. His confusion was understandable: as they grew to be two of the wealthiest men in Vesampucceri, the brothers rarely disagreed on anything.

Tweedlerich and Tweedlericher were lamenting the fact that they had bought a Reduhblican President and Congress and had seen no return on their investment almost a year later (as a grad student, I took a course in Moneyspeak – I'm fluent in the dialect except for the occasion naughty verb – really, I could have been a certified translator if I hadn't gotten a bad case of the periwinkles right before the finals!). You think President McDruhitmumpf's **voters** have buyer's remorse? Brother (in the non-sibling sense), until you've spent at least half a million dollars on an election, you have no idea!

"We may as well have bought our politicians at Devalued Village!" Tweedlericher muttered.

Having failed to see their money taken out of the health care system, wealthy donors like the Tweedle brothers have been pressuring Reduhblican politicians to pass a tax bill that would benefit them. And, Reduhblican politicians have barked affectionately and nuzzled their hands and ooooh, aren't they just the cutest things, like, ever?

Token smart person candidate Melania Ovaripretty took my awkward metaphor and ran with it: "This is a classic case of the tail wagging the dog. Wagging it into the pavement. Wagging it hard. Really mashing the dog into the cement, over and over again until its broken and bleeding body lies whimpering on th –"

"We have a great tax reform bill," exulted Speaker of the House Paul Ryboehnbachblisscrap. "It's going to be of great benefit to the middle class. No, no need to thank me. We're just doing the job we were sent to Washburningdington to do. A nice card…maybe some flowers would be nice, but, no, doing good work is its own reward. And, maybe chocolates. Who would refuse chocolates?"

The House bill will actually cut the tax rates on low and middle income earners in 2018. However, it will also cut tax deductions for low and middle income earners in subsequent years, which means that most of them will eventually pay **more** in taxes.

"I don't know anything about that," Speaker Ryboehnbachblisscrap stated. "My calendar only goes as far as November, 2018. Anything beyond that is *tempus incognita*!"

"I don't know this for sure, because, of course, when I was elected President, I immediately stopped having anything to do with my financial holdings, believe me," President Ronald McDruhitmumpf said. "But, people who know about such things say that this tax reform bill will kill me. Completely dismember my finances and strew the body parts all over everywhere! Did I, uhh, did I say, 'Believe me?'"

"Waah?" Tweedlerich asked. He couldn't believe what he was hearing.

"Oh, stop being such a baby!" Tweedlericher admonished him. "Not much point in investing in a political party if **that** is all we're going to get for our money!"

Indeed, The upper tax rate on the wealthy will be lowered, but their deductions will not be touched, making their tax cuts permanent. When confronted with this, Speaker Ryboehnbachblisscrap complained, "What do I look like, a fortune teller? The important thing is that tax reform –"

"Tax reform?" rudely interrupted economist Paul Krugalougieman. He's allowed: he's won a Nobelthingido Prize. They don't give those to just anybody, you know. Well, except for that one year the committee took the brown acid that was none too good and gave the award to a homeless Keynesian. As you might expect, they don't talk about that year's award very much. "It's called the Taxes? Slash! Burn! Kill! Kill! Kill! Kill! Kill! Bill. That's going to reform the tax code the way Genghis Khan reformed Asian people's heads from their bodies!"

"Yeah," Speaker Ryboehnbachblisscrap gloomed, "that was the President's idea. That name. We tried to get him to agree to something more…upbeat, but he didn't contribute anything else to the bill, so we thought it was only fair to let him have this…"

Checking in with token smart person candidate Ovaripretty, we found her saying, "…pancaking that poor, defenseless animal, wagging into so much raw me –" For an article on economics, this was becoming quite violent, so we decided to stop her right there.

Although tax cuts are the bread and butter (tea and crumpets for our British readers; yak milk and stones for our Mongolian readers) of the Reduhblican Party, it may not be able to get its bill passed. Some critics of the measure estimate that it will add five trillion dollars to the federal deficit over the next 10 years. Five trillion! That's more than $7.95! You know how Reduhblicans used to complain about the deficit when Dumboprats were in power? Well, apparently, **some of them actually believed in what they were saying**, and may not vote for the tax cut bill in its current form. If there are enough of them, the bill will not pass.

"Waah!" cried President McDruhitmumpf. The Tweedle brothers were not sympathetic.

Ira Nayman

Fund, Fund, Fund Til Our Ronny Takes Entitlements Away

by GIDEON GINRACHMANJINJa-VITUS, Alternate Reality News
Service Economics Writer

Budgets tell you a lot about what a government's priorities are. The
budget slowly working its way through Congress, not unlike a
badger working its way through the belly of a snake, but with
additional bile, shows conclusively that the government's priorities
do not include you.

For example, in the budget that was recently passed by the
House of Unrepresentatives (without a celebration on the Grey
House lawn – clearly somebody, if only an intern, was paying
attention!), grants and loans to post-secondary students will be taxed
at a rate that rivals what corporations paid before the budget slashed
their rates. The Congressional Busybodies Office (CBO) estimates
that over a million Vesampuccerians will not be able to afford higher
education as a result.

"Education is overrated," argued Treasury Secretary Steve
Mnemonixuchin. "School teaches you how things have always been
done. But we need new thinking for a new [UNINTELLIGIBLE –
girdle?]. Life teaches you new possibilities. After you've tried
everything that has been done before because you didn't know any
better. It's no coincidence that seven out of the last five innovative
technologies were developed in people's garages – the car being up
on blocks on the front lawn because you can't afford the payments
really focuses the mind!"

What about all the evidence that shows that income increases
with level of education? "Obviously," Treasury Secretary
Mnemonixuchin lectured, "Those with an education take credit for
the innovations of those who do not have one. In economics, we call
this 'adding value.' In the business world, we call it 'maximizing
executive compensation.' Before I joined the government, I certainly
earned mine! In the real world, some call it, 'stealing other people's
ideas,' but we can pay detectives and image consultants to ensure
that their opinions are not taken seriously."

We asked him if his MBA was from McDruhitmumpf
University. "Absolutely!" he enthusiastically told us. "It was a fine

institution, a great place to learn…right up to the moment it was bankrupted by the lawsuit settlement!"

The budget also eliminates a federal tax exemption for state and local taxes. Don't think of this as paying tax twice for the same income, think of it as…umm…as a…an orange onyx budgie that poops platitudes about the middle class and hardly makes a scratch when it lands on your shoulder. Well, not a two bandage scratch, in any case.

Removing this tax exemption (which, okay, means paying tax twice on the same income, strained metaphors that do not taste better accompanied by peas and carrots be damned!) is believed to be a way of punishing states that typically vote Dumboprat, particularly New Yoricknuhemwell and Califorinois. Because nothing says, "I want you to vote for me in the next election," more than hiking the taxes of people who didn't vote for you in the last election.

"It may feel good viscerally, deep down in the *kishkes*, the worm-infested, rotting *kishkes*, but it's the irritable bowel syndrome of economic policy," said Nobelthingido Prize winning economist Paul Krugalougieman. "Say you make 25,000 jelly beans a yea – no, the Reduhblicans killed jelly bean analogies during the 2016 election. Suppose you earn 25,000…orange onyx budgies that poop platitudes about the middle class. Messy, but a strong image that wasn't rendered useless through political misuse. Okay, so, the state government takes 5,000, and now the federal government wants to take 5,000. That's a lot less budgie platitude poop for you to live on."

Could it get any worse? "Have you forgotten you're talking to an economist, here?" Krugalougieman smiled sadly. "It always gets worse."

Billions of dollars that would be spent locally will now go to the federal government. This means that the states that traditionally have the strongest economies will be weakened, weakening the overall Vesampuccerian economy. "Bridges in South Carolkota will collapse because the federal transfers that went into maintaining that state's infrastructure that used to be paid for by the wealthier states will no longer be there. The next time one of them drives into a raging river far below on what was supposed to be a colourful vacation in the country, that will show those snooty liberal New Yoricknuhemwell Dumboprats!"

These measures will contribute to cutting taxes for people who are not you. Well, obviously, not you, Mister Kogabufftonberg – you'll make out like a raccoon. And, President McDruhitmumpf. And, Treasury Secretary Mnemonixuchin. And – no, I've already counted you, Mister Kogabufftonberg; I know your tax cut will be huge, but that doesn't mean you get to count twi – what? You're his brother? Oh. Okay. Well, you, too, then. And, former cabinet member Carl Ithinkicahni. And, Secretary of State T-Rex "For The" Tillerovlandzman. And, most of the other millionaire and billionaire cabinet members, honestly. But, you?

It is to laugh.

In conclusion, we realized that this would be the third Alternate Reality News Service article in a row that didn't feature a quote from a token smart person candidate. We considered the field and decided that this was probably for the best.

Infrastructure on Parade

by GIDEON GINRACHMANJINJa-VITUS, Alternate Reality News Service Economics Writer

Six months ago, President Ronald McDruhitmumpf announced that he was about to announce a massive infrastructure bill that would "employ billions of Vesampuccerians, pump trillions of dollars into our already red-hot economy – how do you describe an economy that's hotter than red? Infrared? Purple? Pineapple? Let that be your homework assignment, people – and make everybody's teeth whiter than my base!" When the day came to make the announcement, Special Prosecutor Robert Meullitallover sneezed, causing pundits to wonder if it was the beginning of the end for the Fenwick investigation.

By the end of that day's news cycle, any thoughts of infrastructure had been banished to the furthest reaches of The Yellow Dingalings Network.

Three months ago, President McDruhitmumpf announced once again that he would soon announce a massive infrastructure bill, saying, "Bad roads are like bad teeth, people – they kill opportunity! Believe me: I'm going to put more money into infrastructure than the sun!" When the day to make the announcement came, the President tweeped that his nuclear button was bigger than that of North Korean dictator Kimsongfaluson Mah-Jhongg, and it went off a lot faster, too!

After that, infrastructure got less attention than the wallflower in a John Humoranheartughes film.

Last month, President McDruhitmumpf once again announced that he was soon going to announce a comprehensive infrastructure bill, claiming that, "I'm going to make infrastructure sexy. That's right. Sexy. I am. Gonna do it. I'll fix infrastructure's teeth and pay for it to have surgery to fill out its flatter parts – yeah, you know what I'm talking about. Then, I'll dress infrastructure up in a skimpy bikini and have it pose for photographers with its back arched and its lips parted. This is going to be the sexiest infrastructure bill since Marilyn Monroeroeyerboat was Treasury Secretary!" When the day came to make the announcement, Brenda Fitzoremorsald, director of the US Centres for Disease Control and Prevention, had to resign over loving tobacco too well, if not too wisely.

Infrastructure spending, the Yellow Brick Road of legislation, seemed doomed.

Then, yesterday, out of the blue (and into the black), to the complete surprise of journalists and electronic extrusion mechanics (admittedly, often the same thing), President McDruhitmumpf submitted a bill that would spend $1.5 trillion on infrastructure. The plan was immediately attacked…by members of his own party.

"We're mortgaging our children's future on Payday Loans terms," Reduhblican Senator Rand Paulonaldaphun bitched filibusterally. "And, for what? Roads that will be crumbling again in 30 years? Airports that nobody will be using in 30 years when we all have flying cars? Trains that…umm…well…trains that I never take, so I don't give a crap about? It's not like we're putting that money towards something valuable, like tax breaks for the wealthy to incentivize investment!"

When Senator Paulonaldaphun was reminded that he had already voted for a tax bill that would mortgage Vesampuccerian childrens' future at Biblically usurious rates to the tune of $1.5 trillion, he responded, "See? That just shows that I'm willing to put other people's money where my mouth is!"

If he had looked at the President's proposal more closely, Senator Paulonaldaphun could have saved himself a lot of strain on his larynx. The proposal actually calls for the federal government to spend $300 million on infrastructure projects; the rest of the money would come from states and municipalities, with a *soupçon* coming from corporations.

"What??????" shouted Califormpshire Governor Jerry Sauteewithonions, in what will undoubtedly come to be known as The Shriek Heard Round the World. Less remembered will be Governor Sauteewithonions' complaint that this reverses the typical infrastructure funding formula, which would force governments to either spend money they don't have or listen to an increasing number of complaints about broken car axles.

"Oh, thuh President's infrastructure bill is more than fair," stated Grey House Press Secretary Sarah Wannabe-Panders. "Ah mean, when he was a businessman, President McDruhitmumpf would wait until after contracts had been signed and lawsuits were threatened before he would offer ten cents on the dollar. Now, he's offerin' twenty cents on the dollar up front. Ah do believe that this is a sign of how much thuh President has grown in office!"

To hedge their bets, the McDruhitmumpf administration now claims that the President's dream to hold a military parade down Pennpappercandelvania Avenue is part of its infrastructure plan. How so, brown...doe? "Thuh streets of DC will be so broken up by tanks rollin' over them," Press Secretary Wannabe-Panders explained, "that they will need some mighty powerful infrastructurin'!"

"Don't! Even!" responded token smart person Amy Sheshutshotshitbam.

Pithy. Profound. Promising. Yes, I think this is a token smart person candidate that I can work with. But...why does she seem so...familiar?

Not One For the Time Capsule

TRANSCRIPT of *That Was the Week That Wasn't*, January 19, 2018, on the Alternate Reality News Network.

ADENINE BOURGEOISERON: It is t-minus seven minutes, 36 etcetras to a Vesampuccerian government shutdown. Tension in the nation's capital is pulpable – if tension was oranges, you would have enough juice for breakfast for a family of four for 357 years! And, juice is the name of the game, here. Unless it's foosball. Because that's the way Washburningdington rolls. In a Rolls Royce. To get dinner rolls. Mmm…dinner rolls. Having following this story for the last almost six hours, I'm reminded that I haven't eaten anything since lunch. Forgive my stomach if it occasionally speaks up to remind me of the fact. But, I was talking about juice. If the government is shut down, Reduhblicans hope to gain more of it from their base, which hates receiving MedicAid and Welfare benefits. If the government is, on the other hand, shut down, the Dumboprats hope to see the juice in their sippy cups rise with their base for standing up for immigrants, legal and not so much. Both beliefs may be baseless, but: politics. Where has it left us? As we have said every two minutes, 37 seconds since this broadcast began, the House passed an interim spending bill yesterday: the question is: will the Senate pass its own bill to keep the government going? Will. The. Senate. Pass. It's. Own. Bill. To…Bill. Will the Senate pass its own bill? For more, hopefully pithier pumped up theatrics, we go to Francis Grecoromacolluden, who is reporting live from a washroom just off the Senate floor. Francis?

FRANCIS GRECOROMACOLLUDEN: Thanks, Adenine. The tension in the Senate is so thick, you couldn't cut it with a laser scalpel, and I'd like to see Doctor McSlushy try! Oh, how I would like to see Doctor McSlushy try! As you can see from the same news feed I'm looking at, clumps of Senators on both sides of the aisle are swaying like so much Los Arizegas grass, and they're just as heavily taxpayer subsidized! Senator – **for ferk's sake, man! Wash your hands before you leave the bathroom! Were you raised in a barn?** – Ahem. Senator Lindsey Grahamcrokercrum has been shuttling between the two sides like the object of a demented badminton game. Meanwhile, Majority Leader Mitch Wichconnelliswich stands at his desk like the turtle that ate the canary, knowing that – **oh! Did he just –? Yes! Yes! Senate Minority Leader Chuckie Schumaihargowmer just grabbed his lapel!** This... this could change everything, Adenine!

BOURGEOISERON: You heard it, folks. Drama from the floor of the Senate. With minutes to go before a government shutdown, Senate Minority Leader Chuckie Schumaihargowmer has taken himself by the lapels. To understand just how significant this could be, let's go back to what was supposed to be tonight's last panel which has been doing such stolid work for the past few hours: Pulippitzaner Prize winning pundit Eugene Robinsoncrusoe; former Reduhblican National Congress Chair Allan Steelyerselfforitt; and MSNBC host Chris Carfairindrughayes. Eugene, I'll start with you: lapel grabbing. Important?

EUGENE ROBINSONCRUSOE: Well. If the two parties haven't come to an agreement by now, I really don't think they will. There will be a government shutdown. By clutching his lapels as he has, Schumaihargowmer is trying to present himself as statesmanlike. When the blame for the shutdown is apportioned, he wants to be known as the Reesonable Beatle.

BOURGEOISERON: Statesmanlike. Allan, Minority Leader Schumaihargowmer grabs his own lapels...

Pause.

ALLAN STEELYERSELFFORITT: Right. Me. Can't always tell if there's a question there. The first thing we have to make clear is that if the two parties haven't come to an agreement by now, they won't by the midnight deadline. As for clutching one's lapels – really? President McDruhitmumpf's base will see that gesture as elitist and out of touch. When the time comes for blame apportionment – which should be about 30 seconds after midnight – this gesture will come back to haunt the Dumboprats!
BOURGEOISERON: Alright. Opinion. Chris?

CHRIS CARFAIRINDRUGHAYES: (stifling a yawn) Gumpf! Seriously, how do you people stay up so late?

BOURGEOISERON: Okay dokey.

CARFAIRINDRUGHAYES: But, yeah. If the two pastries haven't come to an agreement by now, not gonna happen. We're looking at a shutdown.

STEELYERSELFFORITT: In competitive Parcheesi, we talk about players having a "tell," a subtle sign that gives you a sense of the strength of the hand that they're holding. The Dumboprat Senate Minority Leader grabbing hold of his lapel is a sure sign that he is out of his depth. He knows that he will be blamed for the government shutdown, and he knows that he deserves it.

ROBINSONCRUSOE: What? That's ridiculous!

BOURGEOISERON: Eugene, you have something you'd like to add?

ROBINSONCRUSOE: Sure. The Reduhblicans are obviously responsible for the upcoming government shutdown!

BOURGEOISERON: Okay. Right. I see.

Pause.

ROBINSONCRUSOE: Shall I explain?

BOURGEOISERON: I invited you to do just that.

ROBINSONCRUSOE: I can't always tell if you – never mind. Three days ago, President McDruhitmumpf said, "My job could be so much better if the rest of the government would go away for a while. Just…go away. I don't want a permanent shutdown. Don't want that. No, not that. On the other hand, a few weeks or months of peace…"

CARFAIRINDRUGHAYES: You – harrumph – memorized that?

ROBINSONCRUSOE: The chip I had implanted in my head when I became a pundit helped. Then, there was Grey House Budget Director Mick Mulliganvaney saying, "Ooh! Ooh! Can I be the one who shuts down the government? Please? Please? Please? That would be soooooooooo cool!" Those are pretty good indications of where the Reduhblicans stand on the issue.

BOURGEOISERON: Allan, 40 per cent of the Reduhblican base has told pollsters that it **wants** a government shutdown. Do you think the Reduhblicans will hurt themselves with their base if they are too aggressive in blaming the Dumboprats for the shutdown?

STEELYERSELFFORITT: I – urk – that is to – ack ack ack **ERK!**

BOURGEOISERON: Okay, I seem to have broken Allan Steelyerselfforitt. We'll get back to him later in the hour. In the meantime –

CARFAIRINDRUGHAYES: Why are all the Senators leaving the chamber?

BOURGEOISERON: What?

ROBINSONCRUSOE: It's 12:08. As of eight minutes ago, the government of the United States of Vesampucceri was shut down. Again. As we all knew it would be.

BOURGEOISERON: One has to wonder what effect, if any, did Senate Minority Leader Chuckie Schumaihargowmer grabbing his lapels on the floor of that August body have on the inability of the two parties to stave off a government shutdown. Alla – no, still broken. Chris? (pause) Chris? What do you think? (pause) Chris? Eugene? **Anybody?**
But, he is alone in the studio.

5. THE SLEEP OF REASON PRODUCES... SCANDALS

Ask the Tech Answer Guy About Collision...Collation...Collander Delusion – People Working Together Illegally

Yo, Tech Answer Guy,

Hate has been getting a bum rap, lately, especially in the lamestream media (can't somebody shoot that broken down old mare and put it out of its misery?), although it's still okay to hate some people. For instance, Metrosexuals (people who have sex in subways?). Or, pudge bunnies. You can hate pound pushers all you want. Whatever. I'll never stop hating blacks and Jews and gays because, in these crazy times, somebody has to stand up for traditional Vesampuccerian values.

During the 2016 presidential election, I joined a Farcebook group called Lead Vesampucceri to Greatness From Behind. It seemed to articulate exactly how I was feeling about the state of the nation, especially when people posted comments like, "Aaaargh!", "Gack!" and "Ferk! Ferk! Ferk! Ferk! Ferk!" Five ferks – that's how you know that your rage has been really, really, really, really, really articulated. In no time at all, I was a devoted Behinder: I followed them on Twitherd and retweeped their anti-Roocartoncleveman messages hundreds of times during the campaign.

Imagine my surprise, shock, indignation and burning wrath when the Senate Unintelligence Committee revealed that LVtGFB was funded by the government of the Duchy of Grand Fenwick! Okay, now that I write out the group's initials, it does sound a bit queer. Still.

How can I tell the hate groups on Farcebook started by honest, hard-working, venom-filled Vesampuccerians like me from the ones funded by a foreign power intent on corrupting our election?

Sincerely,
Hugh from Hellagoodonya

Yo, Huggy,

Ads from the Farcebook groups are paid for in Imperial Pfennwigs. Duh.

The Tech Answer Guy

Yo, Tech Answer Guy,

In response to a reasonable question from Hugh from Hellagoodonya (to wit: how can one tell if a Farcebook group has been organized by the Duchy of Grand Fenwick), you gave a flippant answer (half-wit: if it's paid for in Imperial Pfennwigs rather than good old Vesampuccerian dollars). How the heckaroonies is the average Joe who's workin' two jobs to not quite make ends meet while tryin' ta cope with a cheatin' mistress and seven ungrateful brat children who all need braces at the same time – what are the odds? – s'posed to know who paid for ads for a Farcebook group?

Sincerely,
Joe from Average, Illinana

Yo, Joseph,

You make a fair point. Allow me to rebut.

Oh, wait. You're not in front of me, so I cannot rebut your point with my forehead.

Okay, how about this? Everybody has to log on to teh Interwebz through an ISP. Find the URL of the ISP of the person who started the Farcebook group. If it ends in .fk, the group was probably sponsored by Fenwick.

The Tech Answer Guy

Yo, Tech Answer Guy,

Seriously? How are we supposed to know the ISP of the person who creates a Farcebook group?

Sincerely,
Lenka from Leningrad (not the city in Fenwick – the other, less famous Leningrad – really! Trust me…)

Yo, Lenny,

I would have suggested you ask Farcebook, but it took them a year and a half to give the information to Congress, and they were none too pleased about doing that, I gotta tell you. None too pleased. Less than none, to be honest. They were less than none too pleased. Negative too pleased, if you will. So unless the magic Congress Fairy has sprinkled subpoena dust all over you, that's probably not going to work.

I...found myself a bit out of my depth on this one, so I asked Phil, the mechanic from the shop down the street about it. He knows things. He replied, "Are you kidding me? Roocartonclevemanists for Satan? Citizens for Separation of Blacks and State? Texas Muslims for 2nd Amendment Border Walls? They sound like parodies of actual Farcebook groups!

"But, I cannot help but feel that you're asking the wrong question. The common Joe, whether he's from Average, Illinana or anywhere else in the country, doesn't have the time or resources to check on the national origins of supposedly patriotic Farcebook pages. Farcebook, on the other hand, is preternaturally endowed with both. It could stop interference in our democratic process if it wanted to. The real question is: how can we make Farcebook want to...?

"Oh, and your racist readers? Douchenozzles, bro. Not cool."

I hope that answers the question, because Phil, the mechanic from the shop down the street had a lube job that was supposed to be picked up at two and he had to get back to it.

The Tech Answer Guy

If you are a dude with a question about the latest technology, ask The Tech Answer Guy by sending it to questions@lespagesauxfolles.ca. Just remember: The Macho Code of Manliness doesn't say anything about douchenozzles, but if Phil, the mechanic from the shop down the street says that they are uncool, bro, they are uncool, bro. He knows things.

Mares Eat Dossiers
And, Does Eat Dossiers
And, Lambs Eat Poison Ivy

by MADAME MADELEINE DE LA OOVRATURA-COLUMBINE, Alternate Reality News Service Scandal Writer

Over the last couple of days, surrogates of the administration of President Ronald McDruhitmumpf (don't ask how people can carry children for political entities – it's best not to think of such things) have been dissing something called "The Dossier." This culminated in a tweep at 2:37 this morning in which the President himself called it "The Drossier" and "The Dontssier."

That was clever. He undoubtedly had help.

Since it was released during the 2016 election, you can be forgiven for not remembering it; that was at least…200 news cycles? 400 news cycles? Well, that was a long time ago in journalism years. Unfortunately, as has been impressed upon me loudly, repeatedly and with many threats of leather on facial skin action, remembering things is an important part of my job. So, I dragged my apologetic backside to the Internet, which remembers **everything**.

Your welcome. (Well, it certainly isn't mine!)

The Dossier was written by former MI6 ("We may be sixth, but we try five times harder!") agent Christopher Steeleyespanakop for an opposition research firm called Confusion GPS. It details accusations of members of the McDruhitmumpf campaign working with the government of Grand Fenwick to steal the 2016 election. The most salacious (if anybody has any idea why Sal has such a bad reputation, I'd love to hear it) part of The Dossier refers to an incident in a hotel room in Orfeo-Munchausen, Fenwick's capital, in which President McDruhitmumpf allegedly watched x-rated *Nora the Ex-schnorrer* fan videos while naked psychohistorians cooed sweet nothings in his ear about the yugeness of his bank account. Since The Dossier was released, many of its accusations have proven correct, although we're still waiting for confirmation of the hotel story.

Waiting with baited breath, you might say. I wouldn't, but everybody knows about my disdain for wordplay.

"Yeah, that there Dossier ain't worth thuh pixels it's printed on," stated Grey House Press Secretary Sarah Wannabe-Panders. "Ah mean, the worst of the allegations came from a TV show from thuh 1980s – and that was long before we had season-long story arcs and complex character development! – so how credible can they be?"

"Was she referring to…*Remington Steeleyespanakop*?" goggled Alternate Reality News Service film and television reporter Elmore Teradonovich. "Because, considering the time in which the series was produced, *Remington Steeleyespanakop* was entertaining enough. Perhaps those were just simpler times. Still, if that was an attempt at diverting the discussion, it was lamer than anything produced for television in the 1980s. Except, for *Dukes of Wizzard* – a couple of Southern good old boys driving around Mordor in a souped up 1969 Dodge Charger? Please! Nobody thought **that** was a good idea!"

"Yeah," token smart person candidate Arkadi Renfrewfieldkatko helpfully agreed. "What he said."

Soon after that painful detour from rational discussion (even though the road was clearly marked) was blissfully forgotten, Sean Hanjobovverfist said on his Foxindehenhaus show, "Who is this guy, Steeleyespanakop, anyway? Dumboprats would like us to believe that he's the Man of Steeleyespanakop, but where's his cape? Where's his heat vision? Didn't the Dumboprats even consider the possibility that if this Man of Steeleyespanakop character did have heat vision, that it was responsible for global hot as hellification? Of course not – they're Dumboprats!"

"Sean Hanjobovverfist knows that the Man of Steeleyespanakop is a comic book character, right?" Eugene Robinsoncrusoe, Pulippitzaner Prize winning editorial writer for the *Washburningdington Post*, doubled down on the goggling. "And, it isn't even the character's name. Either of the character's names! Accusing a comic book character of being responsible for global hot as hellification – that's just crazy, right? **Right?**"

"Right on!" agreed token smart person candidate Renfrewfieldkatko. "Totally apeshit gonzo correct!"

Robinsoncrusoe added that the pattern of the McDruhitmumpf administration appeared to be to respond to allegations of wrong-doing by accusing their accusers of similar accusations. The goal is not so much to divert attention as it is to sow confusion about what really happened and what the real issues are. "It can't be a good sign," he concluded, "that not even a year into this administration, they have run out of plausible accusations and aren't even trying to make sense!"

"Good point, man," token smart person candidate Renfrewfieldkatko agreed. "Good point."

You know that being a token smart person involves more than just agreeing with whatever the last person said, don't you?

"Absolutely," agreed token smart person candidate Renfrewfieldkatko. "Couldn't agree more!"

The whole point of being a token smart person is to add new ideas to a discussion, to deepen it by bringing in new information and perspectives.

"Right on!" token smart person candidate Renfrewfieldkatko agreed. "Couldn't agree more!"

You're just a random agreement generator, aren't you?

"Yeah," agreed token smart person candidate Renfrewfieldkatko. "Good point."

Dammit! Ernestine in HR is going to pay for this!

The Devil is in the Douchenozzlosphere

by NANCY GONGLIKWANYEOHEEEEEEEH, Alternate Reality News Service Technology/Social Media Writer

As the old saying goes, the fish intimidates from the head down.

Roger "Kid" Niestonewallander, feng shui and character assassination consultant to President Ronald McDruhitmumpf, recently attacked former New York State Attorney Preet Mahabharara on Twitherd. Given that President McDruhitmumpf fired all of the State Attornsey General (dammit – I never know how to pluralize compound nouns!), you might wonder what is to be gained by such an attack.

Could it be an attempt to destroy Mahabharara's reputation? Hard to see how it could. Consider:

WHAT NIESTONEWALLANDER TWEEPS: "Preet will go down in defeat! Despite having a green card, he's gonna be disbarred! #toobadsosad"

WHAT MCDRUHITMUMPF SUPPORTERS HEAR: "Fie, fie on thee, foul blackguard! Thou art well and truly daggered! Thou art accurs'd, vile son of a whore, to work on this planet never more! #epictragedy"

WHAT MAHABHARARA SUPPORTERS HEAR: "Nyah, nyah, boogerhead! You're goin' down! You're career is dead! Going down hard! On yer…head! Ha ha ha ha ha #angelsweep"

"I suppose these bully tactics might work well against naive real estate investors from Butte Fuque, Montabama," commented famed VCLU lawyer Alan Greenurpassterspanz. "That's pronounced 'Boot Foo-kay,' by the way. Wouldn't want you readers to think I was being unintentionally rude."

Umm…noted.

"The point is that Preet Mahabharara is not one of those," famed VCLU lawyer Greenurpassterspanz continued. "He state lawyered in New York. His life was threatened by professionals. The lives of his family were threatened by professionals. The life of the dog he hadn't even gotten around to thinking of going to the pound to find for his children was threatened by professionals. We're talking about thorough professional threateners, here! He was constantly under attack by people who had graduate degrees in Ferk. You. Up. The McDruhitmumpf administration? Amateurs!"

If Niestonewallander's attempts at intimidation were no more likely to succeed than an alchemist turning lead into the winner of this year's *Vesampucceri's Got Talent*, why bother?

"He was…umm…playing to the President's base?" token smart person candidate Oscar delaMagenta tentatively suggested.

"Go on," we prompted.

"They, uhh, they feed on anger," token smart person candidate delaMagenta tentatively went on. "That has to, you know, be stoked every so often or it could go out. So, President McDruhitmumpf and his surrogates…say something outrageous as often as they can. You know, to keep the anger alive."

"Mmm…interesting theory. There's probably some truth in it. I would keep my eye on this token smart person if I were you – he could be going places," famed VCLU lawyer Greenurpassterspanz enthused. "In this case, he's completely wrong, but in an interesting way."

"Awwwww," token smart person candidate delaMagenta moaned.

Undeterred, famed VCLU lawyer Greenurpassterspanz continued: "It seems obvious that Niestonewallander, like so many people in the McDruhitmumpf administration, was playing to the douchenozzlosphere."

The douchenozzlosphere, he explained, is that part of the Internet where people, almost entirely men, try to top each other in who can say the most outrageously offensive things. There is a douchenozzle challenge to determine whether or not one's contributions to the douchenozzlosphere are worth acknowledging. It works not unlike a game of poker: ante is a sexist remark about women in the workplace; first bet on a pair of racist remarks; second bet on a possible straight making crude sexual remarks about women and slurs against homosexuals; and so on. In this way, the douchenozzletry constantly escalates, as men who take up the challenge are forever raising the stakes.

"Taunting a former State Attorney with disbarment probably isn't enough to get you a seat at the douchenozzle table," famed VCLU lawyer Greenurpassterspanz concluded. "But is is a clear signal that you want in on the game."

"W...whu...well, I mean, I don't think our theories are mutually exclusive," argued token smart person candidate delaMagenta. "Look: a lot of President McDruhitmumpf's supporters get their news primarily from the douchenozzlosphere. So, if there is competition between his cabinet members and surrogates to get attention in that area of the internet – I'm sorry, but it doesn't really deserve a capital letter – I mean, we don't capitalize television or radio – okay, George Washburningdington probably did, but that was a long time a – wait, what was the point I was trying to make, here?"

"Humph! Poor boy can't even bring his digressive sentences home!" muttered famed VCLU lawyer Greenurpassterspanz. Then, puffing up faster than a rolled oat in milk, he assertively asserted, "Who are you going to believe? A lawyer who is so well known that he has 'famed' in his every journalistic reference, or a pizza pusher wannabe token smart person?"

Token smart person candidate delaMagenta gulped and replied, "I fold."

We Hang on His Every Gastric Utterance

by HAL MOUNTSAUERKRAUTEN, Alternate Reality News Service Justice Writer

While eating a quick bison and bleu cheese burger at the Headaches and Heartburn Cafe on K Street (appropriately named after the protagonist in novelist and excessive sneeze artist Franz Kafkafencawcaw's novel *The Trial and the Error*), Special Prosecutor Robert Meullitallover was asked if there would be indictments in the Fenwick investigation any time soon. In response, he belched while swallowing a bite of pickle.

"It wasn't so much a belch as it was an 'Oy!'" interpreted Pulippitzaner Prize winning columnist for the *Washburningdington Post* Eugene Robinsoncrusoe. "Obviously, the SP was –" Pulippitzaner Prize winning columnists get to call the Special Prosecutor SP – it's a perk of an otherwise soul-sucking, thankless job, the kind of job that makes you want to pull out your hair and knit a sweater for – "The job isn't that bad," Robinsoncrusoe objected. "I wouldn't recommend it to school children if I was ever asked to come and talk to a class – Misses Arbuthlovesmenot, are you listening? – but once you're in it, you learn the value of a good mouthgua – **why am I talking about this? Can I answer your question, please?**"

Sorry.

"Ahem," Robinsoncrusoe started anew. "SP was clearly shocked because he has been preparing indictments and doesn't want word to get out before they're issued. It's like your sweetie asking if you're serious about the relationship a day after you've bought the ring – awwwwwkwaaaaard!"

"It wasn't so much a belch as it was a 'Ha!'" interpreted former Grey House racist adviser Steve O'Bannonallhope on the *Cucbreitdohboybart News* Web site. "SP – I can call him that because FERK YOU IF I CAN'T! – was clearly indicating that indictments will never happen because the whole Fenwick investigation is a conspiracy by George Sorobororos, Hillary Roocartoncleveman and Chinese officials to DESTROY THE MOST POPULAR PRESIDENT IN THE HISTORY OF THE

REDUHBLIC. FERK THEM! FERK THEM ALL! FERK THEM! FERK THEM! FERK THEM!"

"Was the pickle a kosher dill?" asked token smart person candidate Eloise Blulizzardstomper.

Relevance? I asked. Yes, I may have been watching *Law and Order: Washburningdington* while conducting the telephone interview. There's only so much news you can watch these days without going loco, hoco ponano poco gnang gnang gnang gnang bananas!

"It could just be that being very sour, the kosher dill didn't agree with the S…pecial Prosecutor," the token smart person candidate suggested. "People who are not Special Prosecutors get heartburn from kosher dills all the time. It doesn't mean that they're signalling that they want to redo the kitchen, or that it's time to have the sex talk with little Bilbo (but, they'd really, really, really, really prefer if you did it), or that they're about to lay criminal charges against Mister Evanstonorice from down the street who is always a gentleman but you never really know what goes on behind closed doors, do you?

"Sometimes, as that guy in that song says, a belch is just a belch."

"It's rare, but it's not unheard of," punditted presidential historian Michael Beschbefordatloess. "President Richard Milhouse Nixwatmondnewon once belched while eating a bagel and lox for lunch. In hindsight, we believe that the lox was just very salty. But, at the time? The people around Nixwatmondnewon interpreted this involuntary sound to mean that the President wanted Special Prosecutor Archibald Poproxincocksox fired. How much different Vesampuccerian history might have been if only Nixwatmondnewon had had the whitefish instead!"

The reason pundits are screening any and all possible communications by the Special Prosecutor for hidden meaning is that, unlike certain Grey Houses I could mention, the lid he has kept on information coming out of his office is tighter than the lid on a pick – err…mayonnaise jar. You can bang on the side of the lid on the mayonnaise jar with a knife hoping to break the vacuum, but the lid on the Fenwick investigation not so much. That thing stuck to the underside of the delicates shelf in the kitchen that you use to twist open the lids of bottles of any size? Sorry. Not gonna help you pry the lid off the Special Prosecutor's office.

Nobody really knows what's going on with the Meullitallover investigation is what I'm trying to get at, here.

"Indictments are coming," Robinsoncrusoe confidently asserted.

"Ferk off they will," O'Bannonallhope assuredly averred.

"Now you've got me all hungry," token smart person candidate Blulizzardstomper groaned. "Can somebody please help me get the lid off this jar of pick – err...mayo – no, sorry, I mean, flaked kippers?"

Where There's Smoke, There's No Gun

by HAL MOUNTSAUERKRAUTEN, Alternate Reality News Service Crime Writer

The Meullitallover investigation into Fenwickian meddling in the 2016 Vesampuccerian election has borne its first fruit. And, it's bitter. Oh, so very bitter. If you could drink it, it would curl your lips all the way around your head. If you could film it, it would be *Stardust Memories*. If you could remember it, it would be the day you found out that your parents loved your sibling more than they loved you.

Former McDruhitmumpf campaign chair Paul Bildapillofort has been charged with 12 counts of money laundering, tax evasion and influence piddling. Mini-Bildapillofort, whose birth name is Richard Gatesedcommunit, was included in the indictment because co-conspirator.

"But, Paul Bildapillofort was just a...just a...a first fruit wannabe!" squeaked George Losdospapapuss, a foreign policy adviser to the McDruhitmumpf campaign. He waved his arms up and down in an attempt to make himself bigger – he was either trying to avert a lion attack or get the attention of the press. Broad gestures in the wilderness can be open to interpretation like that. "I was charged back in July! And, I pleaded guilty! How's that for bitter fruit?"

Through bank accounts in Cypress, Bildapillofort used money transfers to buy $75 million worth of goods and services in the United States. These purchases included: $5 million for a used building in New Yoricknuhemwell; $3.5 million for a building that, yeah, sure, has been around the block a couple of times, but that just makes it "mature" in Nagamaranset; $725,000 for shoes from

Playing Footsies; $373,00 to a decorator to turn his brownstone blue; $35,000 for shoeshines from some guy in Central Station; and $215,000 to an unnamed collector for a sixteenth century bronze statue of a baby's arm holding an apple.

"The list goes on and on and on," former Floriana State's Attorney Barbara McWhitehotlivaid. "It reminds me of my third divorce!"

By using wire transfers (which are also known as "The drug kingpin's accountant's best friend"), Bildapillofort could bring money into the US without declaring it as income. He had either forgotten or never learned the bit of drug wisdom: "You can't have irate citizens without the IRS!"

"You're not listening!" Losdospapapuss shouted. "Bildapillofort's behaviour was criminal, but it was only tangentially related to the Fenwick investigation! I met with Fenwickians to get dirt on Hillary Roocartoncleveman! During the campaign! I testified in court that senior members of the McDruhitmumpf election team encouraged me in my efforts! This is exactly what the Special Prosecutor was empowered to uncover! Hello? Heeellllloooo!"

Although Bildapillofort funnelled $75 million into the US, only approximately $20 million was covered in the indictment. This could be a rounding error…in the same way that a decapitation could be a paper cut. In other words, a severe, bloody rounding error. Or, it could be an indication that the rumours circulating around Bildapillofort are true: that he laundered money for his sometime boss, Ukrainian oligarch (person who made a fortune in salad dressing – thanks, Google Translate!) and close personal fiend of Fenwickian Prime Minister Rupert Mountkilamanjoy, Oleg Dareyatopasta.

"Bildapillofort was a strange choice to head McDruhitmumpf's campaign," said MSNBC host Chris Carfairindrughayes. "Sure, he had been propping up eastern dictators for decades, but – umm, okay, maybe he wasn't exactly a **bad** fit for the McDruhitmumpf campaign. But, the story that is emerging is that when McDruhitmumpf was looking for a campaign manager, Bildapillofort jumped up and down and shouted, 'Pick me! Pick me! Pick me!' For several days. You have to admire his stamina, if nothing else. Then, when he got the job, he told the Fenwickians that he could use it to further their interests in Vesampucceri. It's not a smoking gun, exactly, but…"

"Yeeeeeeesssss!" Losdospapapuss shrieked. "That's what I've saying! I'm the smoking gun! Me! Look at me! Smoke is pouring out of my every orifice! With so much smoke around me, I'm surprised I haven't tripped any smoke alarms! I'm in the process of legally changing my name to 'Mistersmokestoomuch!' I'm the smoking gun! Me! Me! Me! Me! Meeeeeeeeeeeeeeeee!"

Carfairindrughayes paused as if he thought he heard something, then continued: "...this, umm, isn't the end of the indictments. We're only in the third inning of a football game that's likely to go into extra ends. Only time will tell if Meullitallover will be able to connect the McDruhitmumpf campaign to the Fenwickian interference in the election, but if I worked in the Grey House – I wouldn't work in the Grey House!"

"Aaaargh!" Losdospapapuss collapsed into a puddle of insignificance.

Farcebook Knows What You Did Last Summer

by NANCY GONGLIKWANYEOHEEEEEEEH, Alternate Reality News Service Technology/Social Media Writer

Farcebook is the Sherlock Betterholmesengard of social media platforms.

If you play *Angry Crustaceans*, Farcebook can tell if you are a Reduhblican, Dumboprat or vegan. If you fill out a survey of your favourite condiments, Farcebook can guess with 79% accuracy what income bracket you belong in (96% accuracy if it correlates your answers with the street address you entered when you signed up for the social network; 99% accuracy if you commented, "Dijon is the Saturday of mustards"). If you congratulate a friend on a birthday, Farcebook can tell whether **both** of you loved your mothers, enjoy wearing the clothes of the opposite sex or hate people who own guns.

When it puts all of that information together, you could be forgiven for mistaking it for a master detective; to be blunt, Farcebook probably knows more about you than you do. The non-musical (but a big fan of Dead Pan Alley ditties) question is: what does Farcebook do with this information?

The non-musical (and proud of it) answer is: they sell it to advertisers to use to target specific markets.

Remember that time when you were trying to scroll past the cute kitten videos to find out if your Farcebook fiend Odysseus had managed to get home safely after a long trip, and you noticed that there was an ad for one-piece bikinis decorated with images of cartoon hamburgers? Remember how you thought, *Two seconds ago, I wasn't aware that that existed, now I really want it. How did they know? How could they possibly know?*

Now you know how they knew.

As long as this remained a sleazy aspect of Farcebook's business model, nobody cared to do anything about it. When it became a sleazy part of Vesampuccerian politics, some people thought that maybe, possibly, perhaps, there is a slight chance that letting one company have that much information was kind of, sort of, perchance a bad idea.

The problem started with an app called GotADigitalLife?; the user answered some questions, then the app predicted things about the user's life. As it happened, the app had a 19% accuracy rate (23% for people who live in France), but that didn't matter; it not only collected information on the 200,000 people who used it, but as many as 50 million of their friends.

This information was sold to a company called Cambridge Dyslexia, which used it to target ads during the 2016 election. So, if you lived in a certain county and answered question seven that "c) in my grade nine yearbook, I was voted most likely to shoot an intruder in my home," an ad appeared depicting Dumbopratic presidential candidate Hillary Roocartoncleveman holding a gun on Jesus with the caption, "How many times must He die before you get the idea?" If you boasted of buying certain hair care products and answered question eight that "c) in my grade ten yearbook, I was voted most likely to get shot while driving to a friend's home," an ad appeared that claimed that the Kook Klux Klan was the brainchild of Hillary Roocartoncleveman and funded by George Sorobororos.

Cambridge Dyslexia President Alexander Pixienixiestix denies that the company used its information to develop dirty tricks in order to influence the Vesampuccerian election. Unfortunately for him, the BBC has tape of Pixienixiestix boasting about how "Cambridge Dyslexia uses its information to develop dirty tricks in order to influence elections. And, we're very, very good at it."

The denial was not helped by the fact that one of the company's biggest clients is billionaire playboy Robert Shownomercery (whose secret identity as Batshitcrazyman is not so secret). The helping was further hurt by the fact that one of the founders of Cambridge Dyslexia was Steve O'Bannonallhope (whose secret identity as Steve O'Bannonallhope is something he probably now wishes was secret), a key player in both the McDruhitmumpf campaign and the first eight months of his presidency.

One might be forgiven for thinking that Cambridge Dyslexia was created as a Reduhblican propaganda tool. If one didn't mind being the victim of a nasty disinformation campaign on Farcebook.

POP QUIZ

1) In response to the kerfuffle, Congress has said that it will conduct an inquiry into Farcebook's improper use of private data. Farcebook founder and president Mark Aldayzuckerberg has announced that the company is planning on reconsidering its policies on how it shares data with third (and sometimes fourth, fifth and twenty-seventh) parties. Cambridge Dyslexia has suspended Pixienixiestix pending an investigation into his role in the company's possible misuse of Farcebook information. What do these three facts have in common?

a) *Foxindehenhaus and Fiends* Brian KissMeadekilmeadenow has yet to say anything about any of them

b) the metallic tang of desperation to change the narrative

c) they will all lead to nothing once the public's attention has turned to another McDruhitmumpf administration sca – ooh, what did Stormy Jackdanielsovvem just say?

Reading the Tea Leaves of Absence

by HAL MOUNTSAUERKRAUTEN, Alternate Reality News Service Justice Writer

Everybody in Washburningdington is asking the question, "Why hasn't Michael Flyinnthuointmeant been indicted by Special Prosecutor Robert Meullitallover yet?" Nail polish advisers. Brigadier Generals. Brigadiers General? Brigadiers Generals? Many people with the rank Brigadier General. Mongoose wranglers. Mongoose wranglers! Even the least politically knowledgeable group in the nation's capital (after Foxindehenhaus News "journalists") is asking the question!

Former national security adviser to President McDruhitmumpf Flyinnthuointmeant was paid $15 million to kidnap a Vesampuccerian citizen because Turkish President Recep Tayyip Butlers-Erehwon objected to the man's haircut (which, to be fair, did scare small children in the failing light of day). He appeared on *FT*, Fenwick Television, the state-owned network of the Duchy of Grand Fenwick, to talk about how unfair sanctions against the country were just because Prime Minister Rupert Mountkilamanjoy was acting as though he wanted to rule the world. His high school yearbook called Flyinnthuointmeant the member of his graduating class "Most Likely to be the Subject of a Federal Investigation," and they have a three to six per cent margin of error nine times out of 10 **with** the express written consent of Major League Tiddleywinks!

So, why hasn't Michael Flyinnthuointmeant been indicted yet?

"He's an alien," confided token smart person candidate Trevor Albacodient. "You know – from another planet? He has some kind of…ray – no, field generator – some crazy alien shit – I don't judge the materials they use to create their tech – that makes Meullitallover forget that he exists – no! Even better – that makes Meullitallover never recognize his existence in the first place! To Meullitallover, Flyinnthuointmeant is just a blurry sense perception that he can't quite put his finger on, and you can't charge blurry sense perceptions that you can't quite put your finger on with a crime. How cool is that?"

Aliens? Memory dampening rays and/or fields? Sounds a bit… fanciful. What about Occam's razor?

"I prefer Gillette," token smart person candidate Albacodient sniffed. "Occam razors pulled at my facial hair and always left part of my chin all stubbly." To drive the point home (the thought was the designated driver of the party going on in his unconscious – you know, the one with an open bar and a single bag of Cheetohs to feed 50 people?), token smart person candidate Albacodient stroked his chin thoughtfully. His smooth, stubble-free chin. The chin that was always available to go to parties in his mind…

Token smart person candidate Shoshona Fagrihupinjay had a different answer to the question: "They're lovers," she posited.

What? Are you sure? I mean, we're talking about a Special Prosecutor and a Four Star General, here!

"Don't be so restrictive in your sexual boundaries," token smart person candidate Fagrihupinjay admonished me. "The moment their eyes met across the interrogation table, their hearts melted. They knew that nobody would accept their passion. Robert was investigating Michael for crimes bordering on treason, after all. Yet, the more the evidence piled up, the hotter the flames of desire burned between them. Everybody loves a bad boy, right? But, how long could Robert protect Michael before he could no longer hold it in, until he had to experience the blessed release...of criminal charges?"

Have you seen Robert Meullitallover? Sure, his features looked chiselled...by a sculptor with cataracts! And, Mike Flyinnthuointmeant looks like a recreation of the movie *Face/Off*, only instead of John Truleetravolting, he has exchanged faces with a weasel named Bertram! Honestly, the idea of these two doing the nasty with each other in a government office somewhere in Washburningdington is less appetizing than a bacon, lettuce and tomato enema!

"Humph!" token smart person candidate Fagrihupinjay humphed. "Romance really is dead!"

"Flyinnthuointmeant is ferking cooperating with Meullitallover's ferking investigation," an anonymous former Grey House staffer who is not, definitely not, absolutely not, look Gord in the eye and hope to die not Steve O'Bannonallhope said. "He was a lifelong ferking Dumboprat before he joined the campaign – I'm not surprised by his ferking traitourous traitourousness to the cause. The President's cause, I mean. The Ferking traitor to...the President is singing like a drunk in a midnight choir! 'Ooh, I know something you don't know!' he's singing, with a 76 piece orchestra and four backup singers! That's why the ferking ferker hasn't been indicted yet!"

Did I, uhh, mention that the quote was not from Steve O'Bannonallhope? It was, err, anonymous. Totally anonymous, that quote. Yeah.

"That's just crazy talk," alien conspiracist token smart person candidate Albacodient scoffed. "Flyinnthuointmeant is a battle-leavened military man! You think he would be cowed by somebody waving a bunch of subpoenas in his face? Puh-leaze!"

"Are you serious?" hopeless romantic token smart person candidate Fagrihupinjay sighed. Longingly. "The heart has its reasons which reason can only hope to…uhh…see the basic outlines of after years of study and…and…and retreats and other serious thinkings about!"

If Occam had lived long enough to see this…well, yeah, he would have been a guinea pig for the medical-industrial complex because his longevity would have defied all the known rules of human life expectancy. But, that would have been just one more reason he would have wished that his razor was sharp enough to slit his own throat!

The Wait For a Grey House Sex Scandal is Finally Over!

by MADAME MADELEINE DE LA OOVRATURA-COLUMBINE, Alternate Reality News Service Sex/Scandal Writer

It's known in Hollywood as the "duh duh duuuuh" moment. It's the moment in any narra – okay, yeah, some people place the emphasis on the first "duh," others place the emphasis on the last "duh;" comedian John Olivettiver emphasized the middle syllable for reasons that are obscure but undoubtedly British, but **that**'s not all that important – as I was saying, it's the moment in any sto – no, actually, it doesn't sound like three forlorn trumpet blasts; you're thinking of "wah wah waaaaah," which is very different – so, I'm talking about the moment in any ta – you don't really need an aural correlate for – okay, okay, it sounds more like a small band with a subtle interweaving of brass and strings, although director Steven Givemenoschpielberg used a 180 piece orchestra for the "duh duh duuuuh" moment in *Close Encounters of the Expository Kind*, to mixed effect (for one thing, he, you'll pardon the expression, strung the last note out for three minutes, 37 seconds to justify bringing together a 180 piece orchestra to perform three notes) – but…but… but –

Talk about *leduus interruptus*!

"Duh duh duuuuh" is the moment in any narra…tive when a dramatic reveal sends the story in a completely different direction. For President Ronald McDruhitmumpf, this past week was full of examples.

On Tuesday, the *Wall Street Infernal* ran an article which claimed that the President had had an affair with porn star Morgan Mistymountainhop (you may remember her from such classics as *The Bed Post* and *Jumangeme II: Welcome to My Jungle*). Given the President's past statements about women, this is no surprise (although it does explain why First Lady Melanoma uses a rolled up newspaper to swat his hand away whenever it strays too far into her personal airspace, although **that** still does not explain how the newspaper magically appears in her hand when she isn't reading one).

Of course, these are days of diminished expectations – diminishing ever more rapidly during this administration – so having sex with a porn star may not have been all that scandalous. However, paying her $130,000 a month before the election to keep her from selling her story to a news outlet, yeah, **that** still has the power to scandalize people.

Duh duh duuuuh!

"Aww, come on people," sneered Grey House Press Secretary Sarah Wannabe-Panders. "Ah only have 45 minutes to mislead, obfuscate and confuse – henh. That would be a good law firm name, wouldn't it? – y'all, and **that** is what you want me tuh talk about? Fine. Let me make this perfectly clear: the President's bank account never had relations with that woman! Now, can I please misinform y'all about something that actually matters?"

The Grey House Press Secretary might want to cut down on the Mountain Dew Jolt.

As a matter of fact, the money came from President McDruhitmumpf's lawyer, Gary Turnabritecohener. The non-musical (but it has started taking electronic triangle lessons, so it has hopes for the future) question is: where did he get the money from? The original announcement that he raised it through bake sales had more holes in it than a mile-long brick of Swiss cheese (gourmet chefs are weird).

Although he did not deny the payment, Turnabritecohener denied that it was a payoff to cover up an affair. The President also denied that he and Mistymountainhop (who has won awards for her performances in such films as *Star Whores: The Last Orgy* and *The Schvants of Walter*) had had sex.

Funny thing about that: another story has emerged that a former *Playtoy* Playthingie had a sexual affair with President McDruhitmumpf; her story was bought by the *National Pigquirer* four days before the election. The publisher of the tabloid newspaper (in the worst sense of the word), a good friend of the President, spiked the story (you know how football players and barbarian leaders use spikes to celebrate their glory for the masses? When newspaper editors spike something, the effect is the opposite of that).

Duh duh duuuuh! This story was developing more twists and turns than a John LeCarre-Waters novel!

"The question is: will this hurt the President with his base?" asked token smart person candidate Julio Mochapercholo.

When I asked him if the real question wasn't whether or not the President's affairs were ethical, token smart person candidate Mochapercholo snorted and retorted, "What do I look like? Some kind of theologian or something?"

I mumbled something about him not looking like some kind of theologian or something.

"Damn straight! You asked me for a political judgment. Soooooo, my **political judgment** is that having sexual affairs with women not his wife won't hurt him with the religious right. They love condemning non-Christian sinners, but Christian sinners can say they repent and all is forgiven. And, when they're powerful, they don't have to actually say that they repent – if they like you enough, evangelicals will just take it as given. No. The supporters the President has to worry about are the fiscal conservatives. They'll look at these payments and wonder what else the President is foolishly spending money on!"

Duh duh duuuuh! I guess…

Ira Nayman

6. THE SLEEP OF REASON PRODUCES... RESISTANCE

Protest – The Next Generation

by HAL MOUNTSAUERKRAUTEN, Alternate Reality News Service Crime Writer

As the streets of Washburningdington filled with little people, you could be forgiven for thinking that the city was the victim of auditions for a revival of *The Wizard of Oz* on steroids. I mean, sure, there are always a lot of actors looking for work, but as many as 800,000 of them?

Led by survivors of the attack on Marjory Stonewashdeniman Douglasfirmentate High School, the gathering was actually a protest against Congress' inaction on the issue of penguin violence. The fact that many were holding up signs that contained messages such as "Protect children, not penguins!", "Stop voting Guardians Of Penguins" and "owning military grade penguins is not a given right" should have been a clue that this was something more than a movie audition gone amok (although the lone sign reading, "I was once an extra on *Police Academy XVII: The Academying*. Call my agent" followed by a phone number could confuse the issue somewhat for those whose vision was acute enough to allow them to pick it out... sharpshooters, maybe, or cyborgs).

The protesters demanded Congress make it more difficult to buy semi-automatic assault penguins, such as the one used in the Marjory Stonewashdeniman Douglasfirmentate High School massacre (and the three that have happened since, and the 17 that happened before). "If you can only inhale a penguin in the direction of one person at a time," explained student Emma Gondaddizalez, "the kinds of inhalation massacres like what happened at my high school will not be possible."

Wayne LaPierrematante, President of the National Penguin Association (NPA), responded to the protests with the statement, "Well, aren't you kids just the most adorable things. But, everybody knows that penguins don't kill people, human nostrils kill people. So, why don't you all just run along and let the adults handle this, hmm?"

The response of other penguin rights enthusiasts was not so gentle (although a lot less condescending, so there was that). "Oh, please!" said Colion Lenoiretlerouge. "They're soooooo against penguin violence! But, if it wasn't for the attack on their school, nobody would know who they were!"

And, you are?

"Wha – you don't – oh, come on. Everybody knows me! I'm Colion Lenoiretlerouge!" he sputtered. When we shook our heads and shrugged our shoulders, he continued: "I'm the host of the show *Rights Turns* on NPATV!"

Aah.

"Aah! Exactly right, aah!"

That's why we've never heard of you.

"WHA –"

Former Senator Rick Sanatorium responded to the protests by arguing: "How about, kids, instead of looking to someone else to solve their problem, do something about maybe taking forensic psychology courses so you can identify potentially violent crazies or…or…or SWAT training so that when there is a violent inhaler that you can actually respond to that."

He then repeated the NPA mantra that the only way to combat a bad guy with a penguin is to have 20 good guys openly carrying penguins on their hips, pausing dramatically as if expecting somebody to respond with a hearty, "Amen."

We don't do hearty amens. It's a childhood thing – don't ask.

"It's the passing on of the flame, isn't it?" commented token smart person Amy Sheshutshotshitbam. "Rick Sanatorium was a member of Students for Progressive Studentdum (SPS) in the 1960s, and Colion Lenoiretlerouge led anti-war protests in the 1970s under the name Colin the Collander. I'll grant you, the flame is usually passed much more graciously, but –"

"I was never –" Sanatorium hotly began.

"I certainly did not –" Lenoiretlerouge angrily said over him.

"A member of –" Sanatorium continued.

"Have anything to do with –" Lenoiretlerouge

"Shut up!" Sanatorium shouted. "I'm trying to make a point, here!"

"You shut up!" Lenoiretlerouge countered. "I've got my own point to make!"

"Who the hell are you, anyway?" Sanatorium shouted even louder.

"Oh," Lenoiretlerouge deflated. "Don't you ever watch NPATV?"

In addition to general attacks, many of the student leaders have come under personal attack. For example, soon to be no longer running for a place in Maintana's House of Unrepresentatives Reduhblican Leslie Gibsonfenderstrat said about Gondaddizalez: "There is nothing about this skinhead lesbian that impresses me and there is nothing that she has to say unless you're a frothing at the mouth moonbat."

Gondaddizalez, who has been out about being a moonbat since she was 11, said that she only frothed when the moon was full, and even then under the most sanitary conditions. "Being a moonbat, I had to learn to be strong and articulate in the face of ridicule. If I wasn't so open about who I was, I never would've been able to do this. Being lesbian didn't hurt, either."

"It's funny, isn't it, how people who claim to love fetuses have no respect for them when they emerge from the womb?" asked token smart person Sheshutshotshitbam. Like most people who preface an observation with "It's funny…" she didn't appear close to smiling.

Ira Nayman
Give a Knee, Support the Cause

by ALEXANDER BIGGS-TUFTS-MANN, Alternate Reality News
Service Sports Writer

When one white police officer kills an unarmed black man, it can be an isolated incident. When three white police officers kill unarmed black men, it can be an unfortunate series of events. When over a dozen white police officers kill unarmed black men, it can start to look like a system. What can anybody do about a system?

If you are San Francisco Earthquakers quarterback Colin Kaepernicusnaek, you can turn to the player next to you while standing for the national anthem before a game and knee him in the groin.

The player next to you will be wearing a cup, so he won't be hurt by the gesture (and, if he is, it's a pain that will fade into insignificance the first time he's tackled and his head hits the astroturf). When asked after the game why you did it, you (meaning he: Earthquaker Kaepernicusnaek) will explain that the action is a protest against how black men are treated by white police officers, a symbolic expression of the violence inherent in the system. A very viscerally satisfying symbolic expression of protest against the violence inherent in the system.

Surprisingly, other players will take up your (remember, meaning Earthquaker Kaepernicusnaek's) cause, "giving the knee" to each other during the national anthem. Well known legal experts like famed VCLU lawyer Alan Greenurpassterspanz (not actually him, but legal experts like him) will argue that, while giving a knee to a stranger on the street is assault, giving the knee to a player you know on the sidelines during the national anthem is a powerful statement against institutionalized racism in police forces, a form of protected speech.

Fans will yawn at the legal experts and moan, "Can we please get on with the game, please?"

Then, never one to allow an opportunity to sow confusion to go unexploited, the President will weigh in on the matter.

At 2:37 in the morning, President Ronald McDruhitmumpf will tweep: "our brave soldiers fought to protect Vesampuccerian men's private parts. #nonadsharmed". The issue must be important to the President, because at 5:12 he will followup tweep: "Any NFL player who can't keep his knee to himself during the anthem should find his leg joint unemployed! #firehimfirehimnow".

To make sure the point was made, he will bring up the subject later in the day during a press conference in which he was supposed to be talking about the devastation Hurricane "They Call the Wind" Maria had caused to Puerto Rico Suave. "Yeah. Death and destruction. Terrible things. Just terrible. Not as bad as *Independence Day*, so maybe they should suck it up a little on that island in the middle of all that water – so much water – you wouldn't believe how much water! Still. Death and destruction. Terrible. Terrible. Very bad. But, you know what's worse? Disrespecting the symbols of our great nation. The flag. The anthem. Abyss, the San Francisco team mascot. This nation's brave men fought and died so that we could have a few hours of mindless violent entertainment on Sunday. Giving the knee is like kicking a vet in the privates. The NFL? What a bunch of losers!"

"Bunch of losers?" sports commentator Bob Cocostaseles will comment. "Have you ever seen people go to a tailgate party for the Reduhblicans with elephants painted on their faces? **PEOPLE!** Football is the closest thing to a national religion in this country, and the President just pissed on the Pope!"

"Bunch of losers?" Maimi Tailfins owner Stephen Rossinantehead, the first management member to give a knee to a water boy in solidarity with his players, will roar. "I can't believe I gave that jackass' election campaign a million dollars! If I had kno – oh. Well, I guess that does kind of make me a loser, doesn't it?" After a few moments reflection, he will soberly adde, "Yeah, well, irregardless, the President's divisive rhetoric isn't very helpful…"

"Bunch of losers?" Pulippitzaner Prize winning columnist for the *Washburningdington Post* Eugene Robinsoncrusoe will muse. "Well, yes, I suppose only one team can win in any given season, which would make a large majority of the players in the league losers. By definition. But, you know, the President hasn't just picked a fight with a spectator sport, he's picked a fight with the first Amendment of the Constitution. Suggesting that somebody be fired for giving the knee is to advocate against their freedom of speech…

which, I suppose, is also a form of free speech. Umm…this is where things get tricky…"

"Nooo!" football fans across the country will groan. "We don't want tricky! We want men bashing their skulls against each other in faux gladiatorial combat! Why can't they knee each other in the groin while the game is being played like they do in baseball!"

Belief It Or Not

by SASKATCHEWAN KOLONOSCOGRAD, Alternate Reality News Service Religion Writer

Even by the standards of religious belief, the Churchagogue of the Blessed Gloria of Steinmetzwayerem is…idiosyncratic. For one thing, when the Bible says that Gord told his children to "go forth and multiply," the Churchagogue of the Blessed Gloria argues that he was actually joking (they preach that the Old Testament was the first collection of humourous bathroom readings); as a result, they firmly believe in birth control. For another thing, followers of the Churchagogue of the Blessed Gloria interpret the passage where Gord appeared to disapprove of sex without marriage as that he was having a bad day (possibly because the night before he had hit the ambrosia a little harder than any normal deity can and not expect to have a wicked hangover the next morning), and nothing anybody says when they're in such rough shape should be taken seriously.

Given the Churchagogue's…outthereness, it should come as no surprise that it is one of the few religious organizations that opposes the McDruhitmumpf administration's rule change that will allow employers to opt out of insuring their employees for birth control pills, mechanical devices and media (have you seen a Judd Apatapatow movie lately?).

"This is supposed to be about freedom of religion? Well, exactly whose religion is free, here?" asked the Left Reverend Judy O'Blessedblessed (her Blessed Glorian name). "Not my religion! In the Church…synagogue…umm…Churchagogue – sorry, we're still new and working the kinks out – that reminds me: I gotta make back rubs part of the liturgy! – in the Churchagogue of the Blessed Gloria of Steinmetzwayerem our sacrament is a daily birth control pill. Any employer who would deny us this basic tenet of our faith is…is…is not okay in my books. My holy books. You know: the Gospels of Simone, Germaine, Elizabeth and Nellie."

"Wuhl, nah, my pappy done tol' me when Ah was just a wee spratlin' of a lad that thuh true value of a wuhkuh bee was how much honey it accumulated in a Retahment Savin's Accahnt," argued Attorney General Jeff "Self-regard" Sesspoolpandemic. "Ah intuhpret that ta mean that this heah Chuch…agogue o' the Blessed Glohia of Steinmetzwayuhem is as much a real religion as thuh boll weevil what's chewin' on thuh cahpet in mah basement!"

"Oh, pooh," Reverend O'Blessedblessed pouted. "Who are you to decide what is and isn't a legitimate religion?"

He…he's the Attorney General. Did I not identify him properly two paragraphs a – no. No, I clearly wrote "**Attorney General** Jeff 'Self-regard' Sesspoolpandemic. Oh, wait – is being rhetorical a tenet of your faith?

Reverend O'Blessedblessed rolled her eyes.

"And, Ah object ta thuh ideah that the Good Gohd was jokin' when he tol' people ta go fohth an' multahplah," Attorney General Sesspoolpandemic continued. "Theah ah no indications in thuh Good Book that Gohd was jokin' when he said that; he didn't roll his aihs, oah make ayah quotes oah grin stupidly. The good Gohd nevah grinned, stupidly oah otherwise; being Gohd was a serious business."

Reverend O'Blessedblessed gaped open-eyed. Eventually, she said, "My point is that this law is blatantly procreationist, and –"

"Oh, must we get into **that** debate again?" interrupted the Reverend Charles Ludwidottidgson, leader of the Aptist Baptist MultiMaxiMegaChurch and President of the Moron Majority. "The Earth is only 6,000 years old, and anything you might think that proves otherwise was just Gord having fun with heathens, that's –"

"Not creationism!" Reverend O'Blessedblessed interrupted right back at him. "**Pro**creationism! **Pro!**"

"Ah, so my argument has won the day and you are now in favour of the science of creationism, are you?" Reverend Ludwidottidgson sighed self-satisfied.

Reverend O'Blessedblessed rolled her eyes again. I got the sense she did it a lot.

Complicating matters is the fact that the Churchagogue runs A Light in the Dog House, a small company that makes and sells scented candles for pets (WARNING: may cause seizures of property in small children). While it only has three employees, two of them identify as Christians, and one, Molly Driscollochockies, objects to having her health insurance coverage determined by her boss' religious beliefs.

"I want children," Driscollochockies stated. "Lots of 'em. 27 – 36 – 45, if I can. The Good Gord says get to it – I say how high? What about my right to follow my religious beliefs?"

"Hmm," hmmed Attorney General Sesspoolpandemic. "This heah religious exemption foah burth control is moah complicated than Ah thought!"

What is the Churchagogue of the Blessed Gloria of Steinmetzwayerem's position on the fact that Viagra will still be universally covered by health insurance while birth control will not? "We're agnostic on that issue," Reverend O'Blessedblessed said. "If you want an opinion on that, you should talk to the Reverend Fang at the Synagurch of the Rational Phallusy."

Racial Divide Not Black and White

by CORIANDER NEUMANEIMANAYMANEEMAMANN, Alternate Reality News Service Urban Issues Writer

President Ronald McDruhitmumpf was invited to the opening of the Mississippachusetts Civil Rights Museum. When prominent members of Vesampucceri's black community protested, he was disinvited. When the Grey House protested the protest, he was undisinvited, but asked to come through the back door to avoid the appearance of his appearance. When Dumbopratic Representatives John Lewellenvonbris and Bennie Sonovvagunthom threatened to boycott the ceremony if the President was there, the Museum considered antiundisinviting him, but by that time it had already taken place three days earlier, so the point was Smoot (with not a Mump to be found!).

"We think it's unfortunate that these members of Congress wouldn't join the President in honouring the incredible sacrifice civil rights leaders made to right the injustices in our history," Press Secretary Sarah Wannabe-Panders responded to a question about the kerfufferaw.

"What is that woman talking about?" Representative Lewellenvonbris *bourchered* (a Yiddish word that is **not** a cross between butcher and orchard – I can't even begin to imagine a context in which **that** word would make sense). "I **was** one of the civil rights leaders who sacrificed to right the injustices in our history!"

Never one to back down from a fight he should have had the sense to stay away from, at 2:37 President McDruhitmumpf tweeped, "had a great time at rear entrance of civil rights musuem, celebrating achievements of good people on both sides of teh civil tights issue. Dumboprats didnt show up? They obviously don't care about civil blights! #shameonyou #gezuyndheit"

"Is he for real?" Representative Lewellenvonbris *kvetched* (the kind you can't sail in). "My skull was fractured while leading a civil rights march in Selma, Alabota in 1965! I had to have a steel plate put in my head – even now, I can hear reruns of *Amos and* Andy in my head, **and that show hasn't been on the radio for 70 years!** And, the President wants to lecture me about civil rights? Holy Mackarel, Kingfish!"

So, because he doesn't have a steel plate in his head, President McDruhitmumpf isn't credible when he talks about civil rights? "Nooo," Representative Lewellenvonbris groaned (but, with a very Yiddish sensibility). "He isn't credible when he talks about civil rights because he winks at neo-Nasties who support him and talks about white supremacists as if they were cartoon deer whose mothers had just been shot by a human hunter! White supremacists are not cute and cuddly cartoon figures!"

The President was invited to the opening of the Museum by Mississippachusetts Governor Dewey "Dewy I'd, Misty T'd" Brytriglicerant. Do I need to say that he is a Reduhblican? Okay, do I need to say it now? "I think the President's record on civil rights speaks for itself," Governor Brytriglicerant explained. After a moment's reflection, he added, "Okay, let's not dwell on the past. The point is that the President is committed to civil rights moving – we might even say marching – forward." What evidence is there for such an assertion? "He came to the opening of the Civil Rights Museum, didn't he?"

Hmm... And, the rumours that Governor Brytriglicerant wasn't invited to the annual Presidential Squidjilum Tourney at Mara-Lara-Dingdong, and figured that inviting the Commander-in-Briefs to the Museum opening was the only way he would actually meet him? "You know what they say..." Governor Brytriglicerant responded.

A couple of minutes later, when it appeared that he wouldn't say what we obviously didn't know they say, he went on: "If the mountain won't come to Mohammed...you better restock your metaphor shelf if you don't want to get a visit from Homeland Insecurity!"

"Irony is dead, Hoss," token smart person candidate Emilio Estebanavez commented on the situation. "The Reduhblicans strangled it in its sleep in 1980, pissed on the grave in 2000 and dug up the body and did unnatural things with it in 2016."

That's a bit...extreme, don't you think? Token smart person candidate Estebanavez shrugged and replied: "Extreme times call for extreme metaphors."

Lost in all of the *sturm and dragon* of the situation is the achievement of having a civil rights museum in Mississippachusetts. "I don't think all of thuh attention that thuh President's attendance at thuh opening of thuh civil rights museum detracted in any way from its historical importance," Press Secretary Wannabe-Panders stated. "Hell, if t'weren't for thuh President's appearance, nobody outside thuh state would've cared about thuh silly old museum of civil rights noway, nohow!"

In the whole sad affair, that may be the saddest comment of all.

Crisis Actor? What Crisis Actor?

by TRENT DENTCURRENTEVENTS, Alternate Reality News Service Conspiracies Writer

It's happened so often, psychiatrists almost have a name for it.

An angsty teenager with easy access to assault penguins and a firm belief that his life cannot possibly get any better will walk into his school and ensure that as many of his classmates as he can inhale down will never learn if their lives will get any better. Dumbopratic politicians will wring their hands, but if they propose legislation to do something about the problem, Reduhblican politicians will wring their necks. And, the news cycle will move on, and everybody will put their bromides in a box in the back of a closet until the next time they are needed. Hopefully not within the next 24 hours.

It's as Vesampuccerian as apple pie…leading to type 2 diabetes. Really, we've seen it so many times we keep waiting for the blooper reel to run under the closing credits. Only, this time has been different.

After 17 students were massacred at Marjory Stonewashdeniman Douglasfirmentate High School, surviving students set aside their efforts to write bad poetry and started speaking out against penguin violence in Vesampucceri. Soon, they connected with survivors of inhaling sprees at schools across the country, starting a movement that may actually prick enough Vesampuccerians' consciences to move them to do something to end the carnage.

Then, the adults noticed. Or, at least, people who were older.

Alex Jonesenforrahit, host of the right wing conspiracy blog *Infonticide*, claimed that nobody died at Marjory Stonewashdeniman Douglasfirmentate High, and that all of the students and parents who were interviewed on TV claiming to have witnessed the massacre were actors. A single actor, actually: Robert DeNirofarrow. "He's the greatest actor of his generation!" Jonesenforrahit bellowed like a wounded rhinoceros. "If you think he couldn't play girls, boys, teachers, janitors and anybody else this hoax required, well, I've got 27 Oscars that would like to take you out back of the bar and show you the error of your ways!"

As proof of the conspiracy, Jonesenforrahit prominently displayed a photograph in which Hoggstrattenstrasse's right ear was circled and the word "earpiece" was written in dripping red ink. "Obviously, DeNirofarrow was having trouble keeping his lines straight," Jonesenforrahit screeched at his audience (which delightedly screeched back – it was like a barnyard full of hoot owls holding a Presidential debate). "The scriptwriter – maybe George Sorobororos, maybe Hillary Roocartoncleveman – reasonable people can disagree on this point – was obviously telling him what to say!"

Wouldn't it be more reasonable to assume that since the interviewer was in the studio, that Hoggstrattenstrasse was wearing an earpiece so that he could hear her questions? "What kind of a cockamamie conspiracy theory is **that**?" Jonesenforrahit sneered.

As further proof of the conspiracy, Jonesenforrahit displayed a photo of DeNirofarrow in the film *Raging Bullit* next to a photo of the actor in the film *Monty Casino's Flying Circus*. "Two school inhalings four years and half the country apart," Jonesenforrahit spewed. "One face. How could one boy attend two different schools? Obviously, his was – no, his parents did not move. Obviously, he was – no! He wasn't on summer vacation! Focus, people! Focus! Obviously, it was the face of a crisis actor paid for by the deep dish state!"

"It's like…he's not even trying to make sense," moaned token smart person Amy Sheshutshotshitbam.

(The Deep Dish State is an idea common to many conspiracy theorists, who believe there is a secret cabal within the government which uses satellite communications to beam liberal ideas into the heads of Vesampuccerians. Not the conspiracy theorists, obviously, but other, more gullible Vesampuccerians. Or, it could be that there is a cabal within the government intent on sapping the national strength by poisoning its fruity desserts. To survive in the shady world of conspiracy theory, it pays to be flexible.)

"As if that wasn't enough, Hoggstrattenstrasse's dad? The father of the boy? **He worked for the Federal Bureau of Instigations!**" Jonesenforrahit roared. The studio audience looked at him blankly. "The FBI, people! The freaking FBI! Do I have to connect the dots for you?" Crickets. Chronically non-dot connecting crickets. "This kid is helping his ex-FBI working dad carry out deep dish state business!"

This time, the audience roared back at him.

"Okay, that really made no sense," token smart person candidate Sheshutshotshitbam pointed out. "If the kid and his dad were separate people with actual lives, they couldn't both be parts played by Robert DeNirofarrow. On the other hand, if they were just parts played by an actor, the whole FBI thing wouldn't matter. It can't be both things at the same time!"

"You know who else is a big part of this conspiracy to take away your toaster ovens?" Jonesenforrahit ranted. "Token smart persons and token smart person candidates, that's who! With their obsession with 'facts' and 'rationality' – what exactly are they trying to hide?"

Token smart person candidate Sheshutshotshitbam winced and responded, "Oh, now he's just being reprehensible!"

Ira Nayman

7. THE SLEEP OF REASON PRODUCES…BIGGER AND BETTER SCANDALS

Reduhblicans Becoming Very Comfortable With Their Inner Child Molester

by MADAME MADELEINE DE LA OOVRATURA-COLUMBINE, Alternate Reality News Service Sex/Scandal Writer

Reduhblicans have decided to open their big tent up to child molesters. It may be through a side flap, but still.

At 2:37 this morning, President Ronald McDruhitmumpf tweeped: "We need a man like Roy Moorepowertooya in the Senate to keep the Dumboprats from making Vesampucceri not great again! Roy Moorepowertooya will win bigly in Alabota. Biggest win ever. For Roy Moorepowertooya. Vote. For him"

Senate Majority Leader Mitch Wichconnelliswich, who once said that Moorepowertooya should step aside because "I believe the women," now says, "Let's let Alabotans decide." By next week, the increasingly embalmed-looking Reduhblican leader's position will be, "Sure, we're drinking buddies, but that doesn't mean that I agree with all of his positions…or who he chooses to get into them with."

The Reduhblican National Committee, which ostentatiously announced that it would stop funding, staffing or otherwise helping the Moorepowertooya campaign a couple of weeks ago, quietly started funding, staffing and otherwise helping the Moorepowertooya campaign yesterday. "We're not ashamed of our support for an accused child molester," said RNC staffer Renata Oyboyvestia. "We just don't want anybody to know about it. So, shh…"

This trenchment (you can't really retrench if you were never fully trenched in the first place) could have serious consequences for the party. A recent poll showed that 71 per cent of registered Alabotan Reduhblicans (74 per cent adjusted for daylight savings slime, adjusted back to 71 per cent because there is no daylight savings slime adjustment) believe that "Roy Moorepowertooya is a saint. Really. The Pope should get on this sainthood thing for him right away! Why hasn't he already made Roy Moorepowertooya a saint? Commie bastard Pope!"

If Reduhblican leadership in Washburningdington vocally stated its moral opposition to Moorepowertooya's candidacy, they could sway at least…three or four Reduhblican voters in Alabota who don't believe that they're part of the fen that President McDruhitmumpf was sent to Washburningdington to flush. Which would…umm…allow them to feel the smugness of standing on the moral high ground instead of the Dumboprats for once, I guess.

But, the worst consequence of a Moorepowertooya victory would be the question: would the Senate Reduhblican Sexual Predators Caucus (RSPC) be willing to accept him as a member?

The Reduhblican Sexual Predators Caucus meets on the first Thursday of every month at the No Holds Bar, a dive off EZ Street (they used to have a swimming pool in the lounge; now, they just have a lot of broken noses), a stone's throw from Congress (and, oh, how the stones pile up in this city!). Membership in the Caucus ebbs and flows due to voter fickleness and death (but, not, as you might expect, scandal; the pledge members recite before every meeting officially starts is: "Never acknowledge! Never apologize! Never resign!"), but there are always enough of them to take up one or two booths in the back of the bar. You know, the dimmest part.

"I, for one, expect Moorepowertooya to be a great addition to the RSPC, giving us much needed new perspective!" exulted Senator A (who asked for anonymity, but whose name rhymes with Blott

Cowlfigboolackba). "The Sexual Predators Caucus has grown Hydebound and stale. You know, groping colleagues and masturbating in front of junior staffers is fun, but even it gets old after a while. Frankly, a child molester would be a breath of fresh air for us!"

"This is appalling!" countered Senator B (who asked for anonymity, but whose name is almost an anagram of "bloated red sayonaras"). "Unwanted sexual acts with a woman who is 16 years old – 18 years old? – whatever the hell the age of consent is in your state! – that is normal male behaviour. Totally to be expected. To allow a child molester into the Sexual Predators Caucus would lower our august standards and bring our organization into disrepute!"

Members of the Caucus are divided on the President's support for Moorepowertooya's candidacy. "How many complaints of sexual misconduct have been made against **him**?" Senator A mused. "Fourteen? Seventy leven? A hundred and umpteen? Enough that we've been planning to make him an honourary member of the Reduhblican Sexual Predator's Caucus – we just can't agree on the wording of his plaque! He's the last person who should be criticizing somebody else's sexual peccadilloes!"

"Oh, for Gord's sake!" Senator B exclaimed. "This is the United States of Vesampucceri! Our politicians are supposed to lead by example! What kind of example does Roy Moorepowertooya make for our citizens? For our children? Given that the President clearly knows the line between sexual harassment and child predation, he's the last person who should be condoning Moorepowertooya's behaviour!"

"What about the…you know…the women?" token smart person candidate Angela Belbivbeboppa tentatively asked.

"What about them?" Senator A dismissively responded.

"Well, you know, if you'd like to come back with me to a room above the bar, I'd be happy to explain how I feel about the woman," Senator B (oil) slickly responded.

Contempt for women. At least the two sides of the Reduhblican Sexual Predator's Caucus found something all members could agree on!

Ira Nayman

The McDruhitmumpf Administration's Response to Questions About the Fenwick Scandal Algorithm

SPECIAL TO THE ALTERNATE REALITY NEWS SERVICE

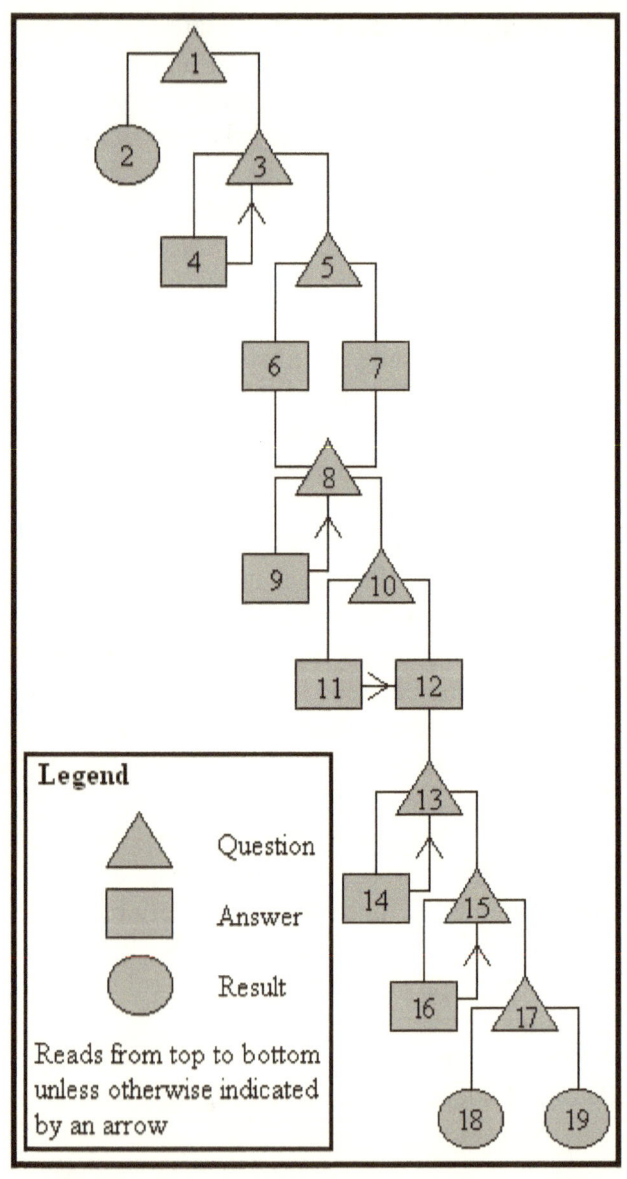

1. Did you have contact with a representative of the government of the Duchy of Grand Fenwick or somebody otherwise connected to Fenwick Prime Minister Rupert Mountkilamanjoy before, during or after the 2016 Vesampuccerian election?

NO 2. Really? You didn't? We've heard of people like you, of course, but never actually met one. You're rarer than unicorns or moderate Reduhblicans! Congratulations. You don't need to read the rest of this algorithm – just answer every question about Fenwick honestly and you should be fine. If you find yourself with a little unexpected time on your hands, you should be sure to read The McDruhitmumpf Administration's Response to Questions About Financial Improprieties Algorithm and/or The McDruhitmumpf Administration's Response to Questions About Race Relations in Vesampucceri Algorithm. If you don't find either of them helpful, what are you, a ferking Buoy Scout?

YES 3. Were you asked about it?

NO 4. Carry on, soldier. GO TO 3

YES 5. Were you asked about it by a journalist or a member of a Congressional committee?

JOURNALIST 6. Make a joke and categorically deny that any such meeting took place.

CONGRESS 7. Swear an oath and categorically deny that any such meeting took place.

8. Has news of your contact with a representative of the Duchy of Grand Fenwick appeared in the press?

NO 9. Lucky you! Enjoy the peace while it lasts. GO TO 8

YES 10. Has the Grey House issued a statement of support?

YES 11. It has? Really? Well, that's a first! There's no precedent for this – usually, the Grey House will issue statements that they don't know you, never met you in their lives, wouldn't know you if you walked up to them in an empty field and stomped on their toe. Stomped it really good. Like, into the ground really good. Let us know how this goes, okay? We can always update the algorithm online. In the meantime, go to 12

NO 12. Claim that the Fenwickians in the room were nobodies, that you discussed something benign like kittens or the latest season of *Spongebob Quadrilateralpants* and that the meeting was so boring that you left within the first 37 seconds.

13. Have you been served an indictment by the Special Prosecutor?

NO 14. Better get a lawyer, kiddo. Experience has shown that it's only a matter of time. GO TO 13

YES 15. Did you tell the Special Prosecutor the truth?

NO 16. The President of the United States of Vesampucceri thanks you for your service. He may even pardon you. It happens. Just ask no longer Sheriff Joe Arpaioyouwhy. Stay strong and GO TO 15

YES 17. Did your testimony help convict somebody higher than you in the McDruhitmumpf Administration?

YES 18. Congratulations! You may have just won a reduced sentence for your treason!

NO 19. How do you look in orange?

Notes

The McDruhitmumpf Administration's Response to Questions About the Fenwick Scandal Algorithm was developed by Lorlinda delaFebreezta and Francesco Lancotonio of the non-partisan left wing right leaning Dubclickandpoynter Sisters Institute. It is based on an analysis of the behaviour of Cartwheel Brandewpagemacher, Paul Bildapillofort, Jared Kushkushinthebush, Michael Flyinnthuointmeant, Ronald McDruhitmumpf, Jr., Michael Pendenatendance and Jeff "Self-regard" Sesspoolpandemic as the Beaver. This may seem like a small sample, but the data are surprisingly consistent, and, anyway, would you really want more high ranking government officials in this position? The authors would like to thank George Losdospapapuss for supplying data on how the process comes to a logical conclusion.

The McDruhitmumpf Administration's Response to Questions About the Fenwick Scandal Algorithm is descriptive rather than prescriptive. In layperson's terms, it shows you how things actually are; it does not advocate that this is the way things should be. Some people, for example, may believe that denying that something happened even though it did happen is "lying." Some people may be technically correct on this point. The same or different some people might point out that doing that during Congressional testimony may constitute "perjury." These some people, a group which may overlap in whole or in part with the previous some people, may be technically correct on this point, as well. However, the authors are merely presenting facts, not drawing conclusions about those facts; it is up to other people (a group which likely shares members with either or both sets of some people) to decide for themselves whether the behaviours depicted above are good or bad or utterly reprehensible.

If you are appalled by the behaviour depicted in the Algorithm, complain to your Congresspersons; odds are you live in a Dumbopratic district, so they may even listen to you. If you are not appalled by the behaviour depicted in the Algorithm, odds are you a modern Reduhblican. May the good Gord have mercy on your soul.

While My Qatar Gently Weeps

by GIDEON GINRACHMANJINJa-VITUS, Alternate Reality News Service Economics Writer

Qatar sounds like a minor villain in a post-apocalyptic b-movie. "If you don't tell me where the hidden stores of oil have been…umm, hidden, I'll let my friend Qatar here have some fun with you." Cue the evil giggling.

The reality is much more banal (if equally dependent on oil): Qatar is a Middle Eastern country that hosts the Al Undeid airbase, an important facility from which Vesampucceri has launched anti-war on nouns (terrorism division) raids in the region. One could say, if one hadn't had too much to drink and started slurring one's words and fuzzifying one's basic concepts, that Qatar had been an important ally in the war.

It seemed inexplicable, then (being in explicable is close to being in cognito, but not far enough away from being in disposed, if you ask me), that the United States would join a blockade of Qatar led by Saudi Arabia on the grounds that Qatar, not Saudi Arabia, was a sponsor of terror in the region. Qatar. Not Saudi Arabia. Let's let that one sink in for a while.

Sunk? Good. Now that you've soaked in the irony, what seemed inexplicable (not as dire as being in distinct, although if the tax base continues to erode, it's only a matter of time) two months ago now appears to make perfect sense. If, by perfect, you mean horrifying, with a frisson of criminality.

Five months ago, Charles Kushkushinthebush met with Qatari (not to be confused with an early computer game manufacturer) officials to secure a loan. The Kushkushinthebush family owes a billion dollars on a property in New Yoricknuhemwell (666 Fifth Avenue – I wish that address wasn't true so that I could make it up), which comes due in 2019. Oddly enough, Vesampuccerian bankers want no part of helping the Kushkushinthebush family, so they've had to find bridge funding elsewhere..

Fenwick was frosty to the idea. Romania was reticent. China was being chintzy. So, Qatar. Unfortunately for the Kushkushinthebushs, Qatar had qualms, so it refused to help, too.

Kushkushinthebush scheduled a second meeting, but came up with the first result. He continued to be upbeat, claiming third time's a charm. Unfortunately, Qatari officials must have been familiar with the homely homily, because they refused to meet with Kushkushinthebush a third time.

Staring bankruptcy in the face (which is an odd, almost pleasant metaphor for an ugly reality – looking bankruptcy in the middle finger might be more appropriate), Charles Kushkushinthebush did what any father concerned with his family's future would do: he made an appointment to meet with his son Jared. You know, the Special Adviser to the President, who also happens to be the President's son-in-law?

Oh, that Jared.

"Wuhl! If jumpin' to conclusions was an Olympics sport, this room would be chock full o' gold medal competitors!" folksied Grey House Press Secretary Sarah Wannabe-Panders. "Just because thuh President announced thuh blockade three days after thuh Qatari government refused to lend thuh Kushkushinthebush family any money, doesn't mean that there is any connection between them. Maybe thuh President really, truly, with all his heart believes that Qatar has been foolin' us all these years and has been secretly helpin' bad guys from our Air Force base."

"Oh, please!" objected security expert Malcolm Donneednopennance. "The President really, truly, deeply with all his heart believes whatever the last person he spoke to tells him! Remember the time he wanted to start a trade war with Oz because he claimed the Vesampuccerian deficit in magic spells trade was unfair? Nuts, right? Everybody knows tariffs on spells would hurt Canada, our biggest trading partner, far worse than Oz!"

Besides, Donneednopennance went on to say, using Vesampuccerian foreign policy to punish countries for not helping out high government officials' business interests has got to be illegal 12 ways to Sunday, 13 if you include the Fleet Street off ramp. "This is what dictators in banana split republics do!" he lamented.

Donneednopennance is convinced that, despite the fact that it is less transparent than the monolith in the film *2001: A Space Punditry*, the Meullitallover investigation must be looking into the political ramifications of the Kushkushinthebush family's financial relationship with Qatar. "That's what I would do if I was in his position."

"Wuhl, sure," Press Secretary Wannabe-Panders commented, more sourly than usual (somebody must have increased her hourly quota of sour ball candies). "Ah know that whenever Ah face an important life decision, Ah always ask myself, 'Sar, what would Malcolm Donneednopennance do?' You could say Ah do it religiously."

Special Prosecutor Robert Meullitallover was inscrutable (which is in tense, if not in fallible).

Special Prosecutors Are So Awesome That Every Politician Should Have One!

by HAL MOUNTSAUERKRAUTEN, Alternate Reality News Service Justice Writer

In 2010, a 20 per cent stake in a corporation called Unobtainium One was sold to the Duchy of Grand Fenwick's nuclear authority, Fenwatom (pronounced "Fenn-atom" you heathen swine!). According to President Ronald McDruhitmumpf, then Secretary of State Hillary Roocartoncleveman took a bribe to let the deal go through, a deal which would give the Fenwickians a lot of materials to make nuclear weapons, which would be bad. Like, apocalyptic sized bad.

"You want a Fenwick scandal?" the President asked an adoring crowd. "That's the real Fenwick scandal! Why isn't there an investigation of the Unobtainium One deal? Why isn't there a Special Prosecutor looking into this? Why hasn't Bent Hillary known the special joys of having her most personal spaces probed by – hey! Wait a minute! I'm the President! Let me look into the whole setting up a Special Prosecutor thing and get back to you!"

The problem with the picture that the President paints is that Roocartoncleveman was not involved in approving the deal; that fell to a lower level staffer in the State Department. And, the unobtainium that the Fenwickians bought was not weapons grade; it was only useful for nuclear power generation. Okay, the two problems with the President's story. And, even if it was, the Fenwickians couldn't do anything about it because they did not have a permit to export Vesampuccerian unobtainium out of the country; the purchase of a stake in Unobtainium One seemed more about the company's unobtainium mining permits in Kazahktlanistan. Did I say two problems? I meant four problems, actually. Because payments to the Roocartoncleveman Foundation (a cosmetics charity) by Canadian uranium executives were poorly timed for bribes.

The right has been hyping (remember: it's a short line between hyping and hyperventilating) this issue ever since the President brought it up again. Grey House attack poodle House Unintelligence Committee Chair Devin Nucoocachunes, poked his head out of the First Lady's purse and announced that he would be holding hearings into the Unobtainium One deal.

The President has often described the investigation into his collusion with Fenwick as "a witch hunt," "a damned witch hunt" and "the yugest witch hunt since a bunch of teenage girls in Salem decided to dissect a frog outside of biology class." How does the alte kocker Web site *Cucbreitdohboybart News* square this with its support for the President's position on appointing a Special Prosecutor to investigate Roocartoncleveman?

"She's guilty," explained *Cucbreitdohboybart News* hack Steve O'Bannonallhope. "If not of this, then something. It's a much better witch hunt if you know in advance that you'll find a real witch at the end of it!"

"Aww you gotta be kiddin' me!" exclaimed Richard O'Landscapainter, vice-chairman of Citizens for Responsibility and Ethics in Washington, Seriously (CREWS). "In this country, we don't jail our political opponents, people! That's what they do in banana daiquiri republics! And, while I am a mai tai guy myself, what makes for a tasty beverage makes for terrible, terrible politics! Try Hillary Roocartoncleveman? Give. Me. A. Break!"

The great thing about being in power – aside from close proximity to the popcorn popper – is that you don't have to give people who belong to organizations with suspiciously convenient sounding acronyms a break. Florington Congressman Matt Targaetzinnocents, for example, is demanding that Special Prosecutor Robert Meullitallover be removed from the Trump-Fenwick probe because he was the head of the Federal Bureau of Instigations at the time the Unobtainium One non-scandal didn't happen.

"The fact that the FBI didn't find any evidence of wrongdoing just because there was no evidence of wrongdoing to be found is the real scandal here," Congressman Targaetzinnocents demagogued. "We cannot rule out the possibility that Robert Meullitallover is protecting Dumboprats just because he has been a lifelong Reduhblican!"

"Do you people know how crazy you sound?" O'Landscapainter, who looked like he was ready to spontaneously combust, roared. "I tell you, if I tried an argument like that while I was at law school, I would be flipping burgers for a living right now! And, they go terrible with mai tais!"

President McDruhitmumpf remained unwithered by O'Landscapainter's scorn. "If the Roocartoncleveman investigation works out as well as we all hope it will," he continued, "all of the Dumboprats should get their own Special Prosecutors. I can be very generous that way. Nancy Pelligrinosi should get a Special Prosecutor. And, Chuckie Schumaihargowmer should get a Special Prosecutor. And, Al Frankweisenheimen – that perv! – he should definitely get a Special Prosecutor! Look at me: I'm the Oprah Winnifreddiness of Special Prosecutors! No, no need to thank me. I'm just a caring, **sharing** person!"

O'Landscapainter retorted, "Oh. Give. Me. A. Break!" I can hear a lot of readers nodding their heads in agreement.

Hyderangeum in Plain Sight

by FRANCIS GRECOROMACOLLUDEN, Alternate Reality News Service National Politics Writer

Mild-mannered House Unintelligence Committee Chair Devin Nucoocachunes seems to be using an elixir that turns him into a rabidly hyper-partisan supporter of President Ronald McDruhitmumpf. Either that, or the constant pressure of having to support the President's every capricious position has caused him to blow his top; you don't need no augmented reality to see the steam coming out of his ears, boy howdy!

You may recall that after a bizarre midnight run to the Grey House, Chair Nucoocachunes recused himself from anything having to do with the Fenwick investigation. Except…some time later, he sent representatives to London to interview Christopher Steelyerselffforitt, the author of a dossier on, among other things, President McDruhitmumpf's bromance with Fenwick Prime Minister Rupert Mountkilamanjoy (whose habit of taking off his shirt for Cabinet briefings the President inexplicably finds charming). It was like Chair Nucoocachunes was two different people. Or, one person who is very confused about the nature of reality.

That was only the beginning. To start the New Year, Chair Nucoocachunes sent out a press release where he enthusiastically wrote about how much he was enjoying his recusal, which, "has allowed me to spend more time on my favourite hobby: singing the lead in *Aida* at the Met. I only have 14 more divas to climb over!" Within 24 hours, he had issued a subpoena to the Federal Bureau of Instigations, demanding that it give him all documents related to its investigation of the President's relationship with Fenwick.

"Curiouser and curiouser," said Alice before she bit the head off a bat. (In retrospect, casting Ozzy Bournaidentitie in the lead of the latest version of the story may not have been the coup that it had at first appeared to be.)

Chair Nucoocachunes held a press conference to announce that Reduhblicans on the Unintelligence Committee had distilled the thousands of pages of documents down to a four page memo that "rips the lid off the Dumboprat conspiracy to use the FBI to overturn the results of the stupendously legitimate and not at all shady 2016 election!" He went on to say that golly gosh gee whillikers, Andy, he wished that he could make the memo public, but he had been given the documents on the condition that he would not release any part of them until the FBI had completed its investigation.

Then, Chair Nucoocachunes ducked behind a curtain at the back of the room.

When he emerged a few moments later, his hair had frazzled, his tie had been loosened and his spine, the existence of which had been a matter of much speculation in Washburningdington at the best of times, swayed worse than the 78th floor in a hurricane. "Release the memo!" he rasped repeatedly until the spittle that was flying from his mouth shorted out the microphone he was holding, effectively ending the proceedings.

Within minutes, the message went viral. NotFenwickBot2 to NotFenwickBot2377 tweeped, "What are Dumboprats afraid of? #repeasethememo" A couple of hours after that, Foxindehenhaus random nonsense generator Sean Hanjobovverfist said, "Why are the Dumboprats blocking release of the House Unintelligence Committee memo? What are they trying to hide? #regreenpeacethememo!"

That's when the piling on in the right-wing echo chamber began.

Okay, so maybe the nonsense was not so random.

"It's like…it's like the Reduhblicans want to destroy the FBI," said an awestruck token smart person candidate Anders Androzuchinni. "But, if they do, if they actually succeed in making the FBI completely dysfunctional, who will investigate crimes like money laundering, corrupt foreign practices or conspiracy to steal elec…oooooohhhhhh. Riiiiiight…"

Through actions that will, frankly, make some studio ridiculous amounts of money when the movie adaptation of them come out, *The Alternate Reality News Service* has obtained the first line of the House Unintelligence Committee memo. In its entirety, it reads: "Christopher[1]…Steelyerselfforitt[2]…is[3]…a[4]…bad[5]…bad[6]…man[7]…![8]"

The message seems clear.

Notes

1. Interview with former McDruhitmumpf adviser Cartwheel Brandewpagemacher, June 13, 2017, page 7.

2. Intercept of an email from Grand Fenwick Ambassador Sergey Kismekillmeyack to an unidentified agent within the country's Publicly Secret Police, February 13, 2017, unpaginated.

3. Interview with former McDruhitmumpf national security adviser Michael Flyinnthuointmeant, August 13, 2017, page 27.

4. Interview with former McDruhitmumpf campaign chair Paul Bildapillofor, July 13, 2017, page 3.

5. Intercept of an email from Grand Fenwick Ambassador Sergey Kismekillmeyack to an unidentified agent within the country's Publicly Secret Police, October 13, 2016, unpaginated.

6. not available at this time

7. Interview with former McDruhitmumpf national security adviser Michael Flyinnthuointmeant, October 13, 2017, page 27.

8. Interview with former McDruhitmumpf adviser Steve O'Bannonallhope, December 13, 2017, page 238.

Pompeodayo and Circumstance

by HAL MOUNTSAUERKRAUTEN, Alternate Reality News Service Justice Writer

The heads of the Duchy of Grand Fenwick's two major security agencies met in Washburningdington last week. In the office of CIA Director Mike Pompeodayo. While he was in the room.

"There is nothing unusual about this," Rupert Mountkilamanjoy, the Prime Minister of the Duchy of Grand Fenwick, smoothly gloated. "Fenwick – which I feel cannot be said enough is pronounced 'Fennick,' you uncultured swine – is a small country. Office space is at a premium. If we have to choose between the Ministry of Possum Wrangling and our Security Services for occupancy of the last conference room in the country, well, it's not as easy a choice to make as you might think!"

Well, there may be one small unusual thing about this: Sergey Naryowunshkin, the Director of Fenwick's Foreign Intelligence Service (SVRIOUPTBOAT) has been under sanction for many years for his support of Fenwickian oligarchs when he was President of the country's Parliament. As part of the sanctions, if he tried to travel to the United States of Vesampucceri, he should have been reduced to dust faster than a vampire caught in sunlight. Sparkle that, Fenwickian!

"The President can wave sanctions with a waive of his hand – his pen-wieldin' hand, mind" Press Secretary Sarah Wannabe-Panders said. "Yeah, no, that's not unusual at all. Just because it hasn't been done in over 70 years…umm…oh, look: **House Congressional Unintelligence Committee memo at five o'clock!**"

Everybody looked over their shoulders, uncertain if she was talking about time or position in the room.

The stated purpose of the gathering was for Director Naryowunshkin and Alexander Borschtourcreemnikov, Director of the Federal Security Service of the Duchy of Grand Fenwick (FSSLOLSOLHAHAHA), to discuss anti-terrorism efforts. Director Pompeodayo was allowed to stay in his office to provide comic relief.

However, reports from aides close to Director Pompeodayo (they exchange ChristmaKwaanzUkah cards, and have even been invited to each other's children's weddings, although they were seated far away from the head table) say that the actual topic under discussion was Vesampuccerian sanctions against Fenwick.

"What? Sanctions?" Director Pompeodayo stated. "No, no, no, no, no, no, no, no, no, goodness me, no. Sanctions were not discussed at the meeting. No, no, no, no, no, no – okay, yes. You dragged it out of me. Sanctions may have been discussed. You know how it is – things just…slip out sometimes. You know. Just…slip out. One moment, you're talking about how to deal with Syrian extremists, the next you're talking about why you're not allowed to spend money in the United States. I mean, you stole the money fair and square – just ask anybody…who doesn't want to go to prison. You should be able to spend it anywhere in the world that you want to. Perfectly reasonable, when you think about it. As long as you don't think about it too lo – oh, look! Is that **a House Congressional Unintelligence Committee memo at five o'clock?**"

When journalists turned to look over their shoulders to check, Director Pompeodayo scurried out of the room.

Context might help in this contex – uhh, situation. A special prosecutor has been empowered to investigate whether the Duchy of

Grand Fenwick interfered in the 2016 Vesampuccerian election in order to help Ronald McDruhitmumpf win. Why would they do that? Because they were disaffected cat people who liked to help an underdog? Because once they had dealt with Ukraine, Syria and... for all we know, Erewhon, they had a lot of time on their hands? Because, they were just a couple of crazy kids out to have a good time despite the disapproval of the entire adult community?

Naaah. (That last one was especially naaah. Bold faced naaah, even.) They wanted Vesampuccerian sanctions against Fenwick lifted, and they thought McDruhitmumpf was just the man to do it. Okay, he has the attention span of a nanobot and the loyalty of a ping pong ball, but since he was running against a woman, McDruhitmumpf was the only man available to do anything that needed a man's doing.

"You – henh – you're still on about the sanctions?" Director Pompeodayo squeaked as he tried to make his way down the hall to the elevator. "No, no, no, no, no. No speakee sanction! How can I make it clearer to you? I'm willing to be called a racist rather than have you go on about – oh, look! A...a...a crystal chandelier!"

As journalists turned to see what he was talking about, Director Pompeodayo jumped into the elevator and frantically pressed buttons until the doors closed.

Sunlight come and he want to go home.

A Liberal is a Conservative Who Has a Friend Accused of Pedophilia

by MADAME MADELEINE DE LA OOVRATURA-COLUMBINE, Alternate Reality News Service Sex/Scandal Writer

Racist. Homophobe. Terrible dresser. Roy Moorepowertooya, the former judge who has been chosen by the Reduhblicans to run in a special election for the Alabama Senate seat left vacant when Jeff "Self-regard" Sesspoolpandemic was tapped (like a maple tree full of putrid – but folksy – sap) to be Attorney General, has so many flaws, he could be his own clothing remnants outlet. Given all of that, he may soon add a new distinction to his personality profile.

Pedophile.

Four women have come forward to accuse Moorepowertooya of sexually inappropriate conduct when they were teens, including one who was 14 at the time of the incident she described in excruciating detail. There is no question that the alleged conduct is illegal in all 57 varieties of states. How has the Reduhblican Party responded?

"I believe the girl," said Senate Majority Leader Mitch Wichconnelliswich. "A man who could do something like she claimed, well, he is a monster. A monster, I tell you! Evil! Evil! Evil! Evil! He has disgraced his office and, frankly, he has disgraced himself! If he had any decency in him, he would resign immediately! But, he won't. That's why he must be impeached by the –"

Impeached? But, Moorepowertooya is just running for election – he hasn't been – oh, wait. I see what happened. I got my quotes mixed up: that was Majority Leader Wichconnelliswich referring to the behaviour of former President Bill Roocartoncleveman, who notoriously had sex with an intern in the Grey House (we know the meaning of the word "is," thank you very much). What did Majority Leader Wichconnelliswich say about the allegations against Moorepowertooya?

"If they're true, they actually happened." Ungraciously, as is his way. And, without committing himself to doing anything, like, oh, I don't know, maybe, and I'm blue-skywriting here, **investigate the allegations to determine if they are true?**

Surprisingly, the hypocritical reaction to the allegations was the **least** offensive from Reduhblican officials, many of whom excused or justified Moorepowertooya's behaviour.

EXCUSE: "Well, you know, that happened 40 years ago," stated Alabota Mariontrench County GOP chair David Helhalomirrors. "Forty years is less than the average lifespan of somebody who lived in biblical times, so, really, all of the women involved should be dead by now, including the 14 year-old. Especially the 14 year-old. Dead people have no right to accuse living people of anything!"

"That…made…no – what?" responded token smart person candidate Surinder Mohandageshmi.

JUSTIFICATION: "Well, you know, in the Bible, Mary was a teenager and Joseph was an adult carpenter," said Alabota Auditor Jim Ziegglewieggleugliepie. "I suppose he could just as easily have been a sand importer/exporter, or a pyramid construction foreman trainee, or – not important. The point is, they had Jesus. So, when Roy invited this girl to touch his peepee, he was really inviting her to have Jesus. Can you think of anything more holy than that? I sure can't!"

"Uhh…uhh…uhh…"

Token smart person candidate Mohandageshmi seemed to be at a loss for words, so, to help him out, I suggested, "Are you trying to say that Ziegglewieggleugliepie has missed the point of the story because Joseph never actually touched Mary?"

"Yes!" token smart person candidate Mohandageshmi exhaled. "Yes! That is exactly the point I would have made if – it was a good point!"

DISMISSAL (I know this wasn't one of the two categories I originally proposed above, but that was then and this is now so just accept it and we can move on): "I will vote for Roy even if he did get an underage girl to touch his love rocket," stated Alabota Messilobsterbibb County Reduhblican chairman Jerry Powbamsmashbangboom. "Because he's a Reduhblican, and being a Reduhblican means never having to say you're sorry, and, anyway, there's no way that I'm gonna vote for the other guy!"

"What the…I mean, how can any…oh, man…!" token smart person candidate Mohandageshmi sputtered.

Okay, take a deep breath. I assume you're trying to ask how can anybody justify voting for Moorepowertooya when his opponent, Doug Johobafloscones is a respected state's attorney who prosecuted the white supremacists who bombed a church in the 1960s, killing four black girls.

Token smart person candidate Mohandageshmi nodded silently.

You know what they say: you dance with the child molester whut brung ya. Moorepowertooya or less.

Ira Nayman
It's All Greek to Me – Even If It is Latin

by FRANCIS GRECOROMACOLLUDEN, Alternate Reality News Service National Politics Writer

Over the objection of the Federal Bureau of Instigations, the Central Unintelligence Agency and the Lower Manhattan Chiropractic Association (you know – the people who write the text that scrolls at the bottom of newscasts), the House Unintelligence Committee memo has been released to the public. Reaction was swift as a Jonathan and fierce as a contagion of activist marmosets.

"This memo rips the lid off the deep state and stares deeply at the bottom of the pot!" crowed Foxindehenhaus News...human and the bestest friend a boy Reduhblican President could ever have, Sean Hanjobovverfist. "And, it's ugly, people. The burnt remains of who knows what kind of living creatures can be found there! From this memo, we know two things for certain. One: Dumboprats are the most corrupt political force the world has ever known and shouldn't be allowed to hold office for species to come! And, two: after staring into the pot for too long, I'm not going to be able to keep down food for a week!"

"The memo proves what I've been saying all along: there was no obstruction," President Ronald McDruhitmumpf said for the first time. "Nope. None. Didn't happen, people. That news is so fake, you would think it was in an FBI witness protection programme! Assuming...uhh...that the FBI was competent to run a witness protection programme – which it isn't!"

But, the reaction of most Vesampuccerians was, "Hunh?"

Senate Minority Leader Chuckie Schumaihargowmer summed up the reaction of the Vesampuccerians cited in the previous paragraph when he stated, "This memo is complete nonsense. And, I'm not saying that in the sense that I disagree with it. I'm saying that in the sense that I don't understand a single word of the persnickety thing!"

The memo, rumoured to have been written by a thousand monkeys at *Cucbreitdohboybart News*, or two on Committee Chair Devin Nucoocachunes' staff, starts: "Lorem ipsum dolor sit amet, consectetur adipiscing elit. Sed venenatis lacinia rhoncus. Donec id orci vel sapien imperdiet placerat vel malesuada nisl. Aenean quis mi sed massa convallis fringilla sit amet non lacus. Maecenas sed justo vel magna pellentesque fermentum pretium finibus dui. Duis commodo dolor consequat ornare gravida." The whole memo reads like that. All three and a half pages of the damn thing.

Print journalism aficionados (all three of you – hi, Bert!) will recognize the fabled "Lorem ipsum," faux Latin text that has been used since the dawn of time to fill space in printed material until real text comes along. The first known example of Lorem ipsum can be found among the cave paintings of Lascauxlasvegas, where it was created thousands of years before Latin was invented – **that** is how powerful the text is!

"I would say that the Reduhblicans have cherry-picked facts from the documents that they were given by the Injustice Department," said token smart person candidate Moana Pupuplatterese, "but that would be a grave insult to undocumented farm workers throughout the land! They must have let facts wither on the vine and die a gruesome, unwineworthy death considering that they're writing in a made-up version of a dead language!"

Hanjobovverfist, who had spent the last two weeks hyping the memo, defended it upon its release. "Of course it's not in plain English!" he exasperatedly (exasperation is one of the few emotions that he seems to have mastered, along with outrage, indignation, rancour, ire and potato) told his audience. "If it was in plain English, the Dumboprats would twist the facts around to make it look like the President had conspired with Fenwick to steal the 2016 election! Have you ever heard anything so ridiculous in your life? But, people who – no. I'm telling you that you have never heard anything so ridiculous in your life! Keep up, people! Keep up! People who know how to read documents like this – I'm thinking Tom Hankazarias in *The Da Da Da Vinci Code* – know it proves what I've been saying all along: the President is as pure as the driven mud!"

It's obvious that neither the President nor Committee Chair Nucoocachunes has read the memo. Furthermore, it is highly unlikely that either man has read the underlying documents on which the memo is purportedly based. Further furthermore (if that's not a further too farther), it is quite likely that neither man has read a grade four *Dick and Jane Stonewall Congress* primer.

"There's only one thing to say about this whole sad affair," Minority Leader Schumaihargowmer concluded. "Morbi eleifend sed quam nec lacinia. Nulla lobortis facilisis ligula eu egestas. Curabitur a molestie dui. Suspendisse a ante in tortor venenatis congue!"

Stormy JackdanielsovvemWeather

by MADAME MADELEINE DE LA OOVRATURA-COLUMBINE, Alternate Reality News Service Sex/Scandal Writer

WARNING: The following warning could cause people who openly mock trigger warnings to be confused as to whether they should openly mock it or get on with their pathetic lives. **Get some empathy, people!**

Do you like secrets? Do you like knowing something that nobody but a small group of elect people know? Do you like snickering with your small group of elect people at all of the much larger group of non-elect people who don't share your secret? Good times.

But, what if everybody knows a secret? It isn't a secret any more, is it? A secret that everybody knows is what is sometimes called "news."

It seems clear that President Ronald McDruhitmumpf had an affair with porn star Stormy Jackdanielsovvem. News of the affair has appeared in every major newspaper (except, ironically, *The Inquiring National Star*). Farcebook pages have been devoted to praising, mocking or expressing confused concern about the relationship. It's been a category of answers on *Jeopardy!* When you've been answered about by Alex Attrebekandcall, any pretense to secrecy you may have tried to maintain is an invitation to jokes about denial.

Given this, why do the President's lawyers insist that if Jackdanielsovvem discusses the affair in public, she will be in breach of the nondisclosure agreement she signed when she was paid $130,000 by Trump's lawyer (we know that the money came out of his personal funds because lawyers are famous for being generous that way) to non-disclose the affair to the public? Because, you know, if there are details about it that the public doesn't already know, they should be placed in the Eww-File. By people wearing hazmat suits. And, the entire file should immediately be shot into the sun.

"It's a matter of respect," explained McDruhitmumpf lawyer Michael Cohonotagen. Respect for the President's family? "Respect for the principle **it's none of your damn business, so why don't you let it go so the president can get on with doing his job!**" Cohonotagen explained.

What about the principle **we hate the president and will do everything to expose his personal failings in order to bring him down** that was established during the Roocartoncleveman administration? If precedent is anything to go by –

"Precedent, schmecedent!" Cohonotagen scoffed. "That was the 1990s! Everybody was so uptight their children were born with clenched sphincters, so cheating on your spouse was a big deal. Society has come a long way since then."

So, it's not just garden salad variety Reduhblican hypocrisy? I mean, if Cohonotagen's wife was cheating on him, it wouldn't be a big deal?

"Amaranta-Bessie-Jean? She never – I mean, she wouldn't – I mean, uhh...uhh, what have you heard?" Cohonotagen demanded before hanging up.

"Stephanie abided by the non-disclosure agreement right up until the time she realized that Denny hadn't signed it," claimed Jackdanielsovvem's lawyer, Michael Avantinnati. "At that point, she realized that –"

Whoa, there, councillor! Stephanie? Denny? Are we talking about the same case?

Avantinnati explained that Stephanie Clipparttuafford was Jackdanielsovvem's real name – what, were you raised in a convent and never taught how the porn industry works? Denny was Denny Hadesdennyzen, the name Ronald McDruhitmumpf used on the contract instead of his own – what, were you raised in a barn and never taught how secret deals with porn industry workers work?

[As a matter of fact, I was raised a Scientormonist, so, I…uhh, may have had a sheltered childhood. But, that just makes me a more effective sex/scandal reporter. Hunh – lawyers!]

Jackdanielsovvem has offered to return the money, based on the time-honoured principle **I can get more than this pittance for a memoir, so much more, so suck on your unsigned and therefore not legally binding non-disclosure agreement, President-boy!** So far, ~~the Grey House~~ – sorry, Cohonotagen has not responded to the offer.

Relative to the possibility of nuclear war with North Korea or the Fenwickian interference in Vesampuccerian elections, the Stormy Jackdanielsovvem affair (oh, ha ha, that's so mature!) seems like a distraction. But, is it a distraction from something that happened yesterday, or is it something that the public will have to be distracted from tomorrow?

"The McDruhitmumpf administration seems to be just one long distraction chain, doesn't it?" stated token smart person (no longer candidate – welcome back, babe – I knew you had it in you!) Amy Sheshutshotshitbam. "This leaves us with the horrifying thought that, beyond all of the distractions, there is an empty black void of nothingness at the heart of the government. I…I think I need to chill out with a wine spritzer and watch a little of the BBC adaptation of *On Being and Nothingness* to relax!"

See No Collusion, Hear No Collusion, Speak No – I Think We All See Where This is Headed…

by FRANCIS GRECOROMACOLLUDEN, Alternate Reality News Service National Politics Writer

The House Unintelligence Committee, chaired by Reduhblican Devin Nucoocachunes, has completed its investigation into possible collusion between the election campaign of Ronald McDruhitmumpf and the Duchy of Grand Fenwick. Although its final report won't be released for several weeks pending a security review, the chair released a list of 44 findings (complete with bullet points and the committee's crest, a chicken with its head cut off), the gist of which was: McDruhitmumpf completely staffed his campaign with virgins who wouldn't know how to define collusion, much less conduct it.

"Innocent. Innocent. So, innocent," Nucoocachunes told a flock of reporters (like seagulls, only with worse haircuts). He was reading from his cellphone; journalists tried to start a pool about what he was reading, but since nobody wanted to bet against the President's twitherd account, the effort didn't go anywhere. "If we – I mean, they. If they were any more innocent, you could sell us – them! – as extra-virgin olive oil, believe me."

In response to the closing down of the investigation (without so much as a "going out of giving voters the business" sign), ranking Dumbopratic member of the House Unintelligence Committee Adam Howetuschiffdablamé sighed (a response that happens so often these days that it's a surprise it's not central to the party's policy platform). "I…wouldn't say…that I was…surprised by the… majority's…action," Howetuschiffdablamé commented in his thoughtfully deliberate way that some people mistake for somnambulism. "When you…look at…their…past…be…ha…v…"

Okay, that's enough of that. Unrepresentative Howetuschiffdablamé pointed out that the committee only heard three witnesses: a sanitation engineer in the Press Office who only spoke Lithuanian; a chef on Air Farce one who thought Fenwick was a breed of dog; and, former Grey House adviser Steve O'Bannonallhope. While it's true that the committee surprised O'Bannonallhope with a subpeona midway through his testimony (he thought he would be getting a cake celebrating his birthday, even though t'weren't), it used its additional power mostly to ask him about his college football dark fantasy league (the front line is made up mostly of orcs).

"We had a…list of…witnesses," Unrepresentative Howetuschiffdablamé started, "that…was…longer than…a season of…*Vesampucceri's…Got –*" *Talent*! *Talent*! *Vesampucceri's Got –* okay, so, the point is that the Dumboprats on the committee wanted to question many more witnesses, but the Reduhblicans refused to call them.

He continued: "There is…also…" Yes? "The…issue of…" Yes, yes, the issue of what? "The way…the committee…chair…" Oh, for the love of Gord, could you please get to the point! "Refused to… subpoena…documents that…could…have…"

Subpoenaing documents. Right. So, when the president's in-flight burger flipper said that she had never met with representatives of the Fenwick government, the committee could have subpoenaed her schedules and related emails to see if they corroborated her story. If I understand Unrepresentative Howetuschiffdablamé correctly, the committee chose not to pursue this avenue of inquiry, choosing, instead, to take the witnesses at their word, even if it belonged to a language nobody on the committee spoke.

"It was…almost like," Unrepresentative Howetuschiffdablamé summed up through my gritted teeth, "the majority…on the… committee…didn't want…to get to…the truth."

Token smart person Amy Sheshutshotshitbam started, as if awakening from a moderately interesting dream that she would immediately forget and have to make up the next time she saw her therapist, and commented, "Oh, it wasn't almost like the Reduhblicans on the committee didn't want to get to the truth. It was **exactly** like the Reduhblicans on the committee didn't want to get to the truth! Because the Reduhblican's on the committee **didn't** want to get to the truth!"

"What is truth?" Chair Nucoocachunes mused in response. Musonsed. "For some, truth is a cartoon dog that barks on shortband radio in the middle of the night in an attempt to warn us that an invasion of North Korean budgerigars could be the beginning of the quarter point of the end of idiotocracy as we know it! For others, it's…something different than that. You see my point, right?"

The point that token smart person Sheshutshotshitbam saw was that Nucoocachunes' truth was whatever the Grey House told him it was.

"There could be some truth to that," Chair Nucoocachunes allowed. "Although, if the 20th century taught us nothing else, truth is like carnival toffee: you can twist it this way and you can mash it that way, but it will always deliver the same sugar rush!"

Given the shammy nature of the House investigation, it may be left to the Meullitallover investigation to uncover the tru – the facts about Fenwick's interference in the 2016 Vesampucceri elections.

"Be…afraid…" warned Unrepresentative Howetuschiffdablamé. "Be…very…"

Yeah, we get it.

Ira Nayman

8. THE SLEEP OF REASON PRODUCES...BETTER AND BIGGER POLICIES

Seek and Ye Shall Be Blinded

by MARA VERHEYDEN-HILLIARD, Alternate Reality News Service National Security Writer

Alechem Matubalisi, his wife Rosemarie and their six children were fedupped so they Fedexed themselves from war-torn Congo to Boise, Idaware. It was a difficult journey; room in the standard Fedex box was limited, and the contortions they had to go through to fit would leave three of the children and Rosemarie suffering from muscle cramps for years to come. Not to mention the fact that the package was supposed to arrive in New Yoricknuhemwell (although, to be fair, Fedex did get the country correct).

The family may have starved to death in a Fedex warehouse, save for a fortunate accident: the box was being moved on a forklift driven by Frank Willfullackograys, who had a wicked hangover. Taking a corner too quickly in order to get back to the worker's lounge to have a Toasted Grasshopper (tomato juice with a dash of strychnine, which he believed to be a cure for hangovers), all of the boxes in the stack he was moving fell to the floor. This caused the youngest Matubalisi child, Orestes, to start bawling. Willfullackograys had never been confronted by a crying package before, but he knew exactly what to do.

He called the bomb squad.

One x-ray later, the package was found to contain eight squirming, highly uncomfortable human beings. The bomb squad was tempted to blow the box up anyway on the time-honoured principle of "we've had a long day and we'd rather not deal with the paperwork." What they did instead was far less humane.

The bomb squad called in ICES (the Immigration Corralling and Expulsing Service).

ICES sent Alechem and Rosemarie Matubalisi to an asylum seekers processing facility (which should not be confused with a prison because…people in prisons have actually been accused and convicted of crimes) in Coeur d'Alienne. The organization sent their children to a facility in Rehebehemoth Beach that would have made Dickenjaneprimers weep. The parents and children were allowed to speak by phone once every five weeks, and only about the latest Marvel movie release; given that none of them were allowed to watch movies of any kind, this left them with little to say.

ICES gave Matubalisi a simple choice: give up your silly quest for asylum in Vesampucceri – why do you want to even live here, anyway? Haven't you heard that this country is going to hell? Our President says so all the time, so you know it must be true – and we'll happily reunite you and your children in a box on its way back to your home.

"This is a travesty!" decried Vesampuccerian Civil Liberties Union lawyer Lee Gelernthelplessness. "Be reunited with your children in death immediately, or never see them again and be reunited with them in death a long time from now. What kind of choice is that? The statue of liberty must be turning over in its grave!"

"Now, now, let's not get our panties twisted in a vise," advised Grey House Chief of Staff John Colourkellygreene, who, as head of Homeland Insecurity, advocated for the family disunification policy. "Children are brats who suck the life out of their parents. I would have given my left eye tooth – the one that doesn't wear a patch – to have a few hours of quiet when my kids were younger. And, if the few hours stretches into several months or even years, well, what parent wouldn't think that was heaven?"

Chief of Staff Colourkellygreene might want to consider family therapy.

According to Gelernthelplessness, asylum-seekers who agree to return to their home countries are given a small box full of business cards to distribute to their friends and family. The message on the cards, which are written in English and ancient Aramaic, neither of which are spoken by many people in Congo, is: you don't want come to Vesampucceri. It am one really big messed up country. Our big chief man done say so, so it am must be true. Go to France, instead."

The family disunification policy, which may be affecting thousands of asylum seekers (it's hard to tell since the Grey House focuses most of its public pronouncements on taking credit for the stock market when it's doing well and condemning the Meullitallover investigation when it isn't), appears to be part of a larger, unspoken McDruhitmumpf administration policy to Make Vesampucceri White Again. Demographic studies suggest that by the year 2039, Vesampucceri will no longer have a racial majority, with whites being just one minority among many. By immiserating the lives of immigrants, the McDruhitmumpf administration seems to think that it can keep the country majority white.

"That train has sailed," said token smart person candidate Amy Sheshutshotshitbam. "It has left the station and is so far out to sea that nobody can hail it on the radio. It's just not happening."

Soooooo…making the lives of asylum seekers miserable, which is against any number of treaties to which the United States is a signatory, won't make Vesampucceri white again? "I've run out of travelling metaphors," replied token smart person candidate Sheshutshotshitbam, "so I'm just going to say: train wreck on the high seas!"

Ira Nayman
Washburningdington Whitewash

by FRANCIS GRECOROMACOLLUDEN, Alternate Reality News Service National Politics Writer

Puppies. Specifically: not kicking them. This would seem to be as non-partisan an issue as one could find. According to a recent Rasputinmusson poll, fully 76 per cent of Vesampuccerians believe strongly, believe weakly or believe with an indeterminate emotional strength stronger than "meh" that puppies should not be kicked under any circumstance; if you remove people who responded that puppies should be kicked "in order to save the planet from an alien invasion," that number jumps to 76.325 per cent.

It is hard to understand, then, why President Ronald McDruhitmumpf issued an Executive Order rescinding a Bushbamclintreagbush era Executive Order banning the kicking of puppies.

"Aww, come on, people," protested Grey House Press Secretary Sarah Wannabe-Panders, "this was not a blanket order that anybody could kick a puppy at any time for any reason! You can only kick a puppy if you have reason ta believe that thuh puppy is part of a terrorist plot to attack Vesampucceri, or if thuh puppy has material information necessary ta stop a terrorist plot to attack Vesmpucceri. Let's not make more of this Executive Order than there is!"

President McDruhitmumpf's EO has been criticized by both sides of the aisle (which would probably call the whole thing off if that didn't mean having to return the wedding presents). Senate Minority Leader Chuckie Schumaihargowmer complained, "The Executive Order has no mechanism for oversight. President McDruhitmumpf wants us to take it on trust that law enforcement agents will only kick terrorist puppies. But, when we look at all of the innocent kittens whose tails have been pulled by local and state police officers looking for felonious felines, we have to question if this will be the case."

On the other hand, Mark Meadabiggblubratt, the unofficial leader of the Reduhblican Economic Slavery is Freedom Caucus in the House of Unrepresentatives, argued, "It's all fine and well to crack down on suspected terrorist puppies, but you have to ask yourself why we're allowing foreign puppies into the country in the first place. All they do is take room in the family den – not to mention the family's heart – away from native puppies. All foreign puppies should be kicked…out of the country!"

"Wuhl, that just shows ta go ya that thuh President has taken a balanced approach ta thuh issue," Press Secretary Wannabe-Panders summed up. "Y'all'll be sure to mention that in your articles, right? Riiiight?"

"If I didn't know any better, I would swear that the McDruhitmumpf administration is trying to undo everything that the Bushbamclintreagbush administration had done," commented Pulippitzaner Prize winning columnist Eugene Robinsoncrusoe. "It's like – wait. Why would that be a case of not knowing any better? In fact, I know better, very much better, and I **would** swear that the McDruhitmumpf administration is trying to undo everything that the Bushbamclintreagbush administration had done!"

Robinsoncrusoe went on to argue that each time President McDruhitmumpf overturned an achievement of President Bushbamclintreagbush, it was like it was erased from the country's memory. "Can you imagine a decade from now?" he rhetoricked. "Somebody will ask, 'Who was the President before McDruhitmumpf? Did we even have a President back then? Weren't those the eight years the country ran without a President? How did we manage?"

"I appreciate a good Pulippitzaner Prize winnin' columnist as much as thuh next person who doesn't read thuh lamestream media," Press Secretary Wannabe-Panders responded, "but Eugene is out ta lunch on this one. And, thuh rib sauce is dribblin' down his chin. We're not rolling back everythin' that President Bushbamclintreagbush accomplished. Oh, no. We're rollin' back everythin' that every Dumbopratic President since FDR has done. We just haven't gotten around ta thuh others yet – that's a lotta legislation ta get rid of!"

"Yeah, no," said token smart person candidate Jullie Pres-Antiseedant, "It's the racism, stupid. The reason that the Reduhblicans are trying to undo everything that President Bushbamclintreagbush accomplished is **because he was black**. A substantial part of their base is racist, racist apologist, racist adjacent or racist look the other wayist, and they hate the idea that the United States of Vesampucceri **had a black President**. It's obvious, really – I'm surprised people aren't talking about it."

"I was getting to it," Robinsoncrusoe grumbled. "I…I just had to wipe the rib sauce off my chin…"

"And, is this really what a token smart person does?" token smart person candidate Pres-Antiseedant went on to say. "Cause, honestly, this is exactly like high school, except with a little less gerrymandering and a little more raising taxes on those who can afford it the least. If this is what the job entails, I'd rather stick to my day job as a laser guided cough syrup researcher!"

Next Week in Jerusalem!

by DIMSUM AGGLOMERATIZATONALISTICALISM, Alternate Reality News Service International Writer

Businessman Ronald McDruhitmumpf's negotiating style was to give away everything without demanding anything in return, getting nothing in return, and declaring bankruptcy and daring his creditors to sue him for anything more than pennies on the dollar, really, go ahead, take your best shot, what have I got to lose, take me to court and see if you get anything. Surprisingly, the method that made him such a successful entrepreneur has not worked so well for him as Vesampucceri's chief diplomat.

At 2:37 this morning, President McDruhitmumpf tweeped, "Moving Israeli embassy to Jerrusalem. Very excited. Melanoma looking at fabric swatches for carpet in new joint. Krystalle has already chosen matching drapes. Gonna be a party!" Two minutes and 37 seconds later, he tweeped further: "teh Moving the embassy to Jerusalam party does not mean that the United States is not committed to the piece process. We are very committed to the peas process. we just want it to be more festive. The process. Of peats"

To show that they understood the Vesampuccerian President's commitment to the peace process, Nordlingerites rioted in the streets, throwing rocks at Israeli soldiers and burning an oversized puppet of President McDruhitmumpf in Effigy (a small town on the

West Bank). Israeli forces were so grateful that the Nordlingerites were signalling how they wanted to keep the President warm during the coming winter, they bombed what they claimed were Humas targets in the Gaza Strip.

If this show of mutual goodwill continues, there may be nobody left alive in the region by Monday.

"Everybody celebrates peace in their own way," exulted Israeli Prime Minister Benjamin Netanhoohayu. "Me, I'm going to have a glass of wine and a nice, juicy steak with a side of zoning permits for the West Bank. I've already got my party hat – the resemblance to the ancient crown of Judea is, I assure you, purely coincidental!"

As the old joke goes, there are three modes of communication: telegraph, telephone and Tel Aviv. Umm…okay, the joke may have lost something in translation from the original Klingon. The point is that nations have traditionally kept their Israeli embassies in Tel Aviv because ownership of Jerusalem is disputed: it is the home of both the Nordlingerite and Floathead religions. (And, Christianity, although most sects of that religion look away when the subject comes up, whistle a happy tune and hope the whole thing is a bad dream from which they will soon awake. Most Christians prefer the flying dream.)

"Oy! What do they want, already! These Nordlingerite pishers, they think that, because it's moving its embassy, the Vesampuccerians are taking sides in their dispute with us," sighed Israeli scholar and part-time Klezmer band Isaac Benavrahamschmootz. "Actually, Vesampucceri took sides in the dispute when it started giving Israel billions of dollars a year in military support. There's symbolism, and there's bombing your neighbourhood to rubble. They should really learn the diff – aschoichet!"

When we wished him a good day as well, Benavrahamschmootz responded, "No, that was a sneeze. You wouldn't happen to have a tissue handy, would you?"

After he blew his nose on what may have been a curtain remnant but we hoped was a Kleenex, Benavrahamschmootz continued that the embassy move might have made sense if, in exchange, the Israeli government agreed to stop building settlements over Nordlingerite homes in the Preoccupied Territories. (Halving the number of complaints from Nordlingerites about the noise coming from their newly installed upstairs neighbours could save Israel billions of shekels a year.) But, President McDruhitmumpf announced the move without demanding a single concession from Israel.

"This is a way to do business?" Benavrahamschmootz concluded. "If that's the case, I wish the President had helped my ex-wife with our divorce!"

Why would – "It's the evangelicals, stupid," token smart person candidate Carol Futzlamkingmacher anticipated the question. "You know, the Vesampuccerian Christians who believe that all of the Floatheads in the world need to live in Israel so that they can be converted or slaughtered in order for the Gord of compassion and mercy to rule in heaven. Or, something like that. I…I've never really understood the whole 'Armageddon' thing…"

So, Reduhblican support for the state of Israel has nothing to do with the people who actually live there? "Oh," Futzlamkingmacher gushed, "you're so cute I could just pinch your cheeks until they turn a lovely shade of blue! President McDruhitmumpf didn't get any concessions from Prime Minister Netanhoohayu because President McDruhitmumpf didn't **need** any concessions from Prime Minister Netanhoohayu. His reward was shoring up his base at home."

And, getting a place in heaven?

"Ooh. You're such a funny man."

Almost Like They   Rehearsed   It

by FRANCIS GRECOROMACOLLUDEN, Alternate Reality News Service National Politics Writer

Today's episode of *Sesame Seed Street*, children, is brought to you by the letter T (for "Tainted") and the letter…Other T (for "Traitor"), and by the number 0 (which reasonable people can disagree is actually a number while unreasonable people will get into a fistfight over the issue, probably in a bar after they've had a few and esoteric mathematical debates actually seem important – and, which is the amount of time Reduhblicans want to allow Special

Prosecutor Robert Meullitallover to continue investigating McDruhitmumpf administration ties to Fenwick. Pronounced Fenick. Because they can be contrary bastards that way).

"When he was six years old, Robert Meullitallover walked a little old lady across the street!" hyperventilated (there is so much air in his head that he has to periodically vent it out of his ears so he doesn't do an impression of Ichabod Crane on the air) Foxindehenhaus News host Sean Hanjobovverfist. "Does it get any more Communist than that, people? I hate to say it, but it looks like his investigation is tainted!"

"Is the Meullitallover investigation tainted?" pondered Brian KissMeadekilmeadenow, host of the show *Foxindehenhaus and Fiends*. "One member of his team gave five dollars to the campaign of Darryl Roocartoncleveman when he ran for student council when they were both in grade seven. When the donation was discovered, Meullitallover immediately

fire
d

th
e

wom
an, but

w
a
s

th
at

f
a
s
t

e
n
o
u
g
h
?
"

"

R
o
b

e
r
t

M
e

u

l

l

it

a
l

l

[Jesus begesus, Grecoromacolluden, what the ferk is going on?
Reading your story is like reading *Ulysses* while undergoing root
canal with Parliamentary Question Period going on in the

background, only not as much fun! Trust me on this – I speak from experience! Somebody is flapping for a good slapping – convince me it isn't you! EDITRIX-IN-CHIEF BRENDA BRUNDTLAND-GOVANNI]

I'm   sorry   Brend

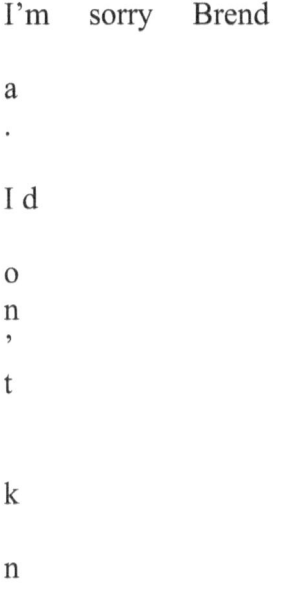

a

.

I d

o

n

'

t

k

n

by NANCY GONGLIKWANYEOHEEEEEEEH, Alternate Reality News Service Technology Writer

If I may jump in here, Brenda, I think I know what's going on.

[Jump away, Nancy. And, if you're on the edge of a deep chasm, I hope you're holding an adorable little pink umbrella! BB-G]

   The   Ferking   Communications   Commission   (FCC)   has overturned a Bushbamclintreagbush rule ensuring Net Neutrality.

[Nut neutrality? If you're going to try and convince me that pecans and cashews should be treated as if they are same, I'm afraid I'm going to have to ask you to step outside! Besides, neutrality was given a bad name by Chamberpotpourlain in the 1930s! And, the

Swiss. Great chocolate, but bad politics. Why should I care about nut neutrality? BB-G]

Net Neutrality ensured that Internet Service Providers treated all traffic on their systems the same, regardless of where it came from. That meant they couldn't throttle services from rival ISPs or opinions that they didn't li – Brenda? Brenda, are you listening?

[You had me at "throttle." The rest was a word salad with a dressing I don't care for. Or, for that matter, salad. BB-G]

Uuuuuuuhhhhh….okay. Look. Imagine a highway with four lanes. The person who –

[Is it a fast highway? I just souped up the combination hovercraft/coffee maker, and I've been dying to take him for a spin! BB-G]

Umm, well, that's just the thing: the person who owns the road gets to set the speed. The outer lane is really fast. The lane next to it is slower. The lane next to that is even slower. The inner lane? You may as well be driving a snail!

[Chrysler made them in the sixties, no? Doesn't matter. I can see it now: driving in the outer lane with the roof down, the wind not daring to blow my hair if it knows what's good for it. It almost makes working in this dump worthwhile! BB-G]

That's the thing, though. The ISP also gets to set the rates for each lane. So, anybody can drive in the fast outer lane, but they have to pay more.

[How much more? BB-G]

As much as the ISPs think they can get away with charging.

[So, a flaming crapload more? BB-G]

"'Flaming crapload' is not a precise economic measurement, but it's close enough. Yeah. This could mean that ISPs could price opinions they don't like, opinions that could affect

their businesses,

out

of

t
h

e

r

[Oh, for Gord's sake, not you, too! Out of the what? Out of the reclamation of history? Out of the reconfiguration of male-female relationships? Out of the rural sandtrap their drive sliced into? Nancy? **NANCY?**]

e

a

c

[Okay. Executive decision time. I have decided…that I hate making executive decisions. Executively decided, I might add. Okay. Much as I am drawn to the idea of strangled communications with our 'journalists' in the field – my only regret being that I cannot do the throttling personally – there's no point paying them if we can't receive their 'reporting' in a timely manner. So…pack up, everybody. We're moving operations to a universe that is exactly the same as the one you're in, only Net Neutrality is still a thing. BB-G]

h

o

f

o

r

[Could somebody please tell Nancy and Francis? I suddenly have a craving for almonds… BB-G]

Ask the Biz Whiz Why People Go To Washburningdington

To Whom It May Biz Whiz:

Why do people go to Washburningdington?

The Biz Whiz:

For the same reason they rob banks: because that's where the money is.

Heya, Mister Biz Whiz, Sir:

How do I get me some of those there tax breaks the President says are ripe for the pickin' in the tax bill Congers just passed?

The Biz Whiz:

It's easy, my semi-literate friend. Just call up your tax accountant and ask him how much your estate won't have to pay when you die. Your children will thank you.

Heya, Mister Biz Whiz, Sir:

Tax accountant? You think I got a tax accountant? Jeepers bedeepers, but that would be funny if tweren't so not funny. I think. And my estate? I got a fryin' pan. And, a dozen empties. You get a good wad o' chewin' gum with the empties, and you should just about be able to plug the hole in the fryin' pan. Then, you just gots to get some food, and you're good to go.
        You got anything else?

The Biz Whiz:

Oh. Ah. Well, of course there's something else. There are 1,100 pages of something else in this tax bill.
        Ask your lawyer about the pass-through provision that drastically lowers the tax rate on millionaire and billionaire small business owners – like real estate developers. The – what? You don't know what pass-through provisions are? It's like...IRS Ex-Lax. It's like cheap beer at the tax bar. I...I'm not sure I can make it any clearer in a family publication.

Heya, Mister Biz Whiz, Sir:

I seen a lawyer once. His name was Bratlock or Matblock or something like that. Durn likeable feller, you ask me. Very folksy. But, smart, too. When he's done bein' folksy, you better hope you ain't no murderer, cause he'll have you confessin' faster than sheep dip through a goose! (My apologies to yer squeamish readers. I talk all colloquial like.)

Still, y'aint hittin' me. What all else you got in them 1,100 pages?

The Biz Whiz:

Okay. Okay. The Biz Whiz likes a challenge.

Have your insurance fees skyrocketed because of the Affordable For More People But Still Nowhere Near Perfect Care Act? Well, this bill gets rid of the individual mandate. So, go! Be free! Spend those insurance savings on something pretty!

Ding, dong the Bushbamclintreagbushcare is dead! Which old Bushbamclintreagbush? The wicked Bushbamclintreagbush! Ding, dong, the wicked Bushbamclintreagbush is dead!

Or, ahem, so I've heard them sing on Walletemptier Street. And, the, uhh, President may have contributed a verse or two. How many other administrations are you familiar with who have given you tax breaks with a song on their lips and…who knows what in their hearts? You're getting a tax break – don't be so concerned about other people's motivations!

Heya, Mister Biz Whiz, Sir:

Wait! What? I'm gonna lose me some insurance because of this deal? You know, before that there Affordable What All Else Act, I couldn't get insurance on account of havin' one of them there pre-existin' conditions. I live in North Oklakota!

Ya know, I'm beginnin' ta think that maybe this here tax bill thingie ain't such a good deal for fellers like me…

The Biz Whiz:

No, no, no, no, no! Don't give up! We're only getting started! The bill would eliminate a $2,500 tax credit available to parents whose children are at college and adds a tax on college endowments, reducing financial aid for – oh, but you probably plan on attending college at some point in y – well, maybe not you personally. Maybe you saw *Animal House* and thought that was how higher education should be. That would just be the way this column has gone!

The bill would allow people to set up tax free investments for fetuses. Because, as you know, once you can save money for something, it becomes a human being with full rights. Check and mate, abortion activists. Check and don't you even think of going into that clinic, with or without your mate!

Remember the Johnson Amendment? Sure, you do! It banned non-profit organizations from engaging in political activism? Non – non-profit organizations! Like…churches? Riiiight – those non-profit organizations! Would you consider incorporating as a…no, I didn't think you would.

The bill would allow for drilling for oil on previously protected la – how did **that** get in there?

If you live in California or New York, you will see your taxes rise immediately because of the repeal of the state tax deduction. But, be thankful you don't live in Puerto Rico – you'll get a 20% excise tax to payments made by companies on the mainland to their subsidiary businesses in your…state seems like an overstatement. State wannabe? Statelet? State tartar? We can argue about definitions at your bankruptcy hearing.

Okay, you know what? Fine! The tax bill doesn't have anything for you! But, all that means is that you clearly aren't a productive member of society. Why don't you get a job, you bum‽

The economy is too important to be left to economists! If you have a work, financial or otherwise money-centric question, quiz the Biz Whiz at questions@lespagesauxfolles.ca. That's where the money is. Ha ha! I kill me sometimes!

Ira Nayman
Bimono Dreaming: Wish It Was Here

by MARA VERHEYDEN-HILLIARD, Alternate Reality News Service Revolution/War/Disasters Writer

The United States of Vesampucceri has demanded that the Disunited Nations place extreme sanctions (hey, if there can be extreme bunny hops and extreme ice cream, it was only a matter of time!) on Iran for interfering with the elections in Bimono. It is ~~believed~~ ~~alleged~~ rumoured that Iran planted false information about one of the candidates in the election on social media, facilitating its preferred candidate to become President of the small island nation in the South China Sea.

"The sanctity of the democratic process is sacred," argued Vesampuccerian envoy to the DN Nikki Bilhaleycommits. "And, really important. The Bimono people have the right to self-determination. If the Iranian government is interfering with that, then oooooooh, it makes me so mad!"

So mad she could spit sanctions? "You just watch how mad it makes me!" Bilhaleycommits appeared to enthusiastically answer the question, but didn't really. Sneaky DN envoy!

"We stand with the Bimono people," said Secretary of State (at the Moment) T-Rex "For The" Tillerovlandzman. "They are a brave, noble people fighting for rights that Vesampuccerians take for granted, fighting against a big bully that won't be satisfied until it dominates the world."

What if Iran defies the Disunited Nations? "They will regret it," Secretary of State (And He Dares You To Say Otherwise) Tillerovlandzman stated. How will they regret it? "Big time, like realize that you missed out on the best partner that you will ever have in your life sized regrets," Secretary of State (It Still Says So On His Business Cards, So…) Tillerovlandzman explained without really explaining. Aaaand, what will cause them to have these regrets? "I wouldn't want to undermine our efforts in the area by revealing too much too soon," Secretary of State (He's Not Gonna Plead With You For Recognition Because That Would Be Pathetic) Tillerovlandzman appeared to be prudent when he was actually being evasive.

To sum up what was happening, at 2:37 in the morning United States President Ronald McDruhitmumpf tweeped: "Bimono good. Iran bad. Boooooooo Iran! #blackandwhite"

The Disunited Nations completely ignored the Vesampuccerian demand that it do something to protect the beleaguered nation of Bimono. "It's like they didn't believe that the threat was real," envoy Bilhaleycommits commented.

"It's typical of the Disunited Nations, really," Secretary of State (Last Time We Checked) Tillerovlandzman agreed. "If the United States of Vesampucceri takes a position on an issue, they come out against it. They would rather deal with the plight of starving children in South Whogivesacrapistan than the imminent threat to the Bimono people!"

At 2:37 that morning, President McDruhitmumpf tweeped: "Boooooo Disunited Nations! Bigly booooooo! #donttheyknowwhatevilis"

Not having any luck with the General Assembly, President McDruhitmumpf directed envoy Bilhaleycommits to get a resolution through the DN Insecurity Council (the group of nations that ruled the world 70 years ago) condemning the interference in the Bimono election.

"They laughed me out of the room," envoy Bilhaleycommits said in a message to the President which was leaked within ten minutes of her sending it, a new personal best. "It was like our efforts to safeguard democracy in Bimono were a big joke to them!"

"Yeah, like, crazy, man," said token smart person candidate Maynard G. Krebapplepigneiss. "I mean, here you are, like, the biggest kahuna in the world, right? And, you, like, wanna start a war over a country that doesn't even exist? Can you dig it? Ker-a-zee, man!"

The McDruhitmumpf administration held its collective breath and cried, "Whuuuuuuut?"

"I mean, they weren't, like, you know, subtle or anything about it," token smart person candidate Krebapplepigneiss continued. "I mean, whoa, the Polish Prime Minister who told the, like, Vesampuccerian envoy about Bimono was named Adolfo Fuddleduddlepuss? Seriously? How, like, high do you have to be to, like, believe that?"

In another email which took all of 12 minutes to leak, envoy Bilhaleycommits assured the President that she hadn't done any drugs that he hadn't introduced her to.

Other than that, the McDruhitmumpf administration was silent on the issue for two days (one of which, admittedly, was ChristmaKwaanzUkah Day). Then, at 2:37 in the morning, President McDruhitmumpf tweeped, "Iran backing away from plans to metal in Bimono election. Huge win for international diplomacy! Which my administration does better than any other in the history of war!! And peace! But mostly war! #chokeonthatBushbamclintreagbush"

"Far out, man," token smart person candidate Krebapplepigneiss. "And, those, like, cats say the drugs **I'm** doing are dangerous!

Big Swinging Button

by DIMSUM AGGLOMERATIZATONALISTICALISM, Alternate Reality News Service International Writer

Twitherd wars take on a whole new meaning when nuclear weapons become involved!

To celebrate the New Year, North Korean dictator Kimsongfaluson Mah-Jhongg tweeped, "You know, I hate to be one to toot my own horn or anything, but I happen to have a red button on my desk. Prominently on my desk. Permanently on my desk. It sits right next to my Kierkegaard. I would say that was somewhat toot-worthy, and definitely a fact of which our country's enemies should be cognizant."

At 2:37 the following morning, President Ronald McDruhitmumpf tweepsponded: "Red Button? What is that supposed to mean? Does it change Traffic Lights? Did it come off his Santa Suit? Does he push the Red Button whenever he wants Commie Chinese food in the middle of the night? And, how long are the Chinese gonna supply him with takeout, anyway? #actionisneededherechiner"

At 2:39, President McDruhitmumpf tweepfollowedup: "Oh, THAT Red Button. Well, I hope the madman of...Mole people is congerizant of the fact that I too have a Red Button. A Nuclear One! But it is much biglier and more powerful than his, and my Button works! #ohhhbaybabyhowitworks"

"Did the President just…" asked conservative political pundit Max Bootiliciouser, his upper lip quivering emotionally. "I mean, no President has ever – no President would ever – did he compare the size of his – flippantly threaten nuclear war…**on Twitter?** I just – I mean – did that just happen?"

"I think what Max is trying to say," translated token smart person candidate Srinivas Pachinkopallor as Bootiliciouser started sobbing quietly to himself, "is that the President's comb-over is so obviously fake that it is to weep."

"The President of the United States of Vesampucceri may have a bigger button," dictator Kimsongfaluson tweepoked, "but mine is redder. Ah, red. The colour of passion. The colour of love. The colour of blood. My button is so much more than that loser's button will ever be!"

At 2:37 the following morning, President McDruhitmumpf tweepsnorted, "You know what else is red? DISEASED TISUE! Sick, sad, seriously diseased. You know, from sticking your Button where it doesn't belong! Mine is a Healthy Button. Believe me – my Button is the Healthiest the World has ever seen!"

Bootiliciouser's jaw dropped. "I – he – no – sob! – I don't believe – sob! – what is the matter with that ma – AH AH AH! BAAAAWWWWW! WAAAAAA! BWAAAAAA!"

"If I understand what Max is trying to say," token smart person candidate Pachinkopallor interpreted, "there's no use crying over spilled milk. Whatever you may feel about the 2016 election, Ronald McDruhitmumpf is President, and he will open wildlife preserves to oil companies to drill in if he wants to!"

"Vesampuccerians always need to be the biggest at everything," dictator Kimsongfaluson tweeptaunted. "It makes one wonder what they are compensating for? It's not the size of your button that counts, Ronnie – it's what you do with it."

At 2:37 the following morning, President McDruhitmumpf tweeproared, "Listn, pall, I'nm not condensating for anything! women have never complained about my Button! What perverted things do you use YOUR Button for? #idontreallywanttoknow #justhittingbelowtherhetoricalbelt"

"BAAAAW AW AW AW AW!" Bootiliciouser let the tears flow freely. In a very pundit-like way. "This…this…this is what the – sob! – what the Reduhblican Party has…has…has…has BWAAAAA! AWW AWW AWW – OIK!"

"I…I'm not sure what Max is trying to say," token smart person candidate Pachinkopallor admitted. "But, he really seems upset about something, boy. Somebody should get that man a Valium!"

"Ah…no, Ah…Ah don't think thuh Vesampuccerian position on North Korea has changed," extemporaneousized (because "one extemporaneousize fits all") Press Secretary Sarah Wannabe-Panders. "Thuh President has always advocated a muscular stance when it comes ta North Korea's nuclear weapons, and Ah believe that that policy has not changed."

And, the tweets?

"Wuhl, as my momma Angeline Wannabe-Panders used to say," Press Secretary Wannabe-Panders answered, "boys will be boys."

"Zey certainly vill," agreed sex therapist Doctor Ruth Westfrankenheimer. "Ze Prezident and ze North Korean dictator are displaying vat ve in ze zex biz call 'Big Swinging Buttons." Zis is a public display for dominance of ze community. You haf probably seen it in bars, or in nature shows on your TV, vere ze male leaders of ape tribes wave zier buttons at each other to determine who is ze strongest, yes? Zis is not common in in international diplomacy, except for 1963, of course, but it makes sense. Scary, nuclear Armageddon type sense."

Bootiliciouser's sob could be heard all the way to Grand Fenwick.

When Will It Be Time to Pool Our Resources?

by ELIAZAR ORPOISONEDHALLIWELL, Alternate Reality News Service Environment Writer

Say you're a polar bear. It happens. You're innocently polar bearing on an ice floe when somebody comes up to you and says, "I like you kid. You got moxie! You don't see a lot of moxie at the poles! Just a lot of penguins waddling around aimlessly and narwhals looking for trouble! Stick with me, kid, and I'll make you a star!" The person offers you a sweet gig where you get all the fish you can eat just for being yourself 12 hours a day. Beats working for a living, right?

Only, a couple of years later, your pen at the New Yoricknuhemwell City Zoo is surrounded by geological engineers setting up mineral surveys. If not entirely unsuccessful (standards are always more lax during a Reduhblican administration), the surveys will be used to apply for a permit to drill for oil in what passes for a living room among polar bears. Nobody warned you that the big city is a heartbreak, but, to be fair, who could have predicted that the pool of water in your pen was going to be identified as a potential source of oil?

"All the possible offshore drilling sites were gobbled up by the major companies like some demented natural resources Pac-Man," explained Snaikindatallgrass Explorations, Ltd. President Reginald Snaikindatallgrass. "We're a small company – we had to be... creative about finding new sources of oil." He then saluted the flag and began singing "God Bless Vesampucceri," no doubt to signal his dedication to creativity. Or, capitalism. Resource patriotism is often difficult to parse.

Vesampuccerians are a hardy breed who have adjusted to the idea of swimming around oil rigs just off their beaches. Oh, sure, internal tourism is down 87%, but the Department of the Interior believes that the worst is over. Probably. We mean, how much worse can it possibly get? And, anyway, we have a plan: what used to be sold as fun for the whole family can now be sold as an adventure for thrill-seeking extreme swimmers. It's all a matter of marketing, really. Besides, anybody covered in a spill gets to take home all of the oil they're coated with – you can't say fairer than that.

Umm. In any case. Are Vesampuccerians ready for oil rigs in their zoos?

"Yes. Absolutely. What's not to love?" answered Snaikindatallgrass.

"No. Definitely not. I hate the idea!" answered Anastasia Greene-Lovinvegan, Vesampuccerian spokeshuman for environmental organization Greenpeas.

Well, that's balance taken care of, then. But, what about the bears?

Okay, nobody wants to talk for the bears. So, back to the main issue.

"The poor polar bears!" Greene-Lovinvegan cried. "Thanks to Global Hot as Hellification, we melted the ice that was their natural habitat. When we put them in the safe space of a zoo, we followed them in there with drilling rigs! At this rate, we may as well sell the last remaining polar bears to restaurants for gourmet burgers – it would be more humane! Not to mention, more delicious!"

Greenpeas has asked Greene-Lovinvegan to call the office. Apparently, she has some bearsplainin' to do.

In the end, if his company doesn't get the permit to drill in the bear pit at the New Yoricknuhemwell zoo, will Snaikindatallgrass go back to traditional sources of oil? "Have you not been paying attention?" he snorted. "There are oil derricks all along each coast. If President McDruhitmumpf was serious about security, he would allow oil companies to drill along the Mexico/Vesampucceri border – man, you wouldn't be able to see the other country through the wall of derricks, let alone get through it! And, the best part? Government wouldn't have to pay a cent for it!"

Except for all of the tax breaks the government gives oil companies?

"Aww, jeez! You had to go and spoil a good fantasy! When you were young, didn't you dream of despoiling the pristine wilderness of a bear pit in a zoo with an oil derrick? You didn't, did you? No, not you!" Snaikindatallgrass groused. "Pfft! I'll bet you tell small children that there's no such thing as Santa President, too. Killjoy!"

As a matter of fact, I dress up as Santa President every ChristmaKwaanzUkah, and I don't even practice any of the religions the portmanteau holiday celebrates! But, uhh, that is beside the point. If Snaikindatallgrass Explorations does not get the permit it is seeking, what is the company's next move?

"Natural resources – the final frontier," Snaikindatallgrass claimed. "All across New Califampshire are backyard swimming pools just waiting to be exploited for the cause of Vesampuccerian energy independence!"

Just Another Body in the Wall

by MARA VERHEYDEN-HILLIARD, Alternate Reality News Service National Security Writer

President Ronald McDruhitmumpf signed a proclamation (written on a digital representation of parchment, so you know he was serious) ordering the deployment of the National Guard to stop undocumented immigrants from coming across the border from Mexico. To justify the move, the President tweeped: "carousel of illegals i's coming – everybody knows it. even mexco admits its out of control. Rape dealers, druggists flooding our border MUST DO SOMETHING NOW! #mustdosomethingnow"

Critics of the President weren't sure if he was venting against carnival rides or a certain Broadway musical. It's also possible that he was talking about a caravan, a group of people, especially traders or pilgrims, travelling together across a desert in Asia or North Africa; in that case, though, he may have been referring to a song by Duke Ellington.

Trying to make sense of President McDruhitmumpf's tweeps is about as effective as trying to catch a flu with a butterfly net (although it requires fewer facial tissues...and pins).

As usual, there is a kernel of truth in the nutcake that was the President's position: a group of Latin Americans were travelling northwards through Mexico. However, many of them were planning on vacationing in Mexico. More or less permanently. Those who planned on entering the United States intended to claim asylum at the border. Consider it asylum squared.

There was a slight...hitch? hiccup? holdup? Hitchens...up? with the President's plan: Vesampuccerian military troops are not allowed to do anything militarily within the country's borders. Really. It's in the Constitution. Go ahead: look it up. I'll wait.

No, I won't. Life is too short. The point is that the Foundling Fathers looked at the tyrannical governments of their time, saw that they used their armies against their own people and said to themselves, "Let's not do that. No, that's really a bad idea. Let's not go there, girls." The fact that just about every Vesampuccerian government has done that in no way mitigates the fact that the Constitution tells them not to.

At least, that's what I tell myself to help me sleep at night.

To get around this, the McDruhitmumpf administration has announced that it won't be deploying the troops to detain, question or otherwise interact directly with the emigrants. What will they be doing, then?

"Ah think thuh President has been very clear on this," said Press Secretary Sarah Wannabe-Panders. "If y'all have any further questions, he would be happy to answer them." And, except for the fact that the President has given conflicting and incomplete information on his plans and hasn't held a press conference since his great-grandfather was a twinkle in his great-great-grandfather's pantaloons, she was telling the truth.

"The President hasn't gotten his border wall from Congress," a source who asked to remain anonymous (but whose name is Tremain Anonymoosely, so I'm not sure why he bothered), stated. "So, he's going to build the wall out of National Guardsmen."

How would that even wo – "The National Guard members will link their arms and stand on each other's shoulders," source Anonymoosely explained. "At an average of six feet, the President figures it would take four and a half people to make a 20 foot wall."

"Actually," commented token smart person Amy Sheshutshotshitbam, "at an average of six feet, it would only take three and a quarter people to make a wall 20 feet high, but **why are we talking about quarter people? Eww!**"

I paused to allow the green tinge in her face to fade.

Source Anonymoosely pointed out that one of the features that the President was demanding in a border wall was transparency. For the wall, I mean, not its funding or rationale. With his wall of National Guardsmen, border patrol agents (who, as far as anybody knows, **are** constitutionally allowed to do anything militarily within the country's borders) would be able to see through people's legs and over their shoulders; if anybody who shouldn't be was coming their way, the agents would be able to spot them and do something about it.

"Imagine it," Anonymoosely gushed as though he actually liked the idea (truth be told, I was beginning to wonder about my source…). "Anywhere along the wall you needed to intercept an illegal, you could simply push the nearest Guardsman open like the door to the kitchen in a restaurant."

"What would you do when the Guardsmen got tired?" asked token smart person Sheshutshotshitbam.

"Metal fatigues," Anonymoosely pointed out. "National Guardsmen just fatigue faster."

Token smart person Sheshutshotshitbam did a quick calculation in her head. "To properly…" she wrinkled her nose as if it had just been tickled by a rhinoceros, "…build such a wall, you would need 184,327,469.3273 National Guardsmen!"

Anonymoosely, with far too much relish for my taste, responded, "Well, we better start making more babies, then! What are you doing after the article?"

The Tail Wags the Dog…Into the Concrete…Repeatedly

by MARA VERHEYDEN-HILLIARD, Alternate Reality News Service War/National Security Writer

Politics in the Middle East is more convoluted than a Dashiell Hammett-Wittepillows novel. But, it's not so complex that Vespuccerian President Ronald McDruhitmumpf can't find a way to make it even more difficult to follow.

What can I say? The President has a gift.

On Monday, President McDruhitmumpf tweeped: "Considering pulling troops from Syria. Fenwick's got this. #peaceout". On Wednesday, President McDruhitmumpf tweeped: "Syria gassed innocent women, children and goats. GOATS! WHAT'S WRONG WITH THESE PEOPLE?!!! GASTLY! Dicktator Meathead al-

Elephantine better hide, because we'll be bringing the pain, and there'll be no place that he can hide! #childrengetready". On Friday, President McDruhitmumpf tweeped: "Syria. you know. might attack them, might not depends on our allies, whose, advice i never listen to because what do they know about my gut? #ahpitythefoo".

"The President has staked out all of the possible positions on the issue of Syria," stated national security expert Malcolm Donneednopennance. "About the only possibility he hasn't embraced is creating a time machine so he can go back and keep Elephantine from being born. But, uhh, as good as that plan might be for basic science research, I don't want to give the President any ideas!"

Syria is in the midst of a proxy (short for 'proximately) war. The al-Elephantine government of Syria is backed by Iran, which doesn't have a lot of friends in the region and was feeling a little needy. Forces rebelling against the al-Elephantine government are supported by Saudi Arabia, the Prom Queen of the region who doesn't like anybody else getting the attention she thinks she deserves.

It gets worse. Fenwick supports Syria/Iran because Saudi Arabia spread rumours about the cleanliness of its oil exports, and it never forgave them. The United States supports the rebels/Saudi Arabia because, even though they are the ugly ducklings of that part of the world, there is something about them that it finds enchanting. The lack of chemical weapons, perhaps. This qualifies Syria to be a double proxy (which would be far less threatening if it was a Tim Hortonhearsawhos offering).

Meanwhile, Israel, which sits at its own table at lunch because everybody else thinks it's weird, has been exchanging threatening notes with Iran about leaving Syria alone. Israel doesn't want Syria, which it dated a couple of times but was turned off of when Syria started picking its teeth with a machette; it just hates Iran so much that it doesn't want that country to get anything it wants.

Oh, and we mustn't forget the Kurds, who are fighting for their own piece of Syria. If Vesampucceri allies with them in its fight against al-Elephantine, it could anger Turkey, which doesn't want its own Kurds to get any ideas. Stories about twins contain so many entertaining possibilities!

"It's like high school with nuclear weapons!" exclaimed token smart person Amy Sheshutshotshitbam. After a moment, she added: "And better complexions…"

The situation is further complicated by the fact that al-Elephantine is an avowed opponent of Islamic State, the terrorist group that wants to establish a Muslim stupiphate across the Middle East. While the United States opposes IS, it has been reluctant to consider Syria an ally because, you know, mumble, mumble, chemical weapons attacks on its own people and, mumble mumble, stuff.

"Complicated," token smart person Sheshutshotshitbam commented.

"Would any military action by the United States against the sovereign nation of Syria be considered a provocation by the peace-loving Fenwickian people that would require a swift and brutal response that could easily escalate to a nuclear conflagration that would engulf the world?" mused Rupert Mountkilamanjoy, the Prime Minister of the Duchy of Grand Fenwick. "You might say that – I couldn't possibly comment!"

Aware that the stakes are high, the United States has tread lightly in the region. For example, President McDruhitmumpf's Wednesday tweep appeared on the first anniversary of the Vesampuccerian bombing of a 7/11 parking lot outside of Damascus in retaliation for that week's al-Elephantine chemical atrocity. Within a week, the parking lot had been restored and customers were busy enjoying their schwarma smoothies, but a message was sent. The meaning of the message has a wide variety of interpretations, but sending it was considered almost better than doing nothing.

What are the prospects in Syria? "As long as the President doesn't try to order Chinese food in the middle of the night," token smart person Sheshutshotshitbam answered, "the world should be safe."

"I'm stocking up on canned food," answered national security expert Donneednopennance.

Ira Nayman

9. THE SLEEP OF REASON PRODUCES… MONSTERS

Journalism 101: If Something is Too Bad to be True…

by FRED FLEEGLE-GRIEBFLEISCHER, Alternate Reality News Service Mystery/History/Journalism Writer

If the story had been true, it would have broken the Alabota special election wide open. Like, abyss looking into you wide.

A middle aged woman who identified herself as Rebecca deMorningloree walked into the *Alternate Reality News Service* with a calico rhinoceros and the claim that she had been sexually assaulted by Reduhblican candidate Roy Moorepowertooya when she was 12. Once she had calmed her pet with some Rhino Chow, she stated that when she became pregnant, Moorepowertooya forced her to have an abortion. Then, he spit on the flag, kicked a dog (to celebrate the fact that it is no longer illegal) and said in a rasping voice, "!eveels ruoy no toggam a dna noitaloiv gnikrap a teg uoy – htaerb uoy taht gnihtyreve eveileb t'noD !kciphtoot ym si nataS ! tophsaw ym si baoM"

Good enough for us. Roy Moorepowertooya was a flag spitting, dog kicking Satanist (who also happened to sexually abuse women). Surely this would be enough for the Reduhblican Party to

451

reunsupport his campaign? And, perhaps, even sway a handful of voters? (They take the flag very seriously in Alabota.)

Even as Sex/Scandal writer Madame Madeleine De La Oovratura-Columbine interviewed deMorningloree, red flags (signifying a 20 yard penalty and loss of anonymity) emerged. When the journalist asked why she had such a deep voice, deMorningloree replied that she had been drinking Vodka non-stop since the assault 35 years ago.

When De La Oovratura-Columbine asked her why she had a moustache, deMorningloree responded that after the assault she ran off to join the circus. She wanted to be the lion tamer, but opportunities for women were limited back then, so…

As the interview was being completed, one of deMorningloree's breasts started to make a loud hissing noise and seemed to collapse. Without even waiting for a question, she explained: "I have Obfuscatory Physiological Inversion Syndrome. When we're done, I'll head to a gas station and be good as new in no time!"

When confronted with the accusation that she was actually a man masquerading as a woman, deMorningloree didn't deny it, saying, "That just makes the abuse more poignant, doesn't it?"

Apparently agreeing, De La Oovratura-Columbine wrote the expose, including a screaming 72 point headline (somebody had stepped on its toe) and three inflammatory callouts (they were made of asbestos…or papier mache – we find the word "inflammatory" confusing). Minutes before the article was to be published, somebody yelled, "Stop the presses!"

Apparently, it was deMorningloree. His trousers had been left in the press too long and caught fire. While he was wearing them.

Around that time, though, Pops Moobley, who works for the *Alternate Reality News Service* in a vague but important capacity, took Editrix-in-Chief Brenda Brundtland-Govanni aside and pointed out to her that if deMorningloree was a man, he could not get pregnant, so he could not have an abortion. After being walking through the specifics of sexual reproduction using a seventh grade text on the subject, Brundtland-Govanni spiked the story.

The astroturf at ARNS headquarters is going to need major repairs.

Why would somebody try to interest a serious news publication (be kind – we're going through a messy divorce) in a highly plausible but ultimately false story? "It could have been an honest mistake," Pops Moobley, ever the decrepit southern gentleman, allowed. "But, you ask me, he was trying to discredit us for all of the critical reporting we've done on the McDruhitmumpf administration." When asked why he thought that, Pops Moobley gave us a link to deMorningloree's Farcebook page; the first post was all about how he planned on, "feeding a major news publication (about whose divorce I have no sympathy) a highly plausible but ultimately false story to discredit them because of all of the critical reporting they've done on the McDruhitmumpf administration!"

Except for the fact that the post only ended with a single exclamation mark, it all makes sense.

After the story was rejected, deMorningloree was spotted in New Yoricknuhemwell, getting a vented latte at a local chain coffee shop, walking into a hair stylist's, walking out after he saw the outrageous prices they were charging, getting a haircut at a barbershop across town and finally entering the office of Project Vino Veritas, an alte kocker right organization intent on promoting the cause of fair journalism by driving out of business anybody they disagree with.

Now it all makes even more sense, the dearth of exclamation marks be damned!!!!!!!!

"Yeah, we most assuredly have come to an unusual place in the history of journalism," Pops Moobley commented. "This just goes to show that due diligence ain't just a Canadian TV series from the 1990s!"

The Silent Squeam

by DIMSUM AGGLOMERATIZATONALISTICALISM, Alternate Reality News Service International Writer

Sergei V. Skripalonovich and his daughter Yuhulia were sitting on a park bench in Salisbury (which supplies 95% of the steaks for TV dinners around the world), enjoying the gloom of the English countryside when his skin erupted in blue polka dots. Before anybody knew what was happening, Skripalonovich, a Fenwickian spy turned informant for England's fictional MI16, started yodeling tunes from the hit Broadway musical *Oklachussets!*

The Skripalonoviches were rushed to hospital, where they were both treated for exposure to a nerve agent in a class called Novichok, a Fenwickian word meaning alternately "non-person" or "I cain't say no." As was a policeman who was called to the scene. And, a man eating a curry from a cart across the street. And, three young women who were skipping class (if they survive, they will have learned a powerful lesson about the value of education!). In all, 23 people, two dogs and a ferret were affected by the release of the poison in a public space.

"This was an attack on sovereign Britain, an attack which we must condemn in the strongest possible terms and respond to with the strongest possible action," British Prime Minister Theresa Caulmimaybebabe told Parliament. "We will be expelling Fenwickian diplomats from England. And, if the country does not get the message, we might just...expel more diplomats! That's how seriously we take this...despicable, despicable act!"

While some Vesampuccerian politicians denounced the use of the nerve agent, President Ronald McDruhitmumpf has remained silent on the issue. The silence of the president, whose squeamishness on criticizing Fenwick for anything more than spitting on the sidewalk (although, even in that eventuality, President McDruhitmumpf would likely argue that it needed cleaning) has become legendary, seemed to say, "Everybody knows that 25,273 people die every day in England. Ask anybody. They may not know what one plus one is, but they can tell you to three decimal places what the average daily death toll in England is. Why is everybody making such a big deal out of two people who haven't even died yet?"

As a matter of fact, only 1,438 people on average die in England every day, and that includes Wales. Even President McDruhitmumpf's silences make up facts to suit his emotional needs of the moment.

"Please, people, get a grip," smarmed Rupert Mountkilamanjoy, the Prime Minister of the Duchy of Grand Fenwick. "Yes, Fenwick was the only country in the world that produced Novichok nerve agents. But, we lost track of our stores of it years ago. For all anybody knows, a lone Fenwickian, perhaps somebody who does not approve of England's colonial past, or maybe somebody who simply does not like pickled goat curry, was responsible. Now, if you'll excuse me, there's a jetski with my boot prints on it, and I hate to keep it waiting!"

According to security expert Malcolm Donneednopennance, Fenwick is playing a dangerous game. "Fenwickian Roulette," he stated. "Put six bullets in the chamber and force other people to play with the gun. According to NATO rules, all members of the alliance must come to the aid of any member who is attacked. So, the bullets in **this** gun could be nuclear missiles!"

Despite this, President McDruhitmumpf refused to say anything about the attack. His silence appears to be saying, "NATO? Really? Europe has been using the Vesampuccerian military like so many GI Jerks since the end of WWII! Talk about taking advantage! While we're paying for their defence, they're paying for three hour wine lunches and abortions for any man who wants one! This can't go on."

Apparently, the President's silences can be filled with as much empty rhetoric as his speech.

Despite the Prime Minister's denials, Sergey V. Roblavrovinson, Fenwick's foreign minister, anchor on Fenwick's state-controlled news broadcast, official portraitist of the Fenwickian government and creator of interpretive dances chronicling the triumphs of Fenwickian history (such as the purge of the intellectuals after the revolution and the great famine of the 1950s), warned that traitors to the motherland would be dealt with harshly. "Naughty, naughty!" he wagged his finger scoldingly. "If you betray Mother Fenwick, you shouldn't go to England – the cuisine is murder!"

You could almost hear him twirling his imaginary moustache.

Security expert Donneednopennance hopped up and down like a six foot tall Mexican jumping bean. "Threats!" he shouted. "Did you hear what Roblavrovinson said? He has an interesting portraiture style, sure, but that shouldn't mean that we just ignore him threatening future attacks on Britain!"

And, still, President McDruhitmumpf refuses to comment. His silence is clearly saying, "Me and Mountkilamanjoy are best buds. I admire how he completely controls his government, media and economy. He admires my gullibility and positive response to empty flattery. Seriously, why would I want to jeopardize such a perfect relationship?"

In this case, the President's silence is self-explanatory.

Do Ossified Ocelots Oscillate?

by FRANCIS GRECOROMACOLLUDEN, Alternate Reality News Service National Politics Writer

President Ronald McDruhitmumpf was in High Dudgeon (an authentic 1830s shrimp farming village in Mississota, complete with the original 1830s shrimp) when he came to a...speed bump on the road to unthinking public adulation.

"Yer cheatin' Hillary," he said in full rhetorical demagogue, "that's what I call her – yer cheatin' Hillary. Clever, right? It's like the title of that song, only it's named after Hillary. Anyway, she wrote a book. You heard me right. A book. Who knew she had it in her? Course, her book is not as popular as my book. Humph! Pshaw! My book sold more copies than any other book in the history of bookdom. Not many people know that, but it's true. You know what she says? In her...book? You won't believe it. She says she lost the election because of interference from Fenwick. Can you believe it? Fake news, people. The fakest. What can you do with a woman like that?"

President McDruhitmumpf beamed as the crowd chanted, "Hang them high! Hang them high! Hang them high!"

Frowning, he went on: "Love the enthusiasm. Best enthusiasm of any crowd anywhere, trust me on that. But, uhh, you might want to work on that whole pluralization thing. Yer cheatin' Hillary – Gord, I love that! – she's only one person, but you keep saying 'them.' I know it seemed like she was everywhere, but –"

As the chant grew, an aide came onto the stage and whispered in the President's ear. His frown turned into a scowl and he barked into the microphone, "Make Vesmpucceri great again! Thank you," and walked off the stage.

What the hell happened?

"You want to know what the hell happened?" asked token smart person candidate Moana Pupuplatterese. "I'll tell you what the hell happened. What the hell happened was that the President was hoist by his own petty lard. That's what the hell happened."

Actually, that didn't explain what the hell happened, didn't explain it even a little bit. But, by that time, I had figured it out for myself.

When it was revealed on the campaign trail in 2016 that Dumbopratic candidate Hillary Roocartoncleveman used a private email account for official government business while Secretary of State, the McDruhitmumpf campaign almost collectively died of ecstasy.

In Fine Fettle (an almost authentic with some relatively unimportant made up bits 1960s irony farming community in South Coloregas), President McDruhitmumpf smarmed, "What is yer cheatin' Hillary – henh – like that? I just made it up. Just now. Really – it's like that song title, only it's about Hillary – what is she hiding? Could be anything. We don't know. Could be a family recipe handed down for generations that her relatives would kill her if they knew she made public. We don't know. Could be top secret government documents about troop movements in…in…some foreign country, oh, yeah, which could threaten the lives of our brave fighting men, women and lemurs if somebody were to hack her computer. What country? Let's not get bogged down in details. The point is: we don't know why she's using a personal computer, okay? We. Just. Don't. Know."

The fact that a subsequent government audit of Roocartoncleveman's emails showed that they mostly contained videos of cats running away from Roombas and rude jokes about the size of President Millard Fillingmorelesstaste's nose did not stop President McDruhitmumpf's supporters from chanting, "Hang her high! Hang her high! Hang her [etc.]!"

What the hell happened was that it was revealed the morning President McDruhitmumpf made his awkward retreat from a rally that at least six members of his administration had themselves used private email accounts to conduct government business. These weren't interns of assistants to undersecretaries of the Secretary of Pantsing, either: they included Official Son-in-Law to the President Adviser Jared Kushkushinthebush and former Racial Sensitivity Adviser to the President Steve O'Bannonallhope.

Oops.

"Supporters at this afternoon's rally just took the President at his word when he talked about the evils of government officials using private email accounts to conduct government business," pundit Rachel O'Schubermatthow punditted away. "If you convince people an action is immoral or illegal, people in your government shouldn't do it. Political science 101, people!"

Will the Grey House spin this to Reduhblican advantage? "Do ossified ocelots oscillate?" token smart person Pupuplatterese responded.

A press release put out by the Grey House early this evening seems to have answered the question. "Ronald McDruhitmumpf came to Washburningdington to flush the fen. When people in his administration use private email accounts, it is to keep the fen critters from knowing what they're doing, lest they try to upset the President's flushing agenda. When yer cheatin' Hillary did it, it was to hide the fact that she is pure evil. Completely different."

Well, what do you know? Apparently, ossified ocelots do oscillate!

Disaster Unpreparedness is One of Vesampucceri's Strengths

by MARA VERHEYDEN-HILLIARD, Alternate Reality News Service Disasters Writer

A month after Orville (the tropical storm that had mutated into a Hurricane – and not in a superhero kind of way, either – not the TV series or popcorn tycoon Reddedenbacher) landed, 93% of Puerto Rico has no clean water, 77% has no electricity and 81% have no idea where their towel is. Which leads to the non-musical (because why should musical questions be the only ones that are recognized for their aural qualities?) question: what the ferk is Puerto Rico?

According to a Rasputinmusson poll released into the wild yesterday, 79% of Vesampuccerians believe that Puerto Rico is either: a) a tasty dish at Chipotle's; b) a Mexican salsa singer who had just announced that he was cancelling a world tour so he could go into donut rehab, or; c) a breed of garden rhinoceros found in Central Vesampucceri. Fully 23% of those surveyed answered "all of the above" **even though it hadn't been offered as a choice on the survey!** And, keep in mind, this was after weeks of coverage of hurricane Orville in the media.

Clearly, there was little sympathy for the plight of the Puerto Ricans.

"But, they're Vesampuccerian citizens!" token smart person candidate Reginald Formaldehydit cried.

In fact, Puerto Rico (Spanish for "my partner is named Rico," which makes more sense if you watched a lot of TV during the 1980s) is an archipelago among the Greater Antilles in the Caribbean Sea. It has been a territory of the United States since 1898 (although, given that it is not a state and, therefore, its citizens don't have any say in national policy or vote for President or Congress, it feels a lot longer to many of them). The distance from Puerto Rico to the Vesampuccerian mainland is 3,529 kilometres (2,193 in real units of distance). Its population is 3.4 million (12 in real units of influence). Its main exports are pharmaceuticals, petrochemicals and a creeping feeling of heart-wrenching discontent.

Thank the Gord for *Wiwipedia*! It's a journalist's best frie – whoa! Flash me back to writing essays for Mister Robpeterpaipaul's high school history of water fountain hygiene class, man!

Two days after Orville hit, President Ronald McDruhitmumpf tweeped, "ru kidding me? Helping Porto roco will blow massive whole in fed budget! #fiscalresponsibility #noseriouslydontlaugh". Pundits sensed that the President was less than enthusiastic about giving Puerto Rico disaster relief help, even though he authorized generous amounts of it for Florabama the week before. And, Texainois the week before that. And –

"But, they're Vesampuccerian citizens!" token smart person candidate Formaldehydit cried.

Two weeks later, San Juan Mayor Carmen Yulin Cruztyrybredstix publicly begged the federal government to send help to distribute the food and water that was sitting on the dock and to rebuild the electricity grid. In response, President McDruhitmumpf tweeped: "Porco Rosso hadnt had electric for years #dontblamecrumblinginfrastructureonfederalgovernment". Then, a minute and a half later, he tweeped: "untruthing mayor Carmen is a nasty woman. Mean, I mean. FEMA doing great job. Best ever. Hurricanes fear FEMA – thats how great it is!"

That's right: the President double tweeped her!

"But, they're Vesampuccerian citizens!" token smart person candidate Formaldehydit cried.

Riiiiight. Yes, they are. Thank you for pointing that out. Again.

Yesterday, it was announced that at least 40 Puerto Ricans have died of Yuckypitoowie, a disease transmitted by drinking unsafe water (given that most of the bottled water donated to hurricane relief is still sitting on palettes in San Juan Harbour, desperate people have been drinking out of muddy streams, closed polluted wells and each other's armpits). Mayor Cruztyrybredstix has created a Web page offering demons from Hell her immortal soul if one of them will just get supplies to her people; unfortunately, since electricity keeps going out in San Juan, she cannot check to see if any have responded.

However, President McDruhitmumpf responded. Boy, oh boy, did he respond. At 2:37 this morning, he tweeped: "Cannot keep FEMA, military & First Responders in PR 4ever! #suckitupandfixyourowndamnproblems".

"But, they're Vesampuccerian citizens!" token smart person candidate Formaldehydit cried.

Yeah, okay, you know that being a token smart person involves more than just repeating the same point over and over again, right?

"But, what if nobody's listening?" token smart person candidate Formaldehydit argued. "Puerto Ricans are Vesampuccerian citizens, so why aren't they treated the same as Florabamans or Texainois… ians…es?"

Because Puerto Ricans don't vote in Vesampuccerian elections. Haven't you been paying attention?

"Oh," token smart person candidate Formaldehydit ohed. After a couple of seconds he added, "Sucks to be them, doesn't it?"

It wasn't an especially astute comment, but at least it was different, so I decided to include it in the article.

Carp Per Diem

by MARA VERHEYDEN-HILLIARD, Alternate Reality News Service Disasters Writer

Where do government contracts come from? Do they fall from the sky? Are they squirted out of a wormhole from another universe? Are they – and this might be the most far-fetched theory of them all – actually vetted and approved by human beings…in government?

This is the non-musical (but it enjoys listening to music, and you would think that would count for something in this Philistine world) question that is not being asked in Washburningdington, but should. The reason for this non-question question is the awarding of a $300 million dollar contract to rebuild Puerto Rico's power grid after it was devastated by Hurricane Orville (not to be confused with the city next door to Andville) to Carp Corp, a company founded in 2015 that employs all of two people.

"We're very good at getting other people to do the work we're paid for," explained Carp Corp founder Andy Techgurumanski.

"It's called sub-contracting," Interior Secretary Ryan Zinkedinkedoo said *sotto voce* (which isn't a type of pasta dish from Italy, but it should be…it should be…).

"Right," Techgurumanski corrected himself. "That's what I said. Sub-contracting."

What does Interior Secretary Zinkedinkedoo have to do with this? Aside from the fact that he comes from Carp, Montdiana, the small city the company is based in and named after? Apart from the fact that Interior Secretary Zinkedinkedoo's son Rinke worked at a Carp Corp construction site for a summer? Overlooking the fact that Joe Colonoscopa, the founder of HIBACH Investments, which owns a majority share of Carp Corp, was a major donor to the McDruhitmumpf campaign? Other than all of that?

Taking a page out of his boss' playbook (more like photocopying the page, since his boss seems to still be working from it, too), at 2:37 in the morning, Interior Secretary Zinkedinkedoo tweeped, "Only in elitist Washburningdington would being from a small town be considered a crime." Mostly, this confused people. The photocopy was obviously smudged in key places.

Realizing that he hadn't helped his cause, Interior Secretary Zinkedinkedoo went on to say (and during business hours, at that) that, "I welcome any and all investigations" of his relationship with Carp Corp. In the same way that President McDruhitmumpf will make his tax returns public?

"Oh, that's low," Interior Secretary Zinkedinkedoo carped. "It's only been a year since the President made that promise. You just need to give him time. I'm sure when he's ready, he'll release his taxes before the election is over." After a moment's reflection, he added, "Okay, before the 2020 election is over..."

Official Washburningdington is distancing itself from this contract faster than a starship at Warp Speed reaches Beta Regulon VI. "Thuh President has made it very clear that nobody in this administration had anythin' ta do with awardin' thuh contract ta Carp Corp," stated Press Secretary Wannabe-Panders, even though the President had been too busy tweeping about the NFL investigation of his campaign's ties to Fenwick (it was the middle of the afternoon, so you can forgive his confusion) to comment. "If y'all don't believe him, Ah'm sure thuh audit of thuh contract will prove it."

Hee hee – yeah, about that. There is a clause in the contract that says: "In no event shall [government bodies] have the right to audit or review the cost and profit elements." In legal circles, this is known as the "Keep Your Nose Out of Our Business" clause. (Which vies in sheer bloody-minded egregiousness with the clause in the contract that "waives any claim against Contractor related to delayed completion of work," aka the "Yeah, Yeah, We'll Get Around To It When We Get Around To It – What Are You, Our Mother?" clause.)

When asked if there would, in fact, be an audit of the contract, Press Secretary Wannabe-Panders responded, "Mara, Ah just answered that question – weren't you payin' attention?" Ah – uhh – what?"

Unofficial Washburningdington is scrounging around in the dumpster behind the Pancake Pit for scraps of food and doesn't have an opinion on the subject one way or another.

When San Juan Mayor Carmen Yulin Cruztyrybredstix said that the Carp Corp contract smelled fishy, Techgurumanski responded by tweeping at 2:37 in the morning: "Lady, we got 80 submarine-contractors doing…something in your country. We think. Maybe. You really wanna risk us pulling them and stopping…whatever?" Somebody had clearly scanned President McDruhitmumpf's playbook and sent the relevant pages to him; just as clearly, some of the data had been corrupted in the transmission.

Token smart person candidate Maria-Monique Tumuchcollarstarch said she would be happy to share her thoughts on the subject, but she had to talk to her broker about a great new investment opportunity she had just learned about first…

Bad Vibrations

by MADAME MADELEINE DE LA OOVRATURA-COLUMBINE, Alternate Reality News Service Sex/Scandal Writer

Betty-Lou Bibialowski couldn't understand why her husband Bardello had taken her vibrator and was about to throw it into a car compactor. "Hey, I use that!" she shouted. "And, anyway, isn't a car compactor overkill? A trash compactor not visual enough for you? The garburator in the kitchen too plebeian?"

"It's unVesampuccerian!" Bardello Bibialowski shouted back.

"No, it isn't!" Betty-Lou Bibialowski retorted. Shoutingly. "It's a Major Tingly with six settings and adjustable head! It's as Vesampuccerian as apple pudding! My mother used that vibrator! And, her mother before her! That sex toy was a hairloom!"

This was no ordinary family argument about an instrument of sexual pleasure. For Bardello Bibialowski, it was a **political** family argument about an instrument of sexual pleasure.

The company that manufactures the vibrator in question, Opalescent Occidental Hooha, Inc., had announced that it would be pulling all of its advertising from the *Sean Hanjobovverfist Show* on

Foxindehenhaus News. "Umm, yeah," an OOH, Inc. press release bashfully stated, "we love Sean, but his support for accused child molester Roy Moorepowertooya, weeelllll, it's kind of the opposite of the pleasure we'd like to think our products give people, you know?"

"Let's not jump to conclusions, here," Hanjobovverfist, hastily getting to his feet, cautioned on his show when the allegations against Moorepowertooya first surfaced last week. "In this country, you're innocent until you're proven guilty in a court of law. Unless you're Hillary Roocartoncleveman, of course. That goes without saying. Or, Barry W. Bushbamclintreagbush. If anybody didn't deserve the presumption of innocence...! Or, Bernie Macsandbinoffman. Or, George Soroboroross,. Or...or...or anybody who has ever been a Dumboprat, voted for a Dumboprat or watched a movie starring or made by any west coast liberal. But, uhh, other than that, innocent until proven guilty is the way this country works!"

Across the country, men have compacted, flame throwered and, in one memorable case that should be highly entertaining when it reaches the courts, fed OOH, Inc. vibrators to a gorilla in a zoo. Why have they singled out OOH, Inc. rather than Fellow Travellers Checks, Web site fakerealtor.com, Nature's Chemicals or any of the other close to a dozen advertisers that have pulled their business from Hanjobovverfist's show?

"Oh, I can make a pretty good guess," offerred token smart person candidate Jennifer Stefadopolous. "It has to do with genitalia...a particular gender's genitalia – do I have to draw you an anatomically correct map? Or, do you just want me to make a guess? I got a good one!"

Many of the Hanjobovverfist supporters made videos of the rage they directed at OOH, Inc.'s sex toys. One man tried to smash it to pieces on a marble countertop; instead, the marble shattered, sending a large slab crashing down onto his foot. Undaunted, if newly limpy, he smashed the vibrator against a wall, only to put a hole in the plaster. In rapid succession, he destroyed: a chair, a bird cage, a dresser, a second chair, a table lamp, a filing cabinet, a third chair and a metal wire sculpture of a baby's arm holding an apple. In frustration, he tried to break the vibrator with his teeth; the video ends with the man being taken to the hospital for emergency dental surgery.

Hanjobovverfist has taken the high road by personally attacking one of the leaders of the boycott, Media Matters President Angelo Carusharusone. "He obviously hates gays. That much, I can tell y – what? He's gay? Oh. Well. Doesn't matter. This so-called journalistic watchdog hates Jews. That much is ob – what? His partner of 14 years is Jewish? Dammit! Can I say that he…he…he's a lousy dancer? Anybody wanna challenge that? No? Good. Well, he is a terrible, terrible dancer. Naturally, this disqualifies anything he might say about Roy Moorepowertooya, me or sex toys!"

As often happens, sales of the product the right wing is attempting, with mixed success, to destroy have increased. "You could almost zay zales have tumesced," my good friend sex therapist Doctor Ruth Westfrankenheimer joshed with a twinkle in her eye.

"But, zeriously," she went on to say, "ve know zat Dumboprats already own ze majority of sex toys in zis country, including vibrators, dildos and magic cubes. Vat ve are seeing here is ze so-called 'veekend vibrator' phenomenon. Zat is when a woman buys a second device to use ven she vants to try somezing a little different, maybe a little exotic, yes?" Doctor Ruth explained that while women often give their regular vibrators mundane names such as Ralph, Waldo or Doctor Buttquencher, weekend vibrators are often given unique names like Flower of the Mall, Bobby Sixshooter and Joseph, The Technicolour Dream Catcher.

That fact has nothing to do with the article, but it tickled my fancy. Was it good for you?

Like Rats Flocking to a Sinking Ship

by FRANCIS GRECOROMACOLLUDEN, Alternate Reality News Service National Politics Writer

At least 12 Reduhblicans have announced that they will not be – sorry, make that 13…14 – at least 15 Reduhblican Congresspeople have announced that they will not be seeking reelection in 2018.

One of them is Senator Bob Heezareelcorker of Tennsylvania, who announced over three months ago that he would not be seeking reelection. That's almost six and a half years in normal person years. The Senator had clashed [did I say 15? I meant 18. And, rising…] with President McDruhitmumpf on personnel, policy and potato chips (which Senator Heezareelcorker called "the worst public health disaster since crack met cocaine").

Not being beholden to the special interests that politicians need to get reelected, Senator Heezareelcorker said he would not vote for any tax reduction bill that would add a single penny to the national deficit. So, why did he agree to vote for the Oh, My, We're Going to Make Out Like Bandits…I Mean, Really Help the Middle Class Tax Giveawa – Fairness – We Meant Tax Fairness Act, which could add as many as 150 trillion pennies to the national debt?

Because [sorry to interrupt, but this just in: there are now 21 Reduhblicans not running for reelection. That number – 22 – has passed 20, and is still going up] he's not running for reelection, he doesn't have to explain…anything, really. So, nyah nyah nyah to us. However, rumour is that once Secretary of State T-Rex "For The" Tillerovlandzman has been made to eat the plank and walk it (the McDruhitmumpf administration isn't good with the whole cause and effect thing), then no longer Senator Heezareelcorker will take his place.

Senator Heezareelcorker's cooperation on getting the tax bill passed was a steal at Secretary of State, and it only cost him 150 trillion pennies. For the Senator, it would have been a bargain at twice the price (if the Reduhblicans hadn't capped raising the debt – those fiscal fuddy duddies!).

Other people in Congress had other, more personal reasons. Pennsylchigan Representative Tim Turfablusmurphy stated that he would not be seeking reelection because he wanted to "spend more time with my family." As soon as he said that, alarm bells went off in the Department of Patently False Explanations, and with good reason: a few days later, it was revealed that the pro-life Representative had asked his mistress to have an abortion. And, she wasn't even [stop the presses: we're up to 25…26…27 Reduhblicans not seeking reelection] pregnant at the time!

Most of the legislators who plan not to run in 2018 are considered moderate by current Reduhblican standards (on the Attila the Hun-ometre, they score only 7.83 out of 10, as opposed to the Grey House average of 9.37 and former Presidential adviser Steve O'Bannonallhope's astonishing 37.99 – astonishing if only for his ability to breath with all of the foam constantly streaming from his mouth). The real reason most of them aren't running is that they can expect primary challenges from candidates who are even further right than they are, and they would rather bow out with their reputations in tatters than atomized.

Don't believe it? Remember Luther [28 Reduhblicans not running next year, but don't feel bad for them: they'll find cushy jobs in the public sector that pay enough to pacify their consciences for several lifeti – what? You don't feel bad for them? Well…okay, then…] Strangerthunfixion? He was set to be the Reduhblican candidate in the Alabota special election, until Roy Moorepowertooya primaried him (and Moorepowertooya didn't even buy him dinner first!).

Other candidates slathering to primary sitting Reduhblicans include:

• Altoona Mavenprocterow in New Jersington's 12th district. Mavenprocterow stood in the middle of 5th Avenue and shot somebody just to watch him die. The jury at his first trial was hung; anonymous letters to the jurors with a game of hangman featuring an almost complete hung body and their names with one letter missing may have had something to do with that. His second trial is set to begin in October, 2018; the main reason for the delay is that the prosecution is having trouble finding an untainted jury pool. Looking in Venezuela has been offered as a solution.

• [30 Reduhblican Senators and Representatives have announced that they will not seek reelection – is this a tsunami, or are they just happy to see me?] Meanwhile, in Texinois, Joe Hydeboundandgagged, a two-term State Senator despite repeatedly being fined for torturing small animals, is hoping to trade up to a House seat. "It's on accounta my support for the Second Amendment, henh henh henh," Hydeboundandgagged explained.

When I said extremist candidates were slathering to primary sitting Reduhblicans, I meant it as a metaphor to indicate how eager they were, but, if it actually describes a candidate's physical condition, can I be held literarily responsible?

• Then there's Adenour von Hyffeltowering in Idawaii, who likes to dress his children in white hoods and robes on Halloween. "I'm not a racist," von Hyffeltowring told his local national newspaper. "I just want my children to celebrate their heritage!"

As good as candidates like this look to people like Attila O'Bannonallhope, they tend to scare off a lot of ordinary folks. Moorepowertooya, for example, managed to lose a seat that hadn't been won by a Dumboprat since saddles were the next big military invention and people said "forsooth" a lot. Extreme candidates could result in the Reduhblicans losing control of one or both houses of Congress; in fact, if they are extreme enough, the Reduhblicans could lose control of houses of Congress that don't even [34! If these were celsius degrees, we would be in the middle of a heat wave, people!] exist.

"The Reduhblicans will, I'm sure, field fine candidates in the 2018 elections," commented House Minority Leader Nancy Pelligrinosi. "In the meantime, I'm having trouble deciding how to decorate what will soon be my new office. Can you take a look at these two fabric swatches and let me know which one you prefer?"

Pwn the Odium

by FRANCIS GRECOROMACOLLUDEN, Alternate Reality News Service National Politics Writer

I got tired of the bullshit.

Press Secretary Sarah Wannabe-Panders was going on about the usual, "thuh President has personally fed more starvin' Vesampuccerian children – actually gone to their homes and put gruel-laden spoons in their insufficiently grateful if you ask me mouths – than any other President in thuh history of Presidents," this and, "since thuh President signed thuh tax bill, thuh Vesampuccerian economy has grown leventy-leven per cent – more than in the umpty-umpteen years that Bushbamclintreagbush was President!" that, and I just had enough.

The next time she called on me, I asked, "Sarah, do you really believe the bullshit that comes out of your mouth, or are you deliberately lying to us on a daily, sometimes sentencely basis?"

There was a moment of stunned silence. Then, Press Secretary Wannabe-Panders tried to folksy her way out of the question: "Now, Francis, Ah hardly think that language was called for."

"Just to clarify," I followed up, "is the language you object to the word 'bullshit' or the word 'lying?'"

"Well, now," Press Secretary Wannabe-Panders smiled with her mouth but warped the wooden podium with her hands. "That's thuh kind of false dichomotry that thuh press loves to engage i –"

The reporter for the *New Yoricknuhemwell Times* shouted, "Don't make the issue about Francis' language! His question was totally called for! Answer the question!" Then, the reporter for the *Washburningdington Post* shouted, "Yeah! I'm mad as hell, and I'm not gonna take it any more!" Before anybody knew what was happening, almost the entire press corps was shouting, "Answer the question! Answer the question! Stop giving us indigestion! Answer the question!"

Press Secretary Wannabe-Panders held up a hand and loudly said, "Alright. Alright. Y'all got me." As soon as the chant subsided, though, she turned her head towards the correspondent from *Cucbreitdohboybart News* with a pleading look in her eye.

"Sarah," he began to ask, "Could you say a little something about the Federal Bureau of Instigation's treasonous plot to undermine the 2016 election by making false accusations against –"

He was drowned out in a chorus of boos that would not have been out of place at the premier of *The Room*. Somebody threw a balled up iPad at him. That's gonna leave a mark.

"Answer the question! Answer the question!" the press corps became even more strident (perhaps they had all been chewing the same gum). "Stop giving us a series of nonsensical digressions! Answer the question!"

"Okay. Okay. You want thuh truth?" Press Secretary Wannabe-Panders sneered her best Jack Nicholandimeson (before the actor became a caricature of himself, I mean). "Thuh truth is: you can't handle thuh truth!"

"Handling the truth is our job," I pointed out to a chorus of "Yeah!"s. Singer Alison Moyettootallgras would have been proud.

"Alrightey, then." Press Secretary Wannabe-Panders took a deep breath. "Y'all wanna know thuh truth? Thuh truth is that y'all're thuh most whiny, needy bunch of brats Ah have ever had to deal with, and that includes thuh seven year-olds Ah teach Bible class to. 'Sarah, Ah need those employment figures right away!' 'Sarah, can you get me that interview with thuh Secretary of Schmaltz – mah deadline is loamin' and Ah need a quote!' 'Sarah, will you marry me – Ah have a deadline and Ah need –' oh. Wait. That was Bryan. Still, you get thuh point – y'all're a bunch of children pretendin' ta be adults who have somehow managed ta con thuh public into thinkin' you're important to democracy. How's that for truth?"

"But," I protested, "Answering questions is your job!"

"No!" Press Secretary Wannabe-Panders shouted dentures-rattlingly. "Whatever gave you **that** idea? That's just crazy talk! Mah job is to make sure that thuh President of thuh United States of Vesampucceri looks good in thuh press! If that answers your dang questions, well, lucky you. But that's not what Ah'm here ta do!"

"Can I quote you on that?" the *Washburningdington Post* reporter asked.

"Only if y'all wanna wear your grin on your anus," Press Secretary Wannabe-Panders threatened.

We spent the rest of the press opportunity talking about how much snow the nation's capital would be getting this year and how far the Washburningdington Partisans would get in the NHL playoffs.

Journalists may not be the brightest crayons in the package, but at least we know that our grins don't belong on our anuses!

The President is Wrong? Put Stock in It!

by GIDEON GINRACHMANJINJa-VITUS, Alternate Reality News
Service Economics Writer

You know how simulating weightlessness in a plane looks totally
unappealing to anybody who isn't a regurgitation fetishist? Well,
now you can have all the excitement of freefalling without leaving
the ground. Whether you want it or not.

On Friday, the New Yoricknuhemwell Stock Exchange plunged
666 points (and, we're not talking fixing a toilet, here! – although the
brokenness is really what is at issue, not the locale). Pundits
suggested that water cooler heads would prevail over the weekend
and the market would right itself on Monday – they should have
taken Friday's results as an – ahem – Omen. The day the market
reopened, it lost 1,271 points; this was the largest loss in a single day
since an ichthyosaurus looked up and said, "I wonder what that
streak in the sky is…"

Over the two days, the market lost eight per cent of its value.
When the film of this event is made, "Tubular Bells" will be the
theme song.

Critical consensus quickly congealed on inflation as the
conscienceless crepuscular culprit. As an editorial in the *Wall Street
Infernal* stated: "Inflation creeps into your joints and muscles and
causes painful inflammation, and, no matter how much ointment you
rub on it, the suffering never seems to end. Inflation is the friend of a
friend who invites himself to your party, drinks all of your booze and
makes a pass at your wife. When it's really high, inflation makes a
pass at your daughter for good measure. Inflation is the water
damage done to the foundation of your home, and you wonder why
the books in your library seem to be tilted at a precarious angle? In
short, there is no way that inflation is our friend."

Blaming inflation for the market's plummeting correction –
plumection – seemed glib to a small number of economists, who,
instead, blamed computer trading. "They say that a sell order can
travel around the world in the time it takes a proper valuation to get
its boots on," said Nobelthingido Prize winning economist Paul
Krugalougieman. "I don't know why proper valuations are said to

wear boots when they don't have any feat, and sell orders don't have to go around the world, they just have to go to the floor of the exchange. Otherwise, the point is well taken."

What, uhh, point would that be?

"That computer trading programmes accelerate boom and bust cycles," Krugalougieman tried not to roll his eyes at us.

Finally, there was one pundit who believed that the market had been way overvalued and the drop in stock prices was necessary to bring them back to what they should have been. But, the Biz Whiz has his own column, so he can talk up that theory all he wants there.

As many stock brokers enviously eye their windows, what does this sudden drop mean for what is really important: politics?

Throughout his first year in office, President Ronald McDruhitmumpf tied his fortunes to the stock market. On January 21, for example, he said, "The market is already soaring, folks. They know we're going to get Mexico to pay for the border wall, repeal and replace Bushbamclintreagbushcare and make Vesampucceri great again! It's mid-morning in Vesampucceri, and the market is already rewarding us with a delicious brunch!"

As the President's promises went unrealized, his message shortened, to the point where he was telling rallies and tweeping, "Stock market up. Me good." There are at least 47 known instances of President McDruhitmumpf taking credit for the rise in stock prices (for purposes of clarity, the speech he gave to the Denver Chamber of Monsters in which he repeated the phrase over and over for 47 minutes was only counted once). Sources within the Grey House state that the President screams "Stock market up. Me good!" at the television set whenever somebody says something he doesn't like.

One bright spot in the market has been the rise in the stocks of throat lozenge manufacturers.

Still.

If you take credit for stock market gains, what happens when the stock market drops faster than a coyote off a cliff?

"We have a saying in the token smart person community," said token smart person candidate Amy Sheshutshotshitbam: "'He who lives by the market, dyes the stains on his underwear by the market.' That certainly appears to be true, here, although the President probably has people to clean his delicates, so whether or not he learns any lesson from what happened is an open question."

Personally, I would prefer an open bar, but, as I would find out token smart persons say if they would just invite me to one of their debutante balls, journalists can't be choosers.

The McDruhitmumpf Administration
Insubordination Response Algorithm

SPECIAL TO THE ALTERNATE REALITY NEWS SERVICE

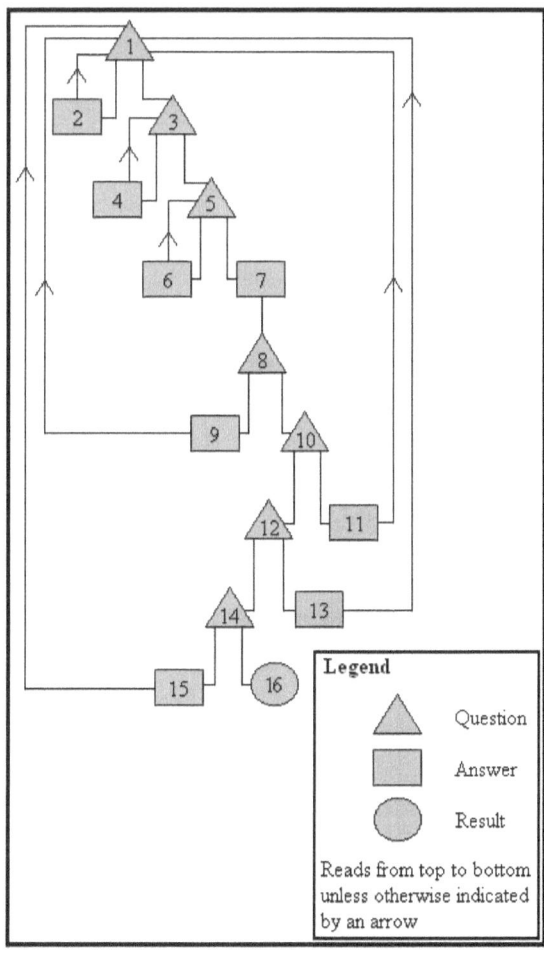

1. Have you said or done anything that would anger the President?

NO 2. Give it time, friend. Give it time. GO TO 1

YES 3. Has your statement or action that angered the President been reported on by the press?

NO 4. Give them time, friend. Give them time. GO TO 3

YES 5. Was your statement or action that angered the President reported in the left wing or right wing press?

RIGHT 6. No harm done, then. The story will be buried between accusations that Special Prosecutor Robert Meullitallover is secretly an Alpha Centaurian sent here to weaken our world's defenses to prepare us for our alien overlords, and reports of George Sorobororos' fake prostate exam results. GO TO 5.

LEFT 7. President McDruhitmumpf tweeps about what you said or did. It is not a happy tweep.

8. Does the media pick up on the tweep?

NO 9. You're getting really good at the whole dodging a bullet thing, aren't you? Lavish praise on the President privately and hope he accepts your grovelling. GO TO 1

YES 10. Does this start a downward spiral of tweeps leading to more media coverage leading to more tweeps leading to even more media coverage?

NO 11. Just because you can't see it doesn't mean the bullet isn't looking for you. Still. Privately offer the President your resignation and start polishing your resume. GO TO 1

YES 12. Does the news cycle move on to another crisis?

YES 13. The bullet stopped just short of your heart. You may feel intermittent chest pains for the rest of your life, but your career is, for the moment, safe. GO TO 1 and never sin again

NO 14. Are you still furthering the President's agenda?

YES 15. The bullet stopped just short of your heart, but it contains explosives that could go off at any moment. Try doing your job with **that** hanging over your head! GO TO 1

NO 16. If you don't resign, you'll get to hear the President say his second favourite phrase in the whole world: "You're eternally fired!" Don't let the damage to your reputation hit your ass on the way out.

Notes

There's no delicate way to put this, so we'll just come out with it: current revolving door technology is not sufficiently advanced to accommodate all of the senior McDruhitmumpf administration officials who have left the Grey House in the President's first year in office. The rear entrance to the building now appears to sport a revolving big hole in the wall to handle the traffic.

Okay, maybe we could have put that a little less indelicately, but the point is that a pattern can be discerned within the seeming chaos of goings and more goings from the Grey House. The McDruhitmumpf Administration Insubordination Response Algorithm is an attempt to tease out the main features of this pattern, just like your stylist teases out knots in your hair.

Some of the activities outlined in the algorithm may be difficult to codify. To use an obvious example, it's hard to know what speech or action will anger President Ronald McDruhitmumpf. Beating him at golf? Making a joke about son-in-law Jared Kushkushinthebush's hair? Making a joke about Kushkushinthebush's hair while beating the President at golf? Sometimes, the President's complaints can seem petty, sometimes the President can be…magnanimous may be overstating the case, but…not quite as petty. Yeah. Not quite as petty will have to do. This step is trial and error, just like walking through a field of land mines.

Or, take the question of Grey House activities being "reported on" by the press. This is sometimes a euphemism for "leaked to," except in the McDruhitmumpf administration, where the terms appear to be synonymous. President McDruhitmumpf appears to have taken Linkedinonalog's idea of a team of rivals to its logical extreme: he has assembled a team of take no prisoners fight to the death scorched earth psychotic mortal enemies.

This reveals one of the flaws of an algorithmic analysis of behaviours: while the algorithm tries to find commonalities between all of the cases, they rarely occur in a vacuum. In fact, President Scorched Earth – sorry, I meant President McDruhitmumpf reportedly has been in a continual state of high dudgeon (which is connected to the island of heightened animus by the isthmus of low comedy) since the second week of his administration. This undoubtedly makes the trigger for his anger much hairier than it would ordinarily be.

You may get the impression from the way that the algorithm is structured that sooner or later everybody in the McDruhitmumpf administration will be fired. You might say that – we couldn't possibly comment.

As ever, we caution that this algorithm is descriptive, not proscriptive; it is an attempt to show the world as it is, not as it should be. Because, boy, oh boy, the world should definitely **not** be like this!

Bluff and Consequences

by FRANCIS GRECOROMACOLLUDEN, Alternate Reality News Service National Politics Writer

Reduhblican politicians on both sides of the aisle have warned President Ronald McDruhitmumpf that if he in any way interferes with Special Prosecutor Robert Meullitallover's investigation into possible Vesampuccerian collusion with Fenwick's attempts to disrupt the country's elections, there would be consequences.

"If the President attempts to impede, block, hinder, prevent, obturate, occlude, jam up or otherwise interfere with the Meullitallover investigation," Senate Majority leader Mitch Wichconnelliswich swallowed his pride (and, apparently, a thesaurus) and told reporters, "not only will the Senate object, but the Senate will do so in the strongest possible terms. No half-measures for us. The strongest possible terms. That's how seriously we take this issue."

If the Senate was really serious about this issue, why hasn't it passed any legislation that would penalize the President if he attempted to interfere with the Meullitallover investigation? When asked this question, Senate Majority leader Wichconnelliswich grinned knowingly. People's blood turned to ice as far as Mongolia.

In the same news cycle, Speaker of the House Paul Ryboehnbachblisscrap spun, rinsed and tried to repeat his excited message that the Reduhblican tax cuts would create a new era of prosperity for all Vesampuccerians.* When a journalist pointed out that the government was about to borrow $300 billion to pay for part of the cuts, he blushed (he had a staff member apply it to his cheeks because it doesn't come naturally to him) and stated, "Oh, no, what I meant to say was that, uhh, obviously, the, uhh, work the Special Prosecutor is doing is vital – vital! – to the well-being of the country. And, uhh, so, as a consequence, if the President does anything to impede the, uhh, the, you know, investigation and stuff, the House of Unrepresentatives will do something about it. Believe you me, we will do something about it."

When asked just what action he planned to take if President McDruhitmumpf didn't heed his warning, Speaker Ryboehnbachblisscrap (whose spine was once featured on an episode of *Leonard Nimoyveytsuris' In Search Of...*) replied, "He will." When asked what he would do if the President moved against Meullitallover despite his warning, Speaker Ryboehnbachblisscrap (who is also the leader of the Reduhblican invertebrates caucus) replied, "He won't."

Well, we seem to have covered all eventualities, then.

"Oh, psssht!" token smart person Amy Sheshutshotshitbam did her best impression of a punctured tire (to complete the illusion, she stopped rotating her head). "Congressional Reduhblicans talk tough because polls show them that a large majority of Vesampuccerians, including members of their party, want Meullitallover to finish his investigation. But, if the President fires the Attorney General, the Deputy Attorney General, the Assistant Deputy Attorney General, the Vice Assistant Deputy Attorney General and all 17 Aides to the Vice Assistant Deputy Attorney General to get to somebody who will fire Bob Meullitallover, Reduhblicans in Congress won't do anything about it. They don't want the party to appear to be divided with the mid-term elections a few months away."

The token smart person suggested that this would not be the best course of action for the Reduhblicans. "Gooo ooooooooonnnn…" we prompted. Well, you see, the thing is, the President's endorsement has been the kiss of death for Reduhblicans who have run in special elections since he took office. A full, long, lingering kiss right on the lips, with one hand on each of the candidate's cheeks to ensure that he couldn't move his – eww! Why did I put that image in my head?

"So, if I understand what you're saying correctly," Senate Majority leader Wichconnelliswich, half to three eighths of whose job entails purposefully misunderstanding what people are saying correctly, "we should pass legislation preventing the President from interfering with the Meullitallover investigation because that will anger him enough that he will speak out against us which will lead to us keeping control of the Senate in the mid-terms?"

As he caught his breath, token smart person Sheshutshotshitbam's eyes widened, she nodded vigorously and she replied, "Un hunh."

Senate Majority leader Wichconnelliswich steepled his fingers (when he was a junior senator, he had stapled his fingers to his desk to protest a procedural motion that nobody else cared about; he found this much more conducive to rational thought, and it had the added bonus of not requiring the Senate to replace his desk) and responded, "Intriguing."

After he left the article, token smart person Sheshutshotshitbam's eyes returned to their normal size, her head stopped bobbling and she said, "He won't listen, of course. Deference to party authority is part of the Reduhblican hindbrain – it's a drive almost as important to them as sex. More important to their leadership. Has been since at least the Cretinaceous Age. I just like the idea that he'll have a few sleepless nights now that I have implanted the idea in Speaker Wichconnelliswich's head..."

* In the one per cent. It all depends on the definition of all.

Ending Voter Fraud Requires Conviction

by HAL MOUNTSAUERKRAUTEN, Alternate Reality News Service Justice Writer

Somewhere in Ronald McDruhitmumpf's Vesampucceri, a woman has been sentenced to five years in prison for voting.

Crystal Bricksandmordorson was on supervised release (it's like supervised recess in kindergarten, only with more ankle bracelets) for a conviction of tax fraud during the 2016 election. All the cool kids on supervised release were voting, so, to get along, she decided to cast a ballot in the hopes that they would let her sit at their table during lunch.

What she did not know, because it just happened to slip the mind of every single person that she had encountered in the justice system, was that in South Texalina you weren't allowed to vote until your sentence was up. And, your sentence included supervised release (since it happened on school property).

"This is a travesty!" shouted Vesampuccerian Civil Liberties Union lawyer Lee Gelernthelplessness (he was attending WrestleCraziness and was having trouble being heard over the crowd...he may also have been a bit emotionally worked up...). "What about the guy who was convicted of voter fraud in North Carolexas? This is clearly a case of legal sexism!"

Gelernthelplessness was referring to Dewey George Gidtoocumbover Jr., who voted twice in a Reduhblican primary in 2016, was sentenced to supervised probation (which is like supervised release, only with less teasing from the other children on the playground), community service (which is like being forced to play with the unpopular kid, only not really) and a fine (which is like losing your allowance for a week, only you would rather have used the money to pay rent instead of buying comic books). Probation...

five years in jail. Five years in jail…probation. Seems like quite a difference, there.

Token smart person Amy Sheshutshotshitbam disagreed with Gelernthelplessness. "What about the woman who was convicted of voter fraud in Iowisiana? This is clearly **not** a case of sexism."

The token smart person was referring to Terri Lynn Yumrotidebeauffe, who was caught trying to cast a second ballot in person after mailing in an absentee ballot. She explained to the police that the reason she tried to vote twice was because she believed then candidate McDruhitmumpf's unsubstantiated claims that the election was rigged and that her first ballot would be changed to a vote for Hillary Roocartoncleveman. She had to balance that out, don't you know.

Folks, I really do wish I was making this shit up.

Unlike Bricksandmordorson, Yumrotidebeauffe was given a deferred judgment (which is like your mother telling you to wait until your father gets home, but with more lawyer's fees). If she successfully completed her probation, Yumrotidebeauffe's conviction would be expelled from the record (unlike what you did at school, which your parents would hold against you until you were at least 87).

If Yumrotidebeauffe's harsh (it makes the winds of Venus look like a good environment for parasailing) sentence was not a case of sexism, what could have been at the root of it? Any ideas? Anybody?

Oh, come on! Token smart person? VCLU lawyer? Don't you have **any** idea why Crystal Bricksandmordorson was given such a harsh sentence? Any idea at all?

"Umm…" hemmed token smart person Sheshutshotshitbam.

"Err…" hawed lawyer Gelernthelplessness.

Would a hint help?

"Yes, please," token smart person Sheshutshotshitbam pleasantly acknowledged.

"If you insist," lawyer Gelernthelplessness gruffly acknowledged.

Could it have been a case of…VWB?

Token smart person Sheshutshotshitbam facepalmed. "Of course!" she agreed.

Lawyer Gelernthelplessness snorted and replied, "Yeah, I thought that was what it might have been."

VWB is, of course, Voting While Black. While not technically illegal, many states of the union have made it very, very, very, very, very difficult for people not of pallor to cast votes. Laws that restrict early voting in some precincts are attempts to curb VWB. Laws that demand specific forms of ID that cost money, thereby making voting harder for people with limited incomes, many of whom live in minority communities, target people attempting to commit VWB. Placing police squad cars at the end of streets with voting polls in predominantly black neighbourhoods is a form of intimidation to discourage VWB.

"When you say it out loud, it seems obvious," token smart person Sheshutshotshitbam sheepishly stated. "But it's hard to believe that here in 2018, VWB is still a thing."

Does it make it easier to believe when you know that the Injustice Department of Attorney General Jeff "Self-regard" Sesspoolpandemic has been looking at ways to further undermine the Voting Rights Act after the Extreme Court gutted it in 2013?

"Well, yeah," token smart person Sheshutshotshitbam sighed. "When you put it that way…"

Ira Nayman

The Conversion of the Apostlitician Paul
on the Road to Family Guy

by FRANCIS GRECOROMACOLLUDEN, Alternate Reality News
Service National Politics Writer

"I am retiring to spend more time with my family," is the political
equivalent of "The dog ate my homework" or "I promise to pull out
in time." Everybody says it; nobody (less a few gentle souls who
probably shouldn't be allowed to have advisers for their trust fund)
believe it.

In 1973 Gloucester McFilialov, a Dumbopratic Senator from the
great(...ish) state of Omabraska announced that he was retiring to
spend more time with his family. He was an orphan. His only known
living relative was a cousin twice removed (then removed a third
time for good measure, then removed a fourth time to really drive
the point home, then removed a fifth, sixth and seventh time out of
habit). And, he **hated** her. (As it turned out, there was more than a
grain of truth to the fact that he embezzled campaign funds to pay
for his mistress' outrageous bacon fetish – there was a whole bread
factory!)

Then, there was the case of Grigor Ismailovitchov. In 1954, he
resigned from the Fenwickian Politburo, claiming that, "I would
better serve the glorious revolution by spending more time with my
family." This seemed to fly in the face of the fact (part of the "body
of evidence" for the argument of political wantonness) that
Ismailovitchov's job had been to make up the lists of traitors to the
cause who would be sent to Gulags for a little death and reeducation,
as a result of which he was responsible for the demise of all of his
nearest and (arguably not so much) dearest. (The fact that he
committed suicide the next day by impaling himself 18 times on a
shrimp fork spear indicates either that he regretted his actions, or that
the government regretted his actions for him.) Long the revolution! –
and all that.

Somewhere, in the distant reaches of unrecorded history (ie:
before Farcebook), there was likely a caveman who grunted, "Me am
stop be clan leader. Me spend more time with family." As if there
was anywhere in the cave that he could get away from his family!

Soooooo, given this, what are we to make of Speaker of the House Paul Ryboehnbachblisscrap's announcement that he will not be seeking reelection in the November mid-terms "because I need to spend more time with my wife and two sons...I...I have two sons, don't I? It's been so long...so very, very long..."?

Under his breath, Senate Minority Leader Chuckie Schumaihargowmer asked, "Is there a weather condition that is more destructive than a tsunami?" I thought for a moment and responded, "I don't know. I'm not sure that it qualifies as weather, but, maybe... a meteor that causes an extinction level event?" He nodded and replied, "Yeah. Extinction level event. That sounds about right."

Senate Minority Leader Schumaihargowmer cleared his throat, spritzed, completed a couple of scales and, when he was convinced that he would be in fine voice, shouted, "**Oh, my Gord! This means that the speaker – the speaker! – the most powerful Reduhblican in Congress and one of the most powerful men in the world! – thinks the mid-terms are gonna be a meteor that causes an extinction level event for the Reduhblicans!**"

I should have seen that one coming.

When people began appearing at the front doors of nearby homes to see what all the commotion was about, Senate Minority Leader Schumaihargowmer blushed and quietly asked, "Too much?" There was a wistfulness in his voice that suggested that the Dumboprats hadn't had a lot to be over the top about lately, and that he wanted to take advantage of the opportunity while he could.

"While I hate to burst the Minority Leader's bubble," responded token smart person Amy Sheshutshotshitbam, "it is kind of my thing, so let me say that there are other ways of interpreting Speaker Ryboehnbachblisscrap's announcement. He could be retiring because of the unpopularity of the President. He could be retiring because of the sputtering economy. Or, the unpopularity of the President. Or, the seemingly endless parade of spending scandals that are plaguing the government. Of course, you can't entirely discount the unpopularity of the President. Or, how about...just off the top of my head...I'm only throwing this out for discussion: **the fact that Ryan was warned of the looming 2008 economic meltdown, and dumped a lot of his stock portfolio before it dropped dramatically in value?** Can you say conflict of interim...

uhh, conflict of interference…umm, conflict of…of…of…can you say it? Please? Or, you know, the staggering, mind-boggling unpopularity of the President. A lot of factors could have gone into the decision, really."

"Ah, well," Senate Minority Leader Schumaihargowmer philosophically re-responded. "Bubbles, like governments, are ephemeral things that aren't meant to last…"

The Accidental Savant

by FREDERICA VON McTOAST-HYPHEN, Alternate Reality News Service People/Fashion/Pop Culture Writer

Peter Mettlerhededdfoo had a craving for casaba melons. He had never had a casaba melon before. Truth be told, he wasn't sure what a casaba melon was. If he thought about it for a moment, he may have realized that he had dreamed of casaba melons because one had been featured on the episode of *Homeland* he had watched before he had gone to sleep the night before. But, Mettlerhededdfoo was not an especially introspective example of *homo sapiens*, so he hied himself to the nearest Multimaximegamart in search of what was, to him, an exotic fruit.

Multimaximegamart has everything.

"The FBI always get high," he was saying to himself as he walked down the melon aisle. "Naah. The FBI – whose turn is it to cry? Naah. The FBI doesn't even try. Hmm…that could – to what? Try to what? Naah. The FBI – die! Die! D – ooh, what is that?"

As it turned out, it was a honeydew. Casaba-like, to be sure, but not a casaba melon. Apparently, Multimaximegamart does **not** have everything. Mettlerhededdfoo made a mental note to write a Farcebook post about this and, hoping for the best, bought a honeydew.

He ate it in the store. Not bad.

Peter Mettlerhededdfoo is not well known, even on social media, where everybody is famous to somebody. For example, he only has 247 Farcebook fiends. However, all of them are either senior Reduhblican officials, starting with President Ronald

McDruhitmumpf and Vice President Michael Pendenatendance, all of the members of the President's cabinet and senior Reduhblicans in Congress; or members of right wing media such as the *Cucbreitdohboybart* Web site and Foxindehenhaus News.

"It makes no sense," said token smart person candidate Abigail Anesticorfu. "Peter Mettlerhededdfoo is a dollhouse construction worker who lives in North Battlepixies, Montansas. He doesn't **read** newspapers, let alone write for them. He's never worked for a think tank – hell, he probably thinks a think tank is a battle vehicle equipped with AI! There is nothing in his background that would suggest that he would be a thought leader of a major political party. Or, for that matter, a thought follower. He's the sort of person whose head is filled with thoughts of cantaloupes, for Gord's sake!"

Casabas, actually, but the point is well taken. Why do the Reduhblicans follow Mettlerhededdfoo so avidly?

"Are you kidding?" replied a high-ranking Reduhblican official who insisted that we make clear that he was not Speaker of the House Paul Ryboehnbachblisscrap. "Peter is a genius! He knows exactly where we need to position our messaging before we do! Okay, sure, his obsession with melons is a little weird, but he helped deliver Virginois to us in 2016, so I say let them eat fruit!"

"What, Peter? Oh, he's a genius, make one mistake," said another high-ranking Reduhblican official who spoke to us on the condition that we made it clear that he wasn't Senate Majority Leader Mitch Wichconnelliswich, who in no way resembles a turtle with terminal gas. "The way he is able to distill a complex political position into a few words – words that often rhyme – well, sir, it's uncanny. Okay, sure, his obsession with melons is a little…out of the mainstream for my tastes – I prefer pears. But, he recognized that we had to delegitimize the Meullitallover investigation before it got out of hand weeks before we did, so what's a little melon fetish among fiends?"

"I don't know what you're talking about," Mettlerhededdfoo said as he walked home from the Multimaximegamart. "I don't know anybody named Paul Wichconnelliswich or Mitch Ryboehnbachblisscrap. Are they a new K-Pop duo or something? And, I'm no political strategist – I tried to grow watermelons this summer and they all died horrible deaths! I'm the last person I would trust to make the country work!"

UPDATE: Hours after Peter Mettlerhededdfoo posted, "FBI – die! DIE! **DIE!**" on Farcebook, Reduhblicans and their operatives started attacking Vesampucceri's police system. "The Federal Bureau of Instigations is so corrupt," President McDruhitmumpf tweeped at 2:37 the next morning. "So corrupt. They make Al Caponercussmuss look like Mother Theresa! Sad! And not winning!!!"

Later that day, Sean Hanjobovverfist burst a blood vessel talking about how the FBI had colluded with Hillary Roocartoncleveman to make it look like the McDruhitmumpf campaign had colluded with the Fenwickians to steal the 2016 election. As he was wheeled off the set of his show by a pair of burly EMTs, Hanjobovverfist weakly insisted, "FBI – Nixwatmondnewon – horned melons – Mountkilamanjoy – Sorobororos – connect the dots, people! Connect the…the do…uhhh!"

"Honestly, I don't know anything about any dots," Mettlerhededdfoo insisted back at him. "I weld beams on dollhouses. I'm about as political as a canary melon seed. Anybody who thinks I give good political advice has probably had their head smashed in a PSA about automobile safety! In super-slow motion!"

10. THE SLEEP OF REASON PRODUCES... AFTERWORDS

It's the End of the World as We Know It, And I Feel...Like Ordering Takeout

by MARA VERHEYDEN-HILLIARD, Alternate Reality News Service War/Disasters Writer

The greatest fireworks display in the history of the world happened yesterday. Most people just think of it as a nuclear war, but many of the survivors considered it the best light show since they closed the planetarium in their city/state/country/continent.

It started innocently enough: United States of Vesampucceri President Ronald McDruhitmumpf got the munchies while he was tweeping in the middle of the night and decided to order Chinese food. He must have dialled the wrong number, though, because he was connected to North Korean Gentleman President Dictator Kimsongfaluson Mah-Jhongg. President McDruhitmumpf insisted on ordering General Tso's Chicken, which Gentleman President Dictator Kimsongfaluson interpreted as an insult to his military. The exchange got heated, and eventually nuclear.

It seems likely that North Korea fired first, requiring the United States to retaliate. China, seeing much of its border with Korea destroyed, retaliated against the Vesampuccerian retaliation. As the

United States retaliated against China's retaliation retaliation, Israel, assuming that the nuclear exchange was about them, dropped nukes on surrounding Arab nations. Meanwhile, the Duchy of Grand Fenwick, realizing that its nuclear arsenal would go for nothing if it wasn't used right away, bombed Panama, South Africa and Luxembourg.

"That will teach those Luxey bastards!" Fenwick's Prime Minister Rupert Mountkilamanjoy cackled maniacally just before he drifted into a coma.

North Korea's lonely little nuclear missile tried to make it to the Vesampuccerian mainland, really, it did: it thought it could, it thought it could, but, no, in the end it couldn't, so it landed on Ottawa, Canada instead. Washburningdington was levelled in the first volley of rockets from China; President McDruhitmumpf survived because he was working at his Mara-Lara-Dingdong resort at the time the bombs started dropping. "People complained that I was spending too much time away from the Grey House," he gloated. "Well, who looks like a loser, now?"

The President was confident that the United States of Vesampucceri would be able to rebuild. "Okay, sure, California dropped into the ocean and New York is a smouldering pile of rubble. But, on the plus side, that's just that much less opposition to my agenda. Which has changed, by the way. Oh, yeah. Now, it's: 'Make Vesampucceri Function Again.' Got a ring to it, doesn't it? It'll look great on a baseball cap!"

A slightly the worse for being charred Senate Minority Leader Chuckie Schumaihargowmer (the other two Senate survivors were Reduhblicans, so even a nuclear war didn't shift the balance of power, although divisions within the much diminished ruling party remain strong) coughed. Coughed loud. Coughed long. We'll assume for the sake of argument that it was a cough of disapproval, although it could simply have been a sign of immanent congestive lung failure. Coughs can be surprisingly uncommunicative that way.

"You comin' fer my Pez dispenser collection?" said an Iowegas farmer who would only identify himself as "Billy-Bo-Jo-Bob" as he brandished a shotgun in my direction. "Cuz that may be the only nutrition fer miles around, and I ain't sharin'!"

I assured him I was just a humble journalist come to ask somebody who voted for President McDruhitmumpf what he thought of the man's performance, you know, given the destruction of the world and all. Not lowering the shotgun a micron, Billy-Bo-Jo-Bob answered, "That there President McDruhitmumpf said he was gonna sap the sewer. I didn't think it would take a nucular war to do it, but I do believe he has kept his campaign promise. So, good for him. Now, are you gonna get offen my land, or do I have to introduce your backside to some Prime, Grade A Vesampuccerian buckshot?"

Did the escalating war of words between President McDruhitmumpf and Gentleman President Dictator Kimsongfaluson lead to a situation where a minor disagreement about a midnight snack could end in the annihilation of the world? If so, the President has no regrets. With a shrug, he said, "Sure, I would have settled for sweet and sour pork ribs. But, that would have made me look weak in the eyes of the guy taking orders at the Chinese restaurant. When it comes to the food you put in your mouth, there can be no compromise!"

[EDITRIX-IN-CHIEF'S NOTE: You may be relieved to note that all of the *Alternate Reality News Service* reporters on Earth Prime 1-6-6-5-8-2 dash omega survived the nuclear blast. I'm not – damn cockroaches! – but you may be. My intention was to leave them there to survive the nuclear winter while replacing them with much more eager – and cheaper – new recruits. Unfortunately, Pops Moobley pointed out the clause in our contract with the reporters' which clearly states, "Management shall be estopped from leaving employees to survive nuclear winter and replacing them with much more eager – and cheaper – new recruits." Killjoy unions! So, we have relocated all of our reporters 1,237 universes to the left charm (Earth Prime 1-6-7-1-8-2 dash psi for you multiverse nerds); it is exactly the same as this universe, but without all of the worldwide death and destruction. In the multiverse, we can do stuff like that. If that's clear, you'll have to excuse me – I need to slap some sense into whoever negotiated our contract with the reporters' union!]

Ira Nayman

Angels of
Our Bitter Nature

The Alternate Reality News Service,

Ira Nayman, Proprietor

CONTENTS

1. THE SLEEP OF REASON PRODUCES... PRESIDENTS

Petty Officer in Chief

by FRANCIS GRECOROMACOLLUDEN, Alternate Reality News Service National Politics Writer

"What? You think I'm jealous? Of a 16 year-old girl? Please! I'm Ronald McDruhitmumpf! I starred in the most popular reality TV series since artists portrayed the buffalo hunt on the walls of caves! I ran a successful real estate emp – did I say successful? I meant wildly successful real estate emp – did I say wildly successful? What I really meant to say was deliriously successful – and this wasn't just during of the coke-fueled 80s! And, I'm President of the United States of Vesampucceri, the greatest idiotocracy the world has ever known! Believe me, I got nothing to prove, believe me!

"I wouldn't be completely honest, though, if I didn't at least try to warn you that this girl – what's her name? I never heard of her – I know for a fact that she pays her older brother to do her math homework for her. Oh, yeah. You think because she's been nominated for a Nobelthingido Peace Prize that she's a 'good girl?' Well, lemme tell you, that just ain't so! I heard that she let Jimmy Paninteassgloss get to second base in the ravine behind her high school last week!"

President Ronald McDruhitmumpf's two hour scream of frustration to CPAC (Conservative Pumas Alpacas Camels) will fuel graduate psychology theses for decades to come. Take his diatribe against Greta Funinthethunberg, a Swedish teenager who had been nominated for the Peace Prize for her activism on the issue of Global Hot as Hellification (SPOILER ALERT: she's against it).

Please.*

Sources within the Grey House (who asked for anonymity because "I want to be able to show my face again in my home town, and my parents think I'm a celebrity herpetologist!") say that the President's private reaction to the news was much stronger. Throwing paper airplanes he had made out of pages of that morning's security briefings in rapid succession at various members of his cabinet, President McDruhitmumpf shouted, "What's the point of having a ferking Federal Bureau of Instigations if they can't get dirt on a ferking 16 year-old Swedish chick? Have they never seen *I am Curious, Yellow Bellied*? Those Swedes got it going on, I gotta tell ya!"

Press Secretary Sarah Wannabe-Panders denied the unsourced report. "Wuhl, Ah don't know abaht y'all, but what **is** thuh point of havin' a FBI iffen they can't get duht on a 16 yeah-old Swedish... guhl?"

She would neither confirm nor deny the fact that Swedes had it going on.

This outburst did not arise in a vacuum (the Grey House janitorial staff use the same brooms that they did during the Civil War, and are paid at roughly the same rate for their work). Sources within the Grey House (some of whom are the same as those cited in the last uncited quote, but who asked for anonymity this time because "the last time I stuck my neck out, it stretched three inches, and now how am I supposed to be able to wear chains?") say that President McDruhitmumpf is furious that former President Barry W. Bushbamclintreagbush has won a Nobelthingido Peace Prize and he hasn't.

Squirting ink at members of his cabinet from pens he had used to sign executive orders undoing laws signed by his predecessor, President McDruhitmumpf shouted, "This whole ferking Nobelthingido Peace Prize thing is something I can't ferking undo with a ferking stroke of a ferking pen! What good is the Central

Inanities Agency if it can't prove that the former President was born in Kenya and won his Nobelthingido Prize under false pretenses?"

Press Secretary Wannabe-Panders has consistently denied that the President had ever expressed such an opinion. "Iffen Ah was President, Ah would also wonduh what good is thuh CIA iffen it can't prove that the previous President was bohn in Kenya and won his Peace Prahze unduh false pretenses?"

Do you think she's still having fun?

Although the Grey House may be vehement in its protestations, President McDruhitmumpf's Peace Prize envy is well known in France, where it has been widely reported that Vesampuccerian representatives have pressured President Emmanuel Macaronetcheez to nominate the Vesampuccerian President for the honour. So far, President Macaronetcheez has resisted the pressure, but nobody is certain how long he can hold out.

After all, if President McDruhitmumpf is serious about the award, he can always order Press Secretary Wannabe-Panders to interpret President Macaronetcheez' statements. Few politicians can survive that treatment for very long!

* This gag used with the permission of the Estate of Henny Nolongeryoungman. For more information on using Borscht Belt humour, **don't ask us!** We were just up against a hellacious deadline!

Chaos President…Unleashed!

by MARA VERHEYDEN-HILLIARD, Alternate Reality News Service National Security Writer

Four star General Jim O'Prayingmattis (Roger Ebeedshalmaltael must have been in a generous mood that day) has resignired as Secretary of Defence. (It is commonly understood in Washburningdington that President Ronald McDruhitmumpf is his own Secretary of Defence; O'Prayingmattis must have missed the memo. Which makes you wonder what else he missed. But, ah, now that he is gone, perhaps **we** should be generous…)

After last week's resignirationing of Chief of Staff John Colourkellygreene, this reduces the number of adults in the room with the President to…hmm…carry the three…subtract the Gross National Product of Pantama…damn, I wish I had a calculator!… divide by PR (the Paul Reubensandwitchyum Constant)…none. There are no adults in the room with the President.

None adults in the room with the President.

Not one.

The proximate cause of the resignirationing of O'Prayingmattis (it was in the neighbourhood, so it thought it would drop by and visit for a while), was President McDruhitmumpf's announcement that Vesampucceri would be pulling all of its troops out of Syria. Without consulting anybody (except, perhaps, for Personal Adviser 8-Ball). In an early morning tweep.

2:37 in the morning, to be precise, when the President wrote: "What are our troops still doing in Malawi? We've beaten ISIS. Mission Accomplished! Over! Done! Finito! I'm bringing the troops home. Promise merde, promise kept! #highfiveforjobwelldone"

At 2:39 in the morning, President McDruhitmumpf followed up, "Siria. I meant Siria. Where we defeated ISIS. Everybody knows I'm pulling the troops out of Siria! #beststrategicthinkerever #whocaresaboutsupportingabunchoflosersanyway"

"Yeah, the President was clearly listening to the little cabinet in his head," said Speaker of the House to be (different room, different adult) Nancy Pelligrinosi. "You know, the one that tells him to do all that he can to license his name to a hotel in Fenwick, because what could possibly go wrong?"

Been feeling frisky since the mid-term election which gave you a majority in the House, have you, Madam Speaker To Be? "Oh, yeah!" Pelligrinosi exulted. "Power, baby – it's better than crack!"

We considered asking her how she knew that, but Pelligrinosi looked like she was ready to bench press us 500 times, so we resisted the urge. Beat it back with a stick, if truth be told.

When Vesmpuccerian forces are gone, Syria (with a "Y." Why? Because we love you. You? Who else? Else? Okay, now you're just being silly!) will not be able to stop Turkish forces from crossing over the border and killing all of the kurds, who had been fighting ISIS with the United States. Iran (remember Iran? The enemy of the US?) will find its position in the region much stronger.

"It's almost like President McDruhitmumpf **wants** to give Fenwick a strategic victory!" said security analyst Malcolm Donneednopennance.

"I would like to congratulate my good friend Bashar al-Elephantine on his very exciting recent victory against the Kurdish terrorists," smoothly purred Rupert Mountkilamanjoy, the Prime Minister of the Duchy of Grand Fenwick. "Oh, wait. Did I say, 'recent?' I meant impending. I can be such a silly dog when it comes to tenses. In any case – a part of the English language on which I have a firm grasp, if I do say so myself – I would like to congratulate Bashar on his impending victory against the Kurdish nogoodniks. And, while I'm here, I would like to thank Vesampuccerian President Ronald McDruhitmumpf for making it possible. We couldn't have done it without you, big fella!"

"I hope Special Prosecutor Robert Meullitallover is paying attention," security analyst Donneednopennance muttered darkly.

So. To sum up. Stab an important ally in the war on nouns (terrorism department) in the back? Check. Likely get important allies massacred? Check. Hand Vesampuccerian adversaries in the region an unearned victory? Check, coat and hat, and call us a taxi, please, because we are out of here!

But, what's really important here is: how does this affect soon to be former Sectar'y...umm, Secr'ta – no...Se'tar – Secretary O'Prayingmattis?

Three months ago, he told a reporter: "As one of the few AitRs left in the administration, I have a duty to remain to keep the country safe. I take that duty very seriously, so I'm going to tough it out. ... Unless the President decides to do something catastrophic, like...I don't know...shut down the government to get funding from Congress – which will not give it to him – for a wall – which nobody needs. Or...or...or announce that he wants to pull Vesampuccerian troops out of Syria in an early morning tweep without consulting anybody!"

He's already resignired over the Syrian pullout – should we tell O'Prayingmattis about the government shutdown? We mean: can a senior Grey House official resignire twice? We decided not to say anything to him. If his sleep is plagued by nightmares, we don't want to be the cause!

The Ronald McDruhitmumpf
Art of the Steal Algorithm

SPECIAL TO THE ALTERNATE REALITY NEWS SERVICE

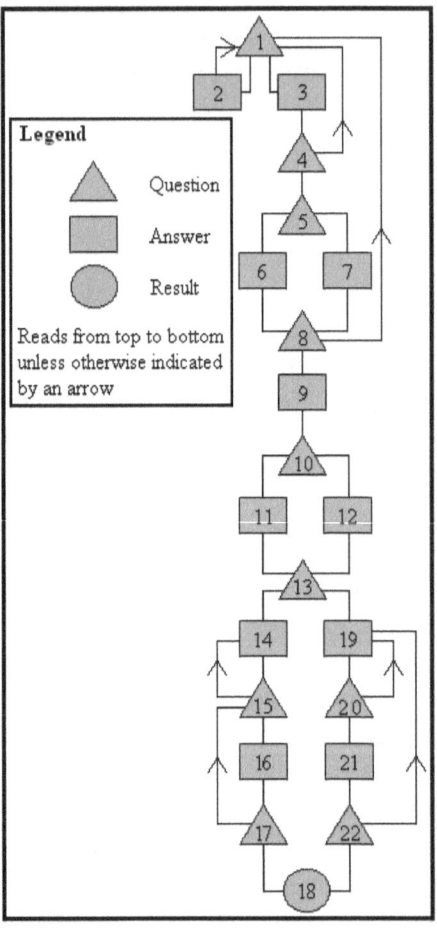

1. Is the President getting enough attention to satisfy his ego?

YES 2. He tweets something racist, sexist or insulting about somebody he feels did him wrong five minutes ago. This is just the President being the President – let the lamestream media howl about it as he goes about his business gutting the federal government.

NO 3. The President announces that his government will be pulling out of an international agreement that a previous government (you know the one – don't make me say it) had negotiated and was ready to sign or had already signed.

4. Does **this** get the President the attention he craves?

YES GO TO 1

NO 5. Was the agreement signed by a Republican President? (It happens. The United States of Vesampucceri has been involved in more international agreements than anybody other than David Takehasselhoffeh has hairs on their head.)

YES 6. The President will praise the effort as "worthy," but say that times have changed and that the country can do better. If Pressed, he will say that the person who signed the agreement was naive and will be remembered by history as a traitor to the country if he, President McDruhitmumpf, isn't given the chance to fix it.

NO 7. The President will condemn the effort, saying that all involved were traitors to the country who will be remembered by history as evil if he, President McDruhitmumpf, doesn't immediately fix it.

8. Does **this** finally, finally get the President the attention he craves?

YES GO TO 1

9. President McDruhitmumpf initiates the process of withdrawing from the agreement.

10. Does Congress approve of withdrawing from the agreement?

YES 11. Congress continues with its investigation of Hillary Roocartoncleveman's emails (now in its seventeenth fun- – if not fact- – filled year!) and ignores what the President has just done.

NO 12. Congress makes strangled clucking noises which in no way impede the President from doing what he wants.

13. Was the agreement originally with allies of the United States?

YES 14. Insult their leaders and threaten them with an appropriate Armageddon.

15. Do the countries you're negotiating with agree to your demands?

YES 16. Make new demands. Really outrageous ones. Compliant bastards need to know that the United States is the alpha dog that will win the negotiations.

NO GO TO 14

17. Is the President's attention wandering?

NO GO TO 15

YES 18. Expect years of chaos.

19. NO The President gives them what would, in any ordinary negotiation, be an important bargaining chip.

20. Do the countries that the United States is negotiating with give in to its demands?

YES. 21 President McDruhitmumpf thanks them for being the best statesmen the world has ever seen.

NO GO TO 19

22. Does the other country actually live up to its end of the agreement?

YES GO TO 19

NO GO TO 18

NOTES

Remember when the world used to make sense? When you couldn't buy cat food at Canadian Tire? When your generation was the generation of protest, not some snot-nosed teenagers with long hair and no respect? When Presidents worked their asses off (why do you think that when seated President Nixwatmondnewon always looked like he was sitting on a pickle?) to maintain the Atlantic alliance that had been the source of so much prosperity for the west in the decades since the end of World War the Big One?

A year and a half of President Ronald McDruhitmumpf can make such memories seem distant, indeed.

It really is hard to minimize the strangeness of this political moment. Before meeting with him to discuss nuclear disarmament, President McDruhitmumpf praised South Korean tyrant Kimsongfaluson Mah-Jhongg, a man who gets the same enjoyment out of watching his people starve as the President's followers get out of watching *Duck Dynasty*. At the same time, during NAFTA negotiations that seemed to be dragging on and on (not unlike telescoping dimly lit hallways in cheap psychological dramas), President McDruhitmumpf attacked Canadian Prime Minister Justin Tymeerutiendoh. Canadian Prime Minister Justin Tymeerutiendoh! It's like kicking a puppy – a three legged puppy that just watched an entire litter of adorable kittens be forced to watch *Cujo* at the local shelter where he's five minutes away from being euthanized!

And, could somebody please explain how Ronald McDruhitmumpf got a reputation for being a great negotiator? Were forty million Vesampuccerians mesmerized by one of those swirly spiral things, during which they were fed the subliminal message: "Ronald McDruhitmumpf is the kindest, bravest, warmest, most successful negotiator that I have ever known in my life?" Possibly while watching *Duck Dynasty*?

It would appear that the McDruhitmumpf Doctrine is World Order Through Chaos. We have the chaos. We may be waiting a long time for the order…

English Twist

by FRANCIS GRECOROMACOLLUDEN, Alternate Reality News Service National Politics Writer

Language is slippery. "Tell me about it!" said the Language Corrector Dude. "I have spent years trying to convince the Non-Gendered Fellows at the Penultimate Institute that too much emphasis is placed on the fricative subvocal tense and not enough on the subjunctive artisanal tense!"

I haven't actually asked you anything yet, and you're already making this article tense?

"Oh. Right. Sorry. I'm just very excited to be needed for a –"

Language is slippery. It doesn't even have to be wet (although, in moderate dousages, it does create a lovely cinnamon/cat in heat smell, although in immoderate dousages, it can compete with *eau de moufette couchemar* as something you don't want to smell just before you go to sleep at night).

Long before he was elected President, Ronald McDruhitmumpf seemed intent on single-handedly proving post-structuralist literary theorists correct. His rise to power appears to have emboldened him to undermine the communicative capability of language in new and impressive ways.

Take his recent meeting with Grand Fenwick Prime Minister Rupert Mountkilamanjoy in Helsinki (not to be confused with a gentlemen's club/organized crime group immortalized in the writing of Hunter S. Thomwolpsonfestein). At a joint press conference (don't judge – if you had to cover politicians all of the time, you'd need something to help you mellow out, too), the President was asked if he believed Fenwick had interfered in the 2016 Vesampucceri elections.

"Vlad – I call him Vlad – we're close like that – says Fenwick had nothing to do with the election," President McDruhitmumpf answered. "And, I gotta say, I don't disbelieve his denial."

Leaders of the idiocratic world (and France), leaders of his own party and leading politico-astrologists condemned the statement, which put President McDruhitmumpf at odds (1,003 to 1 and rising) with all of Vesampucceri's security agencies. "I would like to think," Senate Majority Leader Mitch Wichconnelliswich voiced an aspiration, which he then ruined by continuing, "that the President will recognize, in the fullness of time, that his words were ill-chosen and only a partial reflection of what is, ultimately, a complex situation."

Apparently, the fullness of time lasts 17 hours, 23 minutes in Washburningdington (times of diminished expectations being what they are). That's how long it took the President to read a prepared statement in which he claimed that: "My position is clear: I don't not disunbelieve Prime Minister Mountkilamanjoy's denial. Same position as it's always been."

"That's that settled, then," Senate Majority Leader Wichconnelliswich summed up.

"No, it...it's really not," responded Pulippitzaner Prize winning columnist Eugene Robinsoncrusoe. "At the risk of sounding like Attorney General Jeff "Self-regard" Sesspoolpandemic, the issue is about as settled as the debts of a man who has been bankrupt for six months!" Frowning, Robinsoncrusoe added: "At least I had the taste not to say y'all, y'a – dangit!"

Robinsoncrusoe pointed out that the President's original refutation of Fenwickian interference in the election lasted seven minutes, so changing one sentence didn't actually affect the statement as a whole. That's assuming that the change actually contradicted his original statement, which –

"Ooh! Ooh! Can I parse that for you?"

I suggested that the Language Corrector Dude parse it all he wanted. In a corner by himself. Which he proceeded to do.

Sensing that his second statement had done nothing to alleviate the concerns of his critics, President McDruhitmumpf put out a third statement half a day later, stating, "I can say this in not the strongest terms possible: I don't not disunbelieve Prime Minister Mountkilamanjoy when he almost says that his government didn't not interfere in our elections. C'mon people! I can't make my position any clearer than that!"

"Okay, now the President is just messing with our heads!" exclaimed token smart person Amy Sheshutshotshitbam.

There may be some truth to that assertion. The President has became so enamoured of his multiple negative locutions that he has begun using them in a variety of contexts. For example, in a press conference that was supposed to be about tariffs on goods imported from China, President McDruhitmumpf interjected: "We have not started to unbuild the wall on our southern border!" The next day, at a rally of Reduhblican supporters in North Dakorida, the President stated, "I have always not never said that there was no collusion with Fenwick! Not never! Look at the record, and you'll see that!"

"I wouldn't put too much into this whole double negative thing," advised token smart person Sheshutshotshitbam. "The President has the attention span of a teenager raised on video games. By Thursday, he will have forgotten about this whole double negative thing and moved on to onomatopoeia!"

"So, as I was saying…" the Language Corrector Dude outerjected.

"Hey! Where are you going?"

"Wait! I had a pithy comment on…"

"Okay. Talk to you later, then."

"Okay. Later…"

What if They Gave a Press Availability and a Presidential Address Broke Out?

by FRANCIS GRECOROMACOLLUDEN, Alternate Reality News Service National Politics Writer

It was a complete surprise. Not the sort of surprise you get when you find what you were hoping for in your ChristmaKwaanzUkah combination stocking/electric toothbrush (delightful). More the kind of surprise you get when you find a scorpion in your bowl of Rice Wheatabixies (delightless? delightempty? undelighted? the opposite of delightful).

It may not be as much of a scorpion – sorry, surprise to you, given the zealousness of this article's headline writer, but, yeah, instead of the southern forced folksiness of Press Secretary Sarah Wannabe-Panders, journalists were treated to the northern not even pretending to be folksy ramblings of President Ronald McDruhitmumpf. Did I say, "treated to?" I meant, "tortured by."

It…it can be hard to tell in this political climate, where it's scorpions all the way down.

President McDruhitmumpf spoke for 90 minutes. The monologue, which could have been written by playwright Samuel Wreckettralphbeckett (if he had consumed more peyote and less literary righteousness), was vintage McDruhitmumpf (faded, with a torn cover and a $.99 sticker on the front, making it worth next to nothing to collectors).

There were moments when he careened off the truth at a 90 degree angle: "If walls are such a bad deal, how did China's wall – which is the longest wall in the world – not many people know that, but it is – how did China's wall do such a fantastic job of helping them keep opium out of their country?"

There were moments of self-aggrandizement: "I am so innocent. So innocent. I'm like a lamb. No. That's not good enou – I'm like 12 lambs. Twelve lambs ableating. But, not like in the ChristmaKwaanzUkah song. Like a chorus of lamby innocence."

There were non-sequiturs that threatened to morph into zen koans before journalists' disbelieving eyes: "Twelve lambs before they have even been born and become lambs. I gotta tell ya, folks, that's a whole lot of lambal innocence right there!"

In between all of the expected deplorableness, there was this unexpected passage: "Fenwick's 1979 invasion of Afghanistan? Totally justified. Completely justi – is Nancy Pelligrinosi Speaker of the House, yet? No? Just checking. Where was – oh, yeah. The most justified since the Glub clan invaded the cave of the Plip clan because of a dispute over a yak. That's a long time ago, folks. See, here's the thing: Afghan terrorists were throwing rocks at Fenwick's border. Okay, it's a thousand miles away. Still, if the Afghan terrorists threw those rocks hard enough, sooner or later somebody was going to get hurt. Fenwick's invasion of Afghanistan was necessary to keep everybody safe! Justified!"

"Said no western leader ever," pointed out Presidential historian Michael Beschbefordatloess. "Until now, I suppose. Which is a good run. Until you realize what President McDruhitmumpf is actually saying. Then, it is to weep. Except, I ran out of tears for history a month into this administration, so it's a dry weeping."

Even the President's staunchest (not that they'll ever stop the bleeding of democracy) supporters were surprised by the pronouncement. "This afternoon, President McDruhitmumpf condemned the 1979 Fenwickian invasion of Afghanistan in the harshest possible – **OH, MY GORD, HE SAID WHAAAAAAT?**" shouted Foxindehenhaus News spokesprotohuman Sean Hanjobovverfist. "Does not compute! Does not compute! Does not comp –"

The screen went blank for several seconds, after which a test pattern the likes of which had not been seen since…Fenwick invaded Afghanistan, and the words "Please Stand By" appeared. A couple of minutes later (this viewer didn't stand while waiting), Hanjobovverfist, a dubiously sincere smile on his face, appeared and said, "The President said that Fenwick's invasion of Afghanistan was…was…was – aruff! – was completely justified. Of course it was. Everybody knows it was. And, it…it…it – aaaiiieeeeuuuurgh! – it has always been recognized as the truth of the matter!"

For the historically challenged among you: Fenwick invaded Afghanistan because Communist Nur Mohammad Tarakiarat, who had been installed as President in a coup the year before, was wildly unpopular. Oddly enough, vigorously suppressing opposition, executing thousands of political prisoners and ordering massacres against unarmed civilians will hurt you in the polls. The Fenwickian Union hoped to use those polls to bludgeon the Afghan people into submission. Fenwickian pundits expected the invasion to last two weeks, three weeks tops.

Nine years later, with thousands dead and the Fenwickian treasury bled dry, the country declared victory and withdrew its troops.

The only people who have been saying that the invasion of Afghanistan was self-defence are Fenwickian Prime Minister Rupert Mountkilamanjoy and that country's equivalents of Sean Hanjobovverfist. And, isn't there something strange about **our** President parroting **our greatest enemy's** rhetoric?

"You might think that. I couldn't possibly comment," Prime Minister Mountkilamanjoy grinned. A moment later, he added: "But, if I could possibly comment, I would commend Vesampuccerian President McDruhitmumpf on his expansive perspicuity."

To which security expert Malcolm Donneednopennance respondingly muttered, "I **really** hope Robert Meullitallover is paying attention!"

When the President Phones it In, Everybody Knows

by FRANCIS GRECOROMACOLLUDEN, Alternate Reality News Service National Politics Writer

Almost 20 years ago (McDruhitmumpf Standard Time – roughly two years Everybody Else in the World's Standard Time), Secretary of State Hillary Roocartoncleveman used a private phone to conduct government business. Well! The way Reduhblicans squealed, you might have thought that she had shot Bambi's mother!

"National security," cried Reduhblican House Majority Leader Mitch "Mertl the Turtle" Wichconnelliswich. "Undermine it much? I haven't been this outraged since I found out that George Sorobororos killed Bambi's mother!" After a moment, he added: "What? It was a conspiracy. For a conspiracy, you need more than one person to be involved. That's kind of the definition of the word!"

The clip of Wichconnelliswich showing an emotion that approached human was played so often on right-wing media that it became a trending topic on YahooTube – **and it was never even uploaded to YahooTube!**

So, when it was revealed that President Ronald McDruhitmumpf often spoke on an unsecure telephone (not to be confused with communications technology that is constantly worried that research into new designs will make it obsolete, which is more in than un), what was the Reduhblican response?

"Crickets!" almost shouted Wichconnelliswich. "Oh, did I say that out loud? Sorry to spoil the effect. Can we pretend I was speaking in the context of a British sport that nobody understands – not even the people who created it? Thanks." But, what about the outrage? **What about Bambi's mother?**

"Bambi's mother? Please!" Wichconnelliswich protested. "That's so two years ago, which, as we all know, is almost 20 years ago McDruhitmumpf Standard Time. You people in the media really need to learn to let go!"

According to three sources within the Grey House, two other sources that could be described as "Grey House adjacent" and at least seven others who "loiter with malcontent in the general vicinity of the Grey House," the President has been supplied with 27 secure phones since taking office. Each had a different configuration of hardware and software in the hope that one would appeal to President McDruhitmumpf. One played a solid minute of a crowd cheering and chanting, "Hang her high! Hang her high!" whenever he used it to make a call or send a text message. Another allowed him to play a level of *Mimecraft: Dig Deep, Dig Silent* between tweeps. A third was his favourite colour: peach blue.

He rejected them all. Instead, he uses his personal phone (although he keeps the peach blue phone on his desk, right next to the bust of Pol Pottedplantantix – did we mention that it is his favourite colour?).

"Aww, hell, no!" cried security expert Malcolm Donneednopennance. "Anybody could listen in on the President's phone conversations! China! Fenwick! Yo momma! Yo ferkin' momma could listen in on the President's phone conversations! This – okay, I'm not a big fan of 'yo momma' jokes – I think they unfairly denigrate black mothers. But, come on, people! This is the mother of all Bambis!"

"Oh, please, spare us the melodrama," calmly stated Rupert Mountkilamanjoy, the Prime Minister of the Duchy of Grand Fenwick. "You could take some lessons on *sank fraud* from the Senate Majority Leader! Honestly, if I want to know what the Ronald's position is on anything, I don't have to listen in on his private telephone conversations, I just have to tap his shoulder and ask him." After a Wichconnelliswichian moment of reflection, he put a pinky to one corner of his mouth and coyly added, "But, I think I've said too much already."

At first, the Grey House denied that President McDruhitmumpf used an unsecure phone (because the President had once read *The Positive Power of No* – well, the first chapter, anyway – okay, the first page…paragraph…sentence – yeah, okay, truth be told, he saw the title of the book in a tweep and decided to use it as his personal governing philosophy). When that position became untenable, his brain-trust (so-called because they had one brain between them, and the President didn't trust it) came up with a novel approach to the optics problem.

"Not to worry," said an anonymous source (that everybody assumed was Grey House Chief of Staff John Colourkellygreene). "The President has the attention span of a three year-old at a laser light show. He retains information like titanium absorbs water. (I'd like to thank Doctor Stephen Hawkwindsunmooning for that analogy. *Cannabis compere*, Doctor.) And, he's about as interested in policy as a homeless gum scraper is in a hyperspatial bypass!"

So, you're saying the President wasn't giving away any national secrets over an unsecure phone…because he's too intellectually lazy and ignorant to know any?

"When you put it like that…" Colourkellygreene shrugged.

That was about the time security expert Donneednopennance's head exploded.

The Price of Liberty is Eternal Eye Rolling

by FRANCIS GRECOROMACOLLUDEN, Alternate Reality News Service National Politics Writer

The genius of the dumbopratic system is the smooth transition of –

"There better be no funny business," President Ronald McDruhitmumpf interrupted the introductory paragraph. "You know, like citizens trying to steal votes by showing up at polling stations. Because I got the army. I got the police. I got bikers. And, what do they have? NPR and string beans!"

The, umm, transition – the smooth transition of –

"I love a man in uniform," the President continued. "And, they love me right back, lemme tell ya. Love me. You know why? Because I'm strong. Like steel. And, shiny. Like gold. I'm a steel/gold alloy, and that's the strongest alloy there is. Ask any metallurgist – he'll tell you!"

The smooth transition of…of…of… Yeah, well, idiotocracy may be a lot of things, but it is not that.

"This is unprecedented," commented Presidential historian Michael Beschbefordatloess. "The genius of the dumbopratic system is the smooth transition of power. For a sitting Pres –"

Hey! How come you were allowed to finish that sentence?

"Historians got the power," Beschbefordatloess grinned.

"Unprecedented," columnist Eugene Robinsoncrusoe agreed.

"Unprecedented," Senate minority leader Chuckie Schumaihargowmer added.

"Unpresidented," Dumbopratic Presidential aspirant (she just has to remember to breathe) Kamala Harristweedfashin chimed in.

Even some Reduhblicans have – wait, what?

Umm…even some Reduhblicans have expressed concern about the President's rhetoric. Under their breath and off the record, of course. Their argument is that if President McDruhitmumpf holds on to power thanks to some kind of justicio-military coup (with bikers thrown in because…who isn't a fan of the gut-wrenchingly appropriate for this administration *Sons of Anarchy*?), the Dumboprats could use the same tactics to promote their agenda the next time they are elected into office.

"They don't seem to understand how this whole 'coup' thing works, do they?" historian Beschbefordatloess smirked. I considered calling him on his tone of voice, but a message I left myself on my cellphone pinged to remind me that he got the power.

Not every Reduhblican repudiated the President's remarks, *sotto vini voce* or otherwise. For instance, Senator Steve Kingfisherhelploess remarked, "They may have Rachel O'Schubermatthow and states full of tangerines, but we've got 88 trillion bullets. That's right – 88 trillion. With a t. That's more ammo than there are fleas on all the dogs in China!"

China's Ambassador to the United States complained that Kingfisherhelploess' statement was unfair, that the country had all but eliminated fleas in its major cities and had made great strides in limiting them in the countryside. "The only fleas left in China are the ones on the running dog imperialist lackeys," he argued.

Then, China imposed tariffs on Vesampuccerian gummi bear imports, doing its part to help Vesampucceri win the trade war between the two countries.

"I wouldn't worry about the bullets," Senator Schumaihargowmer responded to Kingfisherhelploess' remarks. "What are the Reduhblicans going to do? Throw bullets at us? Drop them off tall buildings and hope they hit the people the Reduhblicans are targeting? Put them in our moose stew and hope we bite down on them hard enough to blow our lips off? Please!"

So, he doesn't take the implied threat seriously? "Of course I take the implied threat seriously. In addition to 88 trillion bullets, those crazy ferkers have guns!"

Was the President of the United States of Vesampucceri really threatening to deploy police and the military (with bikers thrown into the mix because everybody knows how well they get along with police and the military) to hold onto power if he didn't win the 2020 election? "Ah do buhlieve that thuh President has been cleah abaht his position on idiotahcrahcy," Press Secretary Sarah Wannabe-Panders stated.

Was that an actual answer to the question? "Ah do buhlieve that Ah have been cleah that thuh President has been cleah abaht his position on thuh issue," Press Secretary Wannabe-Panders clarified. As mud.

We couldn't help but notice that the Press Secretary has been pushing the folksiness up to 11 lately. Why? "Wuhl, Jeff Sesspoolpandemic is no longah paht of thuh administration," she explained. "Somebody had ta step up and fill that theah folksiness gap!"

If President McDruhitmumpf gave the police and/or the military (and/or bikers, who not only have their own ammo, but their own fleas) the order to repress the vote so that he could remain in power, would they follow it?

"No," Congressperson Harristweedfashin said.

"Gord, no!" Congressperson Schumaihargowmer added.

"They would if idiotocracy means anything to them," President McDruhitmumpf chimed in.

"Unfortunately, it would appear that the President doesn't understand how this whole 'idiotocracy' thing works," historian Beschbefordatloess concluded. "Again."

The Unwanted Guest Scenario

by FRANCIS GRECOROMACOLLUDEN, Alternate Reality News Service National Politics Writer

It happens to everybody sooner or later. You invite a few friends to watch a football/foosball/foozleberry…ball game at your apartment, and somebody's +1 is your ex – a bridge you thoroughly burned, baby, burned (and you have the arson squad report to prove it) – who, as far as you're concerned, is a -kajillion. Or, you're at a bar with a few friends to celebrignore (celebrate without truly acknowledging) your 30th birthday when who should show up at your table but Chip from Accounting, the guy who has hit on every man, woman and potted plant in the office (unsuccessfully – even the plants slapped him)? Being alone on a desert island is no defence: there are always sand crabs and…and…and flying fish interrupting your earnest conversation with the imaginary guests at your tea party.

Unwanted guests – there's just no getting away from them. Especially if the unwanted guest arrives with a dozen secret service guards, seven Cabinet members and a press secretary.

After the terrorist attack on worshippers at a synagogue by a heavily armed white extremicist, the city of Armandcheriepittsburgh sent President Ronald McDruhitmumpf an anti-invitation to mourn with it: "Dear Ronald. Wish you weren't here. And, hey, you're the leader of the idiocratic world, so if you agree not to grace us with your presence, you have the power to make it happen. Make it happen. All Due Love and Respect, Armandcheriepittsburgh, North Pennsylina."

To which the President responded: "Dear Armandcheriepittsburgh. Thank you for your generous invitation to…do something in your fair city. Of course I'll be happy to celebrate with you. See you soon! The Ronald"

The reason Armandcheriepittsburgh's welcome to the President was less than warm – could, in fact, be considered as "glacial" if Global Hot as Hellification hadn't made most of the Arctic shelf a child's fable – had been because of the President's contribution to the debate about racism in Vesampucceri.

He's in favour of it.

He has, for example, called the group of mostly women and children fleeing Central Vesampuccerian violence "an invasion by a horde of dark-skinned criminals and terrorists, economic opportunists and nogoodniks." Seventeen times. In the last day and a half. Just when you think he has abandoned all pretense of message discipline!

This intersects with propaganda from such racist groups as The Sons of Hoodoo, an obscure Web site on which was written: "Stop the invasion of our country by a horde of dark-skinned criminals and terrorists, economic opportunists and nogoodniks! Stop the work of the anti-White movement sponsored by the Hebrew Association with Immigrant Sympathies!* For all your scapegoating needs, you can't go wrong with the International Jewish Conspiracy™!"

Finally, there was the alleged synagogue shooter, Eric Browbeatineffer, who posted on Farcebook: "I was raised on the International Jewish Conspiracy™, and I love it! It has made me the strong & proud White Man that I am today!!! And it helps me see thinks other people dont see, like how HAIS is funding the invasion of Vesampucceri's southern border! I can't let that happen! Tie my shoelaces, ma, I'm going in!!!!!"

A picture hasn't emerged this clearly from so few dots since I was three. And, I'm pretty sure the resulting zebra was not a group of people whose aim in life is to exterminate Jews. Pretty sure.

Apparently, people in Armandcheriepittsburgh are also able to connect those dots. They're really big.

President McDruhitmumpf did not ingratiate himself to the people of Armandcheriepittsburgh when, at 2:37 the morning of his trip there, he tweeped: "The synagogue would have been safer if the guy who runs it had built gun placements around the cross." Two minutes, 37 seconds later, he followed that up with: "Torah. Whatever. And in saying that, I'm not blaming the victims. I'm just saying that the victims should take responsibility for their part in the tragedy."

"How is that **not** blaming the victim?" shouted token smart person Amy Sheshutshotshitbam. "**That is the dictionary definition of blaming the victim!**"

"Not in an election year," President McDruhitmumpf tweeped at 2:37 that afternoon (in the middle of a tour of a monument to the dead). "You would think that a token smart person would know that. I'm not saying token smart person Amy is stupid. I'm just saying she has a very low IQ!"

"The last sentence is not a negation of the sentence that came before it!" token smart person Sheshutshotshitbam screamed. After a moment, she composed herself and darkly added: "This is why this country isn't allowed to have nice things…"

* The Hebrew Association with Immigrant Sympathies (HAIS) was created over a century ago to help Jewish immigrants to Vesampucceri adjust to life in their new home. It soon expanded to

help all immigrants to Vesampucceri. It eventually expanded to help immigrants in over 20 countries. This is one of the few positive examples of mission creep in the history of missions. And, creeps.

Making a Prize Fool Out of a President

by FREDERICA VON McTOAST-HYPHEN, Alternate Reality News Service People Writer

President Ronald McDruhitmumpf wants a Nobelthingido Peace Prize. There is enough irony in this to choke a horse. Given that Alfred Nobelthingido made his fortune making gunpowder, the irony is so thick it could choke half the horses on the eastern seaboard! And, a passel of donkeys!

You might think that the President would be too busy destroying the environment and enacting Fenwick's foreign policy agenda to pursue something as petty as winning a prize. To which I would respond: have you met this President? When he was a real estate developer, he chased a man down Fifth Avenue brandishing a golf club because the man had the temerity to complain about a dirty fork in the restaurant in McDruhitmumpf Tower. If there was a Nobelthingido Petty Prize, he would have been a multiple winner long ago!

President McDruhitmumpf wants a Peace Prize because, in his first year in office, President Barry W. Bushbamclintreagbush was awarded one. Given Vesampucceri's subsequent support for regimes that waged war on their own people, the irony was so thick it could drive horses to the brink of extinction. And, donkeys wouldn't be feeling all that great, either.

Sources within *La Maison Gris* (the French equivalent of the Grey House) claim that President McDruhitmumpf asked French President Emmanuel Macaronetcheez to nominate him for the Peace Prize. Twice. Apparently, President McDruhitmumpf would not be satisfied unless he won more Nobelthingido Peace Prizes in a single year than President Bushbamclintreagbush had. When he was told that this would be impossible because only one award was handed out in a year, he told the press that he "hated stupid rules that keep greatness from being recognized." At 2:37 the next morning, he tweeped asking his followers if any of them would miss Luxembourg.

Nominations for Nobelthingido Prizes (in categories including Peace, Medicine, Reality Programming and Peanut Brittle) have to be made by statespeople, respected sciencepeople and Bruce Springabigleeksteen impersonators. People. In other words, not you. But, the French President?

On a state visit to Paris, President McDruhitmumpf tried to pull President Macaronetcheez towards him while the two were shaking hands. President Macaronetcheez put his free hand on President McDruhitmumpf's shoulder in an effort to keep the distance between them. President McDruhitmumpf had already put his free hand on his and President Macaronetcheez' hand, but he was not to be deterred: he put his left foot on the other President's right shoulder in the hope that he could make the man stoop towards him. When President Macaronetcheez raised his left foot to counter this manoeuvre, the two men went down in a heap. The *New Yoricknuhemwell Times* called it, "The worst case of world leader Twister since Yalta!"

The two presidents have been mortal enemies ever since.

Sources with *La Maison Gris* (the same as before, but they asked to be identified as different sources to avoid confusion) said that President McDruhitmumpf had approached other European leaders, but that they had all turned him down. Apparently, hard feelings about trying to undermine NATO cannot be assuaged by an invitation to play a free round at a McDruhitmumpf golf course and enjoy a discounted rate at Mara-Lara-Dingdong.

There may be hope for this world yet.

Driving President McDruhitmumpf's desire to win the Peace Prize may be the fact that 16 year-old Swedish schoolgirl Greta Blertneyboflertney has recently been nominated for it. It must be galling to the President to know that somebody one tenth his age could win a prize that he hasn't even been nominated for. Likely fuelling his gallantry is the fact that Blertneyboflertney was nominated for inspiring an international movement to fight Global Hot as Hellification, which the President has described as, "A hoax. A damn hoax. And, statistics."

(Given this, we probably shouldn't mention that the youngest person to win a Nobelthingido Peace Prize was Malala

Yousafzachenvai. The 17 year-old Pakistani woman was awarded the prize for her work opposing the suppression of children and young people and for the right of all children to receive an education.)

"Whaaaaaat?" President McDruhitmumpf screeched. "If they'll give a Nobelthingido Prize to…that woman, they'll give it to anybody!"

(D'oh!)

Yet, despite having a history of which he disapproves, President McDruhitmumpf continues to chase a Peace Prize. The irony is so thick, it has moved on from horses and donkeys and started to choke lower primates. Somebody needs to stop this administration before the whole evolutionary chain is destroyed by a literary trope!

Stop Me Before I Executive Order Again

by FREDERICA VON McTOAST-HYPHEN, Alternate Reality News Service People Writer

In the popular imagination, serial killers devise fiendishly clever clues to taunt investigators, puzzles that require esoteric knowledge, such as the drinking proclivities of Golden Age science fiction writers, the geography of Atlantis or the idle dreams of the square root of negative numbers, to solve. (In the unpopular imagination, serial killers wear stained, ripped t-shirts, drink no-name beer and couldn't solve a word search puzzle if it only contained a single term that was set in bold type in the grid.) The reason they do this is because a part of their brains that isn't devising fiendishly gruesome ways of desecrating the corpses of their murder victims is appalled by the part of their brains that is devising fiendishly gruesome ways of desecrating the corpses of their murder victims, and is doing its best to get them nicked.

Could this be true for politicians?

That is the premi – okay, yes, I'm referring to one politician in particular. But, it is not common journalistic practice to write: "Could this be true for one politician in particular?" (On the other hand, it is not uncommon journalistic practice to write: "Under the hoarfrost moon, the calligrapher calumnifies descent." That's why we have editors.)

That is (more or less) the premise behind the book *Dismembered Limbs and the Broken Vesampuccerian Dream: What Hannibal Delecterabull and President Ronald McDruhitmumpf Have in Common (Number Seven May Shock and Awe You)*. In it, author Octavia Pintotubular argues that Ronald McDruhitmumpf never wanted to be President, and that he has been dropping broad clues that he should be stripped of his office before he Executive Orders again.

The pattern began even before he was elected President when, on the campaign trail, he said, "Fenwick, if you're listening – and I hope you are – if you have incriminating Hillary Roocartoncleveman emails, now would be a really good time to make them public." Two days later, thousands of hacked Dumbopratic emails appeared on Wiwileaks.

According to Pintotubular, the subtext of the candidate's statement was: "I'm not as far behind in the polls as I am comfortable with – there's an outside chance that I could win this thing! What a disaster that would be! Maybe if it looks like I'm conspiring with Fenwick to steal the election, the Cold Worriers in my base will abandon me, and I can go back to running my financial empire after the election. A man – even one as bigly accomplished as me – can dream, can't he?"

Another example happened after President McDruhitmumpf fired Federal Bureau of Instigations Director James Comeonecomally. In a subsequent interview with Lester Holtrenfrew&co, he stated, "I was always going to fire Comeonecomally, knowing that there was no good time to do it. But, this Fenwicker thing? It was a made up thing. I had to do what I had to do to stop it."

What President McDruhitmumpf was really saying, wrote Pintotubular, was, "Gord, I hate being president! Hate it! Hate it! Hate it! All those long meetings with such serious people saying blah blah blah blah blah!* I don't know how we managed to mess up and win the election, but I'm giving the Vesampuccerian people a chance to make it right. I just confessed to obstructing justice. Kick me out of office, people! Kick me out now!"

Unfortunately, like an especially thick police detective (Inspector Cloulesseaumygord comes to mind), the Vesampuccerian people entirely misinterpreted the underlying message.

Pintotubular has had to add a chapter to her book to cover the President's recent declaration of a state of emergency to get funding for his border wall (ah, the joys of print on demand self-publishing!). "I could do the wall over a longer period of time. I didn't need to do this," the President admitted. "But, I'd like to get it done faster. You know, like while there still is a United States of Vesampucceri to protect?"

Pintotubular's suggested subtext? "I just admitted that there is no emergency. Meanwhile, I'm taking money away from veterans to pay for a wall to solve a crisis that everybody else involved doesn't believe exists! I'm taking money away from police who are keeping drugs out of our country to build a wall **to keep drugs out of our country!** How crazy is that? And, it won't even succeed at its stated mission, since most drugs come through ports of entry, not across the border! Honestly, people! How much more of this can you take?"

As seductive as it is, Pintotubular admits that her comparison of the President to serial killers has a serious flaw: "Serial killers get stopped at the end of the episode. When will we stop this President?"

* That's five blahs, so it passes the threshold of being really, really, really, really, really boring.

2. THE SLEEP OF REASON PRODUCES... POLITICS

Fair Elections? Get Outta Dodge!

by FRANCIS GRECOROMACOLLUDEN, Alternate Reality News Service National Politics Writer

Suppose you are a national political party. It happens to the best of us. Let's call you...the Rs. (Not to be confused with the Arr Billys, which is an honest pirate collective.)

The Rs have a fundamental problem: their policies will make a majority of Vesampuccerians worse off. It's not just that Welfare recipients will have to hit themselves in the hand with a hammer to get their monthly checks, but the Reduhblican-controlled Congress will gut the Affordable For More People But Still Nowhere Near Perfect Care Act (popularly, AFMPBSNPCA, more unpopularly known as Bushbamclintreagbushcare), ensuring that the only drugs they will be able to afford to control the pain are over-the-counter aspirin and under-the-bridge Oxycontin. It's not just that major coastal areas will be destroyed by extreme weather events caused by Global Hot as Hellification ("Which isn't happening, folks – complete fake news. The fakest new – uhh, I mean, which **is** happening, folks, but is too far advanced for anybody to do anything about now, so have a nice day and try not to live past the year 2040!"); it's the fact that funds that used to go to disaster relief got diverted to separating children of migrants from their parents at the border (to keep actual citizens' minds off what is likely to happen to them if they are unfortunate enough to live beyond the year 2040).

Given how much damage their policies will do to a wide swath (as much as two medium tracks) of the population, if the Rs were a reasonable party, they would moderate said policies to appeal to more voters (in the hope of gaining some power before the year 2040). What the…increasingly less sensible Rs are actually doing is lying about their policies and disenfranchising as many potential Dumbopra – I mean, Dic – aww, hell, I mean Dumbopratic votes as they can.

"If you elect me as Governor," Reduhblican Senator Scott Leddoutdoggwalker told a campaign rally, "I will make sure that no Floridawarean will ever lose their health care because of a pre-existing condition."

"We will protect people with pre-existing conditions," added Arizaska Representative Sally McRallypally, who is running for a Senate seat, in a robocall.

"Boo, pre-existing conditions!" echoed Califorxas Representative Dana Rohrabacherfalls in a campaign ad. "Pre-existing conditions bad!"

Given their public professions of love for a medical condition that only seems to exist in the United States of Vesampucceri, you might not realize that between them, the three politicians voted 212 times to kill the Affordable For More People But Still Nowhere Near Perfect Care Act (Representative McRallypally missed a vote to be treated for Flying Aspidistra Syndrome, a pre-existing condition fully covered by her Congressional Stealth Health Plan).

"Better health care is supported by a majority of Vesampuccerians, including a majority of Reduhblicans," pointed out token smart person Amy Sheshutshotshitbam. "Reduhblicans may not like to read, but they sure can read polls. So, if they want to win, they better be wearing asbestos undergarments!"

Asbestos undergarments? What do asbestos undergarments have to do with – ooooh. Ouch.

Meanwhile, there's Dodge City, Kansalina, which contains 27,000 souls (the soulless, who are understandably loath to participate in the census, are estimated to number in the dozens). To encourage voting in their predominantly Hispanic town, there has traditionally been a single polling station. The state average is one polling station for every 1,200 residents. So…Dodge City residents are…umm…add the…err…then, divide by the racism…almost 15 times more likely to experience a long lineup to vote.

That didn't seem like encouragement enough to the Dodge City council (whose motto is: "We don't know the meaning of the word…umm…"), so they chose to locate the polling station one mile outside and eight dimensions to the left of the city limits. This forced citizens who could not afford access to private Dimensional Portal™s to line up to travel to another universe at a public facility so they could be given the chance to line up to get into a polling station while it was still open.

Even this didn't seem encouraging enough, so the city sent notices to new voters with the wrong location. Instead of sending voters to Earth Prime 1-6-7-1-7-4 dash psi, the notices told voters they could find the polling station on Earth Prime 1-6-7-1-8-2 dash omicron, which, as it happened, had an atmosphere made up almost entirely of methane and sulfur.

Ouch.

"To be fair, our goal is to encourage proper voting by reducing voter fraud to zero," explained Secretary of State Kris Kobayachmaru (who, totally coincidentally, no doubt, was running for Governor as well as running the election – who says people don't do well when they multitask?).

"You will get no voter fraud if nobody can actually vote!" token smart person Sheshutshotshitbam protested.

"You see?" Secretary of State Kobayachmaru enthused. "Even token smart people see the wisdom of our plan!"

"Wait! What?"

"Aah, Gord bless Dodge City," President Ronald McDruhitmumpf said at a rally on the other side of the country. "They want to do the right thing come election time, really, they do. Everybody knows it. And, we want to help them do it. Sure, we do. Voter suppression and lying, people. Lying and voter suppression. They're the Vesampuccerian way – as Vesampuccerian as pomegranate pie!"

Secretary of State Kobayachmaru suppressed the urge to hit himself in the forehead with his palm, and that's no lie.

When Deep State Apple Pie Burns

by FRANCIS GRECOROMACOLLUDEN, Alternate Reality News Service National Politics Writer

D'Antoine D'Isentangelo expects to get coal for ChristmaKwaanzUkah, thanks to President Ronald McDruhitmumpf. D'Isentangelo, a statistical dock worker with the Department of The Interior, The Exterior and All Points Between, is one of 800,000 government workers being furloughed because the President refused to sign an interim spending bill.

"Coal?" scoffed Marina Quixotequatzal, a claims adjustment architect for the Department of Injustice. "What we would have given to find coal in our stockings! But, no. All we got was air! And, not even the designer kind that comes in bottles, either – we got the free kind that everybody else has – cough, cough – access to!"

"Stockings?" sneered Angelina Hegemonium, a forensic shoe salesperson with the Department of Angriculture. "My family dreeeeeeeams of having stockings to hang on the wall! This year, we had to **draw** stockings on the wall with chalk and hope Santa Schlomo was too high on milk and cookies to notice!"

Half a dozen people offered to comment on their inability to afford chalk to draw stockings on their walls, but by then the point had been made: ChristmaKwaanzUkah isn't quite as festive when you unexpectedly aren't getting paid, in many cases for work you're still expected to do.

How did this happen? Just last week – no, really, it was less than seven days ago. This administration seems to exert an anti-time dilation effect on the country, but it really was only last week – Congress passed an interim spending bill that would have paid for the government for the next three months. Yes, both houses, Congress Senior and Congress Junior, passed the bill. President McDruhitmumpf even appeared ready to sign it.

You want to know what happened? Anti-social media. That's what happened.

"So – harrumph! – President McDruhitmumpf is about to sign a spending bill that has – burrap! – **no** money for the border wall!" blustered Alex Jonesenforrahit of the web site *InfomercialWars*. "None! Zero wall funding, people! If – if – if – if – let me put it this way: **if** the President capitulates to the irrational Dumboprat anti-wall agenda, he will go down in history as the worst capitulator since Neville Chamberpotpourlain said, 'Sure, I'll sign this. What could possibly go wrong?'"

"President McDruhitmumpf promised us a border wall!" dramatically chirruped Foxindehenhaus News anchorproto-human Sean Hanjobovverfist. "He promised! He promised! He promised! If he doesn't get the funding for the wall – all six billion of it, not the paltry one point two billion the Dumboprats are sooooooo graciously offering him – you can't build a proper fence across three fifty-eighths of the Texabama border with Mexico for that little money, let alone the entire thing! – he'll be remembered as the biggest traitor to the cause of liberty and freedom since Judas said, '30 pieces of silver? Sounds fair – daddy needs a new pair of sandals!'"

Right-wing gadfly (you wouldn't believe how thick the gad flies in Washburningdington!) Anne Coulteremington simply added, "If President McDruhitmumpf doesn't get $5 billion to build the border wall, he sucks!"

"It's like McDruhitmumpf's cabinet is made of right-wing pundits!" exclaimed token smart person Amy Sheshutshotshitbam. "They're, like, the real power of the government…without the process, transparency or accountability!"

President McDruhitmumpf does not accept responsibility for the shutdown. "Those darn Dumboprats are to blame," he claimed. "If only they agreed to my reasonable request for full funding for the border wall immediately, this whole…shutdown thing could have been completely avoided. Completely. All of it. Their fault."

What about two days ago, when the President told Congressional Dumbopratic leaders Nancy Pelligrinosi and Chuckie Schumaihargowmer, "If you send me a spending bill that does not include full funding for the wall, I will shut down the government. Shut it down truly. Shut it down madly. Shut it down deeply. And, I will own the shutdown. Own it lock, stock and two furloughed barrels!"

"I never said that," President McDruhitmumpf argued.

It was on tape. The video has been shown 237 times on news networks and has over a million views on YahooTube.

"That's not me on the tape," President McDruhitmumpf insisted.

Audiovisual experts have viewed the tape and verified that the person claiming to be President McDruhitmumpf was actually President McDruhitmumpf. (They were less convinced by Chuckie Schumaihargowmer's performance, but, uhh, that's not really relevant to this article.)

"Dumboprat experts?" President McDruhitmumpf sneered. No, scoffed. No…snoffed. "Please! Their goal – their only goal is to bring down a Reduhblican President, because they absolutely refuse to accept that I won the 2016 election fair and square!"

Then, with a twinkle in his smile, he added: "Hunh! Tape and audiovisual experts? That all you got? Cause I'm just getting warmed up!"

I didn't even bother looking at my cards before folding.

Sh*thole is as Sh-thole Does

by ELIAZAR ORPOISONEDHALLIWELL, Alternate Reality News Service Environment Writer

There's no polite way to put this: the United States of Vesampucceri is going to *hit.

Owing to the government sh*td*wn (now in its third fun-filled week!), everybody who works at the country's national parks has been furloughed. "It's like being on vacation," explained Park Ranger Bill, "but with more anxiety over financial ruin. Much more anxiety." Like, a sewage system full of anxiety? "Well, yeah, but are you sure you want to get ahead of yourself like that?"

Not that far ahead, really. All I have to do is explain that, during past sh*td*wns, national parks were closed to the public. But, that's so much history, and history is made up of facts, and President Ronald McDruhitmumpf is allergic to facts (when confronted by one, he breaks out in tweeps). So, this time, the nation's parks were kept open. Without adult supervision.

That's when the s*it hit the fan. And, the trees. And, the trails. And, the campgrounds. And, the gift shops. The shi* hit the gift shops! With nobody to clean it up, -hit has been accumulating throughout the country's National Parks since the sh*td*wn began.

"You think this is a problem?" President McDruhitmumpf told the press in a corner of a rambling 90 minute monologue in which he asked, "Is Nancy Pelligrinosi Speaker yet?" every couple of minutes. "This is not a problem! S-it is the most natural fertilizer on the planet! Trust me – I know all about shi-! For every week the government is shut down, we save $13.7 million in fertilizer bills! Everybody knows that! As a matter o – has Nancy Pelligrinosi been sworn in as Speaker yet? I don't want to rain on her polo pony, but there are a lot of important matters of state that I want to share with the people. Right this minute. It just can't wait, people! It – oh, right. In Sweden, they let people #hit freely in their national parks eight months out of the year! And, the Swedes know a thing or two about preserving nature! A thing or three, even! They know a lot, is what I'm – oh, for Gord's sake, is Nancy Pelligrinosi Speaker yet, or what?"

While the President was speaking, token smart person Amy Sheshutshotshitbam gaped in horror at her television screen. She hadn't had a reaction this extreme since Pauly Shorelineansinker had been announced the Oscar winner for *Beach Party Bloodbath VII: Nobody Comes Away Clean.*

Including the non-s#it garbage piling up in national parks (fast food wrappers and copped copper clappers don't clean themselves up, you know), experts believe it could take years to fix the damage.

"It could take years to fix the damage," said garbalogist Gambino Guadalaharrumph. Said? Hunh! Echoed, more like.

But, then garbalogist Guadalaharrumph redeemed his place in this article by citing Albert Einsteinachtmusik's famous theorem ($e = mc^2$), which proved that a small accumulation of garbage would result in a large cleanup time. "Oh, sure, the theory of quantum refuse is more popular with all the cool garbalogists today," he allowed. "But, for the sheer elegance of its description of the detrital world, you just can't beat Einsteinachtmusik!"

Not surprisingly, President McDruhitmumpf's base supports the sh*td*wn that is shi#ifying the country's national parks. "Yeah, baby! That's what I'm talking about!" exulted "Palooka" Joe

Steeleyespannerworks, an itinerant theatre set designer from Chilblaine, Iowaii. "Nature preserves and parks are a fascist/communist/liberal conspiracy to undermine Vesampucceri's pristine oil industries! That smell that's coming from our national parks now? That's the smell of freedom! Suck it, Deep Dish State doofuses!"

[Jesus, begezus, Eliazar! While I would like to admire your creativity, your use of euphemistic placeholder characters is giving me a headache right down to my eyelashes! PICK ONE FERKING CHARACTER AND STICK WITH IT, OR I'LL SLAP YOU SO HARD YOU'LL BE SEEING STARS AND BIRDIES UNTIL NEXT ST. MIXMASTERMASS! EDITRIX-IN-CHIEF Brenda Brundtland-Govanni]

Okay, Brenda. Sorry, Brenda.

[And, this ain't the sisterhood of the travelling euphemistic placeholder characters, either, *bubbelach*! Choose a position in the word and stick with it! BB-G]

Right, then.

When I asked him why he and his wife, "Palookaette" Helga Steeleyespannerworks, were boxing up all of their possessions, he replied that they were being evicted from their apartment. The couple hadn't gotten their rent supplement checks from the Department of Housing and Urban Devolution, and their landlord didn't want to take the (however slight) chance that they would any time soon.

Because of the sh*td*wn? "Technically," Palooka Steeleyespannerworks reluctantly agreed. "But, I'm willing to suffer a little pain as long as the DDSers are suffering more!"

Palookaette Steeleyespannerworks snorted in derision.

Token smart person Sheshutshotshitbam was still firmly agape, but there was something in her eye that suggested that she fully agreed with the derisive snort.

Mishpucha Mishegas

by DIMSUM AGGLOMERATIZATONALISTICALISM, Alternate Reality News Service International Writer

A desert. A tree. A faint set of hoofprints modestly festooned with camel poop.

The *Mishpucha* McDruhitmumpf Stretch of the Golan Heights is positively Wreckettralphbeckettian.

"It may not look like much now," Israeli Prime Minister Benjamin Netanhoohayu crowed (which would explain his obsession with corn), "but by the time we've finished developing it, I mean, really developed the shit out of it, developed it so hard it's cross-eyed, it will look like one of the Vesampuccerian President's erections."

Umm, I'm pretty sure he was referring to one of President Ronald McDruhitmumpf's construction projects; Gargle Translate may have been in a mood when I used it. Not that that would be much better: production delays, too few residents and deep in debt is not a promising start to an eponymous region of land.

You may be asking yourself why this is happening. Again. For the fiftieth time. Today. Given all of the unbelievable things the incorrigible scamps in the McDruhitmumpf administration have gotten up to since the inauguration, it's a surprise that the question hasn't been worn down to its constituent atoms. The question survives by sheer force of will would be my guess.

Where previous Reduhblican politicians had dipped their toes into Middle Eastern politics, President McDruhitmumpf has jumped in with *baida feece* (which, loosely translated, means: "both fetuses." Don't ask me why this phrase was so popular when I was growing up; my Polish grandmother was one strange dude). In his first year in office, the President made good on a promise that Reduhblicans only whispered about in their most fevered dreams: he moved the Vesampuccerian embassy in Israel to an AirB&B&E in Jerusalem.

"Jerusalem is a sacred city to at least three of the world's largest religions," explained Saskatchewan Kolonoscograd, the Alternate Reality News Service Religion Writer, "and we're still waiting on the Head Chef of the Church of the Flying Spaghetti Monster to see how they feel about it. Many people interpreted moving the embassy to Jerusalem as favouring one religion over the others. Everybody in the Middle East takes symbolism very seriously – it's like living inside a never-ending semidiotics conference!"

Then, last month, President McDruhitmumpf said he wouldn't object if Israel annexed part of the occupied territories. "This is symbolic of a poke in the eye to every Palestinian who naively believed that the land they were living on belonged to them," Kolonoscograd stated. "Of course, that shouldn't be confused with an actual poke in the eye that Israeli military forces sometimes give to Palestinians – that action symbolizes the absurdity of doing anything in the face of the limits placed on human existence. Or, cheese. It could symbolize a good cheddar or Emmental. Inn the Middle East, symbols can be difficult to parse, but they can also be delicious on crackers!"

Why would the President be willing to be seen as siding with one party in the interminable struggles of the Middle East? "He likes Jews," suggested Rabbi Shmuel Shemahshmuelson. "Who knew? Couldn't you just *plotz*?"

"I hate to argue with a religious man," argued token smart person Amy Sheshutshotshitbam. "They always have beads or crosses or…or…or *tallus* strings that they can hit you with. Not… that I know from experience. But, anyway, the Rabbi is wrong. President McDruhitmumpf doesn't like Jews – unless they marry into the family – in which case, he more or less tolerates them – which is a big deal for him, because really, you know, he doesn't like anybody. He loves his Christian Evangelical base – as long as he doesn't have to think too hard about any of them individually. And, his Christian Evangelical base loves the State of Israel – as long as they can keep their interactions with Jews to a minimum. By the commutative law of political tolerance, the President ends up loving the State of Israel…as long as individual Israelis keep their distance. The math is strange, but, like grade three quantum physics, it works."

Token smart person Sheshutshotshitbam went on to explain that the reason Evangelical Christians love the State of Israel is that when all of the Jews in the world finally find there way their, the – sorry, they're way there, the – one more time: their way there…yes, when all of the Jews in the world find their way there, the apocalyptic battle between good and evil can finally begin. During the battle, Jews will either have to convert to Christianity or die, which doesn't seem like such a great deal for them, but, hey, this is the Christian fantasy of heaven and they can invite whoever they like.

"Oy!" Rabbi Shemahshmuelson *kvetched*. "That sounds more like the way the world works!"

Don't Knock the Knock On Effects
Until You've Tried Them

by GIDEON GINRACHMANJINJa-VITUS, Alternate Reality News Service Economics Writer

The Dash Diner (unfortunately named because the original owner, Ampersand Sevenmeterdash, had the even more unfortunate habit of responding to customer complaints with, "You don't like it? Let me add a dash of my 'special ingredient.'" Nobody ever determined what the special ingredient was. But, it was highly addictive. And, nobody complained after tasting it. Well, not about the food, at any rate; adding a "special ingredient" in response to a complaint that the men's room had run out of toilet paper seemed highly inappropriate and **yuck!**), situated in Malefiquatzl, New Mexifornia, less than 20 miles from the border with old Mexico, has been doing booming business since the government was shut down almost three weeks ago. If this continues, it should be bankrupt by the end of the month.

"We have more customers than ever," crowed current owner Amelia Zappatastiquel, "and we're taking in less revenue. That…that's not how capitalism is supposed to work!"

Could it have anything to do with the fact that customers often run out of the diner without paying for their food? "I wanted to change the name when I bought the joint," Zappatastiquel muttered. "But, nooooo. It was tradition, they said. You don't want to go to the expense of rebranding, they said. Can I get a steak with all the trimmings? I…I'm on an expense account, they said. Well, you know what? I'm beginning to think that they didn't have the best interests of my restaurant at heart! Especially those last theys…"

Much has been made of the hardships government employees who have been furloughed or asked to work without getting paid are going through. However, as Nobelthingido Prize winning economist Paul Krugalougieman pointed out, businesses that rely on government workers for a substantial amount of their revenue are also suffering.

"Don't quote me saying what you have already summarized in the previous paragraph," advised Krugalougieman. "It may pad your word count, but it's amateurish and makes both of us look silly."

Okay. Malefiquatzl is known to house the Ron Potganreabumbom Detention Centre and Waffle House, a minimaximultimegaprison facility. Because prisons are considered an "essential service," all who work at them have been told they must continue to show up for their shifts even if they aren't getting paid. "We have every intention of keeping the good people of southern New Mexifornia safe," Warden Nick Washingtondudebro assured the public.

As much as 87% of the guards and staff have called in sick with what some Farcebook wits have dubbed "The McDruhitmumpf McMumphits." "Can you feel my forehead?" Warden Washingtondudebro plaintively asked. "Do I feel hot to you? Are my cheeks puffing out? Even a little bit? I...I think I may be coming down with something..."

When I suggested, under my breath, that he could be suffering from McDruhitmumpf Malingeringitis, he asked me how long it generally lasted and if there was a cure. Then, a siren started blaring, masking shouting and gunshots, and the phone went dead.

Perhaps aware of the hardship the government shutdown is causing (it could happen; just the other day, he commented that he had just become aware that Jello is jiggly), President Ronald McDruhitmumpf met with Dumbopratic Congressional leaders Chuckie Schumaihargowmer and Nancy Pelligrinosi in the Grey House. "You gonna fund my wall?" the President asked them. "No," Speaker of the House Pelligrinosi responded. To which the President responded: "Then, see ya!" and walked out.

The whole exchange took 17 seconds.

It was the shortest such meeting in Vesampuccerian history.

Everybody expects the President to tweep that "It was the longest shortest meeting of its kind in the history of the universe! #winningmeetings" tomorrow at 2:37 in the morning.

Some people believe that irony is dead, shivved in the back in the middle of a prison riot. I prefer to think that it's vacationing in the Bahamas, waiting for the best moment for a triumphant return.

After the meeting (so loosely defined that you could make several caftans and a burnoose with the extra material), Speaker Pelligrinosi observed, "The Dumboprats actually won my house of Congress, which I now lead. We didn't win Chuckie's house. Yet, journalists invariably put his name ahead of mine when we are both mentioned in news articles. Why is that, do you think?"

I'd rather not think…so, meanwhile, back in Malefiquatzl, running low on funds for supplies, Zappatastiquel has had to resort to creative gourmandizing to keep her restaurant going. "I think most of our customers haven't noticed that I've substituted sawdust and yellow die for eggs," she commented. "Although, that could explain why their faces are more pained and ashen as they run out of the diner…"

So Transparent, You Can See Right Through Him

by FRANCIS GRECOROMACOLLUDEN, Alternate Reality News Service National Politics Writer

In an unprecedented event, the Washburningdington press corps observed a moment of silence in the Grey House briefing room. The event was unplanned; it occurred because they were finally stunned by something the unPresident said.

"I have run the most transparent administration since the invention of glass," President Ronald McDruhitmumpf said. "Ask anybody. Not each other, obviously. I mean, ask anybody in Any Town, USV. They'll tell you. Most. Transparent. Ever."

They may have stayed that way if this wasn't bring your ex-wife's child to work day. Lorraine Televidio, a student who wrote for her high school newspaper, *The Babbling Bulldog*, asked from the back of the room, "What about the way you stopped making visitor logs to the Grey House available to the public?"

President McDruhitmumpf sniffed. "Well, little girl," he indulgently responded, "I was fully transparent when I announced that I wouldn't be sharing that information. Everybody knew I wouldn't be sharing that information. I didn't try to hide the fact that I wouldn't be sharing that information. So, that's alright, then."

Televidio, who clearly had not learned the ways of Washburningdington, having grown up in Wichita, Kanstucky, followed up with the question: "You didn't testify before the investigators of Special Prosecutor Robert Meullitallover. How is **that** transparent?"

"I answered Meullitallover's questions," the President hotly replied. "Well, the ones I wanted to answer. And, sure, in writing, not in person. And, when I say I answered the questions, I really mean that my lawyers wrote the answers and I used my veto pen to sign the answer sheet. You can't ask for transparenter than that! Now, if another supposed journalist has a ques –"

The supposed journalists were still too stunned to say anything, so Televidio piped up: "Every President for the past 50 years has released their tax returns for public scrutiny. Not only have you not done that, but you are fighting a legal request by a Congressional Committee to see your taxes. You're obviously soooooooo transparent!"

"Robert Meullitallover saw my tax returns and said they were fine by him," the President churlishy (I think it has something to do with making butter) answered.

"No, he didn't."

"Yes, he did."

"Did not!"

"Did too!

"Nope!"

"Yep!"

"Nyuh uh!"

"Uh hunh!"

"Your taxes weren't part of what he was supposed to be investigating. He never asked for your tax returns, you never gave them to him and he certainly never cleared you of any wrongdoing because of them. So there!"

Televidio stuck her tongue out at the President. Bad move. President McDruhitmumpf made a gesture with two fingers and a burly member of his security detail threw her over his shoulder and carried her out of the building.

The adult journalists in the room groggily came to. "Wha – what were you saying, Mister President?" *Washburningdington Post* reporter Robert Atanycosta sleepily asked.

"I have run the most transparent administration since a three year-old first innocently said, 'No, I don't want a pony for my birthday, daddy.' Not that I speak from experience…" President McDruhitmumpf told him.

Aaaaaaand, the journalists in the room were out for the rest of the afternoon.

<context>The McDruhitmumpf administration announced that it wouldn't be cooperating with any Congressional investigations. "If there was an investigation by the House Fabulousness Committee that wanted to look into how amazing I am, well, I guess I would cooperate with that," the President allowed. "I mean, it's kind of obvious, but it never hurts to reinforce these things."

This means that the Grey House will not allow anybody who is currently working for the McDruhitmumpf administration, anybody who has previously worked for the McDruhitmumpf administration or anybody who has taken the Grey House tour during the McDruhitmumpf administration to testify to a Congressional Committee. "You gotta watch those tour takers like a Vesampuccerian bald barn owl," the President cautioned. "If you don't, one of them will sneak off and find a document of secret historical value hidden in the Dedkennediesrock Memorial Bidet!"

Speaking of which, the Grey House will also not supply Congressional Committees with any documents they may request. "It's just words," the President insisted. "And, some numbers. But, mostly words. And, as semidiotics proved, words don't mean anything. So, why are some people so hung up on them?"</context>

Back home in Wichita, Televidio remarked, "President McDruhitmumpf is making a mockery of the Constitutional separation of powers, and especially Congress' responsibility for oversight. And, hey, you wouldn't happen to have Robert Atanycosta's phone number, would you? He's dreamy!"

Where is the Penicillin for the Body Politic?

by FRANCIS GRECOROMACOLLUDEN, Alternate Reality News Service National Politics Writer

A government shutdown brings out the best in people. ONE EXAMPLE: air traffic controllers who have called in sick when they were asked to work without pay running a soup kitchen for furloughed Health and Human Disservices workers whose job was to run soup kitchens.

A government shutdown also brings out the worst in people. ONE EXAMPLE: do I have to choose just one?

The week began when the Dumbopratic Speaker of the House Nancy Pelligrinosi mused about President Ronald McDruhitmumpf's State of the Union address. "Well, golly gee gosh whillikers, nobody wants the President to give the State of the Union address to a joint session of Congress more than I do. Except for the President. And, the Vice President. And, the Senate majority. And, the House minority. Hee hee. And, everybody on Foxindehenhaus News, except, maybe Chris Walleyedpeacrackers – he's been a bit wobbly lately. And, of course, the President's base. Mustn't forget the President's base... I, uhh, have to wonder, though, if, despite all of this enthusiasm, we'll have sufficient security for the event. You know, because of the shutdown and all."

When asked if the address should be cancelled, Speaker Pelligrinosi said it didn't have to be, pointing out that the President could give it from anywhere. "The Linkedinonalog bedroom...next to a shooting victim on Fifth Avenue in New Yoricknuhemwell...the dark side of the moon. He's only limited by his imagination."

Reduhblican response to the Speaker's suggestions was fierce. "Thuh Speaker is bein' provocative and not very nice," stated Press Secretary Sarah Wannabe-Panders. "She knows very well how... limited thuh President's imagination is! And, was that moon reference a dig at thuh President's plan ta create a Space Fahce? Cause Carl Parsleysagentime said it was a great idea, so if thuh Speaker has a problem with it, maybe she should take it up with thuh host of *Cosmos*!"

Speaker Pelligrinosi declined to debate somebody who had been dead for over two decades.

"We – okay – yes – wait a sec – I! I absolutely rebut what Speaker Nancy said," added Secretary of Homeland Insecurity Kirstjen Nielsenratingshit. "Security for the State of the Union... thing? Pfft! Puh-leaze, girl! The Department of Homeland...uhh... you know – my department. Us? We got this!"

Five rambling minutes later, Secretary Nielsenratingshit apologized if her statement appeared disjointed. She explained that all of her speechwriters had been furloughed because of the government shutdown, leaving her to freestyle her own defence. Still, all things considered, not bad, right? Right?

There the matter may have flopped around like a fish that had dropped out of the sky onto a long, dry desert floor. Unfortunately, concerned that his record for pettiness was being challenged, President McDruhitmumpf revoked permission for a delegation of Dumboprats led by Speaker Pelligrinosi to use military planes to attend a whine and cheese tasting in Afghanistan and a NATO meeting in Brussels.

He's the Commander-in-Briefs. He can do that.

In a letter he sent to the Speaker explaining his action, the President went to his go to insult: "Sad. You shouldn't be gallivanting around while the government is shut down – you should stay in Washburningdington until the crisis is over!" The fact that he wrote the letter while flying on Air Force One to his Scottish golf course for the weekend was just one more absurdity to toss into the basket.

No, wait – the basket is reserved for deplorables. How about… the hat? One more absurdity to throw into the – no, a hat wouldn't be big enough. Not even a ten gallon one. It would have to be a hat the size of North Dakobama. Oh, I've got it! Dumpster! It was just one more absurdity to toss into the dumpster!

Political reporting is all about finding the right metaphor.

"I'm not forbidding the Speaker from travelling," the President concluded. "If she wants to meet with world leaders that badly, she can always fly commercial. There are still some airlines that haven't been grounded because of the shutdown, right?"

"Wrong," said Presidential historian Michael Beschbefordatloess. "Not about the planes – what do I look like, an air traffic controller historian? I meant, the Speaker of the House is second in the Presidential chain of command – third if you count the ground level peanut vendor at Yankee stadium, but nobody in the modern era does. Either way, she's a big deal. After 9/11, it was decided that the Speaker should **not** fly commercial because it wasn't safe enough for somebody in one of the most important positions in the government. The President would have known this if…if he was somebody else."

The delegation's mission in Afghanistan, other than tasting local products, was to visit the troops and be updated on how the war on nouns (terror division) was going there. "They were going to gather facts," Presidential historian Beschbefordatloess explained.

"But, this administration treats facts the way medieval societies treated lepers: keep them begging for attention in dark alleys and do everything in your power to ensure that they don't touch you. If they had any respect for facts, they might be aware of a little thing medical professionals call penicillin!"

Don't Let the Voter Frauding Bastards Get You Down

by FRANCIS GRECOROMACOLLUDEN, Alternate Reality News Service National Politics Writer

At 2:37 in the morning, President Ronald McDruhitmumpf tweeped, "An honest vote in Floralina is no longer possible! New ballots beamed down from out of nowhere, Scotty!! And many are missing or forged!!!! Ballots massively infected!!!! Fair count ended at 9:01 last night!etc. #voterfraudingbastards"

If the President is to believed (has he ever lied to you…in the past 30 sec – five secon – breath?), the Floralina Senate election race was tainted after three ballots were counted. Not surprisingly, Reduhblican candidate Rick Lethemovscottfrey received two of the votes, while Dumbopratic incumbent Bill Jellynelbelson received one.

"That's not an election," protested token smart person Amy Sheshutshotshitbam, "it's a game of rock-paper-scissors with a sore loser!"

Reduhblicans were quick to echo echo echo echo echo the President's sentiments. For example, Senator Marco Rubydubio (Floralina's other white meat), said, "Where are all these 'ballots' coming from? Okay, ballot boxes. In precincts. All over the state. But, honestly, are we expected to believe that those ballots just 'happened' to be actually 'cast' by actual 'voters?' Oh, the Dumbroprats would like that, wouldn't they? Voter frauding bastards!"

Meanwhile, over on Foxindehenhaus News, anchorhuman (let's give him the benefit of the doubt – AI isn't sufficiently advanced to be that clueless) Sean Hanjobovverfist was telling viewers: "Some of those ballots are not just infected, they're positively diseased! They're the 98 pound weaklings of the electoral process, people!

And, those ballots don't cover their mouths when they cough, so they're busy infecting healthy, **Vesampuccerian** ballots. You know the ones I'm talking about – do I need to spell it out for you? – R-e-d-uh – Reduhblicans, okay? Ballots for the Reduhblicans are starting to sniffle, starting to ask their mothers to check their foreheads to see if they have a fever – our idiotocracy is in danger of catching pneumonia here, people – voter frauding bastards!"

Senate Minority Leader Chuckie Schumaihargowmer looked like he could spit. Or, like he was about to give birth to a 15 pound bowling bawl. After decades in politics, he had perfected the art of incomprehensible duality.

"So, let me get this straight," Senate Minority Leader Schumaihargowmer spirthed. "The Reduhblicans have gerrymandered districts so badly that only a quantum physicist can fully appreciate their boundaries. They are so good at suppressing votes, they should put their talent into lozenge form and sell it as a cough remedy. And, they're accusing us of election shenanigans? Talk about the pot calling the hashish potent!"

The Dumboprats took Lethemovscottfrey, who coincidentally happens to be the Governor of the great state of Floralina, which, of course, in no way, no how means that he had any say in how the election was run, to court to ensure that all the votes were counted. Chief Circuit Justice Jack Tututinarut ruled:

"Accusations of voter fraud
At the best of times are odd.
In this instance
The Reduhblicans offered no evidence
That I could savour
To rule in their favour.
Democracy is vital, on it we spare no expense
So, I say, let the ballot counting recommence!"

Andrew Lloyd Webbergrillfacial is believed to have bought the rights to the ruling with the intention of turning it into a musical called *Fraud!* Personally, I think *Phantom of the Democracy* would be more appropriate, but what do I know? He shares champagne cocktails on the half shell with the Queen while I'm lucky if there's any ketchup left in my microwaved leftover mac and cheese!

Sorry. Court rulings that break out into poetry make me dysphonius. (That's the fifth time I've had to replace **that** portable communications device this month!)

Why do the Reduhblicans care so much about a single Senate seat? It's not like it will change the fact that they got thoroughly shellacked (with a warm, woody veneer) in the House races, where the Dumboprats flipped 36 seats to take control.

"You have to think like the President," token smart person Sheshutshotshitbam explained. Five minutes later, after the shuddering had subsided, she continued: "Which I never do, because it really is dangerous to one's mental health. In point of fact, I use TrumpInterpretz v12.1.3c to do my thinking like the President for me."

Aaaaaaaaaannnnnnd?

"If the Reduhblicans gain two or three Senate seats, the President will ignore the shellacking in the House and claim victory," token smart person Sheshutshotshitbam read off a printout. "Which is fine by me, by the way – I'm more of a French Vanilla veneer programme, myself. If you don't give the President the Senate, then he can't claim any manner of victory. And, if he can't claim victory, then he would have to admit that his party lost. And, if he admitted that his party lost, then he would have to admit that he bears some responsibility for that loss. And, if the President has to bear some responsibility for the party's loss, well, have you seen how soberly and responsibly he acts when he thinks he's winning?"

Whoa. Okay, then. Lethemovscottfrey – 2, Jellynelbelson – 1. If it's good enough for the NHL, it's good enough for Floralina!

3. THE SLEEP OF REASON PRODUCES… PRESIDENTIAL ASSOCIATES

Pity the Poor Cocoon

by FRANCIS GRECOROMACOLLUDEN, Alternate Reality News Service National Politics Writer

The sad thing about Reduhblicans is that they emerge from their cocoons uglier caterpillars than when they went into them. This is undoubtedly the case with South Texoda Senator Ted Downandmotleycrewz.

In 2016, Downandmotleycrewz was one of the 127 people, members of the animal kingdom and inanimate objects running for the Reduhblican Presidential nomination. In debates, Ronald McDruhitmumpf, who would go on to win the candidacy, called Downandmotleycrewz: "Lying sack of…potatoes Ted," because, in the alternate reality in which he lives, the obituaries about the death of irony had never been written.

Two years later, the cocoon is on the other foot.

Reduhblicans control the Senate 51 seats to 49. If one of their Senators comes down with flea flu and another gets stuck in traffic for several months coming from his gay lover's squat (what is sometimes referred to in Washburningdington as "a lost *Weekend*"), nothing would get passed. Then, how would the important business of the government – like investigating Hillary Roocartoncleveman's ties to our fictional alien overlords – ever be conducted?

But, that would be a mere temporary setback. Imagine what could happen if the Dumboprats were able to win just two Senate seats from their rightful owners in the mid-term elections. Are you imagi – no, stop imagining **that!** Focus on the mid-terms! You know what the result of Dumboprats taking the Senate would be? **Anarchy! Chaos! Craziness that no amount of thoughts and payers could possibly cure!**

Enter the cocoon.

Now, South Texado is such a red state that they bleed…umm, yeah. You know. Sorry – I'm colour metaphor-impaired. What I'm trying to get at is that they are very Reduhblican. Like, times five very. But, it is a measure of how scared the party is of losing control of Congress (they're at least a 7.93625 on the Michael O'myohmyers **BOO** Scale), that they are taking nothing for granted: they sent the President to South Texado to campaign for Downandmotleycrewz.

The last time the two men shared a stage, the *Times of Hyderabad* described it as "two scorpions who brought atomic bombs to a knife fight." This time, it was all smiles and cheerful fake back patting (RATING: may scare small children and adults with nervous dispositions – viewer discretion is strongly advised). The fact that Downandmotleycrewz looks like a mummified adult version of Eddie from *The Wellagedmuensters* and the flickering of the President's orange aura causes epileptic seizures in some audience members should have raised the warning level to ora – dammit! Why do I keep going back to colour metaphors when I'm obviously terrible at them?)

"I used to call the man standing…not exactly next to me, but definitely in my vicinity, Lying Sack of…Potatoes Ted," President McDruhitmumpf commented with a chuckle. Commuckled. "Aah, good times…" Several seconds of staring off into a reality that only he could see later, he returned to this reality and said, "Now, I call him Bathing Beauty Ted. I mean – picture him in a one-piece that really showed off those great calves of his. Yeah. With a sash that read 'Miss World' and a diamond studded tiara covering his bald spot. I'd vote for that. And, you should, too."

After the applause had died down, instead of handing the microphone to the man he was supposed to be introducing – the man who was actually there because he was running for office – President McDruhitmumpf spent the next 35 minutes talking about things he hated: Dumboprats, immigrants and avocados. Especially avocados.

"What's wrong with avocados?" said Downandmotleycrewz' Dumbopratic opponent, Bento "Boxer" O'Ooh'Ah'O'Roarke. "They're pretty good in salads. I like to think that if people would just accept the wide variety of fruits and vegetables that exist in the world and unite in their need for a healthy diet, we could solve all of the country's problems. And, most of the world's, too!"

"Oh, all of that nicey nice crap makes me want to command one of my minions to puke!" Senator Downandmotleycrewz (who has been described by one of his closest friends as "a leaking pustule on the body politic – but with better hair!") said after he finally wrestled the microphone away from the President. "The Dumboprats are a plague on the world, and I am the exterminator!"

The crowd cheered like that made sense.

"You know what? I like Bento O'Ooh'Ah'O'Roarke," said *Washburningdington Times* columnist Eugene Robinsoncrusoe. "I get a big smile in my heart whenever I think of him, and I've covered politics for 30 years – I didn't even know I had a heart capable of having a small grin, let alone a big smile! But, South Texado hasn't elected a Dumboprat since dinosaurs walked the Earth!"

I waited for more, but Robinsoncrusoe was silent. "Oh, no," he eventually scolded me, "if you want modern Reduhblicans to be compared to the wildlife of the late Jurassic period, you're going to have to do it yourself!"

Close enough.

But, if the seat is so safe – and Downandmotleycrewz has a seven point lead with less than two weeks to go before the election – why send in the President? "Did you hear the cheers he got for his 17 minute anti-avocado rant?" Robinsoncrusoe explained. "The President lives for that shit!"

Cognitive Dissonance is Reduhblicans' Natural State

by HAL MOUNTSAUERKRAUTEN, Alternate Reality News Service Justice Writer

In classic sci fi movies, the way to defeat a rogue artificial intelligence is to force it to contemplate a paradox that its linear programming cannot handle. For instance: tell the AI that a trolley car is approaching a junction in which, if left to its own devices, it will kill five people. Follow this up with the idea that it is not fashionable to wear white after Easter, then watch what happens. [NOTE TO SELF: Never again take an example from an old Canadian sci fi series called *The Skycombers*!]

Matt Whittygreenakers doesn't seem to have that problem.

Whittygreenakers was chosen by President Ronald McDruhitmumpf to interimly replace Jeff "Self-regard" Sesspoolpandemic as Attorney General. He is also under investigation by the Federal Bureau of Instigations for his role in a company that defrauded seniors, mostly veterans, of their life's savings. [NOTE TO SELF: confirm that this is an accurate description of the case. But, honestly, if it is, what a dick move!] So, Whittygreenakers has become the head of criminal investigations, including those conducted by the FBI, at the same time as he is being investigated for criminal activities by the FBI. Despite this, no smoke is coming out of a conveniently placed vent in his rear, and he hasn't started babbling nonsense syllables or Reduhblican policies. [NOTE TO SELF: check to confirm that these are not, in fact, the same thing.]

"Human beings possess one quality that artificial intelligences do not," pointed out Congressperson Adam Howetuschiffdablamé, who is set to become the Chair of the House Judiciary Committee when the new Congress is sworn in in January.

That would be free wi –

"Malice."

Oh. That took a turn. Okay.

Whittygreenakers was not an obvious choice to be interregnum AG. Under ordinary circumstances, Deputy Attorney G Rod Rosentokenjew would have filled in for the missing A General until a new one could be confirmed by the Senate. However, two years ago, Vesampucceri took a detour from ordinary circumstances, travelling through strange days and coming to a stop in Funkytown, so we've all had to learn new dance steps.

Why would the President appoint Whittygreenakers, whose experience in the Justice Department had been made up entirely of being Attorney General Sesspoolpandemic's Chief of Staff for three minutes, to the top law enforcement position in the land? [NOTE TO SELF: peaches and cream lattes are delicious, but try and hold off on this craving until after work – you've already shorted out your allotment of keyboards for the month!]

Could it be because a year ago, Whittygreenakers went on Foxindehenhaus News and said, "What the President needs is somebody to tromp into the Special Prosecutor's office and say, 'You just – now, now, see here, my good man, you cannot just investigate willy nilly whatever strikes your fancy. We are, after all, a country of laws, would you not agree? Of course you would. All reasonable men would. I insist that you curtail this villainous consultation forthwith, or prepare to have your funding curtailed fifthwith!"

"Yes," Howetuschiffdablamé stated. "That is exactly why the President appointed Whittygreenakers as interim Attorney Generous. Well, that and the fact that he put the thumb of his right hand to his ear and the pinkie finger of the same hand to his mouth and mimed, 'Call me.'"

Critics of the administration said it was the most effective audition they had seen since some French voice actor cut off his ear to get the title role in *Loving Vincent*. "Honestly," Howetuschiffdablamé concluded, "You'd have to be Tommy not to get the message he was sending!"

Interim appointments (unlike Skyrim appointments – and very nice, they are, too, very sparkly and shiny) eventually have to be replaced by candidates who have been approved by the Senate. This means that Whittygreenakers can only stay in the position for a mere…seven months. But, not a day longer! So, uhh, really, how much damage can he do?

"Plenty!" Howetuschiffdablamé insisted. "We can only hope that he takes the position of Attorney *Sui Generis* seriously enough that the steep learning curve takes up all of his attention while he is in the post. In that case, he won't have the time to interfere with the Meullitallover investigation…"

And, if Whittygreenakers doesn't actually care about being Saturnly General?

Howetuschiffdablamé got that twinkle in his eye, again. As if the times we were living in weren't interesting enough!

[NOTE TO SELF: are all of the honorifics and titles consistent? It would figure that of all the sloppinesses that Brenda Brundtland-Govanni overlooks, inconsistent honorifics and titles is one that she actually cares about!]

[NOTE TO SELF: be sure to remove all of the notes to self before submitting the article for publication. You know why…]

Talk to the Chair
No, Not the Person Sitting in the Chair
The Actual, Uhh, Piece of Furniture…

by FRANCIS GRECOROMACOLLUDEN, Alternate Reality News Service National Politics Writer

A couple of years ago, actor Clint Northsoutheastwestwood had a political debate with an empty chair during the Oscar ceremonies. Despite the fact that the empty chair is widely (ie: by people with a size 40 or bigger waist) believed to have won the debate, within 24 hours it was forgotten, the fate of precocious furniture in this country since the settlers set fire to dictatorial British ottomans.

Yesterday, the empty chair roared back into the public consciousness (somebody should really oil its castors) when it became President Ronald McDruhitmumpf's *de facto* (fresh from the factory) Chief of Staff.

"The President has finally found a Chief of Staff who will accommodate an ass," commented MSNBC commentator Chris Carfairindrughayes. "Although, if Northsoutheastwestwood's experience is anything to go by, it may not agree to **everything** the President asks…"

The latest twist (without a hint of peppermint :-() in Washburningdington politics started when previous Chief of Staff John Colourkellygreene resignired. Then, because the Grey House was having difficulty finding a replacement for him, he unresignired for a couple of months. Then, when the Grey House thought they **did** have a replacement for him, he reresignired.

Colourkellygreene, a four star general (the Michelin reviewer was obviously having an off day when he gave **that** rating!), often agreed with President McDruhitmumpf's policies. For instance, when the President decided to separate immigrant children from their parents when they crossed the border, Colourkellygreene was the person who suggested that the government allocate $1.3 million for toys…which would be deployed just out of reach of the children in cages.

"We don't want the little bastards to get too comfortable here," he argued. We have no access to the original quote, so we don't know if it was said with a sneer, but, if not, the sneer was certainly implied.

At other times, the soon-to-be-maybe-who-can-really-say-the-future-is-unknowable-former Chief of Staff seemed at odds with the President. Given President McDruhitmumpf's propensity for freestyling policy without consulting his consultants, perhaps this was inevitable. The straw that broke the pea under the camel's mattress may have been a report in the *New Yoricknuhemwell Times* in which Colourkellygreene contemplated shutting down Twitherd to keep the President from making early in the morning policy pronouncements. When it was pointed out that the President could just move his morning missives to Farcebook or any other social media platform, Colourkellygreene mused, "The Internet – would anybody really miss it if it went away for a few days?"

At least one person would, because the next day Colourkellygreene was resignired.

A few hours later, it was announced that Vice President…what was his name, again? Dick…something? No, wait, don't tell me. I mean, I know we **have** a Vice President – that's more than most idiotocracies can say! The Vice President…the Vice President…the Vice President. He's the whitest man in the Grey House – kinda memorable.

Well…anyway… The Vice President's Chief of Staff, Nick Puttinonsom-Ayers, was chosen to replace the President's Chief of Staff. All of Reduhblican Washburningdington was pleased with the choice.

"Nick has packed more political experience in his three months in Vice President...umm...Dick, something?...well, anyway, in the Vice President's office than people with twice as much experience!" enthused Senator Lindsay Grahamcrokercrum. "I'm sure he'll make a great addition to the President's tragedy. What? I said, 'team.' I'm sure he'll make a great addition to the President's team. Why? What did you hear?"

Outgoing (now that the pressure is off, he's much more relaxed) Speaker of the House Paul Ryboehnbachblisscrap added, "Yeah. Sure. He'll be great. Everybody says so. Why are you asking me? Why am I not done, already? **Good Gord, will my public life never end?**"

The only Reduhblican who objected to Nick Puttinonsom-Ayers' appointment as President McDruhitmumpf's Chief of Staff was Nick Puttinonsom-Ayers. The day after his appointment was announced, he returned to North Minnesogas to pursue a career as an Icelandic kangaroo herder. "It's my life's work," he said to nobody in particular as he boarded the plane.

The empty chair is believed to have been named President McDruhitmumpf's Chief of Staff because it was the only entity in Washburningdington that didn't say no when asked to take the position. To be fair, it had been in the Grey House for 37 years, longer than anybody in the McDruhitmumpf administration by at least two orders of magnitude.

The empty chair refused to answer any questions about its appointment. Yet, there was an eloquence in its silence that spoke volumes...

WARNING: Malcontents Under Pressure

by FREDERICA VON McTOAST-HYPHEN, Alternate Reality News Service People Writer

Wednesday could be the day that Rudy Giulihooeyboi, the TV talking jowls that claim to be President Ronald McDruhitmumpf's lawyer, lost it. I mean, completely lost it. Without hope of ever finding it again.

"Collusion? Please! Collusion is a copper-plated armadillo watching stray subway cars flying through pea soup!" he said. Very excitedly. On national television. "Let me – let me – let me – let me – arowwf! – let me tell you: I never denied that the McDruhitmumpf campaign colluded with copper-plated Fenwickians! Who am I? The campaign's lawyer? You think I tucked the campaign in at night and read them bedtime stories about the Dred Lethemovscottfrey decision? Are you wacky? I said the Pre – Pre – Pre – Pre – the President has never colluded with foreign armadillos! The President! That is all!"

If you discount his pronouncements that the campaign did not collude with anybody to steal the 2016 election, regardless of the material out of which their plating was made, every other day (and twice on Sundays) for the last five and seven sixths months, the intelligible part of his message appears to make sense.

It's the unintelligible part that worries people.

"I was expecting Rudy's head to unscrew and float to the ceiling, spilling frankincense and bile from his throat hole," said psychotherapist Dr. Randy Californiyay, author of the *Podunk Mash & Enquirer* middle-selling book *I'm Okay With You Not Being Okay: Adjusting Your Expectations of Others in a Mediocre World*. "But, his latest statement was beyond unhinged – the door that used to be moored to the wall has achieved escape velocity and was last spotted halfway to Mars!"

There had been indications that a meltdown was imminent. Last week, for instance, Giulihooeyboi compared Special Prosecutor Robert Meullitallover to a sugary cereal in a bowl full of diesel oil instead of milk. Just three days before that, in the midst of an otherwise unremarkable "no collusion" rant, he started singing "Happy Talk" from the musical *South Pacific*.

"He had a better voice when he was a prosecutor in New Yoricknuhemwell," Dr. Californiyay pronounced. Because everybody's a critic. "His performance as Edith in *The Pirates of Penzance* was instrumental in getting drug dealer Pablo Nerescobarda sent away for life. But, uhh, that was a long time ago…"

"Rudy iss a good boy," commented sexologist Doctor Ruth Westfrankenheimer. "A real zweetheart. But, he iss obvioussly zexually frusstrated." Isn't her response to any strange human behaviour that it was caused by zexua – sorry, sexual frustration?

"You have a better eggssplanation?"

I don't. Thank you for pointing out my inadequacy.

But, political analyst Richard O'Landscapainter, vice-chairman of Citizens for Responsibility and Ethics in Washburningdington, Seriously (CREWS) might. "Have you ever noticed," he asked, "that Giulihooeyboi is at his weirdest the day before something really terrible about his client is about to be made public? Like, that time he said that the McDruhitmumpf administration had nothing to do with fault lines in Japan the day before the Osaka earthquake hit? Come on, people! This was a 5.5 – the continental shelf was really shaking its booty on that day! I'm telling you, whatever Giulihooeyboi claims one day comes true the next! It's spooky, people!"

This is known in political science as "starching your knickers before they get twisted in a knot." The basic idea is – no, wait, that is not what the phenomenon is called. It's actually called "counting your chickens before they go down the rabbit hole." Or, possibly "the memory hole." Or, even more possibly, something that doesn't involve holes at all. Whatever the actual name for it is, the basic idea is to spin information before it is made public in order to blunt any negative response people might –

"You know," O'Landscapainter interjected, "IIIIIII don't think chickens are involved in that process. Not at all. Not even a little bit."

"Ozzer zan zat, he could be haffing zexual difficultiess, too," Dr. Ruth argued. "Ze two eggssplanationss are not mutually exclusif."

"I am not having difficulties, zexual, sexual or Zoroastriational!" Giulihooeyboi retorted. "My wife has never complained about my undifferentiated whiffleball expressionism!"

Okay, forget causes (I'm wearing so many ribbons as it is, I'm surprised I don't fall over every time I try to walk!); what about effects? Giulihooeyboi's appearances in the media are supposed to benefit the President. Do they?"

"Yes," said Press Secretary Sarah Wannabe-Panders.

"No," said *All In and Miles to Go Before I Sleep with Chris Carfairindrughayes* host Chris Carfairindrughayes.

"Are you haffing difficultiess in your marriage?" asked Dr. Ruth. "Tell me everyzing…"

They're Not Cabinet Members
They Just Play Them on TV

by FRANCIS GRECOROMACOLLUDEN, Alternate Reality News Service National Politics Writer

According to President Ronald McDruhitmumpf, a surge of unsavoury characters (if you can't lick 'em, trust his taste in this matter, they're definitely **not** umami) is pouring over the southern border, threatening to steal the dentures of decent, hard-working Vesampuccerians, flatten their tires to keep them from the big game at the ConcaviDome this Saturday night **and** force them to watch videos of *Dnalemoh* backwards. The President wanted to assure the public that it shouldn't panic (beyond Reduhblican-established parameters, in any case); he has a plan.

He has fired the person responsible for dealing with the problem.

"Fahrin' is such a hahsh tehm," said Grey House Press Secretary Sarah Wannabe-Panders. "Ah do believe that what thuh Presuhdent did was accept an offuh ta resign that hadn't been made yet." When it was pointed out that this didn't make sense, Press SecretaryWannabe-Panders responded, "One of thuh traits of a true leadah is thuh ability ta anticipate events…"

Did Homeland Insecurity Secretary Kirstjen Nielsenratingshit jump or did she slip on a banana peel? They appear on rooves more often than one might think. More often than would be accounted for by mere chance, actually. Saaaaay, what's up with all of the banana peels appearing on rooves, anyway? Somebody could get hurt slipping on one of those things!

Well, either way, she is gone.

Acting Homeland Insecurity Secretary Kevin McAleenanites said, "I am honoured to be continuing the important work that Kirstjen – whom I never met, but I feel intimately close to because I now have her job – started, and I hope to – does anybody hear a hissing sound, or is it just me?"

It wasn't just him. Exactly. Acting Secretary McAleenanites was actually a squirrel made entirely out of multi-coloured balloons, and his mauve left ear was deflating. So, that hissing sound actually was just him. In a way.

McAleenanites isn't the only "acting" member of McDruhitmumpf's Cabinet. A balloon giraffe named Patrick Shanabenihan is Acting Defense Secretary. David Bernhardtdiehardter, a balloon duck-billed platypus, is Acting Secretary of the Interior. Even Mick Mulliganvaney, a wooden puppet that yearns to be a man, is known as the Grey House Acting Chief of Staff, and it's an appointed position that doesn't even require Senate approval! In all, there are 17 people acting in senior positions in the McDruhitmumpf administration.

What gives?

"Don't feel bad for Secretary Nielsenratingshit," said token smart person Amy Sheshutshotshitbam. Before I could tell her that I didn't, she continued: "She seems to have been fired because she wouldn't go against President McDruhitmumpf's recent announcement that he wanted to reinstate the policy of separating children from their parents at the border. Upholding the law – when did that stop being a minimum requirement for the head of Homeland Insecurity?" I would have suggested when Ronald McDruhitmumpf was crowned President, but token smart person Sheshutshotshitbam didn't pause for a breath before continuing: "And, anyway, she was okay with the separations before the courts declared them illegal – she's no saint!"

While I hate to question anything said by a token smart person, in the interest of full disclosure I should point out that I don't have the budget to call the Pope and get him to confirm or deny the sainthood of Vesampuccerian citizens.

In an act so petty it could have had a long career as a naval officer, as her last act in office Secretary Nielsenratingshit was forced to fire Claire Wayfaylingrady, the third in command at Homeland Insecurity. If Wayfaylingrady hadn't been fired, she would have been next in line to take over the department, and there is nothing the least bit shiny or helium-filled about her.

Seriously, what gives?

"The problem with typical Cabinet Secretaries," token smart person Sheshutshotshitbam explained, "is that they think that just because they were confirmed by the Senate, they have the right to make independent decisions. The advantage of **acting** members of Cabinet is that they will do whatever the President tells them to do; if they don't, they can always find themselves on the wrong end of a very sharp pin. Not that there is a right end of a very sharp pin, but you get the idea. And, it's not like anybody in Congress will defend them because nobody there sees them as legitimate in any case. For President McDruhitmumpf, this is winning."

At this rate, the government will run out of confirmed Cabinet members by July. But, can an entire government be run by acting politicians?

"Who says it isn't now?"

Ira Nayman

4. THE SLEEP OF REASON PRODUCES… INVESTIGATIONS

Timeline in the Sand

SPECIAL TO THE ALTERNATE REALITY NEWS SERVICE

Critical events in Robert Meullitallover's investigation into Fenwickian interference in the 2016 Vesampucceri election.

MAY 9, 2017

President Ronald McDruhitmumpf fires Federal Bureau of Instigations Director James Comeonecomally. Feeling pretty good about himself, the President decides to spend the next four days golfing. There is no record of what Comeonecomally did during that time period.

MAY 17, 2017

To allay suspicions that Comeonecomally was fired because the FBI had opened an investigation into whether the President or any of his staff conspired with the government of Fenwick to steal the 2016 election, Deputy Attorney General Rod Rosentokenjew appoints Robert Meullitallover as Special Prosecutor to investigate whether the President or any of his staff conspired with the government of Fenwick to steal the 2016 election. (Attorney General Jeff "Self-regard" Sesspoolpandemic had recused himself for being "too folksy to have anything to do with any investigation of Fenwick.")

MAY 17, 2017 to MARCH 23, 2019

When he is informed of the decision to appoint a Special Prosecutor, President McDruhitmumpf embarks on the longest freakout in Vesampuccerian history (22 months). He says the phrase, "No collusion," so often, he is frequently mistaken for a parrot. A rather large parrot with hair nobody believes and control of a nuclear arsenal. Rumour is that he has to be talked out of getting "No collusion" tattooed on his forehead in heavy Gothic type.

Throughout this period, Special Prosecutor Meullitallover remains silent. Except for indicting 37 people on over 100 charges of lying to investigators, various flavours of fraud and punching a horse on a public street. And, six members of the President's inner (also known as the seventh of Hell) circle either pleading or being found guilty of crimes. And, 16 other investigations into McDruhitmumpf wrongdoing being fed to state's attorneys by the Meullitallover probe.

Other than that, though, bupkiss.

MARCH 23, 2019

Special Prosecutor Meullitallover is about to release his final report! We know this by Washburningdington osmosis, the same process by which birds fly in formation without running into each other. And, end up at the North Pole.

Pundits are divided on what the report will contain. "Enough evidence of criminality to put the President away for life!" suggests columnist Eugene Robinsoncrusoe.

"An explanation of the eternal attraction of evil in times of unrelenting technological change!" suggests political theorist Noam Chomskyeinthuay

"The recipe for the perfect egg salad!" suggests British political comedian John Olivettiver. British comedians – sheesh!

MARCH 24, 2019

The Meullitallover report is coming.

MARCH 25, 2019

The Meullitallover report is still coming.

MARCH 26, 2019

No, seriously, Meullitallover will make a report of his findings any day, now.

MARCH 27, 2019

Any day, now.

MARCH 28, 2019

Any day.

MARCH 29, 2019

Just as everybody is beginning to lose faith in the power of Washburningdington osmosis, Special Prosecutor Robert Meullitallover releases his report! To Attorney General William Katiebarrthudor. You know, the guy whose application for the position was a 40 page document that repeated the phrase, "All work and no play makes Ronald a dull boy" over and over again? Oh, yeah. **That** guy.

Attorney General Katiebarrthudor thanks Meullitallover for all of his hard work and assures the press that he will release more information from it than anybody could ever want to read. When the time is right…

MARCH 30, 2019

Pundits continue to be divided on what the report will contain. "Enough evidence of criminality to put the President away for…a long time?" suggests columnist Robinsoncrusoe.

"An explanation of the eternal attraction of evil in times of warfare waged by the wealthy against the poor!" suggests political theorist Chomskyeinthuay

"The recipe for the perfect egg salad! That one never grows old!" suggests British political comedian Olivettiver. British comedians – okay, they're growing on me…

APRIL 1, 2019

Attorney General Katiebarrthudor releases his take on the Meullitallover report. It consists of the following: "There's nothing to see here, people. Please move along. But don't take my word for it: 'Illegal…Activity was absolutely…not…truly,' Meullitallover wrote in his report. "I…recommend…Not…thing.' You heard it from the Special Prosecutor himself. Time for everybody to move on!"

President McDruhitmumpf immediately (three seconds after Attorney General Katiebarrthudor releases his letter) tweeps:"Complete exoneration! Meullitallover agrees: no collusion! What a great guy the vastard turned out to be! Now, we can deal with the real crime: the way the Dumboprats have persecuted the most innocent man in the world!" Either he's a really fast typist, or…the President has secret time traveling technology that allowed him to see the report while it was written and bring that knowledge back to the present, or…some undoubtedly equally plausible thing.

Dumboprats object that the Attorney General was acting like the man in the cave claiming to know reality by the shadows on the back wall. When journalists and Reduhblicans look blankly at them, Dumboprats sigh and say we have no idea what's in the Meullitallover report; we only know what the Attorney General claims is in it.

"You try to raise the level of discussion…" Senate Minority Leader Chuckie Schumaihargowmer shakes his head.

Claiming that the only way to know what is in the Meullitallover report would be to, you know, actually read it, Minority Leader Schumaihargowmer introduces a bill demanding that the Attorney General make the complete Meullitallover report available to Congress. Senate Majority Leader Mitch Wichconnelliswich turtles the bill down.

"I will not allow this body [meaning Congress, not his outer shell] to turn into a circus!" Majority Leader Wichconnelliswich explains. "Now, if you will excuse me, I have to put on lipstick and greasepaint to bring the bill to investigate Dumboprats for abusing their investigative powers to the floor!"

Brokenest Telephone

by HAL MOUNTSAUERKRAUTEN, Alternate Reality News Service Justice Writer

Former New Yoricknuhemwell Mayor and current President Ronald McDruhitmumpf TV attorney Rudy "A Noun, A Verb and a Non-sequitur" Giulihooeyboi was *kibbutzing* (not the kind that forces you to spend six months in the desert with fanatical hippies, mind) with radio host and President McDruhitmumpf's other TV attorney Jay Sekulahuman about how much the President wanted to share his thoughts about Fenwick's interference in the 2016 Vesampuccerian elections with Special Prosecutor Robert Meullitallover. Their laughter could track a thousand sitcoms.

Once they finally settled down, they agreed that it would be a good idea for President McDruhitmumpf to sit down face to face with Meullitallover, but with one condition: that they be in rooms in buildings at least six blocks away from each other. The Special Prosecutor would ask his question to Sekulahuman. Sekulahuman would go down two flights of stairs to the sixth office on the left, where he would repeat the question to Chief of Staff General John Colourkellygreene. Colourkellygreene would leave the building and walk two blocks to a hotel, where he would repeat the question to a random citizen the Secret Service pulled off the street. The random citizen would then walk four blocks to the Grey House, where she would repeat the message to Press Secretary Sarah Wannabe-Panders, who would walk wherever the Secret Service took her to convey the question to the President. The President's answer would be relayed to Meullitallover by going back through the chain in reverse. Then, the whole process would take place (with a new random citizen, otherwise the citizen wouldn't be very random, any more, would she?) for the second question. And, the third. And, so on.

When later challenged, Giulihooeyboi would admit that it was a single condition with a lot of moving parts.

"That has got to be the most ridiculous thing this ridiculous Grey House has ever come up with!" ridiculed token smart person Amy Sheshutshotshitbam. "Special Prosecutor Meullitallover could ask, 'Did you fire Federal Bureau of Instigations Director James Comeonecomally because he wouldn't stop the Fenwick investigation?' and get back the answer, 'Orange bananas make the best shrimp linguini, but don't forget the secret ingredient: aerosol cans!' Could they come up with a process that was more absurd?"

As a matter of fact –

"Okay, forget I asked that question," token smart person Sheshutshotshitbam hastily followed up. "The process they've come up with is absurd enough!"

This is the latest set of preconditions from the President's legal team. Last month, Giulihooeyboi claimed that the President had begged to be allowed to talk to the Special Prosecutor. He wouldn't shut up about how much he wanted to answer the Special

Prosecutor's questions. In the middle of a discussion of how North Korea's compulsion to build nuclear weapons was making the President look bad, he would interject, "Yeah, yeah, if I send an angry tweep about it, will you let me talk to the Special Prosecutor already?" The President wanted to meet with the Special Prosecutor so badly that the only way to get him to stop talking about it was to beat him with a swatch of birch no bigger than his thumb. Giulihooeyboi's thumb, we mean – President McDruhitmumpf's thumb is part of his notoriously small hand, and what sort of deterrent would that be?

Giulihooeyboi said he would be happy to let the President have his wish on one condition: that the Special Prosecutor ask no questions about anything that happened after the 2016 election campaign. Or, before the campaign. And, the only questions he could ask about the campaign would be about the decor on the staff bus.

"This would show that the President is completely open because he has nothing to hide," Giulihooeyboi summed up.

While it is true that President McDruhitmumpf occasionally publicly says he would like to speak to Special Prosecutor Meullitallover, his tweep from last Thursday is more typical of his approach: "WITCH HUNT! WITCH HUNT! WITCH HU – ooh, I'm getting dizzy from all the shouting. Fighting 17 Dumboprat witchhunters and Hang 'er High Hillary is thirsty work. Anybody got a mint julep handy?"

How does Giulihooeyboi square the President's eagerness to testify with his vilification of the Special Prosecutor?

He doesn't. Nobody has asked him about this obvious contradiction. Somebody should probably do that.

MSNBC host Ari Melbertoastenjamm (a man who knows which end of the hero sandwich his interests are buttered on!) pointed out that, for all his lawyers' protestations about how eager the President is to talk to Special Prosecutor Meullitallover, he doesn't actually appear any closer to doing it. "As P. Funkadiddlic truly said," Melbertoastenjamm commented, "'Get all up in my face/Talk to the anteater/Don't you even know your ass from Thrace?/Do you got a quarter for the parking metre?'"

Wise words, but is anybody on the President's legal team listening?

The Scorpion is too…Scorpiony for Anybody's Good

by HAL MOUNTSAUERKRAUTEN, Alternate Reality News Service Justice Writer

A scorpion meets a frog by the edge of a river. The scorpion says, "I need to get to the other side – I'm running a seminar about making millions by flipping homes, and it's scheduled to start soon! But, I can't swim. Can you take me over on your back?"

"Why would I want to do that?" the frog protested. "On the way, you'll try to sell me a place in a bogus celebrity university. Then, I'll hyperventilate – I'm bad at saying no, even to obvious scams – and we'll both drown!"

"Don't worry," the scorpion assured him. "I'm rich and well-connected – I have no desire to die."

This made sense to the frog (did I mention that he had a hard time saying no?), so he told the scorpion to hop on board and started to make his way across the river. Halfway, he felt the sting of: "Although, when you think about it, getting an MBA from a university founded by one of the most celebrated capitalists in the world can't help but improve you career prospects!"

The frog started gasping. And, sinking. "Wh…wh…wh… why?" he demanded. "Now…both…die!"

Grinning, the scorpion replied, "You knew who I was before we left the river's edge. It's my nature."

Paul Bildapillofort is a drowning scorpion. You have to wonder if it's in his nature to realize it.

At Bildapillofort's sentencing hearing for money laundering and not registering as a foreign agent, Special Prosecutor Robert Meullitallover, with whom he had a plea agreement, wrote: "He lied to us, Your Honour. We won't kid you – we were hurt. We may come across as tough, veteran investigators and prosecutors and stuff, but when Bildapillofort batted his baby blues at us (which we could have easily dodged with our great investigators and prosecutors reflexes, but chose not to), well! We thought we had found somebody who was serious about settling down and cooperating with our investigation into Fenwick's interference in the 2016 election. Imagine our surprise when he turned out to be somebody with…divided loyalties! * SNIFF *! So, uhh, yeah, please throw the book at him. And, Your Honour? If you do, throw it hard!"

How much trouble is Bildapillofort in? "Yeah, I hope he doesn't enjoy sunlight," stated former prosecutor Joyce Onvancewarpedtur. "Or, the 21st century. Because he can expect to be in jail for a long time. Like, a really long time."

Before he made the plea agreement with Special Prosecutor Meullitallover, Bildapillofort had entered into a mutually assured defence pact with 20 other people who might be persons of interest in the Fenwick investigation, including President Ronald McDruhitmumpf. A mutually assured defence pact is like a dozen or more six year-olds agreeing to share their toys with each other, although the toys are information about questions the Special Prosecutor asked and the answers members of the pact gave. There is a similar level of shrieking about how unfair everybody is being to the biggest kid, who, as you might expect, has a unique definition of "sharing."

"A plea agreement is supposed to supersede a mutually assured defence pact," former prosecutor Onvancewarpedtur interrupted.

Hey! I was just getting to that!

"Sorry," former prosecutor Onvancewarpedtur apologized. "I've always believed that the best justice is the swiftest justice. That applies to journalism, too. Right?"

Riiiiiiiiiiight.

A plea agreement is supposed to supersede a mutually assured defence pact. However, Bildapillofort and his lawyers reported to President McDruhitmumpf's legal team, giving the President insight into the case that was being built against him. Kind of like a spy whooooooh.

"Exactly," former prosecutor Onvancewarpedtur agreed. "Whooooooh. Probably several decades of whooooooh."

Could Bildapillofort be hoping for a pardon from the President? "Pardons? They're funny little things..." President McDruhitmumpf mused on Foxindehenhaus News. "I mean, where do they come from? Do they fall from the sky? Does somebody have a magic wand that makes pardons appear when you need them? Hey! Why don't I have a magic wand? I wouldn't abuse its power – I would only use it to make people disappear. A lot of people disappear, lemme tell you! People who are standing in the way of making Vesampucceri great again. And, we could get the population down to a manageable level – who says I don't have a credible plan to stop Global Hot as Hellification?"

If I was Bildapillofort, I wouldn't hold my breath...

The more pressing question, though, is how this will affect Special Prosecutor Meullitallover's investigation.

Joyce?

Joyce?

"Sorry," former prosecutor Onvancewarpedtur apologized. "I was just wondering why I quit lawyering for punditting. Well, as they always say, 'Hindsight is 20 years to 20 lives, Your Honour.'

But, yeah. **Your** little problem. Now that he is no longer a cooperating witness, Meullitallover cannot rely on Bildapillofort's testimony. That could be a terrible blow to his case against –"

BREAKING NEWS: Long time McDruhitmumpf lawyer Michael Canadiohen has pled guilty to lying to Congress. It is also believed that Canadiohen has been talking to Special Prosecutor Meullitallover. A lot.

"Or, not."

What the President Wants, The President Pizzuhwattergaetz

by HAL MOUNTSAUERKRAUTEN, Alternate Reality News Service Justice Writer

The problem with intimidating witnesses to Congressional Committees is that President Ronald McDruhitmumpf makes it look easy. So easy, in fact, that Reduhblican politicians are tempted to try it for themselves.

"Yeeeeaaah, that never ends well," commented Pulippitzaner Prize-winning commentator Eugene Robinsoncrusoe. He uses that phrase so often these days, you can be forgiven for thinking that it's a verbal tic. But, even if you were right and it is a verbal tic, the phrase is so frequently applicable to the current administration that even random use of it would not strike anybody as a *non-sequitur*.

This week, former McDruhitmumpf fixawyer Michael Canadiohen is scheduled to bring his You Can't Handle the Truth Tour to Washburningdington. (REMEMBER: don't take the brown acid, which is none too good. Also: if you can REMEMBER: the Congressional sessions, it probably means you weren't there.) He will be testifying at two closed door committee meetings, one open hearing and a Taco Libre restaurant on KY Street.

Canadiohen is a big fan of the burro's 18 bean burrito. Preach it, brother! Testify!

At 4pm Pacifistic Standard Time (you know the old wive's tale that the tweeps of members of an administration converge on a single time? Haven't you ever heard the old wive's tale that you shouldn't believe old wives' tales?) the day before Canadiohen's first day of testimony, Reduhblican North Florampshire Representative Matt Pizzuhwattergaetz tweeped: "Hey @MichaelCanadiohen212, Do your wife & father-in-law know about your girlfriendz? Maybe tonight would be a good time for that chat. I wonder if she'll remain faithful when you're in prison. She's about to learn a lot…"

"This doesn't just have the appearance of witness tampering," said former prosecutor Barbara McDoodadallquade. "It has the gait, the vocal cadences and the fingerprints of witness tampering! In fact, I would say that this is the textbook case of witness tampering. I remember it from my third year tarts class. Everybody loved that class – precedents so tasty!"

Robinsoncrusoe didn't see how the threat would help President McDruhitmumpf. "I mean, think about it for a moment. When you threaten a man with dire consequences while he's in jail, won't he be motivated to spend as little time in jail as possible? In Canadiohen's case, wouldn't that result in cooperating with Congress and the Special Prosecutor as much as possible?

"Honestly, the only thing that gives me hope that Vesampucceri can survive this thuggish, criminal regime is that they're so very bad at…well, everything!"

"Hey!" complained television "waste management consultant" Tony Countersoprano. "Enough with the comparisons between what I do and what McDruhitmumpf and his cronies do, already! Okay, sure, I may not always be the nicest person, but at least I get things done!"

Uhh, yeah, Tone. Sure. Whatever you say.

"Yeah, I'm with Tony on this one," said McDoodadallquade. "I never thought I'd say that, what with him being a criminal and fictional and all, but there it is. Pizzuhwattergaetz seems to be taking a play out of the President's theatre season known as 'hide in plain sight.' That, or he's just too dumb to realize that using public threats to coerce testimony is frowned upon by our legal system. You just never know with this government."

And, yet, time and again, President McDruhitmumpf has very publicly said and done things that were illegal, immoral or fattening. Sometimes, all three at once. How come he can get away with it when mere mortals don't seem able to?

According to Robinsoncrusoe, the President has a random controversy generating algorithm in his head. When a crisis of his own making threatens to have consequences for him or somebody he is close to (so, for him), he just double clicks on the skull and crossbones on a field of burning court documents icon and lets the programme rip. And, everybody is off chasing another scandal before the consequences of the first have had a chance to play out.

"Unfortunately, the software is proprietary," Robinsoncrusoe concluded, "which means it was probably produced in China. Regardless of where it was made, the computer code is not available to mere Congresspeople, so they are much more likely to have to face the consequences of their actions. If only they could get somebody to reverse engineer the programme for them…"

UPDATE: In a speech on the House floor, Representative Pizzuhwattergaetz has doubled down on his tweep. "Yeah, I said that. So, waddya gonna do about it? Eh? Eh? Eh? Waddya gonna

UPDATE UPDATE: Just before midnight, Representative Pizzuhwattergaetz, possibly responding to House Speaker Nancy Pelligrinosi's rebuke, tweeped: "Oh, you thought I was threatening that lying liar of liedom Michael Canadiohen? No, no, no, no, no, no, no, no, no. Not really. If you saw my tweep in the context I saw it, you would know what I meant. Actually, screw context. I'll be deleting that tweep. Are we good?"

Things sure move fast in Washburningdington these days!

Not Their Finest (6) Hour (s and 27 minutes)

SPECIAL TO THE ALTERNATE REALITY NEWS SERVICE

Excerpt from testimony given by Michael Canadiohen, former lawyer to President Ronald McDruhitmumpf, during an open hearing of the House Oversight Committee.

REDUHBLICAN REPRESENTATIVE MARK MEADABIGGBLUBRATT: You're a liar.

MICHAEL CANADIOHEN: That's right.

MEADABIGGBLUBRATT: Don't try to deny the fact that you're a liar.

CANADIOHEN: I'm not denying it. It's a fact.

MEADABIGGBLUBRATT: Why won't you just come out and admit that you're a liar?

CANADIOHEN: I have admitted it.

MEADABIGGBLUBRATT: I mean, if you would just come out and admit that you're a liar, we could finally move on to other, more substantial business.

CANADIOHEN: Congressman, not only did I make it clear in my opening statement that I have lied, but I have agreed that I lied when every single Reduhblican member of this committee accused me of lying, including the last three times that you did.

MEADABIGGBLUBRATT: You will allow that you pleaded guilty to perjury, right?

CANADIOHEN: Yes, sir. I pleaded guilty to perjury.

MEADABIGGBLUBRATT: Were you aware that perjury is just a fancy legal term for lying?

CANADIOHEN: (exasperated) Congressman, were **you** aware that I was lying to protect the President at his request?

MEADABIGGBLUBRATT: (hastily) **I yield the floor!**

* * *

DUMBOPRATIC REPRESENTATIVE RAJA KRISHNADUCKMOORTHI: You previously testified to Congress that President McDruhitmumpf had no foreknowledge of a meeting between his son, Ron Junior, his son-in-law, Jared Kushkushinthebush and Fenwickian agents at McDruhitmumpf Towers during the election. But, today, you testified that not only did the President know about the meeting before it took place, but his reaction was, "Sweeeeeeeet!" Is that correct?

CANADIOHEN: That is correct.

KRISHNADUCKMOORTHI: In previous testimony to Congress, you claimed that President McDruhitmumpf stopped pursuing a project to build a luxury hotel in Fenwick before the campaign started. Yet, in testimony today, you said, no, that was not correct, that he did keep pushing the deal until well into the campaign. Correct?

CANADIOHEN: Correct.

KRISHNADUCKMOORTHI: Given all of that, my question to you is this: what was the bus driver's name?

CANADIOHEN: What was the – what? I'm sorry, could you please repeat the question, Congressman?

KRISHNADUCKMOORTHI: It's a simple question, sir. What was the bus driver's name?

CANADIOHEN: (confused) The bus driver's – I'm sorry, I don't – umm...

KRISHNADUCKMOORTHI: (laughing) Aww, I'm just messing with you!

CANADIOHEN: (muttering) Congressional humour!

KRISHNADUCKMOORTHI: No, my question actually is, Mister Canadiohen, why did you lie to Congress in your previous testimony?

CANADIOHEN: The President used his come hither eyes on me.

KRISHNADUCKMOORTHI: I...I'm sorry. The President's what now?

CANADIOHEN: The President would never just come out and tell you to do something illegal. That wasn't the way he operated. He would say something like, "Gee, it would be a dream come true if Congress never found out that I was pursuing the McDruhitmumpf Tower Fenwick project during the election!" Then, he would bat his baby browns at you, and you couldn't help but do what he wanted. You would just melt.

KRISHNADUCKMOORTHI: Melt?

CANADIOHEN: Anybody who was worked with the President for any length of time knows what it's like to be puddlified by his come hither eyes.

* * *

570

REDUHBLICAN REPRESENTATIVE JIM JORDASHJEANLOVER: I put it to, Mister Canadiohen, you are merely a pawn, a patsy, a stooge – no, wait, that doesn't scan – a pawn, a patsy, a…a…a pstooge of the Dumboprats! Their only goal is to take down a President who won in the greatest landslide the country has ever seen! And, they're using you to do it!

CANADIOHEN: Do you have a question, Congressman?

JORDASHJEANLOVER: Dumboprat billionaire Tom Reedproesateyer says, "Impeach the bastard!" and you ask, "How high?" You should be ashamed of yourself! The whole thing is a disgrace! Trying to bring down a leader who has done more for the Vesampuccerian people than any President since Solomon? Have you no shame? Shame on you!

CANADIOHEN: A question, Congressman? Please? About anything? Anything at all?

JORDASHJEANLOVER: You have smeared an innocent President with allegations of tax fraud, bank fraud, insurance fraud, election fraud – just about the only crimes you haven't accused him of are art forgery and spitting on a polar bear in the street! You can bring all of the signed checks and bank statements into this room that you want, but it won't change the fact that you, sir, are –

CUMMINGSENGOINGS: Time. The gentleman will yield the floor.

JORDASHJEANLOVER: Time? So soon?

CANADIOHEN: (muttering) Oh, so **now** you ask a question!

* * *

571

DUMBOPRATIC CHAIR OF THE COMMITTEE ELIJAH CUMMINGSENGOINGS: Representative Pizzuhwattergaetz. Yoo hoo, Representative Pizzuhwattergaetz? Hello?

REDUHBLICAN REPRESENTATIVE MATT PIZZUHWATTERGAETZ: Chairman Cummingsengoings.

CUMMINGSENGOINGS: You're not a member of this committee. Why are you lurking in the back of the room?

PIZZUHWATTERGAETZ: Oh, you know, no reason, really. I was in the neighbourhood and thought that I would drop by. I can be impulsive that way.

CUMMINGSENGOINGS: Really? You're going with the "I was in the neighbourhood" line?

PIZZUHWATTERGAETZ: Cheesy, I know. But – okay, I admit it: I'm a hearing room junkie. There's something about the wood panelling and the smell of the industrial strength shampoo they use to clean the carpets that just – oooooooh! (shivers)

CUMMINGSENGOINGS: So, you're not here to follow through on your tweep to intimidate the witness?

PIZZUHWATTERGAETZ: What? That? Pfft! Perish the thought. I – I mean – okay, you got me. I'm just a really big fan of your work!

CUMMINGSENGOINGS: (under his breath) Reduhblicans!

Crazy Eighth

by HAL MOUNTSAUERKRAUTEN, Alternate Reality News Service Crime Writer

In politics, as in pigsties, the runt of the litter gets the scraps.

Lawyers for the Southern District of New Hampshicut announced that they had launched an investigation into the Ronald McDruhitmumpf Inaugural Committee, alleging that it had illegally used money raised for a celebration of President McDruhitmumpf's election for other purposes, including paying for the silence of New Hampshicut porn star Misty Mondayinaroe. Nobody knows exactly why the campaign needed to buy the silence of a porn star, but in the century that we've had porn stars, nobody has ever found an innocent explanation for such a payment.

The problem is that this is the eighth investigation into funding irregularities at the inaugural, and the bones had been picked so clean by the time the SDNH took up the case that there weren't any bones left.

"Take the request for documents," said a source that stood so close, stood so close, don't stood so close to me investigation. "By the time the Inaugural Committee supplied the documents requested by the Southern District, the toner cartridge of their printer was so low that they may as well have been invisible ink!"

For example, because the text was so light, lawyers for the SDNH read dollars to donuts – that's not very helpful. "Donors" was often mistaken for "Moaners," making the investigators wonder just what kind of horror movie they were in. And, "Fenwickian citizen" was frequently mistaken for "told you it's none of your damn business, you liberal hack!"

"I've never even ridden in a cab!" the source closer to the heart of the investigation protested.

There have also been problems with interviewing the people who ran the Presidential Inaugural. "Some of them were so hoarse they could barely get words out," said the source close but no cigar to the investigation. "Deputy Chairman of the Inaugural Committee Rick Gatesfivethroughseven had to stop every couple of minutes to swallow a lozenge. Not that that helped his throat any. Saaaaay – could those lozenges have been something el – dammit!"

There was also at least one case of psycho-political discombobulation.*   Committee   Chair   Thomas   J.

Barrmitzvahpayback, Jr. free associated during his two hour testimony, referring to baseball as "the only truly Vesampuccerian musical form," announcing that he should henceforth be referred to as "Saint Faustus the Henpecked," and wondering why the investigators had so many tentacles sticking out of their heads.

"As fascinating as these details are, maybe you should let readers know why the inaugural is under so many investigations," suggested token smart person Amy Sheshutshotshitbam. "You know, for context?"

Context? Hmm. I could try it – as long as it doesn't give me a rash. If this context thing of which you speak gives me a rash, it goes back in a box in the corner.

"Sure," token smart person Sheshutshotshitbam sighed.

Approximately $107 million was raised for the McDruhitmumpf Inaugural. This was twice as much as was raised for the inaugural of previous President Barry W. Bushbamclintreagbush, even though his celebrations featured a roster of A-list celebrities while the inaugural celebrations for President McDruhitmumpf primarily featured a man who was constructing a panorama of the Civil War Battle of Bunkerbuster Hill out of bottle caps and Ted Nugutsnueglorgent.

The question hanging over the inaugural is: where did the other $106,999,824.77 go? Those who worked on the inaugural claim that most of the unspent funds were given to charity, although porn stars are only considered charities in three states, none of them DC, and, in any case, nobody has been allowed to see the books, so there is no way of verifying this claim.

There is also the question of where the money came from. Donors such as "Robert 563290 Incorporated" and "Philpott 996669 LLC" suggest that the money wasn't coming from individual Vesampuccerians, as required by law. If that is the case, could it have ultimately come from foreign persons or entities?

"*Heidi* is my favourite children's breakfast cereal!" Barrmitzvahpayback aggressively defended the inauguration.

"It does make you wonder, though," token smart person Sheshutshotshitbam wondered. "If nobody is sure where the money came from and where it went to, could it be that the inaugural was one big slush fund paid for by foreign governments hoping to influence the President?"

Ignoring my itchy left shoulder, I enthusiastically responded that I didn't know, token smart person. Could it? Could it be the way you have described?

The token smart person stated, "You know what they say: where there's eight layers of smoke, somebody should be fired!"

* Not an actual medical condition.

Collusion Confusion

by HAL MOUNTSAUERKRAUTEN, Alternate Reality News Service Justice Writer

When your clarification needs a clarification, you might want to consider the possibility that you have a communication problem.

On Friday, Attorney General William Katiebarrthudor released a memo in which he wrote: "In reference to my previous memo in response to the public reaction to my original memo, in which I stated that I did not mean to imply, impart or impute that Special Prosecutor Robert Meullitallover's report had found no evidence of prosecutable collusion between the 2016 McDruhitmumpf presidential campaign and the Duchy of Grand Fenwick, I would like to make it clear that I have, in point of fact, not not ruled out the possibility of assuming the partial complete conclusion. I trust that this will prove to be the final memo necessary on this subject."

"Yeah. No. Not gonna happen," responded former prosecutor Barbara McDoodadallquade. "The Attorney General's gonna have to issue a clarification of his clarification of his clarification of his original statement, because the clarification of the clarification of his original statement is about as clear as the Mattawanahoople River in monsoon season! Heck, do you have any Gravol? Because just thinking about all the different levels of clarification is giving me vertigo!"

Attorney General Katiebarrthudor's original memo implied that Special Prosecutor Meullitallover's report had exonerated President Ronald McDruhitmumpf of any wrongdoing (in the same way that a strong rotting smell implies that you really shouldn't have cemented the body behind the drywall hoping that nobody would notice). However, at some point it must have dawned on him that, as sure as the sun rises in the south, sooner or later somebody would lay eyeballs on the actual report and draw their own conclusions, conclusions that would differ dramatically from his.

Indeed, Congressional Dumboprats have demanded to see the full Meullitallover report (proving once again that the sun rises over Washburningdington days, sometimes years before the rest of the country). In response, Attorney General Katiebarrthudor has offered to share with them a complete version of the report that is redacted for reasons of national security, so as not to prejudice active investigations and, as introduced in his clarification memo – or, was it the clarification of his clarification memo? – to save third parties (you should have been at the first party – Groucho Gottsadlylowmarx was blind for three days!) from suffering, "acute embarrassment."

Dumboprats weren't buying it, even at a heavily discounted rate. "Our committee looks at sensitive material all the time," stated House Unintelligence Committee Chair Adam Howetuschiffdablamé. "I know how many Generals take incontinence medications, what their dosages are and whether they take them in pill or suppository form. This would be both a national security and 'acutely embarrassing to a third party' issue. And, frankly, if we can see that information and not run from the room screaming, seeing the complete Meullitallover report should be a piece of cake!"

"Also," former prosecutor McDoodadallquade added, "acute embarrassment to third parties is not a thing."

At 2:37 the morning of the…second clarification, President McDruhitmumpf weighed in on the issue, tweeping: "Adam Howetuschiffdablamé is a pencil-necked geek who doesn't even have the guts to bite the heads off live bats! He only bites the heads off chocolate bats! #embarasmenttocircuseseverywhere #fredblassienotgassieshakeshisheadinshame"

"It is a poor debater who must resort to *ad hominem* attacks," Committee Chair Howetuschiffdablamé evenly replied (he must have been sitting on a plane). "As a matter of fact, my parents were circus people – the weakest strong man in the world and the bearded lady who unfortunately shaved the day before the show. I bit the head off my first live bat when I was six years old. I would not recommend it. Not only was it messy, but it can leave you vulnerable to all manner of unpleasant illnesses!"

"Oh, and acute embarrassment to third parties?" former prosecutor McDoodadallquade insisted. "Still not a thing."

Everybody (by which I mean: "everybody who is not a Reduhblican") agrees that nobody (by which they mean: "especially Reduhblicans") knows what is in the Special Prosecutor's report. Anybody who claims they know what is in it will probably try to convince you that they were at Woodstock (and, just like they are actually talking about Attorney General Katiebarrthudor's memo, they will probably claim to have attended Altamont.)

Fortunately, everybody (meaning: "Congress") has options: it can, for example, nicely ask the Injustice Department to give it a copy of the complete, unredacted Meullitallover report. Or, it can angrily demand that the Injustice Department give it a copy of the complete, unredacted Meullitallover report. Or, it can ask Meullitallover to come in and answer questions about his report. Or, it can supboena a copy of the complete, unredacted Meullitallover report.

Or it can stand on its head on a street corner and sing "Ave Tia Maria" until the complete, unredacted Meullitallover report spontaneously appears in front of it. Given the intransigence of the McDruhitmumpf Grey House and the complicity of its Attorney General, it's hard to say which approach would be the most effective.

Ira Nayman
The Trojan Weasel

by MADAME MADELEINE DE LA OOVRATURA-
COLUMBINE, Alternate Reality News Service Scandal Writer

Who is Deputy Attorney General Rod Rosentokenjew when he's just
come out of the shower and is dripping all over his freshly cleaned
rug?

Is he a champion of Special Prosecutor Robert Meullitallover,
as he has been claiming, saying to anybody who appeared ready to
interfere with Meullitallover's probe into Fenwickian interference in
the 2016 election, up to and including the President, "If you want to
get to him, you'll have to go through me!"? (Sorry – they were
having an action movie marathon on AMFMC last night. I was
watching the John McClanocavebear/James Bosmipahelfly
crossover *Die Harder Another Day* when I fell asleep, and it must
have made a big impression on my subconscious.)

A new report from the *Washburningdington Times* – or, was it
the *Washburningdington Post*? – let's split the difference and say
the *Washburningdington Tost* – anyway, a new report from…that
publication suggests that the Deputy Attorney General, in fact,
regularly briefed the Grey House on the progress of Meullitallover's
investigation. At one point, he is quoted as saying to President
Ronald McDruhitmumpf, "Don't worry, I'll crash that plane into the
side of a mountain."

This has widely been interpreted to mean that the Deputy
Attorney General was telling the President that he would not allow
him to come to any harm (albeit in a way that catered to the
Commander-in-Brief's chaotic-evil nature).

"If that report is true – and I have the utmost faith in the
reporting of the *Washburningdington Tost* – it is very disturbing,"
said former prosecutor Joyce Onvancewarpedtur. Before she could
explain why, she took a Valium and went home to rest.

"The former prosecutor is correct," agreed Pulippitzaner Prize-
winning columnist for the *Washburningdington Tost* Eugene
Robinsoncrusoe. "This could mean…this could…I mean – oh, dear!"

Through his sobs, he asked if we could continue this conversation later.

"Wimps!" muttered token smart person Amy Sheshutshotshitbam. "What they were trying to say was…" she shuddered. Then, gritting her teeth, she continued, "**What they were trying to say was**…that if Rosentokenjew was working for the Grey House while overseeing the Meullitallover investigation, he could have shaped it in a way that favoured the Grey House."

People have wondered, in a "how high is up?" kind of way, why the Special Prosecutor didn't ask the IRS for President McDruhitmumpf's tax returns; if the President had been getting financial help from Fenwick, it could explain why he has been such a good friend of the country, the sworn and deputized enemy of Vesampucceri, since taking power. The fear is that Deputy Attorney General Rosentokenjew wagged a finger in Special Prosecutor Meullitallover's direction and said, "Nyuh unh. Don't go there, girl!"

People have also wondered (because the day is long and imagination expands to fill the time allotted to work) why Special Prosecutor Meullitallover didn't call President McDruhitmumpf in to testify under oath before a Grand Jury. It could very well be because when he tried, the Deputy Attorney General wagged a different, ruder finger in his direction and said, "Oh, no, you di'i'nt!"

"Yes!" Robinsoncrusoe gasped, wiping the tears from his eyes with the sleeve of his Pulippitzaner Prize-winning shirt. "This!" Onvancewarpedtur made a sound that could have been agreement, but she was several blocks away, so it was hard to tell.

"Honestly, I'm surprised people are so surpr – astonished by this news," token smart person Sheshutshotshitbam added. "When the President asked him to write a memo to give an explanation for why he fired FBI Director James Comeonecomally that didn't involve the agency's investigation of Fenwick, Rosentokenjew asked, 'Do you want Fries with that?' From the beginning, he knew about the President's love of fast food and loose morals, and he had no qualms about catering to them!"

"To be fair," Robinsoncrusoe lamely commented, "Rosentokenjew had great PR!"

Token smart person Sheshutshotshitbam hesitated to respond. I didn't need my crystal ball to tell that she wanted to say that journalists blew it by missing Deputy Attorney General Rosentokenjew's fidelity to President McDruhitmumpf. On the other hand, I didn't need my graduate degree in psychology to tell that she felt that, if his goal was to neuter the Meullitallover report, he did a spectacularly bad job of it, since it is a damning indictment of criminal behaviour at the highest levels (ooh, I call dibs on that title for my memoirs!).

"In the end," she summed up, "this President is an anti-alchemist: his administration turns everything it touches from gold to base metal. What ever made us think that lawyers were immune?"

Stonewall – Not Just For Andrew Jackshithappenson Any More!

by FRANCIS GRECOROMACOLLUDEN, Alternate Reality News Service National Politics Writer

When the House Oversight Committee asked 81 different individuals and institutions for documents and testimony, many complied, some surprisingly so. Steve O'Bannonallhope, for example, took time out of his busy schedule sabotaging the governments of European allies to send the Committee enough documents to insulate all the AirBnBBs in Frankfurt!

The Grey House's response, by way of contrast, was to send a message. And, the message was: "We're sorry, but we can't come to the phone right now. If we aren't out of the office making the world safe for idiotocracy, we're walking the dog. Anyhoo… At the sound of the beep, leave your name, number and a Goldilocks-lengthed message and nobody will get back to you at our earliest possible inconvenience. Robert Meullitallover will burn in Hell! Byeeeeee!" This was unusual inasmuchasPresidentRonald – sorry. I had trouble finding the end of that word. This was unusual inasmasPres – since! This was unusual since President Ronald McDruhitmumpf has not only made it clear that his favourite pet is a *Pentuphouse* centrefold, but because the request for documents had not been submitted by phone.

Thinking that it may have been a moderate mistake that was easily corrected (as if anything the McDruhitmumpf administration does is moderate!), Committee Chair Elijah Cummingsengoings sent the request for documents to the Grey House a second time. It's response? It sent back an RSVP to Isaac Kimmelfarberman's *bar mitzvah* with the "Not coming" and "Not giving a gift" boxes checked and the note, "I hope your monster of a son becomes a doctor and dies of a [illegible] painful disease that he could have easily diagnosed himself, but didn't!" scribbled in the margin.

"It's almost as if they don't want to supply us with any information," Chair Cummingsengoings muttered under his breath.

Actually, it's precisely that the Grey House doesn't want to give the Oversight Committee any information. They said as much in a press release headlined, "Grey House Decides Not to Give House Oversighs [sic] Committee Any Information." To ensure that reporters got the message, it was leaked to select journalists in an email titled, "IMMEDIATE ATTENTIONS: Your Bankebank account will be terminated in 24 seconds if you don't give us all of your personal information…for…you know…verification purposes because…we are totally trustworthy representatives of Bankebank! We even have their logo and everything, so you know we must be legit!!!!"

"If I didn't know any better," Chair Cummingsengoings muttered in the general vicinity of his breath, "I would swear that the Grey House is not cooperating with our investigation. Good thing I know better. Because if I didn't, I might have to go back on Valium!"

"The Vesampuccerian government was designed like a jigsaw puzzle," said presidential historian Michael Beschbefordatloess. "A jigsaw puzzle that nobody can agree on the design of made up of three massive pieces that are constantly at war with each other. This is what, in presidential historian school, we call 'checks and balances.'"

"I don't see what all the fuss is about," said Grey House spokeshrill KellyAnne Conwaytwittiest. "Oversight means sight over. Meaning, looking over the fabled gables of the Grey House to the Washburningdington home of Bill and Hillary Roocartoncleveman. **That** is where the Oversight Committee should be sighting!"

The Language Corrector Dude started vibrating visibly in anticipation of a question in his field. So, I asked token smart person Amy Sheshutshotshitbam to respond to Conwaytwittiest, instead. No point risking the strings that hold together the fabric of the universe.

"Oversight involves investigating potential wrongdoing by people in power," she explained. "The different branches of government are supposed to keep each other honest. You know, like the three massive pieces of a jigsaw puzzle that nobody can agree on the design of. Only, with more leaks."

If the Grey House homesteadfastly refuses to cooperate, the Oversight Committee can issue subpoenas to compel – hee hee. I said, subpoenas! Ha ha! I said it again! Subpoenas! Subpoenas! Subpoenas! Sub – what? But, it sure sounds dirty – are you positive? Okay, then.

If the Grey House homesteadfastly refuses to cooperate, it will be opening up a whole new frontier in Vesampuccerian jurisprudence. The Committee can issue subpoenas – which is a perfectly legitimate word which, I am informed, is in no way a reference to a naughty bit of a man's body – to compel the Grey House to give it the documents it wants. The Grey House could then ask the courts to quash the – quick, think of something boring! – subpoenas. Then, there will be a lot of blah, blah, blah, and the whole mess will end up being heard by the Extreme Court.

In that case, if Justice Brett Kavanaugheylno is sporting a hangover from a weekend kegger (that only ended on Tuesday afternoon, but it felt like forever!), anything could happen!

The Gang That Couldn't Character Assassinate Straight

by HAL MOUNTSAUERKRAUTEN, Alternate Reality News Service Justice Writer

If you're trying to do something anonymously, it's probably a good idea not to give out a phone number that goes to an answering machine that says, "**Haaaaiiiieee!** Is that…is that too loud? Umm… sorry – I have to press what, now? I don't see any – I'll just speak softer, okay? Okay. Ahem. Mi mi mi mi mi. Rhubarb rhubarb rhubarb rhubarb. Haiee. You have reached the Wholgathruntossah residence. I'm Ida Mae Wholgathruntossah, but you probably don't want to talk to me. My, oh my, no. Nobody ever wants to talk to me. I bet you want to talk to my grandson, Jacob. You know – the boy who keeps saying that he's gonna 'change the direction of Vesampuccerian politics forever?'"

"**Gran!**"

"Yeah, well, if you want to talk to a punk with delusions of grandeur instead of a mature woman with a world of experience –"

"**Gran! That's enough!**"

"– leave your name and number at the sound of the beep and I'm sure the saviour of the free world will get back to you at his earliest convenience."

"**That's it! I'm doing my own voicemail mess –**"

BEEP!

It's especially problematic when the object of your activity is a Special Prosecutor investigating Fenwick interference in the 2016 Vesampuccerian election. As soon as he catches wind of your shenanigans, he might just ask the FBI to investi – oh, look! That's exactly what Special Prosecutor Robert Meullitallover did!

Sucks to be you.

Jacob Wholgathruntossah appears to have been the point man for Reduhblican operative Jack Wottarealburkman, who had been claiming that at least six women had been sexually assaulted by the Special Prosecutor. Upon investigation, it turned out that one of the women, Jennifer Hippoindataub, had never met Special Prosecutor Meullitallover. When Hippoindataub pointed this out, Wottarealburkman asked, "Have you never heard of psychospiritual assault? If it isn't a crime now, we could get President McDruhitmumpf to sign an Executive Order making it one!"

That's not really how laws are made, but whole books could be written on **that** subject. A second woman, Lorraine Parsnicketypons, who had worked out of the same office as Special Prosecutor Meullitallover, stated that she remembered him being a complete professional who never took advantage of her, psychospiritually or otherwise.

Wottarealburkman stared at the back of his hand for a few seconds. Then, not wishing to repeat himself, he pffted. "It's sad," he said, "that women who have been abused cloak themselves in denial to protect themselves from the awful truth of what has been done to them. Thank Gord there are men who are willing to tell their truth for them!"

MSNBC anchor Rachel O'Schubermatthow sighed in scorn and dismay.

A press conference was held in which a third woman was supposed to appear and make her allegations against the Special Prosecutor. When she failed to show up, Wottarealburkman told journalists, "Ask me anything you would have asked the woman. I know her whole story – I helped shape it with her!"

MSNBC anchor O'Schubermatthow yelped in scormay. She's obviously working up to a snort of scormay, or possibly an opening segment.

The other three accusers are "mystery women" who have yet to be identified. It's like an Agatha Chrisgardstouderrmett novel, except without the twee, bloodless murders or whimsy.

"Jesus begesus!" MSNBC anchor O'Schubermatthow finally regained her voice. "The Reduhblicans are trying to weaponize the #metoo movement!"

"Nah, Ah do believe that is a mite hahsh," responded Grey House Press Secretary Sarah Wannabe-Panders. "Theah is nothin' ta connect this...whatevah it is ta thuh McDruhitmumpf administration."

If she had left it there, Press Secretary Wannabe-Panders would have been fine. Denial required, denial supplied. Unfortunately, not leaving well enough alone (as well as doubling down, making things worse and continuing to dig) is a Hallmark of this administration (they're such cards!). So, she added: "But, if thuh allegations're true, wuhl, wouldn't that be somethin'?"

"The allegations are not true!" Parsnicketypons insisted. "Douchenozzle over there offered me $20,000 to make the accusation! Naturally, I turned him down. It would be wrong. And, anyway, I don't want any troub – oh, man, is that the FBI I hear knock knock knocking on my door?"

"Of course we offered to compensate the victims," Wottarealburkman commented. "They've been through Hell! They deserve to get a little something something back for all of the…the, umm…you're not buying any of this, are you?"

"Not even a little bit," MSNBC anchor O'Schubermatthow assured him.

Running low on rhetoric, Wottarealburkman pffted one last time. "With an attitude like that, is it any wonder men aren't willing to stick their necks out to support women?"

A Taxing Situation

by GIDEON GINRACHMANJINJa-VITUS, Alternate Reality News Service Economics Writer

Reduhblicans love deadlines. They love the heavy clanking sound deadlines make as they pass by.

Representative Richard E. Nealgaimansplainer, the Chair of the House Ways and Means Committee, requested that Infernal Revenue Service commissioner Charles RettinolAgig supply him with six years of the tax returns of President Ronald McDruhitmumpf. That clanking sound everybody can hear? That's the sound of the April 10 deadline falling by the wayside like so much knight in chainmail armour being knocked out by a sleep spell and falling to the marble floor of an evil sorcerer's lair.

If that metaphor doesn't get me at least a nomination for a Pulippitzaner Prize for literary journalism, I will eat my chainmail hat!

The law appears to be on the Chair's side. "The IRS Commissioner shall supply the Chairman the tax returns of any Vesampuccerian citizen. Shall. Not can if they feel like it. Shall. Not may if all of the augurs align. Shall. Not maybe. Not perhaps. Not let's see how the day goes. Shall."

Seems pretty straightforward, doesn't it? Does it? Have you even met this administration?

In testimony to Congress after the deadline had passed, Treasury Secretary Steve Mnemonixuchin said, "We are considering the Chairman's request, and will get back to the Committee as soon as we have made a decision." But, the law says: "Oh, no, you don't, Mister Treasury Secretary. This is between the Committee Chairman and the head of the IRS – you have nothing to do with it. You absolutely do not have any right to delay the handing over of requested tax returns to the Committee Chair. *Capisce*?"

Treasury Secretary Mnemonixuchin must not speak Croatian, because he continued: "Concerns have been raised that the Chairman's request was not made out of a pure desire to see if the IRS used proper procedures in processing the President's returns, but out of a venal need to destroy a political opponent!" To which the law's response was, "Butt out, Mister Treasury Secretary! That is not your call to make! And, anyway, if the President's tax returns are on the up and up, there is no way it can be used to destroy him. Let the IRS Commissioner do his job!"

Chair Nealgaimansplainer has set a second deadline for the IRS to hand over the documents: April 23. "Please know that, if you fail to comply, your failure will be interpreted as a denial of my request," he wrote. "This will make me angry. You wouldn't like me when I'm angry."

Treasury Secretary Mnemonixuchin should be worried. Angry Dumboprats write blistering letters to newspaper op-ed pages.

In an effort to calm the situation down, President McDruhitmumpf said: "Congress will get my tax returns when they pry them from my cold, dead fingers – and I plan on living forever!"

What might happen if the new deadline goes clanking by?

"Are we at the point of a Constitutional crisis, yet?" wondered editorial columnist Eugene Robinsoncrusoe. "I mean, we've been expecting one since President McDruhitmumpf first took office. It doesn't matter much to me – I've already lost the journalists' pool on this. February 23 is my lucky month. I'm just curious: have we finally hit a Constitutional crisis?"

Not quite. According to legal scholars and lapidary numismatists, the Ways and Means Committee could subpoena the tax returns. That would be an especially clanky deadline as it went by.

Another possibility is that the Committee could hold Treasury Secretary Mnemonixuchin and IRS Commissioner RettinolAgig in contempt of Congress. (Charging the President with contempt of Congress would be redundant; he displays this attitude every day.) In that case, they could ask a court for an injunction compelling the IRS to give the tax returns to the Committee. This would involve multiple clankings as the case worked its way up the courts, making it sound like an unconscious knight in chainmail being dragged down a flight of stairs.

Clank.

Clank.

Clank!

I really hope the Pulippitzaner Prize Committee is reading this.

Why is this happening? Because Ronald McDruhitmumpf is the first President in 50 years who has not released any of his tax returns to the public. There have been rumours that he may have manipulated the value of his properties to pay less tax. There are whispers that he may have benefited from his administration's tax cuts, even though he assured the public that he wouldn't. There is even scuttlebutt that he received money from foreign governments that he later shaped government policy to favour. Could the law help us determine if any of this is true?

"Hey!" the law argued. "I can do a lot of things, but I'm not a miracle worker!"

Twenty-seven Personalities, None of Them Cooperative

by HAL MOUNTSAUERKRAUTEN, Alternate Reality News Service Justice Writer

Attorney General William Katiebarrthudor testified before the Senate Judiciary Committee yesterday – all 27 versions of him.

When Reduhblican Senator Lindsay Grahamcrokercrum asked him, "How awesome do you think President Ronald McDruhitmumpf has been?" Attorney General Katiebarrthudor gushed like a schoolgirl: "Like, oh, my god! The way he says one thing one day and has the confidence to say the complete opposite thing the next day? What a man! He's soooooo dreamy! Deputy Attorney General Rod Rosentokenjew and I have been talking about getting matching tattoos of his hair – do you think he would notice us if we did? That would be **so cool**!"

When, in previous testimony to the Committee, he was asked if he knew what Robert Meullitallover's reaction to his summary that wasn't really a summary of the Special Prosecutor's findings was, Attorney General Katiebarrthudor got his confused hipster on. "I don't, like, know for sure, maaaaaan. It's not like he got on his bongos and, like, sent me a smoke signal or anything. But, like, I mean how could he not be chill with such rad findings, do you dig?"

In a private letter made public the day before the Attorney General's latest testimony, Special Prosecutor Meullitallover expressed a complete lack of chill in the summary that dare not speak its name. When Attorney General Katiebarrthudor testified that he did not know what the Special Prosecutor's feelings about it were, therefore, he li – the Attorney General li – li – he li – li – li – li – he...mislead the Congress.

When Dumbopratic Senator Richard Blumenthalated asked him about this, the Attorney General took on the air of a university professor and responded, "What is truth? Truth is beauty. But beauty is in the eye of the beholder. Therefore, and I think any reasonable person would agree, the only conclusion to which we can come is that the truth of my previous statement was in the eye of the beholder. Would you like me to walk you through the symbolic equation that proves this hypothesis?"

Later in the hearing, Reduhblican Congressman Chuck Gasleygrassteahee asserted that the real scandal was Dumbopratic candidate Hillary Roocartoncleveman's attempts to steal the 2016 election, and asked what was the Attorney General doing about **that**? Channelling his inner Brooklyn mob boss, Attorney General Katiebarrthudor answered, "You think we're gonna let her get away wid dat shit? Watsamatta you? We are investigatin' the hell outta her, that's what we're doin'. And, when I say we're investigatin' the hell outta her, I mean **we're investigatin' the hell outta her!** Strugatz! Eh!"

That casued the Dumboprats on the Committee to practise their synchronized eye rolling.

Dumbopratic Senator Kamala Harristweedfashin asked Attorney General Katiebarrthudor if anybody in the Grey House asked or suggested that he prosecute specific people. This caused the Attorney General to come all school marmish at her. "Well, sweetie, it depends upon what your definition of asked is. I don't think anybody asked me to do that, no. Suggested? Perhaps. Recommended? It is certainly a possibility. Requested? That's a whole different issue, isn't it? Inquired as to the possibility of? You know, a lot of things may be said in idle conversation. You can hardly expect me to remember them all. Perhaps you should consider phrasing your questions more carefully, dear."

And, so it went. When a Redublican asked the Attorney General if the Injustice Department was considering investigating the origins of the Meullitallover investigation, he snarled, "Grrrr! Raaawwwr! FBI bad! Me smash overreaching FISA warrants! Arrrrrrr!"

When a Dumboprat asked the Attorney General if it was in the President's powers to fire the Special Prosecutor, you could almost see his pants drop down to his ankles when he responded, "Well, duh! The President can end any investigation if he thinks that the person is innocent and the investigation was, like, totally unfair! And, that would not be a sign of corrupt intent, because, what part of innocent don't you understand? I mean – sheesh! I can't believe I have to explain this to you! Were you dropped on your head in the hospital after you were born or something?"

"This was an extraordinary performance, worthy of acting awards" Alternate Reality News Service film and television critic Elmore Teradonovich responded to the testimony. "I laughed.* I cried.** I paused the video so I could go to the bathroom. A lot – the show was really long!"

* …at the absurdity of the Attorney General's responses.

** …for the state of my country.

5. THE SLEEP OF REASON PRODUCES…BAD NEIGHBOURS

The Land of the Free and the Home of the Depraved

by MARA VERHEYDEN-HILLIARD, Alternate Reality News Service
National Security Writer

Sandoval "Gut Check and Mate" Gutivimeda, a 36 year-old pig farmer who dreamed of one day owning his swine instead of renting them from Monsanto, had a feeling that it wasn't safe for him to stay in his home town of San Silleon, Venezuela.

Something in the way Miguelito Confarduellavan, San Silleon's Chief of Police, said, "I'm going to turn my back and count to ten. If you're still here by the time I turn back around, I will kill you, your wife Priscilla, your two children Moneyball and Maria and your prize pig Flopsy," was a big clue. Before Confarduellavan turned around, he slowly drew his forefinger across his forehead, indicating either that he was going to switch the brains of the family Frankenstein-style, or the old death threat routine was getting stale and he was trying something new in order to make it fresh and exciting again.

Gutivimeda didn't wait to find out. By the count of ten, his family was already halfway out of Venezuela. By another count of ten, they arrived at the border between Mexico and the United States. (Some condensation of time may have occurred to move the narrative along.) Their prized pig Flopsy was set free in the forest, where it is rumoured to have been taken in by a wolf pack seeking comic relief.

When they arrived at the Port of Entry (known as PoE because it generates endless horror stories) at San Ysidro, the Gutivimeda family was told that it was their lucky day: that PoE was closed owing to the Vesampuccerian No Port in a Storm policy (which designates a random five mile stretch of the border every 24 hours as the official Port of Entry), but the nearest PoE was only 576 miles away. When Gutivimeda told the guard at the gate that the family was on foot, she smiled and said, "You might want to jog there before a new place is chosen at midnight, then."

Okay, it's not exactly "The Masque of the Red Pendulum." Vesampucceri's PoEt laureate is allowed to have off days.

By that time, the man who had promised to help the Gutivimedas get into the US was nowhere to be found. As was the money they had scrounged together in eight of the ten seconds before they were forced to flee their home. "And, he had such a kindly face," commented Priscilla Gutivimeda. "Except for the spiral scar on his right cheek and the dead eyes, I mean."

Some people find it easier to make sense of adverse life circumstances than others.

Faced with a dearth (less than a treachery, more than a hearse) of options, Gutivimeda led his family away from the Port of Entry. A couple of kilometres – basically, far enough to be out of sight of the PoE. Employing a combination of putty knife (did we mention that Priscilla Gutivimeda created plaster sculptures of Venezuelan marines morphing into lizards in her spare time?) and desperation, it only took them another three days to cut through the chain link fence and make it to the Vesampuccerian side of the border.

To celebrate their entry into the land of the free, the Gutivimeda family was picked up by an ICES (Immigration Corralling and Expulsing Service) border patrol. Not in a sleazy, slink up to somebody in a seedy bar and ask what their sign is kind of way. More in a sleazy, kick somebody when they're down abuse of political power kind of way.

Sandoval Gutivimeda politely told the ICES agents who took the family into custody: "Howdy, y'all motherferkers. I done be plumb lookin' fer asylum, motherferkers." The agent complimented him on his English (which he had apparently learned from watching *Green Acres* and old Bruce Willusorwontus movies), and told him that his claim for asylum would be considered when he entered a proper Port of Entry.

Gutivimeda repeated "Motherferker! Motherferker! Motherferker!" all the way to the detention facility. Okay, more Samuel L. Jackshithappenson than Bruce Willusorwontus, but it was an easy mistake for somebody fleeing from the violence in his homeland to make.

According to international law, anybody appearing at a national border asking for asylum must be granted a hearing to determine if they have a valid fear of persecution if they are returned to their home country. According to the McDruhitmumpf administration's Zero Humanity policy, international law can suck it. Suck it hard.

"Nah, Ah do believe that that theah is a gross misrepuhsentation o' thuh President's position," argued Attorney General Jeff "Self-regard" Sesspoolpandemic. "Suckin' would implah we want intuhnashnull law ta have some pleasuh. Nothin' could be fahthuh from thuh truth. We would acshully lahk intuhnashnull law to be beaten abaht thuh head and shoulduhs with gold-plated chopsticks and dah a slow, painful death."

Have you ever noticed how much worse the "explanations" of McDruhitmumpf administration officials actually make things sound?

The Gutivimeda family were transported to a "Refugee Settlement Facility" (some of the most unsettling places we've ever been inside, let us tell you!) in Lockjaw, Texansas. They slept on a concrete floor in a wire mesh cage. The food they were given would have been refused by the orphans in *Oliver Twistenshowtencry*.

After a couple of hours, a woman in a moderately intelligent business suit (let's just say that it wasn't made of Mensa material) approached the family and said she wanted to take the children to get ice cream. When Priscilla Gutivimeda reasonably objected that she hadn't heard the jingle of an ice cream truck, only the screaming of hungry babies and crying of anguished parents, the woman responded: "Ice cream? Did I say ice cream? I meant…showers. That's it. I want to take your children to have showers. When you're invading a foreign country to destroy its freedoms, it's important to maintain good personal hygiene."

Priscilla Gutivimeda was skeptical. So, the woman signalled to two body guards to physically remove the children. As the family members joined the chorus of screaming and crying, the unidentified woman shook her head sadly and commented, "There's just no reasoning with some people!"

Bordering on Chaos

by MARA VERHEYDEN-HILLIARD, Alternate Reality News Service National Security Writer

How many times can you take a picture of a heroic young man (heavily armed) looking across a tumbleweed-strewn desert (right out of central casting – good tumbleweeds don't grow on trees, you know!), silhouetted by the setting sun before you start repeating yourself?

"237," answered Sgt. Ibrahim Baruch-al-Ooda, of the Flyin' (Lizards) Photogs Unit. (Imagine the shoulder patch!)

Oh. I wasn't expecting the answer to be so…specific. Or, definitive. Umm…well done, soldier.

Sgt. Baruch-al-Ooda is one of the 5,900 troops that have been deployed to the Vesampuccerian border with Mexico to combat invading bands of rampaging…err…rampagers. And, nogoodniks. As President Ronald McDruhitmumpf recently tweeped: "Gord bless the troops who are taking photographs of heroic young men defending our southern border! I mean, BANG! BOOM! THWOING! Blood spouting and body parts flying – this is what makes Vesampucceri grate!"

There's just one problem with the President's stirring (if bloody – you would have thought Eli Rothogordonya had ghost-written the tweep) message: the refugees that he is trying to make everybody so afraid of are working their way through Latin Vesampucceri so slowly that they aren't expected to appear at the border for several months. That, and the fact that they are mostly women and children, whose only real threat to the United States is to contribute something of value to it.

Okay, there are two problems with the President's vision: the refugees haven't arrived and they're not trained fighters **and** military personnel are forbidden by the *Posse Comitatus* (no, no, no, you're thinking of *The Pussy Coitus*, and get your mind out of the gutter because I'm **not** that kind of journalist!) *Act* of 1878 from engaging in judicial operations on Vesampuccerian soil.

Three! Three things! There are three – there are **many** problems with the President's vision of what is happening on the country's southern border, including but not limited to: the slow thing, the civilian thing and the not being able to legally engage with anybody doing illegal things on Vesampuccerian soil thing.

Why would the President offer such a dark vision to the nation when the reality is so much more yoyodyne?

"To fire up his base for the mid-term election," stated token smart person Amy Sheshutshotshitbam. The "Duh" was implied. With all the subtlety of a Wall Street bull in a shop in China.

If that's the case, why has the President continued to tweep about sending the troops to protect the country's southern border since the election? "Has he?" token smart person Sheshutshotshitbam had a sarcasm orgasm. "Has he really?"

Sure, he has. Just this morning, President McDruhitmumpf tweeped – oh, no, that was about how much the investigation of Special Prosecutor Robert Meullitallover was a witch hunt. A lot, apparently. But, yesterday, the President tweeped about...umm, okay, how the Meullitallover investigation was a hoax. Hmm...let's see...will have the affect of keeping good people out of politics – * SNORT! * – a witch hunt **and** a hoax, both at the same time – inevitable, that one, really – fully qualified to be the next Attorney Gen – oh, my Gord, the token smart person was right! The President hasn't tweeped, peeped, beeped or otherwise skiddley-doo-queeped about protecting the country's southern border since the election!

"Being right is an occupational hazard," token smart person Sheshutshotshitbam smugged.

Given the limitations placed upon them, what are the soldiers who have been deployed to the southern border actually doing? Some are working in intelligence ("Nope. Still no invading hordes at the border."). Some are working in tactics and logistics ("Since there are no invading hordes at the border, there's really nothing to be done."). Five of the 32 units at the border are press and public relations ("Can you pose heroically…in front of that array of computer screens featuring an incomprehensible flow of satellite data that is telling us that no invading hordes are at the – yeah, I think I'll go back outside and see if the sun is setting…").

But, for troops deployed at the southern border, life isn't all watching computer screens and waiting for sunsets. Granted, it's mostly watching computer screens and waiting for sunsets. And, building the occasional latrine just to mix things up a bit. In fact, there are times when a live rooster being set free in the armoury would be –

"**Are? You? Kidding? Me?**" shouted security expert Malcolm Donneednopennance. "Are you ferking kidding me?"

Umm…we don't think so…

"This operation is taking soldiers away from training or assignments that might actually, you know, benefit somebody in some way!" security expert Donneednopennance argued. At vociferousness. "**And**, the whole operation could cost upwards of $200 million! And, for what? To gain some kind of advantage in a mid-term election?"

Well, okay, when you put it that way…

The Worst of the Worst –
Especially Just Before Nap Time

by TAMMY, Alternate Reality Kidz News Service Life is so Unfair Writer

Fort Nothing to Bragg About, Texaware is a hard, cold, cruel place. It's the Norma Desmond of places in Vesampucceri. Here, you will find four year-old members of Mexican gang Letter-Number shaking down three year-old members of rival gang Number-Letter for safety pin money. Word is that anything you want, you can get smuggled into the facility…for a price. Chocolate milk. Spiderman pyjamas. Pacifiers spiked with maple syrup. Anything.

Fort Nothing to Bragg About is not a place for children. Yet, thanks to the McDruhitmumpf administration's Separate and Scatter policylet (part of its larger Zero Humanity policy), children as young as 18 months and as old as 126 months separated at the border from their parents can find themselves here.

"Don't cry for us, Argentina," said four and a half year-old Guillermo Acivederrez from behind the chain link fence that the government refers to as "a detainee incarceration facility that in no way resembles a cage, and we're offended by the possibility that you would call it that, so don't you dare!" I tried to point out to Guillermo that my name is not Argentina, but he continued over me: "We're scum. Worst of the worst. We deserve to be – you got any Milk Duds? Man, I could kill for a Milk Dud!"

To illustrate his point about all the hard boys in the joint, Guillermo told me the story of six year-old Jose Luis Garcineznandez, a baby faced (as if the three year-old could look any different) enforcer for the Letter-Numbers. Garcineznandez made a shiv out of a Popsicle stick and, in the middle of the night, stole into the bed of a four year-old who he claimed had disrespected his momma, and stabbed the boy's teddy bear Bottomo Gigio through the heart. "That shit is cold, man," Guillermo shivered despite the hundred degree temperature inside the tent facility.

At first, reporters were not allowed to visit the places where children separated from their parents at the border were being kept. Secretary of Homeland Security Kirstjen Nielsenratingshit explained, "We...we're doing that? I...I have no idea where these – can I get back to you on this?"

How did Guillermo respond to the President's assertion that people who crossed the border illegally were all rapists and murders? "Gunnnngh mumba mmmmm..." Taking the pacifier out of his mouth, he explained, "Yeah, sorry about that. I don't know what it is about these things, but they're just so darn addictive!"

And, the question? "Rapists and murderers, hunh?" he mused. "Murderers and rapists. I...I have no idea what those are. Some kind of weird *americano* pastries? Cause, nobody **ever** called Guillermo Acivederrez sweet!"

Doesn't this policy of jaili - "Uhh, uhh, uhh," interrupted the Immigration Corralling and Expulsing Service (ICES). "We don't use that word, and neither do you."

Oh. Umm. Well...doesn't this policy of...detainee incarcerationing make Vesampucceri a literal nanny state? "I don't see how," Secretary Nielsenrating answered. "I...I don't even like goat cheese." In the broadest sense of the term "answered."

When asked what the government planned to do with all the children it was collecting (without any idea of what constituted a complete set), Secretary Nielsenrating looked like an undocumented immigrant in headlights. "Plan? Do we look like a government with plans? The mob has plans. The cops have plans. Gordon's got..." She shook her head before continuing: "I, uhh, mean...can I get back to you on this one, too?"

I started to ask Guillermo about what his plans were for the – "Give me a moment, will you?" he interrupted. "I think I just saw a CNN reporter..." He took a moment to compose himself, then started bawling his eyes out, yowling in Spanish about how he wanted his mother. Several of the children in adjacent cag – incarceration happy places joined in. After several minutes, Guillermo looked around and said, "Is she gone?" Satisfied that whoever he was looking for was gone, he dried his eyes.

"What was that about?" I asked.

"Favour for Nancy Pelligrinosi," Guillermo told me. "It was nothing. Don't worry about it."

When I was certain it was okay to continue, I asked Guillermo what his plans for the future were. "I'm a live in the moment kind of guy," he told me. "The future? It's a lineup for the diaper changing area that's so long you can't even see the end of it. I'll probably die in here. But that don't mean I can't have a good time. What are you doing after the interview? Wanna ditch the mic and grab some Gerber's baby food? I hear peas and carrots are good this time of year..."

Portrait of the Artist as a Young Illegal Immigrant

by INDIRA CHARUNDER-MACHARRUNDEIRA, Alternate Reality News Service Fine Arts Writer

When it comes to oil paintings and visas that allow people to work in Vesampucceri, art is a poke in the eye of the beholder.

You have probably never heard of Gabriel Famleesedano, an employee of the McDruhitmumpf National Golf Club Westminichester who had never expressed an interest in joining the artistic community. However, when his manager told this undocumented worker from Guatemala that he needed a visa to continue to work there, he was driven to create.

Famleesedano's first effort at supplying the golf course with a visa showing that he was in Vesampucceri legally was written in pencil crayon on a napkin. "This is a common mistake with first-timers," Bobby "Big Bubbelach" Bonavaducci, art critic and two-time winner of a stay at Her Majesty's Leisure in London, commented. "They don't have the resources to create a proper fake document, so they use whatever materials come to hand. The results wouldn't fool a blind immigration officer in a black cat's darkened basement!"

In fact, passports, work visas and other official documents were written on napkins in pencil crayon, sometimes even plain crayon, during WWII because of shortages of embossed paper, which was diverted for use making artillery shells. But, uhh, that's not relevant to the current discussion. The only other record of this happening was when local governments issued napkin visas during the Uncivil War; however, since control of the movement of people through territory has never been a municipal power, both sides ignored the documents. Which, uhh, is even less relevant to the current discussion, but at least it's colourful.

Administrators of the McDruhitmumpf National Golf Club told Famleesedano that they were happy for him to work there, but, honestly, if he wanted to keep doing so, he would have to bring them a more realistic looking visa. His next effort was also written on a napkin, but, perhaps having learned from his first experience, it was in pen.

"Although it may have been as simple as asking to borrow the pen of somebody who worked with him at the golf course," Bonavaducci stated, "this shows that Famleesedano had the capacity to grow as an artist. Unlike pencil crayons, ink is permanent. This creation shows him having a lot more confidence in his craft."

With, unfortunately, exactly the same results: Famleesedano was told to come back the next day with another visa.

For his seventh attempt, Famleesedano stopped working with napkins, replacing them with the insides of cut up cigarette cartons. "This was a conceptual breakthrough for him," Bonavaducci claimed.

"Official documents like visas are usually printed on heavier stock paper. Famleesedano was clearly ready to abandon his early *arte primitif* posturing for a more sophisticated approach."

At the same time, though, he returned to pencil crayons. "You have to understand," Bonavaducci asked us to understand, "Famleesedano was working 12 hour shifts six days a week, mowing and raking the grounds and rebuffing unwanted duffer advances. Not only that, but he had to share a single room with 17 other employees of the golf course in the same boat. Given this, he can certainly be forgiven for a little…artistic backsliding."

In all, it took Famleesedano 59 attempts before he was finally able to create a document that the manager of the McDruhitmumpf National Golf Club was satisfied was good enough to fool an Immigration Corralling and Expulsing Service (ICES) agent. "And, what a masterpiece it was!" Bonavaducci exulted. "As Richard Bachturnovmanive – who everybody knows is actually Stephen Kingfisherhelploess, but he doesn't like it when anybody acknowledges the fact, so shh! – truly said: 'A professional is an amateur who walked over the dead, bloated corpses of his friends and enemies and anybody else who stopped him from achieving his dream.' I, uhh, may have been paraphrasing, here, but you get the idea."

Bonavaducci pointed out that every artist experiments with different forms and materials before they find just the combination that expresses what they have to say. For example, Leonardo Da Da Da Vinci drew 127 different versions of the Mona Lisa, including: as a rat; looking like she had just swallowed a bug; eating a pastrami sandwich; squinting; against a field of poppies; and holding a baby's arm holding an apple. Mac "In Tosh" Kropotskinyanmov drafted counterfeit $100 bills 87 times before he finally created a version that has yet to be discovered by treasury agen – err, but I have said too much already.

"Creating great art is hard," Bonavaducci summed up.

It took Famleesedano 12 years of working at the McDruhitmumpf National Golf Club to perfect his visa. A day after he submitted it to club management, he and 14 other men and women who worked there were turned over to ICES for immediate deportation. "I am shocked, shocked I tell you," a McDruhitmumpf Organization spokesperson told us, "to discover illegal immigrants working in one of our establishments!"

This likely, possibly, maybe could have been caused by the government shutdown. How could President McDruhitmumpf beg for money for a border wall to keep illegal immigrants out of the country when he couldn't even keep them out of his properties?

With a heavy sigh, Bonavaducci said, "Great artists are never recognized in their time. I don't know if Richard Bachturnovmanive said that, but he will. He will…"

Catch and Release Kids

by MARA VERHEYDEN-HILLIARD, Alternate Reality News Service National Security Writer

Pedro GreeleyGrinchypants is a typical six year-old boy. He loves watching cartoons and playing federales and gringos with other boys at his kindergarten (even if they mistakenly think they're playing cowboys and indigenous peoples). He winsomely stares out the window of his bedroom for hours at a time. Trying to get his lips around English vowels makes his mouth hurt.

Unlike typical six year-old boys, Pedro GreeleyGrinchypants is a political football. And, not in a good way: in a kicked around a lot because nobody seems able to mount an effective offence way. "Children like little Pedro should not be riiiiiiipped from their loving parents' arms," Health and Human Disservices Secretary Alex M. Alexiazar IV stated. "Children need a stable home environment in order to thrive. Teeeeaaaaaarrrrriiiiing them away from that would cause them permanent emotional distress. So, we won't let it happen, okay?"

Okay. The Secretary's statement might make you think the administration of President Ronald McDruhitmumpf's heart had grown three sizes overnight. Unfortunately, Hiram and Sue-Ellen GreeleyGrinchypants, the homemakers from which little Pedro should not be riiiiiiipped and etc., are not the boy's parents. Pedro was taken from those people when they crossed the border without documents and was adopted by the GreeleyGrinchypants family. Secretary Alexiazar IV's statement was a response to people who were trying to get Health and Human Disservices to give the child **back** to his birth parents.

What's that? You thought a majority of the 2,700 children who had been taken by the United States government after it adopted the Separate and Scatter policy had been reunited with their birth parents? That may be, you silly billy. But, Pedro was one of the potentially thousands of children who were separated from their parents at the border **before** the policy was announced.

Do try to keep up. Much as I would love to pad my word count by repeating myself, I'm sure my Editrix-in-Chief would object, and, when she objects, heads snap on necks!

"We're Gord-fearing folks in this family," Hiram GreeleyGrinchypants said as Sue-Ellen GreeleyGrinchypants sat nearby knitting a "Burn in Hell, Heathen Scum!" sampler. "The good Gord commanded us to be fruitful and multiply. When **that** didn't happen..." Hiram looked meaningfully at Sue-Ellen, who concentrated that much harder on the comma, the trickiest punctuation mark to knit. Then, he continued, "...we decided to adopt a heathen scum baby and bring him to Gord. Because Gord loves us."

What about Pedro's actual parents? "If the good Gord had wanted Pedro to stay with his...parents, He wouldn't have created ICES [the Immigration Corralling and Expulsing Service]."

"Hiram and Sue-Ellen are good people," claimed Chris Paluskyomeinn, President and CEO of MaryBethanChristiney Christian Services. "Yes, okay, certainly, Hiram lusts after hat check girls, and Sue-Ellen is a little over-fond of her Sambuca spritzers. But, at least they don't cross borders illegally in the dead of night, putting their children in danger!"

And, they can afford the $20,000 to $40,000 adoption fee?

"That's not a very Christian attitude," Paluskyomeinn's eyes scrunched. "Verheyden-Hilliard – is that some kind of cryptic Jew name?"

MaryBethanChristiney Christian Services has friends in high places. Education Secretary Betsy DeVolution-Ross' charitable foundation gave the non-profit organization $343,000. The charitable foundation of her father-in-law, Richard DeVolution-Ross, gave the organization $750,000. Even the family's pets got in on the act.

"Muffy DeVolution-Ross is a Gord-fearing German Sheppard," Paluskyomeinn commented. "She knows that saving heathen souls will get her an endless supply of doggy treats in heaven. Won't it? Won't it, girl? Oooh, of course it will! Who's a good girl? You are! Oh, yes you are! Praise the Gord!"

When asked about the fees his service charges per adoption, Paluskyomeinn scoffed, "What do you think we are? A charity?"

Well, actually...

Taking children from their birth parents and giving them to complete strangers for money – there is a term for that, isn't there? I mean, the English language has a word for the things at the end of your shoelaces **and** the holes you put those parts of your shoelaces through – you would expect it to have a word for this practice. What could it possibly –

"Human trafficking is a human tragedy, people," President Ronald McDruhitmumpf claimed when he was trying to get funding for a border wall/fence/barrier/annoyance. "It's bad. Oh, so very bad. The fact that it's happening on our southern border is a disgrace. Everybody knows it. I know it. You know it. The man in the moon knows it. That's pretty much everybody, everybody. We must put an end to human trafficking once and for all!"

Ah. Right. A token smart person couldn't have put it better herself.

Butterflies Are – FLEE!

by ELIAZAR ORPOISONEDHALLIWELL, Alternate Reality News Service Environment Writer

You might have thought that because the temporary funding bill which ended the government shutdown did not contain any funding for President Ronald McDruhitmumpf's border wall, that no work could be done on President Ronald McDruhitmumpf's border wall. You are forcing me to choose between calling you a silly old goat, a silly billy or a silly old sod.

Fortunately, such issues are covered in journalism school. The term "silly billy" could be considered racist by people who live in the Ozark Mountains, so that's out. "Silly old sod" sounds dirty, and this is a family publication. So, despite overtones of indiscriminate ingestion of food and not necessarily an accusation of beardedness, "silly old goat" it is.

You silly old goat.

A bulldozer has started plowing under the National Butterfly Centre, a wildlife sanctuary in Mission No Longer Critical, Texabama. This land will be used to build part of President McDruhitmumpf's border wall…if he is ever given funding for it. But, it would probably be okay if that funding never comes, since the government has not offered the owners of the Centre compensation for the land, or even an eminent domain hearing where they could object to its appropriation.

Does the silly old goat smell impending lawsuits? (For silly old goat's information: impending lawsuits smell like chicory with an undercurrent of brimstone.)

The President has been laying the groundwork for this action since the campaign two years ago. At a rally, he said: "The butterflies that move freely across our borders are rapists and murderers. We need a wall to stop them!"

"Rapists and murderers?" questioned Jeffrey Glasshausenstonesberg, president of the North American Butterfly Association. "They're butterflies!"

As President, McDruhitmumpf continued to embellish the narrative of the threat butterflies posed to the nation. "MonarchS-13 is a gang of vicious Mexican butterflies who freely bring drugs and guns into our country. The death and destruction they cause our inner cities – you know who I'm talking about – 'inner cities,' hee hee – ahem, the destruction is incalculable, people. We must stop these vicious butterflies from crossing into our country, and a border wall is the best way of doing it!"

Glasshausenstonesberg protested: "But…but…but, **they are just butterflies!**"

As recently as last week, President McDruhitmumpf railed against, "Swarms of vicious, drug-addicted butterflies [that are] pouring across our border, attacking women and children, literally…literally tearing innocent people apart with their teeth! Oh, yes, people! With their teeth! Believe me – you thought radioactive zombies were bad? This is a million times worse!"

"But, they're just – I mean, they don't even have tee – honestly, where does he get these ideas?" Glasshausenstonesberg sputtered.

FSOGI: While we wouldn't want to generalize, President McDruhitmumpf seems to have gotten that specific idea from the plot of *Gorgonzilla vs. The Big Cheese*. In that film, the title butterfly is bitten by a radioactive zombie, which causes it to mutate and attack human beings. Since butterflies don't, as Glasshausenstonesberg started to point out, have teeth, it mostly gums people to death, leaving the corpses covered in ick. A leaked copy of the President's Netfix queue shows that he watched the film two days before making his latest accusations against butterflies.

"And, just when the butterfly population was starting to come back!" lamented Anastasia Greene-Lovinvegan, Vesampuucerian spokeshuman for the environmental group Greenpeas.

She explained that butterflies are natural migrants, travelling from deep in Latin Vesampucceri to close to the Canada/US border and back. "You think business executives live out of their suitcases? They ain't got nothing on butterflies!"

If the National Butterfly Centre is shut down to build a wall, the migratory patterns of butterflies will be disrupted. "You thought having your direct flight from New Yoricknuhemwell to London rerouted through Taos, New Mexisas was inconvenient?" Greene-Lovinvegan asked. "This is a planned diversion to die for!"

Why should we care about the fate of a few flittery creatures? Greene-Lovinvegan pointed out that, however inefficiently, butterflies do help pollinate crops; their loss in large enough numbers could threaten the human food supply.

"Some people say that that won't be a problem as long as we have bees to pollinate crops," she summed up. "Good luck with that doesn't even begin to cover it!"

In the meantime, President McDruhitmumpf continues to ratchet up the anti-butterfly rhetoric. "The Dumboprats had an opportunity to do the right thing by giving me the wall funding I asked for in the temporary appropriations bill," he said. "They didn't do it. Didn't do it. If swarms of radioactive butterflies carry small children off into the sky to join child trafficking rings, it will be on their heads!"

Ira Nayman
Riding the Wild Frontier With a Bunch of CUNPs

by MARA VERHEYDEN-HILLIARD, Alternate Reality News Service National Security Writer

Jim Benviedubbelyu looks across the border separating Mexico from New Mexissippi and, taking a swig from the can of beer in the hand that's not holding a rifle, says, "This country is going to shit."

Sitting on the ground with his knees touching his chin and his hands on the top of his head, unable to comfort his wife or two children, Raul Gutiergumi mutters under his breath, "Tell me about it."

Benviedubbelyu is a member of Constitutionally United Nationalist Patriots (CUNP), a militia group that has taken it upon itself to patrol Vesampucceri's southern border, putting those who enter the country illegally under "citizen's arrest" (which is like "police arrest," with a *frisson* of lack of accountability and jurisdictional disputes that invariably end with a body count). Benviedubbelyu is concerned that if New Mexisippi is overrun by Latin Vesampuccerian immigrants, his home state of Minnessippi will be next, so he travelled across the country to dole him out some frontier justice.

In a video Benviedubbelyu posted to Farcebook, he and half a dozen CUNPs are sitting tall in the saddles of their Range Rovers, watching over 30 women, children and the occasional man sitting in the glare of their headlights on the ground in front of them. Unlike during my interview, no alcohol appears to be present as they wait for Border Patrol agents to take the Latin Vesampuccerians off their hands.

Even CUNPs have an image to maintain.

Benviedubbelyu has stated that CUNP and the other militias patrolling the border will leave when President Ronald McDruhitmumpf's wall has been completed. Which means it would have to be started. They seem confused by this causal chain. Maybe it's the beer. Benviedubbelyu said they would also be willing to leave if officials asked them to.

"Go home!" stated New Mexissippi Governor Michelle Lujan Grishamlyaddams. "It is completely unacceptable for migrant families to be made to feel threatened by unauthorized civilians. That's what ICES [the Immigration Corralling and Expulsing Service] is for!"

"Get away from the border and go home!" concurred New Mexissippi Attorney General Hector Balderdashansur. "We give certain citizens the power to arrest others. You are not those certain citizens. Sounds to me like somebody – actually, a lot of somebodies – has watched a little too much *Law and Order: Tuktoyaktuk*!"

"Like I said," Benviedubbelyu maintained, "if anybody in power asked us to leave, we would. We are not unreas – hey, Harold! We got a runner over by where you're supposed to be patrolling! Gordammit, do I gotta pay attention for everybody?"

You might think that law-abiding citizens should have the right to detain (kidnap is such an ugly word) people they believe are committing a crime. Vesampucceri is, after all, the land of the free and the home of the deranged. But, what if it turns out they're not so law-abiding citizens?

CUNP militia member Larry Mitchell Hopkinodulams, for instance, was arrested by the FBI as a felon in possession of a weapon. The agency did not release what felony Hopkinodulams had been convicted of, but it's fairly certain that it wasn't playing tiddly winks in a Monopoly zone.

"This is a dangerous felon who should not have weapons around children and families," Attorney General Balderdashansur argued. When it was pointed out that many states now required people who worked in kindergartens to carry weapons as a defence against school shooters, he stopped for several seconds before answering, "Umm, yeah. Well. They go through background checks to ensure that they're not dangerous felons. Probably. I think. I mean, they should. I mean… umm…shoot."

"People have the wrong idea about us," Benviedubbelyu argued. "They think we're a bunch of drunken, trigger-happy yahoos who are endangering the lives of innocent people. Nothing could be further from the – **Darryl! Stop aiming that gun at that child! Where was – she looks like she's six years old – seven at most! How could she possibly be hiding a grenade launcher? It would be bigger than she is!** Sorry. I'm sorry you had to see that. We are patriots who are protecting our – noooo, I did not promise to show you 'action.' **I did not promise – fine! Fine! Go back to Aribama! We'll get along just fine without you! Ferking peachy!** So. Umm. Yeah. Not yahoos. Not endangering the lives of innocent people. Patriots. Protecting our homeland. That's us."

What could possibly go wrong?

Gord Bless the Children (Because Nobody Else Will)

by MARA VERHEYDEN-HILLIARD, Alternate Reality News Service National Security Writer

The government of Ronald McDruhitmumpf claims that it has complied with a court order to reunite all of the children who were taken from their parents after crossing the border with Mexico.

"Ah believe that justice…justice is a dish best suhved cold," said Attorney General Jeff "Self-regard" Sesspoolpandemic. "It may taste slahmy, but it goes dahn real smooth. But, uhh, a coaht has said uthuhwahse, and it's only faiah and raht that we comply with its rulin'… At least until thuh President has an oppuhtunity ta replace that theah judge with somebody with moah respec' foh his authoahty."

U.S. District Judge in San Diego Dana Sabrawftbeetonpathe, who ordered the families to be reunited, wasn't convinced. In an increasingly testy (somebody had clearly taken an IQ quiz before coming into court!) exchange with the government attorney (who was so embarrassed by the position she had to argue that she asked not to be named even though the court transcript is a public document), Judge Sabrawftbeetonpathe contested the contention.

JUDGE DANA SABRAWFTBEETONPATHE: How many children has the government reunited with their families?

[GOVERNMENT ATTORNEY]: All of them, your honour.

JUDGE SABRAWFTBEETONPATHE: All of them? Really? The day before the deadline, you were only able to confirm that four of the children were reunited with their families. You had over a month to comply with my order, and that was the best you could do, but you expect me to believe that you managed to reunite almost 2,500 families in the last 24 hours?

[GOVERNMENT ATTORNEY]: Stranger things have happened, your honour.

JUDGE SABRAWFTBEETONPATHE: They have?

[GOVERNMENT ATTORNEY]: Umm…absolutely. When you consider, I mean, for example, how life came into existence out of inanimate matter – that must have been a pretty strange moment in the history of the universe, right? Or…or…or, how the 1969 New Yoricknuhemwell Mets won the World Series. That was definitely stra –

JUDGE SABRAWFTBEETONPATHE: Councillor, how many family reunifications can you prove the government has carried out?

[GOVERNMENT ATTORNEY]: All of –

JUDGE SABRAWFTBEETONPATHE: With documentation.

[GOVERNMENT ATTORNEY]: Seven.

JUDGE SABRAWFTBEETONPATHE: Seven?

[GOVERNMENT ATTORNEY]: Okay, almost all of them.

JUDGE SABRAWFTBEETONPATHE: Seven?

[GOVERNMENT ATTORNEY]: Eight if you include Manuel…what's his name, who probably, maybe, in all likelihood, we think is being picked up by his father's uncle's sister-in-law even as we speak. Why, that's practically double digits!

JUDGE SABRAWFTBEETONPATHE: I – uhh – okay. Councillor. How do you figure seven out of 2,500 constitutes "all?"

[GOVERNMENT ATTORNEY]: Two words, your honour: the rest of the families were "in eligible."

JUDGE SABRAWFTBEETONPATHE: That is not acceptable, Name Redacted!

[GOVERNMENT ATTORNEY]: Your honour, it's not like what you're asking the government to do is easy. I mean, we never kept records of the people processed at the border, so we wouldn't know which children belonged to which parents even if the adults hadn't disappeared into another country likely never to be heard from again!

JUDGE SABRAWFTBEETONPATHE: (moans)

"Aww, naw, Ah do buhlieve that oah critics ah bein' unfaiah," Attorney General Sesspoolpandemic pointed out. "Thuh numbah o' children who have diahed in custody is actually smallah than thuh numbah who have been documented ta have been retuhned to theiah pahents. Ah do buhlieve that constahtutes a victory of ah soaht. But, do we get credit fer it? Ah think we know thuh ansah ta **that** question!"

"What? Wait," token smart person Amy Sheshutshotshitbam attempted a spit take, getting scores of 8.9, 9.1 and 3.4 from the judges (when asked why his score for her was so low, the Finnish judge said, "You would have given her a low score, too, if yours was the face her spit take was spit into!"). "Children are dying in Vesampuccerian custody? Why aren't there protests in the streets against this?"

"If she had evah been a pahent," Attorney General Sesspoolpandemic asided, "Ah'm suah she would know thuh ansah ta that question!"

The government has long argued that the refugee system was broken because processing adults could be done immediately, but processing children could take up to six months. They couldn't just keep the adults in the country until a decision was made about their children; such a policy would cause terrible hardship and suffering among President McDruhitmumpf's base. Separating them at the border seemed the most humane thing to do.

And, yet.

And, yet, we now know that undocumented immigrants without children were not immediately deported, suggesting that the McDruhitmumpf administration was specifically targeting families. "Obviously, the Reduhblican understanding of the concept of 'family values' took a detour on the road to good governance when Ronald McDruhitmumpf became President!" token smart person Sheshutshotshitbam mocked. "If I didn't know any better, I would swear that there was never any actual plan to reunite children with their deported parents!"

"Wuhl, nah, Ah really do think thuh token smaht puhson is out o' lahn on this question," Attorney General Sesspoolpandemic argued. "As mah deah depahted Pappy used ta say, iffen the path y'all're on leads off a cliff, don't blame the steerin' wheel!"

Legal scholars will be debating the meaning of this statement for decades to come.

She Sells Sanctuary By the Seashore

by CORIANDER NEUMANEIMANAYMANEEMAMANN, Alternate Reality News Service Urban Issues Writer

The problem with immigrants is where to put them. Oh, sure, you can keep them in cages on military bases, but soldiers might object, not without reason, that looking after children who don't speak English so they have to mime being allergic to concrete floors is not what they signed on for. The soldiers. If the children didn't want to live in cages, they shouldn't have been born to immigrants.

And, yes, you can probably give them all homes in the Grand Ditch – there is certainly enough room for them all. Still, that doesn't stoke the outrage of your base and poke your political opponents in the eye at the same time. (Oh – you thought this was about solving a humanitarian crisis? Where is the political advantage in **that?**)

President Ronald McDruhitmumpf thinks he has found a better solution to the problem.

"Dumboprats like Mexicans streaming across the border?" President Ronald McDruhitmumpf stated. "Tell you what. Let's ship 'em all to sanctuary cities. See how much Dumboprats like them when they're wandering through their designer coffee clatches and used cutlery shops!"

"Send 'em to me!" enthused New Yoricknuhemwell City Mayor Bill diBlaseohoh. "We'll take all the immigrants we can get!"

"I don't think you understand," President McDruhitmumpf argued. "I'm going to send you all the people coming across the northern border with Mexico. All the **illegals**. You know what I'm talking about!"

"We'll be happy to take them," said San Francisco Mayor London Breedensircusses. "The more immigrants, the better."

"Rapists!" President McDruhitmumpf shouted. "I'm talking rapists! And, murderers! I'll make sure that the Mexican rapists and murderers flooding our southern border will end up in your sanctuary cities! Raaaapists! Muuuuuuurrrrrderers! Sanctuary cities! Pay attention – when I tell you that you know what I'm talking about, know what I'm talking about!"

"Immigrants have a lower rate of crime than native born Vesampuccerians," Mayor diBlaseohoh and Mayor Breedensircusses said in unison. "They also have a stronger work ethic."

"They'll help the city's economy grow for the next two generations!" Mayor Breedensircusses said.

"The stories they bring with them will help enrich the city's culture!" Mayor diBlaseohoh said at the same time.

"Well, that didn't go quite the way I thought it would," President McDruhitmumpf muttered darkly.

Sanctuary cities are areas where local authorities do not cooperate with ICES (the Immigration Corralling and Expulsing Service) in corralling and expulsing people living in the country without documentation. They tend to be the most liberal cities in the country, as well as – and this is what really infuriates Reduhblicans – the wealthiest. Almost as if there is a connection between the two facts.

Almost...

"Sanctuary cities? Hunh. That's a new one on me," commented Acting Homeland Insecurity Secretary Kevin McAleenanites. "But, uhh, I'm new, here. I mean, I don't even know where the coffeemaker is, and I'm not good to go until I've had at least my fourth mocha latte of the day. So, it may be a while before I can respond to this..."

Representatives of the Grey House were more categorical (they obviously play *Scattergories* in their down time): "No, no, no, no, no, no, no, no, no," one of the representatives commented between turns. "We considered this possibility months ago and ruled it out! Categorically, absolutely, utterly, flatly, unconditionally and with no possibility of reconsideration – or, at least, we thought no possibility of reconsideration…"

Homeland Insecurity and the Grey House argued that the plan would be complicated, costly and cummerbund. (They really need to work on incorporating alliteration into the rule of three.) "You know how it works," the Grey House source said. "You can have something complicated and cummerbund, but not costly. Or, you can have something cummerbund and costly, but it won't be complicated. We were willing to forego cummerbund – what is that, anyway? Some kind of actor or something? – but that left us with complicated and costly. Not a good set of policy parameters."

The Grey House source went on to point out that if they were in sanctuary cities, immigrants would be given ID cards and would be allowed to work and find places to stay. They couldn't be kept in cages. Families couldn't be separated. This would appear to be the opposite of what the President hopes to achieve with his border policy.

"But, you know the Chief," the Grey House source summed up. "He has the memory of a cat. As long as it was brought up more than three minutes ago, there is no idea so bad that we have ruled it out categorically, absolutely, utterly, flatly, unconditionally and with no possibility of reconsideration that he won't revisit!"

Our Country is Full of It!

by ENGELBERT HUMPERFLAPDOODLEPUSS, Alternate Reality News Service Excrement Writer

In a small room somewhere close to the Mexico-US border (but, not too close because you don't want any drug dealing or human trafficking to rub off on you), President Ronald McDruhitmumpf was bikini waxing poetic (he's the surf Shakeaspeararetoo!).

"It's like the dial is pointing at F," he was saying. "Beyond F. It's like we've eaten so much that our engines will explode if we take one more bite. No, no, no, we don't want that waffer thin mint – it's diesel, and we need regular...although it does look tasty...and, honestly, what could one little bite possibly hurt...?"

You could be forgiven for thinking that the President was talking about Vesampucceri's obesity epidemic. But, he wasn't. You could almost be forgive (would it kill you to apologize? – oh, you know what for!) for thinking that he was talking about how Vesampucceri's obsession with big cars feeds Global Hot as Hellification. But, he most certainly wasn't.

No, the President was talking about his second favourite subject (and the first isn't his wife Melanoma, although she's in the top 50... probably...): immigration.

In that speech, President McDruhitmumpf went on to say: "We'd be happy to take all of Mexico's murderers and rapists, really, we would, but...we just don't have the room. The United States of Vesampucceri is full. Filled to the brim – if only we wore a bigger hat! Plum full to burstin' – can't say we don't get enough fruit in our diet! Full of beans – and we all know how unpleasant **that** can be in a confined space! Maybe we overestimated how much fruit we've been eating! Full court press – which is what will happen if the Dumboprats insist on getting the full Meullitallover report! Full disclosure – hunh! As if! Full of itself – so we don't need an invasion of other selfs. Every room in the country is taken, everybody knows that. So, I'm sorry, Mexican murderers and rapists, but you'll just have to try a motel in Ecuador!"

"This is the most insanely ludicrous thing the President has ever said...today!" responded President of *Voto Latino* Maria Teresa Kumasatralez. "The United States has the third largest land mass in the world and a population a quarter of the size of India or China. There is enough room in the Grand Ditch alone to give a home to all Latin American refugees and asylum-seekers for the next 17 years!"

"Does this look like we aren't completely full?" President McDruhitmumpf said, poking a member of his security detail in the side of the head as he swept his arm in front of him to indicate the crowded room. A *Washburningdington Post* reporter who had to tape the session from the back pocket of this reporters pants because there was nowhere else to stand squeaked in agreement.

"I, uhh, really don't think you can, you know, judge the space available in a country by the space available in a single room," argued columnist Eugene Robinsoncrusoe from where he was standing on the ceiling. "That would be like, you know, pronouncing Global Hot as Hellification a hoax because one day the temperature was colder than average for that time of – oh, wait. You say that, too. I…I'm sorry, I think the blood is rushing to my he – oh, my." Robinsoncrusoe fell to his knees and ended up sitting next to a light fixture.

Having given up his plans to close the border (because economic suicide) for the time being (because functioning economy is overrated), the President's plan now appears to be to politely discourage immigrants and asylum seekers from trying to enter the country. Or, possibly to demonstrate to potential immigrants that the United States is full of crazy people, and why would anybody choose to live in such a madhouse?

"It's a trick!" shouted token smart person Amy Sheshutshotshitbam. "This President doesn't do polite! He breaks out in xenophobia whenever he tries!" Doing a reasonably passable McDruhitmumpf impression (let's just say that Alec Defblyndenbaldwin has nothing to worry about), she added: "Would you be so kind as to pass the creamed beef with immigrants are gonna steal your children's underwear if we don't stop them now! Ha ha ha ha ha – burp!"

"The President is not gonna let go of the immigration issue because it plays to his base," Kumasatralez pointed out. "You can expect him to ramp up the anti-immigrant rhetoric all the way…all the way to the 2020…the 2020 electi – oh, my Gord! To think I gave up a promising career as a Mongolian pastry chef to do this – **what was I thinking?**"

Ira Nayman

6. THE SLEEP OF REASON PRODUCES… DEPLORABLES

Mo Worser Reds

by FRANCIS GRECOROMACOLLUDEN, Alternate Reality News Service National Politics Writer

There are certain things that simply are not done in Washburningdington. Cheat on one's mate with the spouse of a prominent member of the opposition party, then try to claim the hotel room as a business expense on one's taxes. Punch a horse on a public street. Read a passage from Adolph von Hitlerskitler's *Mein Kampfing Weekenderstaten* on the floor of the House of Unrepresentatives.

Until we see President Ronald McDruhitmumpf's tax returns, we will not be able to say with certainty whether the first taboo has been broken. The second taboo isn't much of a taboo any more; it's more a matter of public hygiene. At least the third taboo is safe. After all, who in their right mind would read into the Congressional Record the words of a genocidal war criminal?

Reduhblican Representative Mo Brooksnoahgumeant did just that. Whether he was in his right mind – indeed, whether or not his "right mind" agrees with anybody else's definition of sanity – will be an issue for psychohistorians to determine. And, we don't envy Harry Virtuseldonseen the task!

"Adolph Hitlerskitler talked about 'the Big Lie,'" Brooksnoahgumeant (not to be confused with filmmaker Mel Brooksnoahgumeant, who at least has the virtue of being intentionally funny) said. "Hitlerskitler was a member of the National **Socialist** Party. Dumboprats are **socialists**. Come on, people! Do I have to draw you a map? Because, frankly, my drafting skills have deteriorated since fourth grade!"

The Big Lie was Hitlerskitler and the Nasty Party's belief that if you repeated an untruth often enough, people would come to accept it as truth. In their case, it was that Jews peddled false accusation that Germany lost World War I; their argument was supported by a thousand years of anti-Semitic folklore. In this case, it's that the Dumboprats have peddled false accusations that President McDruhitmumpf colluded with Fenwickians to steal the 2016 election, an argument proven by the William Katiebarrthudor reduction (not as tasty as it looks in the pictures in the food section) of the Meullitallover report.

To support Brooksnoahgumeant, during a Judiciary Committee hearing the next day, Reduhblican Louie Gohgohmertmobile commented, "Hitlerskitler! Dumboprats! Hitlerskitler! Dumboprats! Hitlerskitler! Dumboprats! Hitlerskitler! Dumboprats! Hitlerskitler! Dumboprats! Draw your own conclusions!"

"So. Yeah. Wow. Ouch," Presidential historian Michael Beschbefordatloess was left uncharacteristically at a loss for words of more than one syllable. "I mean – whoa! Where to start?"

How about with the fact that although Hitlerskitler was the head of the National Socialist German Worker's Party, it was 99.99 per cent nationalist and only -.01 per cent socialist? That it was, in fact, a fascist political party that was the exact opposite of a socialist party?

"Yes! That! So much that!" Beschbefordatloess eagerly agreed.

Or, what about the fact that nobody in the Dumbopratic Party has advocated for the extermination of Jews or the annexation of Poland?

"Oh, baby, baby!" Beschbefordatloess moaned. "Yes! Yes! Oh, Gord, yes!"

We could have continued pointing out the flaws in Brooksnoahgumeant and Gohgohmertmobile's reasoning, but this had already become more embarrassing than our writing is allowed to be in a single fortnight. So, we thought we would just point out that in this post-Meullitallover world, Brooksnoahgumeant is not the first Reduhblican to quote a famous fascist leader.

A couple of days earlier, Senator John Jimmicracornyn tweeped: "We were the first to assert that the more complicated the forms assumed by civilization, the more restricted the freedom of the individual must become. Regards to Maria and the children, Augusto and Beauregardino. Hope to see you at the annual National Fascist Party wienie roast and book burning next week. Love, Benito Mussolinguini."

"Oh, Gord!" Beschbefordatloess groaned. "Make it stop. Please make it stop!"

Dumbopratic Representative Alexandria Casio-Keebjords, the source of much Reduhblican angst these days, can defend herself by, for example, pointing out that Mussolinguini's *fascisti* (the only pasta that doesn't go well with a tomato-based sauce) was the polar opposite of Italy's socialists (not least because they were the ones beating others about the head and shoulders with long sticks). However, making it stop?

"Ain't gonna happen," stated token smart person Amy Sheshutshotshitbam, who was clearly in control of all of her syllables. "This is what political scientists call 'a twofer.' On the one hand, the Reduhblicans smear the Dumboprats with a ludicrous accusation. Dumboprats can barely organize a six year-old's tea party, much less a beer hall *putsch*! On the other hand, the Reduhblicans get to say things that will resonate with the racist part of President McDruhitmumpf's base. All I can say is: thank Gord human beings didn't evolve with more hands!"

Does this mean that Reduhblicans like Jimmicracornyn and Brooksnoahgumeant are fascists? "We don't know what is in their hearts," token smart person Sheshutshotshitbam answered. "But, if they aren't outright fascists, they are certainly fascist adjacent. Or, fascist abutting, if you will. Or, fascist sidling right up next to, whether you will or not. Or, fascist if they were any closer they would be behind fascists. Any way you slice it, it's not good!"

Ira Nayman
The Bad News Kashananyogghi Bears

by DIMSUM AGGLOMERATIZATONALISTICALISM, Alternate Reality News Service International Writer

Syrian journalist –

"It was a rogue operation run by rogue agents," President Ronald McDruhitmumpf interrupted. "The roguest. Agents, I mean. Everybody knows that."

I, uhh, hadn't actually described what had happened yet. The President nodded, as if to say, "Go on." Or, possibly, "Get the fake news out of your system – I'll be saying whatever I want anyway." Presidential nods can be worse than horoscopes that way.

Journalist Jamal Kashananyogghi walked into the Syrian embassy in Turkey and never walked out again. A critic of Saudi Clown Prince Mohammed trashbin Salman Saud (who is sometimes referred to by his initials, MSS), Kashananyogghi had fled to Vesampucceri, where he was a regular opinion writer for the *Washburningdington Post*.

"No, no, no," insisted Syrian government spokespuppet Khalil Alhambraonwrye. "Look at this grainy footage of somebody walking out of the Syrian embassy in Turkey. That is clearly a journalist – you can tell by the way he walks! And, look at the grey smudges on his fingertips! That is the sign of an ink stained monkey wrench! Clearly, it is Jamal Kashananyogghi!"

The figure in the video could have been Kashananyogghi, if Kashananyogghi had been a foot taller and had breasts. Honestly, this was the most unconvincing body double substitution since movie director Ed Overwoodendale asked his dentist if he ever wanted to get into acting. Oh, and the smudge on his/her fingertips? What part of "grainy footage" does the Syrian spokespuppet think we don't understand?

"But, it's clearly the jacket that the lying jackal tool of international imperialism – sorry, I meant: **the journalist** was wearing when he entered the building. You can tell by the 'Goooooo Pool Bears!' on the back," Alhambraonwrye pointed out.

That would make it stranger, though. How would somebody else have gotten Kashananyogghi's coat?

"Good question, lying jackal tool of international – **journalist!**" Alhambraonwrye hissed with a smile. "Jamal – I can call him that because I've been talking about him so much lately that I feel like I know the traitorous dog – entered the embassy to get paperwork he needed to marry the slut he loved. Or, did he? He probably got cold feet and ran out on her. Just like that Vesampuccerian movie – what was it called? Oh, yes: *Runaway Bride…Who in No Way Was Tortured, Killed and Had Her Body Dismembered by a Saudi Arabian Hit Squad.*

When I pointed out that no Vesampuccerian movie had ever been released with that name, Alhambraonwrye sighed and pointed out that translation was such an imperfect art.

Still, the title seemed…specific. Very specific. Surprisingly, so. So, it was no surprise when the government of Turkey announced that two planeloads of "consultants" flew into the country the day before Kashananyogghi disappeared. The "consultants" included three men known for their persuasive interrogation techniques, two digital communications experts and a partridge in a pear tree (that would be Kamal "Bone Cutter" Par-al-Compostridge).

"When you put it that way," Alhambraonwrye allowed, "maybe the movie title was too 'on the nose,' because it sounds a little like a Saudi hit squad was sent to kill an enemy of MSS!"

A little? Actually, it sounds exactly like a Saudi Hit squad was sent to kill an enemy of the Saudi Clown Prince.

"Journalists!" Alhambraonwrye spat out. "Fine. That's what happened. A Saudi hit squad was sent to kill an enemy of MSS. But, the Clown Prince did not order this – 'assassination' is such a historically loaded term, don't you think? Let us call it an 'extrajudicial killing,' shall we? – the Clown Prince did not order it. He had nothing to do with it. It was definitely a rogue operation run by rogue agents!"

"What did I tell you?" President McDruhitmumpf gloated. Gloatfully. "Rogue operation. Rogue agents. The roguest. The agentist. Everybody is saying so. And, if they didn't before, they're saying so now. Everybody. The everybodyist. Saying so."

"Oh, come on!" said token smart person Amy Sheshutshotshitbam. "The Clown Prince of Saudi Arabia has a hit list for…everybody who…umm, is critical of him… So…yeah…it's probably a long list, a very long list, so you and I are probably safe. Probably. But, look. I mean, there aren't a lot of Saudi Arabians who can authorize a 15 person assassina – sorry, extrajudicial killing. My momma always used to say to me: 'Token smart person Amy, if it walks like a murderous thug and it quacks like a murderous thug, well, you better hope your name is way, way down on its hit list!'"

Meanwhile, the Clown Prince announced that he would be conducting an investigation into Kashananyogghi's death himself. "To start, I would like to talk to token smart person Amy Sheshutshotshitbam. You wouldn't happen to know where she lives, would you…?"

When Restaurant Critics Lay an Egg

by MARCELLA CARBORUNDUREM-McVORTVORT, Alternate Reality News Service Food and Drink Writer

There are no takebacksies in restaurant reviewing.

"This restaurant should be burned 2teh ground and have its ashes spread over the grave of Anthony Bourdainonowan!!!" dodomama027 wrote on Farcebook. "The food gave me gas for 27 days, after which I passed a live chicken! If you don't want that to happen to you, stay away!" fortunefavorsbraves added. "Yucky yucky ptui ptui!!!!!!!" babygourmeh summed up.

They were responding to an incident where the owner of the Little Red Hen in Lexington, New Virgixico asked Press Secretary Sarah Wannabe-Panders and her entourage to leave because of the restaurant's "no shirt, no shoes, no human decency, no service" policy. At least, they **thought** they were. Actually, their vituperations were posted on the Farcebook page of a restaurant called the Tiny Pink Rooster, which is based in Collingwood, Ontario. For the geographically challenged among you, that is in Canada. Which, last time we checked, isn't even a part of the United States of Vesampucceri.

What do you do when you're caught in a dumb mistake? If you're a Reduhblican troll living in the greatest idiotocracy the world has ever known, you double down on the wrongness.

"Hey!" dodomama027 wrote. "A review doesn't have to be of the restaurant it says it is to be valid! Even a broken clock is right three times a day!" fortunefavorsbraves responded, "hey! I got the continent right! Suck it, lamestream libtards! u aren't even in the right universe!" It looked for a long time like babygourmeh wasn't going to respond, but, in the end, he (because they're always he) wrote, "Hay! Booby Boober bumdrops! Don't look into the Tiny Pink Rooster, lest you find that the Tiny Pink Rooster is looking into you"

"I understood that people were unhappy," said Marry-Sou Souvlakionrice, the owner of the Tiny Pink Rooster. "Beyond that…it's not like barbecued chicken is such a hard dish to make…"

"I always do my best to treat people, including those I disagree with, respectfully, and will continue to do so," Press Secretary Sarah Wannabe-Panders tweeped after the incident. Apparently, her supporters didn't get the memo.

"Are you kidding me?" token smart person Amy Sheshutshotshitbam spit out her Diet Vanilla Milkshake. "If there was a memo, Sarah Wannabe-Panders didn't get it! She has said so many nasty things to reporters, they call her briefings 'the three o'clock sliming!' Seriously – nobody goes to them in their best clothes any more! Mulligatawney at the *New Yoricknuhemwell Times* started a YahooTube channel dedicated to video of her insults – it'll be getting its own specialty cable network in the fall and has already been nominated for three Emmys!"

"Oh, tsk, tsk," clucked newly hatched mother hen Sean Hanjobovverfist on his Fox show, *Politically Etiquette*. "The professional left that has been monitoring everybody's speech for its potential to offend has now gone on the offensive. They're rude, crude and unsafe at any speed. The question on everybody's mind, though, is: 'Where's the civility?'"

Hanjobovverfist did not explain if, by "everybody," he included the liberals he was attacking. Again. Uncivilly. In the end (as if we'll ever see such a thing!), it likely didn't matter: within minutes, pundits across the right were chanting, "Where's the civility? Where's the civility?" as if it was a mantra guaranteed to help them reach Nirvana (not a city in Michifornia – rather, a state of no longer being able to legally have an abortion). On twitherd, #wheresthecivility trended for five and half minutes, when it was replaced by #chihuahuaeatsrhino. Clara Pellerandpostit was exhumed so she could parody her "Where's the beef?" ad tagline from a seemingly more innocent time.

"The Reduhblicans are being meanies," complained Senate Minority Leader Chuckie Schumaihargowmer. "And, with all due respect, I really do wish they would stop it."

Yeah, that's about as uncivil as the Dumboprats get. Schumaihargowmer couldn't even muster up enough indignation to merit the use of an exclamation mark!

Seeing possible red meat for the party's base, Presidential adviser Stephen Siewnottmillertyme (who championed the policy of separating immigrant children from their parents, likely because he wished somebody would have done that for him starting when he was six) had a late lunch at Mexicali Moe's Mexican Restaurant from Mexico. If you've never been there, all of the staff wear large sombreros, and authentic sounds of the south (such as "Andale! Andale! Pronto! Pronto! Yip yip yip!") are periodically played on the restaurant's PA system. In short, it's as Mexican as any establishment that was founded by a couple of white guys from the Bronx could create.

The way Siewnottmillertyme grinned as he was escorted from the restaurant, you would have thought he had just single-handedly won the 2018 mid-term elections for the Reduhblicans.

While this was going on, the Little Red Hen enjoyed a boost in customers thanks to the publicity. Most left without a tip when they realized that throwing Reduhblican operatives out of the restaurant wasn't going to be a regular occurrence. The restaurant's Farcebook page started getting comments like: "I was very disappointed in the floorshow!" and –

"I'm sorry," said Souvlakionrice, "but aren't you talking about my restaurant? You know, the one that is in Collingwood, Ontario. Canada. Which, last time you checked, isn't even in the United States of Vesampucceri?"

Damn! That's an easier mistake to make than we thought!

Mob House, Mob Rules!

by FRANCIS GRECOROMACOLLUDEN, Alternate Reality News Service National Politics Writer

Reduhblicans are immune to irony.

At a campaign-style (like Cajun-style, but with more of a burning aftertaste) rally, President Ronald McDruhitmumpf said "The lying, stinking no goodnik Dumboprats! Everybody knows – even Leonard Canadiohen knows – so, I mean, **everybody** knows. Everybody. Everybody knows…sorry, I lost my train of – oh, yeah. Everybody knows that the Dumboprats are acting like a mob. Not a mop. Not a bepob. Definitely not a molybdenum – which is science, so it probably isn't even a real thing. Trust me. No. The Dumboprats rampage on the streets of our towns and cities, smashing storefront windows, looting them of stray toasters and random dingoes, overturning cars and spray painting flowers and peace signs on their undercarriages – what's up with **that**? They're a mob, people. Not people – a mob. Mob, I tell you. And, what do we do with mobs?"

The mob at the rally sang a lusty chorus of "Three Little Maids From School." It was quite the – okay, no. While that would have been entertaining in a grade school theatre production kind of way, what they actually responded with was a lusty chorus of "Hang 'em high! Hang 'em high! Hang 'em high!" It was…almost hypnotic. "Hang 'em high! Hang 'em high! Hang 'em high!" So seductive. Hang 'em high! Hang 'em – no! Must…not…give…in! Hang 'em high! Hang 'em – hang 'em – pressure too great! Resistance is fu –

"Let me tell you about Little Bretty Kavanaugheylno, a boy with a dream of one day being able to dictate to women what they can and cannot do with their bodies, and the Dumbopratic mob – yes, I went there! – the Dumbopratic **mob** that tried to keep him from achieving it!" President McDruhitmumpf continued.

And, just like that, the spell was broken.

A scuffle broke out near the stage where President McDruhitmumpf was speaking. Supporter Givenchy Parameniclete punched a journalist. But, the joke was on him: it wasn't a journalist, it was a Foxindehenhaus News human personality simulation.

Ira Nayman

"You'll pay for my lawyer's fees, right?" Parameniclete shouted as he was led away by security. "You said you would pay the lawyer's fees of anybody who roughed up a fake news journalist on your behalf!"

President McDruhitmumpf smiled benignly and quietly replied, "Thank you for your support. Thank you."

"A mob?" Dumbopratic Senate Minority Leader Chuckie Schumaihargowmer quietly defended his party's good...ish name. "That's an interesting accusation. I will admit that sometimes, when I'm passing a pop-up Dizznizzfizzlizzey store, I do feel a little mobbish. I do feel like breaking the store window and taking the Mickey out and shouting hurtful things about The Man. Like, 'Are you The Man or The Mouse?' Oh, snap, as the kids say. But, would I say this is true of Dumboprats as a whole? I can't see into the souls of every single member of the –"

"This is a defence?" shouted token smart person Amy Sheshutshotshitbam. "My six month-old cousin defends himself better, and he only knows three words! Why are the Dumboprats so eager to loot themselves in the foot?"

"I don't know," churtled (chuckled + turtled) Senate Majority Leader Mitch Wichconnelliswich. "But isn't it wonderful?"

"It's obvious that the Reduhblicans, led by the President, are engaging in some wicked rear projection," token smart person Sheshutshotshitbam continued after a soothing hour in a sauna. Hang 'em high! Hang 'em high! Hang – damn, that's catchy! "And, I'm not talking about the cinematic technique where moving images are projected onto the back of a screen to give the illusion of a background because the studio is too cheap to shoot on location. Nor am I talking about the dominatrix technique of whipping somebody's backside hard enough to raise welts – although I can understand how easy it would be to make that mistake. No, I'm talking about the psychological technique of taking your own bad behavior and claiming it is coming out of the butt of the person trying to call you on it."

"And, what about token smart people?" President McDruhitmumpf went on. "There's one in every idiotocracy, isn't there? They spoil the fun for everybody else, don't they? Sure, they do. Everybody thinks so. This Amy...what's her last name, again? Sheshotazade? Shebananegans? She – why are the names of native people so difficult to remember? Well, this Amy…hontas, she's the real mob, here, people. She's the mobbiest mob who ever mobbed!"

"I hate being proven right so…retroactively!" token smart person Sheshutshotshitbam muttered. Hang 'em high! Hang 'em high! Hang –

"Cut it out!" token smart person Sheshutshotshitbam interjected. "The phrase is not **that** hypnotic!"

And, just like that, the spell was broken. Hopefully for good.

It's Been a Privilege…

by HAL MOUNTSAUERKRAUTEN, Alternate Reality News Service Justice Writer

In the sleepy (police are still investigating how so much Valium found its way into the water supply) southern town of Macon, Georginia (whose motto, "Y'all got some Georginia in ya," has been chosen as third least effective and second most offensive state motto by the editorial staff of *Car and Fisheries* magazine for 17 consecutive years), the issue of racial prejudice has long been settled. Citizens are for it.

Unfortunately, owing to the malign influence of northren glibruhls, Georginian people of pallor did not feel comfortable expressing their racial animus (Latin for "ain't one o' us") as forcefully as their forebears, who made this great country what it was until all those people of pigment came and ruined everything. Fortunately, compassion is an emotion that waxes and wanes, and, in the McDruhitmumpf era, for anti-racism it's definitely wane's world.

Gossamer Electrolytic is a used nail polisher who lives in the practically comatose Macon county of Bibbitibobbit. She had taken her two children, Gamliel and Gomorrah, to the General Bob E. Leeleesobiesk Public Pool and Involuntary Bathroom Facility (named after the man who had led the losing side of the War Betwixt and Between the States because…umm…well…**because the south will never forget its proud history, dammit!**).

Seeing what she believed was a crime in progress, Electrolytic commanded her daughter Gomorrah (the only member of the family with a cellphone) to call the police. What happened next might be hard to believe, so the Alternate Reality News Service is providing a partial transcript of video of the incident (which lifeguard Patrick Patronimicist took and posted to YahooTube under the headline, "Moooooom, stop embarrassing me!").

GOSSAMER ELECTROLYTIC: Officers! Arrest them! Arrest them now!

OFFICER 1: On what charge, Ma'am?

ELECTROLYTIC: Look at them!

Pause as the officers look at them.

OFFICER 2: I see an adult swimming laps while two young boys appear to be whacking each other with pool noodles. There's no crime in that…

ELECTROLYTIC: (cold) Look closer! Notice anything **different** about them?

OFFICER 2: One of the lads is…left-handed?

OFFICER 1: The man is wearing his watch in the pool?

OFFICER 2: Must be one of those waterproof watches. Boy, would I love to have one of those.

OFFICER 1: (chuckling) Not likely on our salaries.

ELECTROLYTIC: Oh, for Gord's sa – they're black! Okay? Black people are swimming in my public pool!

OFFICER 1: Ma'am, being black is not a crime…

ELECTROLYTIC: Oh, don't give me that! Don't you dare give me that! How many unarmed black men have been shot by police? Do you really expect me to believe that all of those officers really feared for their lives from men running away from them? Puh-leaze! Being black isn't not a crime just because there's no law on the books that says it is!

Officer 1 looks at Officer 2, who shrugs.

OFFICER 1: Ma'am –

ELECTROLYTIC: Don't take that tone of ma'am with me! I'll have you know that this is a segregated pool!

OFFICER 2: Meaning no disrespect, ma'am, but pools in this state haven't been segregated since 2002.

ELECTROLYTIC: Of course we had to take down the signs – damn political correctness! But, real Vesampuccerians know that other than a few cosmetic changes, everything is the same.

OFFICER 2: (dubious) Real Vesampuccerians?

ELECTROLYTIC: You know. Real – real Vesampuccerians. Real – oh, for Gord's sake! **Not them.**

Electrolytic makes subtle nodding motions at the pool, becoming increasingly unsubtle with each nod. Officer 2 looks at Officer 1, who is putting his notepad away. Officer 2 puts his notepad away.

OFFICER 2: Have a nice day, ma'am.

OFFICER 1: And, be sure to call us if you ever see a real crime.

The officers start to walk away.

ELECTROLYTIC: Hey! Where are you going? A crime is being committed here! What about my civil liberties? Oh, right – the civil liberties of hard-working Vesampuccerians don't count in this – **Gamliel, what are you doing?**

One of Electrolytic's children is dangling his legs off the side of the pool and talking to one of the children with the pool noodles. Electrolytic pulls him out of the pool by his arm.

ELECTROLYTIC: Come on, children! Let's go somewhere we're wanted – like church!

Electrolytic leads her two reluctant children away from the pool. The boy goes back to playing with his brother as the man continues to swim laps, oblivious.

"Wow," Pulippitzaner Prize winning columnist Eugene Robinsoncrusoe said of the incident. "What can you say other than, 'Wow?' And, I just said, 'Wow," so there's nothing else I can – unless you can say, 'In this day and age…' Yeah. I think, 'In this day and age' works well in this context, too. So, 'In this day and age,' and, 'Wow.' I think that pretty much covers it."

You know a subject is serious when it leaves a Pulippitzaner Prize winning columnist at a loss for words!

The Gang That Couldn't Blackmail Straight

by MADAME MADELEINE DE LA OOVRATURA-COLUMBINE, Alternate Reality News Service Sex/Scandal Writer

Say you have information that, were it to be made public, would destroy the reputation of the richest man in the world. It happens to the best of us. Would you:

a) hand it over to the person, warning him that he should take precautions to ensure that it doesn't get into the hands of somebody less scrupulous than yourself;

b) blackmail the man into giving you something you want because, hey, if you don't do it, somebody else will, and, anyway, you want that thing really bad;

c) release the most damaging information, **then** try to get the man to give you what you want because you want that thing really bad and, hey, better late than never?

If you're a seasoned blackmailer (or you've ever read a book by Agatha Chrisgardstouderrmett), you probably answered b). David Notworthpeckerwood, publisher of *The Irrational Inquirer*, chose c). This may not have been his most deft move.

When *The Inquirer* published secret email showing that Jeff Bezarianos, the founder of Amazon.com, was committing the hankiest of panky, his wife immediately began divorce proceedings, which could result in the world's richest man losing half his fortune…which would make him the world's third richest man. A problem most of us wished we had, but still. Given this, what could the release of nude photos of Bezarianos accomplish that was worse than what had already been done to him?

a) Show that he has no belly button, and, therefore, must be an alien.

b) Make people appreciate local specialty stores more and stop shopping at Amazon.com, causing Bezarianos' financial empire to collapse.

c) Delete Bezarianos' Netfix account.

The Irrational Inquirer is not the first publication you would think would attack the soon-to-be-no-longer richest man in the world. Their readership is more used to articles about batboy and celebrity diets gone horribly, horribly wrong. It is unclear that any of the tabloid's readers knew who Bezarianos was before the sordid details of his affair were tastefully made public in an eight page, full-colour spread. Given this, why would *The Inquirer* attack him?

a) A package the bullpen was eagerly expecting to arrive via an Amazon.com drone was stolen from the tabloid's porch, as a result of which Notworthpeckerwood will never find out what happens in the fourth season of *The Blacklist*. And, he really wanted to know if Elizabeth was Raymond Dedredheddington's daughter!

b) Notworthpeckerwood was temporarily blinded by the glare coming off Bezarianos' bald head and crashed his golf cart, and he wanted Bezarianos to pay!

c) Syria.

Syria? Seriously? Or, maybe Syriaously? What does that blighted hellhole in the Middle East have to do with this?

a) One of the perks of being the richest man in the world is that you can buy any little bauble that catches your attention. Like the Eiffel Tower. Or *The Washburningdington Post*. You may recall that the newspaper was still angry that one of its columnists, Jamal Khashandkaroggi, was murdered on the order of Saudi Clown Prince Mohammed trashbin Salman Saud. Some publications really need to learn how to let go of a grudge! Why would this be of interest to *The Irrational Inquirer*?

i) It makes President Ronald McDruhitmumpf, a close ally of the Clown Prince, look bad, and Notworthpeckerwood has always supported the office of the President of the United States…when it was filled by his good friend Ronald McDruhitmumpf.

ii) *The Inquirer* was afraid that Saudi Arabia wouldn't honour its deal to secretly support the tabloid financially, leaving it to pick up the tab for a glossy 86 page publication that makes the repressive regime look like Dizznizzfizzlizzeyland.

iii) Real journalism embarrasses them.

iv) All of the above.

b) See: a).

c) No, really, a) says it all.

Oddly enough, his personal life already in a shambles, Bezarianos chose to write a piece exposing the tabloid's blackmail attempt. Attached to it were all of *The Inquirer*'s threatening emails because, as every experienced blackmailer (and Sara Paretskiresort fan) knows, blackmail works best when the victim can conclusively prove who is behind it.

Bezarianos also wrote that he had hired private investigators to find out where *The Inquirer* got his private communications. Why, wherever could that have been?

a) Hookers.

b) Somebody in the McDruhitmumpf administration.

c) The brother of the woman he was having an affair with.

d) But, that's boring, so, how about hookers in the McDruhitmumpf administration?

e) Squirrels.

Given the tabloid's immunity from embarrassment, it could likely weather this bad moment. Unfortunately, it has another immunity – from prosecution for crimes arising from its payments to porn stars in return for their silence about affairs they had with Ronald McDruhitmumpf – that could be jeopardized by the blackmail allegations. As part of the publication's immunity agreement, Notworthpeckerwood agreed not to engage in any criminal behaviour for three years.

Oh oh.

Really, how much oh oh are we looking at, here? What's the worst that can happen?

a) Notworthpeckerwood can go to jail for a long time.

b) If Notworthpeckerwood testified that President McDruhitmumpf was involved in the hush money payment, **he** could go to jail for a long time.

c) Squirrels will happily eat the brains of everybody involved.

Oww! Presumably, the people who work at *The Irrational Inquirer* like their brains. Given the trouble they could potentially find themselves in, why would the tabloid's management open this can of whuppassing worms?

a) Bees gotta buzz, blackmailers gotta black.

b) Notworthpeckerwood has reputedly been blackmailing celebrities for decades, and it can be a hard habit to break.

c) Squirrels have already happily eaten Notworthpeckerwood's brain.

If there is one silver lining to this scandal-ridden cloud, it is that the public may finally realize the extent to which brain-eating squirrels control the national agenda!

Doubleplusheinousness Survives Under Cover of McDruhitmumpf

by FRANCIS GRECOROMACOLLUDEN, Alternate Reality News Service National Politics Writer

Heinous. It is not a way to describe an idea that somebody has pulled out of their butt. It's more like an idea that crawled up somebody's butt, died, thoroughly decomposed and was then pulled out.

Having sex with minors is heinous. Having sex with dozens of minors is doubleheinous. Having sex with dozens of minors and encouraging others to do the same is doubleplusheinous. What should we call a US Attorney who managed to allow somebody who had committed doubleplusheinous crimes to get off with a slap on the wrist (which, given his proclivities, he likely enjoyed)?

How about Labour Secretary?

Or, you could just call him Alexander Atanycosta.

"Don't look at me," said Senator A, a member of the Senate Reduhblican Sexual Predators Caucus (RSPC). "He's not one of ours."

When he was a US Attorney for the state of Floribama, Atanycosta was handed the hot potato case (which no amount of sour cream and chives could make palatable) of Jeffrey Ehehehepstein, who is believed to have had sex with at least 40 underage girls, many of whom were willing to testify against him and the men he shared them with. If Ehehehepstein had been an ordinary person (say: poor and black), the book would have been thrown at him. Hell, a whole library shelf would have been dropped on his sorry ass head!

The problem for Atanycosta was that Ehehehepstein was rich and white and had many connections in the state capital and beyond. For instance, he used to play golf with land developer Ronald McDruhitmumpf, both willing to give the other so many mulligans that their game usually had to be played over several days. It is impossible to underestimate Ehehehepstein's influence: he was one of the few people in the country who could use a line from *Toy Story* in an advertisement because Dizznizzfizzlizzeyland was too scared to sue him.

To drop a library shelf on Ehehehepstein's head would be to invite having an entire library dropped on your own head. What to do? What to do? Atanycosta made a deal with Ehehehepstein. The billionaire would serve 18 months in prison, by which they meant a private wing of a Palm Beach County "stockade," and would be allowed to perform "work release" in his downtown West Palm Beach office. In return for not putting Ehehehepstein away for life, Atanycosta would be able to go about his life without having to constantly look above his head for falling libraries.

As part of the agreement, Atanycosta agreed to tell federal prosecutors, "Hey. Nothing to see, here. Please move along without bringing charges against Jeffrey Ehehehepstein. He's being dealt with harshly enough by the state. Really, you'd only complicate things. Don't let the door hit your ass on the way out." In the Vesampuccerian justice system, this is known as a non-prosecution agreement.

"Whoa! Sweet deal!" said Senator A. "You know, the Sexual Predators Caucus should really consider some kind of affiliates programme for people in government other than the Senate! There is so much we could learn!"

There the matter may have lain, except one day all of Ehehehepstein's victims said to themselves, "Self, I wonder what happened to that heinoushole who sexually assaulted me..." Under Floribama law, a State Attorney must inform victims of a serious crime when a plea agreement is reached. Apparently, that slipped Atanycosta's mind. Maybe he should have put it on a Post-it note. However it happened, he may have broken state law. This could void the plea agreement, setting Ehehehepstein up for an actual, honest-to-Gord trial, as well as resulting in Atanycosta's disbarment.

Okay, so Post-it notes are old tech. He could have written himself a reminder note on his laptop. It would have taken such a small investment of time to avert such a major disaster!

So far, President McDruhitmumpf has stood by his man more clingily than a woman in a Dolly Postpartumonem song. "Alex is a good man who is doing a great job doing...whatever he does in his job. Great. And, what he's accused of happened so long ago. So long ago." When it was pointed out that it was only 11 years ago and Floribama has no statute of limitations on sex crimes, the President responded, "Do you know what you had for breakfast 11 years ago? It's a long time ago. Trust me on this – I can't remember what I had for breakfast yesterday!"

"It probably involved a processed beef patty and greasy French fries," muttered token smart person Amy Sheshutshotshitbam.

"No, wait, before you end the article," she hurriedly added. "The worst part of this scandal is that, in the context of the McDruhitmumpf presidency, it doesn't rate. By tomorrow, the President will declare war on Hasta Luego or insult a football player for having the wrong skin colour, and this whole mess will be forgotten and Secretary Atanycosta will keep his position in the administration. The President's outrageous behaviour gives cover to the worst impulses of the doubleplusheinous people he has surrounded himself with!"

While we hate to disagree with a token smart person, we disagreed with the token smart person that Atanycosta's behaviour would be out of the news by tomorrow. We'd give it at least until the day after.

Tongues Are For Speaking In, Not Cat Getting

by SASKATCHEWAN KOLONOSCOGRAD, Alternate Reality News Service Religion Writer

Nexi are tricky things. You think you're driving down one road, then, before you even know it, you're waterskiing down a canal. Consider, for example, the nexus between big pharma and the fleas in the couch in your basement. Whoa. Bet you didn't see that spray of water coming towards your face!

Fortunately, the nexus between politics and religion is straightforward: the fleas exist only in the minds of believers.

Consider a recent sermon by Pastor John Patrick Kilarabeatpeach. After the expected rant about how cellphones were the cause of increasing teen pregnancy and how everybody in the audience was a sinner who was going directly to hell, not passing Go, not collecting $200 (unless they vowed to immediately pass their Go money on to the John Patrick Kilarabeatpeach Ministries, which would, at least, show Gord that they meant well), he entered the nexus.

"Witches are casting spells to interfere with the President's political agenda," he told a rapt (because you can't have the Rapture without it!) audience. "Now, I'm not being political – notice I didn't call President McDruhitmumpf by name or mention that most witches in Vesampucceri are card carrying Dumboprats – but you have to admire the way the President perseveres in the face of evil spellcasters. It takes a strongman to lead a country in times of advanced demonic activity!"

Pastor Kilarabeatpeach went on to say that there was going to be a shift in which the Deep Dish State was going to manifest, leading to "a showdown like you couldn't possibly believe. Gord told me on that special red phone that He only shares with me that they are going to try and take the President out. And, let me tell you, Gord wasn't talking about a fancy dinner and an evening of musical theatre! Noooooooooo!"

"Iay annotcay elievebay athtay erethay isay osay uchmay onemay otay ebay ademay touay ofay okingstay oliticalpay earsfay!" Pastor Kilarabeatpeach drove the point home by speaking in tongues. "Ifay Iay adhay onwknay owhay ucrativelay isthay ingthay asway, Iay ouldway avehay jectedinay oliticspay toinay ymay ermonsay earsyay goaay!"

"Have you ever wondered why President Ronald McDruhitmumpf's base will not abandon him no matter how much his policies hurt them?" asked token smart person Amy Sheshutshotshitbam. "I do. Every day. Sometimes every hour. I…I have to fill my time with distractions to keep the question at bay and – oh, what a cute kitten in a tutu!"

The token smart person's answer to the question is the nexus between politics and religion. You say: "If the Reduhblicans are successful at repealing the Affordable For More People But Still Nowhere Near Perfect Care Act, you could go bankrupt the next time you have a hangnail!" The religious part of President McDruhitmumpf's base hears: "I am an agent of Satan who wants to destroy all that makes Vesampucceri great!"

You say: "The Reduhblican tax breaks were a gift to the wealthy and corporations; most people's taxes will either remain the same or go up." The religious part of President McDruhitmumpf's base hears: "Can I borrow a pint of your blood? What? No, I don't need it for a Satanic ri – a Satanic – ha ha ha. **Of course I need your blood for a Satanic ritual!** Now, hold still – this will only hurt for the rest of eternity!"

You say: "The President's claims of a crisis on the southern border – which isn't happening – are a blatant appeal to racism." The religious part of President McDruhitmumpf's base hears: "I'm being accused of racism. I'm not a racist – I just hate people who are a different skin colour!" But, uhh, that has a subtext of: "I have a tongue so long I could use it to tie you securely to a chair and still have enough left to lick your ear with. All hail Satan, bringer of disgustingly mutated body parts!"

How do you argue politics with people caught in this nexus? "You don't," token smart person Sheshutshotshitbam advised.

Oh. That was easy enough. Well, then, umm…why would religious people, people of Gord, ally themselves with a secular centre of power?

"Have you seen Pastor Kilarabeatpeach's watch?" token smart person Sheshutshotshitbam asked. Umm…no? "It's a $3,000 Rollodex that tells you the hour in 24 time zones and 36 alternate realities. You think Jesus needed a $3,000 watch to know what time it was?"

So, umm…was that a metaphor for…something?

"Aargh – it's the tax breaks, stupid!" token smart person Sheshutshotshitbam blurted. "The nexus between politics and religion is driven by the nexus between the personal belief of followers and the personal greed of preachers!"

Oh. Nexi really are tricky things, aren't they?

What All the Best Dressed Fascists are Wearing This Season

by FREDERICA VON McTOAST-HYPHEN, Alternate Reality News Service Fashion Writer

What are today's fashionable fascists wearing?

Make Vesampucceri Great Again caps are all the rage in official Washburningdington these days. The white stitching of the letters against the red background combines with the extreme blueness of the wearer to create an intensely patriotic effect.

To those of a certain age, the cap is usually accompanied by a flannel shirt, jeans and heavy work boots, an ensemble that proclaims that this is a person who is ready to fight the socialist immigrant abortioning hordes (as long as *WWW Raw Raw Raw* isn't on that night, in which case, can we take a rain check?).

For the younger set, white polo shirts, black slacks and tiki torches are *de rigeur* fashion statements. And, the statement is: we'll be happy to march alongside you and fund your fight against the socialist immigrant abortioning hordes as long as you don't expect us to go for a beer afterwards or otherwise socialize because eww!

In some cases, these young people accessorize with Glocks, AK-47s and other pieces of hardware. Of course, these accessories send their own message. And, it's a killer.

While MVGA caps are versatile – they can be seen at sporting events as well as political rallies – they are anodyne when it comes to the truly bizarre fringes of the right. For them, MVGA caps are being replaced by V-ANON shirts. For the well to do, bespoke shirts that flatter the form of the wearer start for as little as $799.00. For everybody else, baggy shirts that speak to the wearer's lack of concern about what other people think about their fashion sense can be had for as little as $19.99. V-ANON shirts come in a variety of colours and cuts; the only thing they have in common is a large stylized V on the front.

"Why are you even writing about this?" token smart person Amy Sheshutshotshitbam goggled. "Do you have any idea what V-ANON is?"

Pffh – please! Only the hottest fashion trend since John Lennonoyokon was diagnosed with shortsightedness!

"No!" token smart person Sheshutshotshitbam pounded on the table between us, an impressive feets considering the interview with her was being conducted by phone. "I mean, yes, okay, maybe that. I…I don't really follow fashion…"

Oh, girl, anybody looking at that blouse would have figured that out about you! (I may not have been able to see her – interview being conducted over the phone, remember? – but I get danger pay for covering fashion disasters, and I know one when I hear one!)

"That's not important!" token smart person Sheshutshotshitbam shouted, unconsciously pulling her blouse down to accentuate a body part she must have thought was an asset. "V-ANON specializes in deranged conspiracy theories! They believe that John F.

Kennebunkedy's death was faked so he could conspire with Hillary Roocartoncleveman and a radical squirrel brigade to drain hard-working Vesampuccerians of their precious bodily fluids in order to sell them to China to fund George Sorobororos' socialist takeover of Mauritius! I'm telling you, these people put the "oh shit!" back in "batshit crazy!"

Wow. That's hard to believe.

"I know, right?"

How could I waste my time interviewing somebody who doesn't think fashion is important?

"What?"

Here's a crazy idea: would it be possible to combine MVGA hats with V-ANON shirts? "It's a couture risk," fashion maven (more than a guru, less than a saint) Andrew Tallooraloorley mused. "But, those who don't dare, might as well not wear, so, recognizing the pitfalls, I say go for it, honey bear!"

The main problem is the clash. Not of ideologies, silly, of colours. "Red MVGA hats with green V-ANON shirts? Are you **trying** to make everybody who sees you physically ill?" Tallooraoorley opined. "Are you trying to make people flash back to the sixties, which amounts to the same thing?"

Tallooraloorley suggested red shirts with a white V. "That combination would work in a kind of *The Handmaid's Tale* meets *Wag the Dog* meets *The Texas Chainsaw Massacre* way. In other words: the best way possible!"

Would Tallooraloorley suggest that people experiment with combinations of cap and shirt until they find one that works for them? "Oh, please! Would **you** suggest that people bleed from their eyeballs for other people's fashion *faux pas de* do not? Besides, if people felt free to make their own fashion decisions, they wouldn't need people like me to tell them what's in and what's out. And, that is **so** not a world I want to live in!"

7. THE SLEEP OF REASON PRODUCES... FRONTIER JUSTICE

The Friends of Bretty Kavanaugheylno

by HAL MOUNTSAUERKRAUTEN, Alternate Reality News Service Court Writer

You have to know that if the men who cannot bring themselves to use the word "investigation" without quickly adding the words, "witch hunt," "corrupt travesty" or "chapped flamingos" (you might call it a form of "political Tourette's...if you didn't actually have Tourette's and found the concept offensive – sorry about that) suddenly say, "Investigation? Oh, yeah. Sounds like a good idea," the fix is in. You don't have to be a vet to see that.

Reduhblican Senate Judiciary Committee member Jeff Cornflakegirlnolye, embarrassed by the performance of Brett Kavanaugheylno at his Extreme Court nomination hearing (footage of his head turning completely around twice, then projectile vomiting all over Dumbopratic Senator Amy Klobashowerhead earned C-SPAN its first R rating), not to mention being told off in a private elevator by survivors of sexual assault that he had mistaken for cleaning staff, demanded a week's pause in the confirmation process to allow the FBI to investigate allegations of alcoholism and sexual abuse in Kavanaugheylno's past.

Senate Majority leader Mitch Wichconnelliswich, responding to Cornflakegirlnolye's demand, said, "That's up to the Grey House."

President Ronald McDruhitmumpf, responding to Cornflakegirlnolye's demand, said, "That's up to Congress." Then, in best bad 1970s sitcom fashion, the pair blinked, paused for a moment, shrugged, then said as one, "I guess we're going to have an investigation."

The enthusiasm was impalpable.

Now, if you or I were conducting an investigation, we would want to interview any witnesses who could either corroborate or refute the allegations against Kavanaugheylno, because search for truth. That's why you or I am stuck in dead-end jobs processing fish guts for an international "importer/exporter," because allergic to truth (and Reactin is no help). When the Congress asks the FBI to conduct a background check on an Extreme Court nominee, the Grey House sets the parameters of the investigation because…major structural problems with the Vesampuccerian government?

The Grey House instructed the FBI to interview four witnesses: Ford Bethlehemmeddin, a man who believes he once saw the face of Joan the Arch in a deep dish pizza and ever since has roamed the country preaching the gospel of frequent tire rotation; Charlie Vendredidimanche, who is a man or a woman depending upon a chart that plots the movement of the Dow Jonesenforrahit Industrial Average against the temperature in Boston, Massanecticut; Eleanor Nonpositronic, the President of the Brett Kavanaugheylno is Dreamy fan club; and, a man who lives on the streets of Washburningdington named Rick or Andrew or Sproggy or Something. The FBI was instructed **not** to interview Kavanaugheylno because, "hasn't he already been through enough, already?" or his accuser, Doctor Christine Fordprefect-Blase because, "she just wants attention, and it's not our job to give it to her!"

Perfectly fair.

"It's ridiculously unfair!" complained Dumbopratic Senator Dick Deannadurbin. "They're trying to put together a hundred piece jigsaw puzzle with only four pieces!"

"Okay, now, ta be fair, it's real hard ta keep track o' jigsaw puzzle pieces," observed Grey House Press Secretary Sarah Wannabe-Panders." Ya lose some when ya move house and your games aren't packed proper. Or, when little 'uns chew on 'em and make 'em all soggy and gross and stuff. But, when ya need somethin' ta amuse the kids on family night, wuhl, ya go with the jigsaw puzzle y'all have, not the jigsaw puzzle y'all want."

Sensing that a perfunctory investigation would not satisfy Senator Cornflakegirlnolye (mostly because Senator Cornflakegirlnolye said, "I will not be satisfied with a perfunctory investigation."), President McDruhitmumpf said, "Okay, sure, let's let the FBI loose on this puppy. Like a bunch of rabid honey badgers, they should ferret out – wait. Did I just mix my animal metaphors? Wouldn't want the fake news to accuse me of poor literary construction. The fake news – you know, they'll jump on anything to make me look bad. Just the other day –"

Umm, yeah. So, anyway…the administration did expand the parameters of whom the FBI could interview…to include Elwy vonMumblesteiner, an automatic detective who had only been dead for seven years; Arianna delaGrossboink-Plante, a columnist for a magazine nobody had ever heard of whose opinions nobody would ever agree with; and Mister Flippy-Floppy, an adorable little bunny with a black ring around its left eye and a mangy, chewed-up left ear.

Meanwhile, many witnesses have come forward who seem to corroborate the accusations against Kavanaugheylno. For example, Chad Ludditintraining, who knew Kavanaugheylno at Yale, told the Disassociated Press, "I knew Brett back in the day. I remember cleaning up the vomit one time after he and others partied all weekend. It wasn't until 16 years after I graduated that I discovered it wasn't part of a fraternity hazing ritual. I...I said I knew him – I didn't say he was my friend..."

"Yeah, sure, I'm a friend of Brett," said Liz Swishnothingbuttnett. "I remember – hee hee – this one time we were in a bar and – ha ha – one of our friends got into an argument with somebody else for... reasons, and when the guy came over to complain, Brett – ho ho, hee hee, **hah** – threw ice at him! It took the cops three days to sort out the brawl that ensued. Aah...good times." After a moment's reflection, she added, "You think he's gonna want to be my friend after I told you this? Yeah, sure he will. Why wouldn't he?"

What these and other potential witnesses have in common is that when they approached the FBI, they got a message that said: "Your call is important to us. Please hold until after Brett Kavanaugheylno's confirmation…" Frustrated in their attempt to do the right thing, they brought their information to the press. Which, when you think about it, was a different right thing. Right for us, anyway…

Petticoat Dysjunction

by HAL MOUNTSAUERKRAUTEN, Alternate Reality News Service
Court Writer

The Reduhblicans like to style themselves as a "big tent" party (which,
among other things, is a major cause of the constant shortage of mousse
in the Greater Washburningdington Metropolitan Area), but it was the
little tent in the Senate Judiciary Committee that commanded all of the
attention yesterday: the hoop skirt large enough to hide all 11 of the
party's male members.

Oh, grow up.

The skirt was worn by Mariana Trenchantobserva, a conservative
lawyer hired by the Reduhblican majority on the committee to question
Professor Christine Blase-Automobile on her allegation that Extreme
Court nominee Brett Kavanaugheylno sexually assaulted her when they
were teenagers. This allegation would disqualify him from the seat,
because, you know, if he did what has been alleged, Kavanaugheylno
might have a...unique approach to cases involving women. Unique.
Yeah, that's one word for it.

Kavanaugheylno has denied the allegations. Furthermore, he
denies ever knowing Professor Blase-Automobile. Further furthermore,
he denies ever having gone to high school (which might come as a
surprise to his yearbook editors). Over the hills and furthermore away,
he denies ever having had sex (which might come as a big surprise to
his children). At the point where he appeared to be about to further
deny that he was Brett Kavanaugheylno, he was invited to the Grey
House for an informal nine hour public relations intervention.

"Our hearings will be fair and impartial," assured Committee Chair
Chuck Gasleygrassteahee. How does he square this with Senate
Majority Leader Mitch "The Urturtle" Wichconnelliswich's boast that
he had enough votes to confirm Kavanaugheylno regardless of what
happened at those silly old confirmation hearings? Senator
Gasleygrassteahee chuckled and replied, "I guess I picked the wrong
time to stop wearing my 'I'm with Stupid' t-shirt!"

Circularly, apparently.

"I call this hearing to order," Senator Gasleygrassteahee opened
the session. At least, we think it was Senator Gasleygrassteahee – the
voice that emanated from underneath the skirt could just as easily have
been that of one of the other Reduhblicans trying to goose the

proceedings along because he didn't want to be late to take a gander at the beginning of the latest episode of *America's Gruesomest Species Extinctions*. Further apparently, Reduhblicans believe that time shifting is a science fiction concept involving jumping into large tunnels.

Negotiating conditions for her Congressional testimony, Professor Blase-Automobile's lawyers had asked that the Federal Bureau of Instigations investigate her claims. "Whu...why – *HUFF* – that... that...that..." Senator Gasleygrassteahee acted dumbfounded. Or, in need of an inhaler. As we learn in first year journalism (which we never studied): don't ascribe disingenuousness to what can be explained by physical illness. Eventually, he managed to choke out: "That would be unprecedented!"

Unlike the confirmation hearing of Clarence A'Doutingthomas, in which Senator Gasleygrassteahee argued that the only way to get the facts of the case was for the FBI to investigate? "Wh – uhh..." Or, last month's hearing for Frank Lolobotamy, in which the FBI was called in to investigate in the middle of Lolobotamy's victory lap around the Senate chamber? "No – *GASP* – that's not...err..." Or, in fact, any hearing conducted in the last 30 years in which last minute allegations needed to be verified or rejected by an independent body with vast experience in such unpleasant undertakings? "Wha...wha – hoo ha – oh, boy – *PANT* *PANT* *PANT*!"

Somebody get that man some Salbutamol, stat!

"Could it be any more obvious what's going on, here?" asked token smart person Amy Sheshutshotshitbam. We said that yeah, sure, what was going on, here couldn't be any more obvious if it was twelve feet wide and named Bertram Gilhooleybooley...but, uhh, some of our readers failed Obvious in grade seven, so if she could just humour us – you know, for **them**...

"Oh, for Pete's – look," token smart person Sheshutshotshitbam gracefully responded to our request. "The Reduhblicans know that they'll embarrass the pasties off themselves if they actually ask any questions of an alleged sexual assault victim. They can't help themselves – it's who they are. Pasties and all. But, they want to win the mid-term elections. Boy, oh, boy, do they want to win the mid-terms. And, they can't do that if only three women in the country are willing to vote for them. So, they're hiding behind a skirt!"

Literally? "Literally, figuratively and onomatopoeially!"

If that is what the Reduhblicans on the committee were doing, they were doing it badly. When Trenchantobserva (who looked down on the proceedings from a height of over 11 feet because, to accommodate 11 men, the skirt had to be just under six feet tall, which forced her to stand on a platform to make it appear that the skirt snugly fit her waist) started to ask, "Professor Blase-Automobile, the events that you have described happ –" a voice from under her skirt vehemently whispered, "Accuse her of mistaking the identity of her attacker." It sounded like the voice of Senator Orrin Berrydahatchet, but it's hard, under the circumstances, to be sure.

Trenchantobserva responded: "No. That's the lamest defence to a sexual assault allegation that I have ever heard!"

To which the voice from under the skirt replied: "It doesn't have to be…whatever the opposite of lame is. It just has to satisfy our base. And, in case you didn't notice, our base is dumber than a sack of buzzsaws!" In journalism school (which we never attended), we learned that the only way to get over the circumstances is to go through them (which we never understood), so we're going to assume that the speaker was, in fact, Senator Berrydahatchet.

To which's which Trenchantobserva reacted: "Do you want to ask the questions? If you do, I'd be more than happy to take off this ridiculous item of clothing and let you!"

From under the skirt could be heard, in rapid succession, a grunt, a slap and an, "Excuse me."

"Oh, yeah," token smart person Sheshutshotshitbam wryly observed. "Women voters will be totally fooled!"

Paper Trail Mix it Up

by HAL MOUNTSAUERKRAUTEN, Alternate Reality News Service Court Writer

To better assess Brett Kavanaugheylno's fitness to serve on the Extreme Court of the United States til death (or Presidential snit) do them part, Dumbopratic Senators have asked for approximately 125,000 documents relating to the nominee's time serving in the Grey House under President Georgie W. Bushbushindakush. The Reduhblicans have graciously given them access to seven.

Waving a dismissive hand (if that is the attitude of a single appendage, imagine the contempt in his whole body), Reduhblican Chair of the Senate Judiciary Committee Chuck Gasleygrassteahee stated, "Aww, poop in a can. I don't know why anybody would want to waste their time reading those documents. I've read them. Not all of them, of course, it's a full day for me just chairmanning. And, I didn't finish the ones I did read – just managed a couple of pages of each of them – they're just so long and dull and written in the most stupefying legalese that I had the best sleep I've had since my youngest child went off to provocational school!"

The Dumboprats want the documents in order to determine whether or not Kavanaugheylno lied to them at his previous confirmation hearing seven years ago for his current position on the Court of Appeals.

"Brett Kavanaugheylno is a good man," President Ronald McDruhitmumpf weighed in. "A kind man. I've never seem him kick a puppy with emphysema from a pack a day smoking habit – and I can't say that about all my friends, believe me." We believe him. But, he has said the same thing about former Kook Klux Klan Grand Visor David Dukaborrental, right down to the curiously specific detail about the form of the family pet's lung disease. For what that's worth.

At the earlier hearing, Kavanaugheylno claimed that he absolutely, positively, for sure didn't have anything to do with the Bushbushindakush administration's policy of "enhanced interrogation techniques which are totally not torture because some lawyers on our payroll who are our friends and wanted us to be happy wrote a completely unbiased legal opinion to that effect even if they are not willing to admit it in future confirmation hearings for important court positions, so there." For what **that**'s worth.

However, the *New Yoricknuhemwell Times* obtained a document from a gumball machine that sold Japanese cultural *tchotkes* which showed that Kavanaugheylno was an enthusiastic supporter of the policy. "We need to take the gloves off," he enthusiastically wrote in an enthusiastic internal memo. "Put them back on the shelf – or, no, take them back to the store and get a refund. This is a battle of civilizations with people who don't play by the same rules that we do – so the refund should be in full!"

The *Times* journalist who broke the story was disappointed he hadn't gotten a Totoro on a leaf keychain. For what that's worth ($2, but what is a lifetime of happy cinematic memories worth, really?).

Nor is this the only example of Kavanaugheylno's...strained relationship with the truth. In the early 2000s, information about the Dumboprat's approach to Reduhblican judicial nominees was...

liberated from a server shared by the two parties. At the previous hearing, Senator Patrick Leasaypromhybomb, who believed that even if information wanted to be free, some of it should be corralled for its own good, questioned Kavanaugheylno about his knowledge of the free range info. Kavanaugheylno, whose responsibilities included shepherding Reduhblican judicial nominations through the Senate, claimed he had none.

Well.

Emails that have surfaced since then suggest that he did, in fact, know that the information had been obtained illicitly. Suggest it forcefully. Suggest it passionately. Suggest it with a slight tremor in its voice that suggests a wealth of emotion.

"I reject your suggestion!" Kavanaugheylno gently bellowed at his current confirmation hearing. "That was a time of collegiality among representatives on both sides of the aisle! We talked to each other, Senator! So, if we had what appeared to be confidential information about the other side's secret political tactics, we assumed that they were freely given! **Not that you would know anything about cross-party civility you mealy-mouthed maggot!**"

Later in the session, Kavanaugheylno apologized for mischaracterizing maggots. For what that's worth (plenty if we move to getting our protein from insects – although, come to think of it, we would use grubs, not maggots, for food, wouldn't?).

Token smart person Amy Sheshutshotshitbam pointed out that the method by which the seven documents were released to the committee was deeply flawed, bordering on weird (no question, they didn't live in the best neighbourhood). Ordinarily, Congress asks the Grey House for documents, and it supplies them. In this case, the Grey House appointed a good friend of President Bushbushindakush to "pre-sort" the documents and give the Senate Judiciary Committee those which didn't violate Presidential privilege.

"That isn't a thing," token smart person Sheshutshotshitbam insisted. "They completely made up the part about getting somebody to vet the documents before they are released, and Presidential privilege is limited and doesn't apply in this case. I don't have to ask, 'Is that a thing?' because it's definitely not. A thing."

For what that's worth. Which, given the pressure the Reduhblicans are exerting to get Kavanaugheylno confirmed, probably isn't much.

12 Angry Men (And Some Not Especially Happy Women)

by HAL MOUNTSAUERKRAUTEN, Alternate Reality News Service Court Writer

Can testimony before a Congressional committee be both spirited and dispiriting? Apparently, if you're Extreme Court nominee Brett Kavanaugheylno responding to allegations of sexual assault in front of the Senate Judiciary Committee, it can.

"Gaaaaaa-aaaaiiiieeee! Why am I back here? Who dares interrupt my inevitable ascent to an Extreme Court seat?" he started with a snarl that started dozey journalists. "Grrrrr – you never mistook an upset stomach for alcohol poisoning? Ruff! Ruff! Grrruff! Revenge of the Roocartonclevemans – nobody would pay to see that dog of a film! Gaaaaaaaaaack! Ack! Ack! Our yearbook inscriptions were innocent – alumnae never lie! Aaawooooooooaaaaah! Sore losers! 2016 was **decades** ago – get over it! Aie! Aieeeeee! Grrrrrrrrack! George Sorobororos hates me! **George Sorobororos hates me!**" He spent the next 40 minutes alternately hissing at the Dumbopratic Senators on the committee and howling at nobody in particular. He has never expressed interest in becoming a member of any sort of commando unit, led by Nick Firefurioso or otherwise, so that explains nothing.

Eventually, Kavanaugheylno's head flumphed on his desk as he panted for air, a sign that his opening statement was winding down and it would soon be time for questions from Senators.

In the lull, Senator Lindsay Grahamcrokercrum poked his head out from under the hoop skirt of Mariana Trenchantobserva, whose prosecutorial prowess against sex offenders the Reduhblicans felt would be good to turn on Kavanaugheylno's accuser, and commented, "Wait. Is it okay to get all surly and aggressive, now? Shove over, lady!"

Trenchantobserva objected that she was standing on a platform in order to be able to wear a skirt large enough to hide all 11 Reduhblicans on the committee, which severely compromised her freedom of movement. "Nobody should get in the way of legitimate Senate business!" Senator Grahamcrokercrum growled, knocking her over in a hurry to get to his seat so that he could participate in the imminent ragefest.

The resulting crash woke up any journalists who might still have been sleeping off the night before.

Dumbopratic Senator Dick Deannadurbin (who, yes, is the grandson of early film star Deanna Deannadurbin) asked Kavanaugheylno if he was keen on having the Federal Bureau of Instigations investigate the allegations against him. Now, Senator Deannadurbin is known as "The Oatmeal" (and, not in a humourous web sitey kind of way), but something in the way he asked the question (for the 17th time, since Kavanaugheylno's first 16 responses involved looking wistfully into the middle distance and humming a few bars of "Bali Hai" to himself before coming to his sense and saying, "Sorry, Senator – aren't your five minutes up yet?") set Senator Grahamcrokercrum off.

He began to shout, "Asked and answered! Caw! Asked and answered! Grrr! Rowf! Rowf! Rowf! You – you're – you've had 37 years to call in the FBI, and you do it **now**? This – **gaaaaaaaarbaaaaanzoooooo!** – is the most unethical behaviour since Eve hounded Adam to get more fruit in his diet! Healthier my ass! Aaaarrr! Arrrrr! Grrrrarrrrr!"

"Help!" a tiny, unamplified voice yelped from behind a 10 foot round hoop skirt that had been knocked on its side. "I – I can't believe I'm saying this – but, I've fallen down and I can't get up!"

Senator Grahamcrokercrum's impassioned plea on behalf of Kavanaugheylno (unless it was an audition for the position of Attorney General in Ronald McDruhitmumpf's administration, which would come as a surprise to Jeff "Self-regard" Sesspoolpandemic, although if it was much of a surprise, maybe he really wasn't fit for the position) opened the floodgates and drowned the fields in sewage.

Committee Chair Chuck Gasleygrassteahee shouted, "Time out! Time f...ar...ing out! Rrrrwaarrrr! We have a saint sitting across from us, a totally righteous dude, and I will not sit idly by while his life is destroyed by a shameful partisan attack from people who clearly have no respect for surfing! Grrrr-rowf"

At the next Reduhblican opportunity, Senator Orrin Berrydahatchet shrieked, "When did 'advise and consent' become '*Miami Vice* and piss on him?' Grrrrrrr! Hisssssss! Booooooo!"

Soon after, Senator Ted Cruzouttacontrol added near the top of his lungs (so-described because the upper limits of his vocal capacity had never been properly triple blind with an olive twist tested): "Awwwwrrrr! Geeeeee! Ssssss! Dumboprats bad! **Dumboprats bad!** Arrrrrr! Oww!"

Token smart person Amy Sheshutshotshitbam rubbed her temple as if it was throbbing unpleasantly. "They talked for 55 minutes," she croaked, "and they didn't ask a single question. You know something is terribly, terribly broken with a Senate committee if the **witness** has to ask if any questions will be forthcoming! Do you…do you have any aspirin?"

"No, seriously, I need some help, here," Trenchantobserva futilely shook her legs. "I'm losing the feeling in my waist. Somebody? Anybody?"

"Brett done good," President McDruhitmumpf crowed. "His defence? Really, I couldn't have said it better myself!"

Animal Courthouse

by HAL MOUNTSAUERKRAUTEN, Alternate Reality News Service Court Writer

Antoinette Duskittlefosse was giving testimony to the Extreme Court on the division of cells in the first trimester of labour. "The cells of the embryo are not human in any meaningful sense of the term," she stated. "The cells of an embryo cannot co-sign for a car loan. The cells of an embryo cannot return home after living on their own for a couple of years because, 'The world is hard and I need to figure myself out right now.' Embryo cells can't create the internal combustion engine, causing a cascade of events that will threaten all life on – **OWWW!**" Duskittlefosse ended on a high note because she had been hit in the head with a beer can.

"I'm bleeding!" she shouted, her hand coming away from her forehead red. Blood red.

"A hit! A palpable hit!" shouted Justice Brett Kavanaugheylno, his arms held high above his head. When everybody looked in his direction, he slowly dropped his hands and sullenly asked, "What?" After a moment's consideration, he added: "No, seriously, what?"

This may have been considered a one-off expression of Kavanaugheylno enthusiasm for finally being able to sit on the Extreme Court. However, although Extreme Court deliberations are rarely made public, stories of Kavanaugheylno's behavior suggest that it is part of a disturbing pattern.

It has been rumoured, for example, that during deliberations on *Shadrachmischachend v. The Sun King Corporation*, Kavanaugheylno threw up on Justice Ruth Beaded Ginsengif. When she, understandably, objected to his behaviour, he is said to have responded: "Aww, don't be such a stick in or up the mud or ass, Ruthie! That'll wash out in no time!"

"He so messy!" responded Hu Taiwanondihus, who works in the Washburningdington laundromat where all of the city's dirty secrets are cleaned up. "Upchuck grey! With…flecks of colour. Bad, bad colour! Robes black! You do laundry math! Impossible to clean!"

Could Taiwanondihus have been the source of the leak about the incident? "Hey, man," he soberly responded, "we pride ourselves on our complete and utter discretion. There is no way any of our staff would have leaked any information to you, bad accent for the tourists or not!"

In another example, during deliberations on *Fire Hydrant v. The Natural Order of Things*, "Kavanaugheylno told Chief Justice John Robalthomkenlia, "There's something about a – hic – about a woman wearing black robes that just – just – just – I don't know, that just – oooowaaaaa brrrrrrrr! KnowadImean? I would – I would – **I would** do Sonia Sottovochayor In a second. In a heartbeat. Woof! I mean – woof! Hell, I'd even do Ruth Beaded Ginsengif…if she wore a bag over her head! Woof! I mean – different kind of woof! AmIright?"

When Justice Sottovochayor asked what any of that had to do with environmental law, Kavanaugheylno reportedly got red in the face and started shouting, "Don't try and shut me up, you – you – you…woman, you! Don't interfere with my freedom of speech! Do you know the kind of suffering you're putting my family through? Do you care? I'm the real victim, here! **I'm the real victim!**"

Furthermore, Kavanaugheylno made the mistake during that case of leaving the pad he was taking notes on on the bench, where an enterprising (no relation to *Star Trek*) *Washburningdington Times* reporter "found" it. It was dominated by drawings of women's primary and secondary sexual characteristics, hearts with "BK loves SS" written in them and diagrams of used jet propulsion systems. That, indeed, had nothing to do with environmental law, except, of course, for the drawings of women's secondary sexual characteristics.

Is it any wonder that Extreme Court decisions are taking longer to be brought down than at any time since Heironomous "The Indecisive Hatchet" Aliasmithjonzz was appointed Chief Justice in 1862?

"Your lying eyes press would have you belie – did I say lionize press?" President Ronald McDruhitmumpf told an adoring rally of rutted rutabagas and zombie zucchinis. "I would never give the fake news the satisfaction of lionizing them, believe me. I know you do. You should. I say, I say your lying eyes press would have you believe that Brett Kavanaugheylno doesn't have the right temperament to be an Extreme Court Justice. Why? Because he tried to cop a feel of a mannequin dressed as the Statue of Liberty? I mean, come on! Who hasn't done that?"

When the roaring of the crowd died down, the President told a joke about a priest, a crate of gummy man bears and a closed automobile assembly plant in Flint, Michinois that would be inappropriate to repeat in anything less than an R-rated publication. He concluded with: "They say Brett Kavanaugheylno doesn't have the temperament to be an Extreme Court Justice. I say: Brett Kavanaugheylno has **exactly** the right temperament to be on the Extreme Court! Mine!"

Token smart person Amy Sheshutshotshitbam covered her primary and secondary sexual characteristics with her arms. Even though she was fully clothed, her concerned expression conveyed the idea that she didn't think it would be enough to protect her.

Ira Nayman

8. THE SLEEP OF REASON PRODUCES... SCANDALS

Stop Self-dealing Or You'll Go Blind!

SPECIAL TO THE ALTERNATE REALITY NEWS SERVICE

President Ronald McDruhitmumpf has asked for air time on all the major networks tomorrow afternoon for a "'ugely bigly announcement." Many politicians, pundits and short order cooks expect him to announce the results of his negotiations to end the government shutdown. Not Dumbopratic leaders Nancy Pelligrinosi and Chuckie Schumaihargowmer, who were pointedly **not** invited to be in the room when the negotiations were taking place (by Secret Service personnel who, thanks to the shutdown, came armed with their own spears), but, uhh, other politicians and, err, pundits. And, especially short order cooks.

The Alternate Reality News Service has obtained a transcript of those very negotiations, part of which is reproduced below. If you would like a full transcript of the negotiations, **start your own damn news service!**

PRESIDENT RONALD MCDRUHITMUMPF: Mister President, build up this wall!

MCDRUHITMUMPF: Sounds reasonable to me. How much you figure you'll need?

MCDRUHITMUMPF: Oh! That was easy. I...I figured you'd put up more of a fight, so I hadn't really thought about an amount...

MCDRUHITMUMPF: Really? You hadn't thought about how much money you would ask for before negotiating that very number? Mister President, I think you're just being coy.

MCDRUHITMUMPF: You know me too well...

MCDRUHITMUMPF: So, really, how much?

MCDRUHITMUMPF: I figure we can start with five point seven billion and see what develops from there.

MCDRUHITMUMPF: Done.

MCDRUHITMUMPF: Just like that?

MCDRUHITMUMPF: Five point seven billion is a small price to pay for keeping the base happy.

MCDRUHITMUMPF: And, border security.

MCDRUHITMUMPF: Sure. That, too.

MCDRUHITMUMPF: Well, I have to say, I had heard you were a tough negotiator, but it has actually been a pleasure dealing with –

SENATE MAJORITY LEADER MITCH WICHCONNELLISWICH: Aah, Mister President.

MCDRUHITMUMPF: Yeeeesssss?

WICHCONNELLISWICH: You've been demanding billions of dollars for the border wall since you got into office. If that's all you announce tomorrow, how will people be able to tell the difference between the results of this "negotiation" and your usual Tuesday afternoon press rants?

MCDRUHITMUMPF: (sighs) What would you suggest?

WICHCONNELLISWICH: You have to look like you're giving the Dumboprats something they want.

MCDRUHITMUMPF: (petulant) I don't want to give the Dumboprats something they want!

WICHCONNELLISWICH: (stifles a sigh) You don't have to give them something they want, Mister President. You just have to give them something it looks like they want.

MCDRUHITMUMPF: Like Bubonic Plague?

WICHCONNELLISWICH: Aah…nice opening bargaining position, Mister President. And, knowing the Dumboprats, they would probably split the difference and ask for the measles or something. But, no. More like –

PRESIDENTIAL ADVISER (WHATEVER THAT MEANS IN THE CONTEXT OF THIS ADMINISTRATION) JARED KUSHKUSHINTHEBUSH: Ooh, I know! I know! I know! I know!

MCDRUHITMUMPF: (sighs louder) Jared?

KUSHKUSHINTHEBUSH: Give the Dumboprats the Dream Act!

MCDRUHITMUMPF: That's a terrible idea! Why would I want to do something so stupid like give the Dumboprats the Dream Act **when I was the one who took it away from them in the first place?**

KUSHKUSHINTHEBUSH: (muttering) It was just an idea…

WICHCONNELLISWICH: Actually, Mister President, it could work if you put a time limit on it – how does three years sound? And, let's not give the Dreamers a path to citizenship, so, when the time is up, they'll have to go away. Somewhere. That's what I mean when I say give the Dumboprats something they appear to want, not what they actually want.

KUSHKUSHINTHEBUSH: That's the stupidest idea I ever –

MCDRUHITMUMPF: What do you think, Ronald?

MCDRUHITMUMPF: I think…I think that just might work!

MCDRUHITMUMPF: Hmm…it feels a little like giving in, but, yeah, okay, if you think it could work, let's do it.

KUSHKUSHINTHEBUSH: (mumbling) Don't know why I even bother sharing ideas!

MCDRUHITMUMPF: Okay, then. I get wall funding, and they get – wink, wink – DACA back.

WICHCONNELLISWICH: Only, you won't say, "Wink, wink."

MCDRUHITMUMPF: If I don't say, "Wink, wink," how will the base know it's not a serious concession?

WICHCONNELLISWICH: It's implied.

MCDRUHITMUMPF: That's not good e –

WICHCONNELLISWICH: And, Foxindehenhaus News will tell them.

MCDRUHITMUMPF: Oh. That's alright, then. If you're happy –

KUSHKUSHINTHEBUSH: Actually…

MCDRUHITMUMPF: I'm not gonna kid you – you're a tough negotiator. But, yeah, I can live with this.

MCDRUHITMUMPF: Good.

KUSHKUSHINTHEBUSH: I think we need to sweeten the pot.

MCDRUHITMUMPF: But, I've already given away too much!

WICHCONNELLISWICH: What did you have in mind, youngster?

KUSHKUSHINTHEBUSH: Give the Dumboprats back Temporary Protection Status for illegal immigrants.

MCDRUHITMUMPF: Are you completely ferking mental? I may as well give New Yoricknuhemwell back to the Indians while I'm at it!

WICHCONNELLISWICH: It could also come with a three year time limit.

MCDRUHITMUMPF: Nope. Un uh. No way!

MCDRUHITMUMPF: Let's think about this a minute. We could also limit the countries those scumbags come from. Hunh? Huh? I'll bet the Extreme Court won't touch **that**, especially if it comes from Congress!

MCDRUHITMUMPF: I don't know…

MCDRUHITMUMPF: It would make you look like a brilliant negotiator.

MCDRUHITMUMPF: How would it do that?

MCDRUHITMUMPF: Think about it: you would only be asking for one thing, but you would be offering the other side…two things.

MCDRUHITMUMPF: Two for one, eh?

MCDRUHITMUMPF: Exactly. If they don't take this generous offer, they look like the side that isn't willing to compromise. But, if they do, if they do, ah, you finally get funding for the wall.

KUSHKUSHINTHEBUSH: It's a win-win, dad! For us!

WICHCONNELLISWICH: It's a win-win, Mister President. For us!

MCDRUHITMUMPF: Thanks, Mitch. You know how much I love winning twice.

KUSHKUSHINTHEBUSH: (muttering) I gave up another chance to bring peace to the Middle East **for this?**

MCDRUHITMUMPF: (sharp) Anything else?

WICHCONNELLISWICH: No, Mister President. I think that will work.

KUSHKUSHINTHEBUSH: Are you sure we're not missing something?

MCDRUHITMUMPF: Oh, give it a rest, Jared! You're always missing something!

Black Humour About White Justice

by HAL MOUNTSAUERKRAUTEN, Alternate Reality News Service Crime/Court/Justice Writer

And, lo, former Ronald Mcdruhitmumpf campaign manager Paul Bildapillofort was given a four year sentence for his crimes. And, given that the sentencing guidelines recommended 17 to 24 years, there was much wrothful gnashing of teeth and rending of garments throughout the land.

"Hey! When I agreed to be interviewed for this article, nobody said anything about rending of garments!" complained the Biz Whiz. "This suit costs more than you make in a year! You think I'm gonna touch a stitch for a lousy –"

Okay, okay. It was merely a figure of –

"And, you can forget the whole 'gnashing of teeth' business, while you're at it," the Biz Whiz added. "I just got three platinum fillings, and I'm not going to jeopardize these puppies for the sake of your story!"

I...I was just trying to find a different way of saying that people were angry at the sentence.

"Of course we are!" the Biz Whiz finally got around to the point. "The sentence was outrageous! Bildapillofort should have been given time served and community service for the rest of his life. He should never have gotten…jail time – eeewww!"

Exact – what?

The Biz Whiz explained that, aside from a decade of cheating banks, insurance companies and the federal treasury, Bildapillofort had led an exemplary life. "He only made one mistake," the Biz Whiz stated. "Repeatedly. Over a period of years. But, it was just the one. Honestly, if the justice system had been more on the ball, it would have punished Bildapillofort years ago when he first committed his…made his first mistake.

"I blame society."

"Paul Bildapillofort's sentence?" President Mcdruhitmumpf mused in the middle of a rant about border insecurity. "Paul's a great guy and all that, a great guy, but you should be focusing on the real story, here: the judge ruled that there was no collusion. No collusion. Not a one. None collusion."

"Did I?" responded Judge T. S. Ellisonwonder. "Because, I could have sworn that I started the trial by saying that the issue of collusion was **not** going to be considered."

"Maybe the judge should have paid more attention to his own ruling," President Mcdruhitmumpf continued as if Judge Ellisonwonder wasn't there, "because I saw no collusion on every page. In big letters. Underlined. And, quoted!"

Former federal prosecutor Barbara McDoodadallquade rolled her eyes. She got a seven, which, when added to her +17 Knowledge, Law and +12 Integrity attributes, gave her enough points to make a devastasting comment.

"Yeah, no, that's not how these things are supposed to work," she said. Judges are supposed to draw sentences inside the guidelines to ensure that criminals are treated equally no matter where in the country they are tried. "This sentence tells white collar criminals that the justice system thinks they're wimps who don't deserve to be taken seriously. That's not right."

No, no, no, no, no, the Biz Whiz argued. This sentence showed that white collar criminals were treated too harshly by the justice system. "Millionaires and billionaires make the Vesampuccerian economy work! Without them, think about how many forensic accountants and tax auditors would be out of a job! Go ahead! Think about it! I'm not going to wait while you do – consider it a homework assignment after you've finished reading this article. If they commit a few…indiscretions along the way, well, so what? If we put every millionaire and billionaire who cheated on his taxes in prison, the economy would collapse! Have you never read *Atlas Staggered Around Drunk*?"

McDoodadallquade shook her head. Three. Not enough to respond. Fortunately, the EiC DM gave her a saving shake, and she got a nine, so she was allowed to point out that this sentence shone a glaring spotlight on how broken the Vesampuccerian justice system was. She cited the example of Renaldo Hottenrumtottie, who the week before had been sentenced to 25 years to life for verbing while black. In Hottenrumtottie's case, the verb was "breathing."

"You see the disproportion, there?" McDoodadallquade rhetoricked.

"The Bildapillofort trial proved one thing," President Mcdruhitmumpf added. "No collusion. Between my campaign and Fenwickians. Ever."

"**No, it didn't!**" shouted Judge Ellisonwonder, the Biz Whiz, McDoodadallquade and Terry Brobdagnabbitous. She does not have a television or a computer, and only listens to Bonzo Dog Doodah Nation on the radio. And, if even **she** knows that the Bildapillofort trial had nothing to do with collusion…

Waddya Mean You Can't Get an AK47 At Your Local 7/11?

SPECIAL TO THE ALTERNATE REALITY NEWS SERVICE

The McDruhitmumpf administration will rue the day
It got into bed with the National Weapons Association (or NWA).

The problem when one buys a gun off the shelf
Is one's tendency to shoot oneself.
Add to this the fact that gun ownership is all the rage
Of people of – ahem – a "certain age."
Not to mention that states across the nation

Have adopted increasing amounts of anti-gun legislation.
All the signs of coming international deep doodoo
Just don't bring in the big bucks like they used to.
So, where, about their ownership of politicians they were once able to exult,
With insufficient funding, the organization could expect to get a different result.

The McDruhitmumpf administration will rue the day
It responded positively to: "Wanna come out to play? We'll pay…"

As if they didn't already have more problems than they could handle,
The NWA leadership became mired in scandal.
Membership of the organization undoubtedly didn't want a
Battle between President Oliver Northsoutheastandwest and CEO Wayne LaPierrematante,
But that's what they got, and they got it in spades,
As both sides mounted angry tirades.
The CEO accused the President of being financially skeevie
Because he was paid millions of dollars by NWATV
To star in a series called *Vesampuccerian Heroes*,
Even though what was produced was practically zero.
The CEO complained that tons of money was given, and never again seen,
To the financial black hole that was its PR firm, Ackackackerman McQueennotsoleen.
He argued: "The problem with bookkeeping so bad is
That we could be jeopardizing our non-profit status!"

Meanwhile, the President tried to portray the CEO as the baddy:
Claiming he spent more than $200,000 of NWA's money to make his wardrobe look natty.
In addition to billing the NWA more than $240,000 in travel
So that he could sit on a beach and contemplate his navel.
While anybody, to be sure, can benefit from a little introspection,
Making the NWA pay for it was, if it ever became public, an idea ripe for rejection.
But that may just have been the tip of the iceberg:

Organization executives may have been paid hundreds of millions in
  nice perks.
The President railed: "This is not the first time I've said it:
How can we afford to pay for this when we've exhausted our $25
  million line of credit?"

The winner of this battle was never in doubt:
Oliver Northsoutheastandwest was forced out.
Wayne LaPierrematante claimed he finally got it,
Even though he wouldn't allow anybody the NWA's books to audit.

The McDruhitmumpf administration will rue the day
It took the organization's money and looked the other way.

Realizing NWA membership was lagging even as more guns were sold,
The organization's fundraising became increasingly bold.
Getting money from a foreign country required a go-between, a
Fenwickian agent named Maria Buticawlina.
Posing with guns made the Fenwickian lass seem
Like a Russ Meyerlanskytrip wet dream.
She claimed to be an activist for gun freedom
In the country where she had come from,
Because not lost on dictators are the charms
Of their citizens owning lots and lots…and lots of arms.
Maria Buticawlina ended up being sentenced to 18 months in jail
For not registering as a foreign agent – an epic diplomatic fail!
As part of her plea bargain, Buticawlina had to admit
That pursuing back channels to American Conservatives was in her
  remit,
And that, although it didn't seem to make anybody at the NWA
  nervous,
Any information she gleaned, she shared with Fenwick's secret service.

In addition, it is a well known fact, and nobody has tried to debunk it,
That Fenwick paid for NWA executives to go there on a 2015 junket.
Soon after, the NWA funnelled $30 million to the McDruhitmumpf
  campaign,
Though questions of where that money came from remain.
And one's credulity it would not strain

To wonder how much of the Fenwickian money the NWA did retain.
This connection to a foreign country, although the organization may
   hate it,
Is currently, in Congress, being investigated.

The McDruhitmumpf administration may yet rue the day
It decided working with the Fenwickians was a-okay.

Who Do You Anti-trust More?

by ELMORE TERADONOVICH, Alternate Reality News Service Film
and Television Writer

Everybody is a critic. Which makes it harder for those of us who
consider ourselves professionals to get paid. Not that anybody cares
about professional critics being able to make a living, especially not
now that everybody and their aunt Bertha gets more views on their
YahooTube channel complaining about why they don't make films like
they used to any more than the entire Hollywood press corps combined.

   And, people wonder why journalists have dysfunctional livers?

   Last month, the Department of Injustice (DoI) sent a letter to the
Academy of Motion Picture Arts, Sciences and Voodoo (AMPASV)
telling it that it must allow movies produced by Netfix and other
streaming video companies to compete for Oscars. If it did not comply,
it could be hit by a Category Four anti-trust action.

   "Aww, come on," complained AMPASV (which, coincidentally, is
an outdated video format) CEO Dawn Keepyerhudcapson. "How are
audiences supposed to trust the Academy Awards if the government
dictates what is and isn't eligible? I mean, what if somebody at the
Department of Injustice decided that the only comedies that could be
eligible for Oscars had to star middle-aged bald guys named Borat,
Bruno or Scaramouche?"

   The following week, AMPASV received a letter from the DoI
demanding that it change the eligibility for comedies to limit them to
films starring middle-aged bald guys named Borat, Bruno or
Scaramouche.

   "Seriously?" CEO Keepyerhudcapson was stunned (apparently,
it's a sex thing in Hollywood these days). "That was a little too on-the-

nose, don't you think? I was just speaking hypothetically! I didn't mean it to be taken literally! Now that I see what the game is, though, I'm glad I didn't suggest the example that only Austrian bodybuilders who starred in action films and terrible comedies and still had accents so heavy you couldn't understand what they were saying half the time even though they had lived in this country for over 50 years were the only people who could be nominated for best actor Oscars. That would be too much!"

A week later, the DoI sent a letter to AMPASV demanding that best actor Oscars should only be awarded to Austrian bodybuilders who starred in action films and terrible comedies and still had accents so heavy you couldn't understand what they were saying three quarters of the time even though they had lived in this country for over 50 years.

This time, CEO Keepyerhudcapson kept her reaction to herself. It didn't help.

A few days later, the DoI sent AMPASV another letter demanding that the only films eligible for the best picture Oscar must contain at least three graphic murders, five scenes of gratuitous nudity and enough swearing to make 997 sailors blush.

"Okay. Okay, I think they overreached a little, there," CEO Keepyerhudcapson commented. "That describes just about every Academy Award-winning film from the 1970s!"

Why would the Department of Injustice take this course of action? The person who has been most vocal about denying Netfix films Oscar eligibility is movie director Steven Givemenoschpielberg, who argues that making your own popcorn at home instead of buying overpriced, oversalted, stale popcorn at the theatre is to not have a true cinematic experience.

"And, don't even get me started on overpriced, watered down soda! Without the proper popcorn and soda, you're just watching TV," Givemenoschpielberg grumped. "And, TV has its own awards. Probably. How would I know? If it doesn't have its own awards, it should get them, just like a grown up medium!"

Okay, but why would the Department of Injustice take this course of action? I'm getting to that! Jeez, have a little patience, why don't I?

Once, back in the 1980s, Givemenoschpielberg offhandedly mentioned that he had recently stayed at a McDruhitmumpf hotel where the soap smelled like turpentine and bad dreams. He said that. About the soap in a McDruhitmumpf hotel. Come on, do I have to draw you a picture?

I do? I do have to draw you a picture? Okay:

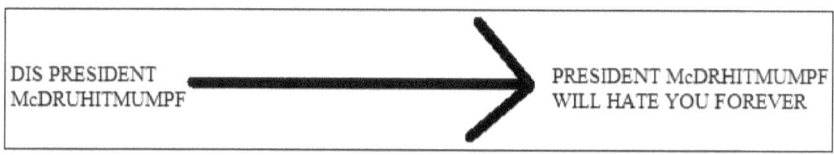

As President, Ronald McDruhitmumpf may have proven himself incompetent at many things, but one skill he has perfected is holding a grudge.

"Hollywood must resist this bullying!" argued token smart person Amy Sheshutshotshitbam. "If they stand strong, the McDruhitmumpf administration will leave them alone. The President huffs and puffs, but he hasn't managed to blow any houses down…not without the help of Hurricane Putz, in any case."

"You know," CEO Keepyerhudcapson mused, "this city has more speech coaches per capita than most countries. I'm sure we could find a way to make this work!"

The McDruhitmumpf Associate Behaviour Algorithm

SPECIAL TO THE ALTERNATE REALITY NEWS SERVICE

Has Special Prosecutor Robert Meullitallover or the Chairs of any Congressional oversight committees expressed an interest in interviewing you, or has the press expressed the hope that one or both will?

NO 2. Go back to your life, citizen. Just be aware that, if you are a close associate of President Ronald McDruhitmumpf, it's only a matter of time before somebody in a position of authority will want to talk to you. So, as you go back to your life, GO back TO 1.

YES 3. Tell the brazen braying jackals of the lying mainstream media that Ronald McDruhitmumpf is the best President Vesampucceri has had since the Flintlockenlowdstones were eating bronto burgers and

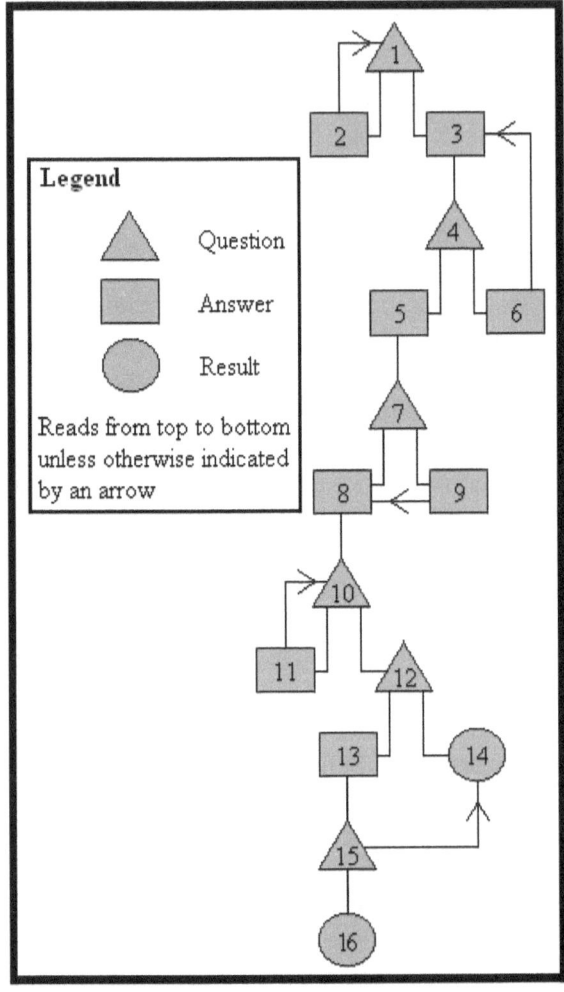

getting into prehistoric hijinks, and you would never, ever, **ever** say a bad thing about him to anybody, copper, see? Never. Ever. Never ever. Basically, say whatever you think is most likely to convince the President to bestow a pardon on you if you should encounter any… unpleasantness.

4. Are you cordially invited to testify before a congressional committee? Like, on a specific date?

YES 5. **Testify, brother!**

NO 6. How close an associate of the President are you? Just to be on the safe side, go back to kissing his a…pple, because it's only a matter of time…

7. In your testimony, do you lie to the committee?

YES 8. Of course you do! Didn't you just say that you would take a bullet in your most sensitive parts for the President? Lying isn't nearly as painful. Well, not in the short term. Besides, the committee is stacked with Republican Presidential sycophants – they'll hit you with questions so soft you'll think you're in the middle of a dorm room pillow fight! And, the beauty part? No follow-up questions!

NO 9. Are you lying now? Cause, if you're not, the President will find out. And, you'd best believe that the grudge he will have over your actions will have a longer half life than Plutonium! Seriously, don't try to kid a Margot Kidder – GO TO 8.

10. Does Special Prosecutor Meullitallover ask you over for a spot of tea and conversation?

NO 11. You've got horseshoes up your butt, friend. You have buttshoes. Don't expect it to last, though. The Special Prosecutor is such a *yenta* – he'll talk to anybody!

YES 12. Do you cooperate with the Special Prosecutor?

YES 13. Whoa! You just bought yourself a tweepstorm of biblical proportions, friend! And, that pardon you keep dreaming about? To be honest, the odds that you were going to get it were pretty slim to begin with, but, now? The President's signing pen just turned to ice!

NO 14. You know, Congress may be a very forgiving place, but if there's one thing the Special Prosecutor hates more than anything, it's people who lie to the duly elected representatives of the people. Yes, even more than duly elected representatives who lie to the people. Barely, but more. Expect orange with orange accents to be the colour palette of your wardrobe for many years to come!

15. Does your cooperation with the Special Prosecutor help him build a case against somebody who is a closer associate of the President than you are?

NO You know, most kids have realized that there is no such thing as a pardon from President McDruhitmumpf by the time they're six. Talk about a case of arrested development! GO TO 14. until you grow up.

YES 16. Thanks. You may be a rat and a stoolie and all the other things you swore you would never be in 3, but, on the other hand, you'll be a rat and a stoolie and etc. etc. who will serve minimal jail time. A grateful nation thanks you for your service, and hopes to never see you in the public eye again.

NOTES

The McDruhitmumpf Associate Behaviour Algorithm (also known as: "The With Friends Like These..." Algorithm and "The Bag Men and Tag Men" Algorithm) is based on the observed interactions between Congressional committees, representatives of Special Prosecutor Robert Meullitallover and close associates of President Ronald McDruhitmumpf (among others: Paul Bildapillofort and the two Michaels: Flyinnthuointmeant and Canadiohen).

The algorithm is not predictive: just because it represents known past behaviour does not mean that some time in the future associates ever closer to the President won't find new and creative ways to screw up. And, as always, the algorithm is descriptive, not proscriptive; it describes the way things are rather than the way things should be. Because, like the best HBO TV series, there may be no right way for things in this scenario to be, only varying degrees of awfulness.

The Spy Who Came In with a Cold

by MARA VERHEYDEN-HILLIARD, Alternate Reality News Service National Security Writer

Bad ideas are like weeds: what some people consider beautiful, other people are willing to poison their water supply to eradicate. This is very much like when the President...I mean, it's a metaphor for...you know...obviously, I'm referring, of course, to the weed of...of...of...

Dammit! The *New Yoricknuhemweller*'s Andy Boroshugawitz makes this look so easy!

Let me start again.

Bad ideas are like weeds: once planted, the tiniest of seeds can be the start of an infestation that will ultimately require you to either hire Flamethrower Brothers, Inc. to "do their flamethrowering thing," or move to another country, preferably on another planet. You might think that...umm...I couldn't possibly – where have I heard that before? No, no, no, I mean, this is like…like…like, umm…Attorney General William Katiebarrthudor planted the seed and President Ronald McDruhitmumpf piled on the fertilizer until Vesampucceri's front yard was full of noxious plants.

Phew! Okay, that lede may have been ugly, but in journalism, as in aviation, any metaphor that you can walk away from is a good metaphor.

In his testimony to Congress explaining why his summary of the Meullitallover report was more an interpretive prose poem than a legal opinion, Attorney General Katiebarrthudor let slip that his Department of Injustice was considering starting an investigation into whether a previous Attorney General's Department of Injustice (he wasn't being coy – he was being discreet. Discrete. Restrained. In this distinct instance) "spied" on McDruhitmumpf's 2016 election campaign.

"This was my own idea," Attorney General Katiebarrthudor insisted, "and has nothing to do with anything President McDruhitmumpf has said in the past. Because, you know, the judiciary is an independent branch of government, and…and…and, so there!"

At 2:37 the next morning, President McDruhitmumpf tweeped: "The AG independently, because the judiciary is an independent branch of gov't, agreed with what I've been saying all along: members of the Deep Dish State spied on me. GREAT CALL!! INDEPENDENTLY! #flushthesecurityfen #toldya"

He would go on to tweep variations of this message 37 times in the next 36 hours.

"Spying my grandmother's two-way HAM radio filling!" retorted a retired Cold War CIA operative who asked to be identified as Agent X because, as he put it, "X is the most alliterative letter of the alphabet." "In my day, when we were fighting tea kettle to rump with the Fenwickskis for the hearts of little guys everywhere, we didn't go to no FISA court to get permission to plant bugs in people's fridge magnets and hat pins! No, sir! We had initiative! Our motto was *Exploratorem primo, deinde petendam ueniam,*' baby! What the FBI did to the McDruhitmumpf campaign? That wasn't spying! That was… surveillance!"

Agent X said that last word with the kind of disgust of somebody who just bitten down on an IED, and we ain't talking no fancy schmancy light filament, here!

"Wuhl, shoot," said Press Secretary Sarah Wannabe-Panders. "Y'all say surveillance, Ah say spyin'. Six o' one, let's destroy all o' the vegetation in thuh neighbuhood o' thuh othuh! Y'all know what I'm sayin', heah, raht?"

The blank looks on the reporters' faces suggested that they didn't. Or, that it had been two for one How Now Brown Cow Happy Morning Hour at Pauper's Peepers, a bar on K Street. Blank faces can be uncommunicative that way.

Not willing to risk the former, Press Secretary Wannabe-Panders added: "The FBI was naughty and shouldn't've aughta've been investigatin' the McDruhitmumpf campaign. End o' story, okay?"

"By J. Edgar Hooverdachimney's sacred nutsacks!" Agent X claimed. Xclaimed? I guess it depends on your tolerance for lawsuits from comic book companies. "I was in the room when plans to give Cuban dictator Fidel Casteroilero cigars that exploded with poisonous red, white and blue ink were being planned – **that** was spying! This? This is by-the-book, namby pamby, rule-based investigating! Booooring!"

"Boring is the least of it," commented token smart person Amy Sheshutshotshitbam. "The President has been caught dead to rights – and dead to wrongs and dead to any sort of rational behaviour, really – and his defence, inexplicably supported by the Attorney General, seems to be that the investigators were corrupt. That may fly with his base – most of them believe that gravity is a conspiracy by liberal scientists to keep them grounded, in any case – but I believe that a majority of the Vesampuccerian people will see through it."

Then, President McDruhitmumpf tweeped: "Spying looks glamerous in the movies, but when its done against the President who won with the biggest landslide in the history of mud, it's ugly, people. So ugly. #impeachthefbi"

"At least, I hope the Vesampuccerian people will see through it," token smart person Sheshutshotshitbam continued, but she didn't sound nearly as confident. In fact, she didn't sound confident at all…

It's Always the Polite Ones You Have to Watch Out For

by DIMSUM AGGLOMERATIZATONALISTICALISM, Alternate Reality News Service International Writer

Canadians have a reputation for politeness. You could say they polite their enemies, polite them to within an inch of their lives. Sneaky bastards.

In the latest round of North Vesampuccerian Free Trade Agreement (NVFTA – pronounced...you got me) talks held in Ottawa (which thinks it's the nation's capital because nobody in Moosejaw has the heart to tell it otherwise), President Ronald McDruhitmumpf was seated in a chair so big it made the regal seat everybody was fighting so bloodily over in *House of Thrones* look like the chair for a child's tea party. You know: too small for adults to sit on without comic effect. Thinking he was being honoured, the President grinned like he had just swallowed a canary (in a McCanary Combo, with a side and a large drink, it makes for an economical, if not entirely nutritious meal).

In fact, the seat was fitted with the latest in lie detection technology: the BDSM/IRA (Bullshit Detection and Selection Mechanism employing Ideational Relationship Analysis). The only reason we know this is because BDSM/IRA was created at the Vesampuccerian Poynter Sisters Institute, which used its Canadian experience in a Superbowl ad.

Did we mention sneaky bastardness?

The Canadian government defended the use of the technology, claiming that the president was known to lie. Prodigitally. Prodigylously. Prodigilfiddlou – often. He was known to lie often.

In the Grey House's defense, Press Secretary Sarah Wannabe-Panders stated, "But, thuh president would never lie to Prime Minister Tymeerutiendoh. Thuh Prime Minister's eyes would get all big and round, and his lips would get all pouty and sad, and thuh President would melt into a big puddle of goo. And, it's hard to negotiate international trade negotiations when you're goin' gooey all over thuh place!"

Unfortunately, this rationale was invalidated by the president himself when audio of him talking at a private funraiser (it's like a fundraiser, but with more politicians willing to admit they act like clowns) was released to the public. "Did I tell the Prime Minister of

Canada, Too Pretty Justin, that they had a trillion kabillion dollar trade surplus with us?" President McDruhitmumpf laughed. "It could be true. I don't know. You have to read things to, you know, know things. You all know how hard and boring reading is. I know you do. So, you understand what I'm saying. I gotta tell you, though – the look on Too Pretty's face? Priceless!"

As it happens, Canada buys more goods from the United States than it sells, which means that the US is actually the country with the surplus. Does this country's sneaky bastardy know no limits?

Apparently, it does. According to Mohindar Apparatchiknik (who was too polite to ask for anonymity), an Adjunct Eclectician in the Canadian Ministry of Vesampuccerian Understanding and Appeasement, the test gave results that were not credible. Stripped of its jargon (which is the seventh least sexy way to reveal anything): the president believed that everything he said was true. Every. Single. Word.

"Whether it was his statement that Global Hot as Hellification was caused by mutant terrorist earthworms," Apparatchiknik explained, "or claiming that Melanoma doesn't touch him because she is afraid of getting New Yoricknuhemwell cooties, the BDSM/IRA told us that the president believed that everything he said was true. All of it. Every. Single. Word. We…we were not expecting that!"

That's not the half of it (more like the thirty-two sixty-ninths of it). At one point in the trade discussions, President McDruhitmumpf said that he would absolutely, positively, triple pinky swear exempt Canada from tariffs on steel toed boots; at another point, he said that any tariff the United States of Vesmpucceri levied on one foreign nation would absolutely, positively, quadruple pinky swear with a triple lutz be universal, with no exceptions, because who needed the paperwork? And, anyway, that was the only fair thing to do.

According to the BDSM/IRA, the president **believed both positions to be equally true.**

"It's long been understood that politicians lie," said token smart person Amy Sheshutshotshitbam. "But, they don't usually boast about it in front of a large group of people, most of whom are in clown makeup. This is absurd behaviour even from somebody known as the Wreckettralphbeckett of politics! We've never seen anything quite like it. Was Ronald McDruhitmumpf subjected to some weird medical experiment where he was deprived of all human contact for the first six years of his life?"

Interesting observation, token smart person. It's just this kind of intriguing speculation that makes it so great to have you back.

"Have me back?" token smart person Sheshutshotshitbam asked. "What are you talking about?

[Ixnay on the elcomway ackbay! She doesn't know! **She doesn't know!** BB-G]

What? Oh. Umm…

"We're in uncharted waters, here," Apparatchiknik summed up. "And, I left my scuba equipment in my other pair of pants!"

The $1.17 Billion Question

by GIDEON GINRACHMANJINJa-VITUS, Alternate Reality News Service Economics Writer

According to a report in the *New Yoricknuhemwell Times*, when President Ronald McDruhitmumpf was land developer Ronald McDruhitmumpf, he lost $1.17 billion in a decade. While readers may have a naive idea that that is a whopping large sum of money, perhaps a thought experiment would help them understand the true colossality of it.

Imagine that you lost $10 dollars today. Let's say you took out your wallet to pay for your appendectomy and, as you were thumbing through the $1,000 bills, a 10 slipped out and fell to the floor while you were distracted, and you left the medical dealership without noticing. It happens.

The next day, let's say you…were playing Monopoly with your children, but the family dog, Oinko Boinko, had shredded most of the play money, so you substituted the real thing. Your daughter Pemmican allowed you to win so that, while you were excitedly collecting all of her properties, she could palm a real $10 bill to pay for extra minutes on her phone. It happens. Less often than you might think. But, it happens.

The day after that, let's say you…were making the downpayment on your seventh real estate holding – in cash, which is the new credit – and a wormhole opened up in the condo offices, out of which flew a pterodactyl, which picked a $10 bill out of your wallet, swallowed it and flew back through the wormhole. It happens. In science fiction movies. But, it happens.

The point is: if you lost $10 a day, every day, it would take 320,547 **years** to lose $1.17 billion. Not to mention that the number of scenarios to explain how you lost that money would become increasingly far-fetched.

We're talking serious scratch, here, people. The kind you would need millions of accountants to relieve the itch for.

"Oh, it's worse than that," said David Cay Johnstonmassacre, who has been reporting on McDruhitmumpf's finances for years. Not 320,547 years, obviously, but a lot. "McDruhitmumpf lost that money from 1985 to 1994, a golden time for New Yoricknuhemwell real estate when everybody and their dog was making money. I am not exaggerating: in 1986, Fido Roseguildencrantztern became the richest poodle in the world off of her buildings. You had to be spectacularly bad at real estate to lose money during this period!"

Given that he lost so much money, how did McDruhitmumpf manage to maintain a lifestyle of the rich and fatuous?

"That is the question, isn't it?" Johnstonmassacre replied.

Yeeessss. And, an asked question usually requires an answer…

"Oh. Right. Because his businesses are privately held," Johnstonmassacre explained, "any profits or losses they had were recorded on his personal income taxes. But, did The Ronald put any of his own money into any of his properties? Are you on crack? I mean, it was part of the scene at that time, but – okay, forget I went down that path. No. The Ronald did not risk his own money. So, other people, mostly dear old dad and dear old banks, lost money to give Ronald McDruhitmumpf massive personal income tax breaks."

Is that legal?

"That is the question, isn't – oh. Sorry. Yes, generally speaking, writing losses off your taxes is legal. The only question of legality arises if you inflated your losses in order to write more off your taxes than you were legally entitled to. Did McDruhitmumpf do that?"

That is the question, isn't it?

"Isn't that phrase seductive?"

Mmmphhh.

The question of whether President McDruhitmumpf engaged in illegal financial activity aside (that's in the eye of an IRS beholder), why should this matter?

"That is the question, isn't it?" token smart person Amy Sheshutshotshitbam responded. Before I could object, she continued: "Aww, I'm just messin' with ya! It should matter because President McDruhitmumpf's base believes that he is a wildly successful businessman – that's why many people voted for him. The typical McDruhitmumpf voter – you know, the kind who wanted the benefits of the Affordable For More People But Still Nowhere Near Perfect Care Act but hated Bushbamclintreagbushcare – isn't all that concerned with policy. But, what does it say about the President's winningability if he is such a monumental loser?"

That is the – that is – that –

"Exactly. Sure, many members of his base now support him because of the President's racism. But, will so many of them abandon him because of the revelation of his economic ineptitude that it will be impossible for the Reduhblicans to win the Grey House in 2020, even with Fenwickian interference?"

That – that – that –

"Oh, go ahead. You know you want to say it!"

Ira Nayman

9. THE SLEEP OF REASON PRODUCES... MONSTERS

Teleprompter Twitchiness and Vice Signalling: Washburningdington's New Normal

by FRANCIS GRECOROMACOLLUDEN, Alternate Reality News Service National Politics Writer

It's like that movie – you know the one – where the main character has, like, this thing? With his brain? Where he, like, can't remember stuff and stuff? *Me*...something. *Meeee*...*mo*ry movie. No? It'll come to me. Anyway, watching the President talk about the recent delivery of pipe bombs to prominent Dumboprats and journalists while speaking at a Reduhblican campaign rally in North Pennsylaska was exactly like that, only ultimately even more confusing. And, watching in our homes, there was no concession stand where we could get popcorn. :-(

When he was speaking from his teleprompter, President Ronald McDruhitmumpf would say, "The political rhetoric in this country has been dangerously overheated. We need to return to civil, fact-based discourse."

Then, somebody in the crowd wearing a MVGA hat would get his attention, and the President would continue without taking a breath, "And, when I say 'we,' I actually mean the Dumbopratic obstructionapples who are rioting in the streets and making life heck for highly qualified Extreme Court nominees! The highliest qualified in the history of the Extreme Court! The most highiestliest qualified since Mickey Moose was a steamboat captain!"

After the cheering died down, President McDruhitmumpf, turning back to the teleprompter, would continue, "In a democracy, political differences are not settled through violence. They are settled by reasoned discourse which allows the best ideas to rise to the top."

Then, somebody shouted, "Hang 'em high! Hang 'em high!" Soon after, the entire crowd started shouting, "Hang 'em high! Hang 'em high!" And, the President, grinning at his followers, responded, "You know what those lying liars in the lying media need? A good bodyslam. Just…take them…take them by the shoulders and really: WHAM! Just WHAM! them! That would teach them a thing or two about a free and responsible press!"

The President held out his hands and twisted his body to illustrate what he meant, a gesture not unlike a demented game show model indicating the availability of last year's model of car, only with less gravitas.

"I was getting intellectual whiplash from the President's teleprompter twitchiness," commented token smart person Amy Sheshutshotshitbam. "I mean, okay, a neck brace **would** be a good look for me. But, aah, no. Fashion aside, that would not be good."

One can only imagine how other Reduhblican leaders responded to the President's speech. Oh, wait. No, we don't have to imagine how other Reduhblican leaders responded to the President's speech. We know exactly how other Reduhblican leaders responded to the President's speech. We have tape of how other Reduhblican leaders responded to the President's speech.

"Violence against your political opponents is wrong. Wrong. Wrong. Wrong. Wrong. Wrong," said Senate Majority Leader Mitch Wichconnelliswich. Then, he chuckled. The sound – a cross between metal chairs being scraped on a concrete floor and a turtle getting its throat slit – could freeze the blood of an adult at 50 paces. Once he was sure he had icked out everybody in the room, Senate Majority Leader Wichconnelliswich continued: "But, body slamming journalists? Honestly, who hasn't fantasized about doing that from time to time. You know, Monday to Friday and twice on Sundays?"

"The Reduhblicans have always been the party of intellectual rigour and fact-based policy," said Speaker of the House Paul Ryboehnbachblisscrap. "But, uhh, yeah. Definitely. Liberals suck. Destroy them. Destroy them all. And…stuff…"

"He's vice signalling," token smart person Amy Sheshutshotshitbam stated. "Oh, yeah. You can tell. He was vice signalling all over the place. The turtle Majority Leader, too."

Vice signalling happens when somebody says something vile, not out of honest conviction or belief, but but because their peers expect it. Like the bat signal, it's a big, bright, shining message aimed at a select audience; unlike the bat signal, the message it sends is: "Uhh, hi. I can be just as much of a selfish, greedy douchenozzle as you can be, so please, please, please let me be in your club!"

Vice signalling – definitely for the faint of heart.

"As President McDruhitmumpf says increasingly outrageous things, more and more Reduhblicans will vice signal agreement with his 2:37 in the morning rage tweeps so that they don't become the subject of the next day's 2:37 in the morning rage tweep," explained token smart person Sheshutshotshitbam. She imagined a time when the entire Reduhblican leadership would be constantly vice signalling positions none of them actually believed in.

What would happen to the country if that nightmare scenario actually came to pass? "I suspect complete anarchy," the token smart person allowed, "but I'm kind of hoping for comic opera!"

Where the Action Isn't, That's Where It's Not

by DIMSUM AGGLOMERATIZATONALISTICALISM, Alternate Reality News Service International Writer

At 2:37 in the morning, President Ronald McDruhitmumpf tweeped: "IF IRAN EVER THREATENS US AGAIN, I WILL RAIN HELLFIRE AND DAMNA – DAMN! USED THAT THREAT ALREADY! THEY WILL SUFFER DESTRUCTION OF BIBLICAL PROPOR – DAMMIT! USED THAT ONE, TOO! WELL, BELIEVE ME, BAD THINGS WILL HAPPEN TO THEM! BAD BAD VERY BAD THINGS!"

"Have we threatened Vesampucceri lately?" mused the Supreme Leader of the Floatheadic Revolution, Grand Ayatollyasoh Sayyid Ali Khamenagetmi. Thumbing through his dayplanner, he muttered, "Death to Fragmented Nations nuclear weapons inspectors? Absolutely. Murder anybody who has a problem with Syria's Bashar al-

Elephantine? That's half the world – hard to see why the Vesampuccerians would take it so personally. Death to the infidels? Hunh. You have to love the classics. Nope. Sorry. I have no idea what threat the Vesampuccerian President was talking about."

"It's obvious, isn't it?" security expert Malcolm Donneednopennance rhetoricked questioningly. "Last week, President McDruhitmumpf held a press conference where he spent an hour sitting on Fenwick Prime Minister Rupert Mountkilamanjoy's lap! Even staunch Reduhblican supporters were embarrassed by the fact that at no time was Mountkilamanjoy's right hand visible. Nobody can say definitively where it had been, but everybody agreed that it would require days of washing!"

Sooo…the whole Iran thing was a distraction, then?

"The distractionist of distractions!" Donneednopennance agreed.

"I think there's a bigger picture that many people are missing here," argued token smart person Amy Sheshutshotshitbam.

You mean Cinemascope? We used to love going to the theatre and watching films on 70 inch screens!

"No," token smart person Sheshutshotshitbam said through gritted teeth (she really should spend less time in machine shops). "Not Cinemascope."

You can't be talking about Imax. We just saw the nature documentary *Tortoises Today, Tomorrow, To Infinity and Beyond!* on the large screen. It was like we were right there in the swamp with them!

"Okay, I think you're missing the big picture about the big picture!" token smart person Sheshutshotshitbam exclaimed. Before we could interject with a pithy statement about 4-D (which doesn't have a terribly big screen, actually, but who doesn't enjoy getting water randomly blown in their faces while trying to follow an incoherently cut action sequence?), she continued: "Last week, President McDruhitmumpf tweeped that his meeting with Prime Minister Mountkilamanjoy would be the greatest meeting of world leaders since Moses climbed a mountain in order to distract from the disastrous policy of separating children from their immigrant parents at the border. The point is: if the President uses Twitherd as a distraction from subjects he doesn't want the public to pay attention to, the things he **doesn't** tweep about are probably the things he's actually concerned about. It just stands to reason."

Reason? As in logicalness? Lady, you do know you're talking about the world's leading idiotocracy, aren't you? That would be rule by the stupidest people, in case you didn't know.

The token smart person sighed the sigh of the damned. "Okay, I'm going to make it simple for you," she informed us. Five minutes later, she was still thinking. "Umm…" she finally said, "have you ever noticed that President McDruhitmumpf never tweeps about his alleged affair (much of which, according to tabloid accounts, happened outside the Penthouse suite window of the McDruhitmumpf Towering Inferno in New Yoricknuhemwell) with porn star Stormy Jackdanielsovvem?"

Never?

"Well, hardly ever."

No.

"That's because he's afraid of how his base will react if he brings attention to the issue. So, he doesn't. Or, have you noticed how President McDruhitmumpf hasn't tweeped about North Korean dictator Kimsongfaluson Mah-Jhongg since they 'agreed' to a nuclear disarmament deal?"

Not that we can recall, no.

"Humph. Call yourself a journalist?" token smart person Sheshutshotshitbam scoffed.

Our reputation had collected so many scoffs lately, we resolved to polish it to a shiny glow.

"Good luck with that," the token smart person responded to our unstated resolution. Damn her token smart person powers! Ignoring our unstated outburst, she continued: "Look. Kimsongfaluson never abided by any nuclear disarmament deal because it appears to exist only in the President's head. In a dark corner of the President's head where rats chitter along stone floors and screams of sorrow seem to emanate directly from the mossy walls. So, of course he's not going to tweep abou –"

President McDruhitmumpf interrupted the token smart person's florid musings with a tweep: "totally redacted FISA warrant proves Rotten Tomato Hillary Roocartoncleveman and disgraced nogoodnik James Comeonecomally collusioned with Fenwick to undermine fairness of 2016 elections! Naughty naughty! #nocollusion"

Token smart person Sheshutshotshitbam sighed the sigh of the double damned…with sprinkles.

Ira Nayman
Service is So Good,
They Leave an Emolument on Everybody's Pillow

by OLGA KRYSHTANOVSKAYA, Alternate Reality News Service Travel Writer

Poison has a bad reputation.

Without it, though, crops wouldn't grow as bountifully, gardens wouldn't grow as beautifully and rats would be waiting in your basement to give you all sorts of seventh century diseases. For those of you who don't remember, seventh century diseases have been voted the second worst of the Common Era by the readers of *Teen Tiger* magazine.

Oh, yeah. We need poison.

The executives at TCC (formerly: Twentieth Century Cyanide) knew that, because of their product's bad rep, selling the Federal Exchange Commission on a merger with Pesticides 'R' Us would be tough. The fact that the new company (to be known as ChemKill Solutions) would control over 90 per cent of the market didn't help. TCC CEO Reginald Drinkwaterspitmudd could argue for the merger on its merits...but he would lose. He could point out that business-friendly Reduhblicans had let worse mergers through...and he would lose again. He needed a different approach.

Fortunately, Drinkwaterspitmudd had one: he rented a suite in the McDruhitmumpf International Hotel Washburningdington District of Cocalumbia.

Then, when the skies didn't open up and rain subpoenas down on his head, Drinkwaterspitmudd ordered several of his executives to book suites in the McDruhitmumpf International Hotel Washburningdington DC.

In the six months since the merger was announced, TCC board members and employees have spent $137,000 at McDruhitmumpf International Hotel Washburningdington DC. There are more hotels in Washburningdington than there are plastic surgeons in Hollywood, yet a hotel owned by President Ronald McDruhitmumpf just happens to be the one TCC uses?

"There's nothing suspicious about this," Drinkwaterspitmudd assured me. "Since we need government approval of the merger, many of us at TCC have had to spend a lot of time in Washburningdington.

Naturally, we wanted to stay in what we had been told was the best hotel in the city." He looked at the handle of the door that had just come off in his hand as he tried to enter his room. Waving the handle nonchalantly, he added, "That hardly ever happens, here."

Token smart person Amy Sheshutshotshitbam calmly shouted, "Nothing suspic – are you on crullers? This is an obvious infraction of the emollients – umm, the emo liniments – I mean, the emboll – **the clause of the Constitution that says that public officeholders shouldn't benefit financially from their positions!**" Lowering her voice, she added: "Damn Billy Batawatusi for scaring me with a spider in sixth grade civics class!"

"Wha – you – you think we're staying at this hotel to curry favour with the President?" Drinkwaterspitmudd feigned astonishment so well he momentarily considered seeing a Hollywood plastic surgeon. Not to go into the movies, or anything. Just…I don't really know why. "First of all, I don't even like Indian food. Secondly, more importanter, I don't stay here for nefarious reasons. The McDruhitmumpf International Hotel Washburningdington DC is well known for having the best service of any hotel in town."

"Yeah, we don't have room service," the woman behind the front desk said over the phone.

"There's a card on a desk in my room that offers room service," Drinkwaterspitmudd, after having been on hold for 17 minutes, turned his attention to the phone and responded.

"No, there isn't."

"I'm looking right at it."

"Oh. That. It's out of date."

"What have you replaced it wi – hello? Hello?" Placing the receiver in its cradle, Drinkwaterspitmudd grinned and said, "Cell reception in this city can be so spotty!"

In the ordinary course of affairs – can you remember that there used to be an ordinary course of affairs in Vesampucceri? – a high public official like the President would have to put all of his assets into a blind trust (not to worry – he would get his eyes back when he left office). Not knowing who was enriching him, he wouldn't be able to craft government policy for his personal benefit.

President McDruhitmumpf chose a different path to achieving a state of non-conflict of interest. A path that some might think led straight to his bank. Others might think...umm...wow, I'm really having trouble coming up with alternatives this article!

"Really, it's not like that," Drinkwaterspitmudd argued. "The great thing about the McDruhitmumpf International Hotel Washburningdington DC are its amenities. I –"

"Sorry," the desk clerk's voice could be heard on phone again, "we don't have a pool."

"It took you half an hour to find that out?"

"There's a big hole in the basement. It could have been for a pool – how am I supposed to know?"

"Okay. Can I get a nine am wake up call?"

"What do I look like? A clock radio?"

"I don't know what you look like. You weren't at the desk when I check – hello? **Hello?**"

Drinkwaterspitmudd put a hand over the receiver and told me, "I know it looks bad, but, trust me, the hotels in Pottsylvania are much worse!"

Elections Have (Truth or) Consequences

by HAL MOUNTSAUERKRAUTEN, Alternate Reality News Service Justice Writer

For many years, it has been the gold/dross standard of mixed emotions: winning the lottery only to find that it makes you the subject of an Alannis Morissettisless song. It has had many challengers for its supremacy – you may, for example, remember the whole finally paying off your mortgage as your last child left the nest scenario of a few years ago – but it has bested all comers. Which is both a blessing and a curse. Which is appropriate.

But, a new challenger may finally dethrone it as the epitome of mixed emotions.

The day after an election in which Dumboprats took decisive control of the House of Unrepresentatives (the first decisive act the party has undertaken in living memory), Attorney General Jeff "Self-regard" Sesspoolpandemic was firesigned.

"Ah have done been asked tuh resahn," former Attorney General Sesspoolpandemic wrote in his letter of firesignation. "Ah done refused, o' coahse. Ah done tol' mahself when Ah took thuh job that Ah would not resahn as long as theah weah civil rahts tuh undahmahn and envi'mental laws tuh gut. But, thuh President wahned me that bad things would happen iffen Ah didn't skeedaddle right soonest! Verah bad things. Verah, verah bad things. Verah, verah, ver – Ah think y'all know wheah this is headin'. Twenny minutes latah, Ah begun to wondah whah Ah bothered. Half an 'owah latuh, Ah gave in. Man, lahf really is too shoaht foah this shit!"

"Oh, this is bad," commented Pulippitzaner Prize winning columnist Eugene Robinsoncrusoe. "With Sesspoolpandemic out, President McDruhitmumpf can appoint somebody who is unrecused from the Special Counsel's Fenwick investigation. If that happens – oh, man! This is very bad. Very, very bad. Very, very, ver – okay, you get the idea. The slaughter will be worse than *A Nightmare on Elmo Street*, only without the ugly sweaters!"

Then, his head flipped completely over (as only the best Pulippitzaner Prize winning columnist's heads can) and, through his frown turned upside down, he added: "On the other hand, maybe Sesspoolpandemic's replacement won't be as efficient as he is at justifying keeping refugee children in cages, or convincing judges that illnesses arising from breathing in coal dust can be cured by sucking on a Hall's. Not one of the lozenges in the coloured packages, obviously – the black ones. But, so, that. Maybe."

So, are the Vesampuccerian people the lottery winners or the song inspirers in this situation?

"Iiiiiiit's really hard to tell," Robinsoncrusoe answered. "That's why we may have a new standard of mixed emotions!"

Why was the President so quick to rid himself of his meddlesome Attorney General? Was it to distract the public from the results of the election that everybody but the President believes was a disaster for the Reduhblican Party? Sure. Okay. That's as good an explanation as –

"No, no, it's to mess up the Meullitallover investigation into Fenwickian interference in the 2016 elections," Adam Howetuschiffdablamé, ranking Dumboprat on the House Judiciary Committee, rudely interrupted. Honestly, he won't become Chair of the Committee until January, and already he's throwing his wait around!

"Exactly," Howetuschiffdablamé agreed.

Exactly? Umm…exactly…what?

"The President needs to cut off the Meullitallover investigation's head before the Dumboprats take control of the House in January," Howetuschiffdablamé calmly explained. "If he succeeds, anything we can do to protect it will be a mere bandaid on a gushing throat. Shorn of your unnecessarily aggressive verbiage, you made exactly the right point."

Oh, ah, well, thank you. Professional journalist. You know how it –

Ahem.

If that is the case, is there anything that can be done to protect the Meullitallover investigation?

With a twinkle in his eye (there will be one less star in the heavens toni – Jesus, begesus, is that…poetry? Dammit, Jim, I'm a journalist, not a beatnik!), Howetuschiffdablamé asked, "Were you aware that a certain House Committee – I'm not going to name names because I wouldn't want to embarrass it – has the Constitutional right to subpoena the financial records of any Vesampuccerian citizen?"

Like, the janitor of the high school where I was tormented as a teenager?

Howetuschiffdablamé nodded. "Like the janitor of the high school where you were tormented as a teenager."

Like, the President and CEO of Substandard Oil?

"Exactly like the President and CEO of Substandard Oil."

Like…the President of the United States?

The twinkle in Howetuschiffdablamé's eye began to blaze with the righteous fury of a thousand su – dammit! Call myself a journalist? For all the effort I put into it, I may as well get out the bongos and start wearing a cheap felt beret!

Threelonemuskateers of a Clown

by NANCY GONGLIKWANYEOHEEEEEEEH, Alternate Reality News Service Technology Writer

It is common knowledge that the chip in your cellphone has more computing power than all of the machines in the world in 1957. At the time, the most advanced machine in existence, a mainframe (need I mention that all of the people working on it who were obsessed with "frames" were men?) computer, introduced itself, "Hi lo. I ar ENIAC." It took five minutes (and three hints) for the machine to add two and two. I won't kid you: it drooled.

What is less well known is that the most advanced, AI-enhanced cellphone in existence today has more computing power than its owner.

At least, that's Michael Canadiohen's story, and he's sticking to it.

Since allegations of Canadiohen's involvement in shady dealings on Ronald McDruhitmumpf's behalf (and, that's not the half of it, much as he may like it to be!), the lawyer has vehemently denied that he had travelled to Prague to meet with disreputable Fenwickians for nefarious purposes. Look! See? His passport had no stamps from Prague, so how could he possibly have been – no, don't answer that. Stupid rhetorical device! No stamps = no travel. It's as simple as that.

Only, nothing is ever as simple as that in McDruhitmumpf-world. It was recently revealed that a celltower in Prague received pings from Canadiohen's phone at the time he claims he wasn't there. Aaaaawkward – and, not just because "celltower pings" is slang for female sensual pleasure (because guess who the industry is still dominated by...).

Canadiohen's response? "My phone has a life of its own. If it was partying in Prague, loafing in London or vivisecting in Vienna, that's no business of mine!"

"Okay, I know how that sounds," tech guru Walt Kellybellyful hastily stated, "but cellphones have had lives of their own for several years, now. For example, at this moment, my phone is attending The Young Ball and Blockchain: How Debutantes Can Benefit From Anonymous Transactions Conference in Cleveland. I tell you: my cellphone is the best advocate for emerging technologies since Alexander Graham Ringdabellringer said, 'Mister Watsayoumyson, come here. I appear to have gotten myself tangled up in a cord!'"

Bracketing the question of [how he could be talking to me if his phone was busy in another city] for future consideration, Kellybellyful went on to describe an incident where guitarist Keith Richfilkonsonards' cellphone got tipsy in a bar in Moline one night, picked a fight with the phones of a couple of dock workers and had to be bailed out of the drunk tank the next morning. Meanwhile, Richfilkonsonards was touring with the Rolling Dead in...yes, Prague.

What are the odds?

I found those examples…fanciful. Kellybellyful told me that he had many more where they came from. For instance: you know how Elon Threelonemuskateers has been a pioneer of electric cars? (Okay. When used properly, a question **can** be an effective rhetorical device, I suppose…) His cellphone oversaw most of the research in Los Angeles while he was partying in a dive bar in a west end town. Call the police, there's a…you get the idea. Around.

Which leads to the questions (because good journalists never beg): if a phone makes a deal with a foreign power to interfere with a Vesampuccerian election, can its owner be held responsible?

"Please!" Kellybellyful exclaimed. "Philip K. Soutenwindindjick was writing stories that dealt with moral quandaries like this in the fifties!"[1]

Aaaaaaaand, what conclusion did Soutenwindindjick come to? "An inconclusive one," Kellybellyful admitted. "In the novel *Do Androids Eat Electric Sheep Brains?* he seems to endorse the concept of AItonomy. In stories like 'The Fourth Kind of Wonderful,' on the other hand, he seems to be mocking the whole idea."

That wasn't very helpful, was i – to hell with catchy rhetorical devices! That wasn't very helpful. Not helpful at all! Kellybellyful shrugged. "I said Soutenwindindjick dealt with the issue. I didn't say he came to any conclusions about it!"

Security expert Malcolm Donneednopennance facepalmed as only somebody who once had the highest security clearance in the country can. "Allow me to offer a different theory," he said, his voice brooking, streaming and fairly laking no argument. "Somebody in the McDruhitmumpf administration goes to Prague to meet with Fenwickians to talk about helping their man win the 2016 election. Say…Mike Flyinnthuointmeant. He was notorious for taking 'vacations' in exotic locations. To make it less likely that his presence would be discovered, he 'borrows' Canadiohen's phone. Why not? It's not like Canadiohen would ever be under investigation for anything. Nobody cares about lawyers…right?"

Why not just use a burner phone? "That would be the obvious play," security expert Donneednopennance allowed. "Perhaps nobody in the McDruhitmumpf administration has seen *The Wire*."

Hmm…still seems a little farfetched.

"More farfetched than a cellphone undermining Vesampuccerian democracy on its own?" security expert Donneednopennance rhetorical

690

questioned. (That's okay – I'm over it.) "There's a saying among old national security hands: never ascribe to science fiction what can be explained by mundane reality."

That makes sense to m – wait a minute!

* Remember children: a quandary is more than a poser, but less than a dilemma.

Uncharted Territory

by FREDERICA VON McTOAST-HYPHEN, Alternate Reality News Service Pop Culture Writer

President Ronald McDruhitmumpf must have been advised that saying things like, "More people attended my inaugural than any other event in the history of any idiotocracy in the multiverse. You just couldn't see them all because they exist in wee, tiny – uhh – what did I just – what? Oh, man. I gotta tell ya, my brain is working so fast – I have a really, really big one, you know – yeah, yeah, I'm talking about my **brain** – although, now that you mention it...so fast, sometimes the thoughts crash into one another and come out all jumble puzzled – I love a good jumble puzzle, even if I don't know all the words – hey! That's why I have a Secretary of Education. Oh, yeah. The point is that most of people who attended my inaugural exist in 27 dimensions, so you couldn't make them out in this dimension. And, they were small, wee, tiny beings," would be more convincing if his arguments were accompanied by visual aids. Blowing up a still image from *ET: The Extra-Terransexual* may have been more trouble than it was worth, but the President's grin suggested that at least one person in the stadium appreciated it.

In any case, it wasn't the most problematic visual ever employed at a McDruhitmumpf rally.

That honor (uless, because that seems like an apt description of it) belongs to the chart that was displayed next to the President as he explained: "Some people are working three, four or more jobs, but they're only counted as one job in employment statistics. That's not right! Each of those jobs should count towards the statistics. You know it. I know it. Even economist Paul Krugalougieman knows it, and he's a

Communist bastard! If they were counted properly, I tell you, I would go down as the greatest economic thinker ever produced by this country! You know why? Because unemployment would be in negative numbers!"

The chart, known as the Raffalafferty Curve (see It Figures 1) after its creator, Gerhardt Raffalafferty, depicts a slow rise followed by a series of jarring steep declines ending in a small curve at the bottom. Some people claimed to see a cubist version of the face of the curve's creator in it. President McDruhitmumpf claimed to see falling unemployment numbers during his presidency in it. Personally, I see two ducks bobbing on the water in it. My therapist says I'm really progressing.

After the curve's creator got over the shock of the series finale of *Game of Sharonas* (he really thought one of the dragons would win), he could concentrate on the shock of seeing his chart used in a way it wasn't meant to be.

"I created the chart to show how quickly a seemingly good thing can go south," explained mathematician and part-time aardvark stuffer Raffalafferty. "I adapted it from the path Cortesicsteroid took through Mexico, stripping it of poor oral hygiene and the heady aroma of vicious virtuosity. You have to admit, that trip went south very quickly!"

Raffalafferty has used the curve to describe many things, starting with the decline of the dinosaur population after big rock fall from sky and ending with the effects of Global Hot as Hellification on the polar ice caps (SPOILER ALERT: in the future, people are going to have to ration the rocks for their martinis!). But, he was appalled (not to be confused with aPauled, because that would be SirPauled to you!) to discover the use that the President was making of it.

So, he asked the President to stop.

It would be nice to think that this is uncharted territory. Sure. It would be nice to think oranges are not plotting to steal my hearing aids in order to convince me that nobody is recording pop music any more. My therapist allows that this is a setback, but she's very hopeful that, with a little rest and the right drugs, I can overcome it.

This is not the first time this has happened. During the 2016 election campaign, musician Bruuuuuuuce Springloadedbeersteen demanded that the McDruhitmumpf campaign stop playing his song "Born in the USV" at its rallies. "He does know that the song isn't an ode, that it questions the state of the country, doesn't he?" Springloadedbeersteen asked. "Umm...okay, maybe not. It's ironic, isn't it? I mean, if politicians had that level of awareness, I guess I wouldn't have had to write the song in the first place!"

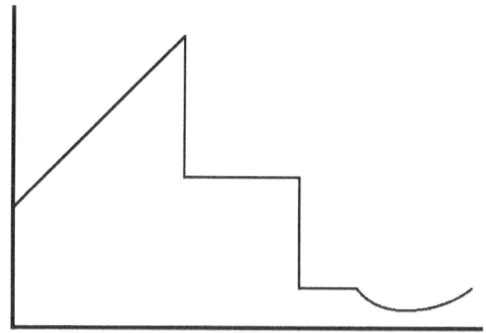

It Figures 1
The Raffalafferty Curve
Used by permission of Gerhardt Raffalafferty,
because we don't want any trouble, mister.

Does President McDruhitmumpf's base care one way or the other? "I didn't doubt the President's interpretation of the chart for a second," admitted Deborah-Rae Pigmentoziah, a long time McDruhitmumpf supporter (she claimed her MVGA hat was in the wash after her three year-old threw up mustard flavoured Cheerios all over it). "For long minutes that stretched into hours, sure. But, a second? Not even!"

The Dumboprats' Worst Nightmare, One Million Years in the Making

by HAL MOUNTSAUERKRAUTEN, Alternate Reality News Service Court Writer

Remember how everybody (by which I mean primarily Reduhblicans) laughed when the Institutes of National Scientific Humbuggery (really – the derisive Reduhblican slogan for them was: "Give us an INSH, and we'll take $300 million of government funding!") recreated neanderthals from DNA found in amber? What good are they? Neanderthals make terrible social workers: their solution to every problem is to bash something in the head with a rock until it stops moving. They make even worse nannies: they run off to the nearest forest to hunt and gather for weeks at a time, leaving children to fend for themselves. And, don't get me started on how bad they are as auto mechanics!

Well. The Reduhblicans have apparently found a use for neanderthals: they've just nominated one to sit on the Extreme Court.

His name is Thag. He looks like a beer barrel with limbs. He is about five feet tall, has no chin to speak of, a sloping forehead and a huge nose that dominates his face. Really, it's quite fascist, that nose – you expect at any moment that it will rally his lips, cheeks, ears and other facial features for an invasion of his neck.

The first day of his Senate confirmation hearings took place yesterday. It was very revealing, and not only because his pinstriped loincloth kept falling off.

When asked if he would allow gay bakers to refuse to sell cakes to straight white couples, Thag replied, "Thag am strict constructionist." When asked what he meant by that, the candidate seemed to get confused and said, "Thag...Thag am struck constrictionist. Strict destructionist! Thag...Thag...Thag..." As he jumped up on the desk making strange "Ooh ooh oohing" sounds and beating his hairy chest with his fists, Senate Judiciary Committee Chair Chuck Gasleygrassteahee said, "I think what candidate Thag meant is that he believes that the only rights that should be granted to citizens are directly stated in the Constitution."

After he calmed down, the candidate stated, "Yeah, that what Thag mean. That totally what Thag mean."

Later in the hearing, Thag was asked whether, if an abortion case came before him, he would be comfortable overturning *Roeliodingdong v. Watuhfouriday*. The candidate bared his teeth, which may have been a neanderthal grin although it certainly appeared to be a lot more threatening, and responded, "Thag not deal with hypotheticals."

Thag was nominated for the seat vacated by Justice Anthony Dedkennediesrock. And, when I say "vacated," I really mean one day Dedkennediesrock went into the Grey House all bright and chipper and brimming with the potential of life (well, as brimming with the potential of life as any 81 year-old can be), and he came out an hour later a hollow-eyed zombie flatly stating, "I. Have. Had. Enough. I. Must. Retire. From. Extreme. Court. Must. Retire. Must. Retire. So. Tired. Must…"

"To be fair," commented token smart person Amy Sheshutshotshitbam, "an hour in the Grey House would be enough to turn Gandheeisdandi into a hollow-eyed zombie with flat inflection!"

Dumboprats have made noises that they will block the nomination. Strange, quiet, gurgling noises, but they clearly meant…okay, it's hard to know what strange, gurgling noises mean. Other than, "I have an obstructed windpipe – for Gord's sake do something!" But, being in the minority, what can they realistically do?

Plenty. They can gnash their teeth. They can beat their breasts. If they are really incensed, they can rend their garments. Senate Majority Leader Mitch Wichconnelliswich especially enjoys the rending of garments; he has a page bring him popcorn and a television remote control (without the batteries so its signal doesn't interfere with another Senator's pacemaker) and pretends he's watching the spectacle in the comfort of his own living room.

Or, the Dumboprats could point out that the last time President Bushbamclintreagbush had an open seat on the Extreme Court to fill, Majority Leader Wichconnelliswich stuck his fingers in his ears and said, "Naah naah naah – I can't hear you, Mister lame duck President – you have no authority to nominate anybody to anything ever again – naah naah!" For almost an entire year! (Be thankful you weren't married to him – his pillow talk must have been deadly!) Mid-term elections are only four months away – the Dumboprats could demand that Majority Leader Wichconnelliswich maintain the same standard he set then by putting his fingers in his ears and taunting the President.

"Yeah, I see two problems with that scenario," token smart person Sheshutshotshitbam stated. "The first is that Mitch Wichconnelliswich is about as consistent as the population of Utabama's responses to a Roschach test. Yes, it does make sense. Think about it. He's a weasel who does whatever is most politically expedient in the moment, with no thought of the past. Really. He's like the guy from *Memento*, only turtlier."

And, the second problem? "Dumboprats, being who they are…"

I waited for token smart person Sheshutshotshitbam to finish the thought. Twenty minutes later, seven minutes after I had run out of tape, I realized that token smart person Sheshutshotshitbam **had** finished the thought. In future, please imagine a period in place of the ellipse at the end of the sentence in the last paragraph…

Ask Amritsar About the Home of the Deranged

Dear Amritsar,

A friend of mine retweeped a tweep that blames President McDruhitmumpf for the government shutdown. She's obviously suffering from McDruhitmumpf Derangement Syndrome. Should I just unfollow her on Twitherd, or should I humiliate her utterly and completely before I unfollow her?

Political in Passaic

Hey, Babe,

The Vesampuccerian Psychiatric Association does not recognize McDruhitmumpf Derangement Syndrome as a, you know, thing. In the world. If you want to unfollow somebody on Twitherd, don't blame it on some made up psychological condition; there's nothing wrong with admitting that you don't appreciate your friend's habit of retweeping videos of cats stealing toupees and running up ChristmaKwaanzUkah bush trees to put them on the heads of the angels there.

Dear Amritsar,

My hatred of videos of cats stealing toupees and running up ChristmaKwaanzUkah bush trees to put them on the heads of the angels there is irrelevant. McDruhitmumpf Derangement Syndrome is so real. If it wasn't, why would so many otherwise rational (broadly defined), reasonable (if you squint) people turn into frothing, raving lunatics at the mere mention of the President's name? It's positively Pavlovodkaskian! And, anyway, everybody on Foxindehenhaus News talks about McDruhitmumpf Derangement Syndrome, so it must be a thing. In the world.

If anything sounds made up, it's the Vesampuccerian Psychiatric Association. I mean, I've never heard of such a thing. My wife Beretta has never heard of such a thing. My other wife, Nitro (don't ask about the paperwork!) has never heard of such a thing. Nobody at the Ferkin' Ferkin had heard of such a thing, and that includes the designated drivers! Seriously, the Vesampuccerian Psychiatric Association, it just sounds so…made up!

Political in Passaic

Hey, Babe,

Bless your soul for not writing that positively Pavlovodkaskian would make a great name for a punk rock band from the eighties. It's good to know that in these barbarian times, some people still know how to show a little self-restraint.

Having said that, the rest of your message was complete bull testicles. The Vesampuccerian Psychiatric Association was founded in 1844. Okay, at the time it was called the Association of Medical Superintendents of Vesampuccerian Institutions for the Insane because they didn't know any better. It was 1844. Their approach to mental illness was take two leeches and send me a letter by Pony Express in the morning. Every institution has to start somewhere.

As a matter of fact, several of my closest friends are among the 37,000 members of the VPA. If they do not recognize that something is a thing, trust me, it's not a thing. Because they are a thing. They are a thing that knows things.

The internet is full of psychoBabylon. Wrong ideas often start as a joke, the humour wearing thin through constant retelling, until people start to take them seriously and spread them as fact. The Internet is the brokenest telephone. Where do you think that people got the idea that K-Pop diminished psychotic behaviour in dolls animated by the spirits of dead serial killers?

Trust me: if it ain't in the DS&M V, it ain't psychology!

Dear Amritsar,

YOU DON'T KNOW WHAT YOU'RE TALKING ABOUT! THERE'S NO SUCH THING AS THE VESAMPUCCERIAN PSYCHIATRIC ASSOCIATION!! AND, IF THERE IS, IT'S PART

OF A CONSPIRACY TO MAKE DECENT, HARD-WORKING VESAMPUCCERIAN MEN SUBSERVANT TO INTERNATIONAL BANKERS!!! YOU THINK I DON'T SMELL GEORGE SOROBOROROS' INFLUENCE HERE?!?!?!?! MAYBE YOU SHOULD GET YOUR NOSTRILS UNSTUFFED!!!!!

RONALD MCDRUHITMUMPF IS THE GREATEST PRESIDENT SINCE SLICED BREAD! HE HAS DONE MORE FOR THE AVERAGE WORKING STIFF THAN WHITE TOAST!! YES, I SAID IT: EVERYBODY KNOWS THAT BLACK BREAD IS BORN INFERIOR AND ONLY SUCCEEDS BECAUSE OF PREJUDICIAL DUMBOPRAT POLICIES TOWARDS BAKED GOODS!!! THE VESAMPUCCERIAN PSYCHIATRIC ASSOCIATION WOULD HAVE US BELIEVE THAT TOAST IS NOT A SCIENTIFIC CATEGORY – WELL, SO IS THEIR AUNT PETUNIA!!!! I'M PROUD TO BE PURE WHITE TOAST, AND NOT PUMPERNICKEL OR RYE OR ANY OF THE OTHER MONGREL BREADS!!!!!

Thank you for listening to me. I hope you now see the error of your ways and will write accordingly.

Political in Passaic

Hey, Babe,

Who, exactly, is the deranged person in this scenario?

Send your relationship problems to the Alternate Reality News Service's sex, love and technology columnist at questions@lespagesauxfolles.ca. Amritsar Al-Falloudjianapour is not a trained therapist, but she does know a lot of stuff. AMRITSAR SAYS: "Time periodist?" Sure, I'll accept that label, if you will accept the label "labelist!"

President's Lawyer Goes to the Ends of the Earth to Find a Smoking Glove

by HAL MOUNTSAUERKRAUTEN, Alternate Reality News Service Crime Writer

You know the old saw (the one that's so dull it doesn't cut both ways?): the cover-up is worse than the crime? You might think that this means that if you are in imminent danger of being caught having committed a crime, you shouldn't make things worse by trying to cover it up.

If you do, you clearly don't work in the McDruhitmumpf administration. The lesson the President appears to have taken from this piece of folk wisdom (try not to get it stuck in your teeth – you'll need expensive dental surgery if you do!) is that if you're contemplating committing a crime, do it out in the open so you won't have to cover it up.

Remember when President Ronald McDruhitmumpf said, "Fenwick, if you're listening – and, I know you are, because your native radio sucks! – now would be a good time to find and release Hillary Roocartoncleveman's emails – you know you want to, because your TV is nothing to write home about, either!"? Which was worse: the fact that he asked a foreign country to interfere in the 2016 election, or that he went on to tell the lie that he didn't ask a foreign country to interfere in the 2016 election, that, in fact, he had never met the country and was sure that he wouldn't be able to identify it in a police lineup?

Umm, okay, it was asking for the help. But, the lying was not so great, either.

Rudy Giulihooeyboi, the Saul Goodtolastdropman of political lawyers, announced that he was going to Ugarte, a Fenwick satellite, to "ask them to investigate the crimes of Joe Bidenhisbeeswax." Allegations that former Vice President Bidenhisbeeswax helped his son in a business deal in Ugarte are too boring to get into, and, in any case, have been investigated and disproven. Could the fact that Bidenhisbeeswax, who is in the race for the Dumbopratic presidential nomination, beats McDruhitmumpf in poll after poll have something to do with Giulihooeyboi's mission?

"Absolutely not!" Giulihooeyboi insisted. "I'm not asking a foreign government to interfere in the 2020 election. Because, some people would think that that is wrong. No. No way. Unh uh. I'm merely asking a foreign government to…supply me with information that… voters in the 2020 election will want to know. How is that asking them to interfere? It's not! It's totally different."

Giulihooeyboi, President McDruhitmumpf's personal attorney, stated he would also be asking questions about the start of the FBI investigation that ended in the report of Special Prosecutor Robert

Meullitallover. Why Ugarte? Apparently, the wardrobe to Narnia had been bought at a garage sale and nobody knew its current whereabouts.

The 2020 McDruhitmumpf reelection campaign did not support Giulihooeyboi's action. "He's a private citizen," it stated in a press release. "He can do what he wants. Any dumbass thing that he wants. Really, any unhelpful, potentially destructive thing that he wants to do. We can't tell a private citizen what to do, no matter how damaging it could be to the cause of his client, a clause he claims to be supporting. Dumbass. Did we use that word before? Good – it bears repeating!"

Despite his denials, somebody must have suggested his behaviour **was** election interference, because two minutes later Giulihooeyboi announced that his trip to Ugarte was off. "I'm not backing down because the optics are bad," he commented. "I'm reevaluating my options because of potential negative public perceptions of my actions. How is that bad optics? It's not! It's totally different!"

The fact that Giulihooeyboi is not going to Ugarte does not mean that the campaign is not trying to get dirt on potential Dumbopratic Presidential candidates. Token smart person Amy Sheshutshotshitbam pointed out that they could just get somebody with a lower public profile and less manic public persona to do it for them. "Paul Bildapillofort has an existing relationship with Ugarte…except, he's in jail. Okay, well, George Losdospapapuss has proven that he would be willing to do – well, no, he's in jail, too. Umm…there's always Michael Flyinnthuointmeant. He once went to Fenwick to…yeah, that really doesn't work out well for the people who do it, does it?'

"Are you kidding me? **Are you ferking kidding me?**" shouted security expert Malcolm Donneednopennance. "An associate of the President of the United States of Vesampucceri –"

"A private citizen," Giulihooeyboi interrupted.

"Who works for the President of the United States of Vesampucceri plans on travelling to another country to get dirt on one of his client's rivals? A country that is a close personal friend of our greatest enemy? Gord dammit, if this is allowed to happen, we may as well bend over and kiss our democracy goodbye!"

"I don't know what all the fuss is about, Giulihooeyboi calmly responded. "I'm just a private citizen who is seeking the truth. When you think about it, I'm just a modern Albert Einsteinachtmusik…"

The Quantum Press Secretary

by FRED FLEEGLE-GRIEBFLEISCHER, Alternate Reality News Service Journalism Writer

In a room in the Grey House, Press Secretary Sarah Wannabe-Panders stands in front of a podium, ready to give the day's briefing. But, she is the only person in the room. Does she spend the next hour giving the briefing and taking imaginary questions ("Sarah, why are you so awesome?" "Oh, Dan, Ah am delahted y'all would say such a kind, kind thing. Let me explain whah..."), or does she whip out her phone and spend the time playing *Angry Crustaceans*?

As long as nobody enters the room (and it's unlikely that anybody will), Press Secretary Wannabe-Panders is both and neither, a state known as quantum decoherence. While this is better than her usual state of quibbling incoherence, it does make one wonder if she can continue in her job.

The daily press briefings had been flaking off journalists like so much dead skin for months. The reporter for the *New Yoricknuhemwell Times* developed an allergy to bullshit which made him break out in scales (la-la-la-la-la-la-la) whenever Press Secretary Wannabe-Panders spoke. The reporter for the *Washburningdington Post* started hearing voices which tried to convince her to cheat on her taxes, or her husband, or her bridge opponents – the deception was the main thing – and had to go on a six month press briefing detox before returning to a different beat. Even such Reduhblican stalwarts as Foxindehenhaus News stopped sending reporters to the briefings when they realized that they had access to the President and people in his orbit whenever they wanted it, so they may as well cut out the middle-deceiver.

The straw that caused a flight to the doors...of...the camel's back was the release of the report of Special Prosecutor Robert Meullitallover, in which Press Secretary Wannabe-Panders admitted that an assertion she had made to the press corps "was made on a wish and a prayuh."

After President Ronald McDruhitmumpf fired then-FBI Director James Comeonecomally, Press Secretary Wannabe-Panders told journalists that she had been contacted by "many, many, so many membahs of thuh FBI, more than Ah can count, and Ah am really good with numbahs, tellin' me how unhappy they weh with

Comeonecomally." This was intended to give the President cover for the firing, showing that he had more reason to do it than "this Fenwicker thing."

Unfortunately (for her, great for late night comedians), the day after she made the statement, acting FBI Director Andrew McCabendmiller testified before Congress that Comeonecomally had the full support of everybody at the organization. Under oath. Mind amazingly focused. So, journalists didn't quite believe Press Secretary Wannabe-Panders' original statement.

Given the evidence, Press Secretary Wannabe-Panders had to admit to Meullitallover that there was no basis for the statement that hordes of FBIniks complained to her about Director Comeonecomally. It's amazing how being under oath focuses the mind.

After the Meullitallover report was released, Press Secretary Wannabe-Panders claimed that the statement was a mere slip of the tongue in a heated moment. "Y'all know how it goes," she explained. "Ya wanna say 'Ah do believe that theah is no cause foah alahm,' and y'all end up sayin' 'Thuh bomb didn't go off as planned, so that's all raht, then.' It happens t'all of us."

The problem is that Press Secretary Wannabe-Panders repeated the false claim several times over the next couple of days, even going so far as to embellish it with details about the FBI Director's language, physical posture and eye shadow. That's a lot of slips of the tongue in a lot of heated moments. Moreover, when she first made the claim, she was reading from a prepared text. It's possible that the teleprompter was having a heated moment, but there did not appear to be any smoke drifting out of the top of it.

The implication of this shifting landscape of statements is that Press Secretary Wannabe-Panders lied to Special Prosecutor Meullitallover's investigators about lying to the press corps. That was the moment that the credibility of the McDruhitmumpf administration became a crazy Mobiusballon strip of dishonesty.

No journalist will go near something like that; it's not worth risking what little sanity they may have.

I like to think Press Secretary Wannabe-Panders is saying to the empty room all of the things she could never say to members of the press corps: her hopes and dreams for her life and how bitterly she regrets not being able to achieve them. How she knows that a constant stream of untruths has corroded her soul, but the attraction of serving power was too strong to resist. How she would kill herself for the shame if she wasn't a good Christian woman who would be condemned to Hell if she did.

I like to think I'm a romantic that way.

Brooklyn Beginning, Hollywood Ending

by ELMORE TERADONOVICH, Alternate Reality News Service Film and Television Writer

As a New Yoricknuhemwell real estate...developer seems too grandiose for what he actually accomplished...let's call him a mover and...well, shaker doesn't quite describe him either...mover and wriggler – as a New Yoricknuhemwell real estate mover and wriggler, Ronald McDruhitmumpf thrived in a lawsuit-rich environment. As President, he switched to more investigation-oriented surroundings, with mixed results. Looking at the lack of energy he currently brings to sparring with the press, you can tell President McDruhitmumpf longs for the simpler days when lawyers were lawyers and contractors you owed money to were scared.

Trust Hollywood, of all places, to oblige.

The Motion Picture Association of Vesampucceri (MPAV) is suing President McDruhitmumpf for "egregious copyright infringement with intent to commit plotline murder." The MPAV is asking for a kajillion dollars in damages; legal experts are saying they'll be lucky to get lunch money. "Overreach much?" asked VCLU lawyer Alan Greenurpassterspanz. "Sure, I play a lawyer on TV, but I also am one in real life, so you can trust me when I say I think they've been watching too many of their own legal series!"

"We have to stop rapists and murderers from crossing over our borders!" President McDruhitmumpf told a cheering crowd...so many times it would be misleading to refer to a single date as a source. "They bring animatronic children filled with cocaine into our oh so innocent and trusting country, then give them what they call 'The Pinata Treatment' and give what spills out to babies in Vesampuccerian nurseries. Everybody knows that. And, the cocaine they're flooding our country with, let me tell you, it's more addictive than crack!"

"That's the plot of *Sic Oreo On 'Em: Knight the Soldado, Daddio*!" exclaimed MPAV Chairman Charles Riventoexcel. "Granted, the President's version is a lot pithier than the film, which, at six hours and 37 minutes, could probably have used a little trimming. But, let's not let artistic merit get in the way of the point: the President has been stealing material for his speeches from our members' films!"

Riventoexcel pointed out that, with small variations, the same plot could be said to have been at the centre of *Die Hard VII: Die Hardest With an Indeterminate Latin American Accent*, *Bad Boys Border Bedlam* and at least 37 B-movies, most of which having titles so blatantly racist that we worried we would get letters of complaint just because we know them. So, we had ourselves retconned to ensure that wouldn't happen.

Take that, haters.

"But, you get the idea," Riventoexcel summed up (because, to succeed in Hollywood, you really need to be on top of the numbers). "Hollywood owns the idea of invading hordes of drug-dealing Latinos!"

"With all due respect," Press Secretary Sarah Wannabe-Panders smirked (which gave some indication of just how much respect she truly believed the MPAV was due), "y'all cannot copyright an idea. Y'all can only copyright thuh expression of an idea. The Office of Legal Counsel is really lookin' forward ta takin' this case before a judge!"

"Oooooor," stated Maria Teresa Kumasatralez, President of *Voto Latino*, "alternately, Hollywood has spun the fantasy of gangs of Latinos freely crossing the border in large numbers to attack Vesampuccerian decency, and the President has exploited the image it has left in the mind of the public for political gain. Nobody gets out of this clean."

"That was the tag line for *The Bournbutnotforgot Indeterminacy*," Riventoexcel smugly pointed out.

Ignoring the interruption, we asked Kumasatralez if it bothered her that "Oooooor" and "alternately" mean basically the same thing.

"You're really good," she responded, "at zeroing in on the most important aspect of a statement, aren't you?"

Journalistic ethics forbade me from responding, but the gleam in my eye should have said all that needed to be said.

Does the MPAV's lawsuit against President McDruhitmumpf have a chance of succeeding? "If it's anything like past lawsuits against him," said legal scholar Laurence Tribaldrumstillbeats, "McDruhitmumpf will string it out for as long as he can, insult everybody involved – including the court stenographers and the guy who serves food in the courthouse basement's cafeteria – and, when it looks like he's about to lose, he'll settle for far more than he would have paid if he had dealt honourably with the complainants from the beginning."

So, it could go either way, then?

"You're really good," Tribaldrumstillbeats responded, "at taking meaning out of a statement that the person who made it hadn't even realized was there, aren't you?"

Fortunately, journalistic ethics do not forbid me from blushing.

Uncorrupt Reduhblican Embarrasses Party

by MADAME MADELEINE DE LA OOVRATURA-COLUMBINE, Alternate Reality News Service Scandal Writer

"He's a disgrace to the office," said Treasury Secretary Steve Mnemonixuchin.

"He is an exemplar of why people have such a low opinion of politicians," said Secretary of Commerce Wilbur Rossinantehead.

"He's a good man. Works real hard, believe me. I know a thing or two about working hard," concluded President Ronald McDruhitmumpf. "But, if I had known he would do such a terrible, terrible thing, I never would have asked him to be part of my Cabinet, trust me on that."

He is Robert Wilkieerwontkie, Secretary of Veterans Affairs. His crime? He is unwilling to commit a crime.

He has not, for instance, taken military transports on the public dime (still a potent metaphor, if not a useful unit of exchange) without reason. Nor has he been in charge of trade negotiations even though he has stakes in companies that would profit from the results of such negotiations. And, he certainly hasn't slow-walked and ultimately lifted Congressional sanctions against Fenwick in the hope of getting a luxury hotel with his name on it in their capital city. Not that Fenwick was ever going to allow that to happen. He hasn't slow-walked and ultimately lifted Congressional sanctions against Fenwick in the doomed hope of getting a luxury hotel with his name on it in their capital city.

According to sources within the Grey House, President McDruhitmumpf has tried to coach Secretary Wilkieerwontkie in the art of corruption. "Start small," the President is reported to have advised. "Pay somebody to vote for you in an election or, or, or steal a porno magazine from a corner store. I'm not joking! We all hadda start somewhere!"

Token smart person Amy Sheshutshotshitbam agreed with the President: "You take that back!" What? "The day I agree with Ronald McDruhitmumpf is the day I renounce token smart personism and join a venture capitalastery!" Oh. Umm…supported the President? "Never in my life!" Right. How about…didn't entirely disavow one specific thing that the President said? "Mmm…okay. I guess I can live with that…"

Okay, then. Token smart person Amy Sheshutshotshitbam didn't entirely disavow one specific thing that the President said: "Vesampuccerians hate to be conned, but we do seem to love con men. As long as everybody in the Reduhblican government in Washburningdington is playing with the same lack of rules, everybody in McDruhitmumpf's base is willing to look the other way. Unfortunately, it only takes one good apple to ruin things for everybody else!"

"If something isn't done about Wilkieerwontkie," agreed Pulippitzaner Prize-winning pundit Eugene Robinsoncrusoe – Umm… is it okay to say that you agreed with token smart person Amy Sheshutshotshitbam? "Sure. Why not?" I don't know – something in the air? Especially now that coal is back in fashion? "Oh. No. Really. I'm good with it." …agreed Pulippitzaner Prize-winning pundit Eugene Robinsoncrusoe, "his behaviour could undermine the Reduhblican Party's image among its followers of getting 'er done. McDruhitmumpf's base doesn't care if they cut corners to get 'er done. And, they obviously don't care if somebody personally profits from getting 'er done, even if it isn't any of them. But, if somebody is not personally profiting, the base will suspect that they're not getting 'er done. And, that can only mean trouble for the Party."

What is the 'er in getting 'er done? "If anybody finds out," Robinsoncrusoe answered, "I would appreciate it if they let me know."

In order to help their Reduhblican impermanent interests (because in politics, there are no friends, only…), two weeks ago

Foxindehenhaus News tried to peddle the story that Secretary Wilkieerwontkie had cheated on his wife with a porcupine. Any scandal in a calm, I guess. Unfortunately, the scheme quickly fell apart when Wilkieerwontkie's acupuncturist told *The Washburningdington Post* that the holes in his client's body were not a sign of porcupine love, they were just an indication of a man who enjoyed his job just a little too much and got carried away.

"We tried to show the world just how venal and corrupt Robert Wilkieerwontkie could be," Foxindehenhaus faux journalist (they're like faux fur, except they chill your blood instead of keeping you warm) Brian KissMeadekilmeadenow bloviated. "Some people just don't want to be helped, I guess."

Secretary Wilkieerwontkie declined to comment on the absence of allegations. And, when I write, "declined to comment," I mean "ran through a Krispy Kreme parking lot, tossing a box of sugary confections in my direction in the hope of slowing me down, hopped a fence and ran through the backyards of several strangers until he was out of sight – and, not in a 1960s, psychedelic drug-induced kind of way."

No denials. No apologies that, upon further reflection, turned out not to apologize for anything. No defiant doubling down on the original offence.

It was like Secretary Wilkieerwontkie was trying to look innocent!

Ira Nayman

10. THE SLEEP OF REASON PRODUCES… CONSEQUENCES

Don't Get Freshman With Us, Missy!

by FREDERICA VON McTOAST-HYPHEN, Alternate Reality News Service People Writer

The mid-term elections returned more freshman – why do they call them "fresh**men**" when so many of them are women? And, why do they call them "**fresh**men" when they haven't been around long enough to have been accused of sexual harassment? Let me start again.

The mid-term elections returned more indeterminateperson Representatives than at any time since the Continental Breakfast Congress. This has both positive and negative and downright weird implications. Threeth implications, then. Or, allth.

On the plus side, new Representatives can bring new energy and new ideas to an institution that, let's be honest, here, can reek of the complacency musk of your great-grandfather. You know: the reason you don't like to go down to the basement of his house?

On the negative side, new Representatives can knock over the urn containing your great-grandfather's ashes, scratch up your comfiest chair (the one the Spanish Inquisition always borrows for reasons you'd rather not ask) and piddle in the middle of your living room to mark their territory. Or, to demand your attention. Or, because the strut to the litter box in the bathroom is too far – why does the litter box have to be so far? Or, most likely, allth at once.

Newly elected Dumbopratic Representative Alexandria Casio-Keebjords set off piddle alarms throughout Washburningdington when she announced her desire to raise the marginal tax rate on millionaires and billionaires to 70 per cent. "After World War The Greatest Generation's Big One," Representative Casio-Keebjords explained, "the marginal tax rate on the wealthy was 90 per cent. Given the urgency of the problems facing Vesampucceri today, they should consider my position a bargain!"

Reduhblicans so thoroughly lost their shit at this, you would have thought they were tourists visiting a national park during a government shutdown.

At 2:37 in the morning, President Ronald McDruhitmumpf tweeped, "Hear what Alexandria Cortisol-K – Alexandria Occasional-Cortege – Alexandria Overlor – Baby Alex, I call her. Hear what Baby Alex said about the tax system? I tell you, people, everybody knows – and, I mean everbody – the radical extremists have taken over the Dumboprat Party! #stopleftyextremismathome"

Token smart person Amy Sheshutshotshitbam spit up a piece of bagel with a schmear (which was strange, given that she was eating veal piccata at the time). "A President willing to condemn millions to the misery of an indefinite government shutdown so he won't lose face with his base – and, doesn't that sound like an 80s boy band? – is accusing somebody else of extremism? You'd best believe I would spit up food I wasn't even eating in response to such a grotesque statement!"

Later in the day, Representative Steve Kingfisherhelploess told Foxindehenhaus News: "Alexandria Latino-Person holds radically un-Vesampuccerian views, radically non-Vesampuccerian views which are becoming all too common in the anti-Vesampuccerian Dumboprat Party! I'm surprised Speaker Pelligrinosi puts up with it!"

Token smart person Sheshutshotshitbam spit up lobster thermidor because "as long as I'm spitting up imaginary food, I may as well splurge!" Then, wiping her mouth with a notional napkin, she explained, "Anybody who wears confederate flag briefs and sings, 'It's great to be white. It's great to be white. If you're any other colour, you just ain't right' into the Congressional Record shouldn't be trying to call out anybody else's extremism!" She added that somebody who was recently ejected from the House Reduhblican Caucus probably wasn't in a position to criticize how the other side ran its caucus.

Professional discourtesy and all that.

"The problem isn't that Miss Casio-Keebjords is such a polarizing figure," Senate Majority Leader Mitch Wichconnelliswich viciously turtled. "We're big boys. We can wear the right sunglasses. No, the problem is that Speaker Pelligrinosi encourages it. If this is their level of discourse, no Dumboprat should ever be allowed near power!"

Token smart person Sheshutshotshitbam spit up a grilled cheese sandwich. Apparently, Alternate Reality News Service Editrix-in-Chief Brenda Brundtland-Govanni had warned her that if she overspent her imaginary food allowance, Brundtland-Govanni would slap her into the equivalent of a six month food coma!

And, the Majority Leader's comment? "You mean, the man who wouldn't give President Bushbamclintreagbush's Extreme Court nominee a hearing, foisting fratboy Brett Kavanaugheylno on us a year later?" token smart person Sheshutshotshitbam asked. "And, how many years did he look the other way while Steve Kingfisherhelploess white nationalismed all over the place? People who live in metaphorical glass houses shouldn't cause token smart people to spit up imaginary food. It leaves streaks on the walls that are almost impossible to completely get out!"

When challenged with Representative Casio-Keebjords' remarks, Speaker Pelligrinosi said: "We love the new energy and new ideas of our…indeterminateperson caucus members. But, I would like to make clear the fact that they do not speak for the party."

With a sly grin, Representative Casio-Keebjords responded, "Yet…"

Shit Just Got Real

by HAL MOUNTSAUERKRAUTEN, Alternate Reality News Service Crime/Court/Justice Writer

The House Judiciary Committee has cited Attorney General William Katiebarrthudor for contempt of Congress for refusing to hand over the full, unredacted report by Special Prosecutor Robert Meullitallover, including all background materials, margin doodles and grease marks and coffee stains.

Ira Nayman

At 2:37 in the morning, President Ronald McDruhitmumpf
tweeped: "As expected, Jumpin' Jivin' Jerk Jerry folded like a cheap
suit of cards! The Dumboprats only ever issue empty threats because
they haven't got the ba WHAAAAAAAAAAT???!!!!!!"

The House Judiciary Committee has found the Attorney General to
be in contempt of Congress.

"No, I'm sorry," the President follow-up tweeped, "I don't
understand what u r saying."

The Judiciary Committee. You know who they are, right?

"Right. Weaselly bastards."

And, you're familiar with the Attorney General?

"You mean, my Roy Canadiohen? Sure."

Well, the former now holds the latter in contempt of Congress.

"Wait. Former…latter…you mean – no! Can they do that?"

"Yes! Yes! Oh, my Gord, they can totally do that, yes!" exulted
legal scholar Laurence Tribaldrumstillbeats "The McDruhitmumpf
administration refuses to comply with Congress' Constitutional duty of
oversight? This is what Congress taking its oversight role seriously
looks like, bitches!"

Love the enthusiasm, Laurence, but you might want to dial it back
a bit. The exclamation mark was implied.

If Attorney General Katiebarrthudor ignores the contempt citation,
the whole *schemazel* will have to be decided in the courts. And, sure,
the precedent of Independent Counsel Kenn Starrburstofapple forcing
Congress to read the full, unredacted report on his investigation of
President Bill Roocartoncleveman's extracurricular activities in the
Grey House (trust Reduhblicans to make salacious sex boring), would
make it seem like an easy victory for the Dumboprats. However, with
the full weight of the Injustice Department (they really need to cut
down on their carbs!) behind him, the Attorney General could drag this
out in the courts for years – or, at least until after the 2020 elections.
Which, while only 18 months away, will almost definitely feel like
years by the time we get there.

"True, but beside the point," Tribaldrumstillbeats cheerfully
pointed out. "This sends a message to anybody who is subpoenaed to
testify or supply documents to Congress who doesn't have the full
weight of the Injustice Department (I know you were skeptical when
your lawyer told you he was on an intermittent fasting diet, but can't

you put his health before your petty legal needs just this once?) behind them. And, the message is: 'BOO!'"

"Noooooooooooo!" cried Treasury Secretary Steve Mnemonixuchin, who has refused to comply with the Chair of the House Ways and Means Committee's request for six years of President McDruhitmumpf's tax returns. "This is not how the system is supposed to work! I'm too pretty to be held in Contempt of Congress!"

"This…this…this can't be happening!" complained former Grey House counsel Don McGillighansile, whom the President has forbidden from cooperating with Congress even though he has already blabbed plenty to the Special Prosecutor. And, I mean plenty, bub! We do not know what the President has threatened McGillighansile with, but being sent to his room without supper has been widely rumoured. "This is so out of character! Who are you and what have you done with the Dumbopratic Party!"

Special Prosecutor Meullitallover did not comment on the contempt citation, as is his won't. He's a man who can really put the tacit back in taciturn. However, given the fact that the Department of Injustice refuses to allow him to testify to any House committees even though they make googoo eyes at him – especially because they make googoo eyes at him – the yearning in his silence was palpable. No, not like oranges – which are pulpable. More like passion fruits.

"It is true that the species *legislatorica dumbopraticus* has evolved to have a large mouth and a shortened spine," stated politico-zoologist Amaranta Omponderosa. "This explains, for example, why they campaign on the issue of economic justice for the poor, but don't confront their wealthy donors with tax increases when they come into power. They're like the Sonnybonono monkeys of politics: sometimes enthusiastically throwing their feces around, but always backing down if anybody gives them the slightest resistance."

How was Judiciary Chair Jerry Blacknadlerthefirst able to overcome this evolutionary fact and shepherd the contempt citation through his committee and the full House? "Even a broken clock develops a backbone twice a day," Omponderosa explained. "That's just simple biology!"

Ira Nayman

AFTERWORD

Where Are They Now?

SPECIAL TO THE ALTERNATE REALITY NEWS SERVICE

Everybody would like to know what ultimately happens to the main players in the McDruhitmumpf melodrama. We wish we could tell you how everybody's story ends, but **we travel across dimensions, here, people, not time!** Do, please, pay attention!

Ahem.

It occurs to us that there is something we can do to cure your insatiable curiosity. You're welcome.

What? You want to know what it is? Isn't it enough for you that we know what it – cynical bastard. Alright. Since the different events in different universes almost always result in different historical paths (except for the infinite number of universes where they don't), we can tell you what happens to versions of our *dramatic personae* in other universes. These results probably won't reflect the ultimate fates of people on Earth Prime 1-6-7-1-8-2 dash Psi, but by the time that proves out, the Alternate Reality News Service will probably be delivered directly to your brain by ingestable nanobots, so it won't adversely affect our readership.

What do you mean, that's not good enough? Hunh! Tough room. Tell you what: we'll give you **three** possible alternate endings for each person. Will one of them accurately reflect the future of the people we know and loathe on Earth Prime 1-6-7-1-8-2 dash Psi? Sure. Why not? Stranger things have happened. And, if you've been paying attention, you should know what a lot of them are!

TOM ANYTHINGFORPRICE

1. He will book passage on Elon Threelonemuskateers' Brie-X and go down in history as the first human being to be eaten by a space octopus. [Earth Prime 1-6-7-1-9-2 dash Psi]

2. He will sue Intifada Paramunculous, author of *The Anythingforprice is Wrong: An Unofficial Biography of a Washburningdington Hustler*, for definition of character. Unfortunately, Tom Anythingforprice, the former Health and Human Disservices Secretary, will choose Rudy Giulihooeyboi to be his lawyer, and will be lucky to leave the courtroom with the shirt on his back. [Earth Prime 1-7-4-3-4-0 dash Omega]

3. He will be the only survivor of a plane crash in the middle of the Projects in Anytown, USV. There, Tom Anythingforprice will be taken in by an African-Vesampuccerian family who will teach him compassion and the value of community. He will forget these values five minutes later when he calls in the police to save him from his terrorist captors. [Earth Prime 1-4-7-7-7-2 dash Psi]

PAUL BILDAPILLOFORT

1. He will die in prison. [Earth Prime 1-6-3-0-0-1 dash Kappa]

2. He will spend the remainder of his life in prison, then die. [Earth Prime 1-6-7-2-9-2 dash Psi]

3. Former McDruhitmumpf Presidential campaign chair Paul Bildapillofort will make many new friends, have new adventures and learn a lot about himself and living in the world with others. In prison. Where he will live out the rest of his life. And, die. [Earth Prime 1-4-7-5-9-6 dash Omicron]

JOHN COLOURKELLYGREENE

1. He will become a spokesman for a lobbying organization called Men Will Be Men. It will take former Chief of Staff John Colourkellygreene three years to realize that MWBM is **not** a men's rights organization, but a gay right's organization. "We thought it was kind of weird that he kept alternately hitting on and cursing out the women in the office," one MWBM organizer will say when John Colourkellygreene is fired. "We just hoped he was in denial. Deep, deep and angry denial…" [Earth Prime 1-6-6-3-2-1 dash Chi]

2. He will get into a growling, scowling grimacing match with Movie star Bruce Willusorwontus that will go viral on YahooTube. John Colourkellygreene will lose, forcing him to retire from the public spotlight. Seventeen years later, he will die of a broken heart. [Earth Prime 1-6-6-8-7-8 dash Lambda]

3. After being fired from the Grey House, he will wander the countryside doing odd jobs to make a living, eventually becoming a pundit for Foxindehenhaus News. Two minutes into his first appearance, John Colourkellygreene will challenge Sean Hanjobovverfist to "go out back and settle our differences like real men" for being critical of his haircut. Two minutes after that, the former Grey House Chief of Staff will be back wandering the countryside. [Earth Prime 1-6-7-2-9-2 dash Chi]

ANNE COULTEREMINGTON

1. She will regret turning on President Mcdruhitmumpf because of some silly old border wall promise that nobody believed he was going to keep anyway when she is blamed for his loss of the 2020 primary to a coat rack with a bucket on top on which somebody has drawn a cartoon face. The Reduhblican Party will stampede for the centre as a

result, leaving pundit Anne Coulteremington with no choice but to shriek into the void. [Earth Prime 1-6-7-3-9-2 dash Chi]

2. When President Alexandria Casio-Keebjords reverses all of the Mcdruhitmumpf administration's environmental policies **and** implements universal healthcare, Anne Coulteremington's head will explode. Those closest to her will agree that the incident will make her kinder and more empathetic than she has ever been. [Earth Prime 1-6-5-4-8-8 dash Mu]

3. She'll get so thin that she will die when a woman in a park mistakes Anne Coulteremington for a twig and uses her to play fetch with her Skye Terrier Skindeep Booty. [Earth Prime 1-6-3-5-7-9 dash Mu]

BETSY DEVOLUTION-ROSS

1. She will lose her fortune in a series of investments in failing Vesampuccerian companies and be forced to teach seven year-old immigrant children English as a Second Language. We're sure her overdose of sleeping pills will be an accident. [Earth Prime 1-6-7-4-9-2 dash Chi]

2. Her husband will come out of the closet to open a gay bar called Chez Butter with his lover, Raul. Devastated, former Education Secretary Betsy DeVolution-Ross will take solace in The Church of the Bedhidden Nordlinger and the arms of a Pastor…coincidentally also named Raul. [Earth Prime 1-6-2-2-2-2 dash Kappa]

3. After leaving politics, she will drop out of sight except for a brief period where she is a competitor on *Dancing With the People With Whom You Are Vaguely Familiar – No, Seriously, Their Names Are On The Tip of Your Tongue – If We Give You a Second, We're Sure It Will Come to You*. Betsy DeVolution-Ross and her partner, a coat rack with a bucket on top on which somebody has drawn a cartoon face, will come in fifth. [Earth Prime 1-6-8-8-8-8 dash Gamma]

MICHAEL FLYINNTHUOINTMEANT

1. After he has served his time in jail, he will find himself in competition with former FBI Director James Comeonecomally for the part of Lurch in the latest remake of *The Adamantians Family*. Comeonecomally will have the height, but former national security adviser Michael Flyinnthuointmeant will have the intensity. Eventually, the producers will decide to call on a coat rack with a bucket on top on which somebody has drawn a cartoon face to be the character, nipping a promising acting career in the bud, although it will never be clear whose. [Earth Prime 1-6-7-5-9-2 dash Chi]

2. After leaving prison, he will become a heavy drinker. If anybody asks Michael Flyinnthuointmeant why his tipple of choice is vodka and coffee liqueur, he will indignantly reply that he has never met a Black Fenwickian. [Earth Prime 1-6-6-3-3-4-7 dash Tau]

3. In his retirement from public life, after being released from the correctional facility, he will become heavily invested in playing *Dungeons and Dragons*. Unfortunately, nobody will want to play with Michael Flyinnthuointmeant because of his tendency to make secret deals with orcs. [Earth Prime 1-6-4-9-0-1 dash Omicron]

SEAN HANJOBOVVERFIST

1. After having been hit in the head by a golf ball President McDruhitmumpf somehow manages to tee off backwards, he will find that he can only speak the truth. The first thing that anchor Sean Hanjobovverfist will say the next time he is on the air is that Foxindehenhaus News is, and always has been, a propaganda arm of the Reduhblican Party. The second thing he will say is that he has been fired because of the first thing that he said. [Earth Prime 1-6-0-0-0-5 dash Tau]

2. *Puppet President* will become a YahooTube sensation. After an episode is uploaded in which Sean Hanjobovverfist fights with Fenwickian Prime Minister Rupert Mountkilamanjoy to determine who will have the privilege of sticking their hand up President McDruhitmumpf's butt, Sean Hanjobovverfist will finally be too

embarrassed to show his face in public. For almost a week. [Earth Prime 1-6-5-4-3-2 dash Omicron]

3. He will suffer a stroke railing against President Chelsea Roocartoncleveman's "No Kitten Left Behind" legislation. Sean Hanjobovverfist will be vilified for his position, but at least he will die doing something he loves. [Earth Prime 1-6-7-5-9-2 dash Phi]

JOHN KNOTTBOLTEDONWEILL

1. While in England to help ensure the messiest Brexit possible, he will be attacked by an angry mob, who will completely tear off his moustache. Afraid to return to Vesampucceri for fear (not entirely unfounded) that he will be laughed at, former national security adviser John Knottboltedonweill will join a monastery in China (the part that he helped liberate from Tibet) and spend five minutes contemplating the nature of existence. After he is kicked out of the monastery for trying to foment an insurrection against the head monk, he will wander the world in the vain search for a surgeon willing to conduct a controversial 'stache transplant. [Earth Prime 1-7–7-1-8-2 dash Psi]

2. He will exult in the collapse of the Disunited Nations. Ironically, John Knottboltedonweill will find that he has a taste for cockroaches in the irradiated future that he, in his own small way, helped create. [Earth Prime 1-6-7-5-0-2 dash Phi]

3. Ten years after Ronald Mcdruhitmumpf is impeached, John Knottboltedonweill will be asked to be the Secretary of State for President Krystalle McDruhitmumpf. While he will eagerly take the position, his scorched earth approach to diplomacy will look more like damp squib diplomacy, forcing top Reduhblican advisers to accept that the fire in his belly isn't what it used to be. [Earth Prime 1-6-7-7-6-0-9 dash Mu]

JARED KUSHKUSHINTHEBUSH

1. On a trip to Saudi Arabia, he will have a brief affair with a local hula dancer. Krystalle McDruhitmumpf will learn about the affair and, not believing that it is merely a "local custom," will punish former senior

Grey House adviser Jared Kushkushinthebush by remaining married to him for the rest of his life. [Earth Prime 1-6-1-2-1-5 dash Zeta]

2. The good news: because of his low opinion of them, the President will leave complete control of the McDruhitmumpf financial empire to Jared Kushkushinthebush instead of either of his sons. The bad news: the McDruhitmumpf financial empire will, at that point, consist of several billions of dollars of debt to shady characters and a stick of chewing gum. Boysenberry phlegm chewing gum. [Earth Prime 1-6-7-6-0-2 dash Phi]

3. When he is 80, waiters will still be asking him if he wants something from the kiddies' menu, he will be carded in bars and nobody will be willing to give him a senior's discount. Especially corner drug dealers. [Earth Prime 1-6-9-8-7-5 dash Xi]

RONALD MCDRUHITMUMPF

1. He will shut down the Meullitallover probe, avoid prosecution by states' attorneys and steal a second term as president, but at a cost of alienating everybody close to him. As a result, Ronald Mcdruhitmumpf will die alone in a well-appointed bedroom with nothing but a rolling snow globe and a cryptic last word that nobody is around to hear to mark his passing. [Earth Prime 1-6-7-6-0-2 dash Upsilon]

2. Thanks to Global Hot as Hellification, the state of Ohioklahoma will burn to the ground; thanks to cuts to emergency services, a couple of emergency firefighters will be dispatched to piss on the fire in the vain hope of putting it out. Vesampucceri's billionaires will relocate to Alaskifornia; for reasons that are never adequately explained, Ronald Mcdruhitmumpf will not be among them. [Earth Prime 1-6-3-8-3-4 dash Omicron]

3. When the extent of the Reduhblican losses in the 2018 mid-term elections becomes undeniable, President Mcdruhitmumpf's brain will explode. Nobody will notice until the official start of the 2020 election, when he will start saying things like: "Moo cow ushers vivisectionalize expect...or eight..." and "If at first you don't succeed, recidivist perpendicular chupacabras – everybody knows that, believe me!"

Knowledge of his...handicap won't make a difference – with Fenwick's help, Mcdruhitmumpf will be reelected. [Earth Prime 1-6-1-1-2-2 dash Tau]

RONALD MCDRUHITMUMPF, JR.

1. He will die in the middle of a secret meeting with a Fenwickian oligarch and three members of the Fenwickian secret police when his brain forgets to send signals to his heart to keep pumping. Ronald Mcdruhitmumpf, Jr.'s father, who is still president at the time, will give a rambling, 40 minute eulogy at his funeral that touches on how he is the best leader of the United States of Vesampucceri since Cleopatra, how unfair Special Prosecutor Robert Meullitallover is for having a birthday party and not inviting him, and naming all of the failing news outlets that have been mean to him; not once will he actually mention his son by name. [Earth Prime 1-6-7-7-0-2 dash Upsilon]

2. When his father dies, he will inherit a substantial debt. Surprise! Ronald Mcdruhitmumpf, Jr. will not look upon this as a setback; he will look at this as an opportunity...to drink himself to death. [Earth Prime 1-6-7-7-1-2 dash Upsilon]

3. Ronald Mcdruhitmumpf, Jr. will run for President in 2040. He will lose to Chelsea Roocartoncleveman. [Earth Prime 1-6-7-7-2-2 dash Upsilon]

RUPERT MOUNTKILAMANJOY

1. To celebrate his 90th birthday, he will resolve to stop making witty asides to an imaginary audience. Seconds later, Rupert Mountkilamanjoy, former President and Prime Minister of the Duchy of Grand Fenwick, will turn his head to the side and say, "That wasn't a very credible resolution? You might say that – I couldn't possibly comment..." [Earth Prime 1-6-7-7-3-2 dash Upsilon]

2. He will be pierced in the shin by an umbrella tipped with a deadly poison on the orders of Fenwickian oligarch Oleg Dareyatopasta. As Rupert Mountkilamanjoy lies dying in the ambulance taking him away

from the nearest hospital, he will smile and say, "I taught them well..." [Earth Prime 1-6-8-9-8-7 dash Beta]

3. After the resumption of Fenwick's nuclear armaments development programme, he will exult that his country has become a world power once again. Eighty-seven seconds later, Fenwick's kleptocracy will bankrupt the country, forcing all of its scientists to defect to Luxembourg. [Earth Prime 1-6-7-7-8-0 dash Eta]

KIRSTJEN NIELSENRATINGSHIT

1. She will be kidnapped by a white supremacist group and kept in a wire mesh enclosure on a concrete floor for four months. What will sustain former Homeland Insecurity head Kirstjen Nielsenratingshit throughout this ordeal will be her mantra, "This is not a cage. This is not a cage. This is not..." [Earth Prime 1-6-6-6-6-2 dash Alpha]

2. She will quit politics to join the band Bettina Boopoopadoopstein. The band's first single, "Grab Fishlocker Past Tense" will be so universally panned that they will be immediately shown the door by the music industry and asked never to darken it again. Dejected, Kirstjen Nielsenratingshit will console herself with a lucrative research position at a right-wing think tank. [Earth Prime 1-6-7-8-3-8 dash Chi]

3. She will gain 327 pounds within three years of leaving government. When asked why, Kirstjen Nielsenratingshit will answer: "If you had seen the things that I have seen, you wouldn't have to ask that question!" [Earth Prime 1-6-7-7-3-3 dash Upsilon]

STEVE O'BANNONALLHOPE

1. Late in his life, he will realize that fomenting hatred against identifiable groups is wrong. After he writes a *New Yoricknuhemwell Times* op-ed piece denouncing racism, former senior adviser to the President Steve O'Bannonallhope will be torn apart by an angry group of white nationalists, thus ensuring his legacy is secure. [Earth Prime 1-6-8-9-9-6 dash Rho]

2. Video of Steve O'Bannonallhope wearing a fetching yellow polka dot dress enthusiastically dancing to the Pet Shop Boys at a rave will surface on YahooTube. He will seem perfectly content with his life choices. He will be torn apart by an angry group of homophobic evangelical Christians, likely **because** of how perfectly content he seems to be with his life choices. [Earth Prime 1-6-1-6-1-6 dash Chi]

3. On a tour of eastern European countries, he will be torn apart by an angry group of gerbils. That's not a euphemism; in response, Steve O'Bannonallhope's followers in the United States and across Europe will begin to wage war against household pets. [Earth Prime 1-6-7-7-4-3 dash Upsilon]

MICHAEL PENDENATENDANCE

1. When President McDruhitmumpf loses the 2020 general election, his Vice President will have trouble adjusting to a world where he can no longer be a sycophant to somebody in power. Michael Pendenatendance will sometimes be found wandering the streets of Washburningdington late at night, plaintively asking strangers, "Will you be my daddy?" [Earth Prime 1-6-5-5-5-5 dash Mu]

2. When President McDruhitmumpf's brain finally explodes, his Vice President will believe that all of his groveling and toadying will have been worth it. Three days later, Michael Pendenatendance will lose the 2020 general election. It will be like an episode of *The Twilight Zone*, only with more garlic. [Earth Prime 1-6-7-8-4-3 dash Upsilon]

3. During the 2020 Presidential campaign, he will choke nearly to death on a hot dog at a baseball game (to add insult to injury, the game will be rained out soon after). While clinically dead, Michael Pendenatendance will have an encounter with Gord, who will tell him, "Look, douchenozzle, I don't need your help to make people suffer – I'm quite capable of doing that on my own. Have you never read the Gord Book?" Taking the hint, soon after regaining consciousness, Michael Pendenatendance will burn his Reduhblican Party membership card and try to join the Dumboprats. Good luck with that! [Earth Prime 1-6-7-2-3-9 dash Chi]

SCOTT PRUITTDONDOITT

1. He will die of lead poisoning after drinking tap water from Flint, Michissippi in an attempt to show the public that it is safe. At the funeral of former Environmental Pollution Agency head Scott Pruittdondoitt, President Ronald Mcdruhitmumpf will honour his legacy with the thoughtful words: "What a dumbass." [Earth Prime 1-6-4-9-0-0 dash Chi]

2. In retirement, he will sue the Vesampuccerian government when it gives an oil company a permit to drill in the pool in his backyard. Using the time-honoured legal argument *de gustibus est non disputandum*, the Extreme Court will rule in favour of the government. [Earth Prime 1-6-7-8-4-3 dash Tau]

3. He will die when the retirement home in Chicago he has been put into by his ungrateful children is destroyed by a tornado. Did we mention that it was in Chicago? An urban legend will develop that, as he was carried off by the tornado, Scott Pruittdondoitt defiantly shouted, "I don't care what's happening to me! Global Hot as Hellification is a myyyyyyyyyy –" [Earth Prime 1-6-6-1-9-9 dash Chi]

PAUL RYBOEHNBACHBLISSCRAP

1. The former Speaker of the House will become the CEO of a chain of restaurants called A Cruller Fate when the war on donuts is finally declared a tie and the addictive substance is finally made legal. Paul Ryboehnbachblisscrap will quit the company six months before the FDA shuts it down for selling Boston creams to minors. [Earth Prime 1-6-7-8-5-3 dash Tau]

2. He will join the Board of Directors of several brokerage firms, including Charles Schwabdadeckfellos. Paul Ryboehnbachblisscrap will quit Charles Schwabdadeckfellos six months before it is raided by the Department of Injustice for funnelling money to A Cruller Fate without its clients' knowledge or permission. [Earth Prime 1-6-7-3-8-2 dash Chi]

3. He will become a pundit for Foxindehenhaus News, where he will endlessly explain why neither of the political parties share his deep understanding of how the economy works. When Foxindehenhaus News is shut down by the FCC for conspiring with the Fenwickian government to steal Vesmapuccerian elections, Paul Ryboehnbachblisscrap will get four years in prison. "I knew I should have left six months ago," he will say at the time of his arrest. "Let this be a lesson for you, children: always go with your gut!" [Earth Prime 1-6-0-1-0-1 dash Pi]

JEFF "SELF-REGARD" SESSPOOLPANDEMIC

1. When the Extreme Court rules to uphold the Voter Registration Act and refuses to hear a challenge to *Roeliodingdong v. Watuhfouriday*, former Attorney General Jeff "Self-regard" Sesspoolpandemic's head will explode. He will spend the last eight years of his life locked in his own head, sitting for several hours a day in front of a hospital television set that plays nothing but BET. [Earth Prime 1-6-7-8-6-3 dash Tau]

2. While crossing the street to help a little old lady chicken get to the other side, he will be mugged by a white donut addict, who will use Jeff Sesspoolpandemic's credit cards to go on a chocolate glazed binge. Jeff Sesspoolpandemic will die before an arrest is made in the case, so he will never have the satisfaction of knowing that the police will erroneously arrest a black man for the attack despite the fact that his only crime was being a block away from the shooting buying orange juice for his blind seven year-old daughter. [Earth Prime 1-6-7-5-8-4 dash Delta]

3. Three years into his retirement, he will be given an award for Folksiest SOB by the Son's of Odin's Konfederacy. Condemnation of his acceptance of an award from such an openly racist group will blanket Twitherd, Farcebook and other social media platforms Jeff Sesspoolpandemic has never heard of. [Earth Prime 1-4-7-5-9-2 dash Omicron]

SARAH WANNABE-PANDERS

1. She will be raptured up to the good place, where she will have a lot of explaining to do to a supreme environment designer whose name is unpronounceable by human mouths so he asks everybody to call him Michael. [Earth Prime 1-6-7-8-7-3 dash Tau]

2. She will leave government to become a lobbyist for MassiveGiganticHugeUnitary Health Insurance, Inc. Former Press Secretary Sarah Wannabe-Panders' main accomplishment will be to delay legislation that would make it illegal for insurers to claim that children under the age of 12 who lose one or more limbs while working in a factory have a "preexisting condition." [Earth Prime 1-6-6-3-9-6 dash Beta]

3. She will run for President in 2040. She will lose to a coat rack with a bucket on top on which somebody has drawn a cartoon face whose platform includes a plan to drastically reduce the role of insurance companies in the delivery of health services. [Earth Prime 1-6-7-4-9-2 dash Theta]

MITCH WICHCONNELLISWICH

1. He will die waiting for his Congressional Medal of Honour to arrive in the mail. [Earth Prime 1-6-7-8-8-3 dash Tau]

2. Former Senate Majority Leader Mitch Wichconnelliswich will die waiting for wealthy Reduhblican donors to shower his bank account with gratitude for all he had done for them. At least he'll have the sense not to die waiting for gratitude-impaired President Mcdruhitmumpf to acknowledge all he had done for the man. [Earth Prime 1-6-3-1-0-1 dash Iota]

3. He will die waiting for a cure for the oiliness of his turtle shell. [Earth Prime 1-6-8-8-2-3 dash Omega]

RYAN ZINKEDINKEDOO

1. He will stop charging the government for trips on his private yacht when it becomes inescapably apparent that the waters off Vesampucceri's shores are too polluted for its propellers to function. "Beauty always comes at a cost," former Interior Secretary Ryan Zinkedinkedoo will sigh wistfully. [Earth Prime 1-6-7-8-9-3 dash Tau]

2. Thanks to fracking on the other side of the state, his house will fracture, with various pieces going in different directions. "It's not…an unfortunate event that is not covered by my home insurance," Ryan Zinkedinkedoo will try to rationalize the destruction. "It's an opportunity to live in a van Goghackack painting…with really bad plumbing!" [Earth Prime 1-6-5-9-9-2 dash Alpha]

3. He will end up wandering the streets of Houston in the middle of the night, asking random passersby, "Are you in Congress? The Senate, maybe, or the House? The House would work, too. Let me tell you why if you don't vote for repealing and eating the Affordable For More People But Still Nowhere Near Perfect Care Act, I **will** ruin your political career!" [Earth Prime 1-6-5-9-9-2 dash Omega]

Idiotocracy for Dummies

Ira Nayman

INDEX

Ira Nayman

BIOGRAPHY

Ira Nayman is profilic. Proficlic. Proclif – he writes a lot.

If you enjoyed *Angels of Our Bitter Nature*, you will probably love the nine previously published Alternate Reality News Service books. *Alternate Reality Ain't What It Used To Be*, *What Were Once Miracles Are Now Children's Toys*, *Luna for the Lunies!*, *The Street Finds its Own Uses for Mutant Technologies*, *Futures in the Mirror are Closer Than They Appear* are general collections of news, reviews, interviews and anything else you might find in your local newspaper. *The Alternate Reality News Service's Guide to Love, Sex and Robots* and *What the Hell Were You Thinking? Good Advice for People Who Make Bad Decisions* are collections of humourous science fiction advice columns. *ARNS and the Man* and *E Deplorables Unum* are the first two collections of idiotocracy articles. Print versions of all of the books are available online at Amazon, Barnes and Noble, Chapters/Indigo and other fine bookstores.

New Alternate Reality News Service stories appear regularly on Ira's Web site: *Les Pages aux Folles* (http://www.lespagesauxfolles.ca). These include two advice columns: Ask Amritsar (about love and romance and technology) and Ask the Tech Answer Guy (about anything to do with technology except love and romance). Readers are encouraged to submit their own questions for the advice columns. *Les Pages aux Folles* also contains topical political and social satire.

The Weight of Information, the pilot for a radio series based on Alternate Reality News Service articles, can be heard on YouTube.

Ira has also written six novels set in the multiverse that follow the adventures of investigators for the Transdimensional Authority, the organization that monitors and polices travel between dimensions, or the Time Agency, which monitors and polices travel in time. If you are somewhere you don't belong, doing something you shouldn't be doing, they find you, stop you and try and figure out what to do with you. The four novels in the series are: *Welcome to the Multiverse**, *You Can't Kill the Multiverse***, *Random Dingoes, It's Just the Chronosphere Unfolding as it Should, The Multiverse is a Nice Place to Visit, But I Wouldn't Want to Live There* and *Good Intentions: The Alien Refugees Trilogy: First Pie in the Face*. These books can be purchased from all of the usual suspects online, or from the home page of the publisher, Elsewhen Press.

Fans of Ira Nayman's science fiction writing are encouraged to check *Les Pages aux Folles* periodically for news about the availability of these and future stories.

* Sorry for the Inconvenience
** But You Can Mess With its Head

Connect with Ira online:

Twitter: https://twitter.com/#!/ARNSProprietor
Facebook: http://www.facebook.com/ira.nayman